ALSO BY WILL HERMES

Love Goes to Buildings on Fire

LOU REED

LOU REED

THE KING OF NEW YORK

WILL HERMES

FARRAR, STRAUS AND GIROUX · NEW YORK

Farrar, Straus and Giroux
120 Broadway, New York 10271

Copyright © 2023 by Will Hermes
Printed in the United States of America
First edition, 2023

Library of Congress Cataloging-in-Publication Data
Names: Hermes, Will, author.
Title: Lou Reed : the King of New York / Will Hermes.
Description: First edition. | New York : Farrar, Straus and Giroux, 2023. |
    Includes bibliographical references and index.
Identifiers: LCCN 2023012589 | ISBN 9780374193393 (hardcover)
Subjects: LCSH: Reed, Lou. | Rock musicians—United States—Biography. |
    Velvet Underground (Musical group) | Warhol, Andy, 1928–1987.
Classification: LCC ML420.R299 H47 2023 | DDC 782.42166092 [B]—dc23/
    eng/20230315
LC record available at https://lccn.loc.gov/2023012589

Designed by Gretchen Achilles

Our books may be purchased in bulk for promotional, educational,
or business use. Please contact your local bookseller or the Macmillan Corporate
and Premium Sales Department at 1-800-221-7945, extension 5442,
or by email at MacmillanSpecialMarkets@macmillan.com.

www.fsgbooks.com
www.twitter.com/fsgbooks • www.facebook.com/fsgbooks

1   3   5   7   9   10   8   6   4   2

Dedicated to my mother, father, and sister—and as always,
to Anne and Gia. Family makes us who we are.

CONTENTS

PREFACE

There's no reason to get into autobiographical things with me, because I'm a writer and a musician.
—**Lou Reed to Jonathan Cott, 1989**

L ike many, perhaps most, writers, Lou Reed didn't especially like being written about. In fact, no popular musician in modern history was more famous for loathing press interviews. A quick YouTube search uncovers Reed coolly eviscerating various interrogators, in scenes hilarious and/or horrifying, depending on your sympathy for journalists. Would-be biographers hardly fared better: one spurred Reed to send a form letter to friends and colleagues asking them not to participate. ("Life is hard enough without an Albert Goldman in your life," he reasoned, referring to the muckraking John Lennon biographer.) And fair enough. Why would anyone—least of all an artist who thrived on fluidity and reinvention—want to be reduced to someone else's story? Reed wanted to control his own narrative.

This is unsurprising, since—besides being one of the most consequential songwriters of the past century—Reed also wrote for the page. He published a tour diary in *The New Yorker*, memoir in *The New York Times Magazine*, poetry in *The Harvard Advocate* and other journals. He published interviews (among them one with the novelist Hubert Selby Jr.), wrote arts criticism (a riff on work by the photographer Robert Frank; a review of Kanye West's *Yeezus*), and penned tributes (David Bowie, Delmore Schwartz). As an undergrad at Syracuse University, Reed took journalism and creative writing classes, and spearheaded a literary zine. When his soon-to-be-legendary band the Velvet Underground broke up, he shopped a book-length poetry manuscript and seriously considered changing careers, returning to the academy.

"I think he'd always fought the idea that he should be a writer and not a rock and roll singer," observed the musician Don Fleming, who helped curate Reed's archives for the New York Public Library.

Still, Reed was chummy with journalists on occasion, and to be sure, benefitted from many who were passionate about his work. Besides Dylan and the Beatles, few songwriters have had more "serious" consideration. In Greil Marcus's canonical essay collection *Stranded*, Ellen Willis—one of America's greatest cultural critics—proposed a playlist of Reed's Velvet Underground songs as the "record" she'd most like to be stranded with on a desert island. Writers and other artists worldwide have waxed worshipful of Reed, with and without "the Velvets," inspired by his creative ambition. Some (most notoriously, Lester Bangs and Peter Laughner) displayed fandom bordering on the pathological. Indeed, Reed's best music, a perfect balance between rock 'n' roll's unhinged id and its intellectual superego, is catnip for a certain kind of mind. And the fact is that, while he resisted listeners reading memoir into his music, that music was nevertheless informed by a life, one that was both conventional and wildly transgressive, and his work deepens—and grows more inspiring still—with a knowledge of that life. As a writer whose own career has been animated by a belief that the best music, "pop" or otherwise, is as rewarding to think about and discuss as the best literature or film, I am in ways a child of Reed myself. Thus, the book you're reading.

Reed began his career writing songs of love, loneliness, and flawed people—familiar topics for rock 'n' roll marketed to teenagers, the music's only presumed audience in the '50s and early '60s. But his early songs also dealt with buying and using drugs, the psychology of addiction, of gender, of intimate-partner violence, of BDSM relationships. This was radical and groundbreaking in 1966, when his band recorded their debut, *The Velvet Underground & Nico*. Nowadays, when such topics make the pop charts (see Rihanna's "S&M" et al.), it's maybe hard to imagine how unprecedented Reed's "guiding-light idea" was: to "take rock & roll, the pop format, and make it for adults. With the subject matter for adults, written so adults, like myself, could listen to it."

By the metrics of their time, the Velvets were not "successful"—

never had a hit single, and never moved much beyond playing small clubs in the United States until a 1990s reunion; their recordings even fell out of print for a time. This made them a shared secret, one that indicated a discerning customer. Or artist: covering a Lou Reed song still suggests membership in an enlightened aesthetic guild of darker arts. David Bowie, always ahead of the curve, and a candidate for foremost Reed superfan, beat even Reed himself by issuing a version of "I'm Waiting for the Man," which he'd heard on an advance acetate, before the Velvets' debut had even been released. The great southern band R.E.M., leading an aesthetic rejig of rock in the '80s that used the Velvets catalog like a Rosetta Stone, issued at least three different Reed songs. The Cowboy Junkies made a "Sweet Jane" as iconic as either of Reed's touchstone versions. A Tribe Called Quest sampled the indelible bass line from Reed's equally iconic picaresque mosaic "Walk on the Wild Side" for their signature "Can I Kick It?," a landmark of early hip-hop. A 2021 Velvets tribute album featured yet another generation of indebted acts, from Courtney Barnett and St. Vincent to Sharon Van Etten and Kurt Vile.

Artists in other disciplines have drawn on Reed's work, too. The breakthrough collection by the influential novelist Denis Johnson, *Jesus' Son*, took its name from "Heroin," one of Reed's defining and most arresting lyrics. Nan Goldin's iconic slide show *The Ballad of Sexual Dependency* was soundtracked to Velvet Underground songs. References to his work were so integral to the memoirist Elizabeth Wurtzel's *Prozac Nation*, he earned a cameo in the film version. Generations of filmmakers, screenwriters, music supervisors, and ad creatives raised on Reed's music used it as emotional shorthand to score a remarkable range of scenarios: straight and queer, transgressive and otherwise. Alongside films by Todd Haynes, whose glam-rock period piece *Velvet Goldmine* features a character based on Reed and whose definitive Velvet Underground documentary made critics' best-of-year lists in 2021, there is work by Danny Boyle (the OD scene in *Trainspotting*, unforgettably set to Reed's "Perfect Day"), Joey Soloway (*Transparent*), Wes Anderson (*The Royal Tenenbaums*), Gus Van Sant (*Last Days*), Lena Dunham (*Girls*), Sharon Horgan (*Bad Sisters*), Reed's friend Julian Schnabel (*The Diving Bell and the Butterfly*), Jenji Kohan (*Orange Is the New Black*),

Wim Wenders (*Faraway, So Close!*), Noah Baumbach (*The Squid and the Whale*), Mike Mills (*C'mon C'mon*), Judd Apatow (*George Carlin's American Dream*), David Lynch (*Lost Highway*, which featured Reed's jauntily snarling take on Doc Pomus's "This Magic Moment"), and many others. More than half a century since he began recording, Reed's work remains in the cultural conversation.

* * *

Reed's supreme muse was New York City: its wild, cacophonous beauty; its lures and dangers; its millions of stories. At the fiftieth-birthday concert David Bowie threw himself in 1997 at Madison Square Garden, he introduced Reed—his main guest of honor—as "the King of New York." It was a mantle Lewis Allan Reed grew into. He was a mirror of post–World War II New York City arts writ large. He fell in love with rock 'n' roll and New York City doo-wop, recording his first single in the late 1950s while still in high school. In college he studied writing with the modernist poet Delmore Schwartz, who became his first creative mentor, and Reed never stopped lauding his memory. (In a preface to a 2012 Schwartz anthology, Reed declaimed, "O Delmore, how I miss you. You inspired me to write. You were the greatest man I ever met.") Reed saw the Ornette Coleman Quartet during their landmark 1959–60 residency at the Five Spot and was deeply affected; he spun early "free jazz" recordings on his college radio show, *Excursions on a Wobbly Rail*, which he named after a Cecil Taylor recording, and launched a literary journal named after Coleman's "Lonely Woman," which he'd often assert was his favorite song of all time. When Reed relocated to New York City after college, he quickly found the avant-garde arts community, working with or in close proximity to pioneers of experimental music (La Monte Young, Tony Conrad), film (Jonas Mekas, Barbara Rubin), and theater (La MaMa Experimental Theatre Club, where his college roommate Lincoln Swados worked). Within eighteen months of graduation, Reed had started a band, the Velvet Underground, and befriended Andy Warhol, his second and maybe most important mentor, model, and muse.

Reed's formal working relationship with Warhol, among the twentieth century's greatest artists and thinkers, was brief—Warhol nominally managed the Velvet Underground for roughly a year and a half between 1966 and 1968, and (sort of) produced their debut LP. Their relationship ran hot and cold, but they kept in touch and the artist's influence on Reed's creative practice persisted well beyond Warhol's death in 1987. He was the subject, explicit or implicit, of a significant number of Reed's works, including the 1990 memorial LP with John Cale, *Songs for Drella*. Aesthetically, Warhol surely confirmed, and likely amplified, Reed's notions about finding beauty in the ugly, banal, reviled, and despised, just as he mirrored Reed's taste for repetition, noise, distortion, cultural provocation, and periodic arcs toward transcendence. Warhol also served as a model (alongside Reed's dad) for how to run a business, especially after Reed got burned a few times; Andy Warhol Enterprises was doubtless a touchstone for Reed's Sister Ray Enterprises. The influence even outlived Reed: in the shadow of the posthumous Warhol industry (including the archival Time Capsules and the Warhol Museum) is Reed's archive at the New York Public Library, and his own posthumous industry. Of course, there were marked differences in sensibility, too, between the men, especially early on: Reed and Warhol were both capable of a cool, voyeuristic remove in their art, but Reed tended toward louder provocations, heart-on-sleeve emoting, and, on occasion, raging self-destructiveness.

Like Warhol, Reed drew extensively on the collaborative talents of other artists. His partners in the Velvet Underground—John Cale, Nico, Sterling Morrison, Moe Tucker, and Doug Yule—facilitated his greatest recordings, and helped shape his musical approach. Before the Velvets, Reed was, frankly, little more than a hack commercial songwriter and folk singer, albeit one with some striking lyric ideas. Cale brought formal music training, and a deep understanding of amplified drones acquired through his work with the pioneering composer La Monte Young. Morrison brought a mastery of R&B and rock guitar styles, along with an instinct for interplay and graceful pivoting between rhythm and lead lines. Moe Tucker brought an utterly unique style, drawing on both rock 'n' roll and West African drumming, that would influence generations of players. Nico gave Reed, a writer whose most memorable characters are generally female or gender-nonconforming, a woman's voice to write for, while Doug Yule (and Tucker, occasionally) gave him another vocal alter ego to play with. On later projects, there were Bowie (*Transformer*), the guitarist Robert Quine (*The Blue Mask*), Anohni (*The Raven*), and others who were alchemically enhanced by the collaborations, just as Reed was.

Years after his studies with Schwartz and Warhol, Reed continued to be shaped by teachers, who found him a devoted, humble student. He took classes with Doc Pomus, Brill Building master songwriter, a kindred Brooklyn kid who wrote many of the doo-wop and R&B hits Reed admired as a teenager. A lifelong spiritual seeker, in his own way, Reed also studied with the martial arts masters Leung Shum and Ren Guang Yi, developing the tai chi practice that was a lodestar in his final decades, and with the Buddhist teacher Yongey Mingyur Rinpoche.

Records and books, too, were his great teachers. Reed crammed on the work of Steve Cropper and James Burton, Ray Charles and Moondog, the Mellows and the Chantels, Dion and the Belmonts, the Byrds and the Rolling Stones, Ornette and Cecil. Notwithstanding unspoken rivalry and doubtless an anxiety of influence, Reed paid close attention to the music of Bob Dylan, covering his songs on more than one occasion. And there were the writers: Schwartz, Selby, William S. Burroughs, John Rechy, Lenny Bruce, Norman Mailer, James Joyce, Leopold von Sacher-Masoch, Virginia Woolf, Alice Bailey, Allen Ginsberg, Rimbaud, Verlaine, Baudelaire, T. S. Eliot, Sylvia Plath, Edgar Allan Poe, Frank Wedekind. All, and more, informed Reed's work.

The single greatest force in Reed's last two decades, in his work and life, was Laurie Anderson, a multimedia artist whose body of work, by the time they partnered in the early '90s, was of Warholian magnitude conceptually, even if her cultural profile was lower (her gender, polyglot creative identity, and tendency to critique oppressive power structures likely slowed her stride into the art world's upper tiers). She'd become a pop star of sorts in the '80s by accident—her single "O Superman," released as a 7-inch 45 on a friend's tiny record label, went to number 2 in the U.K. and charted globally, in a sense becoming her "Walk on the Wild Side." While maintaining separate careers, the couple helped each other with their work, and occasionally performed and recorded together. Reed's interdisciplinary interests bloomed during his years with Anderson, a multimedia artist from the get-go. Together, they became cultural ambassadors, attending art events seemingly every night they weren't performing themselves or otherwise separated by tour demands—the king and queen of a particular New York creative demimonde that over time went uptown and became more than semi-respectable. Reed's public memorial, and a subsequent daylong tribute event, were held at Lincoln Center, the city's high-culture temple. For an artist who once pantomimed injecting himself with heroin on-stage—flinging the hypodermic into the crowd afterward like a guitar pick—and who released a song titled "Sex with Your Parents (Motherfucker) Part II," it was quite a transformation.

Just as Reed drew from many peers, many took inspiration from him. Brian Eno, the visionary musician and sound-production swami, quipped that only thirty thousand people bought the first Velvet Underground record, but each of them started a band. Reed was a key forebear of punk, especially its New York school, and his work with the Velvets coined New York rock's sensibility: lyrically and musically confrontational, intellectual, smart-ass, unabashedly romantic. Patti Smith, in particular, seems to have fashioned her career in large part by Reed's example. He was the cover model on issue 1 of *Punk* magazine. In *Love Goes to Buildings on Fire*, my book about New York City's musical ecosystems in the mid-'70s—a revolutionary period that would alter a wide array of musical genres—I wrote about Reed as a figurehead and (sometimes) absent father. Like Miles Davis, he was a touchstone for all who followed, a measure of excellence and integrity; "What would Lou do?" was an aesthetic question any rock musician worth their salt might ask themselves at one point or another. (Also like Davis, Reed was ornery, struggled with an appetite for drugs, and grew erratic in his creative practice, especially in his later years, when his fame could be as much a disability as an asset.) The "alternative/college rock" of the 1980s was hugely inspired by the Velvets. Matter-of-factly mixed-gender bands emulated Moe Tucker's minimalist stand-up drumming, Reed and Morrison's prismatic guitar trances, Cale's alternately consoling and assaulting viola drones. And they reflected the plainspoken poetry of Reed's best lyrics, by turns tender, winsomely barbed, faux-naive, raging, resigned, cryptic, trying for the kingdom.

Reed's presentation and personae were influential, too. In an era of rock bands wrapped first in matching suits, then hippie cowboy frippery, the Velvets wore urban street clothes, initially basic hipster black, then standard teen nerd (with a brief concession to high-1960s baroque courtesy of the designer Betsey Johnson, Cale's first wife). As an avatar of glam rock, Reed played a proto-goth butch in black leather and matching nail polish to the campy high-femme of Bowie and others, advancing a tradition of rock gender-fucking begun by Reed's beloved Little Richard and others that extended to the present and the future, as trans, nonbinary, gay, and straight artists continue to demonstrate the beautiful diversity of gender identity and sexual orientation. Later in life, Reed's reptilian New York City take on cigarette-sucking cis-male James Dean cool offered yet another archetype.

More significant than mere presentation was how Reed publicly engaged with sexuality. One imagines him laughing at the notion he was some kind of gender studies prophet; in fact, he's been derided on occasion for work deemed retrograde in its attitude toward queer and trans persons. But it can also be argued that he's written some of the most profound music in the English language dealing with fluid identities: "Candy Says," about being uncomfortable in your body, a nod to the trans actor and Warhol Factory superstar Candy Darling; "Some Kinda Love," with its assertions that "no kinds of love / are better than others." There's the original version of "New Age," and the *Berlin* LP, with their bisexual love triangles. And, of course, the signature "Walk on the Wild Side," a set of vignettes informed by both the gender-queer set at Andy Warhol's Factory and Nelson Algren's 1956 novel *A Walk on the Wild Side*, seed of a stillborn musical Reed had been tasked, after he left the Velvets, to write songs for. That seed became a template of pop-song storytelling, and made many marginalized people around the world feel seen.

It's worth noting that the first song on Reed's first proper demo—a tape he recorded, sealed in a box, had notarized, and mailed to himself while in his early twenties to ensure a "poor man's copyright"—was a folk song written in the voice of a young woman, an orphan ballad describing suitors who made her feel "scared" and men in general as "unfaithful" and "ugly," Reed slipping into the persona like a dress in his grandmother's attic. He was clearly fascinated by the feminine. Many of his greatest songs channel feminine or fluid perspectives, so it's no accident many of the greatest Reed covers are by women, queer, and nonbinary artists: alongside Nico's performances, with and without the Velvets, are versions of "Pale Blue Eyes" (Patti Smith, Marisa Monte, Lucinda Williams, Michael Stipe), "Candy Says" (Anohni, Shirley Manson, Thalia Zedek), and others. Much of the best and most insightful writing about Reed has been by women.

Reed claimed his right to self-identify, or not, regarding his sexuality. In an era of digital oversharing, and an exploded LGBTQ+ cultural presence that's now as blessedly commonplace as it is radical, it might seem odd that an artist so lionized for unrestrained expression rarely spoke about it. Reed lived as he pleased, and answered to no one. But as a young man, he came up in a mid-century world that brought violence upon queer bodies even more reliably than today, where loudly "coming out" would have risked physical harm and career repercussions in the rock subculture that, with its rituals of machismo and homophobia, considered him royalty. Without dismissing the importance of articulate queer role models, Reed's insistence on a private life might be read as the empowered, self-caring decision of a public figure to keep parts of themselves off the celebrity trading floor, outside the transactional exchanges considered part of a pop musician's job. Add to that the fact that, like many of us, he enjoyed a fluid sexuality that couldn't be filed under neat definitions, and which changed over time, shaped as much by his partners, no doubt, as other factors. It was certainly nothing about which he cared to get into the weeds with journalists. And here, too, he seemed prescient, employing yet another strategy he'd learned from Warhol, one that can seem counterintuitive as the imperatives of the social media industrial complex try to convince us of the opposite: sometimes, the most powerful act is to say nothing.

Yet there were times in his life when Reed said plenty. In the mid-'70s, his partner was the tall, striking, nonbinary Rachel Humphreys, who accompanied him on tours, to press events, and, on at least one occasion, sang onstage with him (a cover of Chuck Berry's "Little Queenie"). In a 1979 interview around the time Reed was beginning a relationship with Sylvia Morales, an equally striking, strong cis-woman who'd become his second wife, he declared wearily: "I have such a heavy resentment thing because of all the prejudices against me being gay . . . How can anybody gay keep their sanity?"

Combined with his tendency to mess with journalists, Reed's fluidity confused plenty of them, disrupting the standard rock star narrative into which they'd slotted him, and which he performed when he was in the mood, his Christopher Street leather man gear and aviator shades passing for heteronormative cool in mainstream media. Outsiders read a different message. "He was the first queer icon of the 21st century, thirty years before it even began," R.E.M.'s frontman, Michael Stipe, pointed out. "He saw beyond—and lived outside—a society locked into a simplistic straight/gay binary division . . . Every single child of the 21st century who is not square owes him a moment of reflection and thanks." The poet Anne Waldman called him "the non-binary trickster." And Reed's music is a resonant object lesson in the critic Sasha Geffen's truism (echoing Wayne Kostenbaum) in *Glitter Up the Dark: How Pop Music Broke the Binary* that "the division between artist and fan dissolves in the moment of impassioned listening, and with it goes the division between genders . . . In music, people are not separate; they cannot be divided up into two discrete categories."

* * *

Over time, Reed's creative reputation became inextricable from his cultural button-pushing, and there were times that the button-pushing impulse got the better of him. He'd pander to audiences, overplay elements in his music for shock value, and do the same with a lifestyle that became wildly performative. (At one point, he gave a journalist on-the-record tips regarding how best to prepare methamphetamine tablets for injection.) But he recentered himself, and though his past antics cast a shadow, they'd prove the least of his legacy. What defines Reed's best work—besides fearlessness, beauty, intelligence, and switchblade New York City wit—is what for me places it at the highest level of art making: its empathy. Reed wrote his way into other voices, not all of them pretty, some belonging to "the other half / the irredeemable half" that Federico García Lorca, another poet he admired, referred to in "New York (Office and Denunciation)." These kindred humans, regardless of gender, spoke as if with Reed's own voice, a compassionate ventriloquism that always seemed geared toward understanding both the subject and himself. And when you sensed Reed was indeed writing about himself—in a song like, say, "Waves of Fear," as visceral a depiction of end-stage addiction and the panic-attack hellscape of withdrawal as any musician is ever likely to record—he seemed to be doing it to commiserate as much as to exorcise.

Reed also wrote to do battle. As a rule, he wasn't an explicitly political songwriter. But from his earliest work tapes and demos—covering "Blowin' in the Wind" by one of his key influences (and, in a way, rivals), Bob Dylan, or invoking the civil rights struggle in "Put Your Money Down on the Table"—Reed challenged the status quo. Even "Heroin," if you listen closely, is a political song, resonant as ever in an endless era of opioid crises. And, of course, there was New York, his most consistent and satisfying solo LP, which attacked the greed and hypocrisy of America's poisoned political and economic systems as they played out among the haves and have-nots on his hometown streets. Reed wasn't afraid to speak truth to power, quite literally: during a performance at the Clinton White House facilitated by the event's guest of honor, the Czechoslovakian president Václav Havel, Reed's friend and another Velvet Underground superfan, Reed delivered the money shot of his semi-hit single "Dirty Blvd." with relish, despite a White House attempt to vet and censor his set in advance. "Give me your hungry, your tired, your poor, I'll piss on 'em," he sang, "that's what the Statue of Bigotry says." (He chose not to perform "Sick of You," a song from the same 1989 album that, hilariously and presciently, roasted the U.S. attorney–cum–NYC mayoral hopeful Rudolph Giuliani, and imagined a twisted alternative reality in which some craven cabal "ordained the Trumps.")

But certainly, Reed also wrote to confront demons. Insofar as his explorations of the feminine reflected explorations of self, so, too, it would seem, did his writing about masculinity, toxic and otherwise. He dissected abusive psychologies, and those of the abused, with the perspective of someone who harbored both. And though he could be extraordinarily kind, gentle, and generous to both intimates and strangers, impatience and nastiness often shaped his public persona. A notorious perfectionist, he could be tremendously unpleasant when displeased—in a venue during soundcheck, a hotel, a restaurant—especially in his later years, when he suffered from diabetes and other health issues. Tales of his rudeness remain legion among veteran New York City food-service workers, and you did not want to be his personal assistant when his blood sugar level dropped. This aspect of his personality became cemented into myth as a literal and spiritual resting bitch face.

Of course, some of his targets had it coming. As a celebrity, he was no Norma Desmond, and he claimed his space in the city he loved; he was frequently out on the street, walking his dog, going to shows, savoring the town, generally with friends but almost always without a bodyguard, his anger an armor against generic street hustlers and fans who could be intense, when not full-on bat-shit crazy. (Spend a few hours reading the fan mail in his archives and this becomes frighteningly clear.) One might see his default fighter's crouch as the result of growing up a short kid with a reading disability on New York's urban and suburban mean streets, while his knives-out approach to interviewers was also shadowed by early bad experiences, and reflected in part a nonnegotiable demand for high-mindedness. David Marchese, one of American journalism's great interlocutors, wrote a short memorial to Reed reflecting on a not-entirely-cordial interview: "I realized that the reason he did what he did, and acted the way he acted, was because he cared so much—about music, about his ideas, about communicating . . . He belittled and berated me, but I say thank god Lou Reed was here."

As a biographer, I have skin in this game, too. I didn't know Reed personally, though we'd met a couple of times and occasionally crossed paths in the city. I interviewed him for a *New York Times* piece about his wife, Laurie Anderson, during which he grumbled answers into his cell phone while walking their dog Lolabelle in lower Manhattan. ("They should erect a statue to her," he said in reference to his partner, which was true enough.) My interest in Reed's music began when I was a bookishly delinquent teenager in the 1970s, growing up on the eastern edge of Queens, roughly ten miles from where Reed was raised in Freeport, Long Island. I'd hear his songs on WNEW-FM and WLIR-FM, discovering "Sweet Jane" (the glorious *Rock 'n' Roll Animal* version, with its over-the-top guitar-solo intro) and of course "Walk on the Wild Side"—songs that suggested identity was mutable and malleable. When I discovered the Velvet Underground LPs in college, I found those same qualities, and then some. For a young person constructing a self, sexuality included, Reed's words spoke clearly, shrugging off presumed certainties and replacing them with possibilities, a critical perspective-shifting that, as he sang in another signature song, "Rock & Roll," could indeed save your life. I consider the Velvet Underground to be one of the world's greatest rock bands, alongside the Beatles, the Stones, Funkadelic, the Grateful Dead (who, like the Velvets on a good night, could take a jam to the heavens), any you could name—and that Reed's best lyrics are as good as anyone's.

One of the many revelations of this project was reengaging with his large body of solo work. I'd loved much of it for decades: the Bowie-sculpted *Transformer*, *New York*, even *Metal Machine Music*, as much for its fuck-you, mic-drop attitude as for its oceanic, ambient noise swarm. Other albums I'd filed away on grounds of fussy production style or lyrics that seemed tossed-off. But Reed's artistic practice was remarkably consistent from start to finish, whether he was fashioning synth-rock in a mullet with hopes of gaining MTV rotation, or making German-language avant-garde musical theater with Robert Wilson. The goal was nearly always the same: trying to merge the basic, ecstatic joys of rock 'n' roll with lyrics that aspired to do what literature does. Not a single project of his lacked for examples of his creative mastery.

If his work wasn't always successful—and it wasn't—he never stopped trying. And while he understood the reverence people had for the Velvets, he kept moving forward. In hindsight, some of his most maligned work—the *Berlin* LP; *Metal Machine Music*; the Wilson projects, including an imagining of Wedekind's "Lulu" plays never staged in the United States and the Metallica collaboration LP born of it—constitute a significant part of his oeuvre, shaping a modern multimedia song language. Reed's career encompassed virtually the full arc of rock 'n' roll's lifespan, from its 1950s flowering to its twenty-first-century revivals, fusions, and abstractions. He was born with the music, came of age with it, peaked as it peaked, ushered it into its middle age, and watched it take new forms, as he did the same.

NOTES ON PROCESS, MYTH PARSING, AND PRONOUNS

A lot has been written about Lewis Allan Reed, plenty of it dubious. Invented stories and exaggerations, many sowed in the '70s and circulated on the internet, have been accepted as fact. That some were advanced by Reed himself didn't help matters. Even speaking to those who knew him well before he became one of pop music's most notorious drug outlaws—a persona he played to the hilt when it suited him—one gets the sense that memories might be clouded by subsequent myth, every double scotch or methamphetamine injection magnified into more smoking-gun evidence of the "Lou Reed" character he'd blurred into by the mid-'70s. Then again, it was the '70s, and Reed did have an appetite for extremes. I've employed due diligence to get stories straight. Overreporting was easy and entertaining; it seemed at various points in my research that every third person I encountered, especially in the New York circles I move in, had a Lou story to share. This book reflects a lot of them, and if it doesn't capture yours, it will, I hope, complicate it.

If you're hoping for some neat totalizing statement or psychological profile to explain Reed, to fix him like a butterfly specimen, you won't find it here. Somewhat vexingly for a biographer, if thrillingly for a fan, Reed was a shape-shifter who represented the potentialities of identity, one reason why he remains such a compelling figure. "I think everybody has a number of different personalities, just in themselves," he said in an interview. "It's not just people having different personalities. I mean, you wake up in the morning and say '[I] wonder which one of them is around today?' You find out which one and send him out. Fifteen minutes later, someone else shows up."

To be sure, at least one of Reed's personalities was abusive: verbally quite often, by many accounts, and on rare occasions physically. The most credible accounts of the latter—one case involved David Bowie—suggest he was wildly intoxicated, and his verbal abusiveness in later years seems to have increased alongside health problems, including the liver disease that finally killed him. These are not excuses or exonerations, but they're relevant context. Reed battled his darkness throughout his life. And toward the end, in a storybook denouement, he achieved a kind of redemption, and grace, in large part through love. For those whom he accepted as friends, especially in his later years, Reed was among the most loyal, loving, and tender, and generous people they'd ever known.

I've always viewed the topic of music as a portal for writing about the entirety of human experience: love, hate, sex, friendship, community, gender, identity, philosophy, history, psychology, war, politics, the creative impulse and the destructive, ecstasy, sorrow, revenge, forgiveness, transformation. Reed's life story was a vehicle for all these things, but so were the lives of those who were part of it, and I've done my best to disrupt the standard Great Man Narrative, always a suspect concept, devoting space in this biography to those in Reed's orbit without whom he wouldn't have achieved what he did. One of the central fallacies of celebrity culture, politics included, is the primacy of the lone actor. Like most great artists, and accomplished humans in general, Reed was the product of community, and his best work reflects that.

* * *

There were many important nonbinary persons in Reed's circle, and many have passed, which made the issue of gender pronouns tricky. For the late Rachel (deadname Richard) Humphreys, whose family refers to her as Ricky but who was known almost exclusively as Rachel in later years, it was particularly fraught; public records in New York alternately use Richard and Rachel, and most people who knew her stressed that Rachel claimed the right to all her names, and didn't seem to care about gender pronouns. Holly Woodlawn, with whom I spoke near the end of her life, was comfortable with "she," and I found that many trans persons of her generation are less concerned with pronouns than younger people are nowadays. And of course, people's pronoun preferences can change. In every case, insofar as I could establish, I've deferred to the subject's latest preferred pronoun for self-identification during their lifetime. I never spoke with Humphreys, who died in the early '90s, but she was evidently comfortable with she/her—even if I imagine that, given the gender categories of today, she would have identified as nonbinary and used they/their. If there are any lessons to draw from Reed's work and life, any core morality, it's that everyone deserves the dignity of self-definition.

Due to copyright constraints, certain letters, recordings, and other documents of Reed's have been referenced without, or with few, direct quotations. In all other cases, I've tried to root this book in the subject's own words whenever possible. Quotes from author interviews are in present tense, excepting a few with individuals (among them Billy Name and Holly Woodlawn) who passed away before this volume was published. Quotes from other sources are in past tense. For information pertaining to the Velvet Underground, I am indebted to a number of Herculean resources: Richie Unterberger's *White Light/White Heat: The Velvet Underground Day-by-Day*, Johan Kugelberg's *The Velvet Underground: New York Art* (plus his Velvets collection at the Cornell University Library), Alfredo García's *The Inevitable World of the Velvet Underground*, and Olivier Landemaine's ever-evolving *The Velvet Underground Web Page*, olivier.landemaine.free.fr/vu. I drew extensively on John Cale's excellent autobiography, *What's Welsh for Zen*; quotes from Cale are sourced from it unless otherwise noted. Christian Fevret and Carole Mirabello's magnificently curated 2018 pop-up exhibition, *The Velvet Underground Experience* (and the French exhibit that preceded it, *The Velvet Underground New York Extravaganza*), as well as Todd Haynes's beautiful 2021 documentary, *The Velvet Underground*, reassured me that the wide-angle approach to Reed's life story was the way to go, and confirmed that his work remains as resonant, and relevant, as ever. For information about Reed's life beyond that band, I drew on many resources, none more so than the Lou Reed Archive at the New York Public Library for the Performing Arts at Lincoln Center. If you're a Lou fan and you find yourself in New York City, the archive is well worth a visit.

LOU REED

INTRODUCTION

I think it's important that people do not feel alone.

—Lou Reed

Two days before he died, Lou Reed floated in the pale blue water of the heated saltwater swimming pool behind his East Hampton home. He was suffering; had been for a while. His liver, an organ he worked hard over the years, had all but ceased to function. After a waiting period, he'd finally received a transplant. But now that one was failing, too. He knew these were his final hours. But he was with Laurie Anderson, his wife, partner, and soulmate, and a steady stream of close friends had been visiting—to hang out, laugh, weep, eat, drink, and listen to music.

On this afternoon, too weak to swim, Reed was being cradled in the arms of his friend Julian Schnabel. A decade apart in age, the two artists had risen to fame on parallel New York tracks; both frequented Max's Kansas City; both befriended Andy Warhol, and shared his work ethic, making art as reflexively as breathing. In later years, they became close. Schnabel collaborated with Reed on a filmed staging of his *Berlin* LP in 2005, a record the painter and filmmaker loved. Reed was fiercely proud of the project, which was a vindication. When that album—the dark follow-up to his breakout *Transformer* and its radio hit "Walk on the Wild Side"—was first released in 1973, it was vilified by many. A *Rolling Stone* critic called it "a disaster," and "so patently offensive," the writer wanted to take "physical vengeance" on its maker.

But time brought a critical reassessment, as it did again and again with Reed's work. Presenting *Berlin* in opera houses across Europe, its grim song cycle unspooled before magnificent hanging murals by Schnabel ("The *Berlin* Wall," Reed dubbed it), the production turning perhaps the greatest disappointment of Reed's career into one of his greatest personal triumphs.

Reed grew up in a seaside town on Long Island's South Shore; he knew the ocean well, invoked it in songs. Buoyed by the water, looking up at his large, hirsute friend, Reed recalled a moment as a child. "Y'know, I was on the beach with my dad," Reed said, voice diminished to a hoarse whisper. "I put my hand in his hand. And he smacked me in the face."

The recollection—perhaps of a mid-century Jewish dad harshly instructing a son in the fraught matter of how to be a "man" in an anti-Semitic and homophobic culture—might've been accurate. It might also have been delusional hyperbole, born of Reed's failing health and a lifetime of telling stories about himself that were not entirely true. His sister, for one, does not believe her brother's account; she never saw their father raise a hand to him—or anyone, for that matter.

Either way, Reed's friend thought it was a crazy thing: here is a seventy-one-year-old guy about to die, spending his final hours on earth. And this is what he's thinking about.

1.

BROOKLYN > LONG ISLAND > THE BRONX

(1940s–1950s)

DISCUSSED: Beth El Hospital, Białystok, European Jewish immigration, Irving Howe's *World of Our Fathers*, Freeport, Fats Domino, the Chantels, *The Adventures of Ozzie and Harriet*, Murray the K, Jones Beach West Bathhouse, Robert Frank's *The Americans*, NYU, Moondog, Ornette Coleman, electroconvulsive therapy

---

Here comes the ocean and the waves where've they been
—Lou Reed, "Ocean"

The celebrity is a relatable living representative of the spectacle, each offering the individual a possible role . . .
—Guy Debord, *The Society of the Spectacle*

I first became aware of spectacle when I was 9 years old and Rena Cougar showed-me-her-thing if-I-showed-her-mine in the concrete schoolyard of P.S. 192, Kings Highway, Brooklyn during lunch hour, while the older boys fought, urinated in the streets and in other ways made asses out of themselves.
—Lou Reed, "Spectacle and the Single You"

Lou Reed made his life on the island of Manhattan, but he was born and raised on Long Island, whose geographical tip is Brooklyn—with the Narrows and New York Harbor to the west; Jamaica Bay to the east; and beyond, the Atlantic Ocean, the body of water Reed's Eastern European forebears crossed to start new lives.

Brookdale University Hospital and Medical Center—the latest

incarnation of the health-care facility where Reed came into the world—isn't located in the hipster-culture epicenter "Brooklyn" signifies worldwide. It anchors a working-class neighborhood east of Prospect Park, flanked by Church Avenue, now Bob Marley Boulevard, a commercial stretch dotted with bodegas, Caribbean take-out joints, and discount stores. Two-story brick row houses—some kept up, some crumbling—line the side streets. On one, observed shortly after Reed's death, hung a crucifix-shaped sign reading "Baptist Church Redeemer," though behind its iron security bars were stained-glass panels with Star of David symbols, relics from a house of worship likely dating to Reed's Brooklyn days.

When Lewis Allan Reed was born, on March 2, 1942, Brookdale was Beth El Hospital, a voluntary nonprofit developed by the area's then-sizable Jewish community that "pledged to serve all races and religions." At last check, a display case in the lobby housed a bust of Samuel Strausberg, hospital president in the 1940s. "His life and work were dedicated to the forging of a better tomorrow for Beth-El Hospital," read the inscription, "and for all mankind."

That striver's idealism would've impressed Lewis's father, Sidney Rabinowitz, born in 1913 into a Jewish family that emigrated from the region that would become northeastern Poland, then part of Russia in the 1890s. Sidney's father, Mendl, came from a sizable clan: he had at least three children from his first wife in the old country, and three sons, including Sid, with his second wife, Fannie, in America.

An especially colorful member of the extended family was one who would figure in Reed's later life—Sid's paternal cousin, a rebellious young woman named Shulamit "Shirley" Rabinowitz, who was born in a shtetl near Białystok, in April 1909. During World War I, the Germans took control of the town from the Russians; Shirley told a story of a shell crashing through the roof of her house and landing on the kitchen table, unexploded. The Germans often confiscated food, which was scarce, but brought modernization, including running water and a library. The latter was especially welcomed by Shirley, a devoted reader. When the Germans were defeated, a Polish state was formed, which in short order was invaded by the Bolsheviks, who were then driven out in 1920; a crazy quilt of map-making would follow.

Shirley's family were Yiddish-speaking leftists in a newly independent Poland, and she was a committed Communist sympathizer. Fearing for her safety, her father sent her to live with relatives in Białystok, where she learned dressmaking, and by eighteen she was married. But her political involvement put both her and her husband at risk, and she ultimately decided to flee, solo, in 1928, age nineteen. The United States had by then essentially closed its borders to Eastern European Jews, so the young woman obtained passage, alone, to Montreal, later smuggling herself under blankets in a friend's car across the border and into New York City, where she was met at the train station by her uncle Mendl, Lewis Reed's paternal grandfather.

She arrived with two suitcases and a mandolin she'd purchased in Montreal, and soon found work on a sewing machine in the Garment District, earning seven dollars or so for a forty-eight-hour week. The family she left behind, husband and parents, were presumably murdered in the Holocaust.

Shirley never had children, but she taught herself to play the mandolin. She loved literature, and while Jack London and Sinclair Lewis were favorites, Upton Sinclair's *The Jungle*, in particular, darkened her vision of America. But the book that changed her life, she'd claim, was *Jean-Christophe*, the ten-volume novel by the French writer Romain Rolland, who was awarded the Nobel Prize for it in 1915. The book's socialist themes resonated deeply with the young woman. *Jean-Christophe* chronicles the life of a musician-composer (based on Beethoven, whose biography Rolland had written), and addresses the joyful sorrow of day-to-day human experience through an artist-hero who commits himself to absolute truth and individual morality—which, of course, runs him into trouble.

* * *

Shirley's experience mirrored that of countless Jewish immigrants. In *World of Our Fathers*, Irving Howe describes New York's German-Jewish

garment industry when large-scale Eastern European immigration began around the turn of the century. The employers welcomed new ar-
rivals. But work was hard and conditions often unfair. Shirley's third
husband, Paul Novick, nearly twenty years her senior, was editor of
the Yiddish-language Communist Party daily newspaper *Morgen Frei-
heit*, reputedly the largest-circulation Communist newspaper in the
country, in any language, in the 1920s. Shirley became a labor activist
working in Jewish-run shops and, after she began getting blacklisted in
them, Italian ones. She earned herself a nickname: Red Shirley.

Soon a broader cultural movement would begin, as Jewish Americans migrated from blue-collar work into entrepreneurship and degree-
driven professions—what Howe called "the central socioeconomic fact
of American Jewish life." A more privileged, often more intellectually
minded next generation would differentiate themselves from their immigrant parents.

Sidney Rabinowitz was a slight, handsome man with brown hair
and brown eyes who fantasized a career as a writer—or, in more prag-
matic moments, a lawyer. But his parents pushed him toward the nuts
and bolts of business, and, being good with numbers, he became a
certified public accountant. He soon met Toby Futterman, seven years
younger, a dark-haired looker with hazel eyes, also a child of Jewish
immigrants. Her father died of pneumonia when she was sixteen, so
she went to work, landing at United Lawyers Service, a firm that supplied legal support staff.

One day in early 1939, a beauty-pageant scout came by the office, and
though Reed's mom always joked that she was noticed only because the
really pretty girl on staff was out sick that day, the eighteen-year-old soon
found herself being crowned "Queen of the Stenographers of NYC." In
a photo from the ceremony that February, she looks perfectly at home
in an ornate satin gown, stacked heels, and tiara, holding a scepter and
a rose bouquet. A family story suggests Toby subsequently received
a letter from a talent scout inviting her to Hollywood to audition for
films, an idea Toby's protective mom quickly squashed. In any case,
two years later, Toby was a stay-at-home mom herself, raising her infant
son, Lewis, in a Sheepshead Bay apartment at 1620 Avenue V. Five years

later she had a daughter, who was given the somewhat gentile name of Margaret Ellen, perhaps to inoculate her against anti-Semitism. As it turned out, no one was comfortable using her birthname, and she became known to all by her nickname, Bunny.

Sid and Toby made a handsome couple. Family pictures from the 1940s often showed them and their cousin Shirley in swimsuits; in one, Sid poses shirtless, in high-waisted trunks, looking like a bodybuilder. In another, a young Lewis sits on his dad's lap, beaming, Toby and the ocean behind them. In others, Lewis cradles a dog in his arms, and Shirley cradles a baby Lewis. In one of a series with Shirley that might have been taken at a bungalow colony, she stands in a one-piece swimsuit, smiling and bare-legged, mischievously aiming a rifle out of frame. In another, she sits on a porch with a balalaika in her lap, as if in the midst of playing an old melody. The joy in her expression is palpable.

Names were traditionally tricky business for Jewish Americans. Lewis's zayde Mendl owned a stationery store in Lower Manhattan, and according to family legend, Sid was questioned by the FBI one day after doing accounting work for a union the Bureau was investigating. Spooked, he changed his surname from Rabinowitz to Reed, hoping to protect his dad's business from subsequent witch hunts, and no doubt to avoid garden-variety anti-Semitism going forward. Sid's brothers (Stanley and Lew) changed their names to Reed, as well.

Years later, when Bunny began her career, she felt she needed a more serious name, and had never liked Margaret. So she became Merrill, feeling the appellation carried a certain weight.

Sometimes it becomes necessary to reinvent yourself.

* * *

Sid Reed's career as a tax accountant grew, and he became the treasurer of Cellu-Craft, a small Long Island–based company that made bags for Wise potato chips. So in 1953, the year Eisenhower became president and Arthur Miller's *The Crucible* opened on Broadway, he purchased a new home in the suburbs for his family, and they left Brooklyn, moving to the residential north side of Freeport, known as Freeport Village.

Assessed at $9,300, the single-story brick house at 35 Oakfield Avenue, on the corner of Maxson Avenue, was modest but modern: two bathrooms, hot-water radiators, a fireplace, hardwood floors, and an attached garage. This was the culmination of the standard New York City immigrant dream: to trade the paved ethnic inner-city neighborhood, with its tight-packed apartments and shtetl flashbacks, for a state-of-the-art new-construction home, with yard and lawn, in the suburban promised lands east of Brooklyn and Manhattan, in Queens and Long Island.

To friends of their son, the Reeds were familiar and welcoming. "Let me tell you, his mother and father were *terrific* people," says Allan Hyman, probably Lewis Reed's closest friend from elementary through high school and into college. "I spent a lot of time at their house growing up. His mother was the typical American housewife from that period, as middle-class as could possibly be. She'd come in and say, 'You guys want anything to eat? I'll make you a sandwich, some cookies and milk.'"

Reed joined Hyman, who lived around the corner, in the third grade at Atkinson Elementary School. The two boys walked home together and played in the streets, which were wide and quiet, with little traffic. "What do third graders do?" Hyman shrugs. "We'd play stickball, baseball, whatever. My mother said, 'Come back when it's dark.' So we played 'til it got dark."

The Reed house was still standing in the early 2020s, and even with new owners, looked about the same as it did in the early 1950s, renovations and plastic backyard fence notwithstanding. The surrounding homes, mostly modest one-stories, had also changed little, and Freeport Village remained a sleepy bedroom community. The Long Island Rail Road still stops in town; the twenty-five-mile trip to Manhattan's Penn Station takes about forty-five minutes. The conservative Congregation B'nai Israel—where the Reeds attended services led by Rabbi Reuben Katz, and where their son, Lewis, was bar-mitzvahed—is still on Bayview Avenue. In the '50s, the temple had just been built, World War II barely a decade past, and boom times were back. New construction was everywhere. The final stretch of Meadowbrook Parkway, linking nearby Jones Beach to New York City, was being completed, another plume in the cap of the power-hungry technocrat Robert Moses, who transformed the city's park and highway systems.

Part of Queens County until it broke off at the turn of the century, Freeport was an oystering village turned resort town and artists' colony. It became a magnet for the New York theater and vaudeville crowd; the likes of Sophie "Last of the Red Hot Mamas" Tucker, Irving Berlin, and Al Jolson would carouse there alongside neighbors such as Will Rogers and John Philip Souza. During Prohibition, rumrunners darted along the Woodcleft Canal to meet Canadian suppliers out in the bay. Playland Park offered Coney Island–style rides and amusements. The 1939 film *Babes in Arms* takes place in a fictional town, "Seaport," likely inspired by Freeport. Seaport is home to an army of stage brats, led by Mickey Rooney and Judy Garland, who, when the rise of motion pictures threatens their parents' livelihood, rally to save themselves from conventional lifestyles.

By the time the Reeds moved to Freeport, however, the village young Lewis would later describe as "the most boring place on earth" had settled down considerably. Its most famous musician by then was the middlebrow schmaltz king Guy "Auld Lang Syne" Lombardo, a wealthy boating fanatic who held court on his fifty-five-foot cruiser at the marina, and whose twenty-year easy-listening chart run would finally be shut down by the rise of rock 'n' roll.

* * *

Lou Reed's appetite for music developed early. He was devoted to Freeport's WGBB, 1240 AM, at 44 South Grove Street, the station of choice for rock 'n' roll fans. "Movies didn't do it for me. TV didn't do it," Reed said. "It was radio that did."

Reed's first single purchase was "The Fat Man" by Fats Domino, and he haunted the local record shop on Main Street. "Doo-wop, blues stuff, Hank Ballard, the El Dorados, the Cadillacs—all these bands that were doing four-chord music. Four chords: that's all you had to know," Hyman says. "Lou was very, very interested. He got started with guitar; I already played trumpet and started fooling with drums. I got recruited by the Freeport High School marching band, but Lou would never have been involved in an organized group like that, would never have worn a band uniform; he used to kid me about it all the time."

Reed started piano lessons, but "got bored with it," he recalled, despite being engaged enough to start writing short pieces of music. He claimed his formal guitar studies ended the day they started. "[My teacher] wanted to start normal lessons and I said 'no, no, no . . . teach me to play the chords for this record' . . . And that was it . . . There are some advantages to not being schooled."

Sports were also an obsession of Reed's, but similarly on his terms. He was a slight kid, which made certain types of competition challenging; he ran track, but avoided team sports. He once claimed he'd been kicked off the basketball team for throwing a ball at the coach's head, though neither Hyman nor their friend Dickie Green recall this. The three would often shoot hoops at the chain-netted courts near Reed's house after school until nightfall, Hyman says, "but I don't remember him ever playing in any games." Reed also told stories about a pole-vaulting mishap in high school that left him with a back injury, causing him to abandon varsity track and field. In the Freeport High School yearbook for 1958, Reed's junior year, he nevertheless appears in the team photo in a striped polo shirt, hair crew-cut short, smiling broadly. In what's likely a later picture, of his homeroom class (room 220, with Mrs. Woodcock), his dark hair has grown out into something near a pompadour; his head is tilted skeptically, his mouth drawn between smirk and sneer. Change happens fast in high school. "That's Lou," Hyman says with a laugh, looking at the photo. "His expression didn't change much over the years."

The new look may've come from a role model who lived on Reed's block: a central-casting greaser dirtbag in a black leather jacket and engineer's boots, known for petty theft, vandalism, smoking marijuana, and shooting people with his BB gun from the second-floor window of his parents' house. Hyman thought the kid was nuts, but Reed was impressed by his dangerous aura—and maybe for the fear it inspired, as Reed himself was a constant target for bullies.

"Lou spoke of being beaten up routinely after school" during his junior high years, according to his sister. But in later years, he gave as good as he got. "There was this big Italian guy in school who was a pain in the ass," Reed's high school friend Ralph Thayer recalls. "He'd always try to bump you in the hall. He tried to push on Lou, and Lou cleaned his clock right out in front of the school—flew at the guy and started punching. A bunch of people pulled him off. Lou gained a lot of respect for that."

Still, according to his sister, Reed had "a fragile temperament," and suffered from panic attacks. She remembered her brother "locking himself in his room, refusing to meet people," when guests came. "At times, he would hide under his desk." By his own account, Reed also struggled with dyslexia, which made it difficult to read anything involving long paragraphs. He feared he'd never hold a job. Like many neurodiverse kids, he deflected attention from his shortcomings by acting the wiseguy. Anxieties of not measuring up—academically, socially, on the playing field—probably informed his hair-trigger temper and tendency to withdraw.

Reed's anxiety may have also been rooted in sexuality. "I resent it," Reed told a journalist years later, identifying himself unequivocally as a "gay" man and reflecting on his adolescence. "From age 12 on I could have been having a ball and not even thought about this shit . . . If the forbidden thing is love, then you spend most of your time playing with hate. Who needs that? I feel I was gypped." Reed had begun writing about queerness, according to Hyman, who says he was privy to his friend's journals and poetry. "A lot of it was very dark, and very gay-oriented. In those days, if he had given any of it to his English teacher, he probably would have gotten thrown out of school."

How much Reed's sense of otherness fueled his creative drive is an open question. But his sister had no doubt that "his hyperfocus on the things he liked led him to music."

* * *

Hank Ballard was a Detroit church singer who worked the Ford assembly line. In the late '40s he joined an ambitious local R&B group called the Royals. They soon renamed themselves the Midnighters, to avoid confusion with another group, and began recording Ballard's songs for the Cincinnati-based Federal label. They found their first success with a lusty song called "Get It," and expanded on the idea with their second single, titled "Work with Me, Annie," which became the biggest R&B hit of 1954.

Now, if you accept that the term "rock 'n' roll" derives from a literal description of fucking, "Work with Me, Annie" fits the bill. Ballard squeals and sighs and repeats the title over the heaving backdrop of his co-singers; '50s doo-wop never sounded more carnally aspirating than their breathless "HA-um, HA-um, HA-um." And certainly, by the pop standards of the era, Ballard's beseeching couldn't be plainer, imploring in a basic twelve-bar blues to "please don't cheat / give me all my meat." The pianist hammers hot, but the centerpiece, fairly new for R&B, is the electric guitar—on the rapidly strummed opening and especially the solo that jumps off around the 1:30 mark, conjuring the sound of teenage synapses exploding in the back seat of a Bel Air.

"Work with Me, Annie" immediately freaked out the watchdogs at the Federal Communications Commission, who banned it from radio. But it spread like wildfire via jukeboxes and record stores, topped the R&B charts for close to two months, and reportedly sold near a million copies. It soon joined Reed's teenage repertoire. He adored the extravagance, exuberance, and sly humor of the best Black R&B: the Solitaires' "Later for You Baby," Del-Vikings' "Sunday Kind of Love," El Dorados' "At My Front Door," and Elchords' "Peppermint Stick," with its hilariously blatant double entendre. He was moved deeply by the goose-pimpling falsetto flourishes of ballads such as "Gloria" by the Cadillacs and "Baby It's You" by the Spaniels. He was especially struck by certain women's voices in doo-wop. "Smoke from Your Cigarette," by the Mellows, was one of his very favorites, featuring what Reed would later describe as the sad, beautiful, "femme fatale" voice of Lillian Leach.

But perhaps more than any song of the era, the emotional voltage of the Chantels' 1958 "Maybe" cut Reed to the core. It was written by the lead soprano, Arlene Smith, a teenage prodigy who sang Gregorian chant at her Catholic school in the Bronx, St. Anthony of Padua, and by the time she was twelve had performed solo at Carnegie Hall. She formed the group with friends from the school choir, and they recorded the song when she was fourteen. After a piano introduction, the background vocals swoop in on the open-mouthed vowel sound "ah"— it's the sound of vulnerability, of swooning into a deep kiss. And then Arlene Smith plunges "Maybe" into the microphone, in a descending melody that swings up on "I" and up again on "every." It's the first great display of what became known as girl-group pop, and one of the greatest songs in rock history. You can see its effects in a YouTube clip of a teen dance show called *Seventeen* broadcast from Ames, Iowa, around 1958—though it could've been shot in most any middle-class American town. There's a breathtaking disconnect between the song's passion and the corseted displays of the dancers, most if not all of them white, hands awkwardly clasped in closed ballroom style, pelvic girdles orbiting in accordance with unmappable magnetic fields, a palpable exhibition of how rock 'n' roll had shaken American culture.

The music, a racially rebranded form of rhythm and blues, was formally coined in the '40s and early '50s by various artists, most of them Black—Sister Rosetta Tharpe, Louis Jordan, Goree Carter, Roy Brown, Wynonie Harris, Ike Turner, Chuck Berry. Elvis Presley had a regional hit with "That's All Right" in '54. But the music's first crossover hitmaker was Bill Haley—a scrappy white entertainer from Pennsylvania already famed for his yodeling—whose Top 40 version of Big Joe Turner's "Shake, Rattle and Roll" registered as the first nationally recognized rock 'n' roll record that same year, taking its place on the hit parade alongside the Crew Cuts' "Sh'boom (Life Could Be a Dream)," Frank Sinatra's "Young At Heart," and Rosemary Clooney's "Mambo Italiano."

One of Reed's biggest early influences arrived on April 10, 1957, when Ricky Nelson, America's original "teen idol," sang Fats Domino's "I'm Walkin'" on the milquetoast family sitcom *The Adventures of Ozzie and Harriet*. Every Wednesday evening, Reed planted himself in

front of the TV to watch the show, mainly for the musical section at
the end. "There would be this guy in the back doin' these solos," he
remembered, referring to the legendary James Burton, part of Nelson's
on-air band. "I'd run and get my guitar out and try to play 'em. To this
day, I just fall over when I hear him play. And there was a show called
Shindig, and he was one of the Shindogs—I'd watch that, too."

As a white kid from Long Island, Reed was also struck deeply by
"I Wonder Why" by Dion and the Belmonts, a trio of Bronx Italians
steeped in the style of African-American R&B vocal groups ("that great
opening," he'd later say of the song, "engraved in my skull forever").
They were doing what Reed wanted to do. He didn't have much of a
voice, and his guitar playing kinda sucked. But he worked at it. His
first guitar was a Harmony Stella acoustic, which he bought for five
dollars. Then he got a Gretsch hollow-body electric, pretty much the
rock guitar of choice in the '50s, thanks to its association with Chet
Atkins. Not knowing any better, Reed strung it with Black Diamond
acoustic strings. But they worked well enough, and he began figuring
out how songs came together.

* * *

In Reed's junior year at Freeport High, he met Phil Harris, a senior and
fellow rock 'n' roll fan who liked to sing. With another classmate, Al
Walters, they hit on an unsurprising idea for the annual school variety show: a Little Richard act. (It's difficult to overstate the impact the
groundbreaking musician had at the time; in Minnesota the previous
year, a young Jewish man named Robert Zimmerman had a similar notion, and gave a Little Richard–style performance at the Hibbing High
School variety show.) In the auditorium the night of Reed's first band
performance was Elliot Gotfried, a neighbor with connections. He was
impressed, and invited the young men over to his house to audition
their originals (they dutifully worked up a couple one afternoon), then
connected the trio with his friend Bob Shad, an A&R man for Mercury
Records who'd just launched his own imprint, Time Records, a tiny

operation with high hopes and an office on Fifty-seventh Street. "He offered to put us under contract right then, and from what I remember, we didn't hesitate to sign," said Harris.

So one day in the summer of 1958, a sixteen-year-old Lou Reed went into a low-rent studio for his first recording session. Harris sang lead on both songs, standing on a box in the isolation booth to reach the microphone, while Reed and Walters added backup in a separate room. For the instrumental tracks, Reed played guitar with a group of A-list session men, including the guitarist Mickey Baker, saxophonist King Curtis, and arranger Leroy Kirkland. Despite his passion for Black music, working with Black musicians gave Reed immediate perspective. "I can't sing black. I knew that right then. I said 'Don't even try.'"

The trio followed Shad's advice to change their name from the Shades—it was cliché in a pop scene where every young group sported Ray-Bans, and had in any case been claimed by another group—to the Jades. Soon Reed was holding a copy of his first record: an indigo label 7-inch 45.

The A side, "So Blue," is credited to Reed and Harris (though Harris later claimed he wrote it himself). It's a dance number, a proto-"Twist," but a melancholy one, the singer searching the neighborhood for his girl, who isn't home or at the candy store; he knows they're finished. More interesting is the B side, "Leave Her for Me," credited to "Lewis Reed." It's classic, rudimentary doo-wop. "Take away the oceans / take away the seas," begins Harris over a beat that sways like a skiff on choppy water, with King Curtis's sax bobbing alongside, Reed adding "ooh-ooh"s in the background. The singer enumerates all he wants to abandon—in effect, the entire natural world, and all its magnificent but distracting beauty—in order to be left in a blissful void with his beloved. The emotional sentiment is obliteratingly pure. The preoccupation with the ocean, not surprising for a kid raised near the shore, is one Reed would return to over and over.

But then comes the spoken-word midsection, a doo-wop convention pioneered by the Ink Spots, with Harris dropping an octave and talking about nature having its place, which he of course rhymes with "your face." The performance is laughable, nearly a parody, and you can imagine Reed and Harris cracking up in Reed's bedroom as they conjured it, his eleven-year-old sister poking her head in the door asking "What's so funny?" and the boys telling her to get lost—her brother adding, by way of consolation, that she wouldn't understand. And she wouldn't, yet: what Reed was expressing, and simultaneously, perhaps as a safety valve, poking fun at, was the blinding-white hormone-rushing light of romantic love, something sixteen-year-olds are primed for and especially vulnerable to, and which, at its most potent, makes everything else disappear.

Reed saw his record in local diner jukeboxes, but it didn't go much further. His big moment was going to be when the single debuted on the overnight show hosted by Murray the K on WINS 1010 AM. Disappointingly, the host, Murray Kaufman, who would later become one of New York's main rock 'n' roll impresarios after his fellow DJ Alan Freed began having legal troubles, was out sick that night. So the Jades' single was instead presented by a fill-in, Paul Sherman, and as far as Reed knew, it never aired again. Harris got called back to do more recording for Shad. But not Reed. As for royalty earnings, he recalled a check for 67 cents, followed by another for $2.14, after the song got random local traction in Nevada.

But it was a learning experience, and in its way a triumph. Reed wasn't even out of high school yet, and as a bonus, for a while anyway, he had a working band. "We'd open supermarkets, shopping centers, things like that," Harris recalled. "We had glitter jackets." In a DIY publicity still, Reed stands stone-faced in aviator shades, Gretsch strapped over his shoulder, in a striped sports jacket and string bow tie, while Al Walters, in an identical outfit, flanks him, mouth open, as if singing a come-on no woman could resist.

*　*　*

Sex, unsurprisingly, was tied up with music from the start. Reed's first date, in fact, was bartered through WGBB. The station took requests and made dedications, so the switchboards were jammed with kids during certain hours. Sometimes lines would cross, and you could carry on conversations with other random callers over the pulse of the busy signal. This is how Reed met a game tenth-grade girl from Merrick. Reed was still in ninth, and neither could drive. So they made separate plans to get driven to the Freeport Theater on Sunrise Highway, an old movie house with a secluded balcony.

"In those days they used to have a matron in the theater that walked around," recalls Hyman, who later dated the same girl, "and if kids were making out, she'd come over and break them up. Lou's going to town with this girl, kissing and hugging, and the matron walks up with her big flashlight and whacks him in the head with it. Most people would be afraid to take on the matron. But Lou screams, 'Get the fuck out of here, you bitch! Leave us alone!' They both got thrown out."

It was a short-lived romance. "Lou didn't have girlfriends; he had one-night stands," recalls Rich Sigal, another high school friend. "He was good-looking, sexy, appealing to girls. But he never had a relationship." Another friend wrote in his yearbook that he had some claim to the title of "Freeport's gigolo." Sigal recalls Reed saying, as a plain statement of fact, that he considered himself to have a corrupt heart.

* * *

When Harris graduated he joined the navy, ending the Jades. But Reed began senior year as a certified suburban rock 'n' roller, with persona to match. "He was ahead of all of us, on many levels. When we were snagging beers, Lou would find a joint," Sigal says. "Where the hell was he getting dope in those days?! I have no idea. It was all part of his secret life that we didn't really talk about."

Reed was reckless, and liked getting wasted; according to Bunny, he once drove the family car into a tollbooth. At home, he fought fiercely with his parents, who understandably weren't thrilled with their teenage son running around New York until all hours of the morning, playing rock music in dive bars and whatever else he was doing. He and his father could both be verbal bullies, but it never got physical, according to his sister, and home life held together. "Family dinners could be enjoyable," she recalled. "Lou and my father were both extremely witty, with erudite, dry senses of humor and remarkable literary sensibilities. I enjoyed their verbal jousting . . . I was dazzled by it. Their cleverness was something we all enjoyed together."

Reed managed to stay mostly out of trouble at school. Dyslexic or not, he was a devoted reader—Ian Fleming's James Bond series was a favorite, and he raced Sigal to see who could finish books first. For the annual variety show, in the wake of his Little Richard act the previous year, Reed put together two different acts. One was an instrumental rock combo dubbed the Treetoads, with Reed playing electric guitar and Sigal on amplified harmonica; they played a rocked-up version of the *Mickey Mouse Show* theme and two other numbers. The other group was a vocal quartet, with Lou on acoustic. They performed a recent radio single, "I've Had It" by the Bell Notes, a snide mid-tempo rock throwaway about romantic frustration with a chorus that doubled as a high school kiss-off.

The quartet posed for a yearbook shot before the show. Reed looks like a matinee idol in dress slacks, loafers, and a striped cardigan, strumming his unplugged Gretsch hollow body, apparently mid-song, flanked by Sigal and two other classmates, Judy Titus and John DeCam. It's a picture of preppy innocence, except for the name, the C.H.D.s—a reversed acronym for the Dry Hump Club. (Reed's idea, of course.)

"The performance was pretty well received, and we all felt good about it," says Titus. She was Reed's lab partner in physics. "I never sensed anything troublesome about him. He was polite to his teachers, and friendly to everyone else, and good company." In her yearbook, Reed wrote: "I hope you do well at Wheaton. You can come visit me at my pad in New York City some time. Best to a really nice girl, Lou."

The handwritten inscriptions in Reed's junior and senior yearbooks show how he was seen by his peers: a "great guy," "a swell guy," "a real nice kid," "the coolest," "a wild rock and roll singer," "the king of rock and roll," and "a lazy chemistry student." He got praise for his "great personality" and "great voice," was addressed as "Daddio," "Professor," and "Dr. Reed." One kid thanked "Lew Reid M.D." for help with his "phone 'deals.'" He was labeled the "shadiest" of the Shades, urged to "stay sober" and "stop drinking." One woman wrote she was sorry for "that day," hoped he was too, and signed off with "love." Another noted that she didn't know much about him, but that she always looked at him.

A teacher wrote plainly: "You've got it Lew; use it."

His "manager" Elliot Gotfried wished him success in music, but hoped he would attend a good college and make other preparations for the future. Sigal told him to take it slow at NYU, with an apparent allusion to Ramses-brand condoms. One kid wrote brightly, "Good luck in the future—if there is any." This wasn't just flippancy: that April, students across the nation hustled into so-called shelters for Operation Alert 1959, the sixth annual U.S. civil defense maneuvers, designed to simulate a response to nuclear attack—in New York's case, by nine hypothetical hydrogen bombs, including one imagined as detonating directly above Glen Cove, Long Island.

In his senior yearbook portrait, Reed wears a jacket and tie and looks devastatingly handsome—"like Fabian, or a young Dion," Titus says. Or even Ricky Nelson. The description reads: "Tall, dark-haired Lou likes basketball, music, and naturally, girls. He was a valuable participant on the track team. He is one of Freeport's great contributors to the recording world. As for the immediate future, Lou has no plans, but will take life as it comes."

* * *

In the fall of his senior year, Sid Reed drove his son and Allan Hyman six hours north to spend a weekend visiting Syracuse University, where the two had applied. Sid sprang for a room for himself and another for the young men. After Sid went to bed, Lewis and Allan connected with some young women also visiting the school. The two friends soon decided that Syracuse, three hundred miles away from parental supervision, looked like a sweet deal.

They were both accepted and agreed to go. But in late spring, Reed changed his mind. He called Hyman.

"Lewis—you're not going?! Why not?" Hyman protested.

"I can't deal with it. It's too much bullshit. I don't wanna deal with all these phony-ass girls, and the guys . . ."

"But we agreed . . ."

"I just don't wanna go."

"So what are you going to do?"

"I'm gonna go to NYU," Reed told his friend. "I'll be in the city, and I'll be able to get jobs playing guitar."

Or so Hyman recalls. There was likely more to it than that. Reed's anxiety issues might've played a part, along with the simple fear of being too far from home.

That summer, Sigal helped Reed get a job at Jones Beach. For a hormonal eighteen-year-old, being an attendant at the West Bathhouse would seem entertaining enough. But he hated the job, the regimentation of punching in for an eight-hour shift and having to clean up other people's shit, sometimes literally. He also loathed the uniform—a sort of sailor's suit and cap, an image he'd recall in a song years later. He quit before the season finished.

Reed also played music with Sigal—who was just learning guitar—along with Hyman and Bobby Futterman, Reed's cousin on his mother's side. "Lou gave me his Stella, which made my fingers bleed, taught me an E progression, and said, 'Go home and practice it,'" Sigal says. "I got it down, and he said, 'Okay, learn this,' and taught me a four-chord C progression. With seven chords, we started a band." They called themselves the Valets; their business cards read, "Here to serve you and yours."

Reed was singing more; he liked to do fast songs, while Sigal handled slow ones. "You have a sweet voice," Reed told him. "I can't do that." Sometimes a guy named Jerry added conga. They played bars and restaurants, all covers chosen by Reed: Ray Charles's "What'd I Say," which Reed hollered wildly; the Cadillacs' "Gloria"; the Isley Brothers' "Respectable" and "Shout"; "Bony Moronie" by Larry Williams; "Castle in the Sky" by the Bop-Chords.

They did well. Following their set one night, the crowd at Bill's

Meadowbrook Bar would not let them leave, so they played their whole set again. "They held us captive," Sigal says. "I don't recall if they threatened to beat us up, but we could not get off that stage." It was a heady feeling.

*   *   *

"That crazy feeling in America when the sun is hot on the streets and the music comes out of the jukebox . . ."

So begins Jack Kerouac in the introduction to Robert Frank's landmark photo book *The Americans*. Shot in the mid-'50s, it was a national portrait that inescapably lingered on New York City, Frank's home base. Frank was a Jewish émigré from Switzerland whose art was raw, unromantic, and often looked at people on the margins. It was often tremendously beautiful. But at its core it was an art of dissent.

In one shot from the book, a group of kids cluster around an ornate jukebox: listening, vibrating, waiting for something to happen. Frank was fascinated with jukeboxes, and they appear throughout *The Americans*, looking like spaceships, or alien church altars.

In another photo, a sharply dressed trio with striking hairdos—gamine, presenting as men but nonbinary before the term existed—stand before a building. One, with remarkable eyebrows that appear penciled, strikes a pose, hip cocked, and stares down the lens. Another covers their face with their hand, peering between index and middle fingers. The third is frozen, in suspicion or curiosity, on the brink of a smile. Behind them is a sign in a window, partly obscured but for the words "Don't Miss Mister."

In a third picture, taken off the East River on Yom Kippur, you see a group of evidently Jewish men in dark suits and Orthodox hats. Behind them is a man in a pale, modern-cut suit, with a snap brim. He seems to be reading—maybe a prayer book, or *The New York Times*. Behind him is a boy, perhaps seven or eight years old, dressed for temple in a jacket, white shirt, and yarmulke. He has his back to the men, and peers across the gray water toward something out of the frame. Whether it's a plume of smoke curling above a tugboat, or simply the city skyline, with its siren call of infinite possibility, it's hard to know.

You could look at these pictures as a spiritual triangulation of the New York City that Lou Reed stepped into when he began college at NYU in 1959. The university's main campus then was in the Bronx, on a magnificent parcel of hillside parkland nestled between Sedgwick Avenue and 180th Street. The campus boasted Classical Revival buildings designed by Stanford White, who also designed the Washington Square Park arch, and a modernist-brutalist structure by Marcel Breuer, who would soon design the Whitney Museum. The campus centerpiece was the domed Gould Memorial Library and adjacent Hall of Fame for Great Americans, a sculpture garden colonnade lined with bronze busts of scientists, statesmen, and writers. The very first "Hall of Fame" of any kind in America, its assembly included Susan B. Anthony, Ralph Waldo Emerson, Walt Whitman, and Edgar Allan Poe. One can imagine Reed wandering the curved path amid the legends, maybe high on weed, pondering his own trajectory.

Virtually all his friends had left town—among the suburban New York middle class, staying home for college was generally seen as a failure—and it seems Reed knew no one attending NYU. During orientation week, he befriended a kid from Scarsdale, Arthur Littman. Most of the students (including women, first admitted as undergraduates that year) were commuters, but both men lived on campus in the Loew's Hall dorm: Reed in a ground-floor room, Littman on the top floor. The two met in the student union cafeteria. Littman recalls a lanky young man, with matted chestnut hair, "darting, nervous eyes, stovepipe low-rise jeans, a conspiratorial half-smile."

"We were talking about music," says Littman, "and one of the other students said there was a radio station on campus, and you could get your own show if you wanted one." The pair found the studio of WNYU and got slotted for a weekly hour-long program. They called it *Happy Art and Precocious Lou's Hour of Joy and Rebellion*. They played their own records: the bluesmen Big Bill Broonzy and Jimmy Reed, folk-blues singer Odetta, jazz pianists Thelonious Monk and Horace Silver. Their theme was "Up Broadway," a chortling mix of contrapuntal jazz swing, Latin strut, and Manhattan traffic noise from the 1956 *More Moondog* LP.

That choice telegraphs a lot about Reed's taste and value system at the time. Moondog was a singular artist and a quintessentially New York City musician. Born Louis Thomas Hardin in Kansas in 1916, he was blinded as a teen when a blasting cap exploded in his hands. Primarily self-taught, he began making a name for himself as a street musician shortly after arriving in the city, taking his moniker from a mythic canine he once crossed paths with. He played many instruments, including some he invented, such as the trimba, a multivoiced percussion device. He drew inspiration from Native American music he'd encountered in his youth, from European classical music and jazz, and from urban cacophony; he'd duet with tugboat foghorns and bleating taxicabs. The music was unconventional, sophisticated, kooky yet inviting, a mix of found sound, European chamber music, spoken word and global folk that echoed Martin Denny's exotica, Harry Partch's experimentation, and the peregrine spectacle of the Peruvian diva Yma Sumac. Still, it was too weird to get Moondog regular performance bookings, so he began busking on the street in midtown Manhattan—a robed man with long hair and a long beard wearing an elaborate Viking helmet (he admired Norse culture), performing for passersby, generally on Sixth Avenue at the corner of Fifty-third or Fifty-fourth Street. Sometimes, he just stood there silently. But for years he could dependably be found at his post. Reed was fascinated by him, and one day took Littman on a pilgrimage into Manhattan to meet him. "He said he appreciated the attention we'd given him on our show," Littman says. "And he didn't ask for anything. A true gentleman."

Reed's idea of using Moondog's music as a radio show theme song was hardly original. It was lifted shamelessly from Alan Freed, who used "Moondog's Symphony" as the theme for his breakthrough show *The Moondog House*—the rock 'n' roll ambassador/hustler even hijacked the nickname "Moondog" as his personal marketing brand until the blind musician successfully sued him for infringement. In fact, Reed and Littman launched their show the same month Freed was fired from WABC-AM radio in New York amid charges of payola, an event so seismic it made the front page of the *Daily News*. That the music business was a mix of love and theft, it seems, was one of Reed's first college lessons.

Another touchstone of Reed's NYU tenure was seeing the Ornette Coleman Quartet during their legendary first residency at the Five Spot Café, on the Bowery between Fourth and Fifth Streets. Reed was bowled over by Coleman's attack on his plastic alto sax, his tag team with Don Cherry, playing the equally unconventional pocket cornet, backed by the bassist Charlie Haden and drummer Billy Higgins. Littman, who Reed had dragged along, wanted to leave after the first set. But Reed convinced his friend to stay for the late set (riding the subway home alone in the wee hours from the East Village to their Bronx dorm would've been ill-advised).

It's likely that Reed heard Coleman play "Lonely Woman," the ballad he'd recorded in May on *The Shape of Jazz to Come*. One of the most beautiful works in jazz, it was cut in a West Hollywood studio, yet its anxious, hyperactive melancholy feels entirely New York: Higgins laying down a speedy, rattling IRT-train rhythm on his ride cymbal, Haden's bass line moving in slow motion, like a Bowery barfly at closing time, then Coleman and Cherry playing the melody like they're discovering it, note by note, each a reflective cry, as if the players are coming to terms with deep sorrow, turning it over and over again in their minds. But there are no obvious grounding chords to hold on to, just that melodic searching, around which one can imagine steam rising from a manhole up to the streetlights and into the night. Still, the piece feels like a concise complete statement, whole but never predictable, even on repeated listens—deeply felt, simultaneously dissonant and melodically sumptuous, making a profound impact without technical be-bop flashiness.

* * *

Sometimes Reed would bring his acoustic guitar to the cafeteria and play for whoever would watch. "He was a showman," Littman said. "That was really what he was about."

Reed taught his friend some chords. "We tried wailing on 'C.C. Rider,' and 'Gallows Pole' from the Odetta album [*At the Gate of Horn*]," Littman recalls. "We probably sounded like two dogs howling at the moon. I was trying to stay on key; Lou didn't bother to."

Finding things to care about at school was more challenging. In their second semester, Reed and Littman were admitted to an upper-level metaphysics class after Reed decided they should petition the dean in person. "We sat in the front row" for every class, says Littman, who thought the material interesting, though over his head. "Lou thought it was cool. Or maybe he was bluffing. But he always seemed to have his feelers out." Otherwise, little about the school engaged Reed, which must have been troubling for such a restless mind. His friend recalled him as "always a little shaky, which I just attributed to all the coffee we drank."

Predictably, Reed's required military class, with the Reserve Officer's Training Corps, did not go well; he was insubordinate and soon got booted out. Reed would tell stories, almost certainly made up, about threatening to shoot an officer. "ROTC was required. I was a platoon leader. Can you picture this? I marched them into a fence," he joked on a radio show years later.

Whatever actually happened, the demons Reed wrestled with during his freshman year at NYU were no joke. At the cusp of the spring semester, he had a major emotional breakdown.

"Lou announced that he was pulling out of NYU for personal reasons," Littman recalls. "It was a total surprise."

His sister remembers him coming home with his parents one day "dead-eyed" and uncommunicative. "My mother came into my room and told me that they thought he might have schizophrenia," she recalled. "The doctors told her it was because she had not picked him up enough as an infant, but had let him cry in his room . . . It was a belief and a burden she took to her grave."

It's unclear precisely what sort of mental health services Reed's parents sought out for him in early 1960. At the time, the "refrigerator parent" theory, later discredited, attributed certain mental illnesses, including autism and "schizophrenia," to a lack of familial warmth. But the upshot was a recommendation, accepted by his parents, that Lewis Reed receive electroshock therapy.

* * *

> Doctor Gordon was fitting two metal plates on either side of my head. He buckled them into place with a strap that dented my forehead, and gave me a wire to bite.
> I shut my eyes.
> There was a brief silence, like an indrawn breath.
> Then something bent down and took hold of me and shook me like the end of the world. Whee-ee-ee-ee-ee, it shrilled, through an air crackling with blue light, and with each flash a great jolt drubbed me till I thought my bones would break and the sap fly out of me like a split plant.
> I wondered what terrible thing it was that I had done.
> —Sylvia Plath, *The Bell Jar*

Postwar psychiatry in America, like much else, was flush with confidence, and the idea that behavior could be improved through science was a given among the educated and upwardly mobile. These were the early days of "miracle drugs" like Thorazine, widely used in hospitals for subduing schizophrenic patients and, alternately, for treating depression. It was the cutting edge; the best treatment available.

So was electroconvulsive therapy. Developed in Italy in 1938, ECT was widely used by psychiatrists in Nazi Germany and elsewhere, and the American psychiatric establishment, in spite of animal-testing evidence that it destroyed brain cells, went all in. Sam Phillips, the producer who created rock 'n' roll with Elvis Presley, underwent electroshock after a breakdown in 1944, with apparently successful results. Electroshock became part of every psychiatrist's tool bag.

So that spring, Reed began ECT. The sessions likely took place at Creedmoor Psychiatric Center in Queens, a massive facility then housing roughly seven thousand patients. In *The Bell Jar*, a thinly veiled fictionalization of Sylvia Plath's own struggle with mental illness just six years prior, the narrator, Esther, receives electroshock three times a week; Reed's regimen may have been similar, and in time, he'd read Plath's account.

Reed suggested that his treatment was to "cure" his attraction to men. "They put the thing down your throat so you don't swallow your tongue and they put electrodes on your head. That's what was recommended in Rockland County then to discourage homosexual feelings," he told a writer in the late '70s, adding as punch line, "Well, here's an example that it didn't work."

For the most part, psychiatrists of the era used ECT to treat anxiety, depression, rage, and suicidal ideation, not to change a person's sexual orientation per se, though many psychiatrists at the time, most infamously the New York City–based Charles Socarides, were advocates of homosexual conversion therapy. But the stigma and emotional burden of being queer in 1950s America might've triggered any of the above responses. Therapeutic options were limited at the time, and even if Reed was at the age of consent—he turned eighteen in March—he was likely in no position to refuse treatment. In lieu of commitment to a mental hospital, an option that may have also been on the table, outpatient ECT probably seemed the lesser evil.

The treatments left him foggy for a time. "The effect is that you lose your memory and become a vegetable," he told an interviewer, perhaps with some hyperbole. "You can't read a book because you get to page 17 and have to go right back to page one again." His sister thinks it damaged his short-term memory significantly, and gave him lifelong recall problems. Surely, the indignity, shame, and betrayal of the whole affair imprinted him, and it must have left him feeling vulnerable and unsafe. For some time, he seems to have told no one. Allan Hyman, ostensibly his closest friend at the time, says he learned of it only decades later, when reading a magazine profile of Reed.

Yet the treatment would eventually become a battle scar to display, part of Reed's mythology. He made it into a source of strength, one that set him apart from the suburbs, his parents, and the sort of culture that would co-sign it. In his personal narrative, it became, perhaps, like Peter Parker's radioactive spider bite, a source of superpower.

2.

LONG ISLAND > UPSTATE

(1960–1964)

DISCUSSED: Syracuse, Sterling Morrison, Norman Mailer's "The White Negro," Gabriel Vahanian's *The Death of God*, Joan Baez, Delmore Schwartz, Bob Dylan, the assassination of JFK, heroin, William Burroughs's *Naked Lunch*, hepatitis C, "Heroin"

> Hubert Selby, William Burroughs, Allen Ginsberg and Delmore Schwartz . . . To be able to achieve what they did, in such little space, using such simple words. I thought if you could do what those writers did and put it to drums and guitar, you'd have the greatest thing on earth.
>
> **—Lou Reed, 2008**

In the late spring of 1960, Lou Reed was home in Freeport, living with his parents. Art Littman and another friend came out to visit. "He seemed the same," he recalls. "Just a little more shaky than usual. And he had a little quiver in his voice sometimes."

Reed's mother doted on him. She made lunch for the young men, and they hung out and bullshitted, like usual. Reed didn't tell them about the ECT. "He told us about this therapy he was getting for some mental problem, but we couldn't figure out what he was really referring to. He also told us that he was supposed to soak his balls in milk," Littman laughed. "[We thought] maybe he was goofing on us . . ." He assumed Reed would return to NYU. In fact, to his surprise, his brainy, street-smart friend decided to transfer to Syracuse. "It didn't seem like a good fit," he says. "Syracuse was a Division 1 party school. What's Lou Reed doing there?"

In a warm, wisecracking letter Reed wrote Littman after his first semester at Syracuse, Reed didn't disagree. He began by saying he was on the mend: "This school is intolerable in many ways but overall I like it better than N.Y.U. except for the fact that you're down there + I'm up here. The bit with the psycho is over + I am now relatively well adjusted—ha, ha."

Reed chided Littman for not writing, and complained about Syracuse's inescapable fraternity culture, grousing that the students are "narrow," "patriotic," and "not generally bright." He also bragged about his jazz show on the campus radio station WAER, much in the spirit of his WNYU show with Littman. In fact, it had commanded attention straightaway, having already received a complaint from the dean of the music school, who said its mix of cutting-edge jazz, rock 'n' roll, and rhythm and blues was giving his wife a headache.

Still, it must have been a rough reboot for Reed. When he began school in September, he was once again a freshman, having never completed his first year at NYU. Macho fraternity and sports culture indeed defined Syracuse; the school arguably had the nation's greatest collegiate football team at the time, the Orangemen, with the Heisman Trophy winner Ernie Davis and future Hall of Famer John Mackey. Reed had little interest in it. And while he didn't want to join a frat, as he wrote to Littman, he recognized that socially, "you're screwed if you don't."

Though Syracuse University was founded by the Methodist Church, it was by 1960 a nonsectarian institution with a large Jewish student body from downstate—it became known as "The Jewish Harvard" at a time when Ivy League admission policies were perceived, quite accurately, as anti-Semitic. There were even Jewish fraternities. "The ones of rank were all on one strip of Comstock Street," recalls Reed's friend David Weisman. "There was ZBT—Zillions, Billions, and Trillions they called it—the moneyed Jews. The AEPs were the good-looking moneyed Jews, the kind of nouveau-riche cool-ass men from Manhattan and Five Towns; always on the prowl, all very stylish, with mohair sweaters and continental pants and Bonneville convertibles and candy-apple-red Corvettes. The Sammies [Sigma Alpha Mu] were the jock moneyed Jews." It was the Sammies that Allan Hyman pledged to when he arrived in Syracuse. He encouraged Reed to pledge, too, though he'd come to regret it.

Syracuse also had strong academics, and boasted one of the first colleges of fine and performing arts in the country. Crouse College was housed in the campus's most spectacular building, a sort of Romanesque Revival castle built in the 1880s. Reed took classes here, which is where he met Weisman, a handsome, ambitious art student with short dark hair and thick-framed glasses who was escaping his own suffocating childhood in the Southern Tier New York city of Binghamton. "I met him in figure drawing, where we would sit next to each other," Weisman recalls. "Lou couldn't draw very well, I remember that."

Both came from families of modest means, compared with many of their peers. Both were Jewish; both were interested in the arts. Weisman found football deplorable. They clicked immediately, and there was definite chemistry between them.

"We had a shared secret, a sexuality thing," he says. "He was very, very sweet to me. I never saw the nasty Lou; it was all sweetness and googly eyes." Years later, when Reed described falling for a guy when he was nineteen, he was likely referring to Weisman. "It was just the most amazing experience. It was never consummated," Reed said. "I felt very bad about it because I had a girlfriend and I was always going out on the side—and subterfuge is not my hard-on. I couldn't figure out what was wrong. I wanted to fix it up and make it okay. I figured if I sat around and thought about it I could straighten it out . . . so I could 'do it right.'"

Reed and Weisman's other shared secret involved ECT. "My mother had shock treatment a year or two before that. It completely fucked up my life," Weisman says. Reed confessed his shock treatment ordeal "in one of those all night, who-knows-what-the-hell-you're-talking-about conversations, and suddenly there it was."

Sometimes the young men ate at the cheap restaurants on Marshall Street. One evening that fall, they sat at the Savoy counter watching Senator John F. Kennedy debate Vice President Richard Nixon on a black-and-white TV. Kennedy spoke in his resonant New England drawl about raising the minimum wage to $1.25 an hour. Weisman thought that Kennedy, sharp and relaxed in a dark suit, with his robust hair, full lips, and steady gaze, looked like a movie star.

"He can't possibly win," Reed said. "He's too good-looking."

* * *

Reed spent a lot of time in his dorm room with his acoustic guitar. He practiced folk styles, learned Travis picking, and began fooling around with the harmonica. He also had his electric guitar and amplifier, which he'd occasionally plug in and crank up. That's how he met a fellow Long Island guitarist, Sterling Morrison.

"The first sound I ever heard from Lou," Sterling Morrison reflected, "was when the ROTC were marching in the field behind the dorm in their uniforms. First I heard ear-splitting bagpipe music from his hi-fi, then he cranked up his electric guitar and gave a few blasts on that. So I knew there was a guitar player living upstairs."

Morrison grew up in East Meadow, where he studied trumpet, switching to electric guitar after his teacher was drafted, inspired by Chuck Berry, Bo Diddley, T-Bone Walker, and especially Mickey Baker, the A-list session guitarist who'd applied jazz chops to countless rock 'n' roll classics, as well as to Reed's high school recording debut. Morrison liked how Lightnin' Hopkins played, too, though he wasn't much for acoustic music. He liked doo-wop and rockabilly, and the R&B and rock 'n' roll he heard on the Jocko Henderson and Alan Freed radio shows.

Like Reed, Morrison was accepted to Syracuse out of high school but initially passed on it, instead choosing the University of Illinois, where he was asked to leave after two semesters, "mostly for not attending class and for having been drummed out of ROTC, which was compulsory." The two shared that experience, too.

Morrison enrolled in City College briefly, but he'd wind up at Syracuse before long. When they met, Morrison was visiting Reed's downstairs dorm-mate, Jim Tucker, a fellow Long Islander and a blues fan with a big record collection. Unsurprisingly, Reed and Morrison hit it off.

* * *

Reed sunk his teeth into a civics course in his first year that he greatly enjoyed; he advocated "free love" and marijuana legalization in class discussions, hardly populist positions in the early '60s. His young professor evidently appreciated his intelligence and, according to Reed, recommended him for honors.

One of Reed's touchstones at this point, which he'd "quote extensively" in his civics class, as he'd write to Littman, was Norman Mailer's button-pushing essay "The White Negro." A sensation when it was first published in 1957 in Irving Howe's left-radical journal *Dissent*, it was republished as a stand-alone volume by Lawrence Ferlinghetti's City Lights Books, home to Jack Kerouac and other Beat luminaries. Subtitled "Superficial Reflections on the Hipster," it's a nine-thousand-word go-for-broke attempt to out-Beat the Beats, as Mailer's frenemy James Baldwin put it, a dissertation on "American existentialism" full of dubious notions about race, masculinity, and male sexuality. (Baldwin, who found it an infuriating resurrection of damaging Black stereotypes, dismissed it, with a wink perhaps, as "downright impenetrable.") But the appeal of the essay to a certain type of late-1950s white male college student—especially one enthralled by Black culture—is easy to see. Following an epigraph invoking James Dean, Mailer begins, "Probably, we will never be able to determine the psychic havoc of the concentration camps and the atom bomb upon the unconscious mind of almost everyone alive in these years," and goes on to consider the peril of nuclear annihilation alongside "a slow death by conformity with every creative and rebellious instinct stifled." Mailer goes on to analyze the "American existentialist" or white hipster, a marijuana-smoking "sexual outlaw" besotted with the "danger" of the Black American experience, basically a "philosophical psychopath" who, Mailer posits, "may indeed be the perverted and dangerous front-runner of a new kind of personality which could become the central expression of human nature before the twentieth century is over."

Reed was also a passionate fan of J. D. Salinger, and was thrilled when he came upon a stash of old *New Yorker* magazines filled with his stories. Born and bred in Manhattan, Salinger was cool-eyed but deeply empathetic of human failings, with a remarkable ear for the rhythm of vernacular. Salinger also liked to shock; he was skilled with plot twists and not above O. Henry endings. Reed was fascinated by Seymour Glass, the recurring J. D. Salinger character—vaudeville brat, poet, PhD, psychoanalysis patient, war veteran, possible pedophile. Glass is probably best remembered for his stage exit in the final sentence of "A Perfect Day for Bananafish," which described him sitting next to his sleeping wife in a posh Miami Beach hotel room, placing an Ortgies 7.65 mm pistol against his head, and pulling the trigger.

Another class that semester seems to have had a powerful effect on Reed, a religion class with Dr. Gabriel Vahanian. The thirty-four-year-old French-Armenian professor and poet had just published *The Death of God: The Culture of Our Post-Christian Era*, which side-eyed the era's prescriptive proselytizing pop stars, among them Norman Vincent Peale (author of *The Power of Positive Thinking*) and Billy Graham, while suggesting that more authentic Christian spirituality could better be found amid post-Christian cultural enterprise and human creativity. Reed thought Vahanian's book was great, and struck up a friendship with the professor, attending parties at his house and even helping him shop for furniture. Vahanian recalled Reed as a talented student with a "chip on his shoulder" who wasn't averse to an argument, and who wanted to "rewrite" religion, "like everyone in those days."

* * *

Not all Reed's classes went well. Interested in writing, he took a journalism course, which he described to Littman as a "farce." He had a run-in with a professor who accused him of being "insolent" and "arrogant" by writing a piece that attacked the university chancellor; Reed bragged that he "made" a young woman the teacher was attempting to date as revenge. Reed's second semester seems to have been a trainwreck. For starters, he lost his slot on the campus radio station, which mostly programmed classical music and theater tunes, and could not defend his mix of cutting-edge jazz and smart-ass attitude. "The wrath of the faculty and administration rained down on me," said Katharine Barr, the student director of the station at the time. "I had no choice but to let him go."

Meanwhile, after months of badgering, Allan Hyman finally convinced his friend to attend a fraternity recruitment rush. As Hyman tells it, when Reed turned up at the Sammies house party, he was dressed like he'd just crawled out of a dumpster: filthy shirt, tie covered with food stains and knotted askew. People were aghast, assuming a local derelict had wandered in. And Hyman was horrified—he'd pledged to the Sammies and took frat life seriously.

One of the well-dressed brothers shook hands with Hyman, then extended his hand to Reed, who ignored it.

"So, what do you call that outfit?" the young man asked. "Why would you think we'd want you to be a member of this fraternity, dressed that way? You look . . . stupid."

"I wouldn't join this fucking fraternity if you paid me," Reed said. "And you are the biggest asshole that I've ever met. As far as I'm concerned, I hope that you die soon."

"If you propose him for membership, I will blackball him," the young man later told Hyman. "How come you hang out with somebody like that? What's wrong with you?"

Hyman had to escort Reed out of the party. "What were you thinking?" Hyman said. "You're supposed to be my friend."

"You're the one that persuaded me to come," Reed shot back. "I didn't want to. I figured as long as I'm gonna be there, I'm gonna have some fun. There's *no way* I'm joining a fraternity."

* * *

In the summer of 1961, home on Long Island, Reed played a handful of gigs with the Valets. He also began spending time at the Hayloft, a clandestine but widely known gay club in nearby Baldwin that doubled as a hangout for college kids from nearby Hofstra and Adelphi. Men could dance with men at the Hayloft, and women with women, without being harassed. When the poet Rudy Kikel was attending

St. John's University in Queens in the early '60s, he recalled, he brought his straight sister to the Hayloft to introduce her to his world. After seeing him kiss a male friend, she ran out of the bar, crying.

One crowded weekend, Reed met Jehu Martin there, a similarly wide-eyed college student also home for the summer. "Lou was less cruising for guys than just fascinated by gay culture," Martin recalls. The pair became friendly with some of the older regulars. "Lou really wanted to know what the scene was all about." It's possible Reed crossed paths there with a regular who would later become a muse. In 1961, James Lawrence Slattery was beginning to cross-dress, and studying at the nearby DeVern School of Cosmetology; the Hayloft became the future Candy Darling's home away from home.

Barnlike, with a T-shaped interior, the club had a dance floor edged with tables and a small stage abutted by one long bar. Occasionally fights broke out. But the bouncers—male, female, and otherwise— were formidable and it was largely a tame scene. Still, the chutzpah it took for a teen to hang out in a gay club in the early '60s should not be underestimated. Reed bussed tables for a while. "I remember asking him what it was like working there," says Rich Sigal. "He said, 'Oh, it's not bad. When you're walking around, every once in a while somebody will grab your crotch.' He said it kind of laughingly. And I accepted it that way." Years later, Reed would tell a journalist from Long Island's *Newsday* it was the area's best-ever dance floor: "great dancing, great people."

* * *

Writing to Littman during his first year at Syracuse, Reed disparaged the women he'd met as "stupid," "insipid," and "materialistic." But his tune changed at the start of his second year when he met Shelley Albin, a startlingly pretty freshman who was raised in a North Shore suburb of Chicago. Their relationship would be the most consequential romance of his early life.

"I was driving along with some fraternity guy I'd met," Albin recalls, "and he said, 'Oh, there's my friend Lou. I'll give him a ride. He's really dangerous.' And I remember thinking: *This guy is dangerous?* He had the build of a twelve-year-old."

They stopped, flirtation ensued; Reed got Albin's number and called her at her dorm shortly afterward. "It was all pretty fast, pretty direct. And that was that—we were together. Sort of inseparable, for as long as it was." Reed and Albin were a couple for a year and a half. Hook-ups aside, she was his first real girlfriend.

His family and friends were impressed. Sigal described her as "absolutely knock-out gorgeous." For Reed's sister, "it was hero worship at an epic level," she says. "I met her when I was thirteen. She was *so* beautiful. I just thought she was divine and delightful. So did my parents." Reed's parents were so impressed when he brought Albin home over Christmas break, they immediately raised his allowance. "They wanted him to treat her well," his sister says.

Albin wanted to pursue art, and had hoped to go to college at Berkeley, but her parents nixed the idea—too far away, too libertine. Her cousin was an artist-in-residence at Syracuse University, and her brother attended nearby Cornell, so she headed off to upstate New York. "I was supposed to be safe with my big brother watching me," Albin says. "That was the theory, anyway."

As a freshman, Albin's dorm curfew was 9:00 p.m. Men were prohibited from crossing the lobby threshold. "They literally had police at the doors, and if you wanted to go out on the weekends, the school had to have a note from your parents. And you still couldn't go out past nine p.m."

Reed, meanwhile, had switched dorms for his sophomore year, from Watson to a basement room in the newly built Sadler Hall. "I'd talk to [him] through the window; it was below ground level," Albin recalls. "It was like looking into an animal pit."

Reed's pit-mate was Lincoln Swados. Born into a well-to-do Jewish family, Swados grew up in Buffalo, coming of age as an eccentric kid with artistic drive. "As early as eighth grade he began writing prolifically, and his papers were stuffed in sock drawers and shoved under dressers," recounted his sister, the playwright Elizabeth Swados, in her family memoir *The Four of Us*; "the India ink from his drawings spilled into multicolored stains." Her brother also had a major problem with authority. He caused chaos in the private school he attended, and was soon removed: "He sodomized several boys in the locker room. He ran naked through chapel. He sold marijuana at lunch. He stole indiscriminately," his sister wrote. Rejected for a date, Swados put his hand through a window in frustration, needing stitches. He was also a music fanatic. At home, he played Frank Sinatra records around the clock, sometimes at thunderous volume. For his senior variety show, he sang a medley of darkly comic songs by Tom Lehrer, including "Poisoning Pigeons in the Park" and "Masochism Tango."

Reed and Swados were a good match. "Neither one fit in, though Lou fit in more," says Albin, who was also close with Swados. "They both had little sisters they were protective of. Lincoln was quite a sweetheart. We knew he was a little strange. Lou picked up and copied a lot of his behavior. . . . Mannerisms, inflections; things to make himself more interesting, [though] he was interesting enough by himself. Little dramatic touches that Lincoln had but had no clue he had, Lou would make his own. Like an actor."

Their dorm room was a virtual art installation of trash and disorder. Rich Sigal recalls the first time he visited Reed at Syracuse. "The room was pitch black in the middle of the afternoon, and there was stuff all over the floor, books piled up, clothing, just a disaster . . . I see a hand hanging out of the bed, so I peel back the covers and there's Lou. The sheet was covered with writing—like if he'd had a thought in his head, or a poem to write, instead of getting a piece of paper, he'd write it on the sheet."

* * *

In the fall of 1962, Joan Baez was on the cover of *Time*, a remarkable feat for a musician, let alone a woman performing traditional folk songs. She was all of twenty-one, just a year older than Reed. He and Albin saw her perform in Syracuse. Baez sang in a dazzlingly pure alto, an angel chronicling sinners, often in first person. She was also an accomplished fingerpicker; the rushing pattern on her recording of "Silver Dagger," for instance, channeled a fierce pulse of anxiety beneath the measured unspooling of catastrophic news. As Bob Dylan, who released his debut LP that year, would write in his memoir, Baez performed folk music "in an expert way, beyond criticism, beyond category. There was no one in her class. She was far off and unattainable—Cleopatra living in an Italian palace. When she sang, she made your teeth drop."

Despite the school's preppy, frats-and-football culture, the folk music revival had taken root at Syracuse. "There were a couple guys who played banjo and a couple who played guitar who were good," Albin says, adding they played "real folk music—not Peter, Paul and Mary crap." Reed would sometimes take his guitar outside and join them, occasionally singing along. He was briefly part of a quartet that played at the Clam Shack, a local dive. Albin remembers Reed playing harmonica on a rack around his neck. "But he didn't play it in public," she notes, "because Dylan was doing it."

Privately was another story. Reed recorded himself playing a bluesy version of Dylan's "Don't Think Twice, It's All Right" around this time, which showed his harmonica-playing on-point, his Travis-picking technique a bit unsteady. ("Oh, you cock*sucker*!" he mutters in frustration after one flub.) On the same tape, he also made a game attempt at "Blowin' in the Wind" and the spiritual "Michael, Row the Boat Ashore," a recent number 1 pop hit by the milquetoast folkies the Highwaymen. Reed earnestly whispered the "hal-le-lu-jahs" as if hoping not to disturb anyone in the next room, or maybe just from embarrassment.

* * *

Meanwhile, a small rock 'n' roll scene was taking shape in Syracuse. The big band on campus was Felix and the Escorts, an R&B outfit fronted by Felix Cavaliere, a Westchester premed student who'd go on to launch the hit-making Young Rascals of "Good Lovin'" renown.

Rich Sigal recalls Reed raving about a guy named Felix who studied classical piano and could really work a crowd. "In those days he was 'Lewis Allan,'" Cavaliere recalled. "I think he auditioned for the Escorts one time—kind of an odd guy who wasn't all that good on guitar."

Unable to connect with an established band, Reed assembled his own in late '61/early '62 and named it L.A. and the Eldorados, the initials standing for Lewis Allan. A snapshot of a performance in front of the Sammy house shows Reed in a dark cable-knit sweater over a light shirt, playing a hollow-body electric guitar with a tight smile.

"We played a lot of Ray Charles—'What'd I Say,' '(Night Time Is) The Right Time'—and Jimmy Reed," says the bassist, Rich Mishkin. "Half the stuff we'd start, then Lou would just make shit up as we'd go along."

"We got thrown out of a lot of gigs because of Lou," Hyman recalls. "He would never just cover a song. He would always add one of his outrageous lyrics, which usually included the word *fuck*."

Reed was also writing, and was accepted into the English department's new creative writing workshop ("[It] felt great," he wrote to Littman of the validation). But Reed was unimpressed by the student literary journal, *Syracuse 10*, which he thought was too slick and establishment. So Reed, Swados, and a few other coconspirators launched their own samizdat-style publication. The first issue of *The Lonely Woman Quarterly*—named for the Ornette Coleman tune Reed so admired—appeared in early May 1962. It was printed on the mimeograph machine at the Savoy diner, the group's salon when they weren't at the Orange bar down the street. The journal's first run was seventy-five copies, which they sold at the Savoy for twenty-five cents each, banking the money for production of the next issue.

The introduction, bylined "THE EDITORS" but likely written by Reed, invokes a complacent Syracuse art scene and a "vociferous underground . . . gnashing its rabid molars," with a snipe at the conservative activist group Young Americans for Freedom (YAF) and their "navalmesmerized" leader, presumably William F. Buckley Jr. The first piece is a one-page, three-paragraph, untitled sketch credited to "Luis Reed" that begins:

He'd always found the idea of copulation distasteful.

The piece describes an Oedipal-scatalogical drama involving a preadolescent boy who kisses his own image in the mirror and fantasizes about his mother's touch. It also involves domestic abuse; at one point during their embrace, the mother says to her son, "Daddy hurt Mommy last night."

There is also a short untitled poem by Reed, which begins with a narrator and a woman in bed; moves to Washington Square Park, apparently, with its "little cement chess tables"; turns abstract amid pretentious invocations of Dostoyevsky and Sade; and ends at a friend's apartment with a bottle-spinning party game called "truth":

I lie like crazy. You have to it's a matter of discreet protection, but the others have a propensity toward self-exposure, a movement towards the confessional.

The poem's "Epilogue" describes a man who climbs atop a rock, possibly with the intent to commit suicide, but instead floats up to the sky:

there was a man who saw too much

he saw too far too deep

Promoting the *Quarterly*, Swados told a reporter for the student newspaper a bogus story about how the journal's title was inspired by an imaginary beat poet; Reed was identified by the name "Luis" in the article, a "liberal arts student and sometime singer with a campus rock n' roll band." It was apparently Reed's first bit of press, and his first observation of how easy it was to bullshit a journalist.

* * *

Reed tried to play the role of good boyfriend at Syracuse. He even put on a suit and attended a dance at Sigma Delta Tau—Albin had pledged in order to leave the dorms and move into the sorority cottage, which offered fewer social restrictions.

"Shelley and I double-dated to the dance," recalls Patricia Volk, Albin's sorority sister and fellow art student. "We all got in a car together, and Lou looked very pained, sitting there in his suit. He did not want to be there." Volk considered Shelley "the most beautiful girl on campus, in a very unstudied way," and she couldn't understand what she saw in Reed, who was smaller than her. "He was intense. He would have scared me."

Reed had lost touch with David Weisman, who had pledged to AEP and was drawn into frat life. But they reconnected in April to see a new film at the local Regent Theatre: Fellini's *La Dolce Vita*. The men were dazzled, and it fired up their imaginations so much, they stayed awake talking until dawn. Weisman was having a crisis—his mother's mental health situation hadn't improved, and his family had serious money problems. He recalled making the decision that night to drop out of Syracuse, go to Italy, and try to work with Fellini.

"You are really crazy," Reed told him.

But in fact, that's just what Weisman did, successfully. *La Dolce Vita* foretold Reed's future a bit, too. At one point in the film, a beautiful blonde drifts into Marcello Mastroianni's path at a café and spirits him off to a party at her fiancé's castle. In the credits, the actor was identified as Nico Otzak, her character simply as Nico.

Reed attended classes in film and theater directing, though he didn't muster the nerve to take an acting class per se. There's some evidence he directed a modest production of *Le Cimetière des Voitures* (The Automobile Graveyard), a satiric tragedy written by the Spanish surrealist Fernando Arrabal Terán full of sex and cruelty, ending with the crucifixion of a musician. (Reed did not cast himself in the role, though he appeared in another, nonspeaking one.) Around this time Reed also directed a 16mm short for his filmmaking class. Peter Maloney, a *Lonely Woman Quarterly* contributor and one of the theater department's star students, was cast as a clown, "because every student film had to have a carnival and a clown," he says. "It was the Fellini effect."

* * *

The second issue of *The Lonely Woman Quarterly* was published just weeks after the first, and it was a prank from the get-go.

There was a joke about the source of the journal's name (now attributed to "Pliny the elder") and an ostensibly nonfiction piece by "Luis" Reed: an amusingly vicious profile of one of Reed's classmates, "the reptilian treasurer of the Young Democrats," whom he described as a Zionist with an American flag "placed neatly up his rectum." It bore the clear influence of Lenny Bruce, whose LP debut, *The Sick Humor of Lenny Bruce*, had come out in 1959, and whom Reed admired; Rich Sigal recalled him mimicking the comic's outrageous language and jazzbo cadences. Full of grammatical errors, likely dashed off, the essay reportedly set off the student's father, a high-powered lawyer, who contacted the school. Reed was called onto the carpet by the dean and told to watch his step.

Reed's sidekick Swados had two pieces in the issue, both quite dark. A poem titled "The Nightingale" begins "Lost in the land of nighttime / I have crashed into trees." His father soon drove up to Syracuse to fetch his son, who began a journey in and out of mental institutions for the next five years. The diagnosis was schizophrenia with paranoid tendencies; his treatments included electroshock therapy.

That summer, and in the years to come, his sister missed him dearly. As her own therapy, Elizabeth Swados practiced guitar for hours a day in her room, putting to use lessons in Travis picking she'd gotten from Reed in Syracuse when she'd visited. She also began writing songs, and got quite good at it.

* * *

Reed was at loose ends over the 1962 summer break. He wrote to Shelley often. One letter contained a short story of his that he'd repurpose in a number of years. The story involved a young man and woman, presumably dating, who have been separated during the summer and are living in different states. The heartsick and worried young man, Waldo, low on funds, decides to package himself in a box and mail himself to his beloved. When the package arrives, the girl, Marsha, and her friend try to open it, unsuccessfully. Finally, in a fit of frustration, Marsha's friend plunges sheet metal shears through the box and into

Waldo's skull. Shortly after getting the letter, Shelley received a large box from Reed—containing an oversized teddy bear.

"He could be very funny and sweet when he wanted to be," she says.

While Albin was dating boys back home in Chicago, Reed was spending nights at the Hayloft. Albin recalls letters from him detailing the sexual escapades there quite explicitly, perhaps in tit-for-tat gestures of jealousy, to exercise his need to shock, or both. Reed was stirring up trouble elsewhere. Rich Sigal had arranged a double date for himself and Reed one night, and describes Reed arriving at his house with another girl passed out in the back seat of his car. ("Oh, don't worry about her," Reed told his furious friend.) Later that night, when Reed, wasted, broke an expensive cocktail glass belonging to Sigal's parents, his friend nearly pummeled him. "I remember taking a handkerchief out and wrapping it around my knuckles, because I was just going to unload one. Why I didn't hit him, I don't know."

Toward the end of the summer, Reed decided to fly to Chicago to visit Shelley. She tried to discourage him, knowing it would be a disaster. Her mother had found some of Reed's letters, and was not impressed. But Reed would not be deterred. Unsurprisingly, Albin's conservative parents didn't like his shaggy-haired appearance, and Reed got into a political discussion with Albin's father, just to jerk his chain. Reed borrowed her parents' family car to take Shelley out, and ran it into a ditch, half-wrecking it, and not getting Albin home until 1 a.m.

After Reed headed to the airport, Albin's parents forbade her to have anything to do with him ever again.

* * *

In February 1942, just days before Lewis Reed was born, Delmore Schwartz stepped off a train in Penn Station with his pal John Berryman. The poets, both in their twenties, came to town for Presidents Day weekend from Boston, where they taught in Harvard's English department. Schwartz, born in Brooklyn and raised in Washington Heights, was already a literary celebrity, shooting to fame at twenty-five with the story and poem collection *In Dreams Begin Responsibilities*. It was grounded in the New York City immigrant experience. Irving Howe called Schwartz "a comedian of alienation," and described his writing voice as a mix of "the sing-song, slightly pompous intonations of Jewish immigrants educated in night schools [and] the self-conscious affectionate mockery of that speech by American-born sons, its abstraction into the jargon of city intellectuals . . . the whole body of this language flattened into a prose of uneasiness, an anti-rhetoric." Formally, it was a hot-blooded hot-wiring of T. S. Eliot's fastidious modernism (which, twenty-plus years on, was ripe for generational overhaul)—a heady, precociously tragic vision shot through with self-aware irony. One literary macher called it "the first real innovation we've had since Eliot and Pound." Many others followed suit.

The titular story, "In Dreams Begin Responsibilities," had struck a chord when it first appeared in the *Partisan Review*. Nabokov would call it one of his "half a dozen favorites in modern literature"; Reed, given to superlatives, would insist to the end of his life that it was "the greatest short story ever written." Maybe he related to it. The story's surreal conceit, ultimately revealed as a dream, is of a young man in a theater watching a film of his parents' courtship. During a date on the Coney Island boardwalk, his father proposes marriage:

> . . . and it was then that I stood up in the theatre and shouted: "Don't do it. It's not too late to change your minds, both of you. Nothing good will come of it, only remorse, hatred, scandal, and two children whose characters are monstrous." The whole audience turned to look at me, annoyed, the usher came hurrying down the aisle flashing his searchlight, and the old lady next to me tugged me down into my seat, saying: "Be quiet. You'll be put out, and you paid thirty-five cents to come in." And so I shut my eyes because I could not bear to see what was happening.

Schwartz denied the autobiography in this. But he was in fact an obsessive moviegoer, and his parents did have a scandalously turbulent marriage. When he was seven, his mother dragged him into a Long

Island diner to spectacularly confront her husband, there with another woman. They soon separated, but Schwartz still idolized his father, Harry, a very successful businessman who died young. His sixteen-year-old son expected to inherit a huge sum. But between the stock market crash and sketchy estate handling, the presumed million-dollar inheritance turned out to be a mirage.

Schwartz couldn't sustain his initial success. He labored for years on the multivolume *Genesis*, which might have been the longest poem in the English language had it been completed. But Schwartz published only the first volume, two hundred pages' worth, to decidedly mixed reviews. It was failure on a grand scale. In addition to a crisis of confidence, he struggled through two doomed marriages, along with severe manic-depressive bouts, excessive drinking, and a dependence on amphetamines.

By the time Schwartz landed at Syracuse University in August 1962, he was a wreck. He'd gotten the job through the advocacy of Berryman and Saul Bellow, an early protégé of Schwartz's who would base the title character of his Pulitzer Prize–winning novel *Humboldt's Gift* on his mentor. Schwartz arrived in Syracuse alone. He took a room at a hotel, and within days, following a drunken brawl, needed to be bailed out of the county jail.

As a role model, Schwartz was a dubious choice. Reed first encountered him in a bar. "We drank together starting at eight in the morning," Reed recalled. Though decades his senior, Schwartz was similarly the Jewish, Brooklyn-born son of striving, ambitious Eastern European immigrants, extremely articulate and wry. He was diminished, but could still be dazzling, a poète maudit from whom Reed felt he could learn a lot. Reed signed up for his James Joyce class, which consisted largely of Schwartz reading *Ulysses* aloud—Reed claimed he could understand the novel perfectly when he heard Schwartz reading it, but not at all when he read it. Indeed, Schwartz was a terrifically musical and sonorous reader. At the National Poetry Festival in Washington, D.C., that October, he declaimed the lines of "At a Solemn Musick" in wavelike cadences, one moment as if from a mountaintop, the next as if whispering to a partner on their deathbed:

In love's willing river and love's dear discipline:
We wait, silent, in consent and in the penance
Of patience, awaiting the serene exaltation
Which is the liberation and conclusion of expiation.

Hours after that performance, Schwartz trashed his hotel room in a rage and wound up in jail again, delusional. Berryman, weary and gutted, rescued him, and recalled the incident years later in "Dream Song #149":

I got him out of a police-station once, in Washington, the world is tref
and grief too astray for tears.

At the behest of a colleague, Schwartz spent much of his second semester in a private sanatorium near the college. But he left a powerful impression on his students.

* * *

When Allan Hyman left Syracuse to start law school in Brooklyn, Reed's social life realigned. Richie Mishkin, who grew up hunting with the men in his family, took him into dense woods with a pair of shotguns. Hoping for pheasants, they wound up with rabbits. "Lou bitched a lot," Mishkin says. "It was cold. But we were laughing and had a good time." Mishkin recalls the two men bringing home their catch magnanimously, and their girlfriends cooking it. At some point, Reed decided he wanted to ride a motorcycle, a pursuit that didn't fare much better than his drug adventure. "He bought a secondhand piece of shit," recalls another friend, Peter Locke. "An old Indian, maybe. Lou and I tried to get it going. It'd go around the block, then sputter out . . . He was definitely not a bike rider."

Minus Hyman, L.A. and the Eldorados continued—sometimes under an alias, to skirt reports of Reed's bad behavior. The group now had a manager, the Sammy brother Don Schupack, who had a small business booking bands (including Cavaliere's) for frat parties in the region. "I never found Lou difficult," says Schupack, who recalls Reed as smart, sensitive, and intense, clearly with "unevolved talent." On the basis of a demo tape, since lost, Schupack offered to manage Reed as a songwriter. "Some song he wrote and played mournfully, in a minor key, one of those boyfriend/girlfriend, girl-takes-car, gets-stuck-on-railroad-tracks-and-gets-killed songs," Schupack recalls, laughing. "Horrible. [But] it showed what a desire he had."

Two documents of Reed's music circa 1962, likely recorded during winter break, survived: "Your Love" and "Merry Go Round," both undercooked pop informed by doo-wop and rock 'n' roll. The midtempo "Your Love" begins, "I never thought I was a real whole man 'til your love," Reed rhyming *fire* and *desire* against placid backing vocals, snarling and riding vibrato on his vowels. On "Merry Go Round," an organ-driven number with barbed guitar, he's a hopped-up Dion, literary ambitions on a tight leash: "I walk you home yeah every day from school / But still you treat me like I was a fool."

That fall, Reed moved out of the dorms and into an apartment nearby, where he and Shelley played house. Reed also got a dog, the first in a lifelong series of pets who'd provide unconditional love. He named her after Salinger's Seymour Glass, adding an "e" to Seymour to make it feminine. The two would cuddle and play for hours, though Reed wasn't much for taking care of her; Shelley generally got stuck walking Seymoure, and eventually Reed gifted her to his sister.

Reed's apartment generally reeked of weed, which he'd begun smoking with gusto and selling to classmates. He frequently asked Shelley to hold his supply in her room for safekeeping, which she did, stashing sacks in her closet. Reed was getting into other things, too.

"We drove into Harlem one time when we were visiting his parents," Albin says. "We went up to some musician's apartment and [Lou] picked up a package of something. I don't know what it was. I never asked."

* * *

By the end of the fall semester, Shelley Albin had reached her limit with Reed and his dramas, and broke things off. "I'd just had enough," she says. "It was a small campus, we had the same friends, [but] I did not see him if I could avoid it."

When Reed came back from winter break for the spring semester of his junior year in January 1963, there was no Shelley, no Lincoln, no Allan Hyman, and no Delmore Schwartz. In their absence, Reed seems to have focused mostly on drugs, music, and writing. A third issue of *The Lonely Woman Quarterly* included "And What, Little Boy, Will You Trade for Your Horse?" It was written by Reed in third person omniscient, channeling the point of view of "David ———", a college kid in an army surplus jacket who haunts the subway at night:

> *His hair is long. He wears glasses and looks very tired, his eyes closing, head slowly falling between his knees, like someone on junk, jarred back to momentary attention by the trains [sic] jerks and spurts, and then once again to sleep.*

On the street in Times Square, Reed's long-haired character sees an old man pick up a "dungareed boy" and usher him into a cab. He sees another gang of young boys, "very gay . . . mincing and giggling. But they are dangerous." He describes publications in an adult bookstore. He walks into a dive bar and orders a beer. The bartender scoffs at his ID, convinced he is underage—to which he responds, or imagines responding, "You should see me in drag." She serves him anyway, and he drinks his beer, thinking of song lyrics. Suddenly, a barfly seated next to him leans in and pushes her tongue into his ear. Her name is Jane. They banter, she buys him a couple of whiskeys, then tells him he must now do exactly what she wants, "to the letter." To which he replies "Yes, sir," and prepares to leave with her.

The writing had a whiff of Hubert Selby Jr.'s "Tralala," a story Reed had likely encountered (Selby's *Last Exit to Brooklyn* would be published the following year). Reed came to admire Selby's economy of language, and his fearlessness. "Who am I to edit out whatever's coming out of the mind to be written?" Selby would tell Reed years later, discussing his writing process. "Who am I to stand in the way of it, who am I to say 'this is not allowed' or 'this is tasteless'?"

* * *

Reed's final year in school gave him reason to be optimistic, at least at the start. That fall, Schwartz returned to teaching, and Reed enrolled in two courses with him: a writing workshop, and a lecture course focused largely on Eliot and Joyce, titled "Special Problems in English Literature." To cultivate an appreciation for Joyce's mastery of realism, Schwartz suggested that his students simply walk around Syracuse and observe the details. He laid out the idea that art combined lived experience with the fabricated. Speaking with a lisp, smoking like a chimney, wrapped in a rumpled jacket and tie (he sometimes slept off boozing binges on his office couch), he was sharp-tongued, funny, ironic, harsh, and by all accounts dazzling, an ivory-tower mad-hobo genius exalting art's holiness. One imagines Reed hanging on every word.

Schwartz recognized Reed's talent. "Delmore loved Lou, *loved* him," recalls Liz Annas, an art student and single mom who was close to Schwartz at the time. "He knew Lou was going to be famous, and he said so. I looked at this guy sitting on his dirty, disgusting bed strumming his guitar, and thought, *You've got to be kidding!* But Delmore was an incredible judge of character. He knew."

Reed's senior-year classes with Schwartz regularly spilled over into the Orange bar. "We used to meet there every day, four p.m.," said Reed's friend Garland Jeffreys, a student from the Bronx who'd become a successful singer-songwriter himself, with a knack for storytelling he shared with Reed. "Delmore would be the wise old man sitting on the side while we were chattering away—the mohair-sweater-and-Corvette folks, and us, the pre-hippie, funky, faux-songwriters." Schwartz drank copiously at these salons; he once ordered himself five drinks at once (he could hold his liquor, though as one co-ed recalled, he could get handsy when drunk). While Jeffreys and Reed bonded over their love of doo-wop, especially Frankie Lymon, Schwartz had little interest in what he termed "cat-gut music." He thought Reed should set his sights on studying at Harvard.

"I am a writer," Lou would insist over empty glasses in a back booth. "I'm just going to use music."

"No, no, no—you can't stick it in the music, it's worthless!" Delmore would respond, hitting the wooden table.

One night, Schwartz told Albin—still part of the Orange crowd—that she needed to assist Reed. "You have to do whatever he wants. You have to give up your life for him to be famous," she recalls Schwartz insisting. "You have to give up your whole life and be there for Lou."

"No, I don't," she responded.

"Yes, you do!" Schwartz insisted, "You have to! You have to!"

Albin believes Reed had the same idea, but maybe "[didn't] know enough to verbalize it at that point."

There may have been some romantic element to Reed's affection for Schwartz—still a handsome man, over six feet tall and striking, with full lips and a penetrating gaze. Schwartz was at best uneasy with homosexuality, although it held a fascination for him. In any case, Reed loved Schwartz for his wit and intelligence, and marveled at his poetry. At times, he even served as Schwartz's chaperone-nurse-bodyguard, accompanying him to faculty cocktail parties where the poet would come unhinged. Reed imagined himself the animal keeper for the alter ego of Schwartz's poem "The Heavy Bear That Goes with Me," a poem that would linger in his mind:

A stupid clown of the spirit's motive
Perplexes and affronts with his own darkness

Years later, Reed remembered his shame when Schwartz gave a B grade to a story he'd submitted. Reed also recalled a threat. "Lou, I swear—and you know if anyone could I could—you Lou must never write for money or I will haunt you."

* * *

Reed earned decent money as a musician during his senior year. The Eldorados had a standing Friday night gig at the Tecumseh Golf Course, $25 a man. There were out-of-town gigs, too. The group's biggest-ever booking was at St. Lawrence University, a well-heeled private school near the Canadian border in Canton, N.Y. "A thousand bucks for the weekend," Richie Mishkin recalls. "A Friday night mixer, a Saturday day boat party, and the big event Saturday night: homecoming."

They brought their new singer, Nelson Slater, a precocious military brat and Elvis fan from Cincinnati who came to Syracuse on an art scholarship. ("A good-looking tall guy—he could sing his ass off," Mishkin says.) Friday night went well, until Reed started balking about the next day's gig.

"I'm not playing on the fucking boat," Reed said. "I get seasick. And I don't want to get electrocuted."

"Lou, you're from Freeport!" Mishkin argued. "You've been on boats your whole life! You're not going to get seasick, you're not going to get electrocuted. Shut up and do it! We're getting paid a fortune."

"Fuck you," Reed said. "I'm *not* playing on the fucking boat." To drive home his point, Reed punched out a hallway window in the frat house, slicing his left hand up badly.

His bandmates got him to a local ER, where he got stitches in his ring finger. The next day, Reed was on the boat, guitar in hand, somehow forming chords with his unbandaged fingers.

"It didn't affect his playing at all," Slater recalls, still surprised, fifty years later.

* * *

On November 3, having just finished the last sessions for *The Times They Are a-Changin'*, Bob Dylan played the University Regent Theatre in Syracuse. Mishkin and Reed were there, and both were impressed. The Eldorados soon worked up a version of "Baby, Let Me Follow You Down," with Reed playing harmonica.

Later that month, President John F. Kennedy was assassinated. Reed would maintain that the descriptions in his 1982 song "The Day John Kennedy Died" were "literally, exactly what happened." It recalls him sitting in a bar, likely the Orange, with the Orangemen playing on TV, when the news began coming through. "Talking stopped, someone shouted, "what!?" / I ran out to the street," Reed narrates. People compared what they knew, reports were incomplete. He was shot. Maybe dying. Then some trust-fund kid in a Porsche leaned on his horn and announced that the president was indeed dead.

"It was a devastating thing for me," Reed said. "I thought Kennedy could change the world." Indeed, a generation looked to Kennedy—the youngest president in history, elected at forty-three—and Jackie Onassis as a later one would the Obamas. Even that nascent counterculture skeptic Bob Dylan was impressed. "If I had been a voting man," he affirmed in his memoir decades later, "I would have voted for Kennedy."

Reed's soon-to-be mentor, Andy Warhol, star ascendant in New York City, wept at the news in the arms of his boyfriend, John Giorno. And the assassination sent Delmore Schwartz off the rails. Sterling Morrison— who'd returned to Syracuse to try to hustle enough financial aid to enroll and wound up auditing Schwartz's "Significant Modern Writers" class with Reed—recalled Schwartz's paranoid delusions involving Nelson Rockefeller, then governor of New York: "[Delmore] eventually . . . decided that Lou and I were both Rockefeller's spies," Morrison said.

Morrison joined the salon at the Orange, and began playing guitar regularly with Reed. According to Morrison, the first song they did together was Ike and Tina Turner's "It's Gonna Work Out Fine."

* * *

Following winter break, in January 1964, Reed returned to Syracuse for his final semester. One frosty night, he was a few rounds in at the Orange with Schwartz and Jim Gorney, a first-year grad student in creative writing, and a new song came on the jukebox: the Beatles' "I Wanna Hold Your Hand."

"It was so fantastic that we kept throwing nickels in—must have played the damn song ten, fifteen times," Gorney recalls. "The three of us started singing along! It was the first time any of us had heard the Beatles, I think. We left the bar, it was snowing, and we continued singing as we went down the street. It was one of those joyous moments."

It was an out-of-character moment for Schwartz, the pop hater—and

Gorney, a classical music devotee. Gorney recalls a night when he and Reed listened to Alban Berg's dark, war-scarred opera *Wozzeck*. Drawn from an unfinished play by the German romantic Georg Büchner, it was the tale of a disempowered, destitute soldier who, among other degradations, finds himself at the mercy of a doctor's experiments, a scenario that likely struck home for Reed. The 1951 recording was of Dmitri Mitropolous conducting the New York Philharmonic, with its potently dissonant orchestrations and sinewy displays of *sprechstimme*, or speak-singing. "We played it several times, very closely following the words and the music," Gorney recalls; "he was absolutely gripped by [it]." Berg's work was branded "degenerate" by the Nazis, and he died in 1935 in the midst of writing a second opera, an adaptation of two violent, scandalously sexual Frank Wedekind plays, titled *Lulu*, a story Reed would engage with decades later.

At the moment, however, he was trying to graduate, and still dealing weed. He showed up at Gorney's one night with "probably two kilos" stuffed into a suitcase, and asked Gorney to stash it in his basement storage locker. "The deal was he got me to hold this stuff and I got to use some of it," Gorney says, remembering it as a mixed blessing. "I think it somewhat undercut my performance at school."

Gorney doesn't know when Reed first tried heroin, but Shelley Albin heard about it that spring. "He started using [it]. Once or twice, or who knows, not that much—in the end of my junior year, his senior year."

Why did Reed go there? Why not? he might've replied. He'd already learned consciousness was a chemistry set, between booze and cannabis in high school, then ECT and anti-anxiety meds. His impulse may have been basic hedonism, adolescent risk-taking, and/or the desire for bragging rights, informed by the aura of criminal coolness surrounding heroin, and the undying myth linking it to musical creativity, especially in the world of the jazz musicians he admired. It might've been an existential temptation. And it might've been creative writing field research, in service of the sort of "lived experience" Schwartz taught him was at the core of great literature. William S. Burroughs's groundbreaking *Naked Lunch*—a frank dissection of heroin use, among other things, rooted in the author's "lived experience"—was brand-new, published in the United States in 1962 and swiftly banned in Boston for alleged obscenity. Reed had surely read it.

Whatever drew him to try heroin, it didn't go well: in his telling, he contracted hepatitis from sharing a hypodermic needle. Albin remembers him calling to tell her the news. Reed was sick for a while, during which time it's likely he began writing two songs pertinent to the experience: "Heroin" and "I'm Waiting for the Man."

The first centered on the experience of shooting heroin, with precise and fantastical language: the sensation of a needle hitting a vein, the rush of the drug's onset, the ecstatically swaddled nihilism of its effect. The finished lyrics would declare that the act made the narrator feel like "he's a man," and how he hopes to erase the "crazy sounds" made by politicians and visions of dead bodies "piled up in mounds"—a reference to the Holocaust that killed millions of Reed's Jewish kin in Europe, maybe, or any number of atrocities across history—each verse ending with a stoned shrug of "I guess I just don't know."

Reed later explained:

At the time I wrote "Heroin," I felt like a very rather negative, strung-out, violent, aggressive person. I meant [it] to sort of exorcise the darkness, or the self-destructive element in me, and hoped that other people would take [it] the same way. "Heroin" is very close to the feeling you get from smack. It starts on a certain level, it's deceptive. You think you're enjoying it. But by the time it hits you, it's too late. You don't have any choice. It comes at you harder and faster and keeps on coming.

"I'm Waiting for the Man" dramatized the rodent-like ritual of procuring a fix from a dealer, "the man," which Reed rhymed neatly with "twenty-six dollars in my hand." Along with whatever bits of memoir he salted in (e.g., his Harlem shopping trip with Shelley), it reflected the bedrock junkie truth Burroughs laid out in *Naked Lunch*: the two tenets of a pusher's "basic principles of monopoly" are to "always catch the buyer hungry, and always make him wait"—those last words mirrored almost exactly in Reed's verses. "Heroin" similarly echoed

Burroughs in its vivid descriptions; among them, the exchange in the book's opening pages about an unfortunate character who unwittingly fixes up with a poisoned "hot shot."

> *He never got the needle out of his arm. They don't if the shot is right.*
> *That's the way they find them, dropper full of clotted blood hanging out*
> *of a blue arm. The look in his eyes when it hit—Kid, it was tasty . . .*

Reed was luckier, but the hepatitis interrupted his heroin experiments for the moment.

* * *

As Reed was recuperating, Albin was suffering from disabling migraines—and the ailing couple reconnected for a few weeks that spring to take care of each other. With her boyfriend out of town, Reed brought Albin to his apartment to convalesce, and petitioned her English professor, the poet Phillip Booth, to pass her in spite of missing classes. (Reed would even stay past graduation to help her recover and pack for her trip home.) As Shelley recalls, they were "happy as clams" for those few weeks. But her feelings for Reed remained conflicted at best, and when he left school that summer, Albin wasn't sure she'd see him again.

Though he'd managed to graduate, and even made the dean's list in his last semester, Reed departed Syracuse in a cloud of trouble. It was a small city, the police noticed troublemakers, and Reed was on their radar; Albin claims she and a friend flirted with a couple of younger cops one time, hoping to discourage them from hassling Reed. Upon accepting an award from his alma mater decades later, Reed noted he missed graduation, alluding to a claim that the police had threatened to arrest him on the spot if he attended the ceremony. Then again, he may have simply wanted to skip the bogus pageantry.

Either way, Reed never showed up for convocation, and the outlaw tale became part of a mythology whose construction, by the time he landed in New York City, was already under way.

3.

LONG ISLAND > QUEENS (COMMUTING) > LOWER EAST SIDE

(1965)

DISCUSSED: The Vietnam War, Pickwick Records, La Monte Young, John Cale, Tony Conrad, Jack Smith, Piero Heliczer, Angus Mac-Lise, the Film-Makers' Cinematheque, Jonas Mekas, Maureen "Moe" Tucker, Barbara Rubin, Edie Sedgwick, Allen Ginsberg, Summit High School, Max's Kansas City, the Factory, Gerard Malanga

---

Let the musicians begin,
Let every instrument awaken and instruct us
   —Delmore Schwartz, "At a Solemn Musick"

Reed must've had a miserable homecoming: college done, bands shelved, reunion with Albin suspended, no job, and still sick from hepatitis. Furthermore, with his school deferment expired, he had to report to the local draft board. The Vietnam War was heating up, and resistance to it at home was simmering; New York City saw its first notable protest, largely by students, in Times Square that May.

In Reed's telling, he prepped for his draft interview by chewing capsules of Placidyl—a sedative-hypnotic he may have been prescribed by his psychiatrist. When he went to his appointment, he put on a show. "I said I wanted a gun and would shoot anyone or anything in front of me," he'd later write. Ultimately, it was likely the combination of his mental health history and his hepatitis that branded him unfit and saved him from the draft. ("It was the one thing that my shock treatments were good for," he conceded.)

Reed's second lucky break came from his Syracuse band manager, Don Schupack, who'd begun doing business with Philip Teitelbaum, a Brooklyn-born kid who'd worked his way into the songwriting business. After a stint in Jerry Leiber and Mike Stoller's song mill, working alongside up-and-comers like Phil Spector and Paul Simon, Teitelbaum (pen name Terry Philips) signed on with Pickwick Records, a label specializing in reissues and discount knock-offs of popular styles.

Pickwick marketed LPs at around $2 each—standard LPs were $3.98—in supermarkets and discount stores like Woolworth's and Korvettes. They made money; by 1964, they had deals with major labels to press and distribute budget "Best Of" reissues by major acts. The "original" music Pickwick recorded, however, was disposable schlock, but it shifted units. Philips needed hungry songwriters who could work fast and cheap; Schupack thought Reed might be a good fit.

He didn't cut a very impressive figure. Reed "didn't have anything together," Philips recalled. "He was sad. He was this insecure guy. He didn't even believe in his own talent." Philips hired him anyway, maybe in part because Pickwick's owner, Cy Leslie, was a Syracuse alum. Schupack was willing to release Reed from their contract. "I didn't think I could spend the kind of time, or necessarily had the contacts, to help him in the next stage of his career," Reed's first manager recalls. Philips agreed to pay Reed $25 a week, with zero ownership rights to the material he produced. To seal the deal, he paid a visit to the Reed house. "His father wanted to meet me," said Philips, noting that Reed's parents were practically "kissing my ring."

So, like thousands of his suburban neighbors, the newly minted college graduate rode the LIRR from Freeport Station to Penn Station. Then Reed took the subway back across the East River to Long Island City, a desolate industrial enclave on the lip of Queens, across from midtown Manhattan. Pickwick had a primitive studio—basically a concrete bunker with some tape recorders—and its own pressing plant, at 8-16 Forty-third Avenue. Reed reported to the building and sat with his writing team: Philips, Jerry Vance (né Pelligrino), and Jimmie Sims (né Smith). "There were four of us literally locked in a room writing songs," recalled Reed. "They would say, 'Write ten California songs, ten Detroit songs,' then we'd go down into the studio for an hour or two and cut three or four albums really quickly." Authorship was shared by fiat: "It didn't matter who wrote the song; four people got credit for it."

"THE SOUNDS OF SURFING" . . . "THE SOUNDS OF CAMPUS" . . . "THE SOUNDS OF HOT ROD" announced the cover of the *Soundsville!* LP, collecting various genre exercises not without charm. "Johnny Won't Surf No More," which Reed claimed to have written, was a seaside version of the Shangri-Las' 1964 teen tragedy "Leader of the Pack," complete with spoken-word bridge and ghoulish backing vocals that might have included Reed. "I've Got a Tiger in My Tank" is a Beach Boys knock-off echoing the Esso gasoline slogan. The most amusing is "It's Hard for a Girl in a World Full of Men," with one Connie Carson lamenting her boy craziness with double entendres and striking an early blow against slut-shaming. One imagines Reed had a hand in that one, too.

Reed's lead vocals are unmistakable on two tracks. "Cycle Annie" has a nasal, faintly country-western delivery recalling Roger Miller (whose crossover breakthrough "Dang Me" charted that summer), rhyming "Pasadena" with "y'know they don't come any meaner" and dispensing "y'all"s around a fumbling guitar solo. The Roughnecks' "You're Drivin' Me Insane" is less jokey, a hard-charging rockabilly rave-up with hoots and shouts, Reed aping the roughneck vocal style of Mick Jagger (*England's Newest Hit Makers*, their U.S. debut, had been issued in May).

Another Pickwick LP likely featuring Reed was *Swingin' Teen Sounds of Ronnie Dove & Terry Phillips*, a throwback to late '50s/early '60s pop balladry and Pat Boone rock 'n' roll, full of pro-forma dopey clichés. "This Rose" and "Flowers for the Lady" are probable Reed co-writes, the latter with a "roses are red / violets are blue" chorus that would have made Delmore Schwartz choke. "Wild One" has a sung-spoken break worthy of a *MAD* magazine parody: "Music, man, that's wild, y'know what I mean?" declares Dove against what might be Reed's crude rockabilly riffs—"and then there's dancing, baby, and I dig that the most!"

Reed was constantly high at work, according to Philips, on two occasions so wasted he had to be taken to a hospital emergency room. Philips believed in Reed's potential, and like Allan Hyman and others, seemed as attracted to Reed's dark side as repelled by it. So he put up with the bad behavior, though he had his limits: once, after Reed made an offensive comment to his wife, Philips slapped him hard across the face.

Reed's most consequential contribution at Pickwick, also his wildest and funniest, was "The Ostrich." It was another genre knock-off, but a truly remarkable one. The title was inspired by Eugenia Shepherd, the influential New York columnist Andy Warhol once credited with "invent[ing] fashion and gossip together." After getting stoned and reading a Shepherd piece about the ostrich feather craze, Reed came up with a novelty dance number like Marvin Gaye's "Hitch Hike" and Little Eva's "Loco-motion."

"The Ostrich" opens with Reed hollering over grinding noise, like he's trying to be heard on a subway platform as a train hurtles in, followed by a strutting R&B bass line and tambourine—a low-rent take on Phil Spector's Wall of Sound. "All right, everybody get down on your face, man," Reed continues, one part James Brown dance instructional, one part shooting-gallery police raid, adding "put your hands up" for good measure, then shouting, whooping, shrieking soul man "whoa-oo-oo"s and a barking mandate to "do the Ostrich!" Then there's the otherworldly guitar, most audible on the build between 1:25 and 1:35, that steers the whole enterprise thrillingly off the rails. Reed had worked up a shrill riff after tuning all his guitar strings to A# (in three different octaves). It was likely another stoned goof. But the history of pop has been built on jokes, mistakes, and screwing around, and the history of rock 'n' roll was certainly built on displays of theatrical dumbness combined with inspired madness.

None of this is meant to oversell the relatively minor achievement of "The Ostrich." But the song recalls Reed's semi-absurdist *Lonely Woman Quarterly* writing, even his precocious high school single. At the same time, it so closely resembled the sort of thing that might be successful in the crapshoot world of early-to-mid-'60s pop that Philips made a power move—he convinced Cy Leslie to bankroll not only a single release, but the creation of an actual, Beatles-esque band to get on stages and perform "The Ostrich." And so were born the Primitives, who'd lay the foundation for the Velvet Underground.

*　*　*

On a chilly October night in 2015, one week after his eightieth birthday, La Monte Young prepared to perform in the latest iteration of *Dream House*, the composer's long-running installation collaboration with his partner, the musician and visual artist Marian Zazeela. *Dream House* has been the signature expression of Young's interest in drones and extended-duration musical events. Begun under a long-term commission in 1979 and continuing with rare interruptions since, it could be considered a decades-long piece.

In a warehouse space on West Twenty-second Street, warm and suffused with incense, the audience was instructed to remove their shoes. The room was bathed in magenta light; underfoot was plush white carpeting and throw pillows, suitable to sit or lie on, and four white speaker towers were arrayed, one in each corner. *Dream Music* was under way, and the speakers emitted a lowing drone—the "linear superimposition of 77 sine wave frequencies," the program stated—interwoven with diaphanous chanting voices. Given a minute or two, the music became engrossing, then subsuming. The spell broke from time to time, like a wave cresting; attention wandered. Return to the drone, and it pulled you right back under. The visuals were equally hypnotic.

In fact, one barely noticed when six dark-clad musicians filed silently onto the platform. There was no applause—complete silence before, during, and after the performance was insisted upon. Anyone glancing at their phone in the darkened room had a scolding usher immediately at their side.

With his braided white beard, sleeveless denim jacket, and fingerless gloves, Young looked like a combination of grizzled biker and Zen master. Incrementally, with great finesse, the musicians joined the unceasing drone: three voices, fretless guitar, fretless bass, tablas. Their improvisations conjured Indian raga, tracing melodies that rose and fell like breath for well over an hour; it might as easily have been five.

The concert—indeed, Young's entire ongoing *Dream House* project—functioned as a sort of musical opium den: scientifically calibrated, artistically amplified, spiritually fortified, and surprisingly well funded. Its program notes read like a cross between a laboratory report and a spiritual tract. As art, it was deep, solemn, and profound. Yet there was in the presentation a guru's sly wink, and a quiet, yet unmistakable air of showbiz.

This has long been a defining characteristic of the New York aesthetic: radical ideas mixing deep inspiration and outsized ambition with a soupçon of jive. That jive might be delivered as an airtight spiel or in an articulate deadpan to confound naysaying philistines—what Andy Warhol, if one could get him to answer straight, might've called a "put-on." In a town that ultimately respects only the hustle, it's a reasonable approach, and Young's work has remained a transcendent example of it. Credited as the father of the minimalist composition movement, scholar of just intonation, developer of rational number-based tuning systems, and icon of experimental music, Young believes himself to be the most influential composer of the past half-century. "What's more," he told the writer Rob Tannenbaum a few months prior to the performance, "when I die, people will say, 'He was the most important composer since the beginning of music.'"

* * *

John Cale encountered Young's music in the early '60s while attending Goldsmiths' College at the University of London. Born in Wales in 1942 one week after Lou Reed, Cale was the son of an English coal miner and a Welsh schoolteacher, and became an accomplished student of classical music. Close with his mother, he was a troubled kid, who spoke only Welsh growing up; until learning English at school around age seven, he could barely communicate with his dad, who in any case he rarely saw, since he worked overnight shifts at the mine. Cale was hospitalized for a nervous breakdown at sixteen, after his mother's battle with breast cancer left her a semi-invalid. But prior to that, she'd taught him piano, and music became a primary language. He mastered viola in grammar school when she pushed him to join an orchestra; soon, he was playing Paganini's Caprices. As a teen, he had a pivotal encounter with the ideas of John Cage via his book *Silence*, and as a music student at Goldsmiths', began corresponding with both Cage and the composer Aaron Copland. He won a summer scholarship to the prestigious classical music academy at Tanglewood in Massachusetts. For his Goldsmiths' graduation concert, Cale performed a piece by Cage's peer La Monte Young, "X for Henry Flynt," the title a nod to the provocateur who coined the term *concept art*. Its "score" directs the player to repeat a loud sound in a pulse of one- or two-second duration for an unspecified period of time—Cale did so by kneeling at a piano and smashing his elbows on the keys in strict time. It did not earn him a fond farewell.

Cale had flown to the United States and was met by Copland, who accompanied him up to Tanglewood. When the summer program concluded in late August 1963, Cale headed south to New York City, where he exchanged his London return-trip ticket for cash and rented a loft space on Lispenard Street, just below Canal. By September, he was already working with John Cage, signing on for an eighteen-hour-plus performance of Eric Satie's *Vexations*, an eighty-second-long composition that, as the score suggests, is to be repeated 840 times.

The concert, staged at the tiny Pocket Theater, 100 Third Avenue off Thirteenth Street, was a media event. *The New York Times* sent eight critics, working as a tag team, just like Cale and his fellow pianists. The morning the piece concluded, on September 11, 1963, a photo spread on the concert dominated by images of Cale ran alongside coverage of President Kennedy's forced integration of an Alabama high school. The *Vexations* review was mixed at best: the chief critic, Harold C. Schonberg, unconvinced, observed in the group-bylined review that "the listener floated in a suspended animation as seconds flowed into minutes with the idiot repetition of beat after beat." Raymond Ericson was more receptive, comparing its hypnotic quality favorably to the landmark experimental film *Last Year at Marienbad*, which had just opened. Among others in the audience was the up-and-coming art star Andy Warhol, who later claimed, truthfully or not, to have stayed the full eighteen hours.

For an unknown young musician, Cale's first weeks in New York City were going rather well. Shortly after his *Times* spotlight, he was contacted by a TV producer, and Cale turned up a week later as "Mr. X" on the game show *I've Got a Secret*, playing a snatch of *Vexations* for the viewers. His next stop was a pilgrimage to visit La Monte Young on the Lower East Side.

Young had been born into a Mormon family in Idaho and wound up in Los Angeles, where he studied music and played saxophone; he performed with classmate Eric Dolphy, and for a time he led a band with Ornette Coleman's associates Billy Higgins and Don Cherry. In addition to jazz, Young was fascinated by Indian music, especially the droning tamboura, and he listened incessantly to raga recordings by the sarod master Ali Akbar Khan. After doing graduate work at Berkeley in composition, Young came to New York in 1960 and quickly found his footing. He curated the groundbreaking Chambers Street Loft Series with another adventurous artist, Yoko Ono, in her cold-water downtown flat. Like Ono, Young got involved with Fluxus—the process-oriented, highly experimental, often political avant-garde art movement—and was soon pacing John Cage as an avant-garde figurehead.

When Cale met him, Young was leading the Theatre of Eternal Music, a group he'd assembled to explore his ideas about sustained tones. It included Young and Marian Zazeela; a violinist, Tony Conrad; a drummer, Angus MacLise; and almost instantly, Cale. Young "was so flattered that a classical student had come all the way from Wales to sit at his feet that he immediately invited me to come back and play with them," Cale writes. "We created a kind of music that nobody else in the world was making, and that nobody had ever heard before." By Cale's measure, they rehearsed three hours a day for a year and a half.

Tony Conrad was cut from cloth similar to Cale's. After taking a year off to study music in Germany, Conrad graduated from Harvard with a math degree, moved to New York City, and was soon on the frontlines of the avant-garde, collaborating with Young, with his Harvard friend/troublemaker Henry Flynt, and with his roommate Jack Smith, whose touchstone film *Flaming Creatures* he'd soundtrack. Conrad introduced Cale to clip-on electronic pickups for amplifying acoustic instruments, and the two dove into a fantastic noise. Cale filed the bridge off his viola, strung it with guitar strings, and used a bass bow to make it sound heavier still. The result, Cale thought, "sounded like a jet engine." He was delighted.

Cale, too, dove into the multidisciplinary underground scene. He befriended Piero Heliczer, a child-actor-turned-filmmaker whose father, a doctor, participated in the Italian resistance and was killed by the Gestapo, after which the family fled to the United States. Heliczer was a true "multimedia artist" before there was such a term; in addition to filmmaking, he was a musician, poet, visual artist, and publisher, producing small-edition books, pamphlets, posters, and flyers under his Dead Language Press imprint, which he ran out of his apartment at 56 Ludlow Street on the Lower East Side. Heliczer shared the place with Conrad and Angus MacLise, an eccentric polymath from Bridgeport, Connecticut, who knew Heliczer from Forest Hills High School in Queens. MacLise studied jazz and international drumming, and primarily played hand drums. But he was a multitasker too: a soundtrack composer, curator, poet, DIY publisher, occultist, and more.

Cale spent lots of time at 56 Ludlow, a sort of low-rent avant-garde mini-mall. Among the shabby apartment building's other tenants was René Rivera, stage name Mario Montez (in homage to the actor and gay icon Maria Montez), a nonbinary artist and actor who worked with Conrad's roomie the filmmaker Jack Smith, one of the underground's seminal figures. Smith had a rough upbringing, losing his father in a boating accident as a child, and being shuttled between the Midwest and South before reaching New York, where he set up shop as a novelty photographer, shooting portraits of customers playing dress-up. Smith was a magnetic force, drawing together artists from all disciplines. His landmark film *Flaming Creatures* was shot on the roof of a Lower East Side theater with scavenged, fogged 16mm film stock. The result was a fever dream of penis-stroking, breast-jiggling, and bold transgender revelry, with calligraphic credits by the artist (and Young's partner/co-collaborator) Marion Zazeela and a Conrad sound-collage soundtrack that juxtaposed Bartók and Kitty Kallen's sprightly version of "It Wasn't God Who Made Honky-Tonk Angels." *Flaming Creatures* was confiscated and banned after its April 1963 premiere, becoming a cause célèbre and an influential underground film touchstone. Cale and Conrad made a sound-art piece with him in the fall of 1964 that showcased Smith declaiming stoned poetics amid tape effects and other accompaniment; it may have been for Smith's follow-up, *Normal Love*, which along with Ludlow Street regulars showcased Andy Warhol (in full drag), the poet Diane di Prima (very pregnant), and the up-and-coming performer Tiny Tim. Artmaking in the scene was polymorphous and symbiotic; Warhol even shot his own three-minute avant-documentary during the shoot, ultimately titled *Andy Warhol Films Jack Smith Filming Normal Love.*

Lord of his own scene by now, La Monte Young welcomed all sorts of people, including some of the above, to hang out at his group's rehearsal/performances. Drugs were around and, according to Cale, effectively helped fund the work. "La Monte was dealing pounds of marijuana and was very proud of the quality," Cale recalled. "That was where I had my first encounter with [it]. Everybody was smoking." The business was hardly a secret. "At this time, he was the highest quality dope dealer in the avant-garde movement," said Billy Linich, aka Billy Name, a lighting designer who worked with Young. "His place looked like a hashish den or Turkish coffee shop." Young saw this as part of the creative process. "These tools can be used to your advantage if you're a master of [them]," Young said, noting, "There was something in the cannabis experience that probably helped open me up to where I went with [the seminal 1958 work] *Trio for Strings.*"

Cale supplemented his income helping Young move product. "He would call me up using these studio codes," Cale recalled. "O was for opium, 'oboe.' A was for amphetamine. A movement was a pound, sixteen bars in a movement, so two bars meant two ounces. Pot was a piano. He'd say, 'I want six bars of the sonata for oboe.'" Cale used his loft on Lispenard as a stash house. One day, likely set up by another dealer, Cale was arrested, along with Young, and spent the night in the Tombs, aka the Manhattan House of Detention. "[It] was truly horrendous. La Monte paid for the lawyer. The problem was that I had a nickel bag on me. But when they analyzed it, it was nothing, so they let me out the next day."

Sufficiently spooked, Cale sold the lease on his loft and moved into a fourth-floor apartment with Conrad at 56 Ludlow, most likely in the summer of 1964. Rent was $25 a month, which the landlord collected with a gun. While calculating the future of the avant-garde, the young men listened to the radio hits—"A Hard Day's Night" and "Love Me Do," "The Girl from Ipanema," the Beach Boys' "I Get Around," Millie Small's "My Boy Lollipop"—on WINS 1010 AM, the Murray the K show, and other programs. Conrad loved Hank Williams, and both men were besotted by the harmonies of the Everly Brothers. "We played similarly to the way [they] used to sing," Cale recalled. "There was this one song which they sang in which they started with two voices holding one chord. They sang it so perfectly in tune that you could actually hear each voice." To Cale's ear, it wasn't far from the drone experiments he and Conrad were pursuing with Young.

* * *

For Reed, the journey from Pickwick's Brill Building manqué to Ludlow Street would not take long. The Primitives came together at an Upper East Side house party where Philips and Vance were on the prowl for musicians for their "Ostrich" touring band. They struck up a conversation with Cale and Conrad, who looked the part of bohemian "rock and roll" musicians. He invited them to the Pickwick studio, and they showed up with Walter De Maria, a visual artist who shared their interest in outsized minimalism (land art works such as *The Lightning Field* would become his calling card). He also played drums, and had worked with Young over the years.

The three young musicians laughed at the exploitative contracts they were offered, which they declined. But after hearing "The Ostrich," they agreed to play some regional gigs to promote the record. Hell, they'd make some money and, at the very least, it'd be amusing.

As it turned out, they found creative common ground with Reed. Conrad recalled being told that "The Ostrich" was "easy to play because all the strings are tuned to the same note . . . [that] blew our minds, because that was what we were doing with La Monte in the Dream Syndicate. It was pretty amazing, we couldn't believe it."

"That drone stuff was really fun," Reed reflected. "I got into it because of distortion, getting a feedback tone. I didn't know from La Monte Young and all that. I only became aware of that through John."

* * *

Reed and Cale clicked immediately. They had plenty in common, including mental health struggles. And both men had chips on their shoulders. Cale maintains he was voted "most hateful student" by his department heads during college.

"My first impressions of Lou were of a high-strung, intelligent, fragile college kid in a polo neck sweater, rumpled jeans and loafers," Cale recalled. "He had been around and was bruised, trembling, quiet, and insecure. He lived in Freeport, Long Island, with his parents, who kept him on a tight rein . . . He was also seeing a psychiatrist who prescribed a tranquilizer called Placidyl. When I asked why, he said, 'I think I'm crazy.' I told him, 'Fuck, you're not crazy.' I didn't believe in schizophrenia. All I saw in it was a different way of seeing things."

A recording of a wee-hours rehearsal at Walter De Maria's loft at 49 Bond Street showed what the men were up to. Reed, Cale, Conrad, De Maria, and the Pickwick staffer Jimmie Sims worked through "The Ostrich," the bluesman Jimmy Reed's "Shame, Shame, Shame," and a new original called "Won't You Smile." On the latter, Reed seems to be freestyling verses about a "hooker" in the voice of a pimp she has abandoned: "You made me a hundred dollars in a little while / So won't you smile?" At the moment they were rehearsing, rock 'n' roll had just morphed from fad into juggernaut: the Shangri-La's "Leader of the Pack" was in the Top 10, alongside the Zombies' "She's Not There," the Kinks' "You Really Got Me," the Stones' "Time Is on My Side," and assorted Beatles hits. The Primitives seemed to be as much a parody of a rock band as the genuine article.

The band's debut performance was likely December 3 at the Riverside Plaza Hotel, 253 West Seventy-third Street, at a promotional event. Suddenly, they were on a stage, "and we don't know what's going on," Conrad recalled. "None of us have really played this kind of music before, and then there's all this hype and screaming kids and meeting other groups. The whole thing was absolutely unexpected and hypnotizing." Soon he was driving around in a station wagon goofing on the idea of being in a rock 'n' roll band, while actually being in one, albeit briefly. The "tour" amounted to a handful of local dates, including a couple of high schools and a New Jersey shopping mall. Conrad recalled a radio station interview in Reading, Pennsylvania, and a bill shared with the Bronx soul singer Shirley Ellis, who'd scored a hit that year with "The Clapping Song." But "The Ostrich," unsurprisingly, did not become a hit, the gigging came to an end, and the group disbanded. A photo, shot at night, likely mid-tour, shows the men leaning against the car's back bumper. Cale alone looks the role: beatnik goatee, frayed jeans, black boots, a denim jacket under a thrift-store sports coat, and a faintly buzzed expression. Reed, clean-cut in his loafers, white jeans, and crisp overcoat, looks like a wired young preppie from Long Island.

* * *

Reed was working other angles, too. He played what were likely some original folk-style songs on acoustic guitar at a party Cale attended once. "I really didn't pay any attention because I couldn't give a shit about folk music," Cale recalled. "I hated Joan Baez and Dylan—every song was a fucking question!" But later, Reed showed Cale the words to some of his songs, including "Heroin" and "I'm Waiting for the Man," and Cale was stunned.

"He was writing about things other people weren't. These lyrics were literate, well-expressed, tough, novelistic expressions of life. I recognized a tremendous literary quality in his songs, which fascinated me—he had a careful ear." Cale especially admired how Reed could slip into a character in first-person voice, and also his ability to make up lyrics on the fly, as he had during the Primitives' rehearsal—the musical version of his lightning-strike wise-guy conversational ripostes. "At the drop of a hat he would be singing about how we would go and see Walter De Maria in his loft and so on. It was riveting. He had such an ease with language."

Cale was also taken with Reed's fuck-you attitude, and his appetite for drugs.

"I was squeamish about needles. Lou took care of that by shooting me up for the first time. It was an intimate experience, not least because my first reaction was to vomit," Cale recounted. "Shortly after that, though, I would start to feel a lot better because at first heroin makes you feel comfortable and friendly. This was magic for two guys as uptight and distanced from their surroundings as Lou and I."

They shared ideas, intoxicants, illness, hypodermics, eventually hepatitis. They were never lovers, though, and Reed's evident queerness took Cale by surprise. "It wasn't until he gave me a few sexual nudges that it finally clicked that Lou was gay, or at least bisexual. When I told him I was not interested, he mumbled, 'They make them differently in Scotland,' quickly adding that anyway I was not suitable for a marital partner." Cale had had encounters with predatory men when he was younger, including, when he was twelve, his music teacher at the local church ("it certainly took care of my religious sensibility," Cale would later note dryly). Whatever sexual tension remained between Reed and Cale became another facet of a competitive relationship.

The men were so close, Cale conceded, many assumed they were a couple, anyway, albeit a dysfunctional one. In his memoir, *What's Welsh for Zen*, he reflected on their time as roommates: "One of the earliest and most sustaining images I have of our discussions at Ludlow Street while comparing notes in the early days was of Lou's uncanny ability to bring out the worst in people. We would sit in a bar and discuss various gray areas of risk and danger existing in the world, and shock treatment and insanity." Cale believed that Reed's "fears about sanity" led him toward "provocative behavior, actively and purposefully trying his darnedest to set people off. That made him feel he was in control, rather than living in a state of uncertainty or paranoia. This put him in the position of perpetually seeking a kind of advantage for himself by bringing out the worst in people."

Ultimately, though, they remained worlds apart. "Lou and I had one of these rapports where you think the other guy is thinking what you're thinking, but he's not. He couldn't figure me out, and I couldn't figure him out. The only thing we had in common were drugs and an obsession with risk taking. That was the raison d'être for the Velvet Underground."

It was enough for Cale to stop working with Young and devote himself fully to his collaboration with Reed. He was determined to combine the ideas he'd been developing with Reed's songcraft in a sort of aggro-avant-garde take on Phil Spector's pop Wall of Sound—into something both commercially viable and artistically earth-shattering.

* * *

Reed typed a lengthy letter to his troubled mentor Delmore Schwartz around this time. He mentioned his bout with hepatitis after graduation, which kept him in bed over two months. He wrote about the Pickwick job; about the "starving viola player" from Wales and the Harvard grad violinist; about the hysteria of the brief Primitives promotion tour and how he "wasn't up to it I'm afraid, the way I would have been what seems like years ago." He claimed the label was interested in a "folk album" he'd made, but he refused to change his lyrics, "and that was that." He described the record industry as being as "vicious" as most, but "a little more so."

Particularly striking were Reed's descriptions of his adventures in the New York demimonde, which may have been true, invented, or somewhere in between. He noted the "experiences" he'd had since returning to the city, "sick but strange and fascinating and even, some-times ultimately revealing, healing and helpful . . . ny has so many sad, sick people and i have a knack for meeting them. They try to drag you down with them. If you're weak ny has many outlets. I can't resist peering, probing, sometimes participating, other times going right to the edge before sidestepping." He described finding the viciousness and "killer urge" in himself, labeling it "interesting," then conceding "interesting is not the word." He mostly avoided specifics except to mention his discovery of "easy ways" to make money, and the "rich johns" of Park Avenue who would pay between $250 and $700—and up—to watch group sex performances. He admitted to nothing.

Reed still saw himself as a writer; he mentioned he was still consid-ering grad school, and that his Harvard application had been sitting idle "for a while now," adding "maybe I'll teach, maybe Europe. But mainly it must be writing and I think I'm good enough to give it a run for its money." He signed off, hoping Schwartz, his "spiritual godfa-ther," was doing well.

* * *

With the Primitives finished, Walter De Maria returned his attention to visual art. Conrad, who was developing an interest in experimental filmmaking, moved out of the 56 Ludlow Street apartment, leaving it to Cale. Figuring it a dead end, Reed left the Pickwick job, and though nominally living with his parents, he frequently spent nights making music with Cale at the Ludlow space, where Jack Smith edited *Flaming Creatures*. The pair also began busking around town as a sort of urban beatnik Everly Brothers, Cale playing viola and recorder with Reed and his acoustic guitar. A demo tape made in 1965—almost certainly the "folk album" he mentions in his letter to Schwartz—gives an idea of what they might've sounded like on the street. Postmarked May 11 in Freeport and sent by registered mail to his parents' house at 35 Oak-field Avenue, it's the earliest document of what would be the Velvet Underground.

Reed introduces each song on the tape as his original composition.

The first, "Men of Good Fortune," is notably written from a woman's point of view, conjuring a folk ballad not unlike Joan Baez's "Silver Dagger" in its drama of courtship and looming violence. Reed sings as an orphan girl fearing life alone and unmarried, with no trace of parody. "Unfaithful and ugly are the ways of all men," he sings in a shaky tenor, which swoops into a high-lonesome falsetto. It's rather astonishing, given the music he'd go on to record, and as a playacted character study and genre exercise, it drew perhaps from the same creative place as "Heroin."

"Put Your Money Down on the Table" addressed the nation's civil rights struggle, then at a fever pitch (the march on Selma took place that spring). Reed and Cale harmonize in the folk-revival style of Martin & Neil or Gibson & Camp, referring to Sheriff Jim Clark's techniques for subduing protesters: "In Alabama, they use cattle prodders." Given his experience with coercive electricity, Reed must've found the image especially visceral.

Not everything was so serious. "Buttercup Song, or, Never Get Emotionally Involved, with a Man or Woman or Beast or Child" was a vaudeville-style number about a cool character who falls in love with "an androgynous small buttercup" only to become "a fully grown man writing poems at night." "Walk Alone" is wise-guy existentialism with a sophomoric masturbation pun ("you know you gotta beat it alone," Reed sings). More interesting is a song titled "Pale Blue Eyes," a country-folk ballad about jealousy in which the singer lies awake predawn, venting heartache that curdles into anger, wishing his ex "dead" and that she'd "get hit in the head." It'd prove a work in progress.

Also on the tape were early versions of "I'm Waiting for the Man" and "Heroin." The former was a slow blues strut sung in close Everly Brothers harmony, Cale taking the highs. When Reed exclaims, "Hey, white boy!"—the voice of someone about to grill the narrator about his business uptown—Cale answers, sheepishly, "Pardon me, sir." It's tremendously funny, yet hardly comedy. And there's nothing funny at all about "Heroin," a potent folk song that'd largely found its shape on the demo.

A more fleshed-out version was recorded the same month at Pickwick, featuring Reed on acoustic guitar and a bassist, probably Cale. On the tape, someone (Terry Philips perhaps) coached Reed through an intercom.

"Good performance. Do it again, ya blew some words."

"Oh, Jesus Christ . . ." says Reed.

"I need to get a level on this . . . It's not like a performance, baby. You're in a recording studio . . . You don't wanna do it, don't."

"I'm just trying to figure out if I can do it," says Reed without bravado. "All right—ya got time [so] I can run out and get some water?"

Reed begins a slow fingerpicking pattern, with a lilting echo of Rev. Gary Davis's style. The vocal is tender, like a college kid in a coffeehouse:

IIIIIIIIIIIIIII know just where I'm going
IIIIIII-IIIIII-IIIIII'm gonna try . . .

Reed accelerates his delivery to double time, mimicking the drug's rush, words tumbling out in neurochemical mimesis, then settling down for the reprise, language succumbing to opiate blankness.

It was hardly the first time anyone sang about illicit drug use in a commercial setting—jazz and blues acts had been doing that for decades. The Greenwich Village folk scene veterans Eric Von Schmidt and Richard Fariña recorded Davis's "Cocaine Blues" (with Dylan, billed as "Blind Boy Grunt," on harmonica and backing vocals) for an LP Reed was likely familiar with. Then there was "Needle of Death," from the Scottish folk singer/guitarist Bert Jansch's self-titled debut LP, a landmark of the folk revival that would inspire numerous young players in Britain and abroad (Paul Simon and Neil Young among them). Issued there in early 1965 but not in the States, it's not inconceivable a music hound like Reed might've heard it, and that lines like "One grain of pure white snow / Dissolved in blood spread quickly to your brain" might've informed his own writing. Yet "Needle of Death" is a second-person lament to a friend who died of an overdose, where Reed's "Heroin" was something else: a plainspoken character, alternately agitated and benumbed, articulating in first person his anger, his intentions, and the precise arcs of his euphoria. It's chilling, and astonishing.

* * *

The previous September, the Animals' "House of the Rising Sun" became the number 1 pop song in the Unites States—the first British Invasion single not by the Beatles to top the charts. It's a lament by a character ruing his fate, presumably brought on by whoring and drinking. It reimagined a folk song dating back to the early twentieth century, previously recorded by Woody Guthrie, Leadbelly, Joan Baez, and Dylan, who featured it on his debut. But the Animals had plugged in: Hilton Valentine picking out an A-minor arpeggio on electric guitar, Alan Price coaxing *Phantom of the Opera* tones on a Vox Continental, a sharp-toned new transistor combo organ, building the drama as Eric Burdon, a kid from Newcastle just about Reed's age, howls out his regrets. Folk-rock was inevitable and perfectly logical; according to Mishkin, he and Reed had worked up an electric cover of "House of the Rising Sun" back in Syracuse, beating the Animals to it. Now Reed and Cale were determined to create a band to play Reed's "folk" songs louder, and then some.

The pair found a second electric guitarist at the Seventh Avenue stop on the D train. Reed had last seen Sterling Morrison at a Lightnin' Hopkins show in the Village the previous summer; Morrison had been finishing his BA at City College uptown, where he was headed. "[Lou] invited me over to this guy Rick's place to get high and talk/play music," Morrison recalled. "The three of us kept going from that moment."

It's worth noting that just as the trio met, a single block from that same subway stop, Bob Dylan was working out his own folk-rock blueprints aboveground, in Columbia Studio A, 799 Seventh Avenue at Fifty-second Street. He was making what would become *Bringing It All Back Home* with Tom Wilson, an African-American Harvard-grad-cum-record-producer and avant-garde jazz fan. Reed, Cale, and Morrison would meet Wilson soon enough.

Morrison joined Reed and Cale for some final work for Pickwick, and on a tape made at 56 Ludlow in July, Morrison joined in on some new songs including "All Tomorrow's Parties," a tale of a disgraced party girl, possibly suicidal, and by the final verse possibly dead. The track is driven by fingerstyle guitar with high harmonies by Cale. Combining the journalistic morbidity of a murder ballad with a literary third-person POV, it's already a perfect song, although the men can't quite nail a take. "Venus in Furs" is Reed's poetic gloss on Leopold von Sacher-Masoch's 1870 novella of the same name, involving a masochistic man and his dominant mistress. Amusingly, the music conjures an Elizabethan courtship ballad, albeit one colored by the plucking of an Indian sarinda, possibly by Morrison. Cale carries the vocals, queering the book's gender dynamic with lines like "strike, dear master, cure my heart").

There still seemed a question of who would be the lead singer of this enterprise. Recognizing his vocal limitations, Reed was ambivalent, though he'd clearly be the main lyric writer. Cale imagined himself taking charge of the music, with Phil Spector–style orchestrations. But Reed created his songs whole cloth, words and music intertwined, and told his partner bluntly, "I don't think of you as a songwriter."

Cale was hurt. His contributions to Reed's music would be huge. And on the new version of "Heroin," it was unmistakable, Cale's viola adding hair-raising tension to the simple guitar figures, as Reed works on his delivery, veering between comic backwoods mewling and junkie derangement. It would continue to evolve.

On July 25, right about the time of these recordings, Dylan plugged in an electric guitar at the Newport Folk Festival. From then on, folk and rock music wouldn't be quite the same.

* * *

Reed and Cale were busking one night in front of Club Baby Grand at 319 West 125th Street, a fabled nightclub known for jazz (Charlie Parker played there, among others) and comedians (Nipsey Russell launched his career there as a nightly MC); the frontage advertised "ENTERTAINMENT" and "DANCING NIGHTLY" beneath a piano-lid-shaped facade. It was a sketchy neighborhood for two white folk musicians to be busking in; a film clip dated to 1964 showed a window sign up in a nearby bar warning "UN-ESCORTED WOMEN! NOT SERVED—DON'T COME IN." When the duo played "I'm Waiting for the Man," Reed sang about the exact street they were standing on. Cale was amazed at how Reed could parry hecklers. "That was an education," he recalled. "It was beautiful . . . [He could] bring a conversation quietly screeching to a halt. He'd say, 'Are we boooothering you?'"

Eventually a cop shooed them away, and they relocated to Seventy-fifth and Broadway, where they met a woman who introduced herself as Elektrah, though her birth name was Marcia Lobel. An artist and actor involved in the underground film scene, she'd just appeared in two films by Andy Warhol. In *The Life of Juanita Castro* she plays Fidel Castro's brother, Raul. In *Kitchen*, a send-up of heteronormativity and New York City apartment claustrophobia, she played opposite Warhol's new muse and sidekick, Edie Sedgwick.

Lobel also played guitar, and soon she was making music with Reed and Cale. "We played several gigs with her, including a couple at Café Wha?," Cale noted in his autobiography. "She claimed she wanted to be in the band and perform with us, but any time we got close to actually doing anything, she would freak out and delay everything. She had this dazzling smile that would suddenly turn extremely vicious." Cale recalled another woman involved with the group briefly, a single mother with a taste for heroin. But ultimately the band, now called the Falling Spikes, coalesced with Cale, Reed, Morrison, and the drummer Angus MacLise, Cale's colleague in La Monte Young's group.

Their first gig was part of a "ritual happening" organized by Mac-Lise and Heliczer at the Film-Makers Cinematheque ("the Tek"), which had just moved up from 434 Lafayette to 125 West Forty-first Street, just off the movie-palace strip in Times Square. A co-op center for the downtown avant-garde, the Cinematheque was seeded by George Maciunas, a co-founder of Fluxus, which had gained traction in New York City over the past few years due in large part to Maciunas's real estate gaming of abandoned factory loft spaces in SoHo. Among the Fluxus alumni was Jonas Mekas, a filmmaker and cinematic philosopher who wrote a column on experimental cinema in *The Village Voice*, published *Film Culture* magazine, and helmed both the Cinematheque and the Film-makers' Co-op, a combination that made him the godfather of the New York City underground film scene.

Mekas was born in Lithuania in 1922. From a Protestant family, he survived the Nazi occupation, finding work at a couple of weekly newspapers before attempting to flee the country, which landed him in a forced work camp. He and his younger brother immigrated to the United States in 1949, and before long, he secured a 16mm Bolex camera and began making a documentary of his new home base, Williamsburg. He took his skills in publishing and filmmaking and ran with them, developing his critical voice in the quarterly *Film Culture* and at *The Village Voice*, exercizing an aesthetic that hard-pivoted from a sort of passionate, realist universalism to a celebration of a "New American Cinema" centered on the New York underground scene he was part of, in all its abstract, queer, vernacular-creating particularism. His championing of *Flaming Creatures*, in fact, which included both lauding it in the *Voice* and screening it at various events, made it a cause célèbre. It also got him arrested for promoting obscenity, an incident that gave him plenty to write about, and cemented his reputation as a culture warrior.

Mekas had a hand in the Velvets' birth event, which was titled *The Launching of the Dreamweapon*. As Morrison recalled, it was tumultuous:

> In the center of the stage was a movie screen, and between the screen and the audience a number of veils were spread out in different places. These veils were lit variously by lights and slide projectors, as Piero's films shone through them onto the screen. Dancers swirled around, and poetry and song occasionally rose up, while from behind the screen a strange music was being generated by Lou, John, Angus and me; I think Piero was back there sometimes too, playing his saxophone.

The group played other similar events that summer, likely including "an 8 hour spectacle" staged on August 11 at the Broadway Central, a dilapidated luxury hotel on lower Broadway that would soon house the Mercer Arts Center.

The idea for these sorts of "happenings"—unscripted, theatrical, interactive multimedia events—had been bouncing around for a while. There were the "art picnics" held by George Segal on his New Jersey chicken farm in the late '50s and early '60s, social gatherings that featured performance art, and the events staged by Walter De Maria and La Monte Young at various California colleges (including Stanford) around the same time. There had also been the seminal *Theater Piece No. 1*, orchestrated by John Cage in the dining hall of Black Mountain College back in 1952, in which Merce Cunningham danced, David Tudor improvised on piano, the visual artist Robert Rauschenberg played Edith Piaf records, and Cage lectured on Buddhism from a step ladder as films unspooled, slide projections glowed, and boys in white outfits served coffee.

According to Allan Kaprow, the artist generally credited with repurposing the term *happening*, the idea reaches back further, "through Surrealism, Dada, Mime, the circus, carnivals, the traveling saltimbanques, all the way to medieval mystery plays and processions." In a 1961 essay, "Happenings in the New York Scene," he offers a "kaleidoscope sampling" of happening images:

Everybody is crowded into a downtown loft, milling about, like at an opening. It's hot. There are lots of big cartons sitting all over the place. One by one they start to move, sliding drunkenly and careening in every direction, lunging into people and one another, accompanied by loud breathing sounds over four loudspeakers . . . Coughing, you breathe in noxious fumes, or the smell of hospitals and lemon juice. A nude girl runs after the racing pool of a searchlight, throwing spinach greens into it. Slides and movies, projected over walls and people, depict hamburgers: big ones, huge ones, red ones, skinny ones, flat ones, etc. You come in as a spectator and maybe you discover you're caught in it after all, as you push things around like so much furniture . . . You giggle because you're afraid, suffer claustrophobia, talk to someone nonchalantly, but all the time you're *there*, getting into the act.

As this scene might suggest, psychedelics were part of the picture, too. LSD didn't become illegal in the United States until October 1968, and by late '65, the West Coast Acid Tests—basically "happenings" at which LSD was distributed to attendees—were already under way, with overloaded multimedia displays and a young house band, the Warlocks, who by December 1965 would change their name to the Grateful Dead. Coincidentally, the Falling Spikes called themselves the Warlocks, too, for a short while. But around the time of the *Dreamweapon* performance, they changed it again.

Morrison believed it was Angus MacLise who picked up a book titled *The Velvet Underground* at a Times Square newsstand. The 60-cent paperback was a knocked-off bit of hand-wringing softcore sociology that would've been quickly forgotten if not for its repurposed title. Billed as a "documentary on the sexual corruption of our age," it was written by Michael Leigh, a priggish hack describing himself as a neutral "fellow next door." It relayed stories, presumably culled from correspondence with bold men and women, involving spouse-swapping, orgies, queer sex, bondage, and S&M play. "It does not require any expert understanding to know that the activities cited are not only legally but morally wrong and should be exposed," he declares, before describing those activities in hilariously vivid detail, with plenty of scare quotes and pseudo-clinical language. In one passage he describes a photo mailed to him: "a smiling, attractive young brunette posing with a nylon whip . . . ready for 'torture' . . . wearing shoes and hose, a rubber article inserted in the vaginal orifice." The musicians decided the book's title was a perfect band name, telegraphing both the underground art scene and Reed's sexually transgressive lyrics. Thus, the Velvet Underground was christened.

* * *

They set to work straightaway. Needing promotional photos, they dutifully mugged on their Ludlow Street stoop for the photographer Donald Greenhouse, Reed's next-door neighbor in Freeport: Cale in shades and a sport jacket, Reed in a turban. They played more "happenings," and provided live accompaniment to experimental films at the Cinematheque. They also pitched in on various films, including a series of 8mm shorts with Heliczer. One, part of a larger project with the working title *Dirt*, involved two nuns frolicking in a bathtub before heading out to engage a sailor for what seemed prurient activity. The sixteen-minute-long short, later circulated under the title *Venus in Furs*, also spliced in footage from *Bride of Frankenstein*, a 1935 film packed with queer subtext made by James Whale, one of the rare openly gay directors in Hollywood. Finally, Heliczer's film used footage from a remarkably serendipitous shoot, staged at his loft at 450 Grand Street, that was also captured by a WCBS-TV news team—likely tipped off by Mekas—gathering material for a story on New York City's underground film scene. The news package, which would air later that year, featured Cale, Reed, and Morrison playing their instruments on set, shirtless and adorned with body paint; MacLise, in dark sunglasses and a beatnik goatee, sat on the floor playing a hammered dulcimer.

Also on set, dressed in a black mask and a white wedding gown of sorts and tapping a tambourine with a drumstick, is Maureen Tucker. The sister of Jim Tucker, who introduced Reed and Morrison at Syracuse, "Moe" Tucker was born in Queens in 1944, and raised on Long Island. She started playing drums after discovering the Rolling Stones, specifically when she heard their cover of Buddy Holly's beat epiphany "Not Fade Away" on her car radio while driving home from work.

"I was on the Hempstead Turnpike in Levittown and I pulled off the road," Tucker said. "I just couldn't believe this. 'Holy shit,' I thought. 'What's this?'"

She first met Reed when he came to her parents' house to visit her brother. She was still in high school, and she already knew Morrison, who was dating her best friend, Martha. Tucker recalled playing music with Reed once or twice, managing on one occasion to get through a version of the Beatles' "This Boy."

Now, with the Velvet Underground a viable enterprise, Reed and Morrison needed a reliable drummer, and Angus MacLise, for all his creative brilliance, was not that. When the polymath heard the Velvet Underground had a conventional paying rock 'n' roll gig—$75 to play second on a triple bill at a New Jersey high school—MacLise declined on grounds of artistic integrity. "You mean we start when they tell us to and we have to end when they tell us to?" MacLise supposedly said. "I can't work that way." He believed money corrupted creativity.

"The job of a working musician was impossible for [him]," Reed later reflected, adding that MacLise "taught us all a lesson about purity of spirit."

Lesson learned, the band still had a gig to play. So Reed went to Jim Tucker's house to borrow an amp and to see his sister play again. She passed the audition; she even had a car. For her part, Moe Tucker was game. "When he came to see me play, I didn't have enough time to decide if I liked him or not," she said, "but I came to love Lou."

* * *

The group had a new drummer. Now it needed an ambassador. The filmmaker Barbara Rubin played one of the nuns in *Venus in Furs*—an amusing role for the creator of *Christmas on Earth*, a sexually explicit landmark of avant-garde film that had initially been titled *Cocks and Cunts*. She was so impressed by the Velvets that, during the *Venus* shoot, she called her friend Adam Ritchie, an English photographer living on the Lower East Side, and told him to hurry over; he took the first known pictures of the band performing ("They were spellbinding," he says).

Rubin was as much a community-builder as an art-maker, though due to sexism and the art world's fixation on individual achievement, she was often dismissed as a groupie. She was raised in Queens, in the Cambria Heights–St. Albans neighborhood, in a middle-class Jewish family. She ran away at fourteen, hitchhiked to California, took LSD with Aldous Huxley, and generally ran wild until her parents had her committed to Bloomingdale, a Westchester-based mental hospital. There she met a wealthy young California woman, Edie Sedgwick, whose parents had committed her as well. Upon their release, Sedgwick went to Cambridge, Massachusetts, to study art, while Rubin headed to New York City, where she met Jonas Mekas. She began working with him at the Film-Makers' Cooperative, the independent film distribution operation he co-founded. The actor and film critic Amy Taubin recalled meeting her there. "She was on the phone, she had these kind of curlers in her hair, and she was talking to someone in a very heavy New York accent. But otherwise, she seemed totally other worldly. She had the most transcendentally beautiful face I've ever seen. She had this opalescent skin . . . She didn't look like a boy, she didn't look like a girl, but she wasn't androgynous either. She looked like some transcendent creature, like someone decided to paint an angel. It was bizarre."

Rubin swiftly became one of the Cooperative's pivotal figures. She shot *Christmas on Earth* in June 1963, in the same 56 Ludlow Street apartment where Reed and Cale would later record their demos. The film took its name from a line near the end of Arthur Rimbaud's *Une Saison en Enfer* ("When will we go, over mountains and shores, to hail the birth of new labor, new wisdom, the flight of tyrants and demons, the end of superstition—to be the first to adore!—Christmas on earth!") It pushed the formal and sexual transgressions of Jack Smith's *Flaming Creatures* even further: figures covered in body paint, in blackface and whiteface, frolicked, groping breasts, fondling penises in various states of erection; mouths open and close in close-up; a man on his back, legs hoisted, spreads his anus; two men jerk each other off; someone finger-fucks an asshole—explicit sex, much of it queer, enacted as religious ritual. It was conceived for two projectors running simultaneously on the same screen, one set of images centered within another, larger one. In the larger exterior frame, a huge spread vagina, stroked by its apparent owner, would become the functional backdrop for everything— the eternal Mother, the cosmic Yoni, penetrated by ecstatic chaos and birthing it simultaneously. Rubin was eighteen when she filmed it with Mekas's crank-up 16mm Bell & Howell movie camera.

By 1965, Rubin was also functioning as a conduit and creative match-maker. She met Allen Ginsberg, who immediately recognized a kindred spirit. That spring, she helped him organize the International Poetry Incarnation at the Royal Albert Hall, a watershed proto-hippie cultural moment. She was often powered by amphetamines, and she had an effect on people. On the back cover of *Bringing It All Back Home*, Rubin is the handsome woman in the boyish coif standing behind a hunched-over Dylan, hands in his curls, apparently massaging his skull. "I thought of her as one of my gurus," recalled the playwright Richard Foreman. "I thought she was a high spiritual being." To Mekas, she was "always busy, always making peace between the various factions of the Underground art community. We were all bad children to her, not really doing our duties fully, not serving humanity enough, too much in our egos, not serving our art enough, or God, or ourselves. I think she was the most idealistic human I had ever met."

By the end of the year, Rubin would become the Velvets' unofficial advance man, and connect them to their most important booster, Andy Warhol. "Barbara was the moving force and coordinator between us all," Reed said.

* * *

Experimental art was fun, but the band was tired of living on oatmeal. In late summer, Cale traveled back to the United Kingdom for a visit, and took the demos they'd made in July. He knocked on record label doors, even got the tape into the hands of a connected young singer, Marianne Faithfull, but nothing clicked. All he returned with was a stack of records—by the Kinks (who'd released the raga-flavored, proto-psychedelic "See My Friends" in July), the Who, and other bands on a vaguely similar track to the Velvets, matching serious lyrics with druggy, aggro rock 'n' roll.

The Velvets soon connected with Al Aronowitz—the *Saturday Evening Post* writer and pop-music journalist who, at the advanced age of thirty-eight, was launching a side hustle as an artist manager. He was ambitious and successful, with a sound aesthetic compass. As a cub reporter, his *New York Post* editor requested a hatchet job, Aronowitz recalled, on a bunch of "dumb-fuck pansies posing as poets," and the writer spun the assignment into a smart, groundbreaking twelve-part series, "The Beat Generation." A friendship with Allen Ginsberg resulted, followed by a friendship with Dylan, also born of a reporting assignment; in December 1963, Aronowitz introduced the pair, launching an extended creative bromance. In August 1964, he presided over another artistic summit, between Dylan and the Beatles, about whom Aronowitz was writing; though history would give Dylan credit for turning the Fab Four on to marijuana, Aronowitz claimed he supplied the weed and rolled the first joint.

A month later, after a Dylan show in Princeton, Ginsberg brought Barbara Rubin, his nominal girlfriend at the time, to Aronowitz's house (Rubin and Dylan "barricaded themselves into [my] bedroom," Aronowitz recalled). At some point, Rubin urged Aronowitz to check out the Velvet Underground, and introduced him to Reed, who modestly told the writer, "I'm the fastest guitar player in the world!" Aronowitz attended one of their performances, likely at one of the so-called happenings, with Robbie Robertson, one of Dylan's new bandmates. "Robbie sits through one tune," recalled Aronowitz, "and then gets up and walks out in disgust." ("I liked a couple of the songs," the Band's virtuoso guitarist later noted, "but they had a bit of that 'look, we got guitars for Christmas' approach." Robertson was impressed by Nico, though.) Aronowitz thought the Velvets' demo was "a piece of shit." But Rubin kept at him, and eventually he made the band an offer, figuring he could shape them into something marketable.

On the day he came to sign the Velvets, Aronowitz was commandeering a limousine with Carole King, the twenty-four-year-old songwriting prodigy who lived in nearby West Orange with her husband/writing partner Gerry Goffin. Also along for the ride was Aronowitz's new drug buddy, the Rolling Stones' Brian Jones. (Aronowitz was known as a good drug connection, in the wake of the Beatles/Dylan stoner summit; Morrison recalled an earlier encounter with him and Jones when they were looking to score some LSD.) "Brian and Carole wait in the limo while I climb the five flights," Aronowitz wrote. "We talk things over. I tell them I will start them off with gigs in Village clubs that'll tighten and polish them for a rock audience. Lou Reed objects that they want to be overnight stars like the Beatles. 'I can't promise that,' I tell them. 'I can get you exposure. You yourselves have to do the rest.'"

* * *

Aronowitz's first booking for the Velvets was inauspicious—at Summit High School, near his home in suburban New Jersey, on December 11, 1965. They were second on the bill. Opening was a quartet of fourteen-year-olds from nearby Springfield who called themselves, accurately, the Forty Fingers. Headlining were Aronowitz's first management clients, the Myddle Class, a local garage band splitting the difference between Herman's Hermits and the Rolling Stones. They were older—all eighteen—with a strong local following. They'd just released their debut single, "Free as the Wind," a co-write with King and Goffin. King didn't like Aronowitz—she thought he was too old to be hanging out all night with young musicians "like a groupie." But Goffin was wowed by his connections, and the three had gone into business together, launching the short-lived Tomorrow Records in part to release the Myddle Class's debut LP.

Rock 'n' roll concerts were beyond rare in the upscale Jersey suburbs. Accordingly, many kids dressed up: after all, when the Beatles played the Ed Sullivan show in September, they were still wearing suits and ties. Mia Wolff, fifteen, came from nearby Berkeley Heights; she recalled wearing a cranberry-colored corduroy jacket, matching skirt, and a lacy white shirt. Other girls came in brightly patterned blouses, dress slacks, go-go boots or stylish loafers. Kids swigged liquor in the parking lot; bolder ones maybe took a few puffs on a joint.

Rob Norris was sixteen, and hadn't smoked weed yet. But he was a longhair, in fact had been kicked out of New Providence High School for violating the dress code. (When his parents had a lawyer threaten to sue the school, the dress code was modified and Norris was back in.) He also had a pipeline for rock 'n' roll gossip: a friend's sister was Al Aronowitz's babysitter. The afternoon of the concert, Norris got a call from the Summit High School pay phone about this strange band who had just arrived, every one of them dressed in black.

Roughly a thousand kids packed into the Summit High School auditorium that night, with hired security guards to keep order. King, Goffin, and Aronowitz mingled alongside Ken Jacobs—a young filmmaker in Mekas's circle—and his wife, Flo; Barbara Rubin roamed with her camera. "There was such an energy," recalls Stephen Philp. He was twelve, and his brother Rick played guitar in the Myddle Class; he'd even caught a ride that night in King's white Cadillac. The crowd was mainly there for the Myddle Class, and they were restless. The Forty Fingers played two songs and bailed. Then came the Velvet Underground.

"Two of them were wearing sunglasses," Norris recalled. "One of the guys with the shades had *very* long hair and was wearing silver jewelry. He was holding a large violin. The drummer had a Beatle haircut and was standing at a small, oddly arranged drum kit. Was it a boy or a girl?" Norris couldn't tell.

"Before we could take it all in, everyone was hit by a screeching surge of sound," he remembered, "with a pounding beat louder than anything we had ever heard."

The Velvets played three songs. Tucker recalled opening with "I'm Waiting for the Man," though other accounts have the first song as "There She Goes Again"—a chiming folk-rock melody attached to chord changes apparently lifted from Marvin Gaye's 1963 hit "Hitch Hike." If you don't listen too closely, it might sound like a generic teenage relationship plaint. But the description of a woman "down on her knees" and the reprise "you'd better hit her!" suggest something darker, conjuring violence in a way James Brown's "Hit me!" exhortations never did. It had more in common with the threateningly sexualized innuendo of Big Joe Turner's "Honey Hush," whose narrator threatens a woman with the "baseball bat" in his hands, or "He Hit Me (and It Felt Like a Kiss)," the startling 1962 song about domestic abuse written by King and Goffin and recorded by the Crystals, something a pop song student like Reed would have noted, maybe hearing the sort of nonjudgmental emotional documentation he was pursuing in his own writing. Years later Reed noted how his song in part reflected "just how violent America is," and stressed that "for me it's just a song, an attitude. It's got nothing to do with me. Look, I write songs I don't agree with . . . It has to do with a movie I saw, or a character who was a certain way. Or somebody I read about in the paper, or met at a party. I put him in a song and act him out."

Next, the Velvets played "Venus in Furs." Mia Wolff was with a group of fellow students. "I was mesmerized by the sound," she recalls. "The droning quality of it, the deep beat, the downstroke of the chords. We were probably high. I have a visceral memory of sitting there and just being erased by the music." Rob Norris recalled that the song "swelled and accelerated like a giant tidal wave which was threatening to engulf us all."

Sterling Morrison remembered "the murmur of surprise that greeted our appearance . . . increased to a roar of disbelief once we started to play 'Venus in Furs,' and swelled to a mighty howl of outrage and bewilderment by the end of 'Heroin.'" As Cale saw it from his spot on the stage, "we were so loud and horrifying to the high school audience that the majority of them, teachers, students and parents, fled screaming." Moe Tucker recalled the night's cultural revolution in more pedestrian terms. "I was a nervous wreck when we played that show," she said, adding that Reed probably was, too. "Our set was only about 15 minutes at the most and in each song something of mine broke. All my stuff was falling apart! The foot pedal broke in one song; the leg of the floor tom started going loose. I thought, 'Oh shit, I'm going to ruin this!'"

When the Velvets came offstage, it was clear to Cale that the headliners "were really pissed off . . . I tried to apologize to the lead singer, but secretly I was exhilarated." After a break, the Myddle Class took the stage, their fans cheered, and relative order was restored.

For his part, Al Aronowitz had been recording the show on his new Wollensack reel-to-reel tape machine, but in the hustle of the postshow load-out, the $300 unit went missing. Aronowitz was convinced the Velvets stole it; the mystery was never solved. A shame, because the machine probably contained a recording of the Velvet Underground's first show with Moe Tucker, and the first time they shared their worldview outside of the bohemian snowglobe of downtown Manhattan.

In the aftermath, a flame war erupted in the local paper that marked the start of the Velvets cult-hero standing. After the local paper's teen columnist, "Suzie Surfer," praised the Myddle Class and disparaged the Velvets, a group identified as "Some 'Velvet Underground' fans" wrote, "Why don't you stick to your surfboard, Suzie. You're no music critic!" To which she responded: "Stickin' to my surfboard is more fun than hearing about heroin and dope addicts."

* * *

Across the Hudson River, Max's Kansas City opened on December 6 at 213 Park Avenue South, between Seventeenth and Eighteenth Streets, in the space formerly occupied by a restaurant called the Southern. Max's proprietor was Mickey Ruskin, an ex-lawyer with a knack for transforming downtown venues into bohemian salons. The Tenth Street Coffeehouse and Les Deux Mégots (a play on the Parisian literary hangout Café des Deux Magots), on East Seventh, both his, were tag-team birthplaces of the Lower East Side poetry scene, hosting the likes of Allen Ginsberg, LeRoi Jones, Diane di Prima, Denise Levertov, and Ted Berrigan. Soon realizing that "poets aren't really drinkers, and artists are," Ruskin launched the Ninth Circle, a West Village beatnik bar that became an art-crowd magnet. He eventually sold his share to bum around Europe and North Africa. When he returned to New York, he hit on what he hoped was a reasonably lucrative concept: a combination bar/restaurant that could serve business lunches during the day, and become a hipster destination after dark.

The name was concocted by Ruskin's pal, the Black Mountain poet Joel Oppenheimer, who simply liked the sound of "Max's" and figured "all the steakhouses had Kansas City on the menu because the best steak was Kansas City–cut." An air of nighttime exclusivity was cultivated from the get-go. At the opening-night party in January, Ruskin half-jokingly told an *East Village Other* reporter: "Please don't do a story [on Max's]. I'm afraid all those East Village junkies will show up here. This is a high class joint. They won't be able to afford it."

Soon, artists relocated from the Ninth Circle, making Max's their own. The sculptor John Chamberlain, who worked with crushed auto parts, and the musician-turned-abstract-painter Larry Poons were instant regulars. Artists gave Ruskin pieces (some of which he installed in the club) in exchange for a rolling tab. The location—beyond Greenwich Village, above the bohemian border of Fourteenth Street—turned out to be a plus. Lots of New York fashion photographers had studios nearby; artists were also colonizing the neighborhood. "Donald Judd lived across the street, Larry Zox lived across the street, Frosty Myers was there . . . For the first six or seven months, that was the basis of my crowd." Soon, they'd be joined by Andy Warhol.

* * *

Andrew Warhola grew up in Pittsburgh, the child of working-class Eastern Europeans. His father died when he was thirteen, and like Reed, he struggled with mental illness. "I had three nervous breakdowns as a child," Warhol wrote (with ghostwriters) in *The Philosophy of Andy Warhol*. He also suffered a series of illnesses, triggered by a strep infection, that left him battling Sydenham's chorea (aka Saint Vitus's dance), a neurological disorder that confined him to bed for a month and left him nervous, frail, and a natural target for bullies. But Warhol developed other sorts of personal power. "I learned when I was little that whenever I got aggressive and tried to tell someone what to do, nothing happened," he wrote. "I just couldn't carry it off. I learned that you actually have more power when you shut up, because at least that way people will start to maybe doubt themselves." It was a strategy he'd use to great effect throughout his life.

Like Reed with Schwartz, Warhol found a mentor who made him serious about his work: a teacher, Joseph Fitzpatrick, who told his students that art "is not just a subject. It's a way of life." Warhol's creative life began with commercial work, like Reed's at Pickwick. The advertising world introduced Warhol to collaboration, as opposed to the notion of the artist isolated in the studio, a key to his process moving forward. One example of this was a 1951 series of blotted-line drawings for a CBS Radio drug-abuse documentary titled *The Nation's Nightmare*. Warhol based one striking image on photographs of a young man, sleeve rolled up, pantomiming an injection (it was evidently a fun shoot; another contact sheet image shows the same man mugging with a toilet paper roll on his nose).

Warhol shared apartments in his early New York years, also like Reed, with a revolving cast of artists and other oddballs. By 1964, he was successful enough as a commercial artist and emerging fine artist to set up a studio apart from his home, and in January, he secured a large loft on the fourth floor of 231 East Forty-seventh Street, which rented for $200 a month. It was dubbed "The Factory" for its remarkable output and worker-bee vibe; it swiftly became a magnet for collaborators, peers, groupies, fame junkies, speed freaks, and other hangers-on.

Warhol developed his version of "Pop Art" in tandem with other artists, among them his rival art stars Jasper Johns and Robert Rauschenberg. Warhol riffed on corporate logos, package design, news and publicity photos, with both traditional painting and silkscreening. The idea was to reflect the real world with apparent dispassion, allowing people's own attitudes about late-stage capitalist enterprise, mass media, and the art market to fill in the blanks. He was a mirror, depicting car crashes and police violence, movie stars and mass-market soup cans with both a journalist's remove and an artist's curatorial eye, in poker-faced works that could be read as critique or endorsement, or both, or neither. As much for his marketing savvy as his conceptual brilliance, Warhol's "fine art" business soon became wildly successful, influential, inescapable.

By late 1965, when he met Reed, he was an international art star who'd recently pivoted into movie-making. Inspired by the 1959 short *Pull My Daisy*, the Beat Generation object lesson made by Robert Frank and Jack Kerouac, Warhol got hold of a 1929 Bolex 16mm and started making films in earnest. He made the Film-Makers' Cinematheque and Cooperative his film school; the queer surrealism of Kenneth Anger (who shot his landmark *Scorpio Rising* in Brooklyn and Manhattan around this time) was a major influence, along with the work of Mekas, Rubin, and especially Jack Smith. Warhol is said to have seen *Flaming Creatures* at least two dozen times.

Barbara Rubin was among the clearly enthusiastic participants in Warhol's breakthrough film, *Kiss*, a fifty-minute assemblage of face-sucking couples, some of them interracial or same-sex; one take featured Rubin vigorously smooching her fellow filmmaker Naomi Levine. Warhol soon upped the provocation ante with *Blow Job* (a thirty-minute close-up of the face of a man getting his dick sucked) and *Couch*, featuring sex so explicit, Warhol initially screened it only in his studio for friends. Warhol's films may have been "underground" stylistically, but they were made by one of the world's most famous artists. "I can't see how I was ever 'underground,'" he demurred in his book *POPism*, "since I've always wanted people to notice me."

Attention, of course, brought problems. On December 17, 1963, *The New York Times* ran a front-page story, "Growth of Overt Homosexuality in City Provokes Wide Concern." It detailed raids on gay bars and hand-wringing over "the homosexual problem in New York," presenting the case of psychiatrists who believed there was "overwhelming evidence that homosexuals are created—generally by ill-adjusted parents—not born," and asserting that these "deviates" and "inverts" can "be cured by sophisticated analytic and therapeutic techniques." The raids were the opening salvo in a campaign to clean up the city in preparation for the upcoming World's Fair in Queens, a huge event promising to be a civic cash cow. Raids were staged on the Pocket Theater downtown (where Cage had presented *Vexations*) and another underground film house, the Gramercy Arts on 138 East Twenty-seventh Street. The New Bowery Theater on St. Mark's Place was raided in March for screening *Flaming Creatures*, with police confiscating the film along with Warhol's *Filming* Normal Love. In April, Warhol's commission for the World's Fair's New York State Pavilion was nixed at the eleventh hour. *13 Most Wanted Men*—a twenty-foot-square array of mug shots from the New York Police Department's Most Wanted list, silkscreened onto Masonite panels—had already been mounted on the exterior walls. But city administrators, key among them the fair's poobah Robert Moses, found the content inappropriate, for its uncelebratory noir creepiness and perhaps also for its slyly queer title (the unspoken backstory was that the photos came to Warhol via a gay NYC cop dating his friend). Warhol's response was to simply paint over the panels in silver, and declare the monochrome squares a new work.

Indeed, Warhol, like Reed, was a provocateur; his criminal portraits weren't that different from Reed's musical portraits of criminal behavior. Both men wanted to make money. And Warhol was queer, exclusively homosexual by almost all accounts. He was surprisingly upfront about it, swish in presentation even in the '50s, and understood the avant-garde potential of queerness straightaway. He'd tried to show drawings of boys kissing in the early '50s, and his very first gallery show, *Andy Warhol: Fifteen Drawings Based on the Writing of Truman Capote*, connected him to his hero, one of the most famous gay men in America. By the mid-'60s, Warhol was a fixture of gay New York, both tony uptown and artsier downtown, though his Pop Art success traded explicitly gay themes for the coded language of camp: the drag glamour of his Marilyn Monroe silkscreens, and the veiled homoeroticism in his sublimely cheesy Elvis prints, with their six-guns and prominent crotch.

Warhol's filmmaking pivot also begat his systemic creation of "superstars," a term repurposed as readymade from the vernacular of opera fans and Hollywood. One of his first and most well-known was Edie Sedgwick. She'd had a rough upbringing, including sexual abuse. In addition to her own institutionalization (where she met Barbara Rubin), she had a brother who hung himself in a mental hospital, where he was sent for issues supposedly involving his homosexuality. Sedgwick and Warhol connected in March '65, at a birthday party for Tennessee Williams, and soon became inseparable. Her beauty and magnetism were startling. She'd worked as a model, but was too undisciplined to maintain the regimen. It hardly mattered: at twenty-one, she'd come into an inheritance said to have paid her $10,000 a month, which she managed to burn through, fueling endless parties, taking the entire Factory gang to fancy restaurants and footing the bill. She was a beguiling dancer, a big fan of amphetamines, funny and charming— a reality-show natural decades before there was such a thing. She was soon cast by Warhol in her own star vehicle, the fittingly named *Poor Little Rich Girl*. She cut her hair tomboy short, bleached it blond, and started dressing like Warhol, becoming his mirror in a striped Breton sailor's shirt. As a frail, effeminate man deeply troubled by his physical appearance, he couldn't have asked for a more flattering reflection.

The notion of the Factory "superstar" evolved from Sedgwick, and was rooted in Warhol's long obsession with movie stars. He cherished a signed photo of Shirley Temple he got as a child. A 1963 party for Warhol at the Topanga Canyon house of the actor and modern art fan Dennis Hopper drew the likes of Peter Fonda, Sal Mineo, and Suzanne Pleshette, and would be remembered by Warhol years later as "the most exciting thing that had ever happened to me" (despite his drinking too much pink champagne and puking on the drive home). His own superstardom blossomed from his engagement with movie star images—Marilyn, Liz Taylor, Elvis—and the Factory social scene was his attempt to curate, choreograph, aestheticize, and market his own never-ending verité film-shoot. In *The Philosophy of Andy Warhol*, he described superstars as "people who are very talented, but whose talents are hard to define and almost impossible to market." They could, however, be enlisted to market him.

Warhol was a genuine music fan, and saw it as a branding element. Attending the Metropolitan Opera was a key part of his social life, ditto musical theater and the ballet. He had a taste for the raw and the cooked: He adored Bessie Smith's lusty blues, and wore out a recording of Edith Sitwell's *Façade (An Entertainment)*, an avant-pop proto-rap operetta-cum-"happening" from the 1920s. When he pivoted to Pop Art, his studio hi-fi signaled it, blasting 45s by his latest British Invasion faves alongside American girl groups such as the Supremes and the Jaynetts (whose 1963 hit "Sally Go 'Round the Roses" Warhol adored). *Vinyl*, his camp film riff on Anthony Burgess's novel *A Clockwork Orange*, used music by the Kinks and the Rolling Stones. Warhol was even in a rock band himself for a hot minute, an art-star supergroup called the Druds: Warhol sang backup alongside Lucas Samaras and Patti Oldenburg, with Larry Poons on guitar, La Monte Young's sax, and the moonlighting drummer Walter De Maria. (By Warhol's account, he sang badly, Samaras and Oldenburg fought over the music, and the band fell apart after a handful of rehearsals.)

The idea of using a rock band in his art production/promotion stayed with Warhol. In early '65, he connected with the Fugs, a band of provocateur East Village poet-musicians led by Tuli Kupferberg and Ed Sanders. Warhol was a fan of Sanders's 'zine, *Fuck You: A Magazine of the Arts*, and silkscreened banners for his Peace Eye bookstore on East Tenth Street. The Fugs played at the Factory, and Warhol had his assistant, Billy Name, take pictures of them. But the association didn't develop past that.

* * *

While they might've crossed paths at one of the Cinematheque "happenings" that summer, Warhol properly met Reed in December at Café Bizarre, a sleepy tourist trap at 106 West Third Street, just off Washington Square. Al Aronowitz arranged a residency for the Velvets, figuring they could woodshed there, just as the Lovin' Spoonful, another NYC folk-rock group, had earlier that year (they were now touring with the Supremes). The Bizarre had bohemian credentials from its run as a dual-purpose coffeehouse and fringe-theater in the early '60s (it was featured in a 1961 *New Yorker* piece on cabaret licensing). But it was past its prime, and was now decorated in Halloween kitsch, conjuring a set from the new TV series *The Addams Family*, with a riot of candelabras, skulls, shrunken heads, and tribal masks hung on its exposed-brick walls. Its menu featured dubious confections such as "Schizophrenic Sunday" (basically a banana split) and "Voodoo-It-Yourself," which came with a small doll and toothpicks.

"We got six nights a week," according to Sterling Morrison, "some ungodly number of sets, 40 minutes on and 20 minutes off. We played some covers—[Chuck Berry's] 'Little Queenie,' [Jimmy Reed's] 'Bright Lights Big City,' the black R&B songs Lou and I liked—and as many of our songs as we had." Because the stage was so tiny, Moe Tucker used hand percussion. Indeed, the band got better and tighter, which isn't to say they went over well. "We poured our vitriolic sound on the heads of the tourists drinking coffee and looking at their postcards," recalled Cale, "all trying to pretend that they were not hearing somebody say that heroin was his life and his wife." People constantly walked out on their sets.

Barbara Rubin set things in motion. She brought Mekas to see them. She also invited Warhol's silk-screening assistant Gerard Malanga, who'd helped out on *Christmas on Earth*. A strikingly handsome Italian kid from the Bronx, he was a poet who liked to dance; he'd even been invited to show off his rock 'n' roll moves as a regular on Alan Freed's *Big Beat* TV show, an afternoon broadcast in late 1959 on WNEW Channel 5, a local reboot of the national network show canceled when southern affiliates freaked out over interracial dancing. When he was a college student in Staten Island, Malanga met Warhol, who was smitten: the artist wrote Malanga a mash note on the occasion of his twentieth birthday about how "divine" it was to finally kiss him. Malanga was cast as the star of Warhol's *Vinyl*, and soon became the artist's right-hand man—"consigliore to the Godmother of the New York cultural cosa nostra," as the critic Ed McCormack would write.

Rubin, the luminous secretary of state, instructed Malanga to bring his bullwhip, a new dancing prop, to the Velvets show, and he impressed Reed and Cale when he came right up to the front—there was no stage, per se—and gyrated with it provocatively during "Venus in Furs." Cale recalled his performance as "exquisite" and "reptilian."

Rubin wanted Malanga to help her film the Velvets for her planned second film (the never-completed epic *Christmas on Earth Continued*). In turn, he asked Warhol's filmmaking partner Paul Morrissey. The son of a lawyer, Morrissey was a Catholic-school kid from Yonkers, about ten years Warhol's junior, who'd studied filmmaking at Fordham University in the Bronx and served a brief stint in the army—"a thin hyperactive young man with a high-pitched voice and a fast mouth," according to Warhol's biographer Victor Bockris, a cross between "a New England whaling captain and Bob Dylan." Morrissey and Warhol met at a film screening in 1965 and hit it off, and soon Morrissey installed himself at the Factory, ascending from floor sweeper to one of Warhol's main business associates and collaborators. He was by all indications anti-drugs and asexual, characteristics that in fact made him a valuable minority in Warhol's circle.

It was Morrissey who suggested Warhol join them all, and the Factory gang rolled up on the club. "The [Café] Bizarre management wasn't too thrilled with them," Warhol recalled in *POPism*. "Their music was beyond the pale—way too loud and insane for any tourist coffeehouse clientele. People would leave looking dazed and damaged." But he was impressed, especially when Malanga reprised his whip dance. Cale isolated that as the moment "when Andy saw that what he was doing could be connected with what we were doing."

* * *

Warhol invited the band to come by the Factory. The timing was perfect: he'd just been approached by the theater producer Michael Myerberg, who planned to open a huge discotheque in a Queens airplane hangar. They figured they'd call the club Andy Warhol's Up and screen his films alongside rock bands, just like a "happening." The presence of Warhol, Sedgwick, and their media-magnet crew would ensure a draw despite the remote location. It seemed better the band be unknown, rather than an established act, as Warhol would be the main attraction.

Indeed, Warhol's summit with Bob Dylan that winter suggested too many superstars might spoil the broth. Arranged by Barbara Rubin, it was Warhol's first collaboration with a bona fide music celebrity. The newly minted rock star came to the Factory and sat for a pair of Warhol's Screen Tests, his ongoing series of filmed portraits. Shot on single unedited reels of 16mm film, each roughly three minutes long, they were essentially headshots, extended to reveal the sitter's character. "They were like oil and water," Gerard Malanga said. "Just bad friction. Dylan immediately hated Andy and Andy thought Dylan was corny." After the shoot, according to one account, Dylan helped himself to a silk-screened Elvis canvas as payment, tying it to the roof of his car with help from Rubin.

By late '65, Reed surely knew of Warhol as a figure of note. Even Tucker, less of a culture vulture, had read about him ("Of course I knew [who he was]. He was hot shit at the time.") Still, when Reed, Cale, Morrison, and Tucker turned up at Warhol's Factory on Forty-seventh

Street, they entered alien territory: a huge loft space, walls silvered in paint and tinfoil, with busy workers—most likely percolating on amphetamines—attending to one task or another: it was like a theatrical rocket ship careering through space as *La Traviata* blasted on the stereo.

Paul Morrissey sat the band down and laid out Warhol's proposition: the artist would manage the band, buy them new instruments, get them bookings and a record deal in exchange for 25 percent of whatever money they made.

The bandmembers looked at one another. Reed surveyed the silver space.

"This sounds like a lot of fun," he said.

The Velvets' nominal manager, Al Aronowitz, was thus written out of the script ("I am a total asshole and idiot to have put any faith in a handshake deal with a bunch of junkie hustlers," he'd later write). The band also ended their Café Bizarre residency. On what would be their final night, the wife of the manager, Rick Allmen, was displeased with the abrasive "Black Angel's Death Song," and she told them to knock it off.

"The exact words were 'Play one more song like that and you're fired,'" Reed recalled.

"So we led off the next set with it," Morrison said. "A really good version, too."

* * *

Reed and his bandmates lugged their instruments up to the Factory and made it their base camp, folding themselves into the scene. As they learned, it was no twenty-four-hour party, even if its denizens slept little. Warhol was a workaholic who kept close tabs on his finances. He was constantly making, doing. Socializing was networking: courting potential patrons and commissions, seeking out new superstars, looking for ideas to trade, borrow, or steal. As Morrison observed, the Factory "was usually pretty quiet. The noise happened later, after you went somewhere."

Reed, Cale, and Morrison had their first big night out with the Factory crew on New Year's Eve 1965. They began early, unsuccessfully trying to crash a party at the playwright Edward Albee's with Warhol, Sedgwick, Malanga, and the Harvard classics scholar and underground film actor Donald Lyons. One account has them heading up to the Apollo Theater in Harlem to see James Brown. Either way, the crew eventually wound up at Sedgwick's apartment. They'd heard CBS would finally be airing their underground film story on the late-night report, which, with astonishing serendipity, featured the Velvets, from their shoot with Heliczer, as well as Warhol and Sedgwick. The group huddled around her black-and-white TV set.

The segment began with the newscaster Dave Dougan outside the Bridge, a theater space on St. Mark's Place, a banner advertising the Fugs next to his head.

"Not everyone digs underground films," he announces, looking like a complete square, "but those who do can dig them here."

One can imagine everyone in the room exploding with laughter.

There's a clip of Jonas Mekas speaking professorially on the difference between "narrative" and "poetic" cinema. And then the Velvet Underground were on TV. The CBS News crew had trudged up five flights to Heliczer's loft—essentially the Velvets' group home at that point, where Reed generally slept on a ragged mattress on the floor ("It made me nervous because we had rats and I worried about being bit")—and struggled to set up their lights. Reed, Cale, and Morrison were shown getting their faces and torsos painted, like the novitiates in Rubin's *Christmas on Earth*. They performed without singing, Morrison recalled, and no music was audible on the short clip that aired under the newscaster's voice-over. But there was Cale, sawing away at his viola next to Reed, strumming an electric guitar maniacally. Morrison played his coolly; Tucker, masked, whacked a tambourine with a stick; Piero Heliczer gripped a movie camera to his eye; Barbara Rubin, in a nun's habit, watched from the sideline. Then Sedgwick was seen dancing at a party, a vision of mod gracefulness. The interviewer asked what her parents thought about her work with Warhol. "Arghhh! They hate it; they're terrified," she said, laughing. "They hated the idea of my doing any modeling to make my own way. And as soon as I got into this, they're sending telegrams saying 'oh, you've got to go model, please!'" Explaining why he made movies, Warhol offered: "Well, it's just easier to do than, um, painting, because the camera has a motor, and you just turn it on and you walk away."

The newscaster asks if there's anything special he is "trying to say" with his films. Warhol waits a beat, then responds, utterly deadpan, from behind tinted, wrap-around eyeglasses: "No."

It served as a perfect setup for the newscaster's snarky outro ("Andy Warhol tries to say nothing, and succeeds"). But in Sedgwick's living room that night, the kicker was probably lost amid the laughter and amphetamine chatter. The first-ever film document of the Velvet Underground, albeit silent, had landed on the nightly news. Soon, the clock struck midnight, and Reed's thoughts on the new year ahead were no doubt flashing like fireworks.

4.

LOWER EAST SIDE

(1966)

DISCUSSED: Nico, amphetamines, Billy Name, the Exploding Plastic Inevitable, the Dom, the death of God, Tom Wilson, Los Angeles, the Mamas and the Papas, the Grateful Dead, Frank Zappa, Bill Graham, San Francisco, the Fillmore, the death of Delmore Schwartz, the Yardbirds, David Bowie né Jones

---

*It is less a reflection of a period
Than an anticipation of it.*

—Gerard Malanga, "Chanel"

Christa Päffgen was born in 1938 in Germany, and spent the World War II years moving around the country with her mother. Her father, a soldier, died in combat. After the war she wound up in Berlin, where she hung around the elite KaDeWe (aka Kaufhaus des Westens, or Department Store of the West) shopping center, hoping to be noticed. Tall, shapely, with full lips, high cheekbones, fine blond hair, and cool blue eyes, she didn't have to wait long. By her teens she was modeling high fashion for German photographers, and by the time Reed and David Weisman saw her cameo in Fellini's *La Dolce Vita* in Syracuse, she'd already graced magazine covers across Europe. Her style was mutable. In a 1956 shoot with the photographer Jeanloup Sieff, who'd help make Twiggy an icon ten years later, Päffgen sits on a table, nude but for pantyhose, sporting an ultrashort Audrey Hepburn pixie cut. Glancing coolly over her shoulder with an unlit cigarette in her hand, she's a ravishing figure of indeterminate gender.

Relocating to Paris, she listened to jazz and the popular singers of the day, foremost among them Edith Piaf and Jacques Brel. Päffgen wanted to sing, and was determined to move away from modeling, just like her character in the Fellini film. She took her stage name from her lover, Nico Papatakis, a nightclub owner who encouraged her to take voice lessons and brought her to New York, where she studied acting at the Lee Strasberg Studio (Marilyn Monroe, she claimed, was among her classmates). After a fling with the French actor Alain Delon, she gave birth to a son, Christian Aaron, known as Ari. On the 1963 New Year's cover of French *Elle*, Nico held the newborn in a bundle of fleece, the Virgin Mary as a society matron with a blond bouffant. Delon denied paternity (though his mother often took care of Ari). Nico was on her own.

Her voice lessons helped in her biggest film role, the lead in Jacques Poitrenaud's 1963 *Strip-Tease*. Billed as Krista Nico, she played Ariane, a struggling ballet dancer who fumbles into fame as a highbrow stripper before reclaiming her calling. The pianist Joe Turner, an American expat who worked with Louis Armstrong in the 1930s, plays her artistic conscience, Sam, in a nod to *Casablanca*. Nico had limited acting skills, but informed Ariane with strength, agency, and self-respect, humanizing her without cheap moralizing. The film was Serge Gainsbourg's debut soundtrack commission, and Nico recorded his title song, a steamy cha-cha-cha on which she breathily tells off a "voyeur" over bongos and brass (her version was shelved in favor of one by the popular Juliette Gréco, who was involved with Gainsbourg at the time).

Nico's musical ambition was further catalyzed by Bob Dylan. Following his show at London's Royal Festival Hall on May 17, 1964, he traveled to France to meet the singer Hughes Aufray, who was planning an LP of his songs, *Aufre Chante Dylan*. At some point Dylan met Nico, who invited him up to her place; per legend, he emerged one full week later. Nico then accompanied him to Greece, where he'd write songs for his next LP, *Another Side of Bob Dylan*. As Lou Reed was bidding farewell to Shelley Albin, Dylan and Nico parted, as Dylan returned to New York to record some new songs, including "Motorpsycho Nightmare," in which he described being seduced by a farmer's daughter named Rita, who "looked like she stepped out of *La Dolce*

Vita." More significant is a song written in Greece that didn't make the album, "I'll Keep It with Mine." A romantic ballad, then unusual for Dylan, it would seem tailored for Nico's unusual low-register voice. She believed the song was written about her, and though Dylan never copped to it, he apparently had a demo acetate sent to her, fulfilling a promise to write a song for her to sing.

But that summer she'd record another song, her debut for Immediate Records, a label newly launched by the Rolling Stones' manager, Andrew Loog Oldham. "I'm Not Sayin'" is folk-pop just before Dylan's electric transfiguration, wrapped in orchestral strings with guitars and other accompaniment by Brian Jones—with whom Nico had begun a relationship—and a young studio musician named Jimmy Page. Written at the brink of the free-love era by one Gordon Lightfoot, it's about the coexistence of love and unfaithfulness. In a black-and-white promo clip, Nico wanders along the Thames, lip syncing imprecisely, in boots, a mid-length skirt, a tight-fitting shirt, her pale hair cut into stylish bangs. "I may not be alone each time you see me, or show up when I promised that I would," she sings, bobbing as if on a boat, surveying the water and, finally, deigning to look into camera lens, implacable.

Nico met Warhol, Sedgwick, and Malanga in a Paris nightclub during their European gallery blitz in May '65. She was obviously camera-ready "superstar" material, and Malanga invited her to call when she was in New York. That autumn she did. Warhol arranged to meet her at a Mexican restaurant: "She was sitting at a table with a pitcher in front of her, dipping her long beautiful fingers into the sangría, lifting out slices of wine-soaked oranges. When she saw us, she tilted her head to the side and brushed her hair back with her other hand and said very slowly, "I only like the fooood that flooooats in the wiiine."

She'd come prepared. She showed Warhol her single—which had tanked in Britain—and the Dylan acetate, talking of her aspirations. Warhol recalls Morrissey, who accompanied him to the meeting, was stunned, raving that Nico was "the most beautiful creature who ever lived."

Some accounts suggest that Nico saw the Velvets the same night as Warhol did; Nico would later tell a French TV interviewer it was "the most beautiful moment of my life." Psychedelics might've had something to do with her reaction; Al Aronowitz claimed he took her to see the band at Café Bizarre after he and Nico spent an LSD-fueled night in a motel at the Delaware Water Gap. Morrissey claims credit for the idea of pairing Nico with the Velvet Underground. It made sense on a number of levels, not least as a tactic to get the European actor involved in Warhol's film enterprise.

The idea didn't go over well with the band, but must've stung Reed in particular, who was already insecure about his talents as a frontman. "The first thing I realized about the Velvet Underground was that they had no lead singer," said Morrissey, "because Lou Reed was such an uncomfortable performer. I think he forced himself to do it because he was so ambitious, but [he] was not a natural performer." However, Morrissey and Warhol were persuasive, and Cale thought it would work, so Reed conceded and Nico was on board. "I was just this poor little rock and roller," Reed later lamented wryly, "and here was this goddess. We didn't really feel we had a choice. I mean, we could have just walked away from it, or we had a chanteuse. So we had a group meeting and said 'All right, we'll have a chanteuse, and Lou will write a song or two for her, and then we'll still be the Velvet Underground.' Y'know, why not?"

* * *

On January 3, the expanded band—now three men, two women—convened for their first full rehearsal at the Factory. Recorded evidence suggests Nico sat out for most of it. The band warmed up with some instrumentals. A Bo Diddley groove titled "Miss Joanie Lee" stretched out for eleven minutes, strafed with surf-style slide guitar flourishes (likely Morrison's) and outbursts of free-jazz noise (likely Reed's). Another jam began with a riff on the Beatles' "Day Tripper"—a pop radio staple at the time—then segued into a dance-party grind, with more frantic guitar. At one point, Reed recites the lyrics to "Venus in Furs."

"'Shiny, shiny, shiny boots of leather'—t'get right into it, right?" he says, giggling.

Later, Reed sings "Heroin" with riveting new affect: gone are the folkie mannerisms, replaced with a straightforward, streetwise read, a Long Island dirtbag version of Berg's *sprechstimme*. The guitars play off Cale's amplified viola, which shrieks like a faulty turbine, with Moe Tucker keeping time on tambourine, gradually accelerating, then slooowing down, as the drug takes effect. Later, Sterling and Cale riff on Booker T. and the MGs' "Green Onions" as Reed coaches Nico on the lyrics to "There She Goes Again." In her matter-of-factly stoic Germanic delivery, Nico recites the same words Reed sang a month prior at Summit High School, about a girl "down on her knees," but with history unspooling in new associations: war culture, sex as commodity, fear of feminine power, looming threats of assault.

She pauses after a false start. "I have to learn that," she said; "it can be still higher."

The band shifts keys and Reed joins in, with evident frustration, snarling an approximation of duet harmony. But it falls apart, perhaps intentionally.

"I really fucked this up," he says.

* * *

The Velvet Underground's first gig with Nico was at the Hotel Delmonico, 502 Park Avenue at Fifty-ninth Street, on Thursday, January 13. It was a swanky setting with bona fide rock 'n' roll history. Brian Epstein met Ed Sullivan at the Delmonico in November 1963 to plan the Beatles' first appearance on his TV show; the band got stoned with Dylan and Aronowitz there a year later. The occasion for the coming-out party was an unlikely one: the band would be the musical guests at the 43rd Annual Dinner of the New York Society for Clinical Psychiatry.

"I was invited to speak at the [banquet] by the doctor who was the chairman of the event," Warhol explained in *POPism*. "I told him I'd be glad to 'speak,' if I could do it through movies . . . he said fine. Then when I met the Velvets I decided that I wanted to 'speak' with them instead, and he said fine to that, too."

The scruffy Warhol entourage arrived as the black-tie banquet was beginning. Andy played along, in a black tie and jacket over corduroys, plus his signature sunglasses. Nico wore a stylish white pantsuit. Maureen Tucker, behind tiny beatnik sunglasses, looked genderless in slacks and a striped T-shirt. Reed and Cale wore matching black turtlenecks, Cale accessorizing with a thick rhinestone snake necklace, Reed adding a rumpled sports jacket, collar popped Elvis Presley–style. Chewing gum and sipping a martini in a leopard-skin-pattern coat, Edie Sedgwick mingled with the psychiatrists, a species with which she had some experience. Gerard Malanga, in formal attire, brought his bullwhip. And naturally, Warhol brought a film crew: Mekas and Rubin, abetted by Warhol's jack-of-all-trades assistant Billy Name and Warhol's then boyfriend, the Harvard dropout and neophyte filmmaker Danny Williams.

It's a fair bet some of the group was fueled by speed. Cheap, easy to get, and mostly legal, the Factory crew consumed it regularly; Warhol preferred Obetrol, a cocktail of amphetamine, dextroamphetamine, and methamphetamine similar to modern-day Adderall, while Reed preferred Desoxyn, straight methamphetamine, stronger and longer-lasting. Either way, speed was the ideal New York City drug: it kept you awake to work and/or party around the clock, with the extra benefit of keeping you slim (a side effect the eternally body-conscious Warhol valued, as would Reed). More unpleasant side effects ranged from anxiety to full-blown "amphetamine psychosis," as well as psychological addiction and assorted physical maladies.

But these seemed like minor drawbacks to an antidepressant whose popularity rivaled that of modern SSRI drugs like Prozac and Lexapro. Distributed widely via legit prescriptions from psychiatrists and general medical practitioners, as well through gray-market diet clinics and assorted black-market channels, it's estimated that between 8 and 10 billion amphetamine tablets were ingested annually in the United States between 1963 and 1969. Unlike SSRI drugs, they lent themselves to extreme use. Some of the Warhol crew (chief among them the actor Robert Olivo, aka Ondine or the Pope) took heroic doses of speed and slept rarely, dubbing themselves the Amphetamine Rapture Group, or A-men, a moniker telegraphing their drug-enhanced superiority complex with a tidy sacrilegious punch line. (They were alternately known as the Mole People.) Less-extreme use of amphetamines—by politicians, sports figures, masters of industry, and everyday working joes—was so common as to be utterly unremarkable; President Kennedy got regular fifteen-milligram injections of amphetamines, in a cocktail with hormones and vitamins, to stay on top of his game. Danny Fields, a brilliant pop-music fanatic whom Reed would meet soon enough, helped himself to pills from the thousand-count bottles at the office of his dad's medical practice. "I was on amphetamines my whole life," he said. "On the dining room table there was a bowl of amphetamines—they took them in the morning so they wouldn't overeat."

When the three hundred doctors and their well-dressed partners were seated in the magnificent white-and-gold Hotel Delmonico ballroom and the food was served—roast beef, string beans, baby potatoes—the director of St. Vincent Hospital's in-service psychiatric unit made remarks from the dais. And then a spotlight illuminated the Velvet Underground, who'd set up beneath a pair of candelabra wall sconces. They began "Heroin," Reed working the song's looping riff, describing what happens when the smack begins to flow. It's conceivable that among the hundreds of New York–area psychiatrists in that room was the one that prescribed his electroconvulsive therapy years before. No recordings of the performance survive, but one imagines Morrison stretching out the notes, Cale laying into his steel viola strings to generate his infernal howl, and Reed strumming faster, amp cranked, and maybe thinking about being a teenager, electrodes on his skull, bit in his mouth, and maybe he aimed the electricity of his guitar into the darkened ballroom at the candle-lit skulls of the doctors and their dates in their tuxes and their ballgowns, to share a small taste of what New York psychiatry had done for him. During "Venus in Furs," Gerard Malanga reenacted the whip dance he'd improvised at Café Bizarre. Edie Sedgwick danced with him, in her black tank top, bright red skirt, and delicious speed grin, the two of them throwing writhing shadows against the wall, while Reed implored the crowd to taste the whip and "bleeeeeeeeeeeeed for meeeee."

At some point in the set, Barbara Rubin and Billy Name had burst out of the service door with a movie camera and a blinding, hand-held floodlight, training it on people as if conducting interrogations.

"Is his penis big enough?" Rubin asked one well-dressed woman, pointing at her companion. "Do you eat her out?" Rubin asked him, following up with moon-faced curiosity. The man smirked, sneered, recoiled. Rubin chided him. "Why are you getting embarrassed? You're a psychiatrist; you're not supposed to get embarrassed!"

Before the band finished, people had begun heading for the doors, collecting their minks and overcoats. Newspaper reporters, likely tipped in advance by Warhol as well as the organizers' flak, waited in the lobby for feedback on the feedback, and the guests gamely obliged. Dr. Allen Lilienthal told the *New York Times* arts critic Grace Glueck, "I suppose you could call this gathering a spontaneous eruption of the id." Another doctor described the performance as "a repetition of the concrete quite akin to the L.S.D. experience," yet another called it "ridiculous, outrageous, painful . . . it seemed like a whole prison ward had escaped." The event's host, Dr. Campbell, who the *Herald Tribune* described as "a swinging post-Freudian," called the performance "a short-lived torture of cacophony." A colleague of his announced simply, "I'm ready to vomit."

The next day's newspaper headlines were punch lines: "SHOCK TREATMENT FOR PSYCHIATRISTS," declared the *Herald Tribune*. It was good copy and good publicity for all, win-win. Yet for all the column inches, the Velvet Underground's music was mentioned only in passing, overshadowed by Warhol in what would prove a portent. In one paper, Cale was identified as bandleader with no mention whatsoever of Reed. Still, if the debut of the Velvet Underground & Nico was dismissed as "a combination of rock'n'roll and Egyptian bellydance" music in *The New York Times*, it was still covered, and the fact that it was part prank made it sweeter. "It was hilarious," Reed said later. "It was just a big joke."

* * *

Mekas would eventually use footage from the performance in an abstract short. A more vivid film document was shot days later by Warhol at the Factory, apparently intended as motion picture "wallpaper" for his forthcoming multimedia production, which would have the Velvets at its center. The opening shot is an extended close-up of Nico, mostly expressionless. She addresses her son, Ari, age three, off-screen, then taps a tambourine with a maraca as the band triangulates rock thrust, R&B groove, and drone. At one point Ari grabs the maraca and joins in. The film is classic Warholian aimlessness, unedited static shots punctuated with lurching pans and zooms, focus racked in and out seemingly at random. The image might be a postwar parent's nightmare: unreachable young people, eyes hidden behind wraparound shades, playing alien music at ear-bleed volume in an apparently drugged trance, a toddler crawling around at their feet. Ultimately, the police show up, presumably responding to a noise complaint, which may have been called in from the Factory for the camera's benefit ("It's still too loud!" someone hollers off camera). Reed puts down his black Gretsch hollow body, removes his shades, wipes sweat off his face, replaces his shades. The End.

The footage demonstrates one thing clearly: Nico would be the band's centerpiece. Her pitch might waver, but her voice was gripping, grave and girlish, tender and invulnerable. It was ill-suited to most of Reed's songs. But "All Tomorrow's Parties," the country-folk number from the '65 Reed-Cale demos, would become a perfect vehicle, her brooding cantillations transforming the tale of the doomed party girl into a stunning set piece.

Nevertheless, new material was needed. At Warhol's suggestion, Reed wrote a song about Edie Sedgwick, "Femme Fatale." Yet surely Nico was on his mind as well, as he conjured a streetwise woman with "false-colored eyes" who will "break your heart in two." If the girl in "All Tomorrow's Parties" is a victim, the woman here is a mantis, like Keats's *belle dame sans merci* or Alban Berg's Lulu. Nico's performance, an icy seduction over a purring melody, was both come-on and cautionary tale. After his tenure at Pickwick, Reed had clearly mastered the art of writing to order.

The greatest of the songs that became Nico's signatures—and a candidate for Reed's most moving song—is "I'll Be Your Mirror." It's a deceptively simple pledge to cleanse someone's self-loathing with love, to clarify and reflect back their unappreciated beauty, to allay their fears. Yet word choice complicates things. "Please put down your hands" suggests an attempt to comfort a partner racked with shame—i.e., stop hiding yourself. But it also hints at a violent relationship, as in "There She Goes Again." There's a powerful tension between the prettiness of the chord changes and Nico's faintly detached singing—the voice of a nurturing yet remote *Kinderfrau*, or a devoted partner willing to disappear figuratively in support of a lover. "You have to give up your life for him to be famous," Delmore Schwartz had insisted to Shelley Albin. In fact, Albin says the title quotes her. "'I'll be your mirror'—that's our conversation, word for word," she says. The song's conceit also reads as a Warholian notion, referencing the way his work mirrored pop culture. In any case, Reed had hit his full stride as a poetic songwriter. In a rehearsal recording from March, the song is fully shaped but for an odd blues lick jutting off the chorus, and an outro pushing Nico into an uncomfortable upper register—she ends the song in a coughing fit.

An alternate telling of the song's creation has Nico pledging the same words to Reed—"Oh, Lou, I'll be your mirror"—which may well be true. Perhaps unsurprisingly, the two began an affair. "Lou Reed was very soft and lovely," Nico reflected. "Not aggressive at all. You could just cuddle him like a sweet person when I first met him, and he always stayed that way. I used to make pancakes for him. I had subletted a place on Jane Street when he came to stay with me." According to Cale, Reed fell "head over heels" in love, even moving in with her, briefly. Their peers viewed the romance with skepticism, at least in hindsight. "You could say Lou was in love with her," Morrison said archly, "but Lou Reed in love is a kind of abstract concept." Ronnie Cutrone, a teenage Factory assistant around that time, characterized Nico as "a weirdo" and suggested love was out of her wheelhouse: "You didn't have a relationship with Nico."

Morrison saw the romance as a political move by Nico, and perhaps it was the same for Reed. He was still ambivalent about having her in the band; he would prank her at rehearsals by cutting off her mic, or drowning her out with noise. "Lou liked to manipulate women, you know, like program them," Nico said years later. "He wanted to do that with me. He told me so." Nico also believed Reed had a grudge against her because of her German heritage, "what my people did to his people." But she gave as good as she got. According to Cale, when the romance between the two ran dry, she "just swatted him like a fly." He described a scene in which she arrived late for rehearsal, and was met by a very chilly Reed. After a stretch of silence, Nico announced: "I cannot make love to Jews anymore" (Reed responded by getting wasted on Placidyl). The affair, about six weeks long, was over by late February, by which point Cale's fling with Edie Sedgwick, begun in earnest on his second day at the Factory, had also run its course.

Reed's most consequential love affair that year, though nonsexual by all accounts, was with Warhol, thirteen years his senior. They were dissimilar, yet had much in common. Warhol was raised religious in a working-class Catholic home during World War II, Reed raised post-war in a mostly secular, middle-class Jewish one. Warhol was an effeminate man who did little to hide his homosexual orientation; Reed was more butch, fluid, and passed for straight. Warhol wielded detachment and passivity as weapons of self-defense; Reed used his razor-edged tongue. And where Warhol made idea-driven art that was cool verging on bloodless, Reed's was largely gut-driven, hot-headed, and blood-splattered, as well as more frankly tender on occasion. But both men had industrious immigrant roots in Eastern Europe; both grew up with doting mothers and fathers with whom, at best, they had trouble connecting. Both were marked by health crises as young men, struggled with depression and dyslexia. Both found salvation, and abiding interest, in modern art-making technology—electric guitar for Reed, ballpoint pens and a $1.25 Brownie camera for Warhol. Both were creatively ambitious in college, if hardly perfect students; both published in student literary magazines they themselves edited (Warhol's very first published image, interestingly, was a drawing of musicians), and both were provocateurs with a taste for the juvenile (Warhol's "Nosepicker" series, worked up while studying in Pittsburgh, caused his first cultural brouhaha). Both were set on pursuing high-art ideals in a pop arena, compensated for limited technical skills with potent ideas, and played with primitive, faux-naïve creative styles; personas, too. Both dabbled in various drugs, including cannabis, but favored alcohol and speed, which they used regularly, sometimes copiously. Both skirted the draft; both touched on progressive ideology in work whose politics were rarely explicit. Both cultivated a journalistic remove in their image-making and storytelling. Both would be skewered by critics and snubbed by institutions. And both made queer-themed art at a time when that was considered beyond the pale, if not illegal. Like millions, they both came out, aesthetically and sexually, in New York City. "I loved him on sight," Reed declared, marveling at the serendipity of it all. "He was driven and he had a vision to fulfill. And I fit in like a hand in a glove."

You can feel their dynamic in the four Screen Tests Reed did for Warhol. In one (ST262), Warhol cast Reed's face half in darkness, shadows accenting the curve of his lips, which he repeatedly wraps around the tip of a Coke bottle as he drinks from it, eyes hidden behind wraparound shades, a hot-cool image of rough-trade flirtation. If it was Reed's decision to use the bottle as a prop, it was an inspired one, simultaneously conjuring fellatio, Warhol's 1962 Coke bottle series, and perhaps the poetry of Frank O'Hara, the New York School icon who died in July, and whose signature "Having a Coke with You" is a sly masterpiece of queer desire wrapped in art-world metaphors. Above all, the reel showed the young musician with a well-developed understanding of how to present himself as a commodity.

Maybe in part because of their similarities, and the potentially destabilizing intensity of their attraction, Reed and Warhol's relationship was fraught from the get-go. "Lou was very suspicious of Andy, but on the other hand, he was in awe of him," Cale writes, adding dismissively, "Andy latched onto [sic] Lou because he was this creature of another part of New York life that he didn't have at the Factory, an example of a Long Island punk." According to Billy Name, Reed was "sort of like Andy's Mickey Mouse." There's a whiff of jealousy, perhaps, in both those descriptions. Warhol certainly recognized in Reed a kindred spirit: queer, or at least very comfortable with queerness, and intensely driven, with an uncompromising vision. Reed became one of his favorites, for his smarts, his wit, and what Warhol considered his "pubescent" good looks. In Warhol, Reed found a new mentor.

Of course, it was the '60s, the sexual revolution was under way, and the Factory was an autonomous zone. Danny Fields, a Queens-bred journalist and budding music industry player and Factory outlier who had his own crush on Reed ("I thought he was the hottest, sexiest thing I had ever seen . . . oh my god, the emotional energy I expended on that person"), was likely closest to the truth when he observed: "Everybody was in love with everybody. We were all kids, and it was like high school . . . who could even fucking keep track?"

* * *

Reed learned plenty from Warhol. He learned how to parry an interview, and to cultivate an imperviousness to criticism. But Reed's biggest takeaway was Warhol's work ethic, which would stick with him for life. "One of the things you can learn from being at the Factory is if you want to do whatever you do, then you should work very, very hard," Reed said. "Work is the whole story. Work is literally everything." Warhol also served as a model for Reed's evolving sexual identity, at a point where his experience with men or anyone gender nonconforming would seem to have been limited. The Factory was a normalizing safe space at a time when you could still be jailed for going to a gay bar at night, let alone presenting as queer in daylight. For Reed, it must have been thrilling, and a huge relief. Like the rest of the Factory crowd, he could create himself as he created art, with few boundaries. Warhol already had: he was the model of a successful gay man who, in the tentative pre-Stonewall years, demonstrated how to live a fabulous life more or less out of the closet while in the public eye, transforming from a suit-wearing uptown commercial artist into a leather-jacketed, flamboyantly wigged, sexually ambiguous celebrity. "I was watching this like a hawk," Reed said.

For his part, Cale was uncomfortable with the Factory's "heavy gay scene," a discomfort Reed, perhaps defensively, preyed on. "He claimed that he had made it with my previous roommate and classical colleague David Del Tredici, and ultimately that he was the first Mrs. La Monte Young—all the time protesting that he couldn't understand why I hadn't made it with both of them!" Cale recalled. "Lou was full of himself and faggy in those days. We called him Lulu, I was Black Jack, Nico was Nico. He wanted to be queen bitch and spit out the sharpest rebukes of anyone around. Lou always ran with the pack and the Factory was full of queens to run with." There was likely jealousy in Cale's take. "Everyone was certainly in love with [Lou]," said Fields, "me, Edie, Andy, everyone."

Billy Name was certainly fond of him. Raised in Poughkeepsie, where the childhood sight of the Mid-Hudson Bridge being painted silver stuck with him, the former Billy Linich came to the city to train as a lighting designer, working with La Monte Young and the Judson Dance Theater. He met Warhol while working as a waiter at Serendipity 3, a fancy café at 225 East Sixtieth Street with a largely queer staff. After seeing Linich's silver-painted East Village apartment, Warhol asked him to work on his new Forty-seventh Street space. And so was born the Silver Factory, covered from floor to ceiling in silver paint and aluminum foil. Warhol and Linich became lovers briefly, then just intimate collaborators. Linich gave up his apartment and moved into the Factory, where he was trusted custodian, caretaker, mascot, assistant, and documentary photographer, shooting with the Pentax SLR Warhol gifted him. Linich's semi-official title was "Factory foreman." As a goof, he changed his last name to Name, and it stuck.

Name clicked with Reed instantly. "I remember the first time we talked, it was like we had always talked," Linich recalls in his apartment in Poughkeepsie, the silver Mid-Hudson Bridge visible from his kitchen window. "We were like two guys from the same neighborhood. He was from Long Island. I was from Hudson Valley. We were both in the metropolitan New York area but outside of the hub. We were the same temperament. The same tonality. Same type of guy. We immediately tuned in to each other. We just looked at each other and said 'Ah-hah.' We were totally in tune." The two became friends, and on occasion, hooked up for sex after a long night out. "We used to play,"

Name says, a smile behind his long biker's beard. "He was open; bisexual, I guess." Reed and Warhol were "strictly comrades," Name believes, never lovers.

"They were both interested in business," he says. "And progressing. Progressing, progressing, progressing; expanding, expanding, expanding."

* * *

The next iteration of that progress was Andy Warhol's *Up-tight*, a multimedia Factory installation—"happening"—with the Velvets as its reactor core, ostensibly preparing for the Queens nightclub arrangement. It was less about conjuring a psychedelic experience, per the early happenings, than an amphetamine rush, "uptight" being Factory slang for speeding, adopted from Stevie Wonder's "Uptight," a Top 5 hit in early 1966. Where the song used it in a positive sense, observed Ronnie Cutrone, who helped crew the shows, "we changed it to mean rigid and paranoid. Hence methedrine."

Staged, with help from Mekas, at the Film-Makers' Cinematheque, the shows were all about agitation and overload. Reed and the Velvets played as loud as possible in the tiny theater, while Warhol's films were projected on and around them, with abstract slide projections on top of that. As Cale recalled, they were "just victimizing the audience more than anything." The idea was not all, or even mostly, Warhol's, but a direct extension of what Reed and the nascent Velvets had been doing at the old Cinematheque on Lafayette. "The underground filmmakers didn't have money for sound," Reed said. "We used to make tapes and give them to people. Our tapes would be the soundtrack for 17 to 20 different movies, and then it got to the point where Piero showed a movie and we just sat behind a screen and played along with it. [It] was a natural step to meet Andy and then say, 'Oh, you've got a week at the new Cinematheque . . . we'll play along with your movies.'"

These abstracted instrumentals, from the raga-rock psychedelia the band rehearsed in Warhol's *Symphony of Sound* to the menacing noise jams used for his film *Hedy the Shoplifter*, wormed their way into Reed's songs. A recording from the Cinematheque that month shows the band sketching the screeching outlines of what would become the song "European Son," veering into "Suzy Q," the Dale Hawkins rocker from the Stones' newly released LP *12 x 5*, then into freestyle electric guitar cluster bombs: high-speed strumming, sliding runs, string-scraping. The recording also shows a cruel dynamic playing out between the band and the new vocalist.

"Now Nico will sing," Reed declares. She attempts to deliver the tender lyrics of Dylan's "I'll Keep It with Mine" over a noisy pimp-roll swagger that vaguely recalls "I'm Waiting for the Man," nearly shouting at points, as the band plows through incongruous changes almost as if she isn't there. In addition to the tension between Nico and Reed, the band wanted no association with Dylan, their main competition in the poetic rock 'n' roll department. "When Nico kept insisting that we work up 'I'll Keep It with Mine,' for a long time we simply refused," Morrison admitted. "When we finally did have a go at it onstage, it was performed poorly [and] we never got any better at it, for some reason." Reed had also refused Nico's requests to sing "I'm Waiting for the Man" and "Heroin"—telling requests given the path her later life took. They might've been interesting versions; in any case, the recording shows the band had perfected "Heroin," with Reed singing. Warhol's notebooks from this period—which among other things kept track of the Velvets' heroin costs—suggest some of them were also walking the walk.

In a foreshadowing of the group's strange relationship with their hometown, the Cinematheque *Up-tight* shows were mostly ignored beyond the downtown scene; they received a slight, snide *New York Post* review focused on Warhol, with no mention of Reed.

Nevertheless, Warhol's next step was to take the show on the road, and the band was all-in. John Wilcock, a *Village Voice* co-founder, was the first journalist to document their sound, describing a show at Rutgers University on March 9. Here, he wrote, was a group "whose most notable attribute is repetitive, howling lamentation which conjures up images of a schooner breaking up on the rocks. Their sound punctuated with whatever screeches, whines, whistles, and wails can be coaxed out of the amplifier, envelops the audience with exploding decibels—a sound two and a half times as loud as anybody thought they could stand. (It bears roughly the same relation to hit-parade rock 'n' roll as does Archie Shepp's to the mainstream of jazz.)"

After Rutgers, the entourage drove a rented bus to Ann Arbor to stage *Up-tight* at a University of Michigan film festival. New York being a harbor for grown-ups who don't drive, mainly Nico was at the wheel, and it was a white-knuckle ride; having driven a lot in England, she occasionally veered into the left, oncoming lane (Warhol "was the only one who wasn't scared," Nico recalled. "He just couldn't care less"). The trip was clearly a bonding experience. Nat Finkelstein, a photo-journalist who often hung out at the Factory, came along for the ride. In one shot, Reed stares dreamily into the camera, Warhol's arm around his waist, the pair in near-matching leather jackets; in another, Warhol smirks, with his hand squarely on Reed's crotch.

The Velvets played a loud, full-bore set in Michigan, including their Café Bizarre kiss-off, "Black Angel's Death Song," and a noise jam finale dubbed "The Nothing Song." The audience was split between hecklers and converts. The band was getting its legs—but it took an extended residency in the East Village for the Velvets to come into their own.

* * *

Gerard raised the oversized pink plastic syringe above his head and slowly started spinning till he dropped to one knee. I held my arm out to him, my hand over the inside of my elbow as my lower body twisted to the rhythm of "Heroin." On the ceiling an old mirror ball turned, its spots of light jumping from one dancer to another like lost souls looking for a host. The enormous faces of demented queens and ravaged superstars filled the wall behind us as if they were giants peering into a box of dancing Lilliputians, but their distorted voices and stunned expressions were only the projections of Warhol's experimental movies. Dwarfed by Mario Montez's lipstick-stained teeth and looking like in-

sects that had just crawled out of his mouth, the Velvet Underground played in their wrap-around shades . . . Gerard
held the syringe out to me like a priest holding the cross to
a sinner and I responded by hooking my fingers under his
belt buckle and slowly grinding my hips lower and lower
down his body to the heavy pulse . . .

—Mary Woronov, *Swimming Underground*

The Exploding Plastic Inevitable—a gibberish name coined by Morrissey, inspired by Dylan's freestyle prosody on the back cover of *Bringing It All Back Home*—was the next edition of *Up-tight*. It was launched
on April Fool's Day 1966 at the Polski Dom Narodowy (Polish National
Home), a triptych of connected buildings housing a ballroom and community hall, located on the north side of St. Mark's Place on the Lower
East Side.

A German cultural center in the late 1800s, the space hosted a talk
by Teddy Roosevelt when he was a young reformer fighting Tammany
Hall. It was a preferred party spot for the Jewish gangster "Dopey"
Benny Fein, whose crew had a shootout there in 1914 with Italian rivals
who'd hired the hall. In *St. Marks Is Dead*, the historian Ada Calhoun
notes that Fein was a pro-union radical who regularly employed
women to carry out his strike mandates, making it possible he crossed
paths with Reed's labor activist cousin, "Red" Shirley Novick. In 1964
the site was purchased by Stanley Tolkin, the Polish owner of Stanley's on Twelfth and B, an artist-friendly bar where Warhol showed
early work. (Confusingly, the downstairs bar in the new space was also
known initially as Stanley's.) The upstairs ballroom was rented out,
variously hosting jazz bands, dances, and the proto-psychedelic "Theater of Light" shows staged by the artists Jackie Cassen and Rudi Stern.

Warhol decided to rent the Polski Dom Narodowy ballroom and
run his own show after the Queens nightclub deal fell through (the
promoter decided to open instead with the Young Rascals, led by
Reed's Syracuse rock 'n' roll rival Felix Cavaliere, though the endeavor
went bust in the end). That the space was known by shorthand as the
Dom was a plus, adding a transgressive whiff of S&M. After signing

the contract on the day of the first show, Warhol rushed an ad into *The Village Voice.* "DO YOU WANT TO DANCE AND BLOW YOUR MIND WITH THE EXPLODING PLASTIC INEVITABLE," it read, minus a question mark, breathlessly promising "ultra sounds, visions, lightworks . . . food, celebrities and movies including Vinyl, Sleep, Eat, Kiss, Empire, Whips, Faces, Harlot, Hedy, Couch, Banana, etc., etc., etc., all in the same place at the same time." Also on the bill was the Velvet Underground and Nico.

Like the Beatles' months at the Cavern Club compressed into thirty days, the Velvets played the Dom nearly every night in April 1966. And like a drug-addled version of Mickey Rooney and Judy Garland's *Let's-put-on-a-show!* spectacle from *Babes in Arms,* everyone worked to make the shows dazzling. Sure, the Dom was run-down and smelled like urine, more like a high school auditorium than a ballroom. But that added to the effect. Malanga whitewashed the walls to make better screening surfaces. Film and carousel projectors, the latter loaded with abstract images, were set up on the balcony, run by Warhol, Rubin, Danny Williams, or whoever could be enlisted. There was a mirror ball, spotlights, and strobes. Outside, a spray-painted banner hung from a third-floor window: "ANDY WARHOL LIVE / THE VELVET UNDERGROUND / LIVE DANCING-FILMS / PARTY EVENT NOW."

The first night drew roughly 750 people at $2.50 a head. Beer was 75 cents, soda 50 cents, sandwiches 50 cents; the "show" ran from 9 p.m. to 2 a.m. Café tables with checkered tablecloths and wooden folding chairs were set around the perimeter of the space, though some chose to lie on the floor. Revelers showed up in boots, bell bottoms, metallic polyester miniskirts, plastic chain-mail dresses, colored fishnets, pencil heels, ostrich feathers. Others came in office clothes: jackets, ties, sensible skirts. College kids came in street clothes, jeans, turtlenecks, loafers. In terms of discotheques or rock 'n' roll concerts, nothing quite like the production had ever been seen. Colored slides projected images on top of films, on top of other films, on top of the band. Between sets, three turntables played rock 'n' roll and other records, often simultaneously, mixed with the already muddled film soundtracks, fed through a jury-rigged sound system utilizing eighteen woofers. The residency blue-printed disco culture in New York some years before pioneers such as David Mancuso and Nicky Siano would refine it: the queer aesthetics, the celebrity fabulousness, the drug use (there was a mattress-covered sideroom for smoking weed and tripping out), the uninhibited dancing. "There wasn't anything like that before," said Mary Woronov, a handsome Brooklyn Heights prep-schooler who'd decamped from her art studies at Cornell to join the Factory clan. "All you could do was go to a cocktail bar that had a little piece of floor for the mambo or the twist."

When the band came onstage, they worked their way through Reed's songs and extended jams, Tucker pounding out time, the room rattling like an old IRT train careering into the future. Cale recalled Nico singing "I'll Be Your Mirror" as the mirrored ball sent strobe-light beams ricocheting around the room, while films provided counternarratives: Reed might appear as an insect singing into Nico's Brobdingnagian cinematic ear. Or she might serenade herself, a small priestess in a pantsuit, like Garbo or Hepburn, dwarfed by her own gorgeousness. Woronov joined Malanga during the run as a stage dancer, a vision of butch resplendence: she recalled the locking mouths of Warhol's *Kiss* projected over her head, "hypnotic as the twisting coils of a snake," as Malanga fondled the whip in her hands, running the lash over his lips while the band played "Black Angel's Death Song." The interracial and pansexual *Kiss*, radical in the Cinematheque in 1963, was no less so here. So was the ensemble's gender-bending presentation, Nico's teutonic contralto croon buoyed by the Bo Diddley beats of the boyish Moe Tucker.

Problems only generated more creativity. One evening, Tucker discovered her drum kit had been stolen. She combed the neighborhood, scavenged a couple of metal trash cans, and upended them onstage, drumming on them for a few days until she could get a new set; there was a small footprint of gunk under each can at the end of the night. In the cruddy, makeshift dressing room, Nico always lit a candle before the show. The habit irritated Reed. But his attitude was equally devotional; they all knew the shows were something special. "Lou and I had an almost religious fervor about what we were doing," Cale recalled.

The Dom shows made money. The first night's take was over $1,000 at the door alone; the first week's, all totaled, $18,000. The Velvets earned

$100 a night. Celebrities and kindred artists turned up, limos pulling to the curb: Jackie Kennedy, Salvador Dalí, Allen Ginsberg, Sammy Davis Jr., Walter Cronkite. There were young people with artistic aspirations: a wannabe filmmaker named John Waters, who'd recently been thrown out of his dorm at NYU for smoking pot; John Zorn, a precocious twelve-year-old attending the United Nations School and already a fan of extreme things; a nascent British music writer, Charlie Gillett, then a grad student at Columbia. Anne Waldman, a young poet who lived down the block, was moved to rapture, describing the Exploding Plastic Inevitable production as "a magnificent god realm of sensuous desire, spectacle of eros and cruelty with mesmerizing power, psychic mystical drone pulsing inside one's own body." Her peer John Ashbery turned up on opening night fresh from nearly ten years abroad. He'd never attended a rock concert, and was so overloaded by the sensory barrage he burst into tears, exclaiming, "I don't understand this at all!" For others, it was just a great night out. Tucker's and Morrison's Long Island friends would come in for the weekend shows and, as she recalled, "it was just like sitting in your living room." The bacchanal continued nightly. In a New York City analogue to the West Coast Acid Tests, begun that winter in Northern California, with LSD on offer as the Grateful Dead played, Factory associates moved through the Dom ballroom, injecting people with speed, according to Warhol, "if they halfway knew them."

At night's end, those still wired might go out cruising the gay bars. Queer culture, still underground, was making moves. The month of the run, a group of men from the Mattachine Society, the pioneering gay rights organization, got coverage in *The New York Times* for challenging State Liquor Authority regulations that enabled bartenders to deny them service (the headline: "3 DEVIATES INVITE EXCLUSION BY BARS"). Reed was familiar with the scene. "A bunch of us would leave the Dom really late and go to the after-hours clubs around the Village— Lou knew them all," Warhol recalled in *POPism*. "At the Tenth of Always (named after the Johnny Mathis song 'The Twelfth of Never') there'd always be one same little blond boy every night who'd get drunk and turn to Lou and demand, 'Well, are you a homosexual or not? I am and

I'm proud of it.' Then he'd smash his glass on the floor and get asked to leave." Warhol also recalled a place called Ernie's: "no liquor, no music, no food—just a back room with jars of Vaseline on the table."

While the Dom shows left an impression on those who attended, they didn't receive much attention. Given the celebrity turnout, *The New York Times* covered them on its fashion page, with photos of Nico "in a white wool pea coat from London" and stylish society types frugging to the beat. Nationally, the shows were beneath notice. *Time*, the country's foremost newsmagazine, ignored them. As it happened, the issue on stands when the Dom run began featured a cover story centered in part on the work of Reed's former professor Gabriel Vahanian. Its all-text cover image caused a sensation among readers: in huge type, stoplight-red-on-black, it asked simply: "IS GOD DEAD?" The sight of that cover, lighting up the newsstand racks, must've amused Reed as he stumbled home in the morning light after a wild night, ready to sleep or, perhaps, to just pop more Desoxyn, head uptown to the Factory, and prepare to do it all again.

* * *

During the night of the first Dom show, Reed's apartment was robbed; among his losses was his cherished collection of doo-wop 45s. But it was now time to start making records with the Velvets. After two weeks of shows, with money banked and songs fairly polished, the Velvets went up to Scepter Sound, at 254 West Fifty-fourth Street, a modestly equipped studio that was not in great shape. But as Reed was surely aware, it was owned by Florence Greenberg, whose imprints issued some of the greatest early rock 'n' roll records: the Isley Brothers' "Twist and Shout," the Shirelles' "Will You Still Love Me Tomorrow," the Kingsmen's "Louie Louie."

Though nominally the Velvets' manager, Warhol knew zilch about the record business, so he turned to Norman Dolph, a twenty-seven-year-old Yale grad working as a sales exec for Columbia Records. He'd met Warhol through his side gig DJing art events—he contributed his mobile disco setup for the Dom shows—and the men agreed to split the $1,500 cost of the studio sessions. Reed and Cale had some studio experience, Nico too, but Dolph and Warhol had next to none; the mostly awful audio quality of Warhol's films testifies to his sound recording skills. Dolph admits his role was limited to making the trains run on time "because they were doing it on my money." John Licata, in-house engineer at Scepter, handled the technical end. Warhol, however, supplied ideas. According to Cale, he insisted they keep the sound of their live performances. Reed recalled Warhol telling him, "You've gotta make sure to use all the dirty words." Morrison said Warhol's main contribution was to give them courage in their conviction: "He argued against restraint."

Reed was stressed. He desperately wanted to make a record that would earn him recognition, to exercise the control he couldn't at Pickwick, or even in the Velvets' performances. Cale had his own ideas, which leaned into his skill set in avant-garde conceptual and symphonic music, and the two locked horns. "Lou turned everybody else from being excited about making a great record into paranoid wrecks," Cale recalled. Reed didn't want Nico on the record at all, but she recorded the songs she usually performed (minus "I'll Keep It with Mine"). Despite Reed's displeasure, everyone "treated [Nico] with great respect" during the sessions, according to Dolph. Nico was very stressed herself; she had so much difficulty nailing "I'll Be Your Mirror," she wept between takes, and fled the studio the moment her parts were voiced. Moe Tucker mostly kept mum and out of the line of fire, trying to get her parts right and keep the drums from rattling on their rickety stands. She thought the time crunch—they had to finish recording in four days—worked to their advantage: "We didn't have time for nonsense."

The session was pressed onto an acetate disc, which Dolph delivered the same day—April 25—to his colleagues in Columbia's A&R department. The song sequence began like a slap in the face, with a dissonant nine-minute rock jam, "European Son (to Delmore Schwartz)," full of squalls, feedback, and musique concrète (including, per lore, the sound of a shopping cart crashing into a stack of dinner plates). "You spit on those under twenty-one," Reed sings, a sly nod to his rock-hating mentor, and maybe a challenge to the suits he imagined releasing the song.

It was followed by "Black Angel's Death Song," with Cale's screeching viola and Reed's bad-trip poetics ("cut mouth bleeding razors," "bowels and a tail of a rat") suggesting horrors personal and cultural. In early 1966, to propose material like this for a pop LP was beyond the pale; to lead with it seems a pitch for instant career suicide. The next song, "All Tomorrow's Parties," with Nico's sweetly mournful vocals, was more comprehensible in terms of current rock 'n' roll, if barely—the raga-ish guitars echoed sounds the Beatles were exploring at the time, albeit here set alongside Cale's jackhammer piano, prepared à la John Cage with a chain of paper clips laid across the strings.

Columbia's verdict was swift: "'There's no way in the world any sane person would buy or want to listen to [this record]" is roughly how the memo read. Other rejections followed. The Atlantic Records guru Ahmet Ertegun liked some songs but objected to others, notably "Venus in Furs." There was evidently a thumbs-down from Elektra Records, too. But MGM/Verve Records made an offer, and by May 2, the five members of the Velvet Underground had signed a contract with them.

The man responsible was the label's new director of pop A&R, Tom Wilson. Wilson had just left Columbia after producing Bob Dylan's "Like a Rolling Stone" (a dress-down of a woman some speculated to be Edie Sedgwick) and *Bringing It All Back Home*. When asked if Wilson started him on the rock 'n' roll path, Dylan told *Rolling Stone*'s Jann Wenner, "He did to a certain extent. That is true. He did. He had a sound in mind." Wilson was an unusual character: a Black man from Waco, Texas, who graduated cum laude with a degree in economics from Harvard, where he'd been president of the Young Republicans club. He launched a jazz label, Transition, that released pioneering LPs by Sun Ra and Cecil Taylor. At MGM, he operated with similarly open ears and creative freedom. He signed Frank Zappa and the Mothers of Invention, dropping $21,000 of company cash to record their unbridled double-LP debut, *Freak Out*. He also signed the visionary singer-songwriter Van Dyke Parks, who recalled Wilson as "an ebullient spirit . . . Charismatic, statuesque, and curiously empowering for those in his orbit." Wilson became an unlikely hitmaker: his rock remix of Simon & Garfunkel's folkie "Sound of Silence" made them stars. It made him a perfect fit for the Velvets. "He understood what we were trying to say," Cale said. "He'd been in the avant-garde . . . We kept pushing and improvising, and he didn't bat an eye."

At the last minute, though, the MGM deal hit a bump. According to Cale, Warhol, Morrissey, and the Velvets had formed "the Warvel Corporation" in January with the understanding that the band's income would be paid to Warhol, who'd take 25 percent off the top for managing the band, buying them equipment, etc., with the remaining 75 percent then going to the Velvets. Now Reed insisted the band should receive all the money; they'd pay Warhol and Morrissey their cut later. The power play may have been spurred by advice from Reed's father, a savvy businessman; it may've been a lack of trust in Warhol, or a fear of ceding control to someone for whom he had strong feelings. Whatever the case, Reed would not budge. "Needless to say," Cale noted, "neither Andy nor Paul ever saw a penny from this deal once they agreed to change the wording to satisfy Lou."

In the end, it was small potatoes: the band got a paltry $3,000 advance, perhaps because the label had burned up so much cash on *Freak Out*. Warhol had capitulated in the end, but it left a scar. "That broke relations between him and Lou," Mary Woronov believed. "Anything to do with money broke Andy's relations."

* * *

I saw a sign in the sky
It said, "T-t-t-trip"

—Donovan, "The Trip"

The day after the contract signing, the Velvets, Warhol, and the rest of the Exploding Plastic Inevitable gang boarded a plane to Los Angeles. They were booked for an eighteen-night run at the Trip on Sunset Strip—the city's counterculture ground zero. The Dom shows had gone so well, everyone figured they could be re-created among the beautiful people of Southern California. After all, back in December, a quartet of transplanted Greenwich Village fixtures who dubbed themselves the Mamas and the Papas released "California Dreamin'," shifting America's pop music center of gravity to the West Coast, where a psychedelicized folk-rock scene was brewing, with the Byrds in L.A. and the newly christened Grateful Dead in San Francisco. In February, after changing their name from the Warlocks, the Dead in fact relocated to L.A. to get in on the gold rush; by May, when the Velvets landed, the Mamas and the Papas' debut LP, *If You Can Believe Your Eyes and Ears*, was just hitting number 1 on the *Billboard* Top 200.

To be sure, the Velvets were making far darker and more confrontational music than that, or the Byrds' new *Mr. Tambourine Man*, or even the Dead, whose first LP was still a year off and whose chemist-turned-soundman Owsley Stanley had, about a month prior to the Velvets' first gig, unleashed three thousand hits of his top-shelf Blue Cheer–brand LSD onto the L.A. scene. Perhaps unsurprisingly, the Velvets' bad-trippy sensory blitzkrieg received a less-than-warm California welcome. As Cale recalled, someone had drawn a gravestone next to the band's name on their dressing room door at the Trip ("We were like, great"). The first night packed in celebrities: Sonny and Cher (quipping that Warhol's next-wave circus "will replace nothing, except maybe suicide," though her husband apparently enjoyed it), David Crosby of the Byrds (who described it as akin to "eating a banana nut Brillo pad"), the future contemporary Christian singer/songwriter Barry McGuire (who suggested the band needed to "go back underground and practice"), and a recent UCLA film school graduate and poet named Jim Morrison, likely taking notes for his own nascent rock band, the Doors. But the club was near-empty the second night, and the Velvets didn't get along with their opening acts, who included label-mates and L.A. freak-rock outliers the Mothers of Invention (despite what would seem a similar aesthetic sensibility, or maybe because of it, the leader, Frank Zappa, loathed the Velvets).

Shortly thereafter, the club was shuttered by the police for reasons that remain unclear, but probably involved open drug use during shows and the club's financial problems; Reed's lyrics and the Exploding Plastic Inevitable's S&M theater probably didn't help matters. Hoping to get their unpaid $3,500 guarantee, and with arrangements already made to stay two more weeks, the band settled in at the Castle, a celebrity guesthouse at 4320 Cedarhurst Circle, in the Los Feliz hills just outside Hollywood. Once home to the Brooklyn-raised silent film star Norma Talmadge, per legend, it now hosted rock royalty; Dylan had been there not long before them. During their stay, the group posed for the photographer Lisa Law, née Bachelis, whose husband, Tom Law, owned the Castle. In one image, eyes hidden behind wrap-around shades, Reed sits beside Nico on a wrought-iron seat beneath a pine bower. In another, the pair appear to be harmonizing, mouths open, eyes locked on each other. Whatever the state of their relationship was by then, they make a striking couple. During the layover, the Velvets lolled about the Castle; Warhol cooked eggs for everyone in the morning; the pragmatic, teetotaling Tucker tried to keep to her normal routines. "They'd tease me," she said, "but every Sunday morning, I'd say, 'I need a car to go to church.'" (Warhol, whose mother was a devout churchgoer, and who would become more devout himself in the coming years, usually obliged.) Morrison soon got antsy and relocated to the Tropicana Hotel on Santa Monica Boulevard, where he partied with the Buffalo Springfield, a folk-rock band whose Canadian co-founder Neil Young was also making moves; just that month, the group landed a gig as the house band of the Whisky-a-Go-Go, another fulcrum of the L.A. scene.

Making use of the time, the Velvets reworked some of the Scepter sessions material at Hollywood's more up-to-date TTG Studios. "Venus in Furs," "I'm Waiting for the Man," and "Heroin" were fully rerecorded. The latter revision is marked: where the Scepter version is a near-angry declamation, ramping up quickly, designed to shock with blunt force, the slow-building new take shows the song's narrator wrestling with an idea: certain, then doubting, nodding into reverie, and finally returning to cold truths.

It was a startling performance. For her part, though, Maureen Tucker was unhappy with the take. At one point in the recording, unable to hear the band, she simply stopped drumming. "When we got to the part where you speed up, you gotta speed up together, or it's not really right," Tucker reasoned. "I couldn't hear shit. I couldn't see Lou to watch his mouth to see where he was in the song. And I just stopped." Yet the rhythmic drop-out is the finale's coup de grace, highlighting Cale's viola-noise whiteout and throwing Reed's vocals into relief.

Another novel aspect of the take was the opening line, which Reed altered from "I know just where I'm going" to "I don't know just where I'm going." Cale was dead-set against it—he felt it altered the whole premise, shifting the narrative tone from conviction to surrender. He recalls telling his partner that he'd "fucked up the whole song."

Yet Reed stood by the change; if it was a hedge against the song being read too much as a drug abuse endorsement, he never copped to it. Cale could take the lead sometimes on musical arrangements. But lyrics, especially when Reed was delivering them, were beyond debate. As Cale would later assert, it was the precise moment their relationship began to fray.

* * *

The Velvets also crossed paths that month with two up-and-coming rock music impresarios who'd have a major impact on them: Steve Sesnick, a smooth New York operator with a connection to Warhol and an interest in artist management; and Bill Graham, a San Francisco promoter who had just begun booking the Fillmore Auditorium in San Francisco. Graham saw the Exploding Plastic Inevitable at the Trip, and while he'd later call the production "the worst piece of entertainment I've ever seen in my life," he knew a publicity magnet when he saw one. After convincing a skeptical Paul Morrissey, Graham brought Warhol and the Velvets north for a three-night stand at the Fillmore over Memorial Day weekend.

San Francisco's rock culture had been transformed in January when the Trips Festival was staged at Longshoreman's Hall. A mass-market version of the "acid tests"—complete with its own Warholian art-star sponsor, Ken Kesey—it saw thousands of kids swigging LSD-dosed fruit punch over its three-day run, dancing to music by the Dead and the Jefferson Airplane while bathed in a state-of-the-art light show, channeling psychedelic bliss like the Exploding Plastic Inevitable

channeled white-light speed rushes. "We spoke two completely different languages," Mary Woronov said. "We were on amphetamine and
they were on acid. They were so slow to speak with these wide eyes—
'oh, wow!'—so into their 'vibrations'; we spoke in rapid machine-gun
fire about books and paintings and movies. They were into 'free' and
the American Indian and going back to the land and trying to be some
kind of true, authentic person; we could not have cared less about that.
They were homophobic; we were homosexual. Their women, they
were these big round-titted girls; you would say hello to them and they
would just flop on the bed and fuck you; we liked sexual tension, S&M,
not fucking. They were barefoot; we had platform boots. They were
eating bread they had baked themselves—and we never ate at all!"

The gigs went off with a modicum of disaster. Morrissey got into
a pissing match with Graham about throwing tangerine peels on the
floor, which the short-handed Graham had to sweep up himself at
the end of the night, ensuring the Velvet Underground a permanent
place on his soon-to-be-bicoastal shit list. Then Malanga was arrested
in a North Beach diner for possession of a weapon (his whip) and spent
the night in jail. Adding fiscal injury to insult, the EPI had to rent lighting equipment, as the Fillmore was only just ramping up as a concert
venue (the Dead wouldn't have their first gig there until the following
week, on June 4).

Thus, the Velvets were in a combative mood, playing ferociously
loud each night and, in what might have been the birth of a signature
rock 'n' roll gesture, leaving their instruments feeding back onstage as
they walked off. It certainly didn't impress Ralph J. Gleason of the *San
Francisco Chronicle*, at the time one of the nation's few established pop
music journalists; within a year, he'd create *Rolling Stone* with a young
Berkeley student, Jann Wenner. Gleason described the Exploding Plastic Inevitable show as "a bad condensation of all the bum trips of the
Trips Festival," labeling Warhol's concept "non-creative" and "non-
artistic," and branding the Velvets "dull," "campy," and "Greenwich
Village sick." His takeaway: it was a "lame" facsimile of the blossoming San Francisco scene.

The new issue of *Life* magazine—the nation's premiere periodical, alongside *Time*—may also have triggered Gleason's hometown boosterism. The cover story, "Wild New Flashy Bedlam of the Discothèque," essentially credited New York with launching the new, immersive club experience. The opening spread featured the Velvets at the Trip, Reed in his wraparounds with Malanga in blurred motion below a projected image of Moe Tucker's gigantic, granny-glassed head. "You had better wear earplugs, dark glasses, and shin guards," the introduction warns. "Otherwise you may be deafened, blinded or bruised in an electronic earthquake that engulfs you completely."

The number 1 book in the country that month was Jacqueline Susann's *Valley of the Dolls*, a roman à clef about a decadent, pill-popping, celebrity-obsessed culture whose author was carpetbombing the country with publicity appearances while roaring on amphetamines. Mainstream American culture was beginning to get strange.

* * *

That summer, the Exploding Plastic Inevitable ran aground, as Warhol turned his attention elsewhere and Nico headed to Ibiza for a holiday. Reed wound up in Beth Israel Medical Center with a flare-up of hep C, by some accounts from a dirty amphetamine shot in San Francisco. The remaining Velvets soldiered on to Chicago for a week of shows in late June at a nightclub called Poor Richard's. Cale and Morrison shared vocals, Tucker played bass, Angus MacLise rejoined briefly for the ride, handling percussion. Afterward, he told Morrison he regretted quitting the band.

While still in the hospital, Reed learned that Delmore Schwartz had died. He was found collapsed in the dingy hallway of the Columbia Hotel, at 70 West Forty-sixth Street, his clothes partly torn off, as if he was trying to escape them. The coroner identified the cause of death as a heart attack. He was fifty-two years old. An obituary in *The New York Times* referred to him as a "poet of the city," citing his accomplishments and reprinting "O City, City," a sonnet in which he describes:

Being amid six million souls, their breath
An empty song suppressed on every side

Despite being offered full tenure at Syracuse, Schwartz had walked off his teaching job in January and had been living in various Manhattan fleabags. When Reed tracked him down at the Dixie Hotel on Forty-second Street and tried to visit, Schwartz turned him away, raving and threatening him. Other friends were similarly scared off; the author Saul Bellow saw him on the street looking "East River gray," but was afraid to approach him. Schwartz had been so estranged from family and friends that his body went unclaimed for days. Eventually an aunt showed up at the Bellevue morgue, and two *New Yorker* staff members—Dwight MacDonald, his longtime champion from the *Partisan Review*, which first published "In Dreams Begin Responsibilities," and William Knapp—came to the hotel to collect his papers. NYU, where Schwartz got his undergraduate degree and taught briefly, picked up the tab for his funeral.

Reed checked himself out of the hospital early to attend the funeral, with help from Schwartz's confidante Liz Annas (she flashed her social services agency ID and did some fast talking to facilitate his release). In a T-shirt, black jeans, and earrings, Reed arrived at the service late, Gerard Malanga in tow, and sat in the rear. When Annas chided Reed for his getup, she recalls him insisting, "I think Delmore would like the way I look."

Reed sat through the service in silence. There were about two hundred people in attendance. Schwartz's aunt Clara talked about their family ("Our house wasn't Jewish in dishes, or in always going to shul," she said, "Jewish is heart. Delmore was Jewish"). MacDonald spoke about the old days, though few of Schwartz's peers were there to hear. John Berryman did not attend. Nor did Robert Lowell, though he sent a telegram. Only a handful of mourners trekked out to Cedar Park Cemetery in Westwood, New Jersey, for the burial. Reed and Annas wound up in a town car with MacDonald, who told one demeaning story after another about Schwartz. "I thought Lou was going to punch him," Annas says.

There was another death that summer in Reed's circle. With the Exploding Plastic Inevitable tour on ice for the moment, and Warhol terminating their affair, the filmmaker and lighting designer Danny Williams, who'd been traveling with the EPI, bailed on the Factory scene and returned home to his family in Massachusetts. After dinner one night, he took his mother's car for a drive. It was later located near the beach at Cape Ann, but Williams was never found—it's speculated he simply walked into the sea and drowned. He left behind a wooden box full of journals and a shaving kit bag full of drugs.

In July, MGM/Verve issued a seven-inch 45 rpm single by the Velvet Underground, their debut release: "All Tomorrow's Parties" backed with "I'll Be Your Mirror." Nico sang both, and the sleeve shows the band illuminated as if by a police-car floodlight, hers the only face fully visible. A promotional item that seems to have barely been circulated, it would have the dubious distinction, in hindsight, of being deemed perhaps the single rarest vinyl artifact of the 1960s. By the standards of the era—the Beatles' *Revolver* wouldn't be issued for another month—it was pretty far out for pop music. It was also haunting and magnificent.

* * *

Like Reed, Bob Dylan also spent time in the hospital that summer, after crashing his Triumph T100 motorcycle up in Woodstock. He'd use it as an excuse to lie low for a while. With time on his hands, Dylan's manager, Albert Grossman, leased the Dom out from under Warhol and rebranded it as a new rock venue called the Balloon Farm. In October, the Exploding Plastic Inevitable did some shows there, which occasioned the first proper magazine profile of the Velvet Underground, in the Sunday section of the *New York World Journal Tribune*. "A Quiet Night at the Balloon Farm" was written by Richard Goldstein, a Columbia journalism grad determined, like Ralph Gleason in San Francisco, to write seriously about rock 'n' roll (Goldstein had just begun his weekly "Pop Eye" column in *The Village Voice* in June). After speaking with Reed and Cale between sets at the club, Goldstein would describe the Velvets as "Andy's rock group" and their music as a "marriage between Bob Dylan and the Marquis de Sade." Nico was "half goddess, half icicle"; the sound of her singing was "something like a cello getting up in the morning." Cale, expounding on the qualities of subsonic sounds, came across as bandleader.

This likely didn't thrill Reed when he read it. But he was creating his own persona, in the Janus-face act of countless rock 'n' roll partnerships, positioning himself as a street punk Everykid. "Let them sing about going steady on the radio. Let the campus types run hootenannies," he told Goldstein. "But it's in holes like this . . . that the real stuff is being born. The university and the radio kill everything, but around here, it's alive. The kids know that."

It was the first time Reed saw himself quoted at length in a major publication, and it no doubt left an impression on him. So too did Warhol's performative interview "Andy Warhol: My True Story," generally regarded as the ur-document of the artist's public self-creation, which appeared two weeks later, in the November 1 issue of *The East Village Other*. It had been created with the journalist Gretchen Berg, who embellished Warhol's responses to her redacted interview questions, presenting them as a startling, stream-of-consciousness, manifesto-manifesting monologue. "I'd prefer to remain a mystery," begins Warhol in the piece, "I never like to give my background and, anyway, I make it all up different every time I'm asked." Later, he offers, "It's too hard to think about things. I think people should think less anyway. I'm not trying to educate people to see things or feel things in my paintings; there's no form of education in them at all." A month later, Reed's essay "A View from the Bandstand," similar in free-associative spirit to Warhol's endeavor, appeared in a special issue of the art magazine *Aspen* devoted to Warhol and "pop" culture. The issue also included a flexidisc single that included a droning feedback instrumental, "Loop," credited to the Velvet Underground. It was indeed a loop, with the disc's final groove circling back on itself when the stylus hit the record's center—a nod to La Monte Young's work in that it could theoretically go on forever.

Reed opened his essay with a scene of cultural torpor being exploded by pop 45s, the poet Robert Lowell squared off against Little Richard:

Writing was dead, movies were dead. Everybody sat like an unpeeled orange. But the music was so beautiful . . . The only decent poetry of this century was that recorded on rock-and-roll records. Everybody knew that. Who you going to rap with. Little Bobby Lowell or Richard Penniman alias Little Richard, our thrice-retired preacher.

Reed went on to sneer at "psychological tests" and "doctors trying to 'cure' the freaks while they gulp pills," insisting, "It's the music that kept us all intact. It's the music that kept us from going crazy."

Meanwhile, the group still had no money, and since Warhol no longer ran the Dom, they were at the mercy of the new management. By mid-October, they'd quit the Balloon Farm, with hopes their fortunes would change when the album was released.

It was decided that Warhol would do the cover design. He'd done a number in the past, among them Kenny Burrell's self-titled 1957 LP (a blotted-line image of Burrell playing guitar) and Johnny Griffin's *The Congregation* (the saxophonist rendered in a similar style), both for Blue Note. He also illustrated *The Story of Moondog*, which Reed likely played on his Syracuse radio show; the cover, all text, was in fact penned in flowery cursive by Warhol's mom, Julia, a frequent collaborator in his early commercial art. His cover for *The Velvet Underground & Nico*, however, reflected his current approach to image-making, and would become one of the most iconic LP images of all time: a silk-screened photograph of a banana, printed a bit larger than life-size on a sticker, which peeled off to reveal a similar silk-screened image of the fruit's interior, suggestively tinted pink—as Reed described it, "a very sexy, groovy banana."

* * *

Nico's connection with the band remained tense, a situation exacerbated by her extracurricular involvement with Warhol. Right after the Fillmore shows, the pair split to fly to Boston to host a campy film series for WNAC-TV called *Pop Art Theater*. In one intro segment, the "All Tomorrow's Parties" single was played. "I'm Nico," she announced, "and I sang it with the Velvet Underground, the new, uhh, exciting rock'n'roll group of tomorrow." More significant was her screen time in Warhol's film *The Chelsea Girls*, which premiered at the Cinematheque in September. It was actually a shuffle-mix of shorter films shot over many months at various locations, including the titular Chelsea Hotel, the Factory, and one of the Velvet Underground's crash pads. The narrative, insofar as there was one, spotlit various women in the Factory tribe, including Mary Woronov as a character called Hanoi Hannah. But Nico was the main attraction, blondly dominating the two scenes that generally served as the film's beginning and end (Warhol's initial intent was for the film's multiple reels to be shown in random order, on two projectors running simultaneously side-by-side). Despite its unconventional format and three-hour-plus length, it became an art-house success, generating real money for Warhol. Nico, however, saw little of it, so with a child to support and the Velvets on hold, she took up the Balloon Farm's offer of a solo residency in the basement lounge. Reed, irritated by her growing fame, refused to perform with her, eventually recording a tape of guitar tracks that she used for a while as onstage accompaniment. But in time she met kindred musicians to back her, among them the folk singers Tim Buckley, Tim Hardin, and a precocious sixteen-year-old from California named Jackson Browne.

Meanwhile, the Velvet Underground's debut LP sat in the can. In the wake of the nonstarter "All Tomorrow's Parties" release, Tom Wilson wanted another song that might be a viable single, and he wanted it sung by Nico. Reed's response was "Sunday Morning." The song grew from a Warhol request to write a song about paranoia, an emotion speed aficionados like Reed knew well. "What a great thing to write about," he said. "All of us are so paranoid anyway. It's like the Great Subject." Reed shaped the song with Cale sitting around a piano at a friend's apartment on a Sunday morning, the story goes, taking evident inspiration from the Mamas and the Papas' "Monday, Monday," a number 1 pop hit that spring. But when the band assembled with Tom Wilson to record it at Mayfair Sound Studios on Seventh Avenue— a better facility than Scepter, hired no doubt in hopes of engineering a gem—Reed pulled another eleventh-hour power play: he announced that he would be singing it, not Nico.

When Wilson heard the result, he was satisfied. Sweet and haunted, Reed's vocals in the final mix recount restlessness and wasted years against a celeste melody, ghosted by Cale's viola and Nico's "la-la-la"s. It was slated as the album's lead song, and released as a single in December, with "Femme Fatale" as the B side. Finally, the LP was done.

The band wound down its first year as avant-garde commandos by dipping their toes into the mainstream. They played some Midwest dates, including a "Mod Wedding Happening," a marriage ceremony between an artist and a dancer at which Warhol autographed Campbell soup cans and Nico, in a lavender pantsuit, sang "Here Comes the Bride." The Velvets also joined Dick Clark's Caravan of Stars teen tour for some one-offs in Detroit alongside Gary Lewis and the Playboys, Sam the Sham and the Pharoahs, and, from England, the Yardbirds, whose guitarist Jimmy Page had played on Nico's solo single. There was admiration between the Yardbirds and the Velvets; Page described the latter's live sets as "phenomenal" and "intense," and the Yardbirds would soon cover "I'm Waiting for the Man" in their live sets. They were among the first-ever artists to cover a Velvet Underground song.

But probably not the very first. By the end of 1966, Reed's work probably made its greatest impact on a nineteen-year-old British singer just finishing his own debut LP. During a trip to New York in November, Kenneth Pitt, a music publicist turned artist manager, got ahold of an advance acetate of the Velvet Underground's album and passed it on to a client—the former David Jones, who'd just changed his last name to Bowie, in homage to the American actor Jim Bowie. Instead of a circular label, the LP acetate had a small rectangular sticker in the center with "WARHOL" scrawled on it in pen. David Bowie dropped the needle onto side one, and his ideas about what rock music could be were transformed.

"I was hearing a degree of cool that I had no idea was humanly sustainable," he recalled years later. "Ravishing. One after another, tracks squirmed and slid their tentacles around my mind . . . By the time 'European Son' was done, I was so excited I couldn't move. It was late in the evening and I couldn't think of anyone to call, so I played it again and again and again."

5.

LOWER EAST SIDE > UPPER EAST SIDE > LOS ANGELES > BOSTON

(1967–1968)

DISCUSSED: *The Velvet Underground & Nico*, Leonard Cohen, the Gymnasium, the Boston Tea Party, Nico is fired, Warhol is fired, Candy Darling, Jackie Curtis, Betsey Johnson, Alice Bailey's *A Treatise on White Magic*, *White Light/White Heat*, Valerie Solanas, Warhol is shot, Martin Luther King Jr. is shot, Robert Kennedy is shot, Cale gets fired, Doug Yule, *The Velvet Underground*

> [Lou] was always trying to move, mentally and spiritually, to some place where no one had ever gotten before.
>
> **—Sterling Morrison**

> "It's aggressive, yes. But it's not aggressive bad. This is aggressive going to God."
>
> **—Lou Reed on *White Light/White Heat***

*T*he Velvet Underground & Nico was listed as a new release in the January 28 *Billboard,* but the LP's actual birth was difficult. The first ad for it appeared in the small New York weekly *The Village Voice* with no legible image of the band, just a shot of Warhol's head peeking up over the album jacket and the headlines "SO FAR UNDERGROUND YOU GET THE BENDS!" and "WHAT HAPPENS WHEN THE DADDY OF POP ART GOES POP MUSIC?" Even in the marketing of their own LP, the Velvets played second fiddle to their mentor. The slight continued with the package: Warhol's Cavendish banana sticker, bright yellow against a blank white background, with his signature stamp displayed prominently beneath it and, in minuscule type, the instruction "PEEL SLOWLY AND SEE" near the fruit's tip. The band's name? Nowhere on the cover.

But that wasn't the only problem. Inside the gatefold jacket were a variety of press quotes, most fairly negative (Reed thought printing them would be funny; "the flowers of evil are in bloom" was his favorite). The positive ones were supposedly slipped in at the eleventh hour by Verve. The biggest issue, however, was the back cover photo of the band during an Exploding Plastic Inevitable performance, with the barely distinguishable, upside-down image of Eric Emerson projected above them. Emerson, a beautiful wild child with dance moves and a creative bent, was cast in *The Chelsea Girls* after Warhol saw him leap across the room at one of the Dom shows. Unfortunately, no one at Verve had asked the young artist's permission to use his image, and, smelling opportunity, he claimed damages of $500,000. Instead of cutting a deal with Emerson, who likely could have been bought off for a fraction of that, the label pulled the record out of stores, eventually reshipping it with black stickers over the contentious image (and in later printings, with Emerson's photo obscured). In the end, the case was dismissed when Emerson failed to show up for a hearing. But the damage was done.

The Velvet Underground & Nico peaked at number 171 on the *Billboard* chart, and generated no hits, not even the exquisite "Sunday Morning." Nevertheless, the album existed. Moe Tucker went into a store to buy one, just for the thrill of it. Sterling Morrison called up *Cashbox* magazine every week to get word on how it was selling. And Reed took the Long Island Rail Road home to Freeport in his black leather motorcycle jacket with an armload of LPs—the prodigal rock 'n' roll son.

But his frustration with the group's situation was growing, and though he joked about it, the bad reviews hurt. He saw Zappa get his band's debut released ahead of the Velvets, with a better reception and what seemed like more promotion. To add insult to injury, Zappa and the Mothers had moved to New York and begun a six-month residency in the Village at the Garrick Theatre, 152 Bleecker Street, far outlasting the Exploding Plastic Inevitable's Dom run.

Reed was also increasingly estranged from his bandmates. The pre-vious fall, he took an apartment of his own, on Tenth Street between First and Second: tiny, noisy, bug-infested, $65 a month. His conflicts with Cale, who'd moved in with Morrison between First and Av-enue A, increased. They were both involved with the Factory ancil-lary Susan Bottomly, and their drug-buddy interests diverged, given Reed's preference for amphetamines (which Cale avoided) over her-oin. Reed's discomfort with Nico was magnified by her relationship with Cale, who'd moved in with her briefly early in the year, when she got an apartment near Lincoln Center. Reed purportedly stormed into the Factory one day shouting about his ex-lover: "So she photographs great in high-contrast black and white! I'm not playing with her any-more!" He would, though; in fact, he and Morrison began accompany-ing her on guitar from time to time for her gigs at the Balloon Farm's ground-floor bar (known as "the New Mod-Dom," or just "the Dom"), where she'd often perform alongside Warhol films in a folk-club ver-sion of the Exploding Plastic Inevitable; in one account, Reed silently nuzzled a Hershey's bar in a Screen Test above her while she crooned to the rubberneckers.

As it happened, another Jewish singer-songwriter/poet/fiction writer, Leonard Cohen, met Nico at the Dom around this time. "She was a sight to behold. I suppose the most beautiful woman I'd ever seen up to that moment," he recalled. "I just walked up and stood in front of her until people pushed me aside. I started writing songs for her then." Nico introduced Cohen to Reed, who was familiar with his writing. "[He] surprised me greatly because he had a book of my po-ems," Cohen recalled. "I hadn't been published in America, and I had a very small audience even in Canada. So when Lou asked me to sign *Flowers for Hitler*, I thought it was an extremely friendly gesture of his." Another night, in Max's Kansas City's back room, someone hassled Cohen; Reed said to him, "Man, you don't have to take that kind of shit. You wrote *Beautiful Losers*." For his part, Cohen praised Reed's songwriting, and one imagines Reed and Nico had some influence on *The Songs of Leonard Cohen*, which Cohen began recording that August.

Cohen may have spurred Reed to think more about his own poetry, which had taken a back seat to music since he left Syracuse. When Gerard Malanga was invited to guest-edit an issue of the West Coast literary magazine *Intransit*, he and Warhol assembled a 220-page tome, publishing many in the Factory extended family (Cale, Nico, Jonas Mekas, Angus MacLise, Piero Heliczer) alongside the New York School stars Frank O'Hara (who'd just died), John Ashbery, Anne Waldman, and Ron Padgett. Warhol contributed "Cock," a transcription of amphetamine babble recorded at the Factory.

Reed contributed a long poem, "The People Must Have to Die for the Music." Over four pages that seemed to incorporate similar Factory chatter, Reed praised Rimbaud, dissed Robert Lowell (again), noted the difference between "rimming" and "reaming," and professed a hatred for psychiatrists in a remarkable shock-spiel that also invoked clogged hypodermics, scatological play over a glass table, and turning tricks on Union Turnpike. The poem ended with a rejection of pessimism and a paean to the greatness of rock 'n' roll, praising the Moonglows, the Paragons, and the Jesters while memorializing James Dean and Johnny Ace, the Memphis singer who accidently shot himself in the head on Christmas Day in 1954. It was a tour de force, sketching out themes that would inform Reed's work for years to come.

* * *

On Easter Sunday 1966, approximately ten thousand people attended a Be-In at the Sheep Meadow in Central Park. It had been staged, with stealth, by a collective including the writer Paul Williams—who had launched the first-ever rock 'n' roll journal, *Crawdaddy*, as a college student the previous year—and a young actor, Jim Fouratt, who helped distribute thousands of handbills, designed by the up-and-coming psychedelic poster artist Peter Max. Fouratt's response to anyone asking who the organizer was was a grinning "YOU are." There was no scheduled entertainment. But people sang, danced, strummed guitars, and plucked banjos; meditated, blew bubbles, jumped rope, climbed trees, and waved peace-sign flags. Balloons were everywhere. Shaggy-haired young people distributed flowers and candy. Straights, many strolling after Easter mass, gawked and giggled. Someone led a procession with an outsized papier mâché banana.

The latter must've amused Reed, who came uptown to take it all in. Billy Name was there, ditto Danny Fields, who was working with the British band Cream, in New York for their debut U.S. shows. Fields was babysitting the bassist, Jack Bruce, who'd eaten a fistful of popcorn handed to him by a wide-eyed "Technicolor girl," unintentionally embarking on his first acid trip. ("Eric [Clapton] was like "What the fuck did you do to my bass player?" said Fields, recalling the guitarist's reaction when he returned Bruce for the show.) Hippie skepticism notwithstanding, Reed was impressed. "No one wanted to leave," he told the actor and Factory regular Ondine, marveling about it subsequently at Max's Kansas City. "We should have just camped there together and stayed." Later that day, Reed met Jackson Browne at a session for Nico's forthcoming solo LP, *Chelsea Girl*, and caught a set by Cream at the RKO Theater on Fifty-eighth Street at Third Avenue, where the band was part of a show called *Music in the Fifth Dimension* (the bill also featured the U.S. debut of the Who). The revue was hosted by Murray the K, the DJ who didn't premier Reed's high school single roughly ten years earlier.

* * *

Reed wrote or co-wrote four of the songs on Nico's debut LP. Written for Warhol's film but not finished until it had already come out, "Chelsea Girls" was a paean-requiem for a cast of characters based on the Factory crew. In a motif echoing Dylan's "Desolation Row" or "Highway 61 Revisited," they emerge verse by verse—among them Ondine, Woronov, and Brigid Berlin—as Reed's verses rhyme "room 115" with "S&M queens" and "room 506" with "it's enough to make you sick." The music faintly echoed "Ruby Tuesday," the baroque folk-rock B side released by the Rolling Stones in January. The album also featured "Wrap Your Troubles in Dreams," from Reed and Cale's '65 demo, perfectly suited to Nico's low register, and "It Was a Pleasure Then," an eight-minute meditation on "bitter-tasting hatefulness" and "shattered minds" credited to Reed, Cale, and Nico, with ghostly incantations set against folk-rock guitar and harrowing feedback. Jackson Browne wrote three songs, including the shimmeringly rueful "These Days," and Tim Hardin contributed "Eulogy for Lenny Bruce," a tribute to Reed's hero, who'd OD'd in his bathroom the previous summer—the bell toll finale of an album even darker than the Velvets' debut.

Meanwhile, the band scrounged for shows. Morrissey, now effectively the Velvets' manager, worked out a deal through the Dom's owner to rent a cavernous gymnasium inside Sokol Hall, a Czechoslovakian cultural outpost uptown, at 420 East Seventy-first Street off First Avenue in Yorkville. Complete with trampolines and other accessories potentially useful for a roomful of druggy rock 'n' roll fans, the Gymnasium was an interesting space for what turned out to be a month-long residency.

"I'd only seen a handful of electric bands at that time," says Chris Stein, a nascent Brooklyn hippie whose fledgling band lucked into an opening slot. "We're in this big echoey fucking gymnasium . . . [the Velvets] came on, using the echoes and feedback and the reverb of the room as part of their sound. I'd never heard that before. It was awesome."

Indeed, the Velvets had developed into a powerful machine onstage, and had worked up some new songs. On a Cale tape dated April 30, "Guess I'm Falling in Love" comes off like a Rolling Stones single: upbeat, hook-filled, with straightforward hot-shit rock 'n' roll guitar breaks and a faintly lewd central verse ("I got the fever down in my pockets") that recalled Dylan's "Absolutely Sweet Marie" from *Blonde on Blonde*, just issued that spring. Two instrumental jams also felt derivative: "Booker T," an obvious nod to the R&B masters Booker T and the MGs, and "The Gift," a two-chord saunter with droning solos that threatens to break into Them's 1964 single "Gloria" for ten minutes straight. But the standout, being performed publicly for maybe the first time, is "Sister Ray," which sounded like little that came before—a nineteen-minute groove monster that hurtled forward with the breathlessness of a meth rush while feedback squalls flashed like heat lightning and Reed hollered out scenes of what sounded like a party to end all parties: gender-fluid blow jobs, drug injecting, and a murder no one seems especially bothered by. Like the rest of the new songs, it was a work in progress. But it'd be a keeper.

* * *

Warhol's waning interest in the Exploding Plastic Inevitable, and his strained relationship with Reed, came to a head in 1967, just before the Summer of Love. The EPI performed its final show in May at the Scene, a basement rock venue run by the precocious Westchester hot boy Steve Paul at 301 West Forty-sixth Street at Times Square, just around the block from the Factory. The novelty of playing rock 'n' roll amid projections and films was gone—even Murray the K's revues had half-assed light shows. Moreover, the Velvets' fan base was expanding beyond the art-world chin-scratchers, poets, and society voyeurs, a change that didn't please everyone. Ronnie Cutrone recalled dancing onstage with Woronov and Malanga as a mob of uninvited audience members came up to dance onstage with them. "Everybody was liberated to be as sick as we were acting," he said.

The same month, on May 26 and 27, the Velvets played their first dates at the Boston Tea Party, a new arts venue that had been conceived as an outpost of Mekas's Cinematheque.

The shows would prove pivotal. On the first night, Nico didn't turn up at all, maybe due to a Dom commitment, or jet lag—she'd just been in Europe with Warhol for a screening of *The Chelsea Girls* at the Cannes Film Festival. With national distribution, the film was giving them all a palpable sense of mass-culture fame, heady even for Warhol and Nico, who'd tasted it in the past. (The film was ultimately cut from the Cannes schedule due to concern over its content, but it screened in Paris some days later.)

The Velvets had been pissed off that Warhol took off to the continent with Nico and left them behind—understandably enough—which might have contributed to how things panned out. When she arrived at the Tea Party near the end of the Velvets' set on the second night, Reed and his bandmates refused to let her onstage. She never performed with the band again.

Three days later, coincidentally, the vice squad raided the Symphony Cinema, where *The Chelsea Girls* had been screening; in short order, the film was officially banned in Boston. Nevertheless, the Velvets would end up making the city their default home base for the next few years.

* * *

Things might have played out very differently. In London after the Cannes dustup, Warhol told a journalist about some upcoming gigs there for the Velvet Underground. But they never happened, nor did other potential European engagements with the EPI. Warhol was frozen out of the Venice Biennale that year by his former comrade Henry Geldzahler, then curating American artists for the event from his post at the Metropolitan Museum of Art; he wouldn't go out on a professional limb to back Warhol's new multimedia direction, which his high-art world saw as even more suspect than his canvases. Other Exploding Plastic Inevitable gigs failed to materialize, including one at the prestigious Spoleto Festival, either from curatorial cold feet or Warhol's diminished interest. There was even talk of a "rock opera" version of *The Chelsea Girls* for a big Warhol retrospective in early '68 at Sweden's Moderna Museet, though in the end it came to nothing. It's hard to know the trajectory the Velvets might have taken if Warhol had gotten them to Europe; in later years, their profile there, along with Reed's, grew to be much larger than in the States.

On June 3, a week after Nico's excommunication from the band, the Velvets played a benefit for Merce Cunningham's dance company at the Glass House, the famed Modernist building designed by the architect Philip Johnson in the wooded suburbs of New Canaan, Connecticut. No light show, no films, no Nico; just Gerard Malanga, with his whip; Billy Name, helping with setup; and Warhol, who spent most of the evening chatting up Johnson, one of his major patrons. Guests, including Jacob Javits, the Republican senator from New York, paid $75 a head; society-page swells in blazers and party dresses lounged on the grass watching lithe modern dancers on a wide wooden stage, which became a discotheque platform when the Velvets plugged in after dinner. Before long, the music was shut down, after police received noise complaints from the neighbors.

On the limo ride back to New York City, the group discussed their future. Their album was getting no radio play; according to Morrison, the only New York station that had been airing it, the countercultural community outlet WBAI, stopped when the band refused to play a benefit concert.

Could a proper manager achieve what Warhol and Morrissey had not? At Max's in May, Danny Fields had introduced Reed to the Beatles' manager, Brian Epstein, who "sticks his head out of [his limousine] window," Reed recalled, "says, 'Get in,' and offers me a joint." Reed got in with Fields, and Epstein informed them that he'd taken the Velvets' LP on vacation, listened to it repeatedly, and "liked it very much." With the Beatles having abandoned touring the previous summer, he was nosing around for new acts. In fact, Warhol and Epstein apparently discussed a British Velvets tour at some point, though the shows never happened. Epstein was gay, which may have helped or hindered a connection with Warhol's less closeted world. In any case, nothing more came of the connection; by late summer, Epstein would be dead of a barbiturate overdose.

Meanwhile, Reed had been speaking with Steve Sesnick, the macher the band met in Los Angeles and reconnected with at the Boston Tea Party. Sesnick was interested in managing the band, and Reed liked the idea, as did Tucker, who was impressed by his enthusiasm; she thought he was "more our style . . . much more our type of person" than others they'd crossed paths with. Even Warhol's point man Billy Name thought they should enlist him as a proper manager, one who seemed to actually know the business.

The come-to-Jesus session with Warhol likely happened in early summer. According to Reed, Warhol sat him down and said, "You gotta decide what you want to do. Do you want to keep just playing museums from now on and the art festivals? Or do you want to start moving into other areas? Lou, don't you think you should think about it?"

"So I thought about it," Reed said, "and I fired him. Because I thought that was one of the things to do if we were going to move away from that."

Warhol was furious. "I'd never seen Andy angry, but I did that day," Reed said. "He was really mad. Called me a rat. That was the worst thing he could think of."

In later years, Reed spoke matter-of-factly about it. But however much sense it made from a business perspective, and however much the men's friendship had cooled after their clash over the management contract, it must've been a traumatic split—especially given Warhol's anger, which doesn't quite jibe with Reed's suggestion that Warhol encouraged the break. The art-incubating, queer-friendly sanctuary of the Factory would never feel as welcoming. Legal documents suggest the Velvets' separation from Warhol was made official by July, and Steve Sesnick became their new manager. In a broader sense, Reed was on his own.

* * *

There are four or five bars a nervous square might relax in, but one is a Lesbian place, another is a hangout for brutal-looking leather fetishists and the others are old neighborhood taverns full of brooding middle-aged drunks. Prior to the hippy era there were three good Negro-run jazz bars on Haight Street, but they soon went out of style. Who needs jazz, or even beer, when you can sit down on a public curbstone, drop a pill in your mouth, and hear fantastic music for hours at a time in your own head? A cap of good acid costs $5, and for that you can hear the Universal Symphony, with God singing solo and the Holy Ghost on drums.
　　　　　　　　　　　　　　　　　—Hunter S. Thompson
　　　　　"The 'Hashbury' Is the Capital of the Hippies,"
　　　　　　　　　The New York Times Magazine, May 14, 1967

A couple of months or so after the release of *The Velvet Underground & Nico*, on June 1, the Beatles released *Sgt. Pepper's Lonely Hearts Club*

Band. Nico had attended a promotional dinner party at Brian Epstein's London home a couple of weeks prior, with other insiders and journalists, and was treated to a preview hearing of the LP. (She's said to have told Paul McCartney she liked "A Day in the Life," except for the stupid little pop song in the middle.) When Nico parted ways with the Velvets days before the release of *Sgt. Pepper's*, she couldn't know that the album she'd made with them would stand alongside the Beatles' release as one of the most influential albums ever. However, at that precise moment, the creative hotspot of rock music was not in London, or in New York, but in San Francisco.

Hell's Angels, published in 1967, established twenty-nine-year-old Hunter S. Thompson as a rising star of journalism; dealing with the West Coast motorcycle gang, it profiled a reviled subculture in a way that bore kinship with Reed's work. In May, *The New York Times Magazine* published a piece by Thompson describing a New Left political movement that had begun in earnest at the University of California, Berkeley, then changed tone and relocated to the Haight-Ashbury neighborhood of San Francisco after the 1966 election of Governor Ronald Reagan. Thompson described a scene where "marijuana is everywhere," and "at-home entertainment is nude parties at which celebrants paint designs on each other." He predicted that when the school year ended, given the media hoopla that he was now amplifying, between "50,000 and 200,000" young people would descend on the neighborhood in a national summer-break bacchanal. It turned out to be around 100,000.

"The Summer of Love" was mirrored to an extent in London. But New York City seemed instead to empty out. "Teenage ninnies flocked from Middle America out to the coast; hot on their heels came a predatory mob from NYC," Morrison observed. "Roughly speaking, every creep, every degenerate, every hustler, booster and rip-off artist, every wasted weirdo packed up his or her clap, crabs and cons and headed off to the Promised Land." (This may have had something to do with the destabilizing flood of speed into the once-mellow "Hashbury" scene that summer.) The Velvets sat it out.

Nico, however, newly untethered, headed west, attending the landmark Monterey Pop festival in June on the arm of the Rolling Stone Brian Jones. She then returned to the Castle in Los Angeles, where she had an intense hookup with Jim Morrison, who was just tasting stardom (the Doors' "Light My Fire" single would reach number 1 in July). Next, it was up to San Francisco for the belated local premiere of *The Chelsea Girls*. She also appeared in a new film with Warhol, *I, a Man*, shot in Los Angeles and New York in July, featuring a young actor and playwright, Valerie Solanas, who'd soon play a major role in Warhol's life story.

Two new superstars came onto the scene as well. Warhol recalled picking up a pair of custom-made pants at the Leather Man on Christopher Street in August, where he met a couple of young charmers, Candy Darling and Jackie Curtis, who invited him to a production of Curtis's stage production *Glamour, Glory and Gold* at the Playwrights' Workshop at Bastiano's Cellar Studio on Waverly. Curtis presented variously, while Darling was ultra-femme and very beautiful. She'd also have a role in Warhol's life; Reed's, too.

The remaining Velvets spent the Summer of Love learning to play nastier. Reed hot-rodded his Gretsch Country Gentleman—the model George Harrison played—with four pickups, one lifted off a Fender Stratocaster. He made his sound cut deeper, with a built-in pre-amp, tremolo and speed controls, and stereo electronics allowing him separate channel feeds. Like the Yardbirds and the Who, Reed used a Vox distortion box (a Tone Bender) and an AC100 amp with a mid-range booster. He was determined to make a noise supreme.

The band played shows on Cape Cod, did a residency in Philadelphia, and played a couple of weekends at the Tea Party. For one of the latter gigs, on August 11, Warhol came to town to film the show. The result was thirty-three minutes of 16mm color film of the Velvets performing, a barrage of over- and underexposed images with terribly distorted sync sound; speedy jump cuts alternated with images of the band onstage, crotch shots of bare-chested men, and someone manipulating a clear plate of colored liquid atop an overhead projector. Still, it channeled the Velvets' overwhelming power—Cale dragging a bow across his viola in the shadows during "Venus in Furs" while dancing fans snaked around one another, Reed searching for a metaphoric mainline while preppies and hipsters frugged furiously to "Sister Ray." But the footage was lost in the flood of Warhol's film projects, and nothing of significance to the struggling Velvets was ever done with it.

Love was, however, in the New York air that summer. Cale began a relationship with Betsey Johnson, a rising-star clothing designer who'd attended Syracuse with Reed and briefly dated Morrison. The relationship took a toll on the Reed-Cale partnership, as did Steve Sesnick. Cale disliked their new manager straightaway, taking him for "a snake" who viewed him and the other Velvets merely as Reed's sidemen. "Sesnick fucked up my relationship with Lou," Cale stated plainly. "And I was angry at Lou for letting him do it."

Meanwhile, Shelley Albin had moved into Washington Square Village with her new husband, who taught at NYU. Reed had remained in touch ("He always knew where to find me," she recalls) and still carried a torch. He'd been opposed to her marriage, and told her so. But Albin had no interest in rekindling the flame. Nevertheless, they still saw each other on occasion.

In another college flashback that summer, Reed's old friend and roommate Lincoln Swados—no longer institutionalized, but still battling demons—threw himself in front of a subway train. He survived, but lost his right arm and leg. His parents loathed Reed, considering him a bad influence. But he visited his friend. "Lincoln had an outpatient apartment in Gramercy and Lou was over, just hanging out," recalls his sister Liz, who was sixteen and crushed-out on Reed, who'd come a long way since she'd met him in Syracuse. "They were smoking dope and talking, and my brother was hopping around on one foot and they were both laughing hysterically at that." Later that day, Reed took them both to a head shop near Tompkins Square. It was the first time Liz Swados ever saw someone shoot up.

* * *

The Velvets began recording *White Light/White Heat* in September. They'd been woodshedding material onstage for months. Aside from the brief "Here She Comes Now," tender songs were shelved; the intent was to assault, to capture their live energy, per Cale, "to keep that animalism there."

With its mandate to "Watch that speed freak!" the title track obviously deals with methamphetamine. But Reed was also interested in "white light" as a spiritual metaphor. He wasn't bullshitting: in interviews he referred to Japanese Johrei (white light) healing practice, which he'd experienced, and to the work of the esoteric English theosophist Alice Bailey, the late author of *A Treatise on White Magic*, which he considered "an incredible book." Bailey describes a process of wresting back control of "the astral body" in the midst of mindsets like panic attacks—which Reed had certainly wrestled with—by summoning an incandescently meditative state: "[You] will with deliberation call down a stream of pure white light, and, pouring it through your lower vehicles, you will cleanse away all that hinders."

Rob Norris, who saw the Velvets' first show with Moe Tucker at Summit High School, often caught the band when they played in Boston, his new hometown, and recalls backstage conversations with Reed focused on astrology, the occult, and Bailey's theories of healing, particularly the one she referred to as the Seven Rays of Energy, ideas that may also have been coded in the *White Light/White Heat* songs "Sister Ray" and "I Heard Her Call My Name." Reed "was very emphatic that 'White Light/White Heat' could be taken two different ways," Norris said.

If there's stealth spirituality to *White Light/White Heat*, there was also stealth heartbreak. "The Gift" combined the menacing R&B instrumental they'd been sculpting for a while with the short story Reed sent Albin in college about Waldo, a lovesick "schmuck" who winds up dead in pursuit of his beloved. (It's read by Cale, perhaps as a dodge, as Reed was evidently still besotted with Albin.) The stuttered, two-minute "Here She Comes Now" conjures a woman who can't quite be moved to orgasm, or who is perhaps a lover's proxy: a guitar. "I Heard Her Call My Name" suggests a dead lover or spiritual teacher— "everybody has a 'her,'" Reed admitted—while his scrapyard noise-guitar freakout, translating the cries of his free-jazz heroes, is one of his greatest moments as a player in terms of pure sound, standing with Roger McGuinn's on "Eight Miles High" (a song Reed greatly admired) and Jimi Hendrix's excursions on *Are You Experienced?*, issued in the spring, recordings by guitarists with what most would consider far greater technical skills. Yet the intensity of Reed's performance was no less thrilling, a lesson in less-is-more that the Velvet Underground would impart to many.

And this was just prelude to "Sister Ray," which would run almost the length of side two. The lyrics are a burst of flash fiction that amplifies the transgressions of the first LP—there's a sketchy sailor from Alabama, a gun, a variety of sex acts, and an evidently incapacitated narrator attempting to find a vein to jam a hypodermic into. Reed referred to it on one occasion as "a novel," and another occasion as "a joke"; he recalled writing the lyrics on a train ride back from a Velvets show, and suggested a flamboyant Black trans woman was the source for the song's titular character. The song, with pronouns that became unstable in concert, may have been influenced as well by the 1967 appearance of *Christine Jorgensen: A Personal Autobiography*, a publishing sensation that returned its glamorous author to a notoriety begun in the early 1950s, when she returned from sex-reassignment surgery in Denmark as a transgender celebrity (the *Daily News*, known for page-one headline wit, went with "EX-GI BECOMES BLOND BOMBSHELL" for a story in late '52). For some years Jorgensen had been living not far from Reed's parents, in Massapequa, and it's hard to imagine he wasn't aware of her as a teen. Reed also knew trans folks at the Factory and in the underground film scene, so it's not surprising he'd write a song with what seems a transgender lead character.

Reed had refined the lyrics from the earliest versions, but it was hardly cleaned up; in fact, the partial shift to first person often puts the singer and their "ding-dong" at the center of the action. Musically, per Reed, the song was another attempt to capture the sound of Cecil Taylor and Ornette Coleman, while it also conjured meth's surging intensity. As organized guitar-rock chaos, "Sister Ray" has rarely been bettered. With writing credited to all four band members, it reflected its making: three musicians staring one another down, each determined to drown out the others, with a fourth keeping time on a drum and holding it all together. According to Reed, the amps were all cranked to ten. Cale recalled it as straight-up competition: his distorted electric organ elbows through the guitars, the Phantom of the Opera having a seizure on a circus calliope, while Morrison creates a stroboscopic din and Reed yells for someone named Jim to "whip it on me!" spitting out lyric fragments, slurring and snarling, instruments hurtling forward in screaming unison until, after seventeen breathtaking minutes, they drive the riff over a cliff.

Despite the potent performances, the recorded sound was questionable at best. Playing together in real time in the studio, at maximum volume, created tremendous leakage across tracks. The levels were too high, and the band didn't understand the limits of the technology; Reed claimed that Mayfair's house engineer, Gary Kellgren, walked out of the "Sister Ray" session, telling the band, "You do this. When you're done, call me." The *White Light/White Heat* sessions lasted just under a week and were fueled by "a great deal of chemicals," according to Cale, including heroin. Tom Wilson was on hand, but was less than detail-oriented in the studio; by most accounts, he largely spent his time there sweet-talking the girlfriends he always seemed to have on hand.

The finished *White Light/White Heat* cover image was shot by Billy Name: a skull with a sword through it. This was actually a tattoo on the arm of Joe Spencer, star of Warhol's homoerotic film *Bike Boy*, printed black on black and nearly illegible unless you hold it to the light at a certain angle. The cover was the precise inverse of the album title, and of countless brightly colored 1967 psychedelic LP jackets—another high-concept art gesture that was no marketing asset. For promo shots, the band posed in an empty conference room at the Verve offices, in outfits designed by Betsey Johnson—Cale in a sort of "Little Lord Fauntleroy meets Alice in Wonderland" Victorian dandy suit with jumbo collar flaps, Reed in leather jacket and paisley scarf, Sterling Morrison in a Sir Lancelot–cum–heavy metal outfit with a studded turtleneck, Moe Tucker in an androgynous low-key sports jacket and dress shirt combo. It was a game gesture toward the baroque costuming that was becoming common rock parlance, and even Reed, never much of a clotheshorse, was on board. "Lou said I cut a really good crotch," Johnson recalled.

Waiting for the album's release and the requisite promotional dates, Tucker picked up temp gigs as a typist (she got some work from Warhol, who had her transcribing the Factory amphetamine-babble conversations that became his verité *a: A Novel*, though she complained about having to type the obscene words). Cale traveled to the Virgin Islands and then to Europe with Johnson. Morrison moved in with his girlfriend Martha, Tucker's pal from Levittown. Reed, unattached, wrote poetry. In November, Verve released "White Light/White Heat" as a lead single, with "Here She Comes Now" as the B side, and, once again, as with their previous releases, virtually no radio stations played it.

* * *

When the *White Light/White Heat* LP was released in January, it wasn't especially well received, either. *Rolling Stone* didn't run a review, though a Detroit writer named Lester Bangs claimed to have written one for the magazine that was rejected, declaring the LP "the best album of 1968." In Britain, *Melody Maker* called *White Light/White Heat* "utterly pretentious, unbelievably monotonous," while *New Musical Express* dismissed it as "weirdo stuff." The *Los Angeles Free Press*, accurately if not admiringly, described it as "a ruthless howling cry swirling up from the bottomless neon depths of East Village speed dens and Jack Smith's transvestite orgies," summing it up as the "noise of nihilism." It was not exactly the makings of a successful promo campaign in 1968. But it found its small audience. In New Jersey, an up-and-coming musician named Debbie Harry played it incessantly, driving her parents crazy.

For marketing, Verve took out a few ads and issued a double-LP label sampler for radio, featuring Wilson interviewing Reed. Sesnick asked Verve to shift the publicity budget to further fund their touring, which probably seemed a better investment. Live, the band grew increasingly experimental. "Sister Ray" spawned variants and sequels.

One, known as "Sweet Sister Ray" and documented on a bootleg from a Cleveland show in late April, was a sprawling thirty-nine-minute slow-jam blues-rock journey with free-jazzy soloing and freestyled lyrics. At one point during that version, Reed described an electroshock session: a doctor entering the room, the feeling of Vaseline on the forehead, of hair standing on end. In another variant of the song, "Sister Ray Part 3," Reed became a southern preacher, "telling stories and just inventing these fantastic characters as we played," Cale recalled.

Amid this experimenting, Reed was rethinking the Velvets' music. He wanted to sell records. In February, the band recorded two songs more commercial-sounding than anything on *White Light/White Heat*, perhaps thinking of a follow-up single. "Temptation Inside of Your Heart" was bubblegummy pop-rock with scruffy Motown-style backing vocals. "Stephanie Says" was a cryptically tender song about a girl, possibly based on Nico, who takes phone calls from "across the world," is "not afraid to die," and whose apparent coldness earned her the nickname Alaska. Colored with Cale's gorgeous viola, it's a folk-rock character profile of a sort that Reed would return to.

Both recordings would be shelved. But Reed's interest in simple, marketable, lyric-driven songs grew, and Cale began feeling edged out of the creative process. Tucker never took sides, but recalled that "at certain times, there'd be a lot of tension" between the two. Morrison recalled Reed and Cale coming to blows on one occasion.

When Cale and Betsey Johnson announced their wedding plans, it didn't improve matters. Johnson was a strong, successful woman making better money than the Velvets—by Cale's account, she'd often spirit him off to an upgraded hotel when she met up with the group on tour; when the couple moved into a spacious loft on LaGuardia Place, he was further isolated from the band. If Reed resented the relationship, he still participated in the wedding at City Hall in April. Naturally, Johnson designed the outfits. She wore a bright red velvet jacket and matching scarf, a white blouse with ruffled sleeves, and a corsage; Cale wore a black jacket and corsage, Reed a wide-collared dark blue jacket, bright yellow shirt, and shades. He got a corsage, too.

When the band returned to the road in May, the internecine tension was channeled into phosphorescent music. At the Shrine in Los Angeles, performing on a bill with the Chambers Brothers and Dr. John, "Sister Ray" sounded like "the roof of the building was cracking open," according to one awed observer. The Velvets made time for some recording at TTG Studios in L.A., working on a couple of Reed songs that didn't make much room for Cale. "Hey Mr. Rain" is a jaunty folk-rock tune—a nod to the traditional "Baby, Let Me Follow You Down," a Dylan staple—that Cale warps nicely with dissonant viola. "I'm Beginning to See the Light" is catchier still, with some Dylan in its delivery as well, plus Tucker's snappy drumming. The latter song would evolve, but its sound, and title, suggest a change coming. They're the last studio recordings Cale made with the group.

* * *

On June 3, after picking up an Obetrol prescription, Andy Warhol returned to the Factory, which had relocated to the sixth floor of 33 Union Square West, just down from Max's Kansas City. Outside the building was Valerie Solanas, the actor who appeared with Nico in Warhol's *I, a Man* the previous year, work for which Warhol paid her $25. She got on the elevator with him. She was wearing makeup, unusual for someone who usually presented butch, and a heavy winter coat, odd given the season.

Upstairs, the office was bustling. Warhol got on the phone with Viva, one of his "superstars." She was preparing for a cameo in *Midnight Cowboy*, a film about a male prostitute, whose director wanted a Warhol-style party scene with actual Factory scenesters. As Warhol handed the phone to a colleague, he saw Solanas pointing a gun at him. He screamed for her not to shoot. But she did. Warhol later described it feeling "like a cherry bomb exploding inside me," and seeing his black T-shirt soaked in blood. When Billy Name, alerted by the commotion, came out of the darkroom, he saw Warhol lying in a dark red pool. He knelt, took Warhol in his arms, and held him, weeping; a pietà.

Around the time Warhol met her, Solanas had been distributing mimeographed copies of her feminist tract, *SCUM Manifesto*—the title connected to the acronym for a group she imagined, the Society for Cutting Up Men. Warhol thought Solanas an interesting character, but after casting her in *I, a Man*, his interest in her waned, as it did with many he'd drawn into the Factory solar system. She grew angry at him for snubbing her, evading her phone calls, and losing a typescript she'd given him, titled *Up Your Ass*, that she hoped he might film; she became obsessed with avenging herself. According to the *Daily News*, when she turned herself in to a police officer just after the shooting, she handed over her .32 automatic and explained, "I am a flower child. He had too much control over my life." It wasn't the first time a gun had been discharged at the Factory. In the fall of '64, a woman named Dorothy Podber came into Warhol's studio dressed in black, accompanied by a great dane, took a pistol from her purse, and put a bullet in the forehead of a Marilyn Monroe canvas. A supermarket heir Warhol hoped to enlist in a film project, Huntington Hartford, drunkenly fired some rounds into the Factory ceiling in 1966, and just prior to the Union Square move, in November '67, an Ondine associate known as Sammy the Italian fired a gun during a fumbled robbery attempt, fortunately injuring no one. But as the art-making at the Factory pushed speed-fueled extremes, playacted film violence was turning real. Ondine's face-slapping in *The Chelsea Girls* and other cruel dramas were mirrored off-camera in abusive relationships, including one of Warhol's. In hindsight, a stage had been set for the Solanas shooting.

The attempted murder made national news, which reached Reed at the Beverly Wilshire Hotel in Los Angeles, where he saw a newspaper headline in the lobby the following morning. It shook him to his core. He saw it as an assassination, like President Kennedy's and Martin Luther King Jr.'s, the latter occurring just two months prior to Warhol's (Bobby Kennedy's assassination would follow, and supersede Warhol's two days after). Estranged or not, Warhol remained Reed's mentor and peer, a friend and soulmate, a genius and a visionary. Delmore Schwartz was dead; now this. Whatever ugliness Reed reflected in his lyrics, real life continually made it pale by comparison.

* * *

The Velvets stayed out west for much of the summer. Opening for Quicksilver Messenger Service in July at San Diego's Hippodrome, Cale, Morrison, Reed, and Tucker played a set Lester Bangs would declare "the ultimate Velvet Underground concert," singling out the epic "Sister Ray, Part 2" as "one of the most incredible musical experiences of my concert career." The band's powers had reached a new peak.

Which makes the group meeting Reed called in late September so hard to comprehend. When Tucker and Morrison arrived at Café Riviera at 255 West Fourth Street at Seventh Avenue—a bohemian bar Jack Kerouac had frequented in the '50s—they were met only by Reed, who informed them that Cale was now out of the band.

There was arguing; Morrison recalled a lot of banging on the table. He felt Cale had been performing brilliantly. But Reed would not budge. The choice he presented was stark: continue without Cale, or Reed would bail on their forthcoming Midwest shows and dissolve the band. Moe Tucker claimed she never understood what the problem was between Reed and Cale. Morrison, too, was baffled, because the music they were making was so great. For his part, Cale felt Sesnick had driven a wedge between him and Reed to consolidate power. Cale believed his marriage had something to do with it, too, as did Betsey Johnson, who also chalked the split up to professional jealousy. Morrison acknowledged Reed had increasingly little patience with Cale's avant-garde pursuits, which included spending band money on an expensive bass amplifier project. Cale's close work with Nico on her second solo LP, *The Marble Index*, which Reed was not involved in, probably stuck in his craw. Reed's paranoia, speed-induced or as default mind state, likely drove the decision to oust Cale, as well. Cale suggested the drug use that once bonded them fostered miscommunication and distrust as they retreated into their preferred substances. "If all those drugs hadn't been around," he said, "we would've all been pushing for something. It was the time to really back off for a minute. Because the trust was gone."

When journalists asked Reed about the split, he generally dodged the question, or claimed his reasons were "really personal" and "very private," declining to explain beyond that it was time for a change. If he'd have confided in anyone at this point, it probably would've been Tucker. "We were very close, a brother-sister relationship," she says. "Total trust." In her mind, Reed "really wanted to get some success going—real success. Maybe he wanted to make it less 'avant-garde' or whatever the word is . . . y'know, more normal." But fifty-some years later, she remains reluctant to guess Reed's mindset, as he never explained it to her. "I shouldn't even say this," she says when pressed, "because I don't know what the story is. I really don't."

In any case, Reed tasked Morrison with delivering the bad news to Cale, which the forthright Morrison did in person, showing up at his bandmate's apartment. "Lou always got other people to do his dirty work for him," Cale said.

* * *

It may not have been coincidental that Reed's move shadowed Warhol's pivot from avant-garde provocation to more mainstream product, in the wake of his shooting, from "art" to something more like entertainment or decoration. The Factory's move to Union Square, and the transformation of its office culture into something nearer an ad agency than an artist's studio, reflected a more conventional taking-care-of-business attitude telegraphed in Warhol self-promotional soundbites of the time, including his famous quip "The new art is business." The Silver Factory's cast of characters was largely displaced to Max's Kansas City around the corner as some, like Mary Woronov, peeled off from the scene, tired of not getting paid for their work and ready to move on. Equally indicative of the new order was Warhol's decision to mass-market his "greatest hits," selling silkscreened remakes of his Marilyn Monroe and Campbell's Soup images under the brand name Factory Additions. Warhol's society portraiture also ramped up, a money engine that required him to dial back his more extreme creative tendencies.

Within a couple weeks of Cale's departure, Reed, Morrison, Tucker, and Sesnick were at Max's talking terms with Doug Yule. A twenty-one-year-old Long Islander based in Boston, Yule played with the local

Grass Menagerie; the Velvets had met him previously at the Tea Party when they'd crashed at his manager's apartment. A day after the Max's meeting, Yule rehearsed their entire back catalog in a marathon session at Reed's loft on West Twenty-eighth Street, just off Seventh Avenue, and the day after that he was onstage with the band in Cleveland at La Cave, navigating chord changes on bass and organ. Yule was a capable, versatile musician who seemed very unlikely to challenge Reed's leadership.

The Velvets' transformation was remarkable: in little more than a year, they'd gone from being the fulcrum of a multimedia art extravaganza with Warhol, their sound defined by John Cale's screeching drones and Nico's It Girl European sangfroid, to a dark-matter psychedelic juggernaut navigating the outer limits of free-form improvisation and lock-groove hypnotics, to their current incarnation: a fairly straightforward rock band jamming in hippie dance halls. On record, propelled by Reed's latest batch of writing, they were about to make yet another transformation.

After a five-night run at the Whiskey a Go Go—the most important rock venue in L.A., having launched the Doors and put an early spotlight on artists from Cream to Jimi Hendrix—the Velvets returned to the neighboring TTG studios. As it happened, Hendrix was also recording there that month; he caught a Velvets set at the Whiskey, and came backstage to praise the band. (Jim Morrison supposedly caught a set, too.) The Velvets also landed a gig at nearby Beverly Hills High School, booked by the student body president, the future journalist Mickey Kaus. They played to a mostly empty auditorium, followed by a panel discussion that included the school psychologist, who complained the music was too loud. "Lou Reed and [he] got into an incredible pissing match," recalled Kaus. "It was considered a disaster."

At TTG, the band worked on a remarkable batch of new songs they'd been sculpting live: reflective and celebratory, lovelorn and yearning, confused and searching, philosophical and spiritual. Taken together, they were nearly a 180-degree departure from the harsh vibe of *White Light/White Heat*. First was the sound: mostly ballads and mid-tempo rockers, cleanly recorded, with space around each instrument. Gone was the tsunami of fuzz tones and feedback, replaced by the pastoral guitar breeze of twelve-string Fender Electric XIIs and Gibson hollow bodies. According to Morrison, their effects pedals and devices were stolen at the airport en route to California, which might further explain the new sonics. The band was now nominally producing themselves (Tom Wilson left MGM/Verve in January to start his own company), aided by the engineer Val Valentin, who'd helmed Astrud Gilberto and Stan Getz's 1964 megahit "The Girl from Ipanema," a benchmark of pop intimacy that's one reference point for the more hushed music Reed was cultivating. So, too, were LPs marking the start of the singer-songwriter movement in rock: debuts by Joni Mitchell, Neil Young, and Randy Newman—all artists to whom Reed would pay attention—were released in 1968, as was the atmospheric *Astral Weeks* by Van Morrison, an Irish singer-songwriter with interests in poetry and occult litera-ture who'd recently become a presence on the Boston scene revolving around the Tea Party.

Where *White Light/White Heat* opened with Reed at his most ecstat-ically deranged, the Velvets' third LP, simply titled *The Velvet Under-ground*, opens with him at his most tender and empathetic, though in fact the voice was not his. "Candy Says" was in Reed's mind "probably the best song I've written." And indeed, the recording is sublime, mov-ing quickly from heartbreaking to uplifting and back again, gentle guitar strums and arpeggios behind a boyish high tenor voice, like something you'd catch in a half-dreaming state on a distant radio. The lyrics draw a portrait of someone—there's no gendered pronoun—who hates their body and "all that it requires," hates their endless internal chatter of indecision, who looks to the sky at a limitless beauty that still fails to settle their mind, and wonders, in a marvelous metaphor that rises up the scale to join the bluebirds in the chorus's final line: what it would be like to simply walk away from oneself, to actually *be* someone else. The song's marvelously simple third-person sleight of hand, the "she says" framing of each verse, like that of "Sister Ray," allows its singer to do just that. And while the lyrics feel universal, the backstory deep-ens them. The song's clear inspiration is Candy Darling, who'd just made her film debut that September in Warhol and Paul Morrissey's

Flesh. As a high-femme trans woman, Darling's body hatred was of a particular sort; according to Warhol, she often referred to her genitals as "my flaw."

Reed said of the song: "We look in the mirror and we don't like what we see . . . All of us have said at some point 'I wish I was different' . . . I don't know a person alive who doesn't feel that way. That's what the song is really about—and not only in looks, but in what you require." Those "requirements" might be sexual, emotional, presentational, or sartorial. Certainly, the amount of time and effort Darling put into her appearance struck both Reed and Warhol. Warhol likely identified with her to an extent, as a fairly swish gay man very attuned to the feminine, who was drawn to trans women and cross-dressed himself on occasion. It's hard to know if Reed ever experienced gender dysphoria (a term that wasn't even coined yet), as he seems never to have spoken of such feelings, at least publicly. But for a song so tenderly empathetic, it hardly matters. Unspooled over a time-suspending four minutes, the song resolves with a chain of ghostly "doo-doo-wah"s, a flashback to the doo-wop boy ballads and girl-group laments both Reed and Darling had probably heard at the Hayloft as teens, watching same-sex couples slow-dance across the floor.

Why did Reed assign the singing to Yule? In strictly musical terms, Yule's voice was higher and prettier than his. Reed might've also wanted to distance himself from lyrics he was uncomfortable voicing himself. And he seemed to like having a body double: with their similar facial features and matching afro-like crowns of dark curls, Yule and Reed looked enough alike that fans sometimes asked if they were brothers. (It's interesting to note that in late '67, Warhol modeled a similarly public ruse, employing his doppelgänger actor Allen Midgette to deliver a series of college lectures masquerading as Warhol, complete with blond wig.) In any case, the vocal shape-shifting added another layer to the song's notions of transformation.

"Pale Blue Eyes," meanwhile, had been evolving from the wiseass country-blues revenge ballad Reed demoed in '65. Onstage in October, it was a seven-minute exercise in Dylanesque surrealism featuring a globetrotting character named Jenny ("shot full of holes"), a narrator who hangs out in graveyards, and a woman frozen into ice. A month or so later in the studio, this freestyle vehicle crystallized into one of Reed's most profound and complicated love songs, tinged with anger, failure, and loss, each major-key verse pivoting to minor, the sentiment souring in synch with the melody, irresistibly, like the curdling sensation that drives someone back to their ex's bed. Like "I'll Be Your Mirror" (and Ingmar Bergman's *Persona*, which had debuted in New York the previous year), the song plays with the idea of being reflected by, and merging with, another. More cryptically, there are lines about lies, time, a life "skipped completely," and a confession of adultery that triangulates justification, contrition, and heartfelt horndog come-on. Sterling Morrison's immaculate solo, a Mickey Baker fever dream, traps the wild abandon of love and lust and rock 'n' roll in amber, and turns it all into a perfect memory of something irretrievably past.

According to Shelley Albin, whose eyes are brown, the title was an in-joke for her, albeit a loaded one. She'd still meet up with Reed occasionally, and it was clear he was still hung up on her. "I wrote this for someone I missed very much," he confessed years later in a volume of his lyrics—adding, no doubt with a chuckle: "Her eyes were hazel."

Completing side one's ballad trifecta was "Jesus," a combination hymn, prayer, and confessional that seems less written than handed down, or overheard in a chapel. Echoing ideas Reed encountered back in Gabriel Vahanian's class, no doubt, it also seemed in part a mash note to Warhol, who'd begun exploring Catholic themes in his work (including a '68 commission for a Vatican pavilion at a World's Fair in Texas) and seemed to be rethinking his relationship to his religion. A skeletal weave of guitars, bass, and voices, "Jesus" was another example of Reed's ability to conjure character and mindset with the simplest of lines, and sell it even if it might run counter to a listener's sensibility. And to be sure, in 1968, a song that quietly called on Jesus for guidance—as Reed does in his slightly shaky high tenor, plaintively and achingly—might have been expected to run counter to the sensibility of many rock fans, let alone Velvet Underground fans (though

Reed would've certainly noted the invocation of Jesus's love in Simon & Garfunkel's "Mrs. Robinson," which had been an unlikely number 1 pop hit that spring).

But *The Velvet Underground* wasn't just ballads. Reed continued experimenting with noise and harmonics in "What Goes On," the clearest bridge between Velvets past and present (the band had been playing it live with Cale). The guitar break at its heart is one of the most exhilarating in the rock canon. Triple-tracked, it was stumbled on when someone—Yule and Tucker have both taken credit—suggested Reed play the multitrack recording back with all three of his alternate solo takes punched up and layered on top of one another, so they unspooled simultaneously, shimmering in and out of sync like silver light beaming down from a sci-fi mothership. The magic continued on "Some Kinda Love," driven by Tucker with just a muffled kick drum and cowbell— Reed considered Morrison's deceptively elastic guitar riff "one of the greatest parts he ever did . . . It's like a perfect clock . . . even though it's repeated, it seems to change as you listen to it." A playful song with a giddy-up groove, it would seem to advocate for sexual fluidity decades before the notion became cultural lingua franca, Reed's delightful lewdness all the more impressive for its abstraction into elements like donning red pajamas and "putting jelly on your shoulder," combining the absurd and the vulgar, as the lyrics suggest, like "a dirty French novel." Delivered, like "Candy Says," in third person, it channels a conversation between "Marguerita" and "Tom" that marvels at love's "endless" possibilities, posits how "groundless" it seems to miss even one of them, and settles the matter by declaring that "no kinds of love are better" than any others. In its understated way, it was Reed's queerest song to date.

The album's most formally extreme piece is "The Murder Mystery," a nine-minute poetry slam with all four members of the Velvets reciting and/or singing parallel texts in opposite stereo channels. "It was supposed to be fun with words, fun with rhymes and sounds," Reed said—but as Morrison conceded, there's a "bit of band autobiography" in there, too. Mention of a "toothless wigged laureate" and a reference to Dylan Thomas's "Do not go gentle into that good night" conjure Delmore Schwartz's final days; mention of a party, carpet, "pigs," "jissom," and murder echo "Sister Ray." "The Murder Mystery" has plenty in common with the Beatles' "Revolution 9," released that November— although with its allusion to Lee Harvey Oswald and invocations of "corpulent filth," it's a more decidedly bad trip. Given the horrors of 1968, however, it was fitting.

* * *

On December 14, the Velvet Underground were back at the Boston Tea Party for the last of their fifteen shows there that year. The opening act, Detroit's MC5, had just signed with Elektra Records via Danny Fields, who'd landed an A&R gig there. The MC5 were serious about their politics; they were the only rock band with the chutzpah to actually show up and play at the violence-scarred Democratic National Convention protests that summer in Chicago. After the MC5's Tea Party set, some of their entourage—members of the East Village Motherfuckers, an agitprop group in town to fundraise and make trouble—took the stage and instructed the crowd to burn down the venue as a show of power. Before any matches got lit, however, they were hustled off their soapbox.

The Velvets had always kept explicit politics out of their music, and Reed disavowed any connection with the agitation—the Tea Party was the band's favorite place to play, he told the crowd, and they'd hate to see it harmed. The venue occupied what had been a Unitarian meeting house in the late 1800s, though its Star of David window design earned it the nickname of "the old synagogue," an identity Reed probably appreciated. Located at 53 Berkeley Street, the Tea Party was named in tribute to both dopers' slang and Boston's revolutionary history. By now, its original connection to Jonas Mekas and the Cinematheque was vestigial, like the Velvets' connection to Warhol; rock 'n' roll paid the bills. The scene was casual, with little division between performers and fans. The dressing room "backstage" area was just a room at the rear of the hall. And with fewer cultural options than in New York City, the audience was a broad mix: students and professors, dropouts and drug dealers, artists, fashionistas, and music fiends.

Postshow, the Velvets would often end up at the apartment of Ed Hood, a perpetual Harvard grad student who came from southern money. Hood had a fondness for books—he had probably two thousand filed on floor-to-ceiling shelves along three walls, and liked holding forth on literature, ethics, and philosophy. He also had a fondness for young men, and a connection to the Factory's Boston contingent. The journalist Robert Somma called these late-night salons "séances," with stoned Boston hipsters eating Chinese food and bullshitting all night. "Lou was a key part of that," Somma recalls. "He was really fun, I might add. Onstage he was more serious; in person he was kind of wacky. On the whole, I found him to be a terrific guy."

Despite Cale's departure and the divorce from Warhol—or maybe in part because of them—the Velvet Underground were thriving, and Reed was at a creative peak. That year, 1969, would be the band's greatest, marked by the release of their finest LP, their most consistent live shows, and the writing of many of Reed's most enduring songs. And then, before 1970 was out, they'd be history.

6.

NYC > SAN FRANCISCO > MAX'S KANSAS CITY > LONG ISLAND

(1969–1970)

DISCUSSED: The Grateful Dead, the Stonewall riots, Woodstock, the Matrix, Moe Tucker's maternity leave, the Max's residency, the end of the Velvets, Lewis moves back home, Bettye Kronstad

---

And there's even some evil mothers / Well, they're gonna tell you that everything is just dirt

—Lou Reed, "Sweet Jane"

She started dancin' to that fine, fine music / You know her life was saved by rock 'n' roll

—Lou Reed, "Rock & Roll"

Valerie Solanas was transferred from Matteawan State Hospital for the Criminally Insane in Dutchess County back to jail, and then, astonishingly, released when a friend posted her $10,000 bail in December 1968. She promptly phoned the Factory and threatened Warhol, demanding roles in his forthcoming movies and that all charges against her be dropped. By the end of January, she was back in jail. But the Factory clan was freaked out, Reed especially.

"Lou said Solanas was after him next," says Shelley Albin. Reed often talked shit just to wind people up, including "anti-women bullshit," she recalls, and he imagined that might've made him a target. Albin remembers him holed up in Max's one night, figuring Solanas wouldn't show her face there. "We couldn't leave," she says. "He'd be in there for hours and hours. I'd be getting really frightened." Solanas was soon sentenced to three years in prison, less time served. Warhol had declined to testify in person; with severe organ damage and a bullet wound in his gut that wasn't healing, he just didn't feel up to it. Reed was outraged by the light sentence. "You get more for stealing a car," he noted bitterly, convinced "the hatred directed towards [Andy] by society was obviously reflected in the judgment."

Reed was still estranged from Warhol, and between touring and his anxieties, Reed apparently never visited him during his long recovery. With Cale gone, and Albin keeping her ex at arm's length, Reed was in many ways alone, and a sense of isolation seems to suffuse *The Velvet Underground*, released in March. His final mix of the album, on a tape dated December 20, heightened that impression; it would become known as "the closet mix," a reference to Morrison's comment about its dry, intimate sound: with Reed's vocals pushed to the fore, it indeed sounded like it was tracked in a closet.

It was a striking effect, especially on the ballads. But it was not "radio-friendly," and the high-concept cover art once again did the Velvets no favors: in an age of Day-Glo color, it featured a dark, grainy black-and-white image of the band arrayed on the Factory's iconic sofa, shot by Billy Name. Reed holds up the October 1968 issue of *Harper's Bazaar*, the fashion magazine that was central to launching Warhol's commercial art career in his early days, an inexplicable gesture in context (the magazine's cover was obscured in the final image, likely for copyright reasons). *The Velvet Underground* was a love letter to Warhol and the old Factory scene, and an elegy for the band the Velvets no longer were. But that was hardly a marketing hook.

Once again, the label seemed to have no clue what to do with the album. The ad campaigns were hapless. Perhaps working off Reed's interest in astrology, one ad indicated each band member's sign in cheeky biographical blurbs; Reed was "a true blue Piscean and a secret sensualist." More dubious still was the radio ad voiced by the New York rock DJ Rosko of WNEW-FM:

How do you feel? You don't really know how you feel . . . Here
are expressions of a new dimension in honesty, purity, and feeling . . . The Velvet Underground. This is you. You'll find your
love, your hope, your reality. The Velvet Underground on MGM
Records will tell you how to feel. Listen.

The review in *Rolling Stone*, the band's first in the magazine, was
written by the increasingly notable Lester Bangs, and was maybe a
better sales pitch. "How do you define a group like this, who moved
from 'Heroin' to 'Jesus' in two short-years?" he asked. "Can this be that
same bunch of junkie–faggot–sadomasochist–speed-freaks who roared
their anger and their pain in storms of screaming feedback and words
spat out like strings of epithets? Yes. Yes, it can, and this is perhaps the
most important lesson [of] the Velvet Underground: the power of the
human soul to transcend its darker levels."

The album was well-reviewed elsewhere, too. Yet for all its piercing
beauty, it sold poorly, failing even to crack the *Billboard* 200; *White Light/
White Heat* had at least made it to number 199. The label's distribution
evidently didn't help: the month of the release, before a show in St.
Louis, the band scoured music shops for a copy and couldn't find one.
Tucker recalled, "One guy who owned a record store, who had come
backstage to talk to us, said, 'Gee, you know, I can't get your record. I
called.'"

In some ways, the cultural disconnect was hard to fathom. The arc
of the band's three records shows a band with its ears to the ground the
whole way: the Dylanesque poetics, Motown-Stax thrust, and proto-
psychedelic sound experiments of the debut; the thrillingly overmodu-
lated jamming of *White Light/White Heat*, not far from what Cream and
Hendrix were doing; and now the magnificent pivot to straightforward
songcraft, in the wake of the Band's *Music from Big Pink* and the sea
change of singer-songwriter-driven folk-rock, however different its
lyrical concerns. Reed saw the post-Cale transformation as essential.
"I thought we had to demonstrate the other side of us. Otherwise, we
would become this one-dimensional thing, and that had to be avoided

at all costs." On the occasion of the album's release in early March, hopes still high, Reed told a radio interviewer at Boston's progressive rock station WBCN, "I think it's just fantastic that we can play this stuff in public, and that people like it."

*　*　*

In April, in an accidental summit meeting of two of America's greatest rock bands, the Velvets were booked for two nights with the Grateful Dead at Chicago's Kinetic Playground, aka the Electric Theater. The Velvets loathed the Dead for a number of reasons. One was surely their connection with their nemesis, the concert promoter Bill Graham; two, the West Coast hippie culture the Dead epitomized; three, perhaps, was how much their music had in common. Both bands were informed by folk and free jazz and devoted to transcendental guitar jams. Both had connections to the classical avant-garde—the Velvets through Cale and La Monte Young, the Dead through its bassist, Phil Lesh, who'd studied with Luciano Berio and collaborated with Steve Reich, a fellow student pushing the boundaries of new music. Both bands had poet-lyricists. Both were briefly named the Warlocks. And both were at the top of their game as live performers; the Dead had just recorded the performances that became *Live/Dead*, arguably their finest recorded document.

"We had vast objections to the whole San Francisco scene," Reed said in a radio interview around that time. "It's just tedious, a lie, and untalented. They can't play and they certainly can't write. The Airplane, the Dead, all of them . . . they can't play. Jerry [Garcia] is not a good guitar player. It's a joke." In some ways, it was an east-west aesthetic turf war not unlike those in the underground film world (Warhol vs. Kenneth Anger) or art world (Warhol vs. Ed Ruscha; New York Minimalism vs. Los Angeles Light and Space), fueled by the Velvets' inability to catch a commercial break. Nevertheless, here they were on a bill that also featured the Dead, their Bay Area brethren Quicksilver Messenger Service, and Detroit psychedelic rockers SRC.

The Dead and the Velvets agreed to alternate their sets each night, so each got to headline. According to Doug Yule, the Dead went long on April 25, cutting into the Velvets' time; one fan recalled Reed coming onstage and gesturing for them to wrap it up, to which Pigpen, the Dead's burly keyboardist, responded with a middle finger. The next night, the Velvets retaliated. "We did 'Sister Ray' for like an hour," he recalled. "Lou was out to prove that he could do it." According to Scott Richardson of SRC, there was also a trip to the ER with Reed to get a tranquilizer when he accidentally ingested some LSD.

The following month, the Velvets were back at the Boston Tea Party with the Allman Brothers Band, who were playing their first-ever shows outside the South; their debut LP was still unreleased. During that May weekend, the two guitar bands might've learned a few tricks from each other.

* * *

A week prior, the Velvets had been in New York at the Record Plant, working on new recordings. Reed already had enough songs for a fourth LP, and though the band's relationship with MGM was curdling due to poor sales, they were still able to secure studio time. Morrison and Tucker thought the tracks would be for their next album; Yule recalled them as demos and work tapes. In any case, the material was strong enough to justify the pressing of a seven-song acetate, a prototype for a fourth LP that would never be released.

Reed often suggested, a bit cheekily, that his albums constituted his own Great American Novel "when you play [them] all in a row." So it's telling that the acetate of the Velvets' fourth LP prototype begins with Tucker singing "I'm Sticking with You," since *The Velvet Underground* ended with "After Hours," her only other lead vocal to date. Set to waltz-tempo piano and acoustic guitar, and sung by Tucker with a beautifully tender Reed duet bit at the end, "I'm Sticking with You" landed like a half-remembered nursery rhyme touched by Beatles-style whimsy. With its double-tracked vocals, Morrison saw it as "a bridge between what we'd been doing" and what came next.

"I'm Sticking with You" was followed by "Sally May," a rock 'n'

roll malt shop boogie with slashing guitar parts and whooping, giggling vocals by Reed, lyrics apparently flipped from John Lee Hooker's
"Sally Mae" and the Solitaires deep-catalog 1955 doo-wop single "Later
for You Baby." (It would eventually be rejigged and renamed "Foggy
Notion.") "Coney Island Steeplechase" was another good-time number, which stressed its point by repeating "good time." Reed's celebration of the Brooklyn shore would've read as nostalgia to an attentive
New Yorker: in 1966, the real estate mogul Fred Trump had bought
and bulldozed Coney Island's Steeplechase amusement park, hoping
to flip it and cash in on Robert Moses's development of low-income
housing in the area. With nonsensical lyrics involving a paraphrase
of the Del-Vikings' doo-wop classic "Come Go with Me," plus a nod to
the beat poet Lawrence Ferlinghetti's "A Coney Island of the Mind,"
Reed's song rode a loopy groove with minimalist organ swirls echoing
the music of La Monte Young's associate Terry Riley, who'd just secured
Walter De Maria's old loft on Grand Street.

Reed's songwriting was pushing in new directions, especially in
terms of memoirish specificity. The title of "Andy's Chest" referred to
Warhol's scarred torso in the wake of his shooting; a revealing Richard
Avedon photograph of Warhol inspired the song, according to Reed
(the New York artist Alice Neel, similarly inspired, would paint Warhol
shirtless the following year, his scars radiant stigmata). In this early
version, "Andy's Chest" is giddy, with a faintly Caribbean bounce and
second-person lyrics directed at Warhol, perhaps in hopes of cheering
him up. Reed sings tenderly about wanting to be a kite "tied to the end
of your string / Flying in the air at night."

Two songs from the sessions appeared to address Shelley Albin.
"She's My Best Friend" is an AM-radio-style shout-out to a soulmate,
full of shining vocal harmonies yet hinting at more complicated emotions: queer self-loathing ("Oh it hurts to know that you're that kind
of fellah"), friend-zone stasis, and the magic of discovering a true kindred spirit. Sexual innuendos involving jelly rolls and amputations
would've surely kept it off the hit parade, had the band bothered to
release it as a single, and the song would ultimately be mothballed.
"I Can't Stand It," a finished track that didn't make the acetate, was a

kinetic tantrum over ping-ponging guitars that swelled into breathtaking thunderheads, with lyrics veering in and out of the absurd—a man living in a garbage pail, a landlady who tries to assault him with a mop, a purple dog wearing spats—alongside clichés about "being a man." Reed explodes into the chorus like he's having a panic attack, declaring his salvation dependent on one person, his mood and the music calming abruptly at a thought: "If Shelley would just come back," he sang, "it'd be all right." Reed had written autobiographically in the past, but never this explicitly.

"Ocean," meanwhile, was something else entirely, a hypnotically down-tempo number that unfurled to Moe Tucker's rolling-surf cymbals, with an incantatory vocal by Reed and lyrics tilting toward abstract poetry. Evil thoughts are insects; the earth is a "hollow hair" on a cosmic head. The song pivots nicely on the word *harmoniums*, conjuring both the drone instrument and Wallace Stevens's debut poetry volume in its four-beat cadence, resolving in a dreamy outro driven by churchy organ and ceremonial tom-toms.

Best, however, was "Rock & Roll." A tribute to a poor little rich girl named Jenny (repurposed, perhaps, from her "Pale Blue Eyes" cameo) who tuned in to a mythic New York radio station and found herself "saved" by the music, it's a song so immaculately plainspoken—"Two TV sets and two Cadillac cars / Well, you know, babe, that's not gonna help us at all!"—it seems less written than found. In truth, the song was memoir: "about me," as Reed said years later. "If I hadn't heard rock'n'roll on the radio, I would have no idea there was life on this planet. You know what I'm saying?" The guitar riff was equally primordial and undeniable, although Reed's vocals overdo the southern soul affect, and the Jordanaires-style "it was all riiiight"s are too cheeky by half. It was another work in progress.

* * *

As the 1960s rushed toward to the decade's finale, queer culture was finally kicking its way out of the underground. *Lonesome Cowboys*, Warhol's deadpan homoerotic Western, had been doing quite well since it opened in May. It was the most "mainstream" film yet to come out of the Factory, a gender-inverted *Romeo and Juliet* spoof featuring Eric Emerson, Viva, and Little Joe Dallesandro that'd been shot in full color on location in Arizona on a proper film set (for one day, anyway) with actors' cabins and an actual budget. Striking while the iron was hot, Warhol backed *Gerard Malanga's Male Magazine*, a morning-to-midnight film program of gay porn that opened on June 25 at a rented theater at 62 East Fourth Street. The copy in one ad read "15,000,000 homosexuals in America? FACT: According to police records and statistics compiled by health officials and doctors—every 6th man in America today is a homosexual."

A few days later, in the early morning hours of June 28, some of those men, evidently, alongside trans persons and others, fought back against a police raid at the Stonewall Inn, a gay bar in the West Village at 51–53 Christopher Street. Owned by the Genovese crime family, it'd been a fairly safe space for the homeless young genderqueers who hung out there, who might otherwise be arrested at any moment on the street for a perceived violation of the city's antiquated "masquerade laws"; originally used to arrest protesters who wore costumes to conceal their identities, they'd been repurposed, alongside other laws, to harass the gender-nonconforming. The Stonewall riots, as they came to be known, would help launch a global civil rights movement, as well as birthing the Pride Parade (which began as "Christopher Street Liberation Day" on the uprising's one-year anniversary).

Years later, Reed would move into an apartment in the building. The weekend of the uprising, however, he was in Philly, playing two nights at the Electric Factory with the Velvets, who reportedly did a forty-five-minute "Sister Ray" during the run, possibly the longest version ever outside the one unfurled in Chicago in competition with the Dead. Whether it was in tribute or in synchronicity with the Stonewall incident is unknown, but the image of Reed careening through his anthem of cocksucking and violence while queers battled police in the New York streets a hundred miles away is a powerful one.

* * *

The Velvets weren't invited to the Woodstock Festival on the weekend of August 15, although their old friend and percussionist Angus Mac-Lise reportedly convened a "Free Tribal Orchestra" there. Instead, they were back at the Tea Party, recently relocated to a short-lived new space at 15 Lansdowne Street, in the shadow of Fenway Park. It would be the Velvets' final gig there, as the club would soon fold. The rock jugger-naut advancing on mainstream American culture seemed to be passing over the Velvet Underground. As the summer ended, their third album having clearly tanked and their future with MGM in limbo, things did not look promising.

Nevertheless, in September, the band managed to knock out a handful of new songs at the Record Plant, among them the celebratory "We're Gonna Have a Real Good Time Together," with its breakneck hot-rod thrust, surf-guitar flash, and handclaps—an odd throwback for 1969, craftier than the '50s greasers in Sha-Na-Na (who did get invited to Woodstock), but no less nostalgic, like a cover of a lost classic except for the line about "shooting" together. Another gem was "Lisa Says"—third in Reed's "She Says" series, not counting the third-person attri-butions of "Sister Ray" and "Rock & Roll"—about a party girl trying to outrun heartache who would "do it with just about anyone." The way Reed's voice breaks at the end of the phrase "what do you find . . . ?" in the midst of the swooning bridge is one of his most indelibly empa-thetic moments, the precise opposite of slut-shaming. But along with the rest of the songs the band had recorded since May, it would wind up on the shelf. Meanwhile, the bootstrap gigging continued.

* * *

Reed sat in front of a packed lecture hall at the University of Texas in Austin. He was responding to a vague, likely stoned question.

"What do you think about, um, nature?" a student asked him. "Should it be preserved?"

Reed pounded the microphone with the palm of his hand. The speakers shuddered: WHOOOMP . . . WHOOOMP . . . WHOOOMP . . .

Perhaps stoned himself, Reed clarified.

"This," he said, "is my nature."

Reed was speaking to a class called "20th Century Literature and Electronic Media," taught by Joe Kruppa, a young English professor inspired by Marshall McLuhan's ideas about media environments. McLuhan's bestselling *The Medium Is the Message*, published in 1967, featured a photo of the Exploding Plastic Inevitable—the author saw the connection between its multimedia assault and his theories—and when Kruppa saw the Velvets were booked in Austin, he made some calls.

"Lou was in a kind of snarly mood," Kruppa recalls. "I loaded up on Warhol slides from the art slide library, and we talked about the [*Death and*] *Disaster* series, and the Electric Chairs series. It was really fun." Reed's cryptic response during the Q&A "was exactly what I'd been teaching the students, that they lived in a different kind of nature now—the nature of the electronic environment and mass media. They didn't quite get it. But I think they got it later on."

The band's first southern "tour" had begun in Dallas some days earlier, with the Velvets performing in a glorified hash den, a converted strip mall storefront decorated with rugs and pillows called End of Cole Ave. Reed recalled the club, as it were, belonging to "some rich kid . . . If he liked a group, he'd bring them into the club and invite friends over. It was insane." The shows, played over two nights, were particularly laid-back, and notable for what the mic-shy Tucker recalled as her live singing debut, on "After Hours." Following the LP recording session, she told Reed she'd never sing it live unless a fan specifically asked her to; in Dallas, "some creep requested it," and she kept her word. Another highlight was a shaggy acoustic version of "Rock & Roll," Reed and Tucker trying to remember the words while attempting Everly Brothers harmonies.

On the afternoon of the final show, a Sunday, the band took a field trip to the Cotton Bowl to watch the Dallas Cowboys trounce the Philadelphia Eagles. That night, in a cowboy hat and bell-bottoms, Reed asked if people had school tomorrow, and if they wanted two short sets or one long one; consensus was the latter. "Okay, then this is gonna go on for a while," he said. "So we should get used to one another . . . settle back, pull up your cushions, and whatever else you have with you that makes life bearable in Texas.

"We saw your Cowboys today, and they never let Philadelphia have the ball for a minute. It was forty-two to seven by the half, it was ridiculous." Reed felt it was cruel, humiliating. "You should give other people just a little chance—in football, anyway."

In November, after shows in L.A. at the Whiskey and a stay at the Chateau Marmont on the Sunset Strip, the Velvets arrived in San Francisco. Given their distaste for the hippie scene, it would seem an unlikely place for them to settle in for a month, let alone reach their apex as a live act—this was the city where they'd locked horns with Bill Graham in 1966, and been skewered by Ralph J. Gleason's withering review. Perhaps the challenge brought out the underdog fight in them.

They began their run of shows on November 7 at the Family Dog on the Great Highway, a new club run by the local promoter and Bill Graham competitor Chet Helms with the hippie dance-party commune the Family Dog in a converted slot-car racetrack at the Playland amusement park. On the first night, the Velvets sounded sluggish. But the next was an entirely different vibe—breakneck ballroom rock 'n' roll, with songs that built to frenzied peaks. On "I Can't Stand It," Reed threw himself into guitar-hero mode à la Hendrix and Townshend, dashing across the stage, humping his amplifier, and dancing wildly. "He'd do a straight run into the audience, right in my direction," recalled Aral Sezen, a nineteen-year-old fan who drove more than a hundred miles from Carmel with friends for the show, "then he would stop, bug his eyes out insanely . . . then turn to face Maureen on his right and start to bring his guitar down on her head. He would suddenly crumple, face the amp and begin this again." Reed ended the song with a frantic, shouted southern-soul breakdown, articulating everything that made rock 'n' roll, at that moment in time, incandescent: the guitar-noise virtuosity, rhythmic fission-chain volatility, musk, vulgarity, absurdity, desperation, and ecstasy.

After the first weekend, the Velvets moved to the Matrix, a smaller club at 3138 Fillmore Street in North Beach that'd been launched by the Jefferson Airplane's Marty Balin and co-owner Peter Abram, who'd just installed a four-track half-inch reel-to-reel to record shows. The club's capacity was only one hundred, and it generally charged two dollars at the door, so the band probably split a hundred dollars a night. They weren't staying in fancy hotels anymore; for a while, they crashed on the floor at the apartment of one of the waitresses. Steve Sesnick was trying to extricate the band from their contract with MGM, who were cleaning house, so tour support had shriveled up. Their albums were still hard to find in stores, and the label had issued only one single from the latest, a 2:40 edit of "What Goes On" backed with "Jesus." Even that was nowhere to be heard. Yet musically, onstage, the band was soaring. They knew they were being recorded at the Matrix, and rose to the occasion.

Despite being in San Francisco, America's supposed drug-taking capital, Reed was not overindulging. There was occasional weed smoking, but Yule claimed he partook only if Reed did. "I didn't want to be stoned when he was straight," Yule said; "there were times when he would invent or put together songs on the fly in a performance, and he'd just turn around and say 'Follow me' . . . you want to be on your toes." Yule recalled one time after getting high with Reed and Morrison when it took them twenty minutes to tune up. The audience, likely just as spaced out, didn't seem to mind at all.

Once in tune, however, the guitar interplay would be dazzling. On one night, a wild, ricocheting exchange through nine minutes of "What Goes On" was paced by Moe Tucker's relentless stutter and Yule's swarming organ, while Reed's soloing pushed an elastic, wildly accelerated "White Light/White Heat" into straight-up noise territory, capped by a white-out ending. But there was more going on than instrumental pyrotechnics. On another night, Reed introduced what he called "a very interesting" new song titled "New Age." A tender ballad, it begins with the singer confessing his desire to "go naked" with "Frank and Nancy." As the forenames of father-and-daughter Sinatras, the line was funny. But the delivery, and the aching chorus about the universal search for love, couldn't seem more sincere. The song was still evolving; in a version recorded later that week, Reed doubled down on the suggestion of bisexuality, declaring it his fancy to "make it" with Frank and Nancy, and shifting verses from Elmore Leonard noir (a man with a gun on his shoulder; the narrator being touched by someone with "hands of ivory") toward reflections on death and marriage (perhaps Delmore Schwartz's and Shelley Albin's, respectively). In terms of queer subtext, the Stonewall uprising might've informed the ideas on display as much as the utopian free-love haze of San Francisco. In any case, the anthemic chorus-coda heralded the birth of "a new age," and on a version dated November 24, tried to musically will it into being, as guitars ascended through a majestic five-minute jam conjuring esoteric renaissance as inspiringly as any so-called hippie band ever did.

Mid-month, the Velvets traveled north for two shows in Oregon, where Reed sat for an interview at KVAN-FM. Reed's banter, amphetamine-fast, touches on meditation, getting his aura read, and how what he does onstage is "a form of yoga." He also talked about *Hamlet*, and how James Joyce and John Cage figured in the recording of "The Murder Mystery." He noted the narrative through-line connecting the Velvets albums, and how each record "reads in order." He suggested the questions raised in "Candy Says," the first song on *The Velvet Underground*, are partly answered in "Some Kinda Love" and "Pale Blue Eyes," and that the opening lines of "Candy Says"—about how Candy has come to hate her body, and all that it requires—are the key to the LP's meaning. "The whole rest of the third album," Reed said, "is just about that."

Returning to San Francisco to finish their Matrix residency, the Velvets gave maybe the greatest single week of performances in their history. On some nights during the residency, they'd begin their first set with only four or five people in the club. But by the final weekend, word had spread, and the room was full. Abram was recording the shows, Reed was in high spirits, and the band was getting along well, playing new songs they'd rehearsed in the club during their off hours. The music was tonic against horrific news: reports on the My Lai massacre had just broken, and President Nixon was initiating a draft lottery to begin the following Monday. During their final weekend of shows, Thanksgiving weekend, the Velvets played "Heroin" again and again, Reed singing with fervor about dead bodies piled up in mounds and politicians making crazy sounds. His stage banter, meanwhile, veered between yogic and comic:

"Good evening. We're your local Velvet Underground. We're glad to see you. [Smattering of applause.] Thank you. We're particularly glad on a serious day like today, that people could find, y'know, a little time to come out and have some fun with some rock 'n' roll. 'Cause these are serious times, or I've been told they are. And since they're serious, we felt impelled to do a very serious set . . . I don't want any of you to enjoy the songs frivolously, because it'll run against national policy—which rhymes, by the way. This is the way poets are."

The band frequently opened with "I'm Waiting for the Man." A version that weekend was far slower than the album version, menacing and slinky, Reed and Yule harmonizing the line "feel sick and dirty, more dead than alive" like they're singing an old blues about aching for a lover—which in a sense, they are. Reed sings blissful "ooo-ooo-woo"s and whistles like Otis Redding on "(Sittin' on) The Dock of the Bay," a song released the previous year whose lazy groove the Velvets echo.

Reed sang about lost love in various guises. "Naturally, when I had it / I treated it like dirt," he points out on the bridge of "Over You," a pop ballad in the Latin-tinged vein of early Beatles hits such as "And I Love Her" and "Do You Wanna Know a Secret." And he gave a lengthy introduction to "I Can't Stand It," his thrilling rant involving a girl named Shelley, that reflected on his time in Syracuse:

This is a song about the sorrows of the contemporary world, of which I know we all know so well. At least I read about it all the time. It's like, one day—this is when I was in college, right?— and I woke up, six thirty in the morning because I get up early, and I put on the radio and they said, y'know, so-and-so truck driver today ran over his baby son's head and it burst like a watermelon. And then they said it's twenty-two degrees out. So I figured, on all levels, there was no reason ever to go out again. I stayed indoors for about eight months. Also passed with honors in Kierkegaard—that's 'cause I understand, y'know, the existential leap. Anyone who lies in bed at six thirty in the morning listening to that *has to.*

Also that weekend, possibly for the first time, Reed played a song with lyrics he seemed largely to be making up as he sang. One version involved characters named Jimmy, Miss Ann, Billy, and the latter's "strange friends." Another, performed the same weekend, was more sparsely populated. Both versions of the song featured a super-catchy riff, a deliciously dreamy bridge, a winning la-la sing-along outro, and a central figure named Sweet Jane. It was definitely a keeper.

The Velvets ended their residency on December 3 with an epic "Sister Ray." In another rock 'n' roll murder narrative three days later, sixty miles east on Highway 580, Meredith Hunter was stabbed to death at Altamont Speedway as the Rolling Stones played "Under My Thumb." Three weeks after that, the '60s ended, and the '70s began.

* * *

The Velvet Underground might not have had a large following, but they had a devoted one. Among them were superfans who, in addition to spreading the gospel, encouraged the underdog band. A number of them would figure in Reed's future life.

In early 1969, Robert Quine was a law student in St. Louis who'd begun recording concerts with a Sony cassette recorder and a hand-held microphone—he taped the Velvets' show there in May. Quine was also a guitarist, a lover of Richie Valens, John Lee Hooker, Jeff Beck, the Stones, and jazz, Coltrane in particular. After finishing his degree, he moved to San Francisco and was a regular at the Matrix during the Velvets' residency, recorder in tow. He met Reed and the men bonded; when time allowed, they'd duck out to the hot-dog stand across the street to rhapsodize about the music they loved, Reed going on about early rock 'n' roll, rockabilly, and doo-wop; their shared love of the Stones; the wild "Eight Miles High" guitar solo Reed saw Roger McGuinn play with the Byrds one night at the Village Gate in 1966.

Another such fan was a teenager named Jonathan Richman. Raised in the Boston suburbs, he fell hard for the Velvets' debut LP, attended Tea Party shows religiously, wrote about the band for the local magazines *Fusion* and *Vibrations*, and hung out with them when they were in town. Richman found the Velvets mesmerizing, not just for Reed's lyrics but for the sound they generated in that particular room. "[They] were unusual in putting a mic in front of Maureen Tucker's snare," recalls Richman, who notes that even miking guitar amps in a medium-sized ballroom was unusual for the era. The result was a spacious, vivid sound mix "very colorful to hear, and it would often hypnotize the crowd of dancers. I mean, after they'd finish 'Sister Ray,' you'd have total silence."

Like Reed, Richman was a singer-songwriter; he'd play outside at the Boston Common open mic in his signature white plastic motorcycle jacket on Sunday afternoons. Sterling Morrison recalled "an alert little kid" with a big grin who would turn up at gigs early and—if given a chance and a guitar—play his latest song. "If the [Velvets] had a protégé," Morrison said, "it would be Jonathan." Moe Tucker was equally fond of him. Ditto Reed. "There's something about Jonathan," he said admiringly. Richman, who considered himself not a mere fan but a "student" of the band, was particularly obsessed with Reed. "It was really funny seeing him mimic—to a T—all of Lou's physical gestures and facial expressions," says Robert Somma, who often encountered Richman at Ed Hood's after-show salons. "He was going to be Lou Reed if it killed him."

Richman still marvels at how the band accepted him as a sixteen-year-old. "They saw how important they were to me, and they acted accordingly," he says. In fact, they facilitated his first proper concert gig, at the Paramount Theater in Springfield, Massachusetts. It wasn't planned. Richman had caught a ride out to the show with Morrison, who was driving the equipment U-Haul. When they arrived, they discovered the openers had bailed. Richman recalls seeing his moment. "I borrowed Lou Reed's Gibson ES-345 stereo electric guitar, plugged into his Sunn-brand amps, and did fifteen or twenty minutes." He played his plainspoken, faux-naif songs, likely including early versions of songs that became his signatures, "Roadrunner" and "Girlfriend." Afterward, as he remembers it, his friends had no criticisms, but didn't offer false praise, either. Reed had no comment at all. Morrison did, offering "with maybe a touch of archness, 'Jonathan, I must say that was quite remarkable.'"

Meanwhile, in London on February 5, another Velvets superfan, David Bowie, was recording "I'm Waiting for the Man" for a BBC radio show. The performance was strutting and raw, with the twenty-three-year-old virtuoso Mick Ronson strangling his guitar as Bowie complicated Reed's drug-deal narrative with an outré rentboy outro: "waiting for the man to walk me home . . . back door man!" he yelps.

Bowie knew the song well: in fact, he'd already recorded it, back in early '67, during his short stint as lead singer with the Riot Squad, mimicking Reed's New York snarl and queering it there, too, as he claimed to be looking not just for "a very good friend of mine" but for "a good friendly behind." Bowie also recorded a song with the group that lifted a couplet verbatim from "Venus in Furs"—an original titled "Little Toy Soldier," involving a character dubbed "little Sadie" and her whip-wielding wind-up toy. Bowie was unafraid to steal, and had no qualms about presenting as queer or nonbinary: Following his U.K. hit "Space Oddity" the previous year, he'd changed his style from hippie-dandy to ultra-femme, with long hair, eye shadow, and "man-dresses," like the one he'd wear on the cover of *The Man Who Sold the World*, which he'd begun recording in April.

Reed's own style at the moment continued the Betsey Johnson Victorian hipster vibe with some hippie-proto-glam flourishes: at Chicago's Quiet Knight in January, he sported a ruffled shirt under a black jacket, a black scarf printed with roses, bell-bottoms, and boots. In a series of publicity stills taken during the L.A. recording sessions in November, he wore a floral-print blouse of sorts, and the band posed for stereotypical shots: huddled together at the center of a fish-eye lens; in a circular formation beneath palm trees; seated on rocks near a waterfall. Angling for a market niche, they were trying to look the part of the laid-back, soul-deep West Coast bands still dominating the rock scene. But it felt a little forced.

* * *

After the modest glory of the West Coast run, the band's business headaches resumed. Their record label, MGM, was having troubles; *Rolling Stone* reported in March that it had lost $17 million over the past twelve months. The imprint's twenty-five-year-old whiz kid president, Mike Curb, responded by firing 250 employees—including the A&R, production, promotion, and support staff—and effectively closing the New York offices. He also claimed he'd be cutting eighty bands from the roster, and unsurprisingly, the Velvets turned out to be one of them.

This was a stroke of good luck, as it freed them from their contract, and soon they'd signed a deal with Ahmet Ertegun at Atlantic, helped along by the advocacy of Danny Fields, who now worked there. This was huge. Ertegun, who'd begun the label in the late '40s and was behind many landmark R&B and rock recordings, was a legend and no one's fool; Fields believed the band's connection with Warhol was part of the appeal. (Atlantic's historic deal with the Rolling Stones, already in the works, would effectively be launched by Warhol's famous jean-zipper crotch on *Sticky Fingers*.) The Velvets met Ertegun for the first time at Salvation, a reputedly mob-owned gay club and celebrity hangout at 1 Sheridan Square, where they played an industry show with the Chambers Brothers; Morrison recalled the label chief complimenting the Velvets on their "excellent rock sensibilities."

And so, when the Velvets walked into Atlantic Studios at 1841 Broadway, just off Columbus Circle near Central Park, on April 15, with the support of maybe the most discerning businessman-aesthete in rock 'n' roll history, it was with the empowered intention of making a commercially successful pop album. Reed had a basketful of unreleased songs. Many they'd worked up and recorded in 1969 on MGM's dime—"I Can't Stand It," "Lisa Says," and "She's My Best Friend" certainly could've been contenders. MGM's claim on them, however, was an open question, and ultimately they'd rerecord just two of the tracks: "Ocean" and "Rock & Roll."

But trouble struck almost immediately once the Velvets had settled in behind their instruments. Moe Tucker had gotten pregnant and decided to keep the child, and over the four months since the Velvets' triumphant final show at the Matrix, she'd begun showing prominently.

"I couldn't reach the drums, I was so fat," she said, recalling a failed attempt to play through a demo take of "Ocean." Doug Yule wound up taking over for her. She was heartbroken. The fourth Velvet Underground album would be recorded without her.

It's hard to overstate the significance of her absence. Her minimalist pulse, influenced by Bo Diddley and Charlie Watts and the Yoruba beat of Babatunde Olatunji's unlikely 1960 hit LP *Drums of Passion* (a record she loved and practiced to) was low-end focused, alternately galloping and funereal, and telepathically attuned to the other players, especially Morrison's exacting rhythm guitar. Both driving and subordinate, it gave the band a heartbeat different from any of their peers. Her exit was also a personal loss; she was Reed's closest friend in the band, and their relationship was mostly conflict-free. By Morrison's account, he and Reed were by then barely speaking. Having decided to finally finish his BA, which he'd abandoned in 1966, Morrison had begun attending City College; he was generally burrowed in a book between takes during the Atlantic sessions. And Reed's friendship with Yule, never one of equals, was straining, as Yule forged an alliance with Sesnick apart from Reed. There'd been some competition between Yule and Reed from the start—like Cale, Yule was a more versatile musician, and younger than Reed at that—and as tensions between them grew, the idea of having a doppelganger may have lost its appeal.

Another pregnancy of note that spring—the sound of another door closing for Reed—was Shelley Albin's. She'd been distancing herself from him. "I purposely didn't have his phone number, or know where his apartments were," she says. "I didn't have any real interest in getting back together with him, living that life I knew he was going to have." Albin was Reed's great muse, his Beatrice, his Guinevere, his Fanny Brawne and Daisy Fay Buchanan. She was a woman he might've considered having a child with, if he'd ever considered such a possibility. Whatever hopes he might've held out for their reunion, it was clear now that she would not be leaving her husband anytime soon.

Reed lost contact with another close friend around this time. Billy Name hadn't been doing well. He was quite literally living in the Factory darkroom: he'd withdrawn from the day-to-day of the place so completely, he virtually never left the room except late at night. Reed was among the few who visited him. Warhol recalled one time in particular, during which Reed emerged after hours in the darkroom with Name. "Lou came out regretting that he had given him three Alice Bailey books on witchcraft. Billy had shaved his head completely because he believed the hairs were growing in, not out—and was only eating whole-wheat wafers and rice crackers now—following the white magic book that shows you how to rebuild your cell structure." One day, without explanation, Name quietly abandoned the darkroom, and never returned. He left a note for Warhol, scrawled in lipstick-red, which said simply: "Andy—I am not here anymore but I am fine. Love, Billy."

Reed's social isolation would be mirrored in the recording process for the new LP, which would be titled *Loaded*. In part due to Doug Yule's instrumental multitasking, as well as the evolution of what was by then common studio practice, songs were not performed in real time by the group, but by tracking parts individually or in clusters. On about half the songs, drums were added last. Tucker's drumming replacements—Doug Yule, his sixteen-year-old brother Billy Yule, the engineer-producer Adrian Barber—didn't approximate her style, and probably couldn't. All played conventional kits, which fit the mission: a more conventional sound that would appeal to radio programmers.

These changes may have contributed to a change in Reed's vocal approach. On the demo of "Rock & Roll," recorded during the first two days in the studio, he nailed a different sort of delivery, a sort of deadpan speak-singing that delivered the lyrics from a cool remove, building tension over the sinewy guitar riffs. On this take, tellingly, he conjured the cadences of a radio DJ. It was near-rapping, a style gestating in other parts of New York City, and it bubbled up from the same well, from smooth-rhyming, pre-rap emcees like Jocko Henderson, whose *Rocket Ship* show on WADO 1280 AM was a fixture of New York rock 'n' roll radio in the mid-'60s. Reed's delivery on this demo would go on to define him over the years, and he'd refine it over the summer.

* * *

When work began on *Loaded*, the Beatles were breaking up. Paul McCartney had released his first solo record, and Simon and Garfunkel's "Bridge over Troubled Water" had finished a six-week run as the number 1 song in America, bumped in April by the Beatles' "Let It Be." Insofar as you could diagnose a national mood by the *Billboard* Hot 100, these songs might suggest a sad country, one in need of consolation.

The Velvets worked hard on what would turn out to be an upbeat album about the redemptive powers of rock 'n' roll. Sad songs were shelved, including a demo titled "Sad Song" (set in 1493 and anachronistically involving Mary, Queen of Scots) and another called "Satellite of Love" (with a doo-wop-styled spoken intro about sorrow and the human race putting "its footprint on the moon's face," as Neil Armstrong had done quite literally the previous summer).

"New Age" made the cut, but minus the bisexual POV of the versions Reed sang in November at the Matrix. The song now involved a fan, presumably male, pledging devotion to an over-the-hill actor "looking for love," with a line about kissing Robert Mitchum. Reed's description suggests Shelley Winters, both in the 1966 film *Harper*—in which she plays a washed-up actor—and in the 1955 noir *Night of the Hunter*, in which her character weds Mitchum's preacher, a serial killer sexually repulsed by women. It was a remarkable poetic slight-of-hand that also conjured Andy Warhol's obsession with actors, and his self-consciousness about his appearance. At forty, disabled from the shooting, Warhol surely felt over the hill consorting with a generation whose motto remained "Don't trust anyone over thirty"; Reed, at the seasoned age of twenty-eight, was likely feeling old himself.

More on theme, if less poetic, was "Lonesome Cowboy Bill," a hyperactive nod to "Ragtime Cowboy Joe," a 1912 pop number 1 in sheet music form, which returned in 1959 as an unlikely Top 40 novelty single by the Chipmunks. "Head Held High" channeled the choogling hard rock of Grand Funk Railroad, a hit generator whose second album had just gone gold, as did the midtempo "Train Round the Bend," while the seven-minute "Oh! Sweet Nuthin'," a laid-back jam, was less "Sister Ray" than Allman Brothers (the Georgia band was working on the *Idlewild South* LP in New York while *Loaded* was being tracked).

But the standouts would be "Rock & Roll" and the finished version of "Sweet Jane," the song Reed had been working on at the Matrix. Built on a D-A-G riff accented with a fourth chord, B minor, the latter was utterly simple and irresistible. "I loved that lick," Reed would declare. "You can make lyrics up to it all day long." He did, revising the words over and over. By May, the cast of characters from the Matrix in November—Jimmy, Miss Anne, Billy, etc.—had become a trio: Jane, wearing a vest; Jack, in a corset; and the narrator, who is in a rock 'n' roll band.

In the studio, Reed delivered the verses with a new theatricality, full of indelible asides. One involved a direct address to the "protest kids" in a tone that might seem to posit '60s activism as ancient history. Another was the "Hah!" he spits out after identifying himself as being in a rock 'n' roll band. It's an amazing, archetypal, Warholian moment: Reed creating a larger-than-life rock star while simultaneously undercutting the whole business as a charade. In effect, this was the formal coming-out of Lou Reed as "Lou Reed."

Reed genuinely believed he was making Atlantic Records an album full of hits; it was one reason the album was titled *Loaded*.

* * *

On June 24, midway through the recording, the Velvets played the first night of what turned out to be a ten-week residency at Max's Kansas City. It was woodshedding, and a homecoming: aside from a couple of one-offs, the band, astonishingly, hadn't played a show in New York City since 1967. Partly this was due to their feud with Bill Graham, whose Fillmore East, on Second Avenue, had become the city's premier rock venue. It was also due to Reed's discomfort with performing "in front of his past," as Yule put it. And indeed, he recalled, people Reed had no desire to deal with showed up during the Max's run.

But times had changed. The Velvets didn't play the ground-floor back room, where Warhol held court in more halcyon days, but upstairs, in a small space where the owner, Mickey Ruskin, had begun staging music events. For the first set, people generally sat at tables, cabaret-style. Later in the evening, tables were pushed aside for dancing. During the residency, the Velvets came off as a cross between a bar band and house party entertainers. Up-tempo versions of "I'm Waiting for the Man" kick-started dancing; new songs like "Oh! Sweet Nuthin'" were cheered wildly. Overcoming skepticism at the band's prodigal return, *The Village Voice*'s Richard Nusser called the shows "exhilarating." A *New York Times* critic heard a sound as "powerful and tight as a raised fist." A writer at *Gay Power*, a new publication launched in the wake of the Stonewall riots, marveled at Reed's guitar theatrics, "camping on Pete Townshend," and the scent of the room, "sweaty armpits mixed with the sweet-and-pungent aroma of vaginal juices." The mood was laid-back, sexy, and goofy, even more so than at the Matrix shows.

"We once did an album with a Pop painter, because we wanted to help him out," Reed quipped on opening night.

"You're doing better without him!" someone hollered.

That was questionable. Some nights the crowd was small. Billy Altman, a student at the State University of Buffalo, recalls a Sunday night show that drew about thirty people. Some slow-danced to the ballads. Between sets, "Sunday Morning" came on the jukebox. Reed plugged in his guitar and played along.

As with the Dom residency, the crowd was a future Who's Who. In April, the writer Lenny Kaye had published a history of the Velvet Underground in the underground paper *New Times*, noting a cult grown "almost religious" in their fandom. At Max's, he danced to "Sweet Jane" and chatted with Reed after the show. A young poet from New Jersey, Patti Smith, turned up with her friend Robert Mapplethorpe, who had just gotten his nipple pierced. Smith adored the band's "dissonant surf beat—they were just fantastic to dance to." Wayne County, an actor sharing an East Village apartment with Jackie Curtis and the go-go dancer Holly Woodlawn—part of the new genderqueer Factory crowd—turned out. County (who later changed their stage name to Jayne) and Curtis had just finished a two-week run of Curtis's *Femme Fatale: The Three Faces of Gloria* at La Mama Experimental Theatre, a play featuring Smith, per County, as "a mafia dyke with a moustache" with "a big phallus hanging between her legs."

Doug Yule recalled being dazzled by it all. "Walking into Max's for the first time was like walking into the bar scene in *Star Wars*," he said.

Over the next two months, the band spent afternoons painstakingly working on *Loaded* in hopes of creating a pop masterpiece, then headed downtown to Max's for their 11 p.m. set. The scene on a random night: Billy Yule, Tucker's replacement, takes the Long Island Rail Road into Manhattan after a day of summer school in Great Neck, where he's making up two eleventh-grade classes. (He plays the Max's gigs mainly for free meals, and is often hearing songs for the first time as he plays them.) Morrison arrives, having just biked over from his place on Christopher Street. Then comes Reed, in a windbreaker and tennis shoes, lugging his Epiphone Riviera up the stairs. He tunes up and chats with a journalist—about his love of playing in a rock 'n' roll band, and how hearing someone singing a song you wrote is like they're "humming your name."

"I'm not a star," Reed demurs, a little apologetically.

The band opens with "I'm Waiting for the Man." There are no spot-lights, and virtually no stage lighting. By the time the band is loping through "Oh! Sweet Nuthin'," about two dozen people are dancing in front of the stage. A dark-skinned woman smiles, bumps her hips salsa-style on alternate beats. The late set ends around 3 a.m. Reed might linger, or head to an after-hours place.

The regimen—five nights a week, two sets a night, Wednesday through Sunday—took its toll on Reed, and trashed his voice, forcing him to hand off more lead vocals to Yule in the studio: "Who Loves the Sun," "Lonesome Cowboy Bill," "Oh! Sweet Nuthin'," the revised "New Age." His voice worked well for the songs. But it no doubt increased Reed's feeling of disconnection with the Velvets.

Home in New York after five years of not quite becoming a rock star, Reed was pushing thirty, living alone in a barren apartment he could barely afford on the Upper East Side, and playing to half-empty rooms upstairs at Max's, where he once sat at Warhol's right hand. The '60s, quite literally, were over.

Despite the promise of the new Atlantic deal, Reed began pulling back from the band. Sesnick, protecting his investment, turned to Yule, who was eager and competent. Yule started running the sessions, adding bass, organ, piano, drums, acoustic guitar, even lead guitar.

Morrison recalled Reed being in a bad way, barely sleeping, due to anxiety and/or speed intake. It might also have involved Reed's diet, which he'd been experimenting with like a lab scientist to maximize his energy, inspired by Alice Bailey's writings—alternately sipping from jars of honey, eating wheat husks, chugging papaya juice, or trying to subsist entirely on lettuce. Morrison, meanwhile, felt increasingly marginalized, too. Trying to keep up with college work, he'd quit both smoking and drug-taking, and was keeping to himself.

Things came to a head one day during a heated argument between Reed and Sesnick, who, according to Morrison, told Reed, "I don't care if you live or die." Reed was stunned. Despite their conflicts, they'd been friends.

* * *

Moe Tucker gave birth to a daughter, Kerry, in June. The drummer was now a single mom, back on Long Island, living with her parents. One night in August, she came to see her band at Max's. She found Reed sitting on the staircase to the second floor, alone in the shadows. She put her arm around him.

"Louie. What's the matter?" she asked.

He told her he was quitting the Velvet Underground. "I knew something must have been terribly wrong," she said, "that he had to leave in order to survive the thing." She was heartbroken. But he'd clearly made up his mind. Tucker watched the show that night, bemused. It was decent, she thought. But it wasn't the Velvets.

* * *

Reed's last show with the Velvet Underground at Max's was Sunday, August 23, though the band still had one more week in the residency.

Morrison was upstairs eating his usual preshow cheeseburger. Reed came in and, for the first time, introduced him to his parents, Sid and Toby.

There was quite a crowd that night. Danny Fields was there, as he was virtually every night. Up front near the left side of stage was Brigid Berlin, Warhol's nominal receptionist and daughter of the Hearst Corporation president Richard E. Berlin. A society girl whose parents encouraged her to take amphetamines to control her weight, she earned herself the nickname "Brigid Polk" for her habit of poking people with speed-filled hypodermics; she was the first character name-checked in Reed's song "Chelsea Girls." Like Warhol, she was an obsessive taper, and had recorded a number of Velvets shows that summer. She had her trusty Sony mono TC-120 cassette recorder with her. Holding the microphone for her was Jim Carroll, a beautiful young poet. In his poem "10 Things I Do When I Shoot Up," listening to the Velvet Underground is listed as one item.

Warhol was nowhere to be seen.

"Good evening," Reed says. "We're called the Velvet Underground. You're allowed to dance, in case you don't know. And, uh, that's about it." He introduces "I'm Waiting for the Man" as "a tender folk song from the early '50s about love between man and subway . . . I'm sure you'll all enjoy it."

Reed stomps out the beat and the band leans into a rousing version, one designed for doing the Monkey, the Watusi, the Mashed Potato. "All right, Sterl!" Reed yells before his bandmate peels off a solo.

Then it's "White Light/White Heat," all speed and esoteric spirituality, Reed making a crack, no doubt for Morrison's English-major benefit, about it coming from a "romantic novel of the 1840s." Billy Yule pushes fills everywhere, riding the cymbal bells, the antithesis of Tucker's style, his brother galloping alongside, Reed launching a free-noise guitar salvo, then cutting it short.

"I'm set free," Reed declares on the next song, "to find a new illusion."

The group launches into "Sweet Jane" with a guitar intro that seems informed by "Uncle John's Band," the first song on the Grateful Dead's brand-new album. Reed sings about Jack, who is now wearing the vest instead of the corset. Perhaps the change is for his family's benefit. In any case, the performance is joyous; some rhythm-impaired fans, perhaps his parents, try to clap along, and Reed says, "C'mon, you can do better than that!" One imagines dancers hopping and gyrating in the low-ceilinged room: humid, hot, packed, redolent of sweat, cigarettes, and weed.

"Go get me a double Pernod," Carroll instructs someone.

"What are ya lookin' for?" a guy inquires, with a classic New York drug-hustle cadence.

"You got a down?" Carroll asks slurrily. "What is it? A Tuinal? Gimme it immediately."

Finishing up the first set, Reed hollers, "It's the beginning of a new age" alongside Yule, then follows "New Age" with "Beginning to See the Light."

A man who sees each of his albums as sequential chapters of a novel does not draft his final set list randomly.

During the second set, someone calls for "I've Found a Reason." Reed asks for a show of hands to indicate how many know the unissued ballad. Two, apparently, of which Fields is probably one. A tender song about love as a reason to go on living, the band demoed it as a folk-rock number in late '69 with Reed playing harmonica, and had recently rerecorded it in a more retro style. It always reminded Morrison of the late-'50s hit "Chanson d'Amour." Its central declaration is Reed crooning, "I do believe / if you don't like things you leave."

But Reed doesn't sing "I've Found a Reason," however resonant its lyrics may be. Instead, he does "Pale Blue Eyes," which he mostly speaks, doo-wop-style, lamenting the things he had but couldn't keep, crooning the "linger oooooon . . ." chorus in a shaky voice. He prefaces Morrison's tender solo with the aside "This is what she said."

He introduces "Candy Says" as "my favorite song, and we hardly ever get to do it." As on the album, Yule channels Candy hating her body, yearning to transcend, dreaming a startlingly potent cliché of bluebirds. Notes and lyrics are flubbed; near the front of the stage, a couple chats obliviously about the new George C. Scott war film, *Patton* ("My father thinks it's one of the greatest movies he's ever seen").

"This is a song about . . . when you've done something so sad, and you wake up the next day and you remember it," Reed says. "Not to sound grim or anything, but . . . just once in a while you have one of those days. I seem to have them regularly." Or maybe he says "rarely"— it's hard to discern.

The band begins "Sunday Morning." Reed botches the lyrics, but sings with heart about a feeling he "doesn't want to know." Then he sings Tucker's showcase "After Hours," noting the person who usually sings it is "home sick." He delivers it like a vaudeville soft-shoe, agoraphobia and loveless nihilism played for laughs. You could imagine Rudy Vallée crooning it through a megaphone. A couple of fans shout requests for "Heroin."

"We don't play 'Heroin' anymore," he says.

Reed plays "Some Kinda Love," declaring the "possibilities are endless," and it unravels into a meandering blues jam. By now, the yammering crowd seems to barely be paying attention. Reed plays his final number with the Velvet Underground, a ramshackle rave-up of the throwaway "Lonesome Cowboy Bill," sung uneventfully by Yule. The song ends. Reed unplugs his guitar.

Backstage, Morrison argued with Reed about his decision to quit the band. They still had a week of shows to do, and the album wasn't even finished. Reed wouldn't budge.

Word spread quickly as people lingered over drinks. "Someone came out and said, 'Lou just quit,'" Fields recalled. He rushed to find Berlin. "Did you get that?" he asked her, gesturing to her recorder.

"Yeah!" she said. He informed her that she'd just recorded the final Velvet Underground performance.

"What do we do with it?" she asked.

Reed clomped down the staircase and out onto Park Avenue. He stowed his guitar in the trunk of his parents' car, and Sid Reed drove home to the old house in Freeport, where his son would be staying for a while.

* * *

Beginning as the bourgeois adolescent who finds his family intolerable, Rimbaud moved with great speed to a recognition of his essential enemy, the whole bourgeois culture.
—**Delmore Schwartz**

Earlier in the year, the University of Chicago Press published *Selected Essays of Delmore Schwartz*, a volume the author had begun compiling in his final years. It includes critical meditations on Rimbaud and other artists. In "The Fabulous Example of Andre Gidé," Schwartz brands the writer "a very complicated human being" who "wrestled with the labyrinthine complications of his being, self-doubting, self-questioning, self-tormented and above all honest." It ends by ruing the direction of pop culture, purposefully mistranslating "ars gratia artis," the maxim branded above the roaring lion head in the MGM film production logo—"which, as everyone knows, means Art for the sake of the Almighty Dollar."

Shortly after his departure from the Velvets, playing an acoustic guitar in his childhood bedroom, Reed sang:

Do you remember the shape I was in?
I was covered with sin.

The sentiment of the song's title, "I'm So Free," was probably wishful thinking. But the reference to "Saint Germain"—the eighteenth-century composer, alchemist, patron saint of the abused, and master of transformation—suggests he was making plans.

Reed spent his first days at home holed up in his room, sleeping. He confessed his depression to friends; his sister believes he was suffering a nervous breakdown. Whether the crisis triggered or followed his decision to leave the Velvets is an open question. He started therapy again, possibly meds, too. He'd take long beach walks with Seymoure, his and Albin's adoption from Syracuse, now the Reed family mascot. He began working part-time as a typist for his dad's accounting firm for forty dollars a week. His mom, one-time Queen of the Stenographers, had always said typing was a good fallback skill.

Loaded was released in late September, and Reed was startled when he first heard it. There'd been some changes from what he'd recalled as the final recordings. The majestic, incantatory coda to "New Age" had been shortened, and the bridge to "Sweet Jane" had been cut entirely, the song ending in a radio-friendly fade at 3:15. In its original versions, "Sweet Jane" hinged on that bridge—the "heavenly wine and roses" section—which amplified the song's self-consciousness with flowery phrases that sound lifted from a greeting card, followed by an irresistible string of sing-along-ready "la-la-la"s. It's the rock 'n' roll equivalent of a Brechtian device, like Jean Seberg's camera stare-down in Godard's *Breathless*. Anyone who "ever played a part," posited Reed in the song, wouldn't "turn around and hate it." He might've been referring to his own performance as "Lou Reed," rock star.

Reed would rail at these edits, which he claimed were released without his consent, although Yule would maintain Reed made them himself. "He edited it. You have to understand, at the time, the motivation," Yule said. "Lou was, and all of us were, intent on one thing: to be successful . . . You had to have a hit, and a hit had to be uptempo, short, with no digressions . . . you wanted a hook and something to feed the hook and that was it."

In any case, Reed was also furious at what he saw on the album jacket. Just one person appeared on the back cover—Doug Yule, hunched over a piano at the far end of an empty recording studio. In the credits, Reed's name was listed third, after Yule and Morrison, and in both jacket and label copy, songwriting credit was assigned collectively to "The Velvet Underground," not to Reed.

No doubt with input from his dad, Reed lawyered up, and after a protracted legal fight, he got his songwriting credits back. But Sesnick laid claim to "The Velvet Underground," which enabled the band to continue as such, fronted by Yule. *Loaded* was released that fall to little fanfare. Label promotion was minimal, unsurprising for a band whose front man and primary songwriter had just quit. There were no hits, as the issuing of singles was half-hearted—"Head Held High," with the B side "Train Round the Bend" (prominently misspelled as "Train Round the Bond" on the picture sleeve), didn't appear until 1971. By November, Reed's bandmates were back at the Atlantic Records studios working on a new "Velvet Underground" album.

Reed, meanwhile, recorded demos in his childhood bedroom. Around the same time, he called Shelley Albin, wanting to reconnect. When she heard his voice on the line, she was in a room with her new baby and her family.

"You must have the wrong number," she told him, and hung up. The two never spoke again, and Albin destroyed all the letters Reed had sent her over the years. She didn't want to be tempted to share them once he became famous.

* * *

Reed first met Bettye Kronstad in the spring of 1968. She was visiting their mutual friend Lincoln Swados at Mount Sinai Hospital's psychiatric ward. Reed was sauntering out of the elevator as Kronstad was leaving Swados's room. "Hey, you! Beautiful!" Reed snapped as she breezed past him. He reached out and swatted her ass.

She turned, angry, and sized him up. Reed was dressed head to toe in denim, with pearl-snap buttons on his shirt, frayed bell-bottoms, and a tumescent air of rock star entitlement. His hair, in a well-groomed afro, added a couple of inches to his height.

He asked what she was doing in a psych ward. "You look normal," he said.

After learning of their shared connection to Swados and flirting a bit more, Kronstad agreed to meet Reed for a drink at the West End Bar, on Broadway off 114th Street in Morningside Heights, near her apartment and Columbia University, where she was working as a research assistant. Reed got hammered on scotch, ranting about his problems with Cale and the Velvets. Kronstad walked him to the subway, not expecting to see him again. But Reed didn't forget her, and in a gesture that suggested he was already planning his second act, he invited her to his final Velvets show at Max's. Seeing him perform, from her spot in the crowd midway back, she felt him singing certain songs directly to her, and after the show, she got a sweaty kiss and a promise he'd call her. She recalled the look on his face as "wild" and "almost pleading." The following week, Reed called her from his parents' house. They soon began seeing each other regularly.

Kronstad was slim, with sparkling blue eyes and dirty blond hair, which she cut short. She came from German-Scandinavian stock and a broken home with an abusive father, a World War II vet who fought at Normandy and suffered severe anxiety likely due to PTSD, although it had yet to become a diagnostic classification. Like Reed, he'd received electroconvulsive therapy as part of his treatment.

Kronstad was smart but restless. After receiving a scholarship to study at Columbia, she'd begun taking acting classes with Sanford Meisner at the Playhouse on Fifty-fourth Street. She lived in Manhattan with a couple of roommates; on weekends, Reed met her in the city, or she'd take the Long Island Rail Road to his parents' house. Her style was preppy, and she impressed Reed's parents. She was Protestant, but came across, in Long Island Jewish parlance, as "a very nice goil."

Amid this throwback into his family and his childhood culture, Reed was rethinking his entire identity. Before the Velvets, he'd thought of returning to school. Now, five years later, he turned his attention back to literature. "He was writing poetry and seriously reflecting," Kronstad says. "He was very disappointed about the Velvet Underground not being as successful as they should be. He did want to continue in the music business. But while he was living at home, he was trying poetry. That was the guy I fell in love with."

His first significant publication came through *Fusion*, the Boston-based music and politics magazine that had always supported the Velvets. When *Fusion* launched a book series (which included *Feel Like Going Home*, a landmark blues study by a Boston University creative writing student, Peter Guralnick), the editor, Robert Somma, had the idea for an essay collection around the theme of rock 'n' roll deaths. Jimi Hendrix had asphyxiated after ingesting a massive quantity of barbiturates in mid-September. Janis Joplin died of a heroin overdose not three weeks later. Brian Jones had drowned in his swimming pool the previous summer. "Why don't you take a shot at writing an essay?" Somma asked Reed over the phone. Reed agreed in an instant.

"It wasn't like I had to cajole him into it, believe me," says Somma, who'd already agreed to publish some of Reed's poems. "I don't think we paid him for it. I don't think he cared."

With the poet Frank O'Hara's slice-of-New-York-life meditation on Billie Holiday's death ("The Day Lady Died") serving as frontpiece (O'Hara died in a car crash in 1966, age forty), *No One Waved Goodbye: A Casualty Report on Rock and Roll* was a landmark of pop-music criticism. It included work by the pioneering Australian music journalist Lillian Roxon, an early Velvets champion; a Q&A with Danny Fields regarding Rilke, O'Hara, Carmen Miranda, and Jimi Hendrix's cock; even an essay by the Velvets' former manager, Al Aronowitz. Reed's "Fallen Knights and Fallen Ladies," however, is the book's only essay by a musician, and he showed a remarkable dual consciousness, as both artist and fan:

"At the age when identity is a problem some people join rock and roll bands and perform for other people who share the same difficulties. The age difference between performer and beholder in rock is not large. But, unfortunately, those in the fourth tier assume those on stage know something they don't. Which is not true. It simply requires a very secure ego to allow yourself to be loved for what you do rather than what you are, and an even larger one to realize you are what you do. The singer has a soul but feels he isn't loved off stage. Or, perhaps worse, feels he shines only on stage and off is wilted, a shell as common as the garden gardenia. But we are all as common as snowflakes, aren't we?"

More than seven pages long, it was an impressive mix of cultural criticism and memoir, both disarming and self-mythologizing (discovering the Beatles in Syracuse while studying Kierkegaard; getting hepatitis from, then writing a song about, shooting heroin). He addresses rock's ongoing race problem ("Hendrix could never have been accepted in white America as a first-rate phenomenon had he had an all-Black band") and tendency to favor burlesque over art. It was not lost on Reed that Joplin and Hendrix, deeply emotive virtuosos, had recently broken up bands to begin new, potentially less lucrative projects. He noted the emptiness of road life and its temptations (at one point quoting his beloved Salinger from *The Catcher in the Rye*), and located the implicit death wish in rock's romanticized doomed-bluesman persona. Also striking was Reed's nod to "the blessing" of a nine-to-five regimen, how it "masters" and "protects" the human mind. It suggested a man working things out on the couch with his analyst—who, according to the essay, advised Reed to depend on no one, "not your lover, your friend, or your doctor."

Reed was proud of "Fallen Knights and Fallen Ladies," which he worked on with Somma. "I did edit it," he says. "My recollection was that he didn't object at all. He thought the process was interesting, thought it improved things."

As the year came to a close, Reed was leading something like a mainstream suburban lifestyle—working a day job, seeing his girlfriend on the weekend. But it was a more unsettled situation than it appeared. Bickering with his father, who was now his employer, too, sometimes got heated. "If we went out to dinner with his parents, Chinese food on a Sunday night, Lou just started drinking and couldn't stop," Bettye says. "I'd try to keep up with him. It was just ridiculous."

The December 24 *Rolling Stone* ran a review of *Loaded*. In it, Lenny Kaye praised Reed's "incredible finesse" as a songwriter, and called it "easily one of the best albums to show up this or any year." He writes with even greater enthusiasm about the farewell run at Max's, noting Brigid Berlin's recordings in particular, then circulating as a bootleg. On paper, the Velvets still existed—but their posthumous apotheosis had already begun.

7.

LONG ISLAND > LONDON > UPPER EAST SIDE

(1971–1973)

DISCUSSED: St. Mark's Poetry Project, *A Walk on the Wild Side* (Nelson Algren novel), David Bowie, *Lou Reed*, *Transformer*, marriage, Lester Bangs, bisexual chic, divorce, *Berlin*, *Rock 'n' Roll Animal*

[It] asks why lost people sometimes develop into greater human beings than those who have never been lost in their whole lives. Why men who have suffered at the hands of other men are the natural believers in humanity, while those whose part has been simply to acquire, to take all and give nothing, are the most contemptuous of mankind.

—Nelson Algren on his 1956 novel
A Walk on the Wild Side

In his works, [he] enjoys constructing aberrant notions whose only goal is to rattle the confidence of plain folks . . . he's amused himself at our expense . . . he has sought to scandalize us.

—Jean Paul Sartre on Jean Genet, from *Saint Genet*

Perhaps I should die, after all, they all (the great blues singers) *did* die, didn't they? But life is getting better now, I don't want to die. Do I?

—Lou Reed, "Fallen Knights and Fallen Ladies"

Danny Fields adored Lou Reed from the get-go, as both an artist and a friend. So becoming Reed's manager seemed like a good idea.

It wasn't. The arrangement lasted two weeks. Fields tried to convince his Atlantic bosses to sign his new client as a solo act, but considering Reed torpedoed the Velvet Underground just after the label signed them, that didn't go well. So Fields shopped him around. Reed obsessed over Fields's progress, calling him at all hours, demanding constant reports, giving orders (like Warhol, Reed had a serious telephone addiction). Fields bowed out.

"I couldn't take it," Fields said. "It was horrible."

Reed's suburban rewind became a double life. Home on Long Island, he avoided the New York scene's pressures. Kronstad slept on a fold-out couch in the den, which Reed's mom made up for her; on Sunday, they'd all have brunch with bagels and whitefish. Reed taught Kronstad to play tennis, de rigueur among aspirational Long Islanders. But he was an impatient teacher, and the first lesson ended in a fight. Kronstad shared her interests in turn. She'd grown up riding horses on her father's farm in western Pennsylvania, and one weekend took Reed to the Equestrian Center in Hempstead. He failed the riding test, and had to remain in the corral while his girlfriend cantered down the trail without him. ("He was humiliated," she recalls.)

Sometimes they'd spend weekends at her place in Manhattan, and he'd introduce her to his friends. She felt the condescension. She was dismissed as "straight," and snidely referred to as "the cocktail waitress," according to Fields. Reed tried to forge a bond between her and Brigid Polk, given the latter's upscale pedigree. But it never took. So Reed largely remained in retreat on Long Island, and doubled down on his writing.

* * *

St. Mark's Church in-the-Bowery was founded in Lower Manhattan via the Dutch governor Peter Stuyvesant. The Stuyvesant family chapel, built in 1660, was replaced in 1799 after it was sold to the Episcopal Church; over the decades, in service to its neighborhood—a perpetual hub for European immigrants and, by the 1950s, a magnet for artists priced out of the West Village—St. Mark's evolved into an unorthodox, activist parish. Edna St. Vincent Millay and Kahlil Gibran served on the church's arts committee; Martha Graham danced there. Though W. H. Auden favored the traditional Latin mass, he worked on an English one with the church's progressive pastor, Michael Allen, brought on in 1959. Archie Shepp organized jazz shows in the west courtyard. In April 1966, as the Velvets blew minds around the corner at the Dom, Allen Ginsberg incanted "Wichita Vortex Sutra" in the parish hall at an antiwar benefit, and his lover Peter Orlovsky read an unambiguous piece about the two men fucking. As one parishioner observed at the time, the St. Mark's Christ was not "the Christ of little old ladies in white Sunday hats, but the vigorous Christ of rebellion."

The St. Mark's Poetry Project was run by Anne Waldman, a latter-day heir to the Beats and the New York School interested in new spoken-word traditions. The project was an offshoot of a social program, Creative Arts for Alienated Youth. One such youth, Patti Smith, made her semi-musical debut there in February. She recited "Oath," a poem that began "Christ died for somebody's sins but not mine" and invoked "every Johnny Ace song I've balled to." She also sang Hank Ballard's "Annie Had a Baby" and Kurt Weill's "Mack the Knife," and read a poem about a car crash accompanied on electric guitar by Lenny Kaye. It was a striking display, and people were buzzing about it.

When Reed appeared on the same altar the following month, it was with a sheaf of poems and no guitar. It was his first public appearance since the Max's farewell, and his first ever poetry reading, sharing a bill with Allen Ginsberg and the Velvets fan Jim Carroll. Gerard Malanga, Danny Fields, and others from the Factory scene turned out to witness the transmogrification, or whatever it was that Reed had in store. Reed was anxious but worked the room like a pro, flirting and gladhanding, Bettye hovering patiently nearby.

At the podium, Reed recited the lyrics to "Sister Ray." He read "The Murder Mystery," framing it in terms of concrete poetry. He read "Heroin," after which Ginsberg clapped vigorously. Reed sounded nervous at points, rushing through endings, knocking into the tape recorder as he turned pages. He introduced new material as his "gay poems," specifying that they were "pro-" gay. There was a paean to dancing with a man ("the grip . . . so strong"), with an aside noting "my father will not speak to me." Another poem suggested cruising a long-haired boy at the library. Reed described the choice between presenting straight or not, and he imagined how nice it would be to just linger outside of a movie theater, "arm in arm," in a world where no one would take any special notice. He noted that John Rechy's pioneering 1963 novel, *City of Night*, was one of his favorite books, and read a wistful prose fragment written from "out-and-out admiration" of it, in which a man, feeling over-the-hill, cruises men on a rainy night, then returns home to his girlfriend. Reed followed it with "Bettye," an evident celebration of his girlfriend, and the lyrics to "Andy's Chest," professing his love for Warhol.

Reed paused to light a cigarette. The remainder of the reading continued mixing memoir and metaphor. "Spirited Leaves of Autumn" conjured his college days, with clear references to Liz Annas's baby, Lincoln Swados's suicide attempt, and Delmore Schwartz "alone and raving." Finally, Reed introduced "a song" titled "The Coach and Glory of Love"; it involved a character wrestling with depression, guilt, and self-loathing who longs, in a resonant and gently provocative American image, to "play football for the coach"—and believes a particular kind of love might save him from the darkness of his own mind.

Reed didn't mention his intention to submit the latter poem to *The Harvard Advocate*, the college's esteemed undergraduate literary magazine (it would be accepted, with seven other poems of his, for the fall issue). What he did say was more startling: he was giving up music entirely to focus on poetry.

How much truth was in the declaration, only Reed knew. But the crowd was stunned by his earnestness. "Rather than being the 'cool' Lou Reed everyone expected to entertain them, he was sincere," recalls Kronstad. "People seemed embarrassed for him."

At Max's after the reading, Reed tried to put on a good face, at one point challenging the rock critic Richard Meltzer to a drinking contest. But he felt the response to his reading was decidedly lukewarm, and by the night's end, Reed was drunk and miserable. Kronstad recalls him "with his head in his arms on a table in the back room, incredibly sad. He felt totally rejected."

* * *

Soon after the event, Reed decided to double down on his music career. Kronstad remembers a night of heavy drinking that ended at "a Long Island gay bar," probably the Hayloft, where Reed was received as prodigal royalty. They closed the place, and she drove them home in his dad's Mercedes; they both passed out in his parents' den. The next morning, Reed laid out his new career plans to Kronstad. He also proposed marriage.

Startled, Kronstad declined, asking for time to think about it. She figured Reed was an alcoholic. But she also figured he was a genius, and was confident that, for better or worse, he was en route to becoming a very famous, paid-in-full rock star.

* * *

The title of Nelson Algren's 1956 novel *A Walk on the Wild Side* was inspired by a song: Hank Thompson's 1952 "Wild Side of Life," one of the biggest hits in country music history (so popular, in fact, it spawned an answer record that became the first country number 1 by a woman, Kitty Wells's "It Wasn't God Who Made Honky Tonk Angels"). Algren's characters might've stepped out of Reed's own imagination: Fitz Linkhorn, cesspool cleaner, street-corner preacher, and drunk; his son Dove, a drifter employed variously as peep-show performer and maker of novelty condoms, blinded in a brawl with a paraplegic; Kitty Twist, a scheming runaway-turned-prostitute. It was a vivid text, and would-be producers came running. One proposed film, which would've starred Elvis Presley and been directed by Elia Kazan, with songs by Leiber and Stoller, never got past Presley's management. Following the 1962 screen adaptation with Barbara Stanwyck and a young Jane Fonda, the off-Broadway director Carmen Capalbo revived the idea of a musical *Wild Side*, albeit in this case for the stage. The notion wasn't so far-fetched; the novel's narrative was frequently punctuated by jukebox-music quotes. Somehow Capalbo connected with Reed, who was instructed to mark spots in the text where he might insert music.

Capalbo had made his name directing Lotte Lenya in the long-running revival of *The Threepenny Opera*. But his staging of another Brecht/Weill musical, *Rise and Fall of the City of Mahagonny*, lasted just eight performances in 1970, and in its doomed wake the Algren project fizzled. But the book's themes, and its title, stuck with Reed.

The first to hear what he'd do with them were Lisa and Richard Robinson. They were a rock 'n' roll power couple: she an ambitious up-and-coming music journalist, he a youth-culture barometer and A&R man at RCA Records, what his wife referred to as the company's "house hippie." They both revered the Velvets, and after meeting Reed through Fields, hosted a dinner for him that spring at their Upper West Side apartment. That night, and on subsequent ones, they recorded him playing songs on acoustic guitar. Some were Velvets-era, such as "Ocean" and "Walk and Talk It." There was new material, too, including a giddy sketch about Manhattan life with a hooky chorus revolving around the phrase "take a walk on the wild side." Richard liked what he heard, and thought he could get Reed a deal.

Thinking the past might abet the present, the Robinsons also hosted a reunion between Reed and Nico that spring. She was in New York to promote *Desertshore*, her new album with John Cale. She'd planned a one-week residency at the Gaslight on Bleecker Street, where Dylan did some early shows. But the club was shuttered in April and she was in bad shape. Her mother had just died, she was using heroin, and she was facing possible legal threats involving a bar fight in El Quijote, the restaurant at the Chelsea Hotel, in which she cut a woman's face so badly with a broken glass, the woman required stitches. It was hard to recognize Nico as the blond goddess of five years ago; she looked haggard, and had hennaed her hair dark red. Still, it was a tender meeting between the former lovers and bandmates, according to Fields. Reed and Nico laughed and played songs together; she'd forget the words and Reed would prompt her, just like the old days.

Any Velvet Underground reunion, however, seemed unlikely. That spring, the remaining members gigged the country, with Tucker back behind her drums and Doug Yule singing Reed's old songs alongside his own. But after finishing a date in Houston, Sterling Morrison announced that he was done, and would not be returning to New York with them: he'd been accepted to grad school for English literature at the University of Texas, Austin, and he was heading there.

"I was going through teaching assistant applications, and I saw one from 'Holmes S. Morrison,'" recalls Joe Kruppa, whose class Morrison and Reed visited in '69. "There was a note saying he'd been traveling and performing with a 'musical ensemble' the past few years—no mention that it was the Velvet Underground [laughs]. When I realized who it was, I said, 'Holy shit! I'm gonna help this guy get an assistant-ship, that's for *damn* sure.'"

* * *

Building up RCA's rock roster with Richard Robinson was Dennis Katz, a thirty-year-old lawyer with the title of vice president of A&R for contemporary music. He'd just signed David Bowie to a three-album deal, advancing him $37,500 against *Hunky Dory*, which he'd already recorded on his own dime. He didn't seem like a sure shot in America, and neither did Reed, whose RCA deal was even smaller. The signed contract in Reed's files, dated October 1, 1971, stipulated a two-year, two-record deal, with a $900 signing advance, and $6,600 upon delivery of the first album, with advances on subsequent recordings modestly laddered up. The royalty rate would be 10 percent, or less if any label A&R staff were enlisted as producers. Mechanical copyright royalties for Reed's compositions would be paid at the rate of 3.5 cents for each two-sided 45 rpm single, and 18 cents per LP (13.5 cents if it was sold at a record club discount). All the studio costs of recording would be recoupable, i.e., charged against Reed's earnings, and the master recordings would be RCA's property "exclusively and perpetually." A clause noted that if Reed was convicted of a felony, the company could terminate the contract with five days' written notice.

It was a start. His solo career had officially begun.

* * *

When David Bowie swept into New York for a promotional visit in September, he planned on meeting two of his heroes. First was Warhol. Bowie had recorded a tribute song, "Andy Warhol," on *Hunky Dory*, but his reception at the Factory was decidedly lukewarm; Warhol apparently disliked the song, and the two didn't click. Warhol retreated behind his lens—in this case, a brand-new video camera with a half-inch black-and-white open reel recorder—and rolled tape. Bowie, never one to ignore a camera, did a short mime performance that involved ripping his beating heart out of his chest.

His next meeting, convened by Danny Fields and the Robinsons, was at the Ginger Man, a French bistro on Amsterdam Avenue, across from Lincoln Center, that was named for J. P. Donleavy's raunchy mid-'50s roman à clef. This meeting was more successful: Bowie looked every inch the gender-fluid starlet, halfway between flower child and glam rocker, hair flowing past his shoulders from beneath a floppy wide-brimmed hat, in yellow Mary Jane shoes and a touch of blue eye shadow.

Lou Reed arrived in jeans, denim shirt, and black leather jacket, with his hair cut short: a butch androgyne with a dollop of Long Island rock fan commoner. They made a striking pair, and spent much of the night whispering to each other over filet mignon while Kronstad and Bowie's wife, Angie, watched them bond. "Lou did kinda fall in love with him," Kronstad says.

After dinner, the couples headed to Max's, where they met Jim Osterberg, otherwise known as Iggy Pop. His band, the Stooges, a wild Michigan hard-rock outfit that Fields had signed to Elektra and whose debut was produced by Cale, had imploded that summer, and Pop was crashing on Fields's couch. It was a meeting of three extraordinary minds—David Bowie, Lou Reed, Iggy Pop—and over the next few days, the trio functioned as a rock 'n' roll think tank. Gatherings often took place at the Robinsons'. One night, Reed and Bowie slipped into a back room and locked the door. After a while, Angie began banging on it, demanding, unsuccessfully, to be let in. The two may have merely been sharing book-nerd observations on T. S. Eliot. But they knew how to get people talking.

* * *

The youth culture of the 1960s had begun mutating in the '70s. Arriving right on time were the Cockettes, an outrageous hippie drag troupe based in San Francisco who made their debut on New Year's Eve 1969. In the wake of Stonewall, they neatly marked a cultural tipping point from flower power into queer power. After the critic Rex Reed wrote about their revue *Tinsel Tarts in a Hot Coma* in his nationally syndicated column ("a landmark in the history of new, liberated theater"), they brought it to New York City's Anderson Theater, at 66 Second Avenue between Third and Fourth, where it ran for three weeks in the fall of '71. Danny Fields did PR, and it was a lowbrow high-society spectacle—opening night drew a Hollywood A-list alongside John Lennon, Yoko Ono, Gore Vidal, Warhol and his superstars. Warhol was trying his hand at anarcho-sexual theater, too, staging his first play, the semi-autobiographical *Pork*, with the actors Wayne County and Tony Zanetta at La Mama, the experimental theater that produced *Femme Fatale*. A minor hit in New York (the *Times* deemed it "good, dirty fun"), it was exported in August to London, where Bowie and his wife saw it twice and hung out with the cast.

Rock 'n' roll was mutating, too. The New York Dolls played their first show in early 1971 at the Mercer Arts Center, a performance space in the old Broadway Central Hotel, where Reed and Cale had played back in the summer of 1965. Their music was rooted in Stones-style blues-rock but cruder, and their stage outfits leaned toward roughneck drag in the vein of Jackie Curtis's gender-fuck street style—they looked like a scene from "Sister Ray" come to life. Nearer the mainstream, psychedelic rock's spangled noodling had branched into two main schools. "Progressive rock" was about complex songwriting that often reflected European classical music structures with over-the-top virtuoso musicianship. Jethro Tull, with the lead singer and flute player Ian Anderson, had a Top 10 U.S. hit with *Aqualung*, issued in March, while the English band Yes made the U.S. Top 5 in November with *Fragile*. "Glam rock," meanwhile, had leaped out of the closet in March with T. Rex's performances of "Hot Love" on British national television, the singer, Marc Bolan, decked out on *Top of the Pops* in a silvery femme sailor suit, looking like a space-age Victorian courtesan. London was home to both schools, so Reed decided he would record his album there.

In December he touched down at Heathrow Airport with Richard and Lisa Robinson to start work. RCA set the trio up for a month at the top-flight Inn on the Park, near Hyde Park, where, despite Reed's small advance, they promptly ran up a huge bill, in fake-it-till-you-make-it rock star style. It was Reed's first time abroad, and he was finally living the life, although bouts of anxiety might have been undercutting him. For much of the trip, Reed stayed holed up at the hotel. "Lou's room was down the hall from ours," Lisa Robinson recalled, "and there were many—many—long nights when he just sat in our room, droning on for hours. As I recall, he was drinking a lot."

There was merriment. One night the three attended a birthday party for Bowie at his house, with Angie cooking, then decamped to El Sombrero, a tony gay-friendly Kensington High Street discotheque, where Bowie and Reed slow-danced together. Reed also did his first international press, speaking with the English journalist John Tobler. "We were listening to some English records and said 'very interesting sound they seem to be getting over there,'" Reed said, explaining why he'd decided to record in London. He also spoke reverently about the Stones' version of "Little Queenie" ("when all is said and done, you can always listen to the Stones, they never let you down") and John Lennon's "Mother" ("The first time I heard it, I didn't know it was Lennon; I ran up to the jukebox and was like 'what the FUCK is THAT? I LOVE that song'").

While in the U.K., Reed got news of a left-field success back home: a new band fronted by the white soul singer Mitch Ryder, called Detroit, had recorded a version of "Rock & Roll" for their new album. Butched up with hollered vocals, hard-rock lead guitar, and a prominent cowbell (echoing the Stones' "Honky Tonk Women" and Led Zeppelin's "Moby Dick"), it'd become a minor hit, landing on the *Billboard* "Bubbling Under the Hot 100" chart in early January. When Richard Robinson told Reed about it, he was over the moon.

"Isn't that just great!" Reed said, slapping his leg, shaking his head, and grinning. "The hot hundred! . . . God help us."

"I'd love to have a number one," he said.

* * *

Reed had no band yet, so he enlisted a crew of English session men to record his solo debut. The guitarist Steve Howe and keyboardist Rick Wakeman had just joined the prog-rock juggernaut Yes and were about to become superstars; the journeyman multi-instrumentalist Caleb Quaye had just finished working alongside Wakeman on Elton John's *Madman Across the Water*. Reed didn't interact much with the hired guns, but found directing them "far more efficient and better in every conceivable way" than his studio experiences with the Velvets. The album was knocked out in two weeks.

Robinson was a novice producer, and mistakes were made. The sound was flat, the arrangements were somewhat bloodless. But the songs were good. Most were first performed with the Velvets, though all got rethought. Reed's singing had gotten flashier, campier. "I Can't Stand It" added R&B-style backing vocals on the chorus, which now invoked "Candy" instead of "Shelley" as absent savior. "Lisa Says" is less emotional and more upbeat than the heartbreaking 3 a.m. version he'd cut with the Velvets two years earlier, its lead character apparently no longer willing to "do it with just about anyone." The album ends with another stab at "Ocean," one of Reed's best and most unstable songs, reimagined here as prog rock, with a gong crash and horror-fantasy imagery buoyed by Rick Wakeman's churning piano: a reeking castle, bloodthirsty warlocks, and the Shakespearean Malcolm, who now "serves your brain on a plate."

How to package Reed evidently baffled everyone. Prototype sleeve art was about as far from glam as one could get: one rough featured a photo of Reed sitting on the beach in a football jersey (number 37, likely in homage to the 1960s San Francisco All-Pro Jimmy Johnson), with his arm around Seymoure, the family dog. In the end, the cover was a punt, an unintelligible illustration depicting a small bird on the sidewalk, having just emerged, presumably, from a Fabergé egg. It was as disappointing as the cover art of *Loaded*, with its cartoon subway signage misspelling "downtown" as "dowtow."

At the start of 1972, the promise of a Velvets reunion was dangled, although Reed likely saw it solely as a way to promote his nascent solo career. Nico had planned some European shows with John Cale. With Reed in London, plans were hashed out for a show by the three of them on January 28 at Le Bataclan, a venerable Parisian nightclub located at 50 Boulevard Voltaire in the busy eleventh arrondissement. Opened in 1864, it was named for the French operetta *Ba-Ta-Clan*, a popular chinoiserie political satire; the building, a magnificent space, resembled a pagoda. Edith Piaf performed there frequently in her day, as did other French stars, and it had recently begun presenting rock acts.

At rehearsals, Reed taught Cale and Nico "Pale Blue Eyes" and "Candy Says," which both postdated their Velvets tenure; Cale added viola to the former, while Nico provided "doo-doo-wah"s on the latter. In the end, regrettably, they'd perform neither. But the show was enough of an event to be filmed for French television, and it was a moving glimpse of roads not taken. It was Reed's first time on a European stage.

"Hello. Took us a while to get here," he tells the audience. "This is a song about copping drugs in New York."

The audience roars at the outset of "I'm Waiting for the Man," which Reed delivers like a cabaret blues, smirking slyly on the line "Hey, white boy." He introduces "Berlin," one of two new songs on *Lou Reed*, as "my Barbra Streisand song," singing it to Cale's piano accompaniment like a European crooner: licking his lips, stroking his hair, lighting a cigarette as Cale takes a solo. After a potent duet of "Heroin," Nico steps to the microphone at the lip of the stage and begins "Femme Fatale," flashing a smile toward Reed as fleeting as a matchstick flare, simultaneously a lost girl and a destroying siren.

It was marvelous. But plans for a replay in London quickly fell apart. Reed had no interest in replaying his past. Two days later, he was back in New York, ready to reinvent himself.

* * *

That summer, Reed signed a management contract with Fred Heller, who'd been managing the successful Blood, Sweat & Tears. Dated June 1, it guaranteed Heller 20 percent of Reed's gross income and locked Reed into a three-year contract. Since he now needed a touring band, Heller connected him with a precocious group of teenagers from Yonkers, just north of the city.

All four were students at Gorton High School; the guitarist Vinnie LaPorta still had braces. Reed auditioned them in the basement of the bassist's parents' house. Their playing was solid—barely—but they took direction well. As with the U.K. session men, there'd be no battles over creative control. The Tots, as he cheekily named the teens, were also cheap; given Reed's small advance, money was tight. He and Kronstad had just moved into a tiny studio on East Seventy-eighth Street at First Avenue, a neighborhood known as "the airline stewardess ghetto," full of compact rentals perfect for those who lived on the road. Reed furnished the place sparsely: TV, stereo, a fold-out couch that doubled as the couple's bed, a rocking chair inherited from his grandmother. It was a far cry from his deluxe accommodations in London.

So was the experience of his first solo tour. The debut show was staged, inauspiciously, in the Millard Fillmore Room at the State University of New York in Buffalo, booked by a student who'd seen the Velvets at Max's. It went passably well. Reed's spirits lifted when a messenger turned up at his motel door the next day bearing a dozen roses, spray-painted gold, and a card from David Bowie. Reed and the Tots stayed at chain hotels for much of the tour, driving equipment from show to show and setting it up themselves, like he did with the Velvets; eventually they got a roadie. When the distance was far, the band drove ahead while Reed and Kronstad flew, coach.

Lou Reed was released in May to lukewarm reviews. Charlie Gillett, the English critic who'd caught the Velvets at the Dom, described it as "pale rock'n'roll." Greg Shaw, writing in *Phonograph Record* magazine, called it "an album of Velvet Underground songs without the Velvet Underground . . . [a] Lou Reed album with an inferior backing group." Not helping matters, perhaps, was the near-simultaneous release of Brigid Berlin's bootleg tapes of the final Velvet Underground show. *Live at Max's Kansas City* was one of the worst-sounding albums ever released, in terms of audio quality, but the music and spirit made Reed's solo debut seem weak by comparison.

Reed read his reviews, and did not take bad ones well. He spent much of the tour in a funk. Kronstad recalled one night in a hotel bar postshow, when Reed, a few drinks in, began shouting that he needed to fire the Tots. ("They're . . . just . . . SO . . . UGLY!" he yelled, after she'd dragged him into the elevator.) According to Kronstad, he could be abusive to everyone, herself included. "If you were the woman in his life, you were as intergral to him as an arm or a leg, and would be treated with as much respect and abuse as he treated himself," she reflected. "That's just the way it was."

Yet he could be a tender, inclusive partner. A striking home recording, likely made after the tour ended, shows Reed working up new songs with Kronstad singing harmonies. Kronstad even sings two songs on her own. "Going Down," redolent of Burt Bacharach's work with Dionne Warwick, suggests a mental collapse in dreamlike images of falling that flicker alongside a euphemism for oral sex. More impressive was the second, which Reed identifies as "Just a Summer's Day," inspired by a day the couple spent in Central Park. Kronstad recalls they drank sangria, argued about their engagement plans and Reed's excessive drinking, then went to the movies. In the song, Reed sketched an unsteadily blissful scene that flickered with self-loathing, eddying around the lines "You made me think I was someone else / Someone good," as he thumped out a waltz in simple chords at an upright piano.

"'Just a Summer's Day' featuring Bettye Kronstad!" Reed crowed at the end of the take, playing emcee. The song would be a keeper, though he would change the name.

Reed worked through another song on the recording by himself, an untitled ballad that may have had a similar element of memoir. It's voiced by a conflicted character whose world, despite the pleasures he's known, seems overwhelmed by sin and pain, a situation he hopes to remedy by abandoning certain friends, or possibly lovers. "I'll say goodbye to Jim," Reed sings gently on the chorus, bidding farewell to "Sam" and "Kim" as well.

Kronstad wondered about Reed's sexual interest in men, but they rarely discussed it and she didn't press him about it. What they had together was genuine. "I think that sometimes, what we allow ourselves to be attracted to physically is something that we're safe with emotionally," she says. "And actually, the emotion and the psychology behind your attraction often is coming first, and the physical attraction is coming afterward."

* * *

In London, meanwhile, David Bowie's star was ascendant, and he continued acting as Reed's booster. In the January 22 issue of *Melody Maker*, Bowie declared that he, Reed, and Iggy Pop were going to take over the rock 'n' roll world. He also announced, "I'm gay, and always have been, even when I was David Jones." He went on to compare his craft to "talking to a psychoanalyst. My act is my couch." The writer, with a suggestion of both homophobic bafflement and valid journalistic skepticism, given Bowie's performative tendencies, wondered if the singer's coming-out was part put-on; the front-page teaser labeled Bowie "rock's swishiest outrage." Despite the 1967 Sexual Offences Act, which decriminalized "homosexual acts" for men over twenty-one, British culture was still deeply homophobic, and Bowie's declaration was a moment that surely shook the nation's teens—gay, straight, and otherwise. Whether his summitry with Reed the previous fall had anything to do with it is an open question.

In any case, their artistic relationship deepened in 1972. In May, Bowie performed "White Light/White Heat" on two BBC live-in-the-studio broadcasts, using airtime slated to promote his new album, *The Rise and Fall of Ziggy Stardust and the Spiders from Mars*, to call attention to his friend as well. "White light makes me feel like Lou Reed!" he sang on one version. And after discussions with their management teams, it was decided that Bowie would produce Reed's next LP, *Transformer*.

Back in London on July 8, Reed found himself singing "White Light/White Heat" and "Sweet Jane" with Bowie at a benefit concert Bowie was headlining at the Royal Festival Hall, two-thousand-plus fans whooping and clapping along. It was Reed's first-ever stage performance in Britain. Bowie was now a full-bore rock star. "Starman"—the breakout single from *Ziggy Stardust*, a concept album about a bisexual alien who comes to Earth and becomes a pop icon—made the U.K. Top 10, and two days before Reed shared the Royal Festival Hall stage with him, Bowie delivered it to maybe 15 million TV viewers on *Top of the Pops*. In a harlequin catsuit with smoky eye shadow, lipstick, white nail polish, and a rooster hairdo, Bowie draped his arm around the guitarist Mick Ronson, whose long blond hair spilled over his gold jumper. "Don't tell your papa or he'll get us locked up," Bowie crooned. It was possibly the most radically queer moment that had ever occurred on British national television.

Reed and Bowie had plenty in common aside from their ambition. Both struggled as teens who felt marginalized. Bowie had a history of mental illness in his family; his older half-brother, with whom he was very close, battled schizophrenia, and like Reed, Bowie kept in check a fear of losing control. Bowie had also lost his father recently, and likely saw in Reed, with five years and a legendary, full-arc musical career already behind him, an older brother/father figure. The two shared interests in literature, film, and theater as well as spiritual pursuits: Bowie studied Buddhism when he was younger, and even considered becoming a monk before his stage hunger changed his plans. Also, they both liked drinking and taking drugs.

Though he didn't show it, Reed was thrilled to be working with Bowie. Bowie was equally thrilled, if a bit rattled, at how much creative control Reed willingly ceded. "I was petrified that he said yes," Bowie said of his offer to help produce Reed. "He just gave the whole project over to me." Bowie had so many ideas, knew the Velvets so well, he was intimidated; he felt it would be "impertinent" of him to suggest Reed try a song in one style or another. But they brainstormed, and Reed trusted his new friend wholeheartedly. He knew he was working with an artistic equal, and importantly, a successful one.

"I really hoped that I wouldn't let him down, and [that it would] be a memorable album that people wouldn't forget," Bowie recalled. He needn't have worried. Bowie chose all the session musicians. There were no ex-Velvets, as revisiting Reed's past wasn't the plan. Still, two old songs made the cut, "Andy's Chest" and "Satellite of Love." Reed sang the latter with trembling vibrato, while Bowie's vocal arrangement veers from Jordanaires allusions to the spectacular glam-gospel high-note swoon at the end. ("What a move," Reed said, marveling at Bowie's contribution. "Very few people could do that. Really pure and beautiful.")

Warhol's influence loomed over *Transformer*. "Vicious," with its fey declaration "You hit me with a flower," came from an idea Warhol gave Reed. "New York Telephone Conversation" was a withering parody of the Max's scene set as an afternoon-after gossip swap among phone addicts, Warhol and Reed surely among them. On "Make Up," a soulful slow jam with a tuba bass line, the singer observes a "slick little girl" putting on her face with a mixture of lust and envy, while the chorus suggests she might be one of the Factory's trans superstars: "Now we're comin' out, out of our closets," Reed declared. Three years past Stonewall and the launch of *Come Out!*, New York City's gay liberation newspaper, the lines' context was obvious, though it would go over the heads of most rock fans.

The most site-specific lyrics, however, and the most indelible, turned up on the song Reed had begun for the aborted *Walk on the Wild Side* musical.

"I re-wrote it and put in everybody from the Factory," Reed explained. The cast was familiar. Reed had already written about Candy Darling, albeit with far more empathy, in "Candy Says." Here he sets her up as a fixture in Max's back room, tossing in a flippant blow job reference. Holly Woodlawn had by now appeared in a couple of Warhol films; as Reed sang, she did indeed come to New York from Miami, and did indeed shave her legs along the way (in a roadside motel in New Brunswick, Georgia, to be precise). Jackie Curtis, who had recently appeared alongside Darling and Woodlawn in Andy Warhol's *Women in Revolt*, a women's lib send-up with allusions to Valerie Solanas, also gets name-checked, suggesting a nonbinary character with a taste for amphetamines, not far from the truth. Joe Dallesandro, a hunky Italian-American model who'd made his Warhol film debut in *Lonesome Cowboys*, was conjured as "Little Joe," a composite of his film characters. "Sugar Plum Fairy" was the nickname of Joe Campbell, a Factory satellite who'd decamped to the Bay Area, where his ex-boyfriend Harvey Milk was a rising star in local politics; in Warhol's *My Hustler*, Campbell played a seasoned hustler called "Sugar Plum Fairy" and, according to Warhol, may have had a hand in dosing the production team on LSD while shooting the film on Fire Island.

Reed first turned heads with first-person monologues: "twenty-five dollars in my hand"; "it's my wife and it's my life." But from the get-go, he was also daisy-chaining third-person character sketches into song: Teenage Mary, Uncle Dave, Seasick Sarah, and Margarita Passion in "Run Run Run"; Duck, Sally, Rosie, Miss Rayon, and Cecil in "Sister Ray"; Jack and Jane in "Sweet Jane"; Jimmy and Ginger Brown, Pearly Mae, and Joanie Love in "Oh! Sweet Nuthin'"; and, perhaps most presciently, in the Factory roll call—Brigid, Rona, Ondine, Pepper, Ingrid, Mary, Susan, Johnny Bore—that Reed gifted Nico in "Chelsea Girls." The technique was hardly new, traceable to seventeenth-century English balladry and earlier; Dylan used it journalistically to tell of Emmett Till and Hattie Carroll, abstractly with the likes of Johnny and Maggie in "Subterranean Homesick Blues." But with "Walk on the Wild Side," a vividly telegraphed theatrical miniature delivered in the tuneful *sprechstimme* Reed had hit on with "Sweet Jane," he made a formal breakthrough. Perhaps it was the vestigial conceit of stage writing that crystalized it. Decades later, in a preface to his collected lyrics, Reed described songwriting as a sort of dramaturgy, and his desire to "write the play with the music of my heart."

The engine of "Walk on the Wild Side" was a gentle funk guitar strum that echoed the Staple Singers' "I'll Take You There," a radio hit that winter. But Reed's song was most clearly defined by its bass line, which was in fact two lines: one played on acoustic double bass, the other on a 1960 electric Fender Jazz Bass. The session player Herbie Flowers played both, inspired to overdub the lines in part so that he could get paid twice for the same song. (At going rates, he recalled earning £17 for both parts.) For Reed, it was money well spent. The effect, in tandem with brush drumming, was a gentle whirlpool of noir cool, magnified by the baritone sax solo of Ronnie Ross, a British jazzman who happened to be Bowie's sax tutor. No less indelible than the lyrics or the bass lines, in a gesture that could be read as wry social commentary, racist arrogance, or both, the vocal trio Thunderthighs—white women all—invoked the singing "colored girls" on the chorus.

Like most every LP Reed would ever make, *Transformer* included a masterful ballad, an exercise in sentimentality illuminated with a twist. Here, it was "Perfect Day," a retooled take on "Just a Summer's Day," the song Bettye Kronstad sang with Reed in their apartment. Here, wrapped in orchestral strings arranged by Bowie's wingman Mick Ronson, it became one of Reed's most convincing performances, his contrite gratitude to a partner for making him think he was "someone else, someone good" recalling a similar glimpse of love's salvation in "I'll Be Your Mirror." The album ended with "Goodnight Ladies," a wistfully literary song nearly as pretty as "Perfect Day," which feels like Reed's fond farewell to the genderqueer, halcyon-in-hindsight Factory scene.

* * *

Though great music was made, *Transformer* was uneven, and Reed was a hot mess during the sessions. "I think he was on heroin," recalled Tony Visconti, the glam-rock sculptor who produced T. Rex's *Electric Warrior*, of meeting Reed for the first time. "He was just sitting in the corner on the floor kind of nodding off. I remember kneeling down and shaking his hand and saying 'hello' and he just looked up and was all glazed over." For Reed, the stress of what he knew was a make-

or-break album must have been overwhelming, and the extent of his self-medication might also explain the extent to which he handed off creative control to Bowie.

In any case, throwaway songs notwithstanding, *Transformer* would be a landmark of both glam rock and queer art, just as the so-called sexual revolution was reaching a peak, an album addressing gay culture, nonbinary gender identity, and all-around otherness writ large. The packaging telegraphed as much. The cover was a high-contrast, intentionally blurred shot of Reed by the English photographer Mick Rock, taken in July during Reed's first U.K. concert, staged in a converted movie theater in King's Cross, London. Reed's glam-ghoul look, which came together when Angie Bowie took him shopping, was a macabre spin on the mime whiteface her husband wore in a 1969 promo short, and perhaps on the perception of New York demimonders as vampiric cadavers who only come out at night. The image, of Reed's masklike face looking wistfully to the sky as he cradled his guitar, would become iconic, and shape his stage persona for a while. It also marked the start of a long creative alliance with Mick Rock.

Transformer's back cover image was no less powerful. Considered for the front but demoted for marketing reasons, it was conceived by Reed as a send-up of binary sexuality, a tableau of a butch man seeing/imagining himself in the mirror as an ultra-femme woman. It was shot by Karl Stoecker, one of Reed's *Lonely Woman Quarterly* sidekicks back in Syracuse, now a fashion photographer in London known for his Vargas Girl pinup aesthetic who'd just shot the cover of Roxy Music's debut LP. The *Transformer* diptych featured the English model Gala in black lingerie, heels, and makeup, opposite Ernie Thormahlen, Reed's sometimes road manager, in a T-shirt and tight jeans apparently concealing a huge hard-on (in a hilarious nod to the Velvets' debut, it was actually a plastic banana). Given *Transformer*'s themes, many fans thought these were pictures of the same person, perhaps even of Reed himself. Around the world, questioning adolescents doubtlessly studied the images, dazzled, discomfited, aroused, and confused.

* * *

Released on November 8, *Transformer* didn't immediately transform Reed's career. In *The New Yorker*, the critic and Velvet Underground champion Ellen Willis described the album as "terrible—lame, pseudo-decadent lyrics, lame, pseudo-something-or-other-singing, and a just plain lame band." *The New York Times* dismissed the album as "flaccid"—amusing in light of Thormahlen's banana bulge—and noted that, Velvets notwithstanding, "the public has never discovered [Reed] and, unfortunately, 'Transformer' will not help his cause." In *Rolling Stone*, Nick Tosches praised the Velvets ("some of the most amazing stuff ever to be etched in vinyl") but was mixed on *Transformer*, insisting with a distinct note of queerphobic macho posturing that Reed should "forget this artsyfartsy kind of homo stuff and just go in there with a bad hangover and start blaring out his visions of lunar assfuck."

Reed's relationship with the rock journalism world, already strange, was getting stranger. He'd surely damaged his relationship with the influential Lisa Robinson when he chose Bowie over her husband, Richard, as *Transformer*'s producer. That falling-out was alluded to by another journalist, Ed McCormack, in a cover story for *Fusion* that fall. As it happened, McCormack and his wife lived near Reed and Kronstad on the Upper East Side, and the couples hit it off. (Kronstad recalls a double date one night that ended with Reed drunkenly proposing the four of them jump in bed together; Kronstad declined.) Reed's friendship with McCormack showed how self-disclosing he could still be with a journalist. Out drinking with him one night until late, Reed spoke in a troubled whirlwind about his Velvets legacy ("I'm in the odd position of having to compete with myself"), self-doubt, and self-loathing. In his published story, McCormack collaged Reed's end of the conversation:

> Sometimes I have this horrible nightmare that I'm not really what I think I am . . . That I'm just a completely decadent egotist . . . Do you have any idea what it's like to be in my shoes? . . . I mean, I have made every hip scene . . . known . . . everyone . . . everyone! . . . and sometimes I think I'm just a phony cocksucker like the rest of them . . . I mean, Bettye is not hip at all . . .

and that's why I love her . . . I want to keep her that way . . . ha! . . . Lou Reed, bi-sexual chauvinist pig . . . I mean, she is so . . . pure . . . And I believe in sparrows . . . I believe in pretty princesses . . . there are hip people, brilliant people, people I absolutely love . . . Yet on another level they are the scum of the earth . . . and in so many ways I am like them, I am no different, no better, so how can what I've done mean anything . . . But I love rock and roll . . ."

The Velvets' legacy continued shadowing Reed. A September show at London's Sundown Theater was reviewed in *Melody Maker* by Richard Williams, a longtime Velvets booster who had once described their third album as a "suite" that was "so far ahead of *Sgt. Pepper* that it makes the album sound like a series of nursery rhymes." Now he ridiculed Reed's "unconvincing" new stage persona, including makeup and silver platform shoes that "forced him to totter on and off-stage like a sad, ageing whore." For a subsequent U.K. show, a perhaps conflicted Reed played nothing but Velvet Underground songs. The audience response was enthusiastic, but for Reed it must've been at best a mixed pleasure.

Back in the States, he turned his attention yet again to poetry. *The Paris Review* published the lengthy, double-columned text of the Velvets' "The Murder Mystery" in the Winter issue. The piece was probably part of a manuscript of poems, prose, and lyrics Reed was assembling. Records suggest the working title was *We the People*, from his poem of the same name, and that he sent a copy of it to Knopf, one of the country's most prestigious publishers, in December.

The dedication on a somewhat later, probably expanded version of Reed's manuscript, retitled *All the Pretty People*, was "To A.W."—Andy Warhol—and the work was parsed into four sections: "Men, Women, Drugs & Parties," "Drugs, Regret & Murder," "Release & Surprise," and "Attitudes," language and content becoming cruder with each chapter. The first section opens with the Whitmanesque declaration "I AM THE CHEMICAL MAN / THE HAMLET OF ELECTRICITY." The narrator of "A Night at the Prom" tells a sixteen-year-old boy that he takes "15 milligram Desoxyn every three hours" and advises "anti-depressants are better than sedatives." His poem about wanting "to play football for the coach," published as "The Coach and Glory of Love" in *The Harvard Advocate*, appears with that title crossed out, renamed "Coney Island Baby." Echoing Reed's post-college letter to Delmore Schwartz, "Dirt" is about hustling on the Lower East Side, keeping out of debt by catering to "a rich cunt's D. H. Lawrence trip." A character named Renee—"a walking hormone shot"—turns up in "Street Hassling," alongside "patrolmen on their knees" and a bloody street fight scenario. "Kicks" considers the sex-like thrill of stabbing someone. The collection's sole prose piece, cryptically titled "Do Angels Need Haircuts?," was the John Rechy–inspired short story Reed had read at St. Mark's Church, about the aging guy cruising for men before returning to his girlfriend and anxiously contemplating marriage.

Apparently, Knopf rejected and returned *We the People*, which probably stung. But with album promotion to do for *Transformer*, which was beginning to get commercial traction, there was little time for Reed to dwell on it.

On December 26, about fifteen minutes from his parents' house, Reed played a live-in-studio set for the progressive Long Island rock station WLIR-FM. After eight months of touring, the Tots were a fairly tight, powerful unit. Reed played to his suburban audience, dialing down the camp. "Vicious" is more fierce than fey. Instead of introducing "Berlin" as his "Barbra Streisand" song, he says, "We're gonna make believe we're in Casablanca, and I'm Humphrey Bogart, and this is what I'm gonna sing to Lauren Bacall." Reed says little about "Walk on the Wild Side," which wasn't a hit yet, but was getting noticed; when he delivers the line about "giving head," the studio audience cheers.

Between sets, the DJ asks about Reed's time in England. Reed praised Bowie for his "empathy," and disparaged Doug Yule, with whom the DJ claimed to have attended high school. Reed says there's "no chance" that he'll ever play with the Velvets again. Then, to begin the second set, he introduced "Heroin," noting wryly that when it was first released, "not only was it banned, but they wouldn't take advertisements for our album because of it. Now here we are doing it over the radio . . . [it's] very funny."

* * *

In January, Reed and Kronstad were married in their apartment at 402 East Seventy-fourth Street, two blocks from the Sokol Hall gymnasium, where the Velvets held court in '67. The couple had upgraded with the help of Reed's $15,000 *Transformer* advance: their new place had a small foyer, parquet wood floors, a large living room, separate bedroom and dining rooms, and an eat-in kitchen with a street view.

Kronstad's family, not thrilled with their daughter's choice of husband, declined to attend, so Reed chose not to invite his family. (His sister was especially upset; Reed and Kronstadt had attended her wedding the previous year.) Reed's manager, Fred Heller, arranged for a Roman Catholic officiant of some sort (Kronstad recalls him as a bishop) to officiate, a compromise between Kronstad's Presbyterianism and Reed's Judaism. The groom wore a white suit with a pale blue shirt, open at the collar. The bride wore white satin slacks, a navy cashmere top, pearls, and navy blue flats, so she wouldn't tower over her husband. The soundtrack was Stevie Wonder's new LP, *Talking Book*, and the ceremony began after the final notes of "I Believe (When I Fall in Love It Will Be Forever)." The couple said their vows, Heller took Polaroids, Reed flirted with the supposed bishop, and the couple headed off to a reception dinner of mainly RCA executives and their wives, where conversations revolved largely around Reed's career.

He hadn't performed in New York City since the Velvets' farewell run at Max's, and it was decided his return would be an Event: one night only, January 27 at Lincoln Center's lavish Alice Tully Hall, a sparkling thousand-seat venue designed for classical music that opened in 1969.

Kronstad pressed Reed into taking a week off before the show for a honeymoon, and his management arranged a trip for the newlyweds to Montego Bay. They had a cabin on the beach. They rode motorcycles and toured the island. Their guide helped them score cocaine, they went out clubbing, and Reed overindulged; the night ended with him passed out on their cabin floor. Angrily, Kronstad smashed a lamp, then sobbed on the phone to her grandmother as the sun came up.

* * *

The Lincoln Center show sold out, and a late show was added. The night was a parade of Reed's past. His Syracuse pal Garland Jeffreys opened both shows; he'd gotten a deal with Atlantic and had just finished his debut LP. Reed drank a lot before the first show. It went well enough. Backstage, Warhol congratulated him, along with Danny Fields and others; Kronstad laid cold washcloths on his face to revive him for the late show. The Tots played with swagger, barreling through the songs with brawn but less nuance than the Velvets. Fans yelled repeatedly for "Heroin," and Reed eventually complied, to the crowd's delight. It was strange to hear people roaring lustily at lines about nullifying one's life, clapping in time to Reed's description of blood shooting up the neck of a homemade hypodermic. When Reed sang about the sailor in leather sucking his ding dong—from the same stage where the Julliard Quartet premiered Elliott Carter's String Quartet no. 3 earlier that week—he articulated his words with clear pleasure.

The tour was off to a good start. In Boston at the New England Conservatory's Jordan Hall, Reed received a hero's welcome from a dozen or so young men up front, who stripped off their shirts to display letters painted on their backs collectively spelling WE LOVE YOU LOU! As part of their promo campaign, RCA had Reed handwrite a concise version of his life story. It was an opportunity to sculpt the emerging persona of "Lou Reed," a savvy street urchin who bore a strong resemblance to Lewis Reed of Freeport, Long Island.

MY BIOGRAPHY

1. Played in Long Island hoodlum bands where there were fights
2. Attended many schools—always had bands i.e. Pasha and the Prophets; L.A. + The Eldorados

3. Expelled from R.O.T.C. for threatening to shoot officer
4. Rejected from Army—deemed mentally unfit
5. Worked as songwriter and met rejection
6. with Warhol and Velvet Underground through various permutations + helped create earlier "mixed media environment" also known in happy sixties as "psychedelic"
7. Left Warhol, realigned band + ultimately realigned self
8. EXILE + GREAT PONDERING
9. LAWSUITS + DEPRESSION
10. R.C.A., solo albums, satisfaction

[Signed] Lou Reed

The label was marketing Reed as the "Phantom of Rock," a sort of zombie-drag harlequin of decadence. On a radio ad, a baritone announcer rumbled: "In the midst of all the make-believe madness, the mock-depravity, and the pseudo-sexual anarchists, Lou Reed is the real thing." Just what sort of "real thing" was hard to pin down. Reed was continuing to fine-tune his persona in the press. In Warhol's newly launched *Interview* magazine, Reed discussed gay clubs in London, taking evident pride in being an ambassador for queer culture without identifying as queer per se. "I dig the gay people and the glitter people. I make up songs for 'em," he said. "I was doing that in '66, except that people were a lot more uptight then. They weren't into it. Now they are, so I drag them out of those dingy little clubs they go to, and I can get them into a concert hall where they can do any fucking thing they want, and the straight people are getting as off on it as anybody else. So it's great."

Reed was also rethinking the reputation he'd developed as a drug guru. In a 1970 interview for *Third Ear* magazine, he advocated on-stage sobriety ("There's nothing higher than actually playing . . . When you're wrecked, you play bad"), and told a writer for New York's *Metropolitan Review*, "I don't think drugs were very helpful to me . . . you don't have to take drugs to write. So I don't. I personally think drugs are shit." Speaking to Lester Bangs in 1971 for a requiem in the Detroit-based music fanzine *Creem* titled "Dead Lie the Velvets, Underground

R.I.P. Long Live Lou Reed," the singer pointed to the change in the group's music after *White Light/White Heat*. "People would come up and say 'I shot up to "Heroin,"' things like that. For a while, I was even thinking that some of my songs might have contributed formatively to the consciousness of all these addictions and things going down with the kids today. But I don't think that anymore; it's really too awful a thing to consider . . . All of a sudden we started looking out when we went on stage and seeing audiences full of stoned-out, violent people asking for those songs. We didn't want to appear to be supporting that . . ." He concluded, "Drugs are bad for Lou Reed," and with respect to his own self-care and spiritual development, informed by Alice Bailey's writing, his interest in reiki healing, and other routes toward mastering his mind and body, he told Bangs, "When you find that they don't really work very good, you move on to something else. Like I haven't got any answers but the same ones everybody else has: yoga, health foods, all of that."

He was, however, in a different place on March 9, 1973, at the Detroit Holiday Inn. He had a show that evening at the Ford Auditorium and was holding court with journalists, including Nick Kent from Britain's *NME* and Bangs, who, after meeting Reed briefly in 1969 at a Velvets show and interviewing him over the phone, was finally having face time with his hero.

The two had things in common. Bangs was raised in a burgeoning San Diego suburb not dissimilar to parts of Long Island, albeit in a devout Jehovah's Witness home. He chafed against religion and '50s suburban morality, and had family issues, too, among them an absent dad and a mom who would periodically destroy his comic book stashes, sure of their corrupting influence. Nevertheless, Bangs gorged on culture—jazz and film, sci-fi and the Stooges, seeing all as equally valid roads to a transcendence he did not find in the Witnesses. He became a cutting, potent, funny, voice-driven writer, channeling his skills through record reviews and pop music journalism in *Creem* and *Rolling Stone*. Like Reed, he had a weakness for speed and booze.

Given the pedestal Bangs had placed Reed and the Velvet Underground on, it was perhaps inevitable that he'd be crestfallen. The writer arrived early for his audience, sat down, and watched Reed from across the room.

> You become aware pretty fast that there's this vaguely unpleasant fat man sitting over there with a table full of people including his blond bride. Pretty soon he comes over to join you and the tic becomes focused too sharply for comfort. It's not just that Lou Reed doesn't look like a rock'n'roll star anymore. His face has a nursing-home pallor, and the fat girdles his sides. He drinks double Johnnie Walker Blacks all afternoon, his hands shake constantly and when he lifts his glass to drink he has to bend his head as though he couldn't possibly get it to his mouth otherwise. As he gets drunker, his left eyeball begins to slide out of sync.

Reed was evidently a mess. He was also performing a new role as solo artist, with a new persona, perhaps applying lessons Kronstad had shared from her acting classes and interview strategies he'd gleaned from Warhol. Reed began riffing—on alcohol and drugs ("I take drugs just because in the twentieth century in a technological age living in the city there are certain drugs you have to take just to keep yourself normal like a caveman"); on the glam-rock embrace of queer chic ("You can't fake being gay, because being gay means you're going to have to suck cock, or get fucked . . . The notion that everybody's bisexual is a very popular line right now, but I think its validity is limited") and cross-dressing ("Guys walking around in makeup is just fun. Why shouldn't men be able to put on makeup and have fun like women have?"); and on his unruly creativity ("I may come out with a hardhat album. Come out with an anti-gay song, saying 'Get back in your closets, you fuckin' queers!' That'll really do it!").

After the show, Bangs followed Reed back to the hotel, got drunk, and began baiting Reed, who rose to it.

"Doncha think David Bowie's a no-talent asshole?" Bangs goaded.

"No! He's a genius! He's brilliant!"

"Hey Lou, why doncha start shooting speed again? Then you could come up with something good!"

"I still do shoot it . . . My doctor gives it to me . . . Well, no actually they're just shots of meth mixed with vitamins . . ."

Bangs's gonzo-fanboy take on statue-toppling New Journalism, titled "Lou Reed: A Deaf Mute in a Telephone Booth," was right on time in a year that saw Hunter S. Thompson's *Fear and Loathing on the Campaign Trail '72* and the Woodward/Bernstein Watergate exposés. And while Reed was clearly winding Bangs up, his responses were not all fiction. The passage of the Comprehensive Drug Abuse Prevention and Control Act of 1970, which classified methamphetamine as a Schedule II controlled substance, made it more difficult for doctors to prescribe, but it was still legal. Among other sources, Reed availed himself of it through Dr. Robert Freymann, a speed missionary who regularly treated an A-list of celebrity patients to cocktail injections of meth and vitamin B_{12}. He was a celebrity himself; Paul McCartney once suggested the Beatles' "Dr. Robert" was in fact about him.

"There were countless mornings I found myself sitting, half-awake, on the concrete steps of Dr. Freymann's office," Kronstad recalled, "to get his famous injection of vitamins laced with amphetamine. Lou loved them more than any other drug he took."

* * *

Meanwhile, Reed was finally getting his wish for chart success. Months after its release, *Transformer* had finally entered the U.S. Top 40, propelled by "Walk on the Wild Side," which was climbing the *Billboard* Hot 100: it hit number 31 during the week ending March 30, number 28 the next week, then 24, peaking at 16 on April 28, where it held for two weeks. It did even better in the U.K., where it hit number 10 in May. Astonishingly, given its lyrics, it was green-lighted by radio programmers. "The simple answer is nobody noticed. He wasn't using one of the seven deadly words," says Dennis Elsas, music director for New York's progressive rock station WNEW-FM at the time, referring to censor red flags such as *fuck*, *shit*, and so on. "It didn't say 'stick a needle in your arm.' The kind of people who would complain about the 'giving head' line probably didn't know what it meant. The 'God damn' in the Grateful Dead's 'Uncle John's Band' caused us more trouble. But we aired that, too."

In late March, at the Century Theater in Buffalo, success bit Reed in the ass—literally, when a deranged fan jumped onstage and sank his teeth into his butt, hollering "Leather!" Reed's custom trousers were undamaged, and he laughed about it later, savoring the publicity. But it was creepy, and it shook him up. Back in New York City, he fretted over how the real-life subjects of "Walk on the Wild Side," none of whom he knew especially well, would take to his pop song profiles of them. "I thought they were going to claw my eyes out when I got back to New York," Reed said, "but Candy Darling came up to me and said she'd memorized all the [Transformer] songs, and that she wanted to make a 'Candy Darling sings Lou Reed' album. That would be great." Woodlawn was also delighted. "Honestly, I'd never met [Lou]," she says, "but I was a fan of his music. A friend called me up one night and said, 'Holly! Turn on the radio! There's a song about you!' So I turned it on, and the commercial ended, and the DJ announced he was now going to play the new Lou Reed song. And there it was: 'doot-doo-doot-doot-doo-doot." While Darling never made her LP, Woodlawn used the song to springboard a cabaret act, which Reed caught more than once, slipping in and out through the kitchen of the Thirteenth Street cabaret Reno Sweeney's to avoid stealing her spotlight. "He'd sit discreetly in the back," Woodlawn says. "I'd promised him I wouldn't say 'And let me welcome Lou Reed!'"

* * *

On a day off after a show in Toronto, with thoughts of his next LP, Reed met with the Canadian producer Bob Ezrin, who'd produced Mitch Ryder's semi-hit version of Reed's "Rock & Roll," and grew his Midas reputation via another Detroit act, Alice Cooper. Working similar ground to Reed, Bowie, and his fellow Michigander Iggy Pop, Alice Cooper had been serving up hard rock in silver jump suits, straitjackets, and fright-mask makeup, with lyrics designed to shock parents, in concerts enhanced by fake electric chairs, guillotines, gallows, and a live boa constrictor. It was shamelessly calculated, and way more commercially successful than the music of their glammy peers. Bowie caught Alice Cooper's show at London's Rainbow Theatre a day or two before recording began on *Ziggy Stardust* in late '71, and maybe learned a trick or two. In '72, Alice Cooper's *School's Out* sold a million copies; *Billion Dollar Babies*, released in February, would top the U.S. charts by spring.

Reed wanted some of this Detroit hard-rock butch-glam chart magic, but on his own terms, and Ezrin understood his fear of being reduced to a puddle-deep pop star. "I expressed my interest in Lou as a poet, and Lou as an artist," Ezrin recalled. Reed and Kronstad wound up spending a couple of days with Ezrin and his family. Reed confessed to Ezrin he'd hit a wall with his writing. "The problem was he didn't know how to follow *Transformer* . . . the direction of [it] hadn't been his in the first place," said Kronstad, referring to Bowie's role.

Ezrin, twenty-four, brainstormed with Reed, and pushed him to do a character-driven project, figuring it would play to his writing strengths. He considered Reed's back catalog, and was curious about the couple in the song "Berlin." What was their story?

The mythic decadence of Weimar-era Berlin was resonant in 1973. Alongside the withering of the libertine 1960s, the U.S. economy had ended its halcyon years. And Christopher Isherwood's semi-autobiographical 1939 novel *Goodbye to Berlin*, about the end of Weimar gay culture, had experienced a revival post-Stonewall thanks to the musical *Cabaret*, which was based on it. The stage production starring Judy Dench impressed Bowie deeply when he saw it in London in 1968, and Bob Fosse's 1972 film version, with Michael York as Isherwood's queer alter ego and Joel Grey as the nightclub emcee, was a monster hit worldwide, controversy and X ratings notwithstanding. Two weeks before Reed and Ezrin's meeting, in fact, it swept the Academy Awards, taking home eight.

Reed and Ezrin decided "it would be really great to create the soundtrack to a non-existent movie where all of the elements within the film were contained in the album." Reed told Ezrin to "give me a month," and he'd be back in Toronto with songs. A few days later, he fired the Tots. The disappointed young men smoked hash in their hotel room with Ezrin after their final show, in Santa Monica on April 20. They were bummed out, but figured they'd had a pretty good run.

That weekend, Reed had a rangy conversation with the veteran DJ Martin Perlich on his signature *Electric Tongue* show at KMET, a progressive radio station in Los Angeles. Reed spoke about fame's wages and their effects ("My relationships to people have changed . . . people want money and favors . . . [but] I've just cut those people out of my life"), and shouted out the Gay Activist Alliance, the civil rights group that pushed Mayor John Lindsay of New York to sign an executive order in 1972 to prohibit discrimination based on sexual orientation. Perlich asked him if he was a kind of "court composer" for the gay community. "Court composer? No. You just write a song," Reed said, snorting. Explaining and defending *Transformer*, and dodging implied questions regarding his own sexuality, had become a part of his job. "I don't think [*Transformer* is] a decadent album," he told Nick Kent. "Singing about hustlers and gay people isn't decadent, is it?"

* * *

Not everyone agreed. On June 2, Reed did a concert at Miami Beach Auditorium, a medium-sized theater-cum-soundstage that had hosted *The Jackie Gleason Show* until it was canceled in 1970. Thanks to his transgressive radio hit, the gig was flagged by local police, and by the time he was detailing the story of Sister Ray with his newly assembled band, a phalanx of cops was in the house, some in riot gear. Accounts vary. The most amusing has Reed singing the line about the police knocking on his chamber door, and then, for emphasis, rapping his microphone against the helmet of a cop standing in front of the stage. When the song ended and Reed walked offstage, he was handcuffed and taken away, in makeup and black leather.

Kronstad feared he'd be roughed up. But Reed was polite and cooperative, albeit amused; for their part, the police processed him quickly and without incident—he was out within an hour, with help from his lawyer-manager. The court summons charged Reed with performing "in an 'obscene' manner by using obscene language and making obscene gestures while entertaining the public at Miami Beach Auditorium."

For Barbara Fulk, a former employee of Dennis Katz's at RCA who'd just been hired as Reed's road manager and caretaker, the night was quite an induction. She's convinced he got himself busted on purpose, figuring the publicity would be worth it. "Lou had this whole notion of how Jim Morrison got arrested in Miami," she recalls, referring to the 1969 incident when the late singer supposedly pulled out his cock onstage. "I think he pushed it [with the cops] until they arrested him, too." Afterward, everyone had a good laugh about it, and the entourage went out to dinner and a late-night drag cabaret to celebrate.

It was also an induction for his new sidemen, hired on the fly to replace the Tots. The band was led by Reed's fellow Long Islander Mark "Moogy" Klingman, a jazz-schooled keyboardist and studio wiz who'd worked with Todd Rundgren. He had a taste for New Orleans grooves, which he grafted into performances of "White Light/White Heat" and "Make Up," the latter becoming a Mardi-Gras strut, while "Heroin" became an R&B slow jam. Reed had wanted to up his game musically, but it wasn't a great fit. At a show in Norfolk, Virginia, Reed berated the band during an extended "Sister Ray" jam that descended into jazz-funk noodling. "Can't you do it any louder than that? C'mon!" he barked. "I can't keep the beat if I can't hear it!"

Riding the biggest success of his career, with less than a month to write a follow-up, and struggling with a new road band, Reed was drinking heavily on the tour. One night, following a particularly serious postshow bender, Kronstad had to steer him back to their hotel room, where he inexplicably turned around, hit her, then fell backward onto the bed, laughing. Furious, Kronstad jumped on him, slapping him repeatedly. The next day, they both had black eyes. The physical abusiveness echoed what Allan Hyman witnessed between Reed and a girlfriend in high school. It also cast the violence in certain lyrics, especially the Velvets' "There She Goes Again" and *Transformer*'s "Wagon Wheel" ("just kick her in the head"), in a new light.

* * *

Home in New York, Reed's promise to deliver Ezrin a concept record based on the song "Berlin" had come due. According to Kronstad, he was suffering from severe writer's block that, alongside the hotel incident, had him shaken. So Reed sat down in his writing chair with his notebook and a bottle of Johnnie Walker Black. The next morning, Kronstad found him in the chair, still awake, with a near-empty bottle.

"I wrote the album," Reed said, tossing his notebook across the room for her to catch.

The story Reed conjured was a tragedy based around a couple: Caroline, a drug-taking "Germanic Queen" who sleeps around with assorted characters (one of them "a Welshman"), and her partner, Jim, an abusive speed freak who would stay up "for five days" at a time, makes love "by proxy," and evidently beats her "black and blue." She loses her children, and in the end, she kills herself, slitting her wrists on the bed the couple once shared.

Reed had never actually been to Berlin. But he'd been wowed by Berg's *Wozzeck* in Syracuse, and was likely familiar with Alfred Döblin's *Berlin Alexanderplatz*, Isherwood's *Goodbye to Berlin*, and *Cabaret*—all works that churned with violence, substance abuse, and sexual transgression. To be sure, there was memoir in Reed's finished verses—glints of Nico in the character of Caroline ("my Germanic Queen"), and of Cale in "the Welshman" from "The Kids." And in particular, the story seemed to hold a mirror up to Reed's and Kronstad's lives, reflected in Jim's physical abusiveness and Caroline's family drama. By Kronstad's measure, Reed "used a lot of the information that he knew about my mother and my father" in the Berlin narrative, alongside "what was happening with us, and a little bit of Nico thrown in."

Kronstad was not pleased. She made Reed coffee as he played her the songs he'd just written from his reclining chair in their living room, with the high ceiling and the parquet floors. He cradled his guitar, shaped chords, sang "black and blue." When he finished, she felt gutted. She went into their bedroom and closed the door, wanting to be alone. Reed begged her to please understand his creative process. But it was a big ask.

* * *

A week later, after discovering Reed injecting drugs, Kronstad reached her limit, and demanded a divorce. Not wanting to involve her family, she allowed Reed's legal team to arrange a flight to the Dominican Republic, where she checked into a hotel, and a day later had secured legally binding divorce papers, albeit in Spanish. She was home that night. They'd been married less than a year.

The next evening, Reed phoned, and a day later, came to the apartment with roses, wine, and take-out from a favorite restaurant. He pleaded his case, made an impression, and before the month was out, the couple were both on a plane to London for the *Berlin* sessions. The divorce would stand, Kronstad was certain. But she also thought her ex-husband had made a great work of art, and that it was her duty to help him see it through.

* * *

The *Berlin* sessions were a rough ride, though everyone went in style: between *Transformer*'s success and Ezrin's hit-making cred, Reed convinced RCA to fund an elaborate production at Morgan Studios, one of England's most prestigious facilities, home to a cutting-edge twenty-four-track recorder. Reed and Ezrin assembled an all-star team: the ex-Cream bassist Jack Bruce, Traffic keyboardist Steve Winwood, drummer Aynsley Dunbar (a vet of Zappa's Mothers of Invention), and a pair of Detroit guitarists, Steve Hunter and Dick Wagner, whose hot-shit style had branded Alice Cooper's *Billion Dollar Babies*.

Reed was envisioning *Berlin* as a "rock opera," determined to be seen as an auteur, while Ezrin was hoping for his George Martin–*Sgt. Pepper's* moment as a producer. Ezrin enlisted horn players, convened a choir, deployed synthesizers and a mellotron. It was in step with the times; prog rock was in full flower. In fact, Reed's former sidemen Steve Howe and Rick Wakeman were working with Yes on *Tales from Topographic Oceans*, a high-concept double LP, at Morgan around the same time, decorating the studio with hay, shrubbery, and farm animal cutouts for ambience. Reed's studio vibe was decidedly less pastoral. Yet he, too, was envisioning an elaborate double LP, with gatefold sleeve, illustrated booklet, and lyrics. Reed also believed *Berlin* would be staged, possibly on Broadway; one idea involved him as narrator, standing under a streetlight outside Jim and Caroline's house.

There were plenty of stimulants and partying, and sessions ran around the clock. According to the photographer Mick Rock, Reed stayed awake for days at a time. Worried about his client, Dennis Katz, who in addition to being Reed's lawyer had recently become his manager as well, replacing Fred Heller, encouraged Kronstad to stay close to Reed, though she was having a rough time herself. Mostly, she kept to her hotel room, watching Wimbledon tennis, staying out of the line of fire.

There was extracurricular revelry, too. On July 4, following his farewell show as the bisexual alien rock star Ziggy Stardust, Bowie threw a star-studded "retirement" party at the Café Royal on Regent Street, and Reed was there. An artfully framed shot by Mick Rock showed the pair leaning in as if kissing, though they were probably just trying to hear each other over the din. But that didn't stop the press from captioning the photo suggestively. And of course, there was no "retirement" for Bowie—before the month was out, he'd be in France recording songs, "White Light/White Heat" among them, for a covers LP.

Bowie was among the parade of visitors in the studio; Ezrin recalled being unnerved at having Bowie watch him while he worked. Ezrin described the *Berlin* sessions as drug-addled and emotionally torturous. "We were in London, it was rainy and dark," he said. "There were a lot of tensions in the room, between Lou and other musicians; not so much between Lou and me, as between Lou and life." Nevertheless, there were moments of thrillingly dark invention. The most indelible was the shrieking children in "The Kids"—they were Ezrin's, recorded by him at home with a Nagra portable. The desperate shouts of "Mommy" were his five-year-old, following his dad's direction; the mournful crying was Ezrin's one-and-a-half-year-old after being told it was bedtime.

Ezrin thought the finished album was "genius." But it took its toll on him; by the time *Berlin* was mastered, he was in the hospital. "It was a heroin rebound . . . I didn't know what heroin was till I went to England on this gig," the producer recalled. "We were all seriously ill." Reed, meanwhile, turned the session's dramas into part of the album's myth, telling a journalist that Kronstad attempted suicide in the hotel bathtub during the sessions, though she denies it.

In the end, no one at RCA was clamoring to bankroll a *Berlin* musical, and the idea was shelved, along with the double-LP concept. Songs were shortened, instrumental outros cut, and the proposed playbill insert scrapped. RCA translated Reed's "film for the ears" ideas tepidly in art-house-cinema-style promo posters: in one, he cradled his hollow-body guitar like a rock Fellini, as a nude, androgynous couple embraced amid faux-movie stills.

* * *

In the run-up to the album release, Reed rehearsed a new road band, fortunately securing the services of Hunter and Wagner. Reed and his team set up camp a few hours north of New York City in the Berkshire Mountains at the Music Inn, a sort of counterculture version of Tanglewood, the famed classical music center nearby that had brought John Cale to the States a decade earlier. Begun in the 1950s, the inn housed the Lenox School of Jazz, whose alumni included Ornette Coleman, and hosted shows at the adjacent Berkshire Music Barn. In August 1963, Joan Baez and Bob Dylan played there, while Cale worked with Aaron Copland just down the road; by 1973, the Music Inn was a full-service hippie retreat, an outdoor concert venue and hotel with a movie theater, two bars, a restaurant, and a head shop.

On September 1, Reed's new band made its debut on the inn's outdoor stage, opening with a majestic five-minute guitar jam cooked up by Hunter, Wagner, and Reed in rehearsals—an exploded version of the teasing fifteen-second intro to "Sweet Jane" on *Loaded*. By some measures, Reed's biggest success the previous year had been a hard-rock cover of "Sweet Jane" by Mott the Hoople, from their David Bowie–produced album *All the Young Dudes*, which had reached number 21 on the British charts and cracked the U.S. Top 100. Reed's new arrangement nodded to it, and when Hunter's solo finally resolved into the song's signature riff, the crowd howled with pleasure.

The following week, the band began the Rock 'n' Roll Animal Tour, which lived up to its name. Reed largely ceded guitar duties to his new wingmen, whose arena-scaled virtuosity fit his new drawing power. He played to fifty thousand at the Scheessel Festival in Germany, sharing the bill with Chuck Berry and Jerry Lee Lewis, childhood heroes Reed was thrilled to meet. He played to maybe thousands more at the Crystal Palace Bowl Celebration Garden Party in Bromley, London, set in a ruined Victorian pleasure garden, with an outdoor stage bizarrely separated from the crowd by a large, stagnant pool. Reed performed a daytime set woozily in black leather and whiteface, crouched near the lip of the stage, surrounded by shirtless hippies standing in waist-deep water. Though the band was sharp, Reed seemed a mess. Freed from playing guitar, he could take the stage as wasted as he dared, and it likely didn't help matters that his ex-wife was his companion and caretaker. According to Kronstad, Reed added heroin to his diet of scotch and cocaine. It was as if, in advance of the album drop, he was determined to stage *Berlin* as a reality show.

The drama peaked in Paris on September 17. Nico, never a stabilizing presence, came to see Reed perform, and there were plenty of drugs. By Kronstad's account, Reed threw a drunken tantrum preshow, accusing her of depleting the coke stash. She tossed a glass of milk in his face and stormed out of their hotel room. The next day, she was on a flight home to New York, and never spoke to him again.

That night in Paris, Reed took the stage hours late, and appeared shaken in his death mask makeup and head-to-toe black leather. He fumbled lyrics and dropped the microphone. During "Walk on the

Wild Side," he crouched on the stage, stroking the mic between his legs; during "Heroin," he collapsed, as if he'd injected himself with a hot shot. Tightroping between performative and lived debauchery, Reed got through the show, which was enthusiastically received. As always, poetically self-destructive artists were in season; that spring, press photos circulated of the singer-songwriter and beloved rake Serge Gainsbourg smoking Gauloises in his hospital bed after a heart attack. The writer Lisa Robinson quipped that Reed's French fans "would've been even happier if he had come onstage with a needle sticking out of his arm."

The next day, Reed continued on to Amsterdam, where he visited the Anne Frank House, did a show, then partied hard with an old friend. He was still in rough shape the next night in Brussels. According to an assistant, he had a severe reaction to some speed, and, unwisely, took more before his show began. Midway through, he split his leather pants; one of the crew dashed out with gaffer tape to strap his balls back in. Reed tried to continue but was too fucked up, and bolted from the stage.

Panicking, with his heart punching against his ribs and his musculature seized up, Reed could not calm himself. There was no way he was going back onstage. With Kronstad gone, a bodyguard barricaded the dressing room and talked Reed down. The crowd, meanwhile, outraged by the thirty-minute set, began tearing up the seats. Reed refused to come out of his dressing room, or let anyone in, and he stayed there until it seemed safe to leave and return to the hotel.

After that night, Reed promised to cool it with the drugs and booze, and largely kept his word. The shows raged, as did the crowds. His fans, a new generation of young glam rockers and heavy metal kids, were intense. They mobbed him after a show at the Empire Theatre in Liverpool, and his driver somehow managed to navigate down a flight of stairs to escape the venue area. In Glasgow, after a show capped by a high-torque "Sister Ray," a pumped-up mob nearly rolled the bus.

The European tour ended in London at the Rainbow on October 10. Reed had invited the Persuasions, the virtuosic R&B vocal group, to open most of the U.K. shows because he adored their harmony singing. But he was caught up in his own affairs, and he mostly ignored them. "He's a strange cat," the group's Sweet Joe Russell told a journalist.

* * *

Having changed his fortunes by performing rock 'n' roll decadence, Reed hoped the release of *Berlin* that month would establish him as a serious artist. However, it was not universally heralded as the work of a great dramatic poet. Reviews were mixed, though, as is often the case, the harshest would be more memorable. In *Rolling Stone*, Stephen Davis placed it among "certain records that are so patently offensive that one wishes to take some kind of physical vengeance on the artists that perpetrate them" and dismissed it with a curt "Goodbye, Lou." The New York City critic and Velvet Underground fan Robert Christgau, writing in his "Consumer Guide" in *Creem*, graded the album a C, calling *Berlin*'s story "lousy" and its creator "washed-out."

Yet others praised the album and Reed's ambition. John Rockwell called *Berlin* "one of the strongest, most original rock records in years" in *The New York Times*. In *The Village Voice*, W. M. Gurvitch called it "a concept album of the highest order." In the December *Creem*, offering counterpoint to Christgau's harsh grade, Lester Bangs called it "the most disgusting brilliant album of the year . . . the bastard progeny of a drunken flaccid tumble between Tennessee Williams and Hubert . . . Selby Jr," also noting, with apparent admiration, that it was "very funny." *Berlin* would also end up on numerous best-of-the-year lists, including that of the *Los Angeles Times*, whose Robert Hilburn ranked it alongside Bowie's similarly madness-shadowed *Aladdin Sane*, the Allman Brothers' *Eat a Peach*, and Paul Simon's *There Goes Rhymin' Simon*.

Still, with no hits, minimal to nonexistent radio play, and weak sales, the takeaway for Reed would be the negative criticism, and he took it hard—which made his achievement on December 21 all the more remarkable. On a bitterly cold night, with recent reviews ringing in his ears, Reed played what might've been the most significant gigs of his professional life, at the Academy of Music on Fourteenth Street in New York City. The money wasn't great: his contract guaranteed him $5,000 for the early show, plus 50 percent of gross after $17,300, and a straight 50 percent for the late show. At five or six dollars, tickets sold well enough: 2,900 of 3,396 seats for the early show, 879 for the late, with a $21,885 total gross. But far more important, the shows were being recorded for a live album. Reed was focused and on point, super-sizing Velvets songs and hard-selling new ones, while the band killed it, Wagner and Hunter's outrageous dual leads—in unison, trading phrases, harmonizing—making a case for them as the greatest hard-rock guitar team in the business. "Sometimes you get into this zone, where it's like you're onstage listening to yourself play," Hunter said of playing with Wagner. "It's a wonderful feeling. And I don't think you can do that in other forms of soloing. I think it has to be that kind of melodic improv." Aside from a malfunctioning audience mic (crowd noise would be dubbed in for the live album using massed cheers from a John Denver concert recording), everything went beautifully.

Reed unveiled a startling new look onstage: hair shaved into a se-vere, ultra-short pixie cut (Ed McCormack called it his "Jean Genet prisoner haircut"), with studded leather wristbands, a BDSM-style dog collar, and an eagle-head belt buckle, gear he'd picked up the previous week at the Pleasure Chest, the pioneering West Village sex toy shop on Seventh Avenue. His look was uncut gay leather bar. But to most straight rock fans it simply read as post-glam hypermachismo.

Offstage, Reed was in full-on bad-boy mode. Duncan Hannah, a twenty-year-old artist so gorgeous he set everyone he met swooning, recalled being drunkenly cruised at Max's by Reed around this time, though it wasn't 100 percent clear if "the avatar of decadence and per-version" was really trying to hook up or just to freak him out when he invited Hannah to join him in a hotel room and "be my little David Cas-sidy," referring to the twinky pop star who'd recently posed naked on the cover of *Rolling Stone*. When Hannah declined, Reed whispered in his ear: "You can shit in my mouth. Would you like that?" (Unsurpris-ingly, the answer was no.)

Ending the year with a bang, Reed was busted on Christmas Eve in Riverhead, Long Island, for trying to pass a fake amphetamine script.

His assistant Barbara Fulk came to bail him out in the only rental she could secure on short notice: a white stretch limo with a horn that played "Here Comes the Bride." Slumped in the back as they cruised back toward the New York City skyline, Reed had plenty to think about. He'd been arrested twice in 1973. His wife had left him, twice. And despite the praise for *Berlin*, the most ambitious writing project he'd ever attempted was shaping up to be a failure. And yet playing the role of a debauched rock star caricature, it seemed he was becoming more popular than ever.

On Christmas Day, his parents likely read the belated review of the Academy of Music show in the Long Island *Newsday* by Dave Marsh, who disparaged Reed's haircut while suggesting his onstage performance was "much more successful" than *Berlin*, and declaring him "one of the most interesting . . . has-been, would-be, never-was geniuses in rock."

* * *

Speaking with Steven Gaines, a writer for the New York *Daily News*, Reed sipped a double tequila. His skin was pale, near-white, his hair freshly dyed black. His fingers were tipped in nail polish—Biba black was his favorite—and they trembled when he lit a cigarette. He was distancing himself from *Berlin*.

"I can't listen to it anymore. It makes me too taut, too nervous," he said. "If people don't like [it], it's because it's too real. It's not like a TV program where all the bad things that happen to people are tolerable. Life isn't that way, and neither is the album." He also copped to an element of memoir in it. "Part of it happened, or it happened to a lesser degree. There was a girl like the girl in the album, but she was right here in New York," Reed said. "And she didn't have any kids, but she almost did kill herself."

Still, Reed could not let go of his hopes for staging *Berlin*. He may have felt competition with Bowie, who was working on "Hunger City," a film-cum-stage project riffing on the future dystopias of *1984* and *A Clockwork Orange*. In any case, Reed knew Warhol was nurturing interest in producing a musical, possibly with Reed's involvement, as far back as *The Chelsea Girls*, for which Reed's belated song "Chelsea Girls" might've served as set piece. In 1972, as *Transformer* was taking off, Warhol was talking about a musical with a working title of "Vicious." In January, around the time the *Daily News* story ran, Reed sat down with Warhol and some associates for dinner at Reno Sweeney's to discuss the notion of Warhol producing a Broadway musical version of *Berlin*, along the lines of *The Threepenny Opera*. "I want *you*, Andy, *your* ideas—not Paul's or Brigid's," Reed told Warhol, in hopes that he might invest himself personally in the project, rather than farming it out to Morrissey or Berlin. Warhol was evidently open to the idea, which may in fact have been initiated by him; he floated ideas for investors, they ball-parked costs, Reed talked about staging the show with an elaborate sound system. Afterward, Reed took Warhol to the Ninth Circle, a West Village gay bar where Reed claimed "all the young beauties are," to give his friend a feel for the characters who inspired the songs, and maybe to cruise, too, Reed comfortably code-switching with successful queer friends. He met with Warhol at least twice more over the next few months, according to Warhol's records, but for whatever reasons, nothing came of the plan. Warhol wouldn't abandon the idea of producing a musical, however: his collaboration with John Phillips of the Mamas and the Papas, *Man on the Moon*, would be in previews by December, closing two days after *The New York Times*'s Clive Barnes described it as "the kind of show that can leave a strong man a little numb and a little dumb," adding, "for connoisseurs of the truly bad, *Man on the Moon* may be a small milestone."

* * *

Despite its underwhelming sales, at least by *Transformer*'s yardstick, *Berlin* had been well-timed in a banner year for prog-rock concept LPs, the most prominent being Pink Floyd's *Dark Side of the Moon*. Reed's *Rock 'n' Roll Animal*, rush-released in February 1974, was also ahead of the curve for rock's next boomlet, the live album. Dylan (*Before the Flood*), Bowie (*David Live*), Van Morrison (*It's Too Late to Stop Now*), and

Joni Mitchell (*Miles of Aisles*) all issued remarkable ones that year. Even John Cale and Nico joined the scrum on the LP *June 1, 1974*, from a concert with Brian Eno and Kevin Ayers informed by the Reed-Cale-Nico reunion at the Bataclan. (The Eno-Ayers-Cale-Nico project verged on a Velvet Underground reunion when the participation of Morrison and Tucker was proposed, though, for various reasons, it never panned out).

Initially planned as a double LP, but ultimately scaled back to a single, perhaps due to label cold feet post-*Berlin*, *Rock 'n' Roll Animal* was a slow-burning success that would spend twenty-eight weeks on the Billboard album charts. Free-form FM rock radio, an ascendent market force, gave it heavy airplay, especially the magnificent hard-rock overhaul of "Sweet Jane," and a savage thirteen-minute version of "Heroin." The cover was a near-facsimile of *Transformer*'s iconic goth-androgyne onstage portrait—a blurred, high-contrast shot of a bare-armed Reed in dark lipstick and eye shadow, the stage lights glistening on his studded wrist restraints and dog collar. Opening the album's gatefold sleeve revealed a BDSM update of Warhol's banana that echoed *Transformer*'s back cover photo—an evident close-up of Reed's crotch bulging beneath his black leather jean zipper and eagle-head belt buckle. If the dazzling intro to "Sweet Jane" would inspire a generation of heavy metal guitarists, and its disturbingly magnificent "Heroin" a generation of curious drug users, its hot-switch sleeve art would, like *Transformer*'s genderfluid fantasia, speak to a generation of horny teens, queer and otherwise. And if there was any lingering question as to which version of Reed would find more commercial success—the "dramatic poet" of *Berlin*, or the id monster he was performing live, *Rock 'n' Roll Animal* laid it to rest. But it was notable, and perhaps not incidental, that, except for the brief take on *Berlin*'s "Lady Day," the entire *Rock 'n' Roll Animal* album was Velvet Underground songs.

8.

UPPER EAST SIDE > WEST VILLAGE

(1974–1979)

DISCUSSED: The cult of the Velvets, Rachel Humphreys, *Sally Can't Dance*, a press conference in Sydney, *Metal Machine Music*, financial troubles, *Looking for Mr. Goodbar*, *Querelle*, *Dog Day Afternoon*, "FORD TO CITY: DROP DEAD," drug injecting (real and staged), *Frankenstein*, *Punk* magazine, the Ramones, Talking Heads, *Coney Island Baby*, Clive Davis, the bicentennial, *Rock and Roll Heart*, Peter Laughner, the Mineshaft, Sylvia Morales, *Street Hassle*, *Live: Take No Prisoners*, *The Bells*, belting Bowie, bottoming out

---

And maybe . . . some kid is borrowing his parents' car and driving into the city and doing things he'd never done before and getting home later than he's supposed to and getting into trouble, but it's all right because he knows he'll never be the same again. (That's what this album is about.)
—Elliot Murphy, liner notes to *1969: The Velvet Underground Live with Lou Reed*

I n early 1973, a Doug Yule solo project titled *Squeeze* was released in Europe as a Velvet Underground album. Tucker, Morrison, Cale, and Reed had no involvement in the LP; it was mostly ignored, and Yule soon ceased trading on the name. But a year later, in 1974, an album titled *1969: Velvet Underground Live with Lou Reed* marked the rebirth of the increasingly mythic band in abstentia. Sourced from recordings of the band's potent latter-day shows in Texas and San Francisco, the bootleg-reclamation project was shepherded by Paul Nelson, a Minnesotan who'd written for *Rolling Stone*, landed a job at Mercury Records, and insisted that the label, whose parent company controlled most of the Velvets' catalog, release the tapes as a double LP.

It did, in a budget package with a chintzy illustration of an ass peeking out from a miniskirt, panties pulled snugly into the crack (on some pressings, a label discreetly obscured the butt). The selections were outstanding: A bluesy "I'm Waiting for the Man," prototypes of "New Age" (with its original bisexual ménage à trois) and "Sweet Jane" (with alternate lyrics and the "heavenly wine and roses" bridge, supposedly performed the day Reed wrote it). The rousing "We're Gonna Have a Real Good Time Together" and the melancholic "Over You" were among the backlog of Velvets songs that had never been released. Maybe most surprising of all, for those who'd missed seeing the Velvets, was Reed's funny, intimate stage banter, as if from an entirely different person from the *Rock 'n' Roll Animal* character he was currently performing.

Elliott Murphy, a Long Island singer-songwriter who'd just released his debut LP, was assisting Nelson with song selection, and penned liner notes that would become the bedrock document of the growing cult of the Velvets. They began: "It's one hundred years from today, and everyone who is reading this is dead. I'm dead. You're dead. And some kid is taking a music course in junior high, and maybe he's listening to the Velvet Underground because he's got to write a report on classical rock and roll and I wonder what that kid is thinking."

1969: The Velvet Underground Live was received with reverence and reverie. Chrissie Hynde, a young American expat living in London and writing for the *NME*, rhapsodized about how the set "takes me right back to the teenage years of my virginal innocence; the evening I spent in some dingy hall, eyes fixed on the cat in the striped T-shirt and wraparound shades, those songs made my eyes water like I was chewing on a wad of aluminium foil, me hoping I could score some dope after the show; me wishing I could be like them." Patti Smith riffed in *Creem*: "I love this record so much . . . Dig it submit put your hands down your pants and play side C . . . the head cracks like intellectual egg spewing liquid gold . . . Lou is so elegantly restrained. It nearly drives me crazy." She also noted, memorably, "a chord so direct it eel fucks you in the heart."

Yet much of the praise for *1969* was backhanded. Dave Marsh's *Rolling Stone* review stressed how superior the Velvets' work was to Reed's current music. Robert Christgau declared it "a more impressive testimonial to Reed than any of his solo LPs," while a reviewer in *Phonograph Record* determined that it rendered *Rock 'n' Roll Animal* "pointless." That was certainly not true from a sales perspective—*Rock 'n' Roll Animal* became Reed's first gold record, then likely besting the entire Velvets catalog combined. But it was thus that Reed found himself at the crossroads of an aesthetic battle between mass-market, big-money rock and the scrappier approach the Velvets epitomized.

The latter would seed a new generation of musicians in New York City. Smith had already begun conceiving of her poetry as songs during a residency at Reno Sweeney's in April, opening for Holly Woodlawn; by summer, she'd have a residency at Max's, like the Velvets had four years prior, and a debut single. Smith's fashion sense was androgynous—she often wore a man's vest, like the heroine of "Sweet Jane"—and she'd regularly cover Velvets songs.

Patti Smith would prove the iceberg tip in an aesthetic sea change and back-to-basics revival that epitomized the same rock 'n' roll battle Reed was internalizing. Along with the Velvets' 1969 set, one of Paul Nelson's first Mercury signings was the New York Dolls. Their music was in some ways the ramshackle hard-rock opposite of Reed's virtuosic new band. But that was central to the Dolls' charm: it seemed like something anyone could do, provided they had the balls to get up onstage in platforms and a blouse and yowl about being a Frankenstein. Aspiring musicians and critics loved them, but professionally, they were a train wreck. Their drummer Billy Murcia died after combining alcohol and pills during an otherwise career-making trip to England in '72, before they'd even recorded their debut LP, *New York Dolls*, a thrilling set that barely sold. But they were the toast of a growing downtown music scene begun at the crumbling Mercer Arts Center that, after the building literally collapsed in '73, shifted to a new venue on the Bowery called CBGB.

Insofar as he noticed the new New York rock scene, involved as he was with his own career, Reed seemed dismissive of it. His peers, though, were taking notes and connecting the dots. In early '74, David Bowie sat for a Q&A with William S. Burroughs hosted by *Rolling Stone*. After years of living abroad, Burroughs had just returned to New York City to teach creative writing at City College at the invitation of his old friend Allen Ginsberg. Bowie talks about the vitality of the new New York rock scene, of which he basically annoints Reed the father, calling him "the most important, definitive writer in modern rock."

"The movement that Lou's stuff has created is amazing," he tells Burroughs. "New York City is Lou Reed."

* * *

And no kinds of love
are better than others
   —"Some Kinda Love," the Velvet Underground

On March 21, 1974, Candy Darling died of lymphoma, possibly a result of the transitioning hormones she'd been taking. She was twenty-nine. During her last months, friends came by Cabrini Hospital on East Nineteenth Street—a short walk from Max's—to say goodbye. There's no record of Reed visiting her. She was a muse to him, but the two had never been close. Holly Woodlawn and Jackie Curtis did visit. The trio shared some laughs, perhaps recalling the photo shoot they all did for *Vogue* in '72, or singing bits of "Walk on the Wild Side." Woodlawn and Curtis tried to hustle the nurse for free food, and swiped some of Darling's expensive makeup, just like the old days.

Before she died, she posed for her photographer friend Peter Hujar in a faintly macabre twist on a Hollywood glamour shot, reclining languorously on her hospital bed amid her get-well bouquets, perfectly made up. In her final days, a friend recalled her half-paralyzed, with a ghost of a mustache and her hair gone from chemo, taking bouillon from a syringe held by her mom, like a baby bird.

After Darling's death, her boyfriend, Jeremiah Newton, visited her mother, who invited him to go through Candy's belongings and take what he could carry. (Darling's mother promised to forward some remaining items to him, but according to Newton, she wound up burning them, afraid her homosexual-hating new husband would find them.) Newton took home Candy's ashes. The body she might indeed have hated for all the things it required, as Reed sang, now required nothing. In her diary, she'd insisted: "You must always be yourself, no matter what the price. It is the highest form of morality."

* * *

Back in New York and on the rebound after his final split with Kronstad, Reed moved in with Barbara Hodes, a clothing designer and Factory-scene satellite he'd met in the Velvet Underground days. He settled into her nicely appointed apartment at 45 Fifth Avenue—just off Eleventh Street, four blocks from the Washington Square Park arch—with a few personal items, shelving his inscribed Delmore Schwartz volumes and first-edition Raymond Chandlers alongside Hodes's art books and international copies of *Vogue*. The relationship was romantic—Reed even took her to meet his parents—but never quite took off. Reed bought her a garter snake for Valentine's Day, which they named Edgar Allan Snake and which he, in a pattern he'd established with his pets, rarely took care of; friends would have to come by and feed it goldfish when they were away. When Reed and Hodes were up late, he'd take her to his beloved Bickford's Coffee Shop, on the northeast corner of Seventh Avenue and Fourteenth Street, a former Beat hangout name-checked by Allen Ginsberg in "Howl," commemorating his generation's best minds roaring on benzedrine and sunk in the restaurant's "submarine light."

They were up late a lot. Reed had acquired an extended family of drug buddies, and as his amphetamine use escalated, he began sourcing it from sketchy suppliers. He lost a startling amount of weight, going from plump to drawn and gaunt, and played with his physical presentation in other ways. He got symmetrical crosses bleached into his dark monk's tonsure, something between a Maltese cross and a pattée, conjuring the Iron Cross of Nazi war decoration. It might have been a riff on the symbol's biker connotations, an extension of his leather man persona, and/or a nod to Warhol's silver wig. Reed liked the look's shock effect so much, he arranged to sit for the superstar portrait photographer Francesco Scavullo, who'd taken some iconic images of Candy Darling the previous year.

* * *

With cash coming in, Reed soon rented a ground-floor apartment at 405 East Sixty-third Street, near where he'd lived with Kronstad. His building was two doors down from a pioneering singles bar, T.G.I. Friday's, which made the neighborhood a pickup scene most nights. Otherwise, it was a cultural dead zone where he was unlikely to run into people he knew from the downtown scene. One exception was his neighbor Ed McCormack, who recounted a night when the two found themselves at a lesbian discotheque, and Reed challenged him to slow dance. Reed led, and the pair moved across the floor to a Françoise Hardy song. "The good thing about dancing with a guy," Reed told him, "is guys have shoulders you can lean on."

Reed also liked hanging out at Club 82, the city's best showplace for drag and trans performers. A 350-seat venue located at 82 East Fourth Street, it opened in 1950 and became renowned for its elaborate stage shows of "femme impersonators," with a waitstaff that was apparently a mix of trans men and male impersonators. Over the years, celebrities flocked to the red-velvet-draped basement: Sinatra, Garland, Liz Taylor, and various Kennedys made the pilgrimage, and a descent down its staircase, lined with photos of past performers, was a journey through time. By the mid-'70s, its shine had tarnished, but under the management of two formidable figures, Butchie and Tommy, and a waitstaff of mostly drag kings, it was reborn as a part-time rock club, featuring local bands. By the spring of '74 it had become a bona fide scene again with a new crop of celebrities, Bowie, Jagger, and Reed among them. Between 3 and 4 a.m., Butch and Tommy would lock the doors and turn up the lights; on certain nights, the revelry continued until dawn.

It was on one such night that Reed met Rachel Humphreys, a gender-nonconforming dazzler. "I'd been up for days as usual and everything was at that super-real, glowing stage," Reed recalled. "I walked in there and there was this amazing person, this incredible head, kind of vibrating out of it all. Rachel was wearing this amazing make-up and dress and was obviously in a different world to anyone else in the place. Eventually I spoke and she came home with me. I rapped for hours and hours, while Rachel just sat there looking at me saying nothing . . . Rachel was completely disinterested in who I was and what I did. Nothing could impress her. He'd hardly heard my music and didn't like it all that much when he did. Rachel knows how to do it for me. No one else ever did before. Rachel's something else."

Humphreys was born in New Jersey in 1952, the fourth of five siblings born to a Mexican mom and an Irish dad. Birth name Richard, often known as Ricky, Rachel presented as a boy growing up—in a studio picture taken for first communion, Rachel was all impish grin and jug ears, in a white suit jacket and black bow tie, an image of Jesus hovering behind. In later years, Rachel sported a mustache, and had a girlfriend briefly. When the family split, they bounced between Texas and New Jersey. Rachel was bullied at school, and eventually left to study cosmetology and hairdressing at a beauty academy in Bayonne, which her mom paid for, and eventually decamped to New York, adopting her little sister Rachel's name. Sometimes presenting femme, sometimes more masculine, nonbinary and gender-nonconforming long before those terms entered the conversation, Rachel cut a striking figure: slim, with dark eyes, a strong chin, full lips, and long black hair. When Reed spoke of his new friend, he used gendered pronouns interchangeably; Rachel went by "Richard" and "Ricky" on occasion.

Barbara Hodes found a pair of false eyelashes on the sink in Reed's apartment, and soon met Rachel. For a while, Reed tried to maintain both relationships; the three of them would end the night at his place on Sixty-third Street. "I kind of wanted us all three to live together," Reed said, noting that the situation was ultimately "too heavy" for the "blond lady" he'd been cohabitating with. Hodes and Reed soon parted ways, and that spring his relationship with Rachel blossomed.

It's worth noting that around the same time as Reed's new romance, Warhol—who'd asserted on at least one occasion "I always wanted to be a girl," though he generally presented as a cis-male—embarked on a major portrait commission devoted to drag queens and trans and otherwise nonbinary persons. *Ladies and Gentlemen* used the same techniques he used for immortalizing Hollywood celebrities and other masters of the universe, and would rank among the greatest of his latter-day works, involving more than 250 canvases. One featured Marsha P. Johnson, the activist whose future was shaped at the Stonewall riots five years prior. As it happened, Reed would soon rent a second apartment, an inexpensive six-room space at 53 Christopher Street, directly above what had been the Stonewall (the bar was shuttered soon after the uprising). And he was already working on his next studio album, which would be informed by gay and drag culture, albeit in a more coded way than Warhol's.

By his own account, Reed wrote the songs for *Sally Can't Dance* quickly, if not as fast as those for *Berlin*. "Ride Sally Ride," a rehash of an old rock 'n' roll trope, would open the album with the lines "Sit yourself down, bang out a tune," and indeed the set would feel banged-out. That song and the title track, which suggested a victimized trans woman turned blade-wielding supermodel, were likely a wink to Sal "Sally" Maggio, manager of another well-known trans hangout, the 220 Club at 220 West Houston Street. The album's sound, meanwhile, was a radical reset. Gone were the metal guitars of Hunter and Wagner, replaced by the soul and funk sound then dominating urban radio and the city's nascent disco and gay club scenes, the sort of music Rachel adored.

Reed had a good team. Co-producing with him was Steve Katz, a founding member of the brassy pop-R&B band Blood, Sweat & Tears and—not incidentally—brother of Reed's manager, Dennis. Prakash John, a Bombay-born Canadian bassist who did time with Funkadelic, signed on with his fellow Canadian the keyboardist Michael Fonfara; both brought legit R&B feel while Reed revisited the Otis Redding vocal moves he'd occasionally break out during Velvets jams. Reed even called in Doug Yule, who was working a day job at a Long Island lithography plant, to help out. The instrumental performances were tasty, but not always convincing behind Reed's delivery, and the songwriting was mostly subpar. An exception was "Kill Your Sons." In a voice alternately deadpan and seething, Reed told a story—his own, pretty much—of family dysfunction and electroconvulsive therapy. A withering indictment of parents handing their kids over to the mental health establishment, it was a survivor's tale imagined as an anthem of suburban teen outrage.

Still, there was an unappealing whiff of cynicism about the project, especially in the wake of *Berlin*'s ambitiousness. The *Sally Can't Dance* packaging suggested a sort of self-aware cartoon, with a cover illustration of Reed that recalled the title graphics of the animated Merrie Melodies/Looney Tunes series; the back cover featured a drawing of a woman, trans perhaps, ostensibly reflected in Reed's shades. The RCA marketing department sprang for a thirty-second TV ad for *Sally Can't Dance*, but the shoot was something of a disaster: Reed arrived clearly too blasted to speak, and after dozens of useless takes, the production team scrapped the script, propped him up in a chair, and took ten wordless minutes of 35mm film stock before sending him home. The finished spot, which probably didn't get a lot of use, featured a bleached-blond Reed in aviator shades and leather jacket, seated with his head in his hand, looking completely wasted. "Sing along with Lou!" boomed the announcer, as the title track played and lyrics scrolled across the screen, an animated ball keeping pace. Reed says nothing, moving only to adjust his sunglasses. Ultimately, the album would squeak into the Top 10 by October and remain on the U.S. charts for fourteen weeks. Reed was proud of it, at least initially, telling friends it was his favorite solo record.

The ad was funny, albeit in a disturbingly exploitative and self-destructive way, playing up the drug fiend persona that had in fact become a reflection of Reed's life. On tour in Europe that summer, one member of his road team recalls him being "a mess" from speed and drinking, up for two or three days straight, then crashing hard. Reed's friend Ernie Thormahlen, *Transformer*'s prosthetically well-hung back-cover model, tried to rein him in. On one occasion he got Reed's hotel room key, found his stash, and gave it to the tour's truck drivers.

The behavior took its toll on his team. One night preshow, Reed was complaining incessantly about his muscles, which had seized up after a speed binge. "I'm not ready to do this," he moaned, as a crew member, Matt Leach, rubbed his shoulders. "I can't go out there." Strategizing, Leach began berating Reed, calling him a "gutless fucking whiny bastard" and ordering him to get dressed "and go put on a halfway fucking decent show!" Furious, Reed stormed off, played a ferocious show, and thanked Leach when he came offstage.

Between shows, his handlers were generally out of the picture. When Reed visited John Cale in London, it was the first time they'd seen each other in years. Reed had Rachel with him, and Cale was with his girlfriend, Cindy Wells, who he met shortly after divorcing Betsey Johnson. The former bandmates marked the occasion by shooting up together. Reed was in the bathroom awhile, so Cale went to check on him; he found his old drug buddy with an evidently clogged needle, rivulets of blood trickling out from multiple holes in his arm, as if Reed was unable to land a good shot. "I quickly tied his arm off, inserted the needle into the best vein I could find, and let it rip," Cale recalled.

Reed's bender continued that summer when, a week after President Nixon resigned on national television, the singer stepped off a plane in Australia, where he was booked for a sold-out nine-show tour. He was received as rock star royalty, and held court at a nationally televised press conference for a group of evidently clueless journalists. Reed's performance was memorable, a mirroring of how Warhol had been script-flipping interviews since the mid-'60s, when he'd tell interviewers to make up the answers to the questions they'd asked him or, as he instructed one writer, "just tell me what to say."

Journalist: What message is it that you're trying to get across?
Reed: I don't have one.
Journalist: Most singers do . . .
Reed: Like who?
Journalist: Well, most singers . . .
Reed: Like who?
Journalist: Would it be right to call your music "gutter rock"?

Reed: Gutter rock?

Journalist: Gutter rock.

Reed: Oh, yeah.

Reed takes a sip of something, perhaps a soft drink, through two colored paper straws.

Journalist: Are you a transvestite or a homosexual?

Reed: Sometimes.

Journalist: Which one?

Reed: I dunno, what's the difference?

Journalist: Is it true . . . that you attacked your fans in England and were arrested for obscenity on the stage?

Reed: No.

Journalist: This is . . . false publicity?

Reed nods.

Journalist: Well, who writes these things about you, if they're not true?

Reed waits a beat and a half. "Journalists," he deadpans.

Speaking later to a Radio JJ host in Sydney, Reed seemed more accommodating, perhaps more intoxicated. "I used to read," he said, mentioning Raymond Chandler and Delmore Schwartz. He woozily sang a bit of the Kinks' "Lola," Ray Davies's hit about hooking up with a trans woman. Asked about *Berlin*, Reed noted "they use it in mental hospitals," claiming that patients find it "calming." He talked about giving up yoga and practicing self-hypnosis, sticking pins in his hands and trying to will himself not to bleed. "My body doesn't seem to belong to me anymore," he said.

Unsurprisingly, Aussie journalists would later have their knives out. Covering his Adelaide performance, a writer noted Reed's "wasted, wan face hiding behind large dark glasses," his "mechanical fag dancing," and the "effeminate assembly" of fans near the front of the stage. Another deemed Reed "the worst imported performer I've seen." One paper awarded him their "Yuuk Award."

Inventing his persona as he circled the globe, Reed was method-acting "Lou Reed" to the hilt. The cover of a tour program featured not Reed but the *Transformer* portrait of Ernie Thormahlen in his banana-stuffed jeans. "Lou Reed is acting the part of a rock and roll singer so well," the program essay declares, "that many say he is the essence of what a rock and roll singer should be."

The essay goes on to quote Reed: "It's like writing a play, and giving yourself the lead part."

* * *

In autumn, Reed was back in the States, and engaged with select journalists more openly. Speaking to *The Aquarian Weekly*, he noted he was reading Sylvia Plath's "scary novel" *The Bell Jar*, and raved about John Schlesinger's queer-themed film *Sunday Bloody Sunday*. Reed also discussed creating characters in his songs, and how their opinions "aren't necessarily mine. I've written songs where I've totally disagreed with the guy who's singing them, but I think it's interesting to put it out there so that people can see it. It's really weird, you create that thing and you really are it, and you yourself wouldn't do it that way or think that way. But he would, and you make him exist and he does it, then you hop out."

Sometimes it was hard hopping out. On October 26, Reed and crew rolled into Detroit for a show at the Masonic Auditorium, and things began going wrong straightaway. First he was refused entry to the hotel restaurant, supposedly due to the dress code. Then, when his frenemy Lester Bangs arrived for a *Creem* feature interview, Reed, possibly in a low-blood-sugar funk, said he wanted to grab a newspaper, then ghosted.

Bangs returned to Reed's hotel suite after the show to try again, and found Reed lounging on his bed with Humphreys. By Bangs's account, he and Reed stayed up until 3:30 a.m. arguing, often shouting, egging each other on, insulting each other brutally, yet apparently enjoying themselves. Bangs was smart, or Reed would never have engaged with him. Bangs suspected he was selling himself short writing about rock music for outlets like *Creem*, which amplified his identification with Reed, who at this precise moment was likely as conflicted as he'd ever been about his own creative compromises.

In the finished piece, Bangs baited Reed with drug questions, and he rose to them. "If you do take speed, you're a good example of why speed freaks have bad names," Reed told Bangs, condescendingly explaining the difference between Desoxyn ("fifteen milligrams of methamphetamine hydrochloride held together with cake paste") and Obetrol.

"Do you ever resent people for the way that you have lived out what they might think of as the dark side of their lives for them, vicariously, in your music or your life?" Bangs asked him.

Reed sidestepped the question, and they veered into a debate about decadence, which Reed denies indulging in, at least in his music.

"Bullshit, man," Bangs said. "When you did *Transformer* you were playing to pseudo-decadence, to an audience that wanted to buy a reprocessed form of decadence."

"Let Us Now Praise Famous Death Dwarves, or, How I Slugged It Out with Lou Reed and Stayed Awake," published in early '75, was one of the most spectacularly twisted pieces of arts journalism ever published, a dirtbag stalker's version of Gay Talese's "Frank Sinatra Has a Cold," a hydrant-gush tirade on the '60s myth of the heroic burnout with Bangs playing a wasted superfan to Reed's debauched rock 'n' roll street poet. The winking art direction similarly played along with Reed's narrative persona, which even by the dubious standards of '70s rock journalism was jaw-dropping: the image of a bleached-blond Reed in a snark-comic, proto-clickbait wanted-poster mock-up: "WANTED: For transforming a whole generation of young Americans into faggot junkies."

Yet for all its entertaining pathology, the feature was horrifically cruel toward Humphreys, who Bangs described as a subhuman grotesque, "beyond the bizarre," and "like something that might have grovelingly scampered in when Lou opened the door to get the milk and papers in the morning." It was a low point of Bangs's career, and Reed was so offended that he never spoke to Bangs again. If any single moment cemented Reed's distrust and loathing of journalists, following the chilly reception for *Berlin*, this was it.

* * *

The fall tour continued in a blur of spectacle. In New York, Reed did a show at the Felt Forum, a smaller sister venue adjacent to Madison Square Garden; it was Reed's biggest hometown show to date. Crouched behind a speaker column, Mick Jagger swigged from a champagne flute, rapt.

"Have you ever played here before?" he asked Reed backstage, afterward.

"How the fuck should I know?" Reed replied, evidently plastered.

In Houston two weeks later, Michael Fonfara introduced the melody of "Heroin" in a *Phantom of the Opera* church organ flourish. In what appears to be a practiced pantomime, Reed wound the mic cable around his bare right arm, over the biceps, and cinched it with his teeth. He studied his forearm, slapped it twice as if to bring up a vein, lowered the aviator shades perched on his head, and began singing, "I . . . don't know . . ." The crowd roars. After spitting out the word *spike*, he produced what looked like a hypodermic, methodically play-acted injecting himself with it, quickly unwound the cable, and began swinging his arm in a windmill—a junkie trick to accelerate the drug's movement into the circulatory system—just as he started singing about the blood flowing through him. He rubbed his hands over his body and through his hair, clutched his arm, and began to sashay, clapping off-beat and singing in a slowed-down slur in case anyone hadn't gotten the gist. His new guitarist Danny Weis slid his fingers ostentatiously along his guitar neck and the band ramped up, Reed moving with them, marching briskly in place, then bumping and grinding until the song reached an epic crescendo. It was ridiculous, horrifying, and awesome; the audience went apeshit.

By the time Reed reached San Francisco later that month—a city with which he'd had a notably complicated professional relationship—the injection pantomime had become routine. Reviewing his show at the Winterland Ballroom, a writer for the *Examiner* declared Reed the "king/queen" of "sick rock," criticized his "repulsive" shooting-up routine, his "pseudo-gay choreography," and his remarkable disengagement. "Reed never seemed last night to have any response to either the music or the crowd," the journalist noted, seemingly puzzled how someone who could come across so "sensitive" in recordings seemed so "distant, dull, and repetitious," in performance, mumbling his lyrics of "loneliness, depression, rejection, and sexual frustration."

"When I'd go see Lou live, he frightened me," recalls Michael Stotter, who worked on Reed's marketing at RCA in the '70s. "I was afraid for him, every time I saw him."

* * *

Back home, Reed liked spending time with Rotten Rita, aka Kenneth Rapp, a good-looking, gangly six-foot-tall semi-criminal opera queen who like Reed adored amphetamines; Rita had an apartment in Queens under a stretch of elevated subway tracks, playing Maria Callas LPs at high volume to drown out the noise. Rita was a Factory veteran. "[He] used to come in with his homemade speed that everyone knew was the worst in the world," Warhol recalled in *POPism*. "Periodically he'd try to upgrade his credibility by giving somebody their money back, but then the next day he'd be in there trying to sell them the exact same stuff back again, telling them that it was a much superior batch so naturally it was more expensive. But as Lou said, 'It's part of the natural environment to have Rotten do things like that. That's why he's "Rotten."'"

Reed evidently still saw Dr. Freymann, to whom he appears to have cut at least $1,300 worth of checks in 1974. But his network of sources for amphetamines had expanded. Reed and his peers swore by high doses of Desoxyn, generally prepped for injection by boiling the tablets in distilled water—optimally the yellow 15 mg ones Reed had lauded to Bangs, the highest potency available, embossed with the stylized "a" for Abbott, the firm that manufactured them. Administered orally, the tablets were time-released, to graduate the onset of effect. Extracted into solution, that safeguard was sidestepped to maximize the rush, and many users, Reed included, went beyond the recommended dosage by orders of magnitude. For Reed it was an intellectualized and obsessive drug experience, not far removed from the exacting extremity of his health-food diets over the years. Given amphetamine's effects on appetite, though, Reed was barely eating at all. According to Hodes, he subsisted for a time almost exclusively on hot dogs—he'd put away four at a sitting—and scotch. The meticulous pharmaceutical connoisseurship was common to the era, as '60s idealism evaporated and only its increasingly sophisticated drug cultures remained. "Better Living Through Chemistry" T-shirts were wardrobe staples for rock fans. Privileged drug fiends kept a copy of the annual doorstop-sized *Physicians' Desk Reference* on hand to help them self-medicate efficiently; Reed's was displayed prominently in his living room.

Yet his supreme obsession, for which speed was a means to an end—increasing endurance, reducing self-doubt, possibly helping him with his dyslexia and other cognitive issues, diagnosed or not—remained work. He cultivated a fetish for cutting-edge music gear and precise sound reproduction. His friend and fellow singer-songwriter Elliott Murphy, who'd secured his own deal with RCA thanks in part to Reed's support, recalls working with him on demos one evening at Reed's apartment until dawn. Murphy went home to crash, only to be awakened by a phone call from Reed a few hours later, asking him if he was ready to come back and work more. Reed had a sophisticated home recording setup: he'd purchased a Uher quarter-inch reel-to-reel with four-track capabilities, likely at Lyric Hi-Fi, the city's premiere audiophile store, whose showroom was just a short walk from his apartment.

With speed-fueled time on his hands, Reed began fooling around with feedback. "I would record tracks of guitar at different speeds," he said, "playing with the reverb, tuning the guitars in unusual ways . . . I would tune all the strings, say, to E, put the guitar a certain distance from the amp, and it would start feeding back." Murphy recalls

The C.H.D.'S

VARIETY Show 1959

march 1959

Rich Sigal

Judy Titus

me

Johnny DeBan

Lewis Reed's first band, the C.H.D.s, 1959 (Courtesy Canal Street Communications, Inc.)

Shelley Albin, 1965
(Courtesy Shelley Albin)

Erin Clermont, Washington Square
Park, 1968 (Courtesy Erin Clermont)

Venus in Furs film shoot at Piero Heliczer's loft, New York City, 1965 (back row, from left to right: Sterling Morrison, Angus MacLise, Reed, Margaret Boyce Cam, John Cale; front row, from left to right: Maureen "Moe" Tucker, Barbara Rubin, Chas Stanley, Heliczer, Julie Garfield) (Courtesy Adam Ritchie)

John Cale, 1966 (© Nat Finkelstein Estate)

Nico and Sterling Morrison at the 43rd Annual Dinner of the New York Society
for Clinical Psychiatry at the Hotel Delmonico, 1966 (Courtesy Adam Ritchie)

Moe Tucker at the 43rd Annual Dinner of the New York Society for Clinical
Psychiatry at the Hotel Delmonico, 1966 (Courtesy Adam Ritchie)

Andy Warhol and Lou Reed with Paul Morrissey in the Exploding Plastic
Inevitable tour bus en route to Ann Arbor, 1966 (© Nat Finkelstein Estate)

The Exploding Plastic Inevitable at the Factory, 1966 (back row, from left to right: Warhol, Tucker, Morrison, Cale; front row, from left to right: Gerard Malanga, Mary Woronov, Reed) (© Nat Finkelstein Estate)

The Exploding Plastic Inevitable at the Dom, 1966 (from left to right: Edie Sedgwick, Malanga, Reed, Morrison, Cale) (Courtesy Adam Ritchie)

The Velvet Underground, 1968 (from left to right: Tucker, Morrison, Doug Yule, Reed)
(Courtesy M.C. Kostek/VUAS)

Reed, 1968
(Courtesy M.C. Kostek/VUAS)

Reed and Bettye Kronstad, 1969
(Courtesy Bettye Kronstad)

David Bowie, Iggy Pop, and Reed, Dorchester Hotel, London, 1972
(© The Estate of Mick Rock)

Reed, Mick Jagger, and Bowie at Café Royal, London, 1973
(© The Estate of Mick Rock)

CLOCKWISE FROM TOP LEFT: Holly Woodlawn, Candy Darling, Lester Bangs, Jackie Curtis (© Bob Gruen / www.bobgruen.com)

Reed in concert at the Winterland Ballroom, San Francisco, 1974
(Courtesy Larry Schorr)

Reed in fresh gear, London, 1975 (© The Estate of Mick Rock)

Reed and Rachel Humphreys, 1975 (© The Estate of Mick Rock)

Patti Smith and Reed, 1976 (© Bob Gruen / www.bobgruen.com)

TOP: Sylvia and Lou Reed, 1986; BOTTOM: Reed and Robert Quine, circa 1981
(Courtesy Sylvia Reed)

Reed and Laurie Anderson, 1996 (© Bob Gruen / www.bobgruen.com)

John Varvatos, Mick Rock, and Reed, 2013 (© Bob Gruen / www.bobgruen.com)

Reed and Anderson, Coney Island, New York City, 1995
(Courtesy Annie Leibovitz / Trunk Archive)

spending "quite a bit of time with Lou and Rachel, sitting around the apartment, listening to the early stages" of what was taking shape as an experimental music project. It was a way to step out of the corner he'd painted himself into, to do something formally transgressive in the mode of serious art music, which would be received as such, but which he could contextualize and market as a sort of ur-rock. The project was already under way during his interview with Bangs. "I could have sold it as electronic classical music," Reed said of his unnamed work, "except the one I've got that I've finished now is heavy metal, no kidding around . . . I'll stick [it] on RCA when the rock 'n' roll shit gets taken care of."

This was hardly new territory for Reed—more like an extension of the noise-drone jams he explored with Cale in the Ludlow Street apartment, and the improvisations the Velvets shaped, first to soundtrack films at the Cinematheque, and later on nightclub stages. One recording, likely made by Reed in 1966 and labeled "Electric Rock Symphony," had him riffing on electric guitar—prettily one moment, harshly frenetic the next, with extended techniques like string scraping and playing below the bridge—for nearly an hour, cutting through a drone haze of reverb, echo, and tape manipulations. It was an approach anticipating techniques other rock musicians would explore more fully in the late '60s, notably those in the German kosmische music scene. Returning to this noise-womb years later, Reed would lean a guitar—plugged in, volume up—against an amp, then a second against another amp, and get lost in the feedback, thick clouds of harmonics conjuring the screech of a thousand subway wheels.

At the moment, however, there was "rock 'n' roll shit" to take care of. On Halloween, the Supreme Court of New York had ruled in favor of Reed's ex-manager in *Fred Heller v. Lou Reed*, the case that arose when Reed changed management. There would be an appeal, but it didn't look good for Reed, and it was probably going to cost him a significant sum of money.

Amid the chaos of touring, Reed had been writing and recording demos. A tape from September '74 featured beautifully reimagined Velvet Underground numbers, suggesting Reed might've had an alternate life as a mid-'70s West Coast singer-songwriter: "She's My Best Friend," "Some Kinda Love," "Candy Says," and "I'm Stickin' with You," the song he'd handed off to Moe Tucker. Among the new songs was "I Couldn't Resist It," a narrative that involved dope dumped on a table, a woman cooking it up in a spoon, and an invitation rhyming "take a little taste" with "a shame to let this stuff go to waste" (the song concluded plaintively as the narrator succumbed to temptation). Another button-pusher, "I Wanna Be Black," was a satire of racialized white male sexual insecurity that scanned as a deliberately offensive joke, rhyming "natural rhythm" with "a lot of jism" and "Martin Luther King" with "wanna get shot in the spring" over a lazy blues shuffle; channeling his collegiate obsession with "The White Negro," it also declared, "I don't want to be a middle-class Jewish student no more." Neither track was likely to put him back on the pop charts.

The standout among the new songs, demoed in December with Steve Katz, wasn't exactly new. "Coney Island Baby" was the name of a 1962 doo-wop single by the Excellents that Allan Hyman recalled playing with Reed's band back in Syracuse. At the St. Mark's Poetry Project in '71, Reed read his poem "The Coach and Glory of Love." Now with tape rolling, and Katz joining in on acoustic guitar, Reed pulled the threads together.

He begins in first person, giving voice to a character who was able to "run the 100 in 9.4 with my clothes on" and who desperately wanted to play football for his high school team, particularly so he could prove himself to the coach, who he imagined would help him "stand up straight." The narrator feared that his soul was up for grabs, and as dawn broke, he was rethinking everything he'd ever done, thinking about the "two-bit friends" who thought he was an animal, and about how he had, in a sense, become one, not knowing why he does the "awful thing" he does. He observes how the city is like "a circus," or "a sewer," and notes how its denizens have "peculiar tastes." And he sang about a princess on a hill, and how the glory of love might save him.

"Rock on, Steve," Reed quietly instructs Katz, who takes a tender, terrifically empathic solo.

"Oh, yeah," Reed says, evidently pleased, continuing the song, and returning to the image of the princess on a hill, who he concedes loved him even though he was often a prick. And—in a striking image that recalls the conceit of "I'll Be Your Mirror"—the narrator hopes that what she loved in him might, at this dark and desperate moment, "come shining through." Reed strums the outro, and Katz lands a perfect note to cap it, chuckling after it fades out.

"Coney Island Baby," Reed says, christening the song, and sounding flush with pride.

* * *

During the first week of January 1975, Reed began recording a new album of songs at Electric Lady, the top-flight recording studio commissioned by Jimi Hendrix in 1970, three weeks before he died. For the initial *Coney Island Baby* sessions, Reed again called on Doug Yule, whom he'd wished dead on a radio show not long ago. Time, and the fact that Reed was finally getting royalties on the Velvets' back catalog—a $40,000 payment had come through the previous spring—probably helped heal the rift. And few players knew Reed's work better. Among the songs he and Yule worked up were the Velvets' "She's My Best Friend," a tribute to someone who's "certainly not your average girl." Yule sang it on the band's '69 demo; this time Reed did, hollering with glam glitz over crunching guitars and barrelhouse piano.

A plan to get Mick Ronson involved as guitarist and arranger on the sessions—his role on *Transformer*—apparently fell apart over money and scheduling. That was hardly Reed's only frustration. Despite their impressive "Coney Island Baby" demo, Reed's working relationship with Steve Katz entered a death spiral, and Katz recused himself as the album's co-producer; he remembers Reed being "totally out of his mind at this point" and "impossible to work with." In late January, the New York Supreme Court upheld the October decision in *Heller v. Reed* on appeal, leaving Reed no options but to wait for the bill. He remained paranoid about his finances, a mind state his amphetamine intake would've amplified, and he'd grown distrustful of his manager, Steve's brother Dennis, a situation that would soon come to a head.

Personnel problems notwithstanding, Reed managed to complete a handful of tracks at Electric Lady. "Crazy Feeling" was a folk-rock love song that, like the revived "She's My Best Friend," seemed to reflect his recent Club 82 meet-cute, from the line about "suit and tie johns" buying drinks, to the one about business ending at 3 a.m. (a likely reference to the club's door-locking ritual), to the hoarsely affectionate declaration "You really really really are a queen, such a queen!," one of Reed's most Bowie moments ever, and an echo of "Queen Bitch," one of Bowie's most Lou Reed moments ever. There was also a beautifully fleshed-out version of "Coney Island Baby," sweetened by Yule's bass lines and a colloquial delivery that recalled the hood rat swagger of Bruce Springsteen. That young singer-songwriter, like Reed a bridge-and-tunnel kid turned self-made New York City street poet, experiencing similar label and management headaches, was fast ascending: a new single, "Born to Run," had just been leaked to radio, and was getting generous airplay on New York's WNEW-FM. As ever, Reed paid close attention to what did well. But by his account, the initial reaction of his management team to his beloved "Coney Island Baby"—whether it was because they felt the song was off-brand, off-trend, too suggestively queer, or some combination of all these things—was roughly "this is one of the worst things we've ever heard in our lives."

* * *

Reed was also burning through road musicians—touring with him was not for the fainthearted. When it came time to assemble a new band, this time he did so with an ear to what his most accomplished singer-songwriter peers were doing, employing players with jazz chops and style. Joni Mitchell had upped her stock by working with the L.A. Express band, first on *Court and Spark* and then with the live *Miles of Aisles*, released in November, which repurposed her early work just like *Rock 'n' Roll Animal* did for Reed. Springsteen had his E Street Band, Van Morrison had his Caledonia Soul Express, and jazz-rock fusion was at its commercial crest following Herbie Hancock's surprise 1973 hit LP *Head Hunters*.

Reed enlisted the Everyman Band, an upstate New York fusion out-fit featuring the saxophonist Marty Fogel (a rangy player in touch with the '50s–'60s free jazz Reed loved) and violinist Larry Packer. At their audition, Reed arrived to meet them in an outfit that made Miles Da-vis's sartorial flamboyance seem tame—Reed had just dropped $600 at Ian's on Grove Street, an edgy retro boutique run by Mariann Mar-lowe, a young fashionista who sourced much of her gear from London, where she'd worked with the upstart designer Vivienne Westwood and her co-conspirator Malcolm McLaren. Mick Rock shot Reed vamping in his new gear: a sheer fuzzy black knit T-shirt with an asymmetrical quarter zip neck; a tighter-weave black tee with a silver-studded crew neck and zippered nipple cutouts; a clear plastic jacket to show off the tops; long, zippered fingerless black plastic gloves; skintight black fab-ric slacks; black winklepickers; and a fresh black-polish manicure, with an extended thumbnail for extra frisson. Rock also shot loving, playful images of Reed and Humphreys.

The ride got rough straightway on February 7, when Reed, Hum-phreys, and his new band landed in Rome to start their European tour, and were greeted at the airport by a baggage handlers' strike. Reed threw tantrums, and later flung a plate of pasta against the wall of the hotel restaurant. Humphreys tried in vain to calm him down. After two days of rehearsals in Rome, their first show was postponed due to labor unrest; in the downtime Reed got an Italian doctor to prescribe him methamphetamine. Traveling north to Milan, the band ran into more trouble via a cadre of young activists with ties to the Situationist International, the art-and-politics movement that informed the '68 stu-dent uprisings in France. Outside the Palalido arena, where Reed was booked, information stalls distributed flyers concerning the *autoridut-tori* movement, which had begun contesting the high cost of entertain-ment events with threats of hit-and-run disruption. (Among the flyers circulating at Reed's show was one accusing the Jewish promoter, Da-vid Zard, of being a "torturer in the Moshe Dayan forces.") Reed was two songs into his set when rioters in masks stormed the stage with clubs and shut it down, trashing equipment and instruments, tearing out seats, hurling stones, bolts, bottles, and petrol cans, and shouting anti-Semitic slurs; according to a newspaper report, two people were injured and tens of millions of lira worth of damage was wreaked. A bootleg recording captured Reed furiously bellowing "You fuckers" before the audio cut out.

A similar scene, complete with riot police and tear gas, played out at the rescheduled Rome concert on February 18 (the show was shut down before Reed could take the stage, and he wept upon being told of the violence outside the arena). With the remaining Italian dates canceled, the group headed to placid Zurich to chill. But Reed was far from chill. He ran up a huge hotel bill, and connected with another doctor. Wired, fretting over his management situation, he reached out to Tony Defries, Bowie's manager, to talk representation. Defries hopped on a plane, but by the time he arrived, Reed had had second thoughts and refused to meet him, sending Fulk to do damage control. Defries was returning to the airport around the time Dennis Katz arrived, hoping to salvage his investment, and he offered Reed a new contract, which would lock in their relationship for three more years, guaranteeing Katz 20 percent of Reed's gross earnings in exchange for overseeing almost every aspect of his career.

Reed remained on a hair trigger. In Sweden, he inexplicably fired Larry Packer. By the time they reached Paris, the remaining musicians threatened to quit when money got held up. Fulk babysat Reed as best she could, seeing to it that the two-bottle Johnnie Walker Black rider mandate was scaled back to one, and making sure the scotch was delivered to her personally for safekeeping. For all this, the music could be powerful, tight, and soulful, with playing geared less toward instrumental grandstanding than collective dynamics.

The crowds, however, didn't always appreciate the nuances. Back in the States in April, as Reed sang an emotional "Coney Island Baby" in Providence, Rhode Island, someone yelled "Shoot up, Lou!" And during an unusually hushed version of "Heroin," which Reed reshaped into something near a spoken-word piece, he stopped to bark "Fuck you!" at a belligerent fan who wouldn't shut up. Yet this was precisely the kind of audience Reed had gone some way to cultivate— vitriol breeds vitriol—and that he continued to bait. On a new song,

"Kicks," where a character finds slitting a man's throat to be "better than sex," Reed invited an audience call-and-response with the chant "kill him" before the song crashed into a guitar-noise finale.

* * *

In March, RCA released a second LP drawn from the '73 *Rock 'n' Roll Animal* tour. *Lou Reed Live* was uneven and didn't represent where Reed was musically anymore, but he was in no position to stop its release. He owed the label more music, and given his growing legal problems, he needed income. He signed off on *Lou Reed Live* with the insistence it conclude with an extended bit of crowd noise where some yob hollers "Lou Reed sucks!" On some level, Reed probably agreed.

Also in March, the Patti Smith Group and Television began a seven-week residency at CBGB. It was the official coming-out event of the New York scene that'd been simmering for a couple of years, led by bands who looked to Reed and the Velvets as forebears. Smith, in fact, usually began her show with "We're Gonna Have a Real Good Time Together," from *1969: The Velvet Underground Live*, the album she'd recently reviewed for *Rolling Stone*; she'd generally end the song by shouting out "Lou Reed!" in homage to its author. Her CBGB residency with Television recalled the 1966 Exploding Plastic Inevitable residency at the Dom, a five-minute walk away. Lines at CBGB ran down the block, and record execs circled; the industry guru Clive Davis, about to launch a new label, cut a deal with Smith. Television, whose thrilling twin-guitar displays recalled the best of the Velvets without sounding too much like them, had recorded demos for Island Records with Brian Eno as producer in December. Two other promising bands, the Ramones and Talking Heads, were getting their acts together at CBGB as well.

It must've been strange for Reed to watch the fuss around bands tapping into his back catalog as he was trying to get a handle on his own career. As always, he was taking notes, sometimes literally. He would often drop by CBGB with Danny Fields, Rachel, and other friends. On at least one occasion he brought a cassette recorder, prompting a run-in with Tom Verlaine and Richard Lloyd, Television's singer-guitarists, who were worried about their ideas being hijacked before they'd even released an album.

"Really nice of you to come down, Lou," said Verlaine, confronting Reed at his table between sets, "but you have to give us the tape recorder you brought."

"I don't have a tape recorder," Reed said, lying.

"Well, we heard that you do," Richard Lloyd said, asking if they could see what was under his jacket.

"Well, there's no batteries in there, and there's no tape," Reed said, lying again—then, finally, smirked and turned over the machine.

Smith, for her part, recalled Reed challenging her one night after seeing her do "Real Good Time."

"What was your intention?" he asked her coolly.

She said, with complete honesty, "Respect."

He studied her.

"Okay," he said.

He may have been revered, but Reed was always looking over his shoulder. And not for no reason. If his post–Velvet Underground musical direction was suspect in the new aesthetic scheme of things, which valorized raw simplicity and anti-virtuosity, his bad behavior hadn't won him many friends among the new guard. The Dictators made knucklehead hard rock with great thrust and comic self-awareness, and their debut album, *The Dictators Go Girl Crazy!*, released in March, sounded alternately like a tribute to, and an Oedipal parody of, *Rock 'n' Roll Animal*. On "Two Tub Man," the singer rhymed "I'm just a clown walking down the street" with "I think Lou Reed is a creep!"

* * *

Early that summer, Reed engaged an idea that must've felt like a lightning strike—a project that could've met his high standards for merging art and commerce, addressed his financial struggles, moved him to the center of the pop culture conversation, and reunited him with a man he loved and admired. Reed's talks about staging *Berlin* with Warhol, whose multifaceted career was as successful as ever, hadn't borne fruit. But after getting an early look at his friend's aphoristic memoir *The Philosophy of Andy Warhol (From A to B and Back Again)*, due that fall, Reed began developing ideas for a musical based on it.

Whether Reed had discussed the project with Warhol or just surprised him with a tape is unclear. But on an undated BASF C-90 cassette titled *Philosophy Songs (From A to B & Back)*, Reed worked through a dozen song sketches, working out lyrics that reflected Warhol's life and ideas over rudimentary acoustic guitar riffs, with traffic noise in the background, as if recording in his apartment with the window open. Some songs conjured his first-person voice, echoing familiar quips about fame, sex, and Coca-Cola. Reed touches on the presentational heroics of "drag queens" ("ambulatory archives of ideal moviestar womanhood," as Warhol described them in *Philosophy*), the artist's notion of a "put-on," and the aestheticization of his hard lean into commerce. ("Being good in business is the most fascinating kind of art," Warhol affirmed in the book, "making money is art and working is art and good business is the best art.") Other songs took a third-person POV. There's humor: Warhol's dog shitting in the aisle of his local Gristedes grocery store; a high-concept Warhol doll that, when you wind it up, does nothing. Other observations are nastier—about Warhol's cheapness, coldness, chronic skin problems, sex life—perhaps channeling Factory characters talking shit about their mentor, or possibly Reed's own venting, at a man with whom he had a complex relationship. Tellingly, Reed offers an apology at the end of the demo, recalling the apologies he made to his ex-wife for the personal details he used in *Berlin*.

With a selection of Reed's recent concert recordings on the B side, the cassette was a thorny blend of artmaking, business proposition, and the sort of mixtape one might make for a lover, to express feelings impossible to articulate in conversation. Warhol's take on the project, or indeed, whether he ever even listened to the tape, is unclear. For his part, Reed bragged about writing it all in a day, telling a writer from *Circus* magazine he had two hours' worth of music, and that Warhol wanted to do the musical with David Cassidy, with whom Reed seemed slightly obsessed at the time. Sometime later, he told his friend

Mick Rock that he'd played the demos for Warhol, and they'd in fact put him off.

"He was fascinated, but horrified," Reed said. "I think they kind of scared him. But I'm thinking of doing it as my next album."

It didn't work out that way, and nothing more came of the project. But Reed would return to the idea of a song cycle based on Warhol's life. He rarely threw anything out; he'd learned that from Warhol.

* * *

In his *Philosophy* riffing, Reed referred to an incident that would've had significance to both him and Warhol. On May 28, Eric Emerson was found dead, next to his trusty bicycle, off the West Side Highway. The *Chelsea Girls* actor and Max's regular, who'd caused them such trouble when he threatened to sue Verve Records for using his image on the back cover of *The Velvet Underground & Nico*, had subsequently become a player in the New York rock scene, fronting a glam band, the Magic Tramps, who played at CBGB. His death was officially listed as a hit-and-run accident. But word on the street was that he'd overdosed, possibly among "friends," who dumped him on the road to avoid being held responsible.

Danny Fields wrote a memorial in the *SoHo Weekly News*. Reed had told him about the rumor.

"They could have put him on a sidewalk bench or something," Reed said ruefully.

"No one does things like that, not even your friends," Fields said.

The death clearly haunted Reed. After all, it might have been him. However invincible he thought himself on meth, however refined his dosing strategies and injection techniques, he knew the risks.

It was the start of a bad summer. In June, Reed received a bill for $174,140 as a result of his losing his breach-of-contract suit with Fred Heller. A private investigator had been chasing Reed down with a subpoena related to the case. A building superintendent at 405 East Sixty-third Street informed him that Reed had moved to a building down the block, and that "Mr. Reed had been seen entering and leaving the apartment building located at 425 East 63rd Street . . . dressed in various wigs and in women's clothing." After staking out the block for days, the investigator finally gave up, leaving the papers taped to Reed's apartment door.

Metal Machine Music, Reed's instrumental album of sculpted guitar-feedback drones, was released the same month, and rather than helping to solve his business problems, the hypnotically assaultive work created new ones. Reed had divided it into four sixteen-minute segments, one for each side of the double LP, and had the mastering engineer Bob Ludwig end side four by unplugging the lathe, rotating the cutting needle manually, and lifting the cutting head at the right moment. The result was a listening experience that would conclude with the turntable stylus literally stuck in a groove, hiccupping an ouroboros fragment of drone, just like the lock-groove "Loop" flexidisc he'd done with Cale for Warhol's '66 *Aspen* magazine commission. *Metal Machine Music*'s multilayered wall of noise, built with guitar outbursts recorded to tape, sped up, slowed down, reversed, and fed through various devices, was also not so far afield for an experimental guitarist who'd come up with the single-note riffs of "The Ostrich" and the layered soloing of "What Goes On." *Metal Machine Music* had a kinship as well with the Stockhausen-inspired tape manipulation on Beatles tracks such as "Revolution 9" and "Tomorrow Never Knows." And the album's liner notes, a mix of fact and fiction with coded references to amphetamine, also acknowledged the influence of La Monte Young in what seemed a send-up of his complex compositional notes, a gesture perhaps intended as an in-joke at Cale's expense. Like Young's work and that of the gathering punk-rock scene—and of course Warhol, whose static films like *Sleep* proffered similar pleasures—*Metal Machine Music* was serious art with a dash of put-on. It might even be read as a radical queer art statement, its wordless roar a shutdown of homophobic interrogation. Finally, and not insignificantly, *Metal Machine Music* was also a quick fix for RCA's product demands, and an avant-garde bitch-slap to all the suits who were sweating him. Reed must have thought it was a brilliant conceptual move.

But it didn't play out well. His management team saw it as a self-destructive joke, and his label, hoping to maximize sales, disingenuously packaged the LP to recall *Rock 'n' Roll Animal*, with a cover image of Reed in studded leather against a black backdrop. A proposed sticker prominently warning potential customers "this record has no vocals" was ditched, along with the idea of releasing the LP on the company's Red Seal classical label, which would have helped signal its content. The upshot was a record that, on top of selling poorly, was returned in droves by angry fans who bought it unwittingly.

Reed would never stop trying to contextualize *Metal Machine Music* as a fusion of "high" and "low" art, which in a sense had been his project all along. He compared it to Warhol's soup can, and his eight-hour single-shot film *Empire*. He'd also describe the LP as "shit on a platter." In any case, Reed's aesthetic impulse proved prescient. In November, Brian Eno released *Discreet Music*, an album of hushed, pulsing electronic drones that was in many ways a quiet *Metal Machine Music*, though it was received very differently. In the end, *Metal Machine Music* was like Dylan's *Self-Portrait*, the double-LP feint released in 1970, born of genuine creative impulse with an agenda that included shaking off a limiting persona and the oppressiveness of certain fan expectations. And like that album, it didn't accomplish the task, though time would.

* * *

"Have I told you the genie jokes?" Reed said to an Australian journalist. "A guy can't pay his taxi fare. So he says to the driver 'Can I pay you with this magic genie bottle?' The driver says 'OK.' So he gets this green bottle with Hebrew writing on it. Rubs it and out comes the Genie. 'I am the Jewish Genie,' he says. 'You can have anything you wish, you can have one wish.' 'Anything?' 'Yes, anything.' 'Oh boy! I'd like to have my dick reach right down to the floor!' And the genie cut his legs off at the thighs."

Reed was dutifully doing his job that summer—touring the world, generating revenue, attempting to promote *Metal Machine Music*, winding up journalists—when the shit well and truly hit the fan. His distrust of his management had reached fever pitch, and in a letter to Dennis Katz dated August 22, he terminated their power-of-attorney agreement and ended Katz's "services as my personal advisor effective immediately." Checks began bouncing. Convinced his tour manager, Barbara Fulk, was helping fleece him, Reed stopped speaking to her in Australia; she hadn't been paid in months, and she soon left the tour. The settlement with Fred Heller hadn't been paid, either, and Reed was found in contempt of court. It also came to light that his taxes hadn't been paid in five years.

Back in New York, Reed discovered he was essentially broke and in debt, a sort of rock bottom the middle-class son of an accountant had never experienced. "I had no money and no guitars," Reed recalled. "The roadies had taken them when they hadn't been paid. I was in debt to everyone, including the musician's union." He moved into room 605 of the Gramercy Park Hotel, 2 Lexington Avenue at Twenty-first Street, thanks to the largesse of the RCA company president, Ken Glancy, a worldly character who bailed on his English lit doctoral work to follow a music biz career and who, fortunately, loved Reed's work. It was a good hideout, at least for a while. On September 30 at 8:30 p.m., Reed answered a knock on his door and was handed a court summons. It concerned a lawsuit Dennis Katz was filing against Reed for unlawful breach of contract, asking for substantial back commissions. Another suit would be filed by Katz's brother, Steve, regarding his contract to produce Reed's next record.

* * *

As it happened, Reed's neighbors in the Gramercy were Bob Dylan and the entourage for his Rolling Thunder Revue tour, set to launch in October; Joan Baez, Reed's guitar hero Roger McGuinn, and the *Transformer* MVP Mick Ronson were all coming and going. Dylan's *Blood on the Tracks* had come out in January, a wholesale reinvention that had been met with hosannas as a return to greatness and an unprecedented display of heart. One imagines it made an impression on Reed when he entered the studio to restart the *Coney Island Baby* sessions, which

Glancy agreed to bankroll. "He asked me if I would promise not to do *Son of Metal Machine Music*. I said sure," Reed recalled. "[He] told me ok, pick a studio and go in and make a rock record."

The sessions began on October 18 and lasted a week. Reed rerecorded "She's My Best Friend," without Doug Yule, but reclaimed some of the tenderness of the Velvets' version, with bubblegummy backing vocals. The album arrangements were playful, warm evocations of AM radio pop-rock conventions. Lyrically, Reed evoked his relationship with Humphreys, juxtaposing romance with darker sentiments, reflecting the near-constant, red-alert levels of danger that characterized trans existence. "Crazy Feeling," strummed on acoustic guitar with chimes, cooing backing vocals, and slithering electric slide guitar, conjured the woozy, after-hours club scene. "Charley's Girl," sweetened with "la la la"s and a clip-clopping cowbell, had Reed describing a sort of police raid and issuing a disturbing pledge that, if he ever saw someone named Sharon again, he would "punch her face in."

This sort of contrast between gently seductive music and harsh imagery reappeared throughout the set. When Reed recorded the unnerving "Kicks," a song whose narrator sees murder as a sort of ultimate fetish, Judith Rossner's grim sexual morality tale *Looking for Mr. Goodbar* was on the *New York Times* bestseller list, a book based on the true story of a schoolteacher and singles bar habitué stabbed to death in her Upper West Side apartment by a man she'd just hooked up with. "Kicks" may also have been informed by Jean Genet's *Querelle*, which made its English-language debut in 1974; in a mirror of the song's key image, the book's protagonist slashes a man's throat, while the song's central verse ("How you get your kicks?") echoes Querelle's banter with the cop he seduces.

But *Coney Island Baby*'s beating heart is its title-track finale, arranged with plaintive backing vocals and guitar notes flashing like fireflies, ramping up gradually through loneliness to the outro, a clear nod to the doo-wop of the Five Keys' exquisite 1951 "Glory of Love," Reed invoking those words in a denouement that emerges like a sunrise, throbbing with hope. Just before the fade-out, Reed becomes a radio DJ, like the ones he grew up hearing in Brooklyn and Freeport.

"I'd like to send this one out to Lou and Rachel, and all the kids at P.S. 192," he says in a lilting voice, name-checking his primary school on Kings Highway in Bensonhurst, then pivoting, it's understood, to address Rachel: "Man, I swear," Reed says, a tremor rolling through his voice like distant thunder, "I'd give the whole thing up for you." It was a helluva love letter. And given the album's completion around the time that Humphreys's little sister committed suicide, it's possible to read *Coney Island Baby* in large part as a gift of compassionate consolation to Reed's deeply grieving partner.

* * *

A few weeks before the final *Coney Island Baby* sessions began, *Dog Day Afternoon* opened in New York City movie theaters. It was based on the true story of John Wojtowicz, a first-time bankrobber whose failed heist was an attempt to raise money that his partner, Elizabeth Eden, needed for gender-reassignment surgery. It was a trans love story, set like Reed's against a backdrop of gritty mid-'70s New York City, where its theme of desperate money-raising was especially resonant. Reed's adopted hometown had finally hit its own fiscal rock bottom, and the federal government refused a bailout. On October 30, the New York *Daily News* memorialized the president's snub in a full-page headline that sounded like something Reed might've thought up, had he gone into journalism: "FORD TO CITY: DROP DEAD."

In December, *The New York Times Magazine* ran a feature titled "The Ghost of Delmore Schwartz." It was occasioned by *Humboldt's Gift*, the year's most celebrated literary novel, whose title character—Von Humboldt Fleisher, a writer who prizes artistic integrity above all else and dies a broken man—was based on Schwartz. The book was written by Saul Bellow, who, like Reed, was mentored by Schwartz. The *Times* piece discussed the early achievement of Schwartz's *In Dreams Begin Responsibilities*, and how the critical adulation he received as a twenty-four-year-old arguably damaged him. "[Schwartz] was terribly self-conscious," the *Times* writer observed; "He knew he was expected to turn out masterpieces and that the critics were laying for him."

Schwartz's later work was considered disappointing, and he became so enraged by his critics that he was once arrested while stalking one at the Chelsea Hotel. The piece quotes "Once and for All," in which Schwartz imagined himself a young man pulled between Apollo and Dionysus, envisioning a god in mourning for "his drunken and fallen princes, the singers and sinners." One imagines Reed reading the piece in his apartment on a Sunday afternoon, and recognizing their kinship anew.

* * *

That month, Reed attended a poetry reading and performance-art show by Camille O'Grady, a self-described "multimedium" artist and regular in otherwise all-male rough-trade sex clubs such as the Eagle and the Spike, where she'd become a gender-outlaw icon. She was a musician, too, and sometimes worked with a band, Leather Secrets, performing poems like "Toilet Kiss" (rhyming the title with "porcelain and piss") in a manner that recalled Patti Smith, albeit more first-person partici- pant than third-person observer. Reed liked her work, and they'd stay in touch.

At the show, Reed ran into the Lower East Side scene vet Peter Stampfel, whose weirdo-folk band the Holy Modal Rounders briefly included O'Grady, and Stamfel's current bandmate Charlie Messing. Reed invited them to visit him sometime at his apartment. Despite fi- nancial woes, he'd been able to leave the Gramercy Park Hotel and return to his apartment. When the men dropped by, Humphreys wel- comed them into a homey holiday scene: a Christmas tree in the living room, vintage wooden furniture, an electric faux-oil lamp, and a stack of records near the futon couch with a copy of Aerosmith's *Toys in the Attic* on top. RCA-brand audio and video gear, a perk of Reed's label affiliation, was scattered about.

Reed came back from running errands; he'd just bought himself a new pair of aviator shades, along with a bow-shaped rawhide chew for his dog. He laughed about *Metal Machine Music*, which he claimed was already a collector's item. And he proudly played the men a test pressing of the finished *Coney Island Baby*, perfect but for a minor vocal phasing issue. "He'd had to call his guy at RCA and get them to stop that plant's production till they fixed [it]," Messing recalled. "He said it was lucky he had good ears, because if he hadn't noticed the mistake, nobody else would have."

Things were looking up. But Reed's speed habit still had a grip on him. His friend Ed McCormack recalled waking up on Reed's leather couch one morning with a blinding hangover. On the coffee table was "a bottle of prescription pills, a circular silver dish with 12 disposable hypodermic needles neatly arranged along its edges in a sort of speed-freakishly compulsive sunbeam pattern, and a row of test tubes filled with water, little white pills dissolving in milky bubbles within each one."

Reed was sleeping off a three-day speed bender in the bedroom, and Humphreys was speaking to her sister Gail on the phone. With her back turned, McCormack swiped the pills—Desoxyns, the gold standard—slipped them into his pocket, and headed for the door. As the saying goes, there's no honor among speed freaks.

* * *

In her 1818 novel *Frankenstein; or, The Modern Prometheus*, Mary Wollstonecraft Shelley imagined an undead human monster that became a Romantic literary figure and an icon, repurposed over generations. Her creature was visualized by the director James Whale and acted by Boris Karloff in the 1931 screen adaptation, with a formidable follow-up franchise, and the creature was strangely resonant in the '70s. His iconic visage was seen regularly on newsstands on the cover of *Famous Monsters of Filmland*, a fanzine that enlisted him as a graphic mascot to target fantasia-hungry adolescents, just like glam rock. The Edgar Winter Group named a 1973 instrumental "Frankenstein," which topped the charts, and David Johansen played the monster as a proto-punk loverman on the New York Dolls' debut, slyly asking if "you think you could make it with Frankenstein." Warhol got in on the act with a sexploitation exercise, *Flesh for Frankenstein*, an Italian film production renamed *Andy Warhol's Frankenstein* for the U.S. market, and was soon followed by Mel Brooks's blockbuster comedy *Young Frankenstein*.

"We are the true children of Frankenstein we were raised on electricity," wrote Patti Smith in her review of *1969: The Velvet Underground Live*. The metaphor had precedent in Reed's stage makeup, and, increasingly, his persona. The act of shooting speed has some metaphoric kinship with Dr. Frankenstein's pumping volts into a cadaver, just as the transmogrification of Shelley's antihero has some metaphoric kinship with the gender mutability that fascinated Reed. In a sense, Lou and Rachel were the original urban goth couple.

Fans made the connection and ran with it. In 1973, a short-lived 'zine called *Punk* featured Reed as the monster, in a comic strip drawn by Tom Toles and written by Billy Altman, the SUNY Buffalo student who booked the first Lou Reed solo performance. In January 1976, another magazine of the same name made its debut in New York City. It featured a cartoon of Reed on its cover, bolts protruding from his square forehead—a rock 'n' roll Frankenstein's monster. The feature story within was hand-drawn in an underground comics style recalling R. Crumb. Its headline read: "LOU REED, ROCK AND ROLL VEGETABLE: AN EXCLUSIVE INTERVIEW WITH THE ORIGINAL STREET PUNK TURNED FINE ARTIST!"

It was based on an interview Reed gave one night at CBGB, after he was bum-rushed at a Ramones show by two of the magazine's founders. Amused by their chutzpah, Reed consented to their interrogation. Eddie "Legs" McNeil asked his opinion of various CBGB bands; Reed praised the Ramones ("Fantastic!"), Television ("I think Tom Verlaine's really nice"), and Patti Smith. Then McNeil asked him his thoughts on Bruce Springsteen.

"He's a shit," Reed snapped, maybe sensing a journalistic setup between established acts and upstarts. "What are you talking about, what kind of stupid question is that?" With knee-jerk New York hustle, Reed insisted the magazine put him on the cover. McNeil agreed.

"Your circulation must be fabulous," Reed sniffed.

In fact, *Punk* would do pretty well. Launched in a former trucking office on the rim of Hell's Kitchen by three Connecticut expats—John Holmstrom, Ged Dunn, and McNeil—the magazine was an aesthetic manifesto in step with the CBGB scene. The sensibility, not unlike *Creem*'s, was sort of tongue-in-cheek, sort of not (*Punk*'s proudly knucklehead debut editorial declared, "DEATH TO DISCO SHIT! LONG LIVE THE ROCK!"), and it aimed to define a musical moment that would ultimately circle the globe, with Reed as its somewhat absent father. It didn't coin "punk" as a term of musical style—the label had been applied to inspiringly amateurish rock music well before Patti Smith's guitarist Lenny Kaye used it to describe the bands on *Nuggets*, the 1972 LP of primitive '60s rock 'n' roll he curated—but *Punk* effectively branded the New York scene with it.

Though he didn't always cop to it, Reed was a genuine fan. The first time he'd heard the Ramones, on a demo cassette in Danny Fields's apartment, he was floored by their face-punch propulsion. "They're CRAZY!" Reed exclaimed to Fields. "That is, y'know, without doubt, the most fantastic thing you've ever played me, bar none. I mean, it makes everybody look so bullshit and wimpy, Patti Smith and me included, man. Wow . . . They are everything everybody worried about— every parent in America would freeze in their tracks if they heard this stuff . . . There they are: their worst dreams come true! That is the greatest thing I've ever heard. Danny—*do* something!" (Fields would in fact wind up managing the band.)

Reed also admired Smith, whose debut album, *Horses*—produced by Cale—had been released in November. Just as the Velvets had channeled post–New York School poetry through early rock 'n' roll, doo-wop, and girl-group pop with a touch of the '60s avant-garde, the Patti Smith Group did much the same thing, drawing landscapes of the city (and occasionally the beach) in which drugs and violence were matters of fact, where desire was sometimes queer, where transcendence was rooted in self-realization as opposed to religious doctrine. Both poets had standout songs invoking Jesus. Where Reed chanted about the ocean and the waves ("Where have they been?"), Smith invoked Redondo Beach and the "sea of possibilities." Where Reed conjured a murderous polymorphous orgy, Smith conjured an encounter between two men blurring rape, knife violence, and consensual bathhouse sex. Where Reed sang about "white light" and "white heat," Smith rhymed "fill my nose with snow" and "go Rimbaud."

The New York scene kept growing. Blondie, a band that evolved from a campy girl group called the Stilettos, was another up-and-coming CBGB act. Their bottle-blond front woman, Debbie Harry, possessed a cool, disarming beauty not unlike Nico's. When Harry sang "Femme Fatale" in between the band's originals, it was a perfect fit.

Then there was Talking Heads, who Reed liked so much, he wanted to produce them, perhaps in part to compete with Cale. One night after catching their set, Reed invited the band up to his place on the Upper East Side. Thrilled, the trio—David Byrne, Tina Weymouth, and Chris Frantz—cabbed it up there, announced themselves to the doorman, and watched the sunrise with Reed as he waxed avuncular, critiqued their music, recommended pills displayed in his copy of the *Physician's Desk Reference*, and ate a quart of Häagen-Dazs ice cream with a bent, blackened spoon. Reed wanted to introduce them to his new manager, Jonny Podell, and discuss working together.

"This was heady stuff for a band that had only played a few shows and were new to New York City," recalled Frantz. "Of course, we told him yes, we'd be happy to see him again." However, as the young band soon learned, Reed's reputation in the industry was not good, and when the production offer was vetted by the Heads' lawyers (a decidedly "shitty deal," as Frantz recalled), the band passed.

And the tributes to Reed's influence were not all flattering. Writing about Smith in *The New York Times*, a besotted John Rockwell drew an extended comparison between Reed and Smith that must have stung. "Although Mr. Reed has managed to turn out some conceptually and verbally interesting material," the critic observed, "he isn't in Smith's league when it comes to words and ideas."

* * *

Yet *Coney Island Baby*, issued in January, was a striking achievement. It sure didn't sound like a punk record—with its slick production, it suggested quite the opposite. But it was plenty punk in spirit, an un-abashedly, if coded, queer record full of camp humor and defiant ro-manticism. The cynicism that diminished *Sally Can't Dance* was largely banished, and *Coney Island Baby*'s doo-wop touches paid homage to the roots of rock 'n' roll just as Patti Smith and the New York Dolls did.

Critics, many sensing an Oedipal moment, ran hot and cold. In a lead review for *Rolling Stone*, Paul Nelson—the same diehard who'd midwifed *1969: The Velvet Underground Live*—praised *Coney Island Baby*, citing its warmth and humanity in the wake of work that had been "a cheap, sensationalized self-parody of the more freakish side of his per-sona." In the U.K., however, where rock was in the throes of imported punk's first flush, critics were unimpressed. "Lou Reed's revolution-ary days are long gone, and the years of his farthood lie heavy upon him," wrote Charles Shaar Murray in the *New Musical Express*. Even at home, young critics were harsh. James Walcott, a sharp writer who'd made the punk scene his beat, marked Reed's return with an essay in *The Village Voice* about his long aesthetic shadow, admiring *Berlin* and *Metal Machine Music* ("a two-record set of such triumphant unlisten-ability that it crowned Reed's reputation as a master of psychopathic insolence"), but rejecting *Coney Island Baby*. "What Reed learned from Warhol (though he could have learned it equally well from Mailer or Capote) is careermanship," he wrote, "making yourself such a com-manding media figure that even when your latest work is a pathetic package of retread riffs and coffee-grind lyrics, people will still be in-trigued by the strategy behind it."

Nevertheless, Reed was thrilled with the album. "This [LP is] just totally the way I want it, from top to bottom," he told Lenny Kaye in an interview that ran in the *New Musical Express*. "I'm as proud of this as I am of anything I did with the Velvets." He was also happy to overhaul his persona. In the Mick Rock cover shot, he's less "Phantom of Rock" Frankenstein monster or *Rock 'n' Roll Animal* leather bar moll than Charlie Chaplin's little tramp gone fey, with a touch of Joel Grey's *Cabaret* master of ceremonies, in black nail polish and a tight tuxedo-front T-shirt, peeking out from behind a bowler hat with his once-again dark hair in a bushy mop.

"No more bullshit," Reed quipped, evidently rejecting not his sexuality so much as the image he'd concocted with fetish gear, hypodermics, and heavy metal theatrics.

Having to do "Heroin" that way, it was so awful. It almost killed me. The worse I was, the more they bought. It was incredible. *Sally Can't Dance* goes to number ten. What a horror. It went top ten and it sucks. People who want more *Rock 'N'Roll Animal*, sorry. I mimic me probably better than anybody, so if everybody else is making money ripping me off, I figured maybe I better get in on it. Why not? I created Lou Reed. I have nothing even faintly in common with that guy, but I can play him well. Really well.

Unfortunately, radio programmers were mostly uninspired by the new Lou, and with no hit single and little significant airplay, *Coney Island Baby* topped out at number 41 on the *Billboard* chart. Still, after the commercial debacle of *Metal Machine Music*, it was enough to redeem him in the eyes of the industry, at least among those attuned to what was shifting in rock culture.

"I got a call from Clive Davis," Reed recalled, "and he said, 'Hey, how ya doing? Haven't seen you for a while.' He knew how I was doing. He said, 'Why don't we have lunch?' I felt like saying, 'You mean you want to be seen with me in public?' If Clive could be seen with me, I had turned the corner. I grabbed Rachel and said, 'Do you know who just called?' I knew then that I'd won."

* * *

Reed's RCA contract was finished with the release of *Coney Island Baby*, and he took the opportunity to switch labels. Reed had known Davis for a while. Both were Brooklyn-born, middle-class, college-educated, ambitious Jewish men in the music industry. They also shared an understanding of queerness (Davis would come out as bisexual later in life). "If you wanted to witness the flip side of New York City nightlife, the seamy underbrush of colorful and sexual goings-on, the transexuals and transvestites, the whole real-life *Rocky Horror* show, Lou was the quintessential guide," Davis recalled. "One night, he took me on a fast-paced tour, not trying to shock me, just to point out this was part of the world he moved in, that these were some of the people he knew. But he would also come to my house to watch the Thanksgiving Parade float down Central Park West, and nosh on bagels and appetizers—just a Jewish guy who grew up in Freeport, except with dyed hair, incredibly long fingernails, and the palest skin, which was not surprising given his nocturnal ways."

For his part, Davis was the quintessential industry macher. A Harvard law grad who segued from a practice into a Columbia Records gig during the folk and rock boom, he soon became president, signing Janis Joplin, Santana, Pink Floyd, and Bruce Springsteen, among others. He was fired from Columbia amid a federal investigation of the label; the web of accusations included, most famously, intentionally billing the label for his son's lavish bar mitzvah at the Plaza Hotel (a charge he denied). By the time Reed reached out to him, or vice versa—their accounts vary—Davis had published his first volume of music biz derring-do memoirs, and launched his own label, Arista, signing Patti Smith right out of the gate. Reed saw Davis as both ally and father figure—ten years his senior, wealthy, highly intelligent. Davis saw Reed as a zeitgeist-perfect imprimatur for his new label, and given Reed's recent track record, an affordable one at that.

* * *

Nevertheless, Reed still had plenty of business woes. The lawsuit Katz filed against him was in play, and while Reed had gotten some pretestimony coaching, it was rough going, to judge from court documents filed in April. "That's bullshit," exclaimed one Katz associate at one point during the hearings, in response to Reed's account of his management travails.

Yet for all his troubles, Reed was feeling optimistic. He was back on track professionally, happy with his work, and, by all indications, in love. His home life, relatively speaking, was remarkably settled. He and Rachel got a puppy: a miniature dachshund Reed named the Baron, who would soon get a companion when Reed bought another dachshund, the Duke. Reed was an inveterate dog lover; savoring the emotional simplicity of relating to animals, he'd play with the two for hours. As with Seymoure, the dog he adopted with Shelley Albin in Syracuse, dogs allowed him to entertain the paternal side of his personality with a partner. ("Maybe they're child substitutes," he'd muse. But again, the parental responsibility of dog-walking was regularly farmed out to his partner, in this case Rachel.)

Humphreys had Reed's back in many ways. On the town or on the road, she played caretaker, and sometimes bodyguard. Humphreys was tall and could come across as menacing. At home, she contentedly played hostess (though her kitchen skills were slight), or sat quietly, fiddling with her long jet-black hair as Reed talked shop with friends, showing them his latest video gear, or playing songs on his Wurlitzer electric piano. The pair were largely inseparable; Humphreys accompanied Reed on tours, to recording sessions, and to interviews. Many journalists, however, seemed to think it a decadent horse-and-pony show, unable or unwilling to believe Reed was in a genuine, satisfying relationship with a nonbinary person. It was a public romance largely unprecedented in mainstream pop culture, and their matter-of-factly out-of-the-closet attitude was not without risk. Yet both came off, at least for a time, as fearless.

Even the punk rock scene, despite enlightened poses and a significant queer constituency, could be hateful. In March, a brawl broke out in CBGB after the Dictators' singer, "Handsome" Dick Manitoba, started heckling the trans rocker Jayne County (who'd changed her stage name from Wayne) with homophobic taunts during her show; Manitoba wound up in an ambulance with a broken collarbone and a gaping head wound after County clobbered him with a mic stand. Shortly thereafter, Lester Bangs drafted a nasty, slur-filled essay about the punk scene's queer and presumably predatory power bloc for *Punk* magazine—partly in solidarity with the Dictators, who'd been subject to local blacklisting after the Jayne County dustup. (When word of the article-in-process surfaced and Bangs got wind of a furious pushback, the piece was shelved.)

* * *

It was a strange summer in New York. The city had been attempting to clean up its act on the eve of America's bicentennial celebrations, which were crowned on July 4 with a nautical parade of tall-masted sailing ships in New York Harbor—not far from the piers where men cruised for blow jobs off the West Side Highway. At the same time, audiences nationwide were flocking to Martin Scorsese's *Taxi Driver*, a film that profiled a city rotted to the core. It was not great civic PR. Likely related to the city's cleanup effort, there'd been a marijuana shortage in town, so severe that the *SoHo Weekly News* ran a cover story on it. At the same time, the city was mysteriously flooded with cheap, remarkably pure Mexican brown heroin—an influx that would be studied by conspiracy theorists for years to come. Reed's drug of choice remained amphetamine, but that, too, was in short supply, as doctors no longer dispensed prescriptions as cavalierly. He did his best to find supplies, though the quality varied.

On July 21, Reed took part in a summit of two generations of New York rock 'n' rollers. The "John Cale and Friends" gig was convened at the Lower Manhattan Ocean Club, a new venue opened at 121 Chambers Street by Mickey Ruskin, who'd cashed out his interest in Max's Kansas City. Cale's friends included Patti Smith (home following her seismic London debut), Talking Heads' David Byrne, and the guitar wiz Mick Ronson. The crowd included a Who's Who of Reed's past, present, and future: Warhol, Danny Fields, Lisa Robinson, Humphreys, Clive Davis, plus the CBGB mishpocha: assorted Ramones, Talking Heads, Smith bandmates, and members of Television. (Cale's attention was also on a young actor, Ellen Barkin.) On "I'm Waiting for the Man," Cale alternated verses with Smith, who hollered "Heeeeey, white boy!" amid her usual poetic freestyling, while David Byrne plinked out chicken-scratch riffs. Reed played guitar and danced a bit, but took no lead vocals. It was a tantalizing evening.

But after a repeat show the following night, it didn't lead to anything more.

Reed would spend a month—twenty-seven days to be exact, by his account—making his Arista-label debut, *Rock and Roll Heart*. Like *Coney Island Baby*, it conjured oldies rock, but without the danger, passion, and frisson of his previous album, and the back-to-basics CBGB acts. Reed kept the lyrics simple. "I guess I'm dumb because I know I ain't smart / But deep down inside I have a rock and roll heart," he sang on the title track ("It'll be one of my most memorable lines," he'd later tell a journalist, wryly). At the same time, maybe to mirror the wiseass humor of the Ramones and the Dictators, he littered verses with dubious in-jokes. On "I Believe in Love," a song invoking "good time rock and roll," he chirped "I believe in the iron cross," an apparent reference to the Nazi iconography of his short-lived hairstyle from a couple of years back. Camping it up lounge lizard–style on the jazzy "A Sheltered Life," he declared, "I've never taken drugs." Elsewhere, the grim "Ladies Pay" conjured cruising sailors, Amsterdam brothel windows, and sad military wives, while "Follow the Leader" paid tribute to New York in the voice of a stuttering speed freak—seemingly half-heartedly if on-brand performances, like a weary character actor dutifully reprising old roles.

One of the record's poignant moments was "You Wear It So Well," on which Reed may've been addressing his lover's hardscrabble life when he sang "All of the pain that you used to tell / You hide it so well." The engineer Corky Stasiak recalls Humphreys at the studio regularly, always ready to calm "Lewis" down with a supportive word or a shoulder massage, otherwise hanging quietly in the background, often with Baron the dachshund. ("She seemed like a great girlfriend," Stasiak recalls.) The sessions were stressful—Godfrey Diamond, the co-producer who pinch-hit on *Coney Island Baby* when Steve Katz bailed, did not return for *Rock and Roll Heart*, so Reed was producing himself, with Stasiak's help, and handling all the guitar parts on top of that. There was plenty of speed, but it didn't always speed things up.

"Okay, session's over. Let's do a playback," Reed might say. "But let's take a break first; I need to go to the bathroom." Forty-five minutes later, he'd emerge from the john, pupils like whirlpools, and yell for the lights to be turned down. Stasiak would cue the tape, press the play button, and turn up the volume high, then higher.

"Ooooooo, yeah," Reed would say, eyes closed, goose bumps rising on his arms. "Yeeeeeaaaaaahhhhhhhh."

Clive Davis hoped his young label's prestige acts could make hits, too. He smelled heat in *Rock and Roll Heart*'s hooky title track, but thought it too sparse-sounding to get radio traction. "I wouldn't and didn't give Lou any specific direction, only asked him to consider fleshing it out, and he refused," Davis recalled. "Not at all surprisingly, he didn't want to hear any suggestions, no matter how well-intentioned." Reed's instincts didn't serve him well saleswise; the record made even less of an impression than his last, reaching only number 64 on the charts before dropping off.

* * *

Like Warhol, Reed had for years been fascinated with the new technology of portable video gear; Nam June Paik's pioneering '60s work cast a long shadow on the New York art scene. Much of the action in this field was at the Kitchen Center for Video and Music, a new space with a rock 'n' roll pedigree: it had begun as part of the Mercer Arts Center in the early '70s, where the New York Dolls and Suicide shaped post–Velvet Underground, proto punk rock; now it showcased emerging video artists. The medium was for '70s artists what Super 8 and 16mm film had been for Warhol and Mekas in the '60s: radically affordable, with a low-fi quality that lent itself to creative abstraction.

Continuing Reed's tendency to harvest ideas from the high-art world, he worked with Mick Rock to develop a video wall for the *Rock and Roll Heart* tour. "I got 60 TVs from a hospital," Reed recalled of the stage setup, twelve stacks of five each arrayed as a cathode-ray Stonehenge, pulsing with feedback loops created by distorted video signals generated by a camera pointed at a monitor. "Every once in a while, something would go wrong and a cable would come loose, so you'd have all these visuals flipping and a Fred Astaire movie in the middle of it." TVs would regularly implode; by the end of the tour, a costly endeavor, they were down to thirty-six monitors, which they dumped when it was time to fly home.

The band was a whiplash blend of the avant-garde and the mainstream. On October 23 at the Akron Civic Center, the second night of the tour, "Lisa Says" and "She's My Best Friend" weren't far from what Reed's fellow Long Island singer-songwriter Billy Joel was doing at the time—or Elton John, for that matter—in terms of instrumentation and arrangements. At the same show, Reed sang "Kill Your Sons" with venom, and delivered "I'm Waiting for the Man" as a twitching jazz-rock seizure, his spasmodic guitar noise solos alternating with Marty Fogel's sax, part noir menace, part Albert Ayler holy shriek of pain, as Reed stuttered out the words like a man in the throes of withdrawal, ready to destroy anyone standing between him and his next fix.

In the audience taking all this in, with a primo orchestra seat, was Peter Laughner. A mightily talented rock guitarist, Laughner had a hand in birthing punk from the outpost of Cleveland—as a founding member of the band Rocket from the Tombs, which evolved into Pere Ubu; as a local scene booster; and as a rock critic. He'd been a major Reed fan since the Velvets days, often covering his songs, and Laughner's own compositions showed the influence, notably "Amphetamine," an artful nod to "Heroin" (in one version, Laughner name-checked Reed and made an oblique reference to "Fallen Knights and Fallen Ladies," his essay on dead rock stars). In a review of *1969: The Velvet Underground Live*, Laughner testified that the band's music "saved my life. It could save yours." His review of *Metal Machine Music* was a three-paragraph-long ellipsis. And he'd interviewed Reed on numerous occasions. In a 1974 profile in the regional music magazine *Exit*, Laughner described a scene in which he gave Reed a copy of John Berryman's *Dream Songs* and three black beauties, then watched Reed snort the contents of the capsules.

Like his friend Lester Bangs, Laughner's obsession with Reed, to put it mildly, verged on the unhealthy. In *Creem*'s March issue, Laughner wrote a savagely unhinged review of *Coney Island Baby*—he claimed the album depressed him so much, he went on a three-day bender, got into a violent fight with his wife, and "ended up the whole debacle passing out stone cold after puking and pissing myself at a band rehearsal."

Laughner outlined his profound love for the Velvet Underground, how he wrote high school papers comparing "Sweet Jane" to work by Alexander Pope and argued how "Some Kinda Love" "lined right up with T. S. Eliot's 'The Hollow Men.'" Reed, Laughner declared, with a nod to Dylan's creation myth, "was my Woody Guthrie . . . and with enough amphetamine I would be the new Lou Reed!" How much was true, and how much authorial hyperbole, was hard to tell. But his fandom was intense. When Laughner's friend and bandmate Adele Bertei first visited his apartment, she recalled a sort of shrine: a photo of an emaciated Reed hung directly above his stereo system, affixed to the wall with a switchblade.

After the Akron show, Laughner went to Reed's hotel under the auspices of doing an interview—although, as the story goes, the meeting was primarily for Laughner to hook Reed up with an ounce of crystal meth.

* * *

As America's so-called sexual revolution was cresting across the board, LGBTQ+ culture in New York City was in full bloom in early 1977. Robert Mapplethorpe—who, with his freshly pierced nipple, danced with his pal Patti Smith to the Velvets at Max's during the band's summer 1970 farewell run—became a star photographer on February 5, 1977, when he opened two simultaneous shows: the straightforward *Portraits* at the Holly Solomon Gallery, and his explicit S&M-themed *Erotic Pictures* at the Kitchen. The way Mapplethorpe aestheticized the extremities of New York queer culture had some things in common with Reed's work, to be sure.

That spring, a feature on Reed in the glossy new gay porn magazine *Mandate*, itself an example of the new semi-mainstreaming, got cover-billing ("THE PRINCE OF DARKNESS . . . LOU REED"). There was no beefcake photo shoot, but it's hard to imagine another mainstream rock musician getting similar attention in that post-glam, punk-ascendent moment. Not even Bowie, who in January released *Low*, the first fruit of his residency in Berlin, where he was trying to kick a cocaine addiction and recenter himself creatively. Bowie's public queerness had become vestigial; in the wake of his star turn as an interplanetary alien in *The Man Who Fell to Earth*—a promotional image from the film graced *Low*'s cover—his persona now tilted toward celestial asexuality. Reed, meanwhile, was still winding up the straights; the previous winter, he'd spent a good deal of his time with a *Rolling Stone* feature writer discussing trans sex workers, when he wasn't rhapsodizing on the glory of Neil Young's guitar work—in particular, "Danger Bird," from Young's new LP *Zuma* ("[It] made me cry," Reed effused).

As heteronormative sex clubs like Plato's Retreat were generating headlines, New York City's gay sex clubs were experiencing a golden era. The Mineshaft had opened the previous fall at 835 Washington Street, to much underground fanfare; a flyer promoting the opening night stressed "a dress code of levi [sic], leather, uniforms, and similar casual attire required at all times. No fluff allowed!" A legendary space with slings for fisting and a bathtub for "water sports," it became a favorite of Mapplethorpe's, who often found photographic models there. Reed told friends he regretted his fame made it difficult to frequent such places, though he managed to visit them on occasion, more as observer than participant.

Erin Clermont recalls going to the Mineshaft with Reed. One of the few relationships he maintained from his Syracuse days (she was a friend of Shelley Albin), Clermont was sometimes a lover, but always a confidant, someone Reed could call at 3 a.m. when he was lonely, to talk or to meet up at some late-night dive. He could count on her as his occasional wingman. "I'd come home and there'd be like thirty-two hang-ups on my answering machine," she says. "I knew then he was trying to get in touch with me, and I'd just have to make up my mind whether I was going to answer [his next call] or just, you know, turn off the phone and get some sleep."

* * *

Humphreys allowed Reed space for these kinds of activities and friendships, it seems, though events that spring suggest the couple were solidifying their relationship. In April, RCA released *Walk on the Wild Side: The Best of Lou Reed*, a cash-in compilation culled from Reed's solo releases to date, on the occasion of his switching labels. The LP cover showed a half-dozen photographs of Reed taken by Mick Rock. Humphreys is in all the shots; in one, she cradles Reed's chin as he tips back his head, evidently awaiting a kiss.

The cover may have been an anniversary gift. Back on tour that month, during a three-night run at London's New Victoria, a 2,300-seat former movie palace in the West End, Reed and Humphreys celebrated their third year together as a couple in a private London club. It was a sort of wedding reception, with an exchange of rings to commemorate their union and a three-tiered cake inscribed "One layer for each year. Hoping for many more. Love Rachel."

"The atmosphere was gentle and happy," recalls the photographer Jill Furmanovsky. One shot of the couple, posed in front of the huge cake, shows them with arms around each other, Reed in a black leather jacket and jeans, Humphreys in slacks and a white blouse, long black hair spilling down, nearly a head taller than Reed. In another, the couple kiss; in another, they cuddle on a couch, Reed's finger idly stroking Humphreys's thigh, head against their chest, while Humphreys runs a hand through his curls.

Furmanovsky recalls Humphreys demanding she hand over the negatives after making her prints. "Rachel wanted them published in the U.K. as a kind of public statement of their wedding."

There was one curious detail visible in some of the shots: Humphreys's free hand was wrapped in a scarf. According to Furmanovsky, "[it] hid a wound that, I remember being told by an aide on the tour, came about because of a fight between them . . . possibly involving a knife." Whatever the circumstances of the injury, Reed's relationship was clearly under strains external and internal. Humphreys was used to violence, transphobic or otherwise. How often she started trouble is harder to say. Some in Reed's circle noted her toughness and quickness with knives. One story had her threatening a girl with a switchblade for flirting with Reed. Another came from a neighbor who saw Humphreys in bad shape one morning, bruised and curled up on the lobby couch, evidently locked out of their apartment. Transphobia, and tendencies to see nonbinary persons as tragic if not deranged, especially at the time, probably informed the stories as well as the incidents.

Home for a tour break in December, Humphreys got roughed up badly; the circumstances of the incident were unclear. Reed called Warhol for help. "He said Rachel had gotten kicked in the balls and was bleeding from the mouth and he wanted the name of a doctor," Warhol recalled in a diary entry. "Lou's doctor had looked at Rachel and said that it was nothing, that it would stop, but Lou wanted another doctor to check. I said I'd get Bianca's. But then Lou called back and said he got Keith Richards's doctor to come over. I told him he should take her to the hospital. I was calling Rachel 'she' because she's always in drag but then Lou calls him 'he.'"

For all the drama, Reed did what he could to protect and take care of Humphreys, as Humphreys did for him. Michael Fonfara lived a few blocks from the couple, and often walked the dogs when they couldn't. He has no doubt how real their relationship was. "Oh yeah," he says with certainty. "They were in love, for sure."

A major issue the couple faced was Humphreys's desire to transition. She began using hormones, and hoped Reed would support her getting surgery, which would include covering the substantial cost. But like many cis partners of trans people, Reed could be less than sympathetic. According to Humphreys's friend Jayne County, Reed liked Rachel as she was, and the couple clashed over it. Then there was the issue of drugs. A recording made in 1977 of Reed's side of a phone conversation captured him and Rachel bickering over cash, though the exact context is unclear. "I know you have money hidden," Reed insisted, exasperated. "I know that! I could get some fucking dope if you just tell me where the money is."

Around this time, a couple of Reed's associates noted a nasty abscess on his forearm, the sort caused by frequent injections, which he made barely any effort to conceal, seeing it as something of a battle scar. One man, who also shot speed, described a harrowing scene in which Reed, in a gesture of bravado and need, stuck a loaded hypodermic into the open wound.

One might imagine that it was at this precise moment, as the meth flushed his consciousness into familiar hyperclarity, that Reed— however much he was method-acting, engaging in embedded journalism, or living his truth—realized things had gotten somewhat out of hand.

* * *

Sylvia Morales was a military kid—her dad, Pete, was a noncommissioned air force officer—and like Humphreys, she had Mexican roots. Morales spent part of her youth in Taiwan, where her dad was based. She attended high school in Hawaii, and in 1974 followed her friend Anya Phillips to New York after graduation. Morales was a good student, and aspired to be a painter; she got into Pratt, and dove into the downtown art and music scene with Phillips, who worked as a stripper and professional dominatrix. At CBGB one night, in the club's neon-beer-sign glow, Morales met Richard Hell, the poet-musician who'd been one of punk rock's aesthetic forefathers. He helped Morales score a cheap tenement apartment at 437 East Twelfth Street, the East Village "Poet's Building," where her neighbors were himself, Allen Ginsberg, the composer Arthur Russell, and others. With her high cheekbones, dark locks, and full lips, she was, alongside Phillips, among the punk scene's iconic beauties.

There are varying accounts of how Morales met Reed. Morales tells the story of meeting him at a bar in June 1977. She was with Phillips, the more outgoing of the two; Phillips introduced herself to Reed, and then called over Morales, who felt an instant chemistry. Morales didn't exchange information with Reed, not wanting to be perceived as a starstruck fangirl. In the following days, though, she got his contact information, and mailed him a letter.

Reed reciprocated, and the two began seeing each other. He was still living with Humphreys, but he'd evidently reached a point where he was considering his options. He understood he was near the end of his rope, and Morales sensed it, too. "I was not a drug taker myself, but I was not a judgmental person. I was surrounded by a bunch of creative types who were already pretty good stoners on their own; Lou did not stand out in that respect," she says. "[But] it was clear to me that he was ready for that part of his life to be over, and to move towards some health and productivity. And I completely understood." By degrees, and with a period of overlap, Reed began separating himself from Humphreys, and before long, Morales moved in with Reed on Christopher Street.

Still, she hedged her bets, like generations of New York apartment dwellers leveraging the real-estate implications of new romances. She remembers a magazine publishing "this nasty schadenfreudey list about rock stars they thought were most likely to die, and he was number one. And it was entirely possible. . . . I kept my Twelfth Street apartment probably longer than I needed to."

* * *

Peter Laughner published a disappointed review of *Rock and Roll Heart* in *Creem*. Writing in epistolary form, he testified he'd listened to the LP "at least 46 times." The result? "I don't feel anything. It's as painless and boring as modern dentistry."

Like Reed, Laughner, too, was at the end of his rope. In June, while staying with his parents, he made a tape of himself performing some originals and favorite covers. It showed the work of a tremendously smart and skillful musician.

"It's real late at night," Laughner says into the microphone. "Everybody's gone to sleep, and I have a six-pack of Genesee, and some Lucky Strikes."

He begins with Television's "See No Evil," hammering out the chords on his acoustic guitar, fingerpicking on the chorus, singing, "I understand all destructive urges / they seem so perfect." He sings Richard Hell's "Blank Generation," the Stones' "Wild Horses," and a rather possessed version of Robert Johnson's "Me and the Devil Blues," played with bottleneck slide.

Then, near the end of the tape, he sings an impeccably raw and gentle rendition of "Pale Blue Eyes." "This is the most beautiful love song I've ever heard," he says, by way of introduction. "And it's very hard for me to do it justice. But I think if you listen to the lyrics, you'll get the idea."

The following morning, his mother found him dead in his bedroom. The autopsy blamed acute pancreatitis, the result of his diligent drug and alcohol abuse. He was twenty-four.

Laughner's was the first death of note in the nascent American punk scene, and to some it was a wake-up call. Bangs wrote a raging, rhapsodic obituary that ran that autumn in *New York Rocker*, a new music newspaper devoted to punk and new wave. It may have been his most moving piece. Bangs wrote about their friendship, which he tried to end when Laughner's drug and alcohol abuse got to a point where even Bangs recognized it as suicidal. He ranted at punk nihilists—"you stupid fuckheads, you who treat life as a camp joke, you who have lost your sense of wonder about the state of being alive." Bangs quoted Laughner's *Coney Island Baby* review at length, and concluded, "Peter Laughner had his private pains and compulsions, but at least in part he died because he wanted to be Lou Reed"—to which Bangs made a point of adding: "That certainly was not Lou's fault; it was Peter's."

* * *

Reed's next album would be shadowed by another death—Eric Emerson's—and if *Rock and Roll Heart* was tepid, *Street Hassle* was anything but. It would be several things: a breakup album, an elegy for love lost, and a time-warping meta-commentary on both a career and an artistic persona grown malevolent—to a point where, like the monster in Mary Wollstonecraft Shelley's book, it seemed poised to kill its creator.

Recording began on the road, with Reed writing and arranging songs on the fly. Bob Ezrin connected him with a German audio engineer, Manfred Schunke, who was working with "binaural" sound recording. The new technique used custom-designed mannequin heads—precisely mapped life-sized models of human heads with multiple pickups arrayed inside—to create vivid, three-dimensional sound imaging that might duplicate the way human beings experience music being made in situ. Schunke recorded Reed's show in Ludwigshafen that spring, and Reed used the live recordings as a starting point for the LP versions.

The swerve between audio realism and fantasy was destabilizing. The *Street Hassle* version of the Velvets outtake "We're Gonna Have a Real Good Time Together" begins as a woozy, drumless studio reverie, with smeared guitar tones similar to those Robert Fripp had unleashed on David Bowie's recent *"Heroes"* LP (Reed got his effect with a vintage Fender Vibroverb amp). The song then morphs into a Reed live performance from Germany—a foggy memory of the Velvets banished in a hot-wired present.

Similarly self-referential was the album opener, "Gimmie Some Good Times," a mash-up with Reed voicing both "Lou Reed" and an ostensible Lou Reed fan. "Hey, if it ain't the Rock 'n' Roll Animal himself," exclaims the latter, who asks Reed what he's doing. Reed responds in ping-pong banter with verses from "Sweet Jane"; when he gets to the bit about Jack and Jane cross-dressing, the fan sneers: "Fuckin' faggot junkie."

Equally startling and offense-courting was "I Wanna Be Black," Reed's acoustic demo now a pimp-swaggering supper-club blues romp, complete with campy backing vocals (performed by both Black and white singers). He'd dialed back the lyrics—the n-word was gone, ditto lines about selling heroin—but its parody of a white hipster still rubbed the listener's face in racist stereotypes without explicitly tipping its hand. A few months before *Street Hassle* came out, Joni Mitchell released *Don Juan's Reckless Daughter*, with its infamous cover photo of the artist in blackface framing the work's complex and similarly problematic engagement with racism. There's no indication that Mitchell's project, or the cultural dustups that followed, played any part in Reed's final decision to feature "I Wanna Be Black" on *Street Hassle*. But as a fan of Mitchell, one of the few English-language songwriters in his league—who identified herself as "a singing playwright and an [actor]," just as Reed described himself—he was surely aware of them.

Ultimately, though, these songs were window-dressing for *Street Hassle*'s titular centerpiece, a ten-minute narrative triptych involving a hookup, an overdose death, and a relationship eulogy. "I wanted to write a song that had a great monologue set to rock," Reed said years later, "something that could've been written by William Burroughs, Hubert Selby, John Rechy, Tennessee Williams, Nelson Algren, maybe a little Raymond Chandler." Given his limited vocal range and his literary ambition, Reed had always been drawn to the combination of spoken word and music, with an appreciation of the *sprechstimme* in *Wozzeck* as well as "top and bottom" doo-wop monologues. The sung-spoke opening of "Street Hassle" conjured Reed's relationship with Humphreys, as "Waltzing Matilda" picks up a "sexy boy" who transports her, with gentle lovemaking, beyond the world they lived in, "despite people's derision." The second section, which echoed the rumors about Eric Emerson's death, was a chilling monologue about a girl who ODs at someone's home, and the decision to dump her body in the street to avoid a police encounter—an option Reed argues for with unnerving cynicism in the voice of a weasley cold-blooded bystander on his way out the door. The dead girl may or may not have been Matilda, though Reed connects the two narratives by repeating the phrase "slip away," alternately conjuring a romantic escape, dodging the police, and someone's final breath.

The song's last section, subtitled "Slip Away," added more layers, Reed channeling the emotional devastation of lost love with one of his most aching vocal performances. The section also included a spoken-word bit involving truth, lies, and "sad songs" that paraphrased the chorus verse of Bruce Springsteen's hit "Born to Run"—and, in fact, was voiced by Springsteen, who was working at the Record Plant at the same time. In spite of having dissed him in *Punk* magazine, maybe partly to make amends, up his own stock, or just fuck with expectations, Reed invited Springsteen to his studio to hear his LP-in-progress and, purportedly, to vet Reed's initial recording of "Street Hassle"'s "tramps like us we were born to pay" passage. By one account, after Springsteen okayed it, Reed asked him on the spot if he'd recite the text himself for the recording, as a replacement for Reed's own. Springsteen agreed, stipulating his appearance would have to be uncredited, and laid it down in one take. The track's other guest-star vocalist was Genya Ravan, a contemporary of Reed's who'd fronted Goldie and the

Gingerbreads, one of the first all-women rock bands, and was currently reinventing herself as a thirty-something punk rock forebear, not unlike Reed. It was all set against elegant string arrangements echoing the work of downtown composers like Philip Glass and Arthur Russell, who Reed likely knew.

"Street Hassle" was an elliptical masterpiece, a sort of parlor room "Sister Ray" that swapped jam-band propulsion for headphone resplendence and sex-noir shock value for deeper emotions, which cast the album's other experiments in a flattering light. In a *Rolling Stone* feature, Mikal Gilmore described the song's narrative as "one of the greatest psychodramas in rock & roll." In their conversation, Reed told Gilmore "Street Hassle"'s protagonist was a real person in his life—"he *did* take the rings right off my fingers, and I do miss him"—and was as frank about his sexuality as he'd ever been to a journalist.

"They're not heterosexual concerns running through that song," Reed told the writer. "I don't make a deal of it, but when I mention a pronoun, its gender is all-important. It's just that my gay people don't lisp. They're not any more affected than the straight world. They just are. That's important to me. I'm one of them and I'm right there, just like anybody else."

* * *

Clive Davis had offered Reed encouragement, but otherwise left him to his own devices for *Street Hassle*. For all the positive press, the record sold poorly. Reed's disappointment was profound. "Lou was crushed," Davis recalled.

One small consolation that year was the "Best New Poet" award Reed received in spring from the Coordinating Council of Literary Magazines. The accolade was for "The Slide," one of eight poems involving violence and queer life Reed published in a small publication, *Cold Spring Journal*. He attended the ceremony at the Gotham Book Mart, a New York literary landmark at 41 West Forty-seventh Street, where his commendation was presented by the maverick presidential candidate and moonlighting poet Eugene McCarthy—the first in a series of political figures to come out publicly as Lou Reed fans. Reed noted the award frequently in conversation, and it seemed to mean as much to him as record sales or radio hits, if not more.

Meanwhile, the Velvet Underground cult continued to grow. A Velvets fanzine called *What Goes On*—unsurprisingly based in Massachusetts, launched by the superfans M. C. Kostek and Phil Milstein—featured Moe Tucker on the cover of its debut issue. Around the same time, the *New Yorker* music critic Ellen Willis wrote a touchstone essay about the band, which also praised *Street Hassle*. Willis's piece was maybe the most powerfully lucid argument to date on the greatness of Reed's writing. "The Velvets were the first important rock-and-roll artists who had no real chance of attracting a mass audience. This was paradoxical," she noted near the start of the piece, connecting Reed's early vision to the present. "Like his punk inheritors, he saw the world as a hostile place, and did not expect it to change. In rejecting the optimistic consensus of the sixties, he prefigured the punks' attack on the smug consensus of the seventies; his thoroughgoing iconoclasm anticipated the punks' contempt for all authority—including the aesthetic and moral authority of rock-and-roll itself." In the end, however, as Willis saw it, Reed's art was about transcendence:

"For the Velvets the aesthete-punk stance was a way of surviving in a world that was out to kill you; the point was not to glorify the punk, or even to say fuck you to the world, but to be honest about the strategies people adopt in a desperate situation. The Velvets were not nihilists but moralists. In their universe nihilism regularly appears as a vivid but unholy temptation, love and its attendant vulnerability as scary and poignant imperatives. Though Lou Reed rejected optimism, he was enough of his time to crave transcendence. And finally—as 'Rock & Roll' makes explicit—the Velvets' use of a mass art form was a metaphor for transcendence, for connection, for resistance to solipsism and despair."

* * *

By 1978, the disconnect between Reed's critical coronation and his ongoing business troubles, including the management lawsuits, made press dealings more turbulent than usual. In February he sat for an interview at the Lion's Head bar on Christopher Street, right next door to his apartment, with a twenty-two-year-old writer on assignment for the *SoHo Weekly News*. Josh Alan Friedman was a fan and a struggling musician, not an expert on his subject, and Reed snapped. "You oughta fuckin' kiss the ground that you're walking on that I'm even talking to you," he barked. "I'll chew you up on any level you want to get to. You're a fucking moron, and you oughta fuckin' know it man, 'cause you don't know what you're talking to, or how you're talking to it. Now I'll go right back into playing Lou Reed for you."

"Lou, that's not fair . . . lighten up," intervened Reed's publicist, who'd accompanied him. Reed later did, contritely offering the writer his fettucine alfredo, then inviting him up to his apartment to listen to *Street Hassle*, singing along to his own recording.

On March 10, Reed began an intermittent residency at the Bottom Line that extended through the spring. The club, at 15 West Fourth Street at the corner of Mercer, a five-minute walk from CBGB, would become his home base in coming years, just as the Tea Party and Max's had been. He rose to the occasion. Sitting in was the jazz trumpeter Don Cherry, among Reed's heroes; Reed had recently buttonholed Cherry in an airport lounge, no doubt with a fanboy account of seeing him with Ornette Coleman at the Five Spot in 1959, and a connection was made. Capping the hometown triumph was the presence of Warhol, who'd reflect that he was now "proud" of Reed, albeit even he measured his friend against his early work. "For once, finally, he's himself, he's not copying anybody," Warhol declared, adding the caveat that "when John Cale and Lou were the Velvets, they really had a style, but when Lou went solo he got bad."

* * *

Reed liked the scale and vibe of the four-hundred-seat venue, though he could play bigger rooms (he described being onstage at the Palladium on Fourteenth Street—the former Academy of Music, where he'd recorded *Rock 'n' Roll Animal*—as "two hours with 14,000 animals throwing beer cans at you"). The Bottom Line was a neighborhood joint where Reed could play for friends and co-conspirators, as well as a music biz schmoozatorium where artists staged coming-out events and career resets. Springsteen's 1975 *Born to Run* residency there announced his breakthrough to megastardom (Reed caught a night with Clive Davis); Patti Smith played a memorable show there the same year, with John Cale as guest, that was broadcast on the influential WNEW-FM and widely bootlegged. Springsteen and Smith were both given to extended stage banter and, in Smith's case, sparring matches with hecklers, which the room's intimacy invited. For the Bottom Line shows Reed recorded that May, for an album he'd eventually title *Live: Take No Prisoners*, Reed took both modes of communication to new heights, in performances that were equal parts music and stand-up comedy. As he quipped during one routine, he'd considered calling it *Lou Reed Talks . . . and Talks . . . and Talks*, which would've been accurate.

Reed insisted on bringing in Manfred Schunke and his binaural mannequin heads to record the performances to multitrack tape, not unreasonable for an artist whose previous live LPs, if legend-building, weren't always flattering. The results on *Take No Prisoners*, however, would be unflattering in their own way. The between-song spiels reflected Reed's satirical writing at Syracuse, his affection for Lenny Bruce, and even his borscht belt hero Henny Youngman, who was name-checked. "The best lack all conviction, and the worst are filled with a passionate intensity—now you figure out where I am," Reed challenged the audience, channeling Yeats, in a bit that opened the LP. That was a tall order. The verbal riffs came fast and furious. "Give me an issue, I'll give you a tissue and you can wipe my ass with it," Reed declared. He mimicked Patti Smith ("Fuck Radio Ethiopia, man, I'm Radio Brooklyn. I ain't no snob, man"), barked at a heckler ("I'll sing when you shut up"), described anal sex. The music, a mix of old and new, was similarly unhinged. A half-mumbled lounge blues "I'm Waiting for the Man" was campy, deranged, excruciatingly slow. "I Wanna Be Black" was performed with a mixed-race band, with Reed ad-libbing T-Bone Walker's "Stormy Monday" (a staple of white blues bands after the Allman Brothers covered it on *Live at the Fillmore East*) and taking mock offense at his backup vocalists when they echo his line about wanting to "fuck up the Jews" ("Hey! You're talking about my people," he interjected). Recasting the song as more overt comedy with Black collaborators in front of an audience clarified its sarcasm, but hardly made it easier to swallow. Reed's response to anyone in the crowd who might've been troubled by it: "What's wrong with cheap dirty jokes? Fuck you. I never said I was tasteful."

At times, the songs seemed beside the point, becoming near-vestigal. The album version of "Walk on the Wild Side" became an embellished monologue, the band comping behind a wired, frequently unintelligible Reed as he roasted celebrities in the audience and spat shrapnel of backstory: about working at Jones Beach as a teenager and quitting the Velvets; about the aborted *Walk on the Wild Side* musical; about Candy Darling at the Hayloft and how he missed her ("and I didn't even know her that well; I'm such a scam artist. She had leukemia from a silicone tit, and I'm supposed to feel sorry?"), about Little Joe ("an idiot . . . has an IQ of 12") and meeting Norman Mailer ("he tries to punch you in the stomach to see how tough you are—he's pathetic . . . somebody step on him, man. Go write a bible"), weaving in and out of the lyrics almost as afterthought. After singing about Jackie Curtis "speeding away," he added: "like me."

By turns absurd, appalling, hilarious, and occasionally touching (a stirring "Coney Island Baby" was personalized with Long Island township shout-outs), the brakes-off flow on *Live: Take No Prisoners* is also a bit frightening. Reed declared he'd "rather have cancer than be a faggot," then backpedaled vaguely; he savaged the critics Robert Christgau and John Rockwell (surmising the former's sexual orientation as "toe fucker," while offering a pair of expletives to the latter) and berated the club's owners for admitting journalists, giving them the best seats, and maybe supplying them with coke.

The cover of *Take No Prisoners* was a cartoon graphic of a bald, buff, bare-chested, hairy-legged character in garters, fishnets, high-heeled boots, bulging briefs, and a studded leather jacket standing in an alleyway next to an up-ended trash can spilling its contents on the ground: banana peels, playing cards, drag queen fetish gear, and a portrait of

Marilyn Monroe in a cracked frame. Perhaps learning from RCA's *Metal Machine Music* marketing mishap, Arista issued *Live: Take No Prisoners* with a small round warning sticker that read simply: "This Album Is Offensive."

* * *

Reed reconnected with Warhol that summer. There was warm feeling between the men. But plenty had happened in the decade since Reed fired him as the Velvets' manager. Reed invited Warhol up to the Christopher Street apartment and showed him around; Warhol offered validation for his efforts to get his life in order.

"When we were going in the kids around were whispering, 'There's Lou Reed.' He tells them, 'Go kill yourself.' Isn't that great?" Warhol recalled in his published diaries. "The two dachshunds he got after he saw me with mine are so adorable—Duke and Baron. He's sort of separated from Rachel the drag queen but not completely, they have separate apartments . . . It's a rent-controlled thing he got from a girlfriend, six rooms and he only pays $485 a month . . . And oh, Lou's life is everything I want my life to be. I mean, every room has every electronic gadget in it—a big big big big TV, a phone answerer that you hear when the phone rings, tapes, TVs, Betamaxes, and he's so sweet and so funny at the same time, so together, it's just incredible. And his house is very neat . . . well, I guess it does smell a little of dog shit, but . . ."

Warhol's images of Reed, taken over the years, were always revealing. In a snapshot taken across a table at the Bottom Line that month at a David Johansen show, Reed looks straight into Andy's lens with a Mona Lisa smile—it's one of the tenderest images ever taken of him. In August, Warhol had a birthday party at the posh 21 Club, at 21 West Fifty-second Street, and Reed was the first to arrive: hair trimmed, in a white suit and bow tie. "He was so adorable, so sober," Warhol exclaimed, with evident surprise. He took a snapshot of Reed, seated at a table in the near-empty room in his jacket and tie, looking like a sulking teenager at a family event. As a present, Reed gave Warhol a cutting-edge television set with a one-inch screen, which delighted his tech-fetishist friend. He also gave Warhol a cassette of Reed covering a song by the English post-punk band Dead Fingers Talk titled "Nobody Loves You When You're Old and Gay."

Reed's split with Humphreys was complete by the end of summer, when Reed's ex finally had to move out of the apartment they'd shared on Sixty-third Street. It was a rough scene. On one occasion, Reed received a late-night call from a mutual friend, who reported Humphreys was living in a hotel, in need of money, sounding suicidal, and complaining that Reed had refused to pay for the transition surgery she wanted. Reed met the friend at an ATM and gave her money to take to Humphreys. But Reed wouldn't go with her to deliver it.

*   *   *

On September 6, 1978, Tom Wilson, the Velvets' early champion and producer, died of a heart attack at age forty-seven. The next day, Keith Moon, drummer for the Who, died of a sedative overdose while trying to kick alcohol. He was thirty-one.

Reed, now thirty-six, surely noted these passings. He was making efforts to get clean, although he was still drinking. And he was making efforts to protect his new relationship with Morales, which was coming into full bloom. There'd already been challenges, including Humphreys, Reed's drug use, and his drinking. That fall, as he and Morales settled into the Christopher Street apartment amid the bustle of the neighborhood's gay cruising scene, they discussed getting a second home outside the city. By December they'd found a place in Blairstown, New Jersey, near the Delaware Water Gap, just under two hours from Lower Manhattan, tucked into the woods alongside a small lake.

Speaking with a journalist from *Creem*—not Bangs, who Reed was done with, but Stephen Demorest—at the Russian Tea Room that winter, Reed was a whirlwind of contradictions. Scarfing down blini and caviar between slugs of Bloody Marys, Reed spoke about his latest health regimen, including a diet heavy on pistachio nuts and orange juice. And the consummate New York City man sang the praises of his new rural lifestyle. "I really love it," Reed said of his Jersey hideaway. "It smells great. Even if you wanted to do something, there's nothing there. It's appalling how much sleep I get . . . Andy used to say you can't see the stars in New York City because they're all on the ground. Well, out there the stars are in the sky."

Reed also used the interview to discuss his sexuality, in a mix of performative button-pushing and heart-bearing that was especially surprising in light of his relationship with Morales, who goes unmentioned in the published article. Reed declared himself a male "chauvinist down to my toes" and made a number of outrageously sexist comments, among them that women were "deluded creatures" who sometimes want to be "smacked across the mouth," and that perhaps "women most appreciate men who ultimately don't need them . . . They want to change you, but if you did change, they'd be horrified and drop you immediately." At the same time, he identified himself unambiguously as "gay" (from "top to bottom"), spoke about falling for a boy at Syracuse (probably David Weisman), and lamented "trying to feel something towards women when you can't."

It's hard to know what was behind this display, and to some extent it may have been the Bloody Marys talking. But whatever pain Reed experienced on breaking with Humphreys was still fresh, and he may have simply wanted to assert his countervailing identity—rather than dismissing it as a stage—as he began a heterosexual relationship.

Recent news, too, likely had an effect. Reed railed to Demorest about the refusal of the New York City Council to consider a homosexual civil rights bill, confessing he sometimes wanted to get a gun and start shooting homophobes. His militancy may have been amped up for the benefit of *Creem*'s editors, who'd published Bangs's hateful words about Humphreys, and may also have been a response to the assassination of the San Francisco city councilor Harvey Milk, which had occurred only days before the interview. (The first openly gay elected official in California history, Milk was a Jewish Long Islander—just like Reed—who'd relocated to San Francisco in 1972.)

* * *

For his next album, *The Bells*, Reed was determined to deliver a commercial success to Clive Davis. Reed made what seemed smart moves. He hired a young guitarist named Chuck Hammer, a Long Island kid who'd written him a letter about loving *Berlin*; Reed gave Hammer a Roland GR-500—a new guitar synthesizer that was coming into vogue—and told him to go home and master it. Uncharacteristically, Reed also enlisted an outside co-writer. Nils Lofgren was a fierce guitarist and deft multi-instrumentalist who had made his name with Neil Young; in 1973, after the guitarist Danny Whitten's overdose, Lofgren stepped into the dead virtuoso's shoes as second guitarist on Young's gutting eulogy, *Tonight's the Night*. As a solo act, Lofgren landed significant airplay on progressive rock radio stations like New York's WNEW-FM; his albums were critically lauded, and they'd charted better than Reed's. After an introduction by Bob Ezrin, the men bonded over *Monday Night Football* at Reed's apartment. Days later, Lofgren followed up with a cassette of thirteen song sketches. For quite some time, he didn't hear back.

"But one night about 4 a.m., the phone rings," recalled Lofgren. "Lou tells me he's been up for three days and nights, really enjoying and working on my tape of song ideas. He informs me he has thirteen complete sets of lyrics finished and if I want to grab a coffee and a pen, he'll dictate them all to me . . . It took hours, but I got them all down." The best of the batch may have been "I Found Her," a junkie *Pygmalion* in which the singer pines for a girl he found "underneath a rock," who was "takin' dope, very sick, almost dead and very crazy," and who he misses badly, even as he blames himself for her downfall.

Reed would ultimately give that one to Lofgren for his forthcoming LP. Reed kept "Stupid Man," in which he described a character trading his "good life" in "Saskatchewan" (a Canadian reference, maybe for the Neil Young sideman's amusement) for a boring, isolated existence, a scenario that also conjured an image of Reed commuting on the Jersey Turnpike between his beloved New York and his Blairstown retreat. Reed arranged it as a sort of disco experiment, taking a similar tack on "Disco Mystic," which channeled affection, and maybe a dollop of contempt, for the music that defined New York's gay clubs, going on to soundtrack the world. ("Disco is pro-sex. I like mindless disco . . . what's wrong with that?" Reed said to a local radio host while promoting the album.) The musical centerpiece of *The Bells*, however, was its title track, featuring the trumpet of Don Cherry, the co-creator, with Ornette Coleman, of Reed's beloved "Lonely Woman." A nine-minute exercise in the sort of "cosmic jazz" that musicians like Cherry and Alice Coltrane were exploring, it was a ritual of drones and searching brass, colored by Michael Fonfara's synth tones and a fifteen-foot gong Reed rented for the occasion. Reed's vocals begin as mostly unintelligible incantations, and end with a chant of "Here comes the bells." Whether Reed had in mind Edgar Allan Poe's night-sweat meditation "The Bells," Albert Ayler's free-jazz landmark *Bells*, wedding bells, funeral bells, or all of the above, was anyone's guess. "The vocal came to me as I sang," Reed would explain in hindsight, "and each year since I wonder at its meaning."

* * *

It was a shaggy set with bursts of brilliance. But when Clive Davis heard the session tapes, he was concerned. Reed recalled a long letter of critique from him, basically saying the album sounded half-finished. Disagreeing, Reed wanted it released as it was, and dug in his heels. *The Bells* was issued in April with little fanfare and evidently minimal marketing, basically "dropped into a dark well," as Reed put it.

The European promo tour, which began that spring, was a shitshow. In Germany, a woman jumped onstage and Reed, startled and apparently drunk, dragged the woman offstage by her hair. He was arrested in the fracas and spent the rest of the night in jail. A week later, he played London's Hammersmith Odeon, and Bowie showed up. Reed was delighted and flattered. After the show, the men and their entourage repaired to a club, where Reed doted on his friend, smothering him with kisses. Sake and Dom Pérignon flowed. At one point, an intoxicated Reed asked Bowie if he'd consider producing Reed's next album.

It was a big ask, and surely a humbling one. Bowie was one of the biggest rock stars on the planet. He was coming off a successful live album, *Stage*. His two previous studio albums, *Low* and *"Heroes,"* while they were experimental collaborations with Brian Eno, were both critically acclaimed and sold well, too. The previous spring, just after Reed played his first three-night run at the four-hundred-seat Bottom Line, Bowie came to town for a three-night run at the twenty-thousand-seat Madison Square Garden.

According to more than one of Reed's bandmates, Bowie responded to his request with something along the lines of "Sure, I'd consider producing your next album, but you'd have to clean up your act," the gist being that Reed would have to seriously cool it with the drugs and drinking. Bowie had moved to Berlin in part to pull himself out of a cocaine addiction, and was trying to stay clean—somewhat, anyway. Memories of the drug-fueled *Transformer* and *Berlin* sessions, along with Reed's recent dustup in Germany, surely gave Bowie pause.

In an instant, Reed reached past Morales and slapped Bowie hard across the face with the back of his right hand—then slapped him again, this time with his palm, grabbed him by the collar, and pulled him across the table. "Don't you ever say that to me," Reed hissed drunkenly into his face.

Within seconds, Bowie's bodyguards broke it up and cleared the room, recalls Chuck Hammer, who was there with his bandmates. "I remember them pushing us up the stairs and out of the restaurant." Reed's entourage perp-walked him back to their hotel rooms, where he soon passed out.

The night did not end there, though. Before long, Bowie, likely pretty lit himself, was banging on room doors in the hotel hallway, yelling, "Lou, come out and fight like a man!"—a line that, under less-charged circumstances, would likely send the two into howls of laughter. Conceivably, Bowie was playacting to sway the press narrative, in an attempt to save face for both himself and his inebriated friend. In any case, Reed's bandmates steered Bowie away from the room where Reed was sleeping, or pretending to.

In the end, art rock's white shark got his payback. During Reed's show, Bowie had his eye on Hammer and his Roland 500. They spoke afterward, and within a year, the pair would collaborate on "Ashes to Ashes," Hammer embellishing Bowie's hit tribute to his enduring junkie Major Tom, strung out in heaven's high while hitting an all-time low.

* * *

Reed was soon back in New York. The fact that he'd in fact been trying to clean up his act must've made the Bowie incident all the more humiliating. Reed was clearly struggling. He'd gained weight, likely from drinking, but was probably off speed—he'd passed a drug test in Germany after being arrested, and in a radio appearance in late May, he sounded much less wired than usual, and in good spirits. He even deigned to take calls from listeners. "Lou, I'd just like to tell ya I like the new album," one fan told him on air, adding, like a ghost of Christmas past, "I hope ya shoot a lotta dope."

"I ask you," Reed deadpanned to the DJs after the caller hung up, "are these my people?"

The following week, Reed sat for an audience with one of his literary heroes, William Burroughs, who'd moved back to New York a few years prior. Reed brought whiskey, and the two hit it off. Reed addressed him as "Mr. Burroughs"; they discussed Beckett, John Rechy, and, perhaps unsurprisingly, heroin, which was at that moment in time flooding into New York City, cheap and fairly pure. It took hold of many in the punk scene: Johnny Thunders, Richard Hell, Richard Lloyd, and Sid Vicious, who'd OD'd on the drug in February in a friend's Greenwich Village apartment. Even Burroughs, after kicking his fabled addiction, had begun using again, as young acolytes gifted him with bags, thrilled at bragging rights for getting high with the Godfather of Junk. One imagines Reed glimpsing the ghost of Christmas future, another artist trapped in their persona.

That night, onstage at the Bottom Line, Reed introduced the song "Heroin" with a more impassioned disclaimer than usual. "When I say 'it's my wife and it's my life,' do you think I'm kidding?" he asks. By some accounts, in fact, he was using again.

Reed was in a state; he'd been arguing with his bandmates, and at one point during the performance he locked eyes with Clive Davis, who was sitting in the crowd, and gave him the finger. "Where's the money, Clive?" Reed said rancorously. "How come I don't hear my album on the radio?" Perhaps it was an attempt to reenact the assault humor of *Live: Take No Prisoners*; Reed must've had a pretty good idea why he didn't hear his album on the radio. But he must also have been ashamed by his inability to sell records for Davis, who he held in such high regard.

The next day, Reed attempted to do damage control. "I just felt like having a business discussion from the stage," he explained in a press release. "Sometimes, out of frustration, you yell at those you love the most. I have a mouth that never sleeps, and I suppose that's why I make rock 'n roll records." He wouldn't, however, be making them for Arista much longer. Reed's contract wouldn't be renewed after his next record, though Davis, always a big-picture guy, never regretted their association. "It was good for the label," he'd write in his memoirs. "He was edgy, farsighted, independent, and hugely influential."

9.

NEW JERSEY > UPPER WEST SIDE

(1980s)

DISCUSSED: Martial arts, getting cleanish, *Growing Up in Public*, getting married, motorcycles, AIDS, Robert Quine, *The Blue Mask*, *Legendary Hearts*, *New Sensations*, *Mistrial*, the death of Warhol, the death of Nico, *New York*, *Songs for Drella*

Reed began the '80s as something of a new man. The dustups with Bowie and Davis, men he loved dearly, shadowed him that summer, which Reed spent off the road, pulling himself together. He dove into a new health regimen, part of which involved martial arts. Michael Fonfara, adept at karate, kung fu, and kickboxing, tells a story of defending Reed on the street in Stockholm when two Russian sailors started harassing him, ostensibly for looking "faggy." Reed wanted Fonfara's fighting skills, and the two began working out together. Sylvia Morales's brother, Peter, an accomplished martial artist, also shared his passion with Reed, traveling out to Blairstown to give him private lessons. Reed liked the yin-yang of the practice. "It's like ballet," he told a journalist in October, "but each move could cripple someone."

Holing up with Sylvia in the New Jersey woods, Reed brought a renewed focus to his guitar playing. Accepting his technical limitations as a player, he burrowed into tone, looking to shape a wall of sound that wasn't deafening, and that would be easier to control than feedback. He'd begun using a custom guitar with a Telecaster neck and a clear Lucite body, played through a Mike Matthews Dirt Road amp, a small, inexpensive unit with a big, gritty tone—Reed boasted he never needed to set the volume past 1. He also bragged about his reformed lifestyle. If fans came to his shows to see their hero court death, they were going to be disappointed. "If I die now," he conceded, "it'll probably be sitting in bed reading a book."

Reed was certainly turning things around. Warhol could see it when he ran into him in the fall. The friends had dinner at One Fifth, off Washington Square Park, and ran into Jackie Curtis and Taylor Mead at the bar. It was almost like the old days. They all planned to continue the night at the Mudd Club, a year-old hot spot at 77 White Street in Tribeca that'd become a sort of Studio 54 for the post-punk scene. "They were having a Dead Rock Stars Night," Warhol recalled. "[Lou] said he would go as himself, but I told him he looks too good for that now."

A happy, apparently sober Lou Reed was a radical notion, but that's what fans got during a holiday run at the Bottom Line. Opening his set on the final night with a doo-wop-tinged "White Christmas," Reed played a new song that set verses of "The Star-Spangled Banner," mostly unchanged, to a pounding rock groove, acknowledging the national patriotic outburst triggered in November when fifty-two Americans were taken hostage at the U.S. Embassy in Tehran. Another new one, "Love Is Here to Stay," was a sort of military wedding march, Reed rhyming "alone" with "telephone" just like Patti Smith had on "Because the Night," her hit co-write with Bruce Springsteen from the previous year. And just as that song was a love letter from Smith to Fred "Sonic" Smith, whom she'd soon marry, "Love Is Here to Stay" was a de facto love song for Sylvia Morales—to whom, as Reed announced onstage that night, he was engaged.

* * *

Before the wedding, however, Reed had an album to make, his final one for Arista. On Clive Davis's dime, Reed went out in style, boarding a plane on January 5 from JFK to Montserrat to record at AIR, a state-of-the-art studio newly built on the island by the Beatles' producer, George Martin. With a swimming pool outside their private villas, a five-star chef preparing frog legs and lobster, and a waitstaff delivering bottomless drinks, Reed and his bandmates lived large. They were the first artists to record an LP at the studio, and Martin took them on a tour of the island; they swam, watched *Fawlty Towers*, and drank prolifically, Reed's self-directed rehab notwithstanding. With Fonfara participating as co-writer and co-producer, the pair wrote "The Power of Positive Drinking" during one of their nightly binges, and the engineer Corky Stasiak recalls enjoying a breakfast banana daiquiri the day they recorded it, as Reed delivered couplets like "some say liquor kills the cells in your head / and for that matter so does getting out of bed." The music was glossy, synth-driven pop-rock reflecting the dance-floor-friendly sounds that were dominating radio, among them the Knack's "My Sharona" (number 1 on *Billboard*'s 1979 Hot 100 year-end chart), the Village People's "Y.M.C.A.," and Blondie's "Heart of Glass."

"The Power of Positive Drinking" took on deeper meaning in the context of an album that reflected Reed's ongoing work with a therapist. On *The Bells*, he'd recorded "Families," which described a man's wholesale estrangement—from the dog that initially no one wanted, but that's now "more a member of this family than I am"; from a little sister who, like his own, recently married and gave birth to a new daughter; from a father who hoped his son would inherit the family business, though his son isn't interested; and a mother equally disappointed in the son, who was still unmarried and childless. *Growing Up in Public* took the approach further, with psychotherapeutic drama that occasionally skirted parody. The album's opening lines sketched a Freudian scenario of a "harridan mother" and a "weak, simpering father" raising a son fated to play out the "classical motives / of filial love and incest." Reed sang of attending public school in Brooklyn and idolizing his dad, who tells him: "Lou, act like a man." Reed further considered what constitutes "being a man" on the title track, which called out "quasieffeminate [*sic*] characters" that "play on your fears" in a passage that conjured any number of Factory characters. "Keep Away" rhymed "MC Escher" with "Shakespeare's *Measure for Measure*" in a song full of pledges that included staying away from "old-time friends" and giving up booze. All told, it was a thematically coherent, if not especially compelling LP that once again suggested a rock musical, *Berlin* recuperating on a West Village analyst's couch. Even Mick Rock's cover shot advanced the theme, a head shot of Reed in a loose V-neck sweater, with tired eyes, a hint of furrow at his brow, mouth near-neutral in a Mona Lisa frown, and no evident makeup. "It's a small arc from the *Transformer* cover, as arcs go," he'd say of the photo years later. But for a guy bearing down on forty, it was maybe a larger one spiritually.

* * *

The real-life Sid and Toby Reed attended their son's wedding on Valentine's Day, which began with a ceremony at the Christopher Street apartment. Corky Staziak took photos with his Polaroid SX-70. Morales, twenty-four to Reed's thirty-eight, wore a lavish white satin gown; Reed a dark suit. A dinner followed at the elegant, of-the-moment restaurant One If by Land, Two If by Sea, located in an old West Village carriage house said to be haunted by Aaron Burr, who once owned it, after which it became a brothel. The reception continued at the Broadway Arcade, a pinball parlor at West Fifty-second Street with a music business pedigree (and where the A&R legend John Hammond, who signed Dylan and Leonard Cohen, among others, still played pinball almost daily).

A tipsy Lisa Robinson testified to Sid Reed that his son's music deserved to be placed in a space capsule to represent the greatness of rock 'n' roll to alien life forms; Sid shared his pleasure that the newlyweds asked him for storm windows as a wedding present. Absent from the festivities was Sylvia's longtime running buddy, Anya Phillips. Absent, too, was Warhol. It was, in many ways, a marriage of reinvention, with much of the past deleted.

* * *

Reed continued signaling his rebrand in the press on the *Growing Up in Public* tour. Speaking to the BBC, he distanced himself from "this thing that's called Lou Reed," talking about his new marriage as an implicit U-turn from his prior relationship ("It's nice to have a trustworthy situation at home") and trumpeting his new sobriety. "I can make this clear to you so there's no possibility of anybody misunderstanding me: I think drugs are the single worst terrible thing, and if there was any single thing that I thought would be effective to stop people from dealing in drugs and taking them, I would do it." He was walking the walk, too, with a zero-tolerance policy regarding drug use for his bandmates and road team.

With hopes of staying clean and minimal support from Arista, Reed kept the tour short, with shows in Chicago and Cleveland, three nights at the Bottom Line, and a short European run. The latter included big venues in Italy, his first shows there since the rioting in Milan and Rome. But in Madrid, at the Román Valero soccer field, history repeated itself. After a long delay, a crowd of about five thousand fans began shooting off bottle rockets and hurling projectiles. About twenty minutes into Reed's set, a partly filled water bottle hit him in the Adam's apple. Reed turned to the band, jutted his thumb offstage, and ended the show, after which angry fans stormed and trashed the stage, leaving an estimated $140,000 worth of damage.

After a handful of West Coast dates, Reed disbanded his group and repaired to his country home to figure out his next move. He wouldn't tour for the next three years.

* * *

Angus MacLise had died the previous summer, on the solstice. The former Velvet Underground drummer had left New York, pursuing the arts on his own terms and by his own compass in Morocco, India, Iraq, Iran, Syria, and Afghanistan, ultimately landing in Kathmandu, where he created handmade chapbooks through his independent publishing project, Dreamweapon. A few years back he'd made a rare appearance Stateside at the Millennium Film Workshop, where he read a poem that invoked "What was heard / In the skeleton's brief aria . . ."

In December, word circulated that Barbara Rubin had died. She, too, had abandoned the city, and after a period of living upstate with Allen Ginsberg (who she'd hoped, in vain, would father children for her), she connected with an Orthodox Jewish community, hoping to become a rabbi (also in vain). She moved abroad, married a religious artist, and had been living in the South of France, where she was known as Bracha Barsacon, or so it was said. She reportedly died giving birth to her fifth child. "Good-bye, Barbara," Jonas Mekas wrote in his diary. "I owe you a lot. And so do many other people."

Reed was one of them, and he'd been facing his own mortality. When he broke up his band, he told Fonfara a doctor had informed him his liver was "the size of a couch" due to hepatitis and substance abuse, and that further drinking could kill him. In New Jersey, Reed pursued self-care with the same intensity he'd brought to his amphetamine habit. He explored biofeedback therapy, attempting to control his anxiety by controlling his own heart rate and blood pressure. And for the first time, he began attending meetings of Alcoholics Anonymous and Narcotics Anonymous. At one in New York, he was reportedly confronted by a fellow addict: "How dare you be here—you're the reason I took heroin!"

Alcohol remained a struggle. Reed's high school pal Rich Sigal, now a New Jersey neighbor, recalls a dinner at the Reed house where the wine flowed freely into everyone's glasses, Reed's included.

Reed got into being out of circulation. He rekindled his collegiate interest in motorbikes, reading *Zen and the Art of Motorcycle Maintenance*. He took apart a Suzuki bike and attempted, unsuccessfully, to rebuild it, then graduated to a more powerful Harley-Davidson V-twin Super Glide, leaving the maintenance to professionals, though he liked to hang around the repair shop. ("Now I'm proud just to take out and recharge the battery without killing myself," he told a journalist.) He bought a chain saw to cut his own wood, but found the machine tougher to control than a guitar, and it left his hands cramped. He had a satellite TV dish installed, uncommon at the time, video game equipment, and a pinball machine. He even purchased a handgun, although never became comfortable with it beyond plinking cans in his eighteen-acre woodland parcel.

Reed's exit from the spotlight coincided with a new era of U.S. conservatism. Ronald Reagan had been inaugurated as president in January, earning the southern evangelical vote via Jerry Falwell, whose Moral Majority assailed the incumbent, President Carter. On the campaign trail, Reagan backpedaled the faint tolerance he'd shown toward California's LGBTQ+ community as governor. He received the first presidential endorsement from the NRA, and he amped up the War on Drugs launched by the disgraced President Nixon, increasing penalties across the board, including for marijuana offenses, as First Lady Nancy Reagan spearheaded the anti-drug "Just Say No" educational campaign.

There was perhaps no more surreal sign of the zeitgeist than the Lou Reed profile in the March 30 issue of *People*. "A Refugee from Rock's Dark Side, Lou Reed Says Goodbye Excess, Hello New Jersey" was written by David Fricke, a young writer with whom Reed would develop a trusting relationship. Pictures of the artist snuggling with his dachshunds and wife were flanked in the two-page magazine spread by a mid-'70s concert photo of him pretending to shoot up. "'Lou Reed' is my protagonist," Reed told Fricke. "Sometimes he's 20-, sometimes 80-percent me, but never 100. He's a vehicle to go places I wouldn't go or say things I don't go along with."

This was a PR coup of questionable value for an artist identified with decadence. But Reed's legal battle with Dennis Katz was still being decided, and the *People* story would be included in the court documents. "To be sure, some revisionism comes with the change," Fricke wrote, gently arching an eyebrow at the tidy rebirth narrative.

Meanwhile, life in New York continued without Reed. A few weeks after the *People* article, Reed and his wife were in town—he'd kept the rent-controlled Christopher Street apartment—and they ran into Warhol in the West Village.

It must've been awkward. Warhol's life had quieted down significantly from the previous decade, but was more unsettled than Reed's. He'd had a falling-out with his boyfriend, Jed Johnson, who'd moved out of his house that winter, and he was in a bad place. "I've got these desperate feelings that nothing means anything," Warhol noted in his diary in April. He was hurt he wasn't invited to Reed's wedding (he'd been snubbed when Reed married Bettye Kronstad, too) and the *People* magazine spread showcasing Reed's happy marriage must've stung. "She's nothing special, just a little sexy girl," he'd later snipe.

Spying Reed from across the street, with his trusty camera as social buffer, Warhol took pictures as Reed approached. In a contact sheet sequence, Reed, wearing jeans and a polo shirt, is unsmiling; his wife, in outsized '70s eyeglasses, is nestled under his arm, looking down.

Warhol asked Reed why he didn't come by the Factory anymore. He said he didn't know anyone in Warhol's circle anymore. Reed asked if Ronnie Cutrone was still around. Warhol said yes. He asked if Warhol's colleague Pat Hackett was around; Warhol again said yes. He asked if Vincent Fremont, Andy's studio manager, was still around. Warhol said yes again, and the two old friends laughed.

There was something going on in the city's queer community at that moment. It came into focus that summer, when an article appeared in *The New York Times* about a rare "and often rapidly fatal" form of cancer, Kaposi's sarcoma, that was dramatically on the rise among gay men. "The cause of the outbreak is unknown, and there is as yet no evidence of contagion," the article explained. "But the doctors who have made the diagnoses, mostly in New York City and the San Francisco Bay area, are alerting other physicians who treat large numbers of homosexual men to the problem in an effort to help identify more cases."

* * *

Weighing options as he cooled his heels, Reed again turned to producing other artists, as Cale had been doing. Reed bounced ideas off Brian Eno, a Velvet Underground fan whose recent production work with Bowie was admired by Reed. But Reed was too controlling to serve other artists' visions. A mid-'70s project with his Syracuse bandmate Nelson Slater, whom Reed helped to ink a deal with RCA, ran off the rails when Reed remixed the final tape without Slater's consent. The guitarist Chuck Hammer decided to pass on Reed's production offer when Reed insisted he ban their former bandmates from the project. Reed was prepared to produce a record by Jim Carroll—the young poet heard asking for Pernod and Tuinal between songs on the Velvets' *Live at Max's Kansas City*, who'd recently scored a near-hit with "People Who Died," a grim laundry list of Carroll's friends that shares formal characteristics with "Walk on the Wild Side"—but plans fell apart when Reed began criticizing Carroll's lyrics and generally trying to hijack the project.

Ready to make his own records again and now a free agent, Reed cut a new deal at his former home, RCA, and began putting a new band together—one that, as it turned out, would reclaim the power of the Velvet Underground. It did so by returning his guitar playing to center stage, an approach instigated in large part by a Velvets fanatic who'd become one of the greatest rock guitarists of all time.

* * *

Robert Quine—the law student who devotedly made audience recordings of the Velvet Underground during the late '60s—had, like Reed, been busy reinventing himself. He'd mostly ditched his law career, and been living in New York City. He remained a music obsessive, and notwithstanding a brief stint at the prestigious Berklee College of Music, was a largely self-taught guitarist, one who practiced obsessively, often six or seven hours a day.

He came from a line of idiosyncratic high achievers. The nephew of Willard Van Orman Quine, the formidable American philosopher and logician, Quine was raised in Akron by parents who loved Brazilian music ("guitars doing a G7/C7 over and over again—that was always my favorite sound in the world," he'd recall). But he was galvanized by rock 'n' roll; he saw Buddy Holly perform, and bought a Stratocaster because Ritchie Valens played one. In the '60s, he spun John Lee Hooker records on his college radio show, took LSD, discovered Coltrane's *Ascension*, and was cracked wide open watching him perform with Pharoah Sanders and Alice Coltrane in San Francisco. When Quine first heard *The Velvet Underground & Nico*, he hated it—"they couldn't play, the guy was trying to sing like *Highway 61 Revisited*, the drummer had a physical disability" was roughly his initial impression. But when *White Light/White Heat* was released, Quine claimed, the LP "completely changed my life."

"I spent thousands of hours on headphones wearing that out . . . [Reed] actually listened to Ornette Coleman, and deliberately did off-harmonic feedback [for] the deliberate monotony of it. This stuff is like Jimmy Reed—it's monotonous or it's hypnotic. For me, it was hypnotic."

After law school in St. Louis, Quine passed the Missouri bar, moved to San Francisco, failed the California bar multiple times, then moved to New York and took a job writing tax law for a publishing house, which he soon left to pursue music. He took a day job at the Strand bookstore, and later Cinemabilia, where he met the musicians Tom Verlaine and Richard Hell. Though Quine had never played his guitar in public, Hell eventually recruited him for the Voidoids, his third great band showcasing virtuosic New York guitarists, following Television and the Heartbreakers. The Voidoids were an ideal pairing of poet and players, and they made "Blank Generation" one of punk rock's defining anthems, with Quine's venom-spitting solo distilling the furious disgust at the core of Richard Hell's junkie ennui.

Among Quine's few close friends were Lester Bangs, who had a short-lived band with him, and Brian Eno, with whom he explored the city's lesser-known Asian restaurants. Quine was also friends with Sylvia Morales, whom he'd met through Hell. "He introduced me to his floor-to-ceiling record collection," she recalls. "If he thought you were one of the people who would understand, he would take you through this scholarly curriculum of guitar riffs. He'd play you one, then he'd be like 'Now, listen to this!' and he took you through twenty or thirty, showing you an evolution of guitar riffs. He was amazing."

After the Voidoids fell apart in 1981, Quine connected with Reed, agreeing to join his new band on the condition that Reed start playing guitar again with gusto. Quine's idea was to re-create a Velvet Underground–style attack, with himself as a post-punk Sterling Morrison. Musically, Reed and Quine were a perfect pair. Temperamentally, as perfectionists who tended toward the egomaniacal, the match was less ideal. Of the four years they managed to work together, Quine recalled drolly, "the first week and a half was really great."

Reed forged a more stable relationship with his virtuoso new bassist, Fernando Saunders, who grew up singing gospel with his family in Detroit. Saunders got his first professional break as a teen, playing bass behind the regional disco hero Bohannon, and soon proved himself a jazz-rock wunderkind, working with the likes of Jeff Beck and John McLaughlin. But Reed seemed most impressed by his club jams. "You played with Bohannon?" Saunders recalls him saying, with a tone of awe. "Then I want you in my band!"

The men worked at RCA Studios at 110 West Forty-fourth Street, in Studio C, a cavernous room that could accommodate a hundred players, setting up in a tight huddle on the orchestra riser and hashing out songs. Saunders was struck by Reed's musical knowledge and his humble demeanor with him, a young hired hand. But the voice-and-guitar cassette demos Reed handed him were baffling at first. "I couldn't understand how this guy got a record deal," Saunders says, laughing. "To me, with my gospel background, that wasn't singing." In session, however, it clicked. "Once I heard his voice in the headphones, it was like he's the narrator, and we're the movie soundtrack. That's how I saw it." Reed even encouraged the ornate embellishments the restless Saunders displayed when he was fooling around between takes, to Saunders's surprise. "He wanted those harmonics, those colors . . . I thought he wanted basic rock. But he wanted art."

For his part, Quine said little, and cut a strange figure—clean-cut, balding, generally in a sports jacket, looking like an accountant but for the dark glasses he wore virtually around the clock, indoors and out. Saunders and the drummer, Doane Perry, were accomplished players with mainstream pedigrees, and Quine recalled them being taken aback by the noisy brutality of the twin guitars. Yet it was a refined brutality, with near-telepathic interplay, lead and rhythm parts constantly shifting, and often turning delicate, just like the Velvets. For the finished LP, Reed would choose first or second takes, recorded after minimal rehearsal, mirroring lyrics with a similarly off-the-cuff feel.

The Blue Mask drew much of its content explicitly from Reed's life, but far more vividly than *Growing Up in Public*. It opens with "My House," Reed counting his blessings with trembling gratitude over atmospheric guitar and fretless bass, sketching a contented writer's life in a beautiful country home while imagining Delmore Schwartz occupying the spare room. "My Daedalus to your Bloom," rhapsodized Reed, reprising a line from his St. Mark's Poetry Project reading in '71, declaring Schwartz "the first great man that I had ever met." "Women" assumes a tone of wonder at the act of heterosexual intimacy, confessing teenage cluelessness ("I was very bitter, all my sex was on the sly") then describing a new love with comic sentimentality, romancing his lady while "a choir of castrati" sing Bach.

But things turn dark fast. "Underneath the Bottle" describes scenes of advanced alcoholism in the first person: mystery bruises, a fall down the stairs, days spent sleeping off benders, shakes so bad that work is impossible. An elliptical rape-murder narrative in "The Gun" is terrifying, all coiled and calm buildup. A similar mindset explodes in the title track, a splatter-painting of psychological extremes: a man raised with brutality to make him tough, hazed with "blood in his coffee" amid sexualized violence that makes "Venus in Furs" seem mild, with an Oedipal murder scene and a closing couplet conjuring the wartime practice of castrating a corpse and stuffing the genitals in its mouth (an image Reed confessed shocked even him when it came out of his pen). The guitar interplay—which seems to take a cue from Television, with Quine staking out the left channel, Reed in the right—is breathtaking, each man slashing and gouging while the other answers, echoes, or sharpens his blade.

Yet even this horror is eclipsed by "Waves of Fear," the ferocious channeling of a panic attack detailed by Reed like a desperate 911 call: chest tightening, heart rate spiking, nose bleeding, trembling, suffocating, "crazy with sweat, spittle on my jaw," out of alcohol, scuttling across the floor in search of a lost pill, spitting out "I hate my own smell," which Reed rhymes with "I must be in hell," as twin guitars churn in spasms, lurching ahead of the song's steamroller groove, then falling behind it, again and again, unable to catch a breath or hold sync, with Quine's instrument like a dental drill jammed into an exposed nerve. How much of it was literal autobiography was unclear. But Reed's struggle with drug and alcohol abuse was ongoing, and one might reasonably imagine much of his life being shaped by the shadow of panicked anxiety: the need to keep it at bay by self-medicating, lashing out at anyone who might trigger it, and making art that muted it, stared it down, or otherwise defused it.

And if "Waves of Fear" was more purely visceral than anything Reed had written to this point, it was at the same time a reminder of the harrowing competition for that honor in the Reed oeuvre: the Auschwitz visions of piled-up corpses in "Heroin"; the woman turning blue in "Run Run Run"; the looming violence of "There She Goes Again"; Waldo Jeffers's blood-spurting skull in "The Gift"; the shaved body strapped to a table in "Lady Godiva's Operation"; the orgiastic dope-shooting murder scene in "Sister Ray"; the self-loathing body hatred of "Candy Says"; the lacerating loss of "Pale Blue Eyes"; the excrement and entrails of "Wrap Your Troubles in Dreams"; the punctured eyeballs and hungry rats of "The Murder Mystery"; the brains served on a plate in "Ocean"; the priest exhuming his dead father in "Hangin' 'Round"; Caroline beaten black and blue in *Berlin*, with her children shrieking and her wrist-slashing suicide; the electroshock treatment in "Kill Your Sons"; the body stuffed in a car trunk in "Sally Can't Dance"; the infernal howls of *Metal Machine Music*; the slit throat in "Kicks"; the overdose victim dragged outside and dumped in the road in "Street Hassle." The list went on.

But for all its horrors, *The Blue Mask* was an album, like so much of Reed's work, about the mythic, and sometimes real, salvation of love. Beyond its titular pun, "The Heroine" posited Reed waiting to be rescued by a figure who "transcends all the men." And the album's final song is a touching doo-wop tribute to "Syl-vi-a," whose name Reed incants, breaking it into syllables until meaning dissolves into longing, a love letter to the former Sylvia Morales, who—were she a lesser woman—might have reasonably, after hearing the album in its entirety, bolted for the door. But she didn't.

Likely as sober as he'd ever been for the making of a record, Reed knew what he'd accomplished. Many would consider *The Blue Mask* his greatest solo album, and even after their falling-out, Quine would consistently note how proud he was to have worked on it. Shortly before its release, Reed spoke with the French author and journalist Bruno Blum, and his excitement was palpable. He described the title track as "very painful . . . very perverse, hopelessly, hopelessly perverse, perverse and doomed forever."

When the interviewer gently pressed Reed on the autobiography in the songs, however, he demurred: "I keep my private life to myself. So if you want to know if I'm an alcoholic and I'm writing personal experience, the answer is no, I'm not, and if I was I wouldn't tell you either."

Reed waited a beat. "But you can send out for a bottle right now and we can really get to know about it a whole lot better." Then he got serious again. "I'm not trying to be a wise guy with you. I'm just sayin' I have to beg off that kind of implied question." They went on to speak at length about "Waves of Fear." "It's about anxiety and terror about which nothing can be done," Reed said. "Terror so strong that the person can't even turn a light on, can't speak, can't make it to a phone. Afraid to turn a light on for what they'll see—for what he is."

"What motivation," Blum asked, with astonishment, "could you [possibly] have to approach that subject?"

Reed responded flatly and plainly, as if there was just one conceivable answer:

"Empathy," he said.

* * *

Press for *The Blue Mask* was fittingly adulatory. Once again, Reed had recorded a "rock masterpiece," and once again, it would sell modestly, reaching number 169 on the pop charts before disappearing.

Though Quine had previewed parts of the album for Lester Bangs during the course of recording it—evidently with Reed's permission—the writer didn't join the chorus of *Blue Mask* hosannas, though he did buy a copy of it for his nephew when it was released. Bangs was trying to finish a rock history book, and to write a novel; he'd also been struggling to get sober—like Reed, he'd begun AA. But on April 30, 1982,

Bangs was found dead in his apartment, of an apparent overdose of pills. Whether it was accidental, as Quine believed, or intentional, no one knew for sure.

Quine considered Bangs one of his few friends, and took his death hard. But Reed's empathy for his guitarist was limited. When Quine delivered the news to Reed, Quine told Bangs's biographer Jim DeRogatis, Reed said, "That's too bad about your friend," but then "[launched] into a forty-five-minute attack on Lester." Reed's anger was rooted in Bangs's hateful writing about Rachel Humphreys, as well as his unsparing critiques of his music. But Quine was hurt by Reed's callousness and, like Reed, was not quick to forgive. While the two continued working together, the relationship never recovered. In Quine's mind, the incident "marked the end of my friendship with Lou Reed."

In Bangs's final months, he'd spent time with Quine, their friend Marcia Resnick, and Resnick's upstairs neighbor Laurie Anderson—a performance artist whose focus had begun veering into recorded music. Her debut LP, *Big Science*, was released the month he died. Bangs had heard an advance copy, and he liked it a lot.

* * *

Reed recorded *Legendary Hearts*, his follow-up to *The Blue Mask*, with most of the same players, again at RCA Studio C. The sessions were marred, however, by Reed's studio tantrums—about room temperatures, technical glitches, and other matters—and constant second-guessing. The session engineer, Corky Stasiak, fielded worried calls from Reed at all hours about rerecording tracks and changing guitar sounds. "I had to turn off my phone," he recalls.

If Reed wasn't living out the scenarios he described in "Waves of Fear," his DIY rehab was nevertheless a rough ride. He hadn't quit drinking entirely: when the recording team went out for Japanese or Korean food, Stasiak recalls, sake flowed and Reed partook. His sidemen noticed his hands often trembled, especially when he first arrived for a session. Reed had worries about his liver, and was always exploring new channels of alternative medicine. "We had a great discussion about Finnbarr Nolan, the faith healer," Stasiak recalls. "Lou was really into what he taught." By all indications, Sylvia was Reed's greatest asset in his struggle to stay healthy. Stasiak is among many who believe she likely saved his life.

Legendary Hearts was released in March 1983, and had plenty of *The Blue Mask*'s emotional rawness. But the glory-of-love idealism that provided a beacon on the earlier LP was barely flickering here; even more than the white-knuckle trials of *The Blue Mask*, the album echoed Sartre's notion that hell is other people. The couple of the sweet, loping "Legendary Hearts" come out fighting, falling woefully short of their titular models. Job stress, maybe writer's block, informs the similarly combative "Don't Talk to Me About Work," while "Martial Law" sketches a wee-hours domestic violence scene in a first responder's voice, warning "don't punch, don't scratch, don't bite." On "Betrayed," a bedroom scene reveals the fallout of paternal sexual abuse against an abstracted country-rock backdrop, while "The Last Shot" and "Bottoming Out" draw frightening images of alcoholism—the former, akin to "Waves of Fear," describes a horrific run-up to a man's attempt to quit drinking (traces of blood in the sink, a chipped tooth) and the seesaw of relapse, while "Bottoming Out" involves a raging quarrel ("if I hadn't left, I would've struck you dead," Reed snarls) and a drunken, maybe suicidal motorcycle ride. Only the closer, the Beatlesque "Rooftop Garden"—a scene taken perhaps from the top of his Christopher Street building—offered a promise of conjugal peace.

The sound of Reed's band, too, had changed. Prince's *1999* had come out in October, and its fusion of rock guitar virtuosity and synth-driven R&B was a game changer; ditto Michael Jackson's *Thriller*, released a month later. Old-school artists were transforming and rebranding. The prog-rock drummer of Genesis, Phil Collins, had become an unlikely pop hit machine by the time of *Hello I Must Be Going!*, with its brittle cover of the Supremes' "You Can't Hurry Love," while Genesis's former singer, Peter Gabriel, issued his fourth album (titled *Security* in North America) around the same time, a synth-driven masterpiece defined by Linn drum programs. Reed was taking notes. He had a new drummer, Fred Maher, a friend of Quine's with a keen interest in the new machines who played his kit with a crisp, clipped new wave feel. The bigger change in Reed's sound on *Legendary Hearts* was the decision to dial back the guitars, with instrumental breaks unspooling in uneventful vamps. The arrangements made some sense in light of groove-centered pop trends, but Reed's falling-out with Quine was probably also a factor. "Every time we did a mix, Quine's guitar would come down a level" per Reed's direction, Stasiak recalls. "It was kind of a childish thing, I thought, like 'I'm mad at you, so I don't want to play with you anymore.'" When Quine heard the final mixes, he was "freaked out," he recalled years later. "[Reed] pretty much mixed me off the record." Quine smashed his copy of the tape to pieces, and didn't speak to Reed for weeks.

Still, Quine swallowed his pride when Reed asked him if he wanted to tour, and when they returned to the road, the result was some of Reed's best-ever live shows. Onstage at the Bottom Line for the first time since 1980, Reed looked healthy, but the tension between the men was palpable. During "Kill Your Sons," Reed played a ferocious passage with his back to Quine; when the latter crafted a majestic solo on "Satellite of Love," Reed stared into the crowd unresponsively, eyes hooded like an iguana.

Saunders saw the Reed-Quine relationship as typical guitar-player competitiveness, albeit worse than most. Quine finished the tour, after which, predictably, Reed cut him loose. "Encouraging him to play guitar again was digging my own grave," Quine reflected with a mix of bitterness, pride, and humility. "But I would have done it again because I owed it to him. This guy changed my life."

* * *

Reed turned forty-one in 1983, an age that put him at a disadvantage with the advent of MTV, the cable channel that precipitated a seismic shift in pop music when it began broadcasting music videos around the clock that summer. Still, he was an icon with an arresting presence, who'd been playing to cameras ever since he sat for Warhol's Screen Tests, and during his recent downtime he'd summoned the rock archetype of "Lou Reed" for a number of films. Paul Simon cast him in *One Trick Pony*, Simon's poison-pen missive to the music industry. Reed plays Steve Kunelian, an oily producer assigned to work with Simon's character, Jonah Levin, a faded '60s singer-songwriter trying to maintain his career. ("Listen, whaddaya think, I'm just a knob turner here?" Reed assures him. "I know what I'm doing.") Reed also informed the leads in two animated features. Ralph Bakshi's *American Pop* involved multiple generations of a Jewish family that emigrates from Russia and ends up in Long Island, where a switchblade-carrying son named Pete, looking much like circa '74 blond Reed, hustles drugs in the big city to a soundtrack of "I'm Waiting for the Man." In the Canadian film *Rock & Rule*, Reed sang parts for Mok Swagger, an aging Nietzschean-androgyn rock star who asserts that humans have "evolved beyond good and evil" and seeks one final gig in postapocalyptic "Nuke York City" to summon an all-powerful dark energy force. ("Your record sales are dropping," warns the Siri-like voice of his supercomputer.) The summer of MTV's launch, Reed appeared in *Get Crazy*, an entertainingly dopey rock musical directed by Allan Arkush in which Reed played Auden, a "metaphysical folk singer" and "anti-social recluse" who'd "invented the seventies" and had been "dropped by six record labels."

There weren't that many clips for MTV to choose from, though the film reel had been gaining traction as a promo tool since Nico wandered along the Thames in 1965 lip-synching "I'm Not Sayin'." To help sell his past two releases, Reed issued a straightforward clip for "Women" featuring him and his band, including Quine, playing on a soundstage, and another for "Legendary Hearts," which had him crooning in tight black leather amid movie stills (Bogart and Bacall, James Dean and Liz Taylor) and cheap computer graphics. When Reed began work on his next album in the spring of 1984, it would be with the intent of repackaging himself for the video age.

As it turned out, the look was not especially flattering, musically or visually. *New Sensations* updated the pop R&B sound of *Sally Can't Dance* for a new decade, with clipped beats, silvery funk grooves, ersatz gospel backing vocals, and effective hooks. The record's catchiest song, "I Love You, Suzanne," featured Saunders's high-stepping bass,

Fred Maher's whip-crack beats, and a guitar riff that Saunders recalled Quine coining during a rehearsal, though Reed didn't credit him or invite him to play on the record. "Suzanne" echoed the early-'60s vocal group sound that Debbie Harry and Chris Stein had updated into a pop juggernaut with Blondie, and it deserved to be a new wave radio hit. It wasn't, despite the video Reed gamely made for it, which was hilariously awful: a perky blond ringer for Bettye Kronstad tries to get a stoic, or stoned, Lou Reed to dance in a club, to no avail. Later, her sketchy beau calls her from a pay phone on a dark street standing beside his motorcycle—a Meatpacking District James Dean—evidently to invite her to his concert, where she shakes it like a frat girl and unsuccessfully attempts to kiss him. Later, she tries communicating with him while he's watching TV, and he pushes her away; out on the street together, Reed's attention drifts from her, possibly to cruise the dude in the phone booth, or cop drugs from him. When she ditches Reed for some slick new wave boys, her jilted paramour surprises everyone by jumping offstage mid-song to demonstrate his outrageously gymnastic dance moves, clearly the work of a stunt double.

The clip for "My Red Joystick"—its title a shameless pun, its lyrics a mash-up of references to "Little Red Corvette" and "Highway 61 Revisited"—was even goofier, Reed and an ex divvying up their belongings after a split, then fighting for the titular game-controlling phallus. As a gearhead, Reed was fascinated by the new technology of gaming; the cover of *New Sensations* showed Reed's outsized image on a TV monitor, seeming to be manipulated by a oddly childlike Reed, sitting on the floor with a joystick game controller in his hand. Another song on the LP, "Down at the Arcade," notes the transformation of Reed's beloved pinball parlors into video-game arcades, with punning tributes to Defender and Robotron 2084 (the latter popularizing the aforementioned red joystick).

As poetry, it was thin stuff. But it was fun, and the LP had its more potent moments. "Fly into the Sun" ("I would not run from the Holocaust / I would not run from the bomb") was a sort of stirringly nihilist gospel song about death as a release. "Doin' the Things That We Want To" was the reverie of a dedicated film- and theatergoer, declaring *Taxi*

Driver's Travis Bickle and *Mean Streets*'s Johnny Boy "the best friends I ever had"—a sad note for anyone, and a telling one for an artist with fans who often seemed unhealthily obsessed with him. And then there was "Turn to Me," its title echoing Bill Withers's indelible 1972 soul hit "Lean on Me." In verses that suggest a mid-'80s Reed consoling '70s fans who unwisely took his lifestyle as a cue for their own, he describes myriad troubles, among them a freebasing dad and a sex-worker mom. One line frets over a wife who wants a child, while another suggests the fallout from amphetamine abuse: teeth ground down "to the bone," the sense that "there's nothing between your legs." And another mentions a friend who "died of something you can't pronounce."

When the song was written, maybe late 1983 or early 1984, it's likely Reed knew someone diagnosed with *Pneumocystis carinii* pneumonia or Kaposi's sarcoma—roughly two thousand cases had been diagnosed in the city, and Reed's neighborhood, the West Village, was an epicenter of what would become the AIDS pandemic. St. Vincent's Hospital, four blocks north of Reed's Christopher Street apartment, on Seventh Avenue at West Eleventh Street, opened the first AIDS ward on the East Coast in 1984, a heartbreaking modern version of the fifteenth-century Venetian lazaretti plague centers; in two years, one-third of the hospital's beds would be occupied by AIDS patients.

*   *   *

New Sensations wasn't exactly a hit, but its bright mix of the glib and the profound did well enough to facilitate a world tour, during which Reed defended his new approach to the press. "I wasn't changing my music . . . I just wanted a sound," Reed explained to a writer for *Musician*, a magazine known for its wonky sensibility, shouting out *New Sensations*'s co-producer John Jansen, who Reed said he'd contacted out of admiration for the drum sound on Air Supply's soft-rock smash "Making Love out of Nothing at All." Reed was playing nice with interviewers. Speaking to New Zealand TV, he was upbeat, praising lowbrow movies like *Police Academy* and the outstanding sound of a brand-new record medium, the compact disc. His attitude toward his songwriting seemed to have relaxed. "I'd hope you could at least get a good laugh out of me, and then if you wanted more than that it'd be there, too . . . not Dostoevsky, but, y'know, there'd be something of substance there," Reed told the reporter, grinning a tight, slightly rictus, but genuine smile.

"I've always been impressed by your sense of humor, actually," the newsman said.

"Yeah, it's dry. I've been told I should smile when I tell a joke. So I've been practicing."

Though he wasn't nominated, Reed attended the first MTV Awards in September 1984. The big winners were Michael Jackson and the ex–Miles Davis sideman Herbie Hancock, reinventing his sound once again on the hip-hop instrumental "Rockit." David Bowie, beamed in via satellite feed from London for a performance of his middling new song "Blue Jean," received a "Video Vanguard" award, which Iggy Pop accepted in person on his friend's behalf. It must have hurt Reed to be left out, and wounded pride might have been the reason he snubbed Warhol, who was at the event, too. "[He] sat in my row but never even looked over," Warhol commented in his diary. "I don't understand Lou, why he doesn't talk to me now."

As it turned out, Reed made his biggest video impression that year not with a promo clip, but, rather startlingly for such an uncompromising artist, with a TV commercial. Honda had launched a witty campaign pushing a vanguard angle for its scooters using musicians, among them Grace Jones, Devo, and Miles Davis. The latter's brief spot features him leaning against a bike in a flamboyant jacket, trumpet in hand, whisper-growling, "I'll play first, and I'll tell you about it later. Maybe." (He does neither.)

But Reed's spot was the most memorable. It was created by the upstart ad agency Wieden & Kennedy, which would soon attach the Beatles' "Revolution" to a Nike commercial, spurring the outrage of boomer music fans. In Reed's spot—a test run for repurposing revered rock songs as branding devices—underexposed street scenes of the Lower East Side were processed to look like grainy Super 8 and edited like a Jonas Mekas reel, peppered with jump cuts into "junk footage" (film stock run-out segments, blurred pans, and flash frames) and set to an edited section of "Walk on the Wild Side." A pair of feet strut in stilettos; two cabbies shoot the shit; a man argues with a cop; pedestrians rush through a crosswalk as a saxophonist leans against a lamppost, blowing in sync with the music. The spot ends with Reed, improbably posed on a Honda scooter outside the Bottom Line. He removes his aviators, looks into the camera, and says, "Hey—don't settle for walkin'," like a Brooklyn wiseguy waiting for a protection payoff.

It didn't blow up the scooter market, but it was a landmark of hip, "ironic" advertising, and in truth, the most aesthetically effective film presentation of Reed's music to date. Where rock musicians and their fans generally saw licensing to advertisers as an unforgivable sellout—Neil Young would release *This Note's for You*, a concept album decrying the practice, in 1988—Reed rejected such purism. Of course, his attitudes toward art and commerce were profoundly shaped by a former adman who painted Campbell's Soup cans and who, even as his art star status made it financially unnecessary, had no qualms taking commissions to produce ads for clients wanting his coolness imprimatur. Before long, Reed cut a deal with American Express, who used his image on cardboard countertop displays to hawk credit card applications for college students. "How to stand out in a crowd," read the copy above Reed's face, eyes hidden behind aviator shades and his signature New York City don't-even-think-of-fucking-with-me expression. "Now it's even easier. Carry the Card."

Reed was open to pretty much anything at this point to get market traction and earn out his advances. He even licensed "I Love You, Suzanne" to a children's TV series, *Kids, Incorporated*, which tracked the lovable hijinks of a young rock 'n' roll band based at a sort of dance club/malt shop. The episode involved Ryan, who gets a crush on the emcee's cousin, Suzanne. When he discovers she's blind, he learns a lesson about relating to people who seem "different," serenading her with Reed's song.

Financially, things began to turn around for Reed in 1984. His lawsuits with his ex-manager Dennis Katz, which had dragged on for nearly a decade and reportedly had Reed enlisting his father for help, were finally settled with the assistance of Reed's new manager, Eric Kronfeld, a successful music industry lawyer. The settlement cost Reed a lot of money, but it did free up royalties from his RCA back catalog, notably for "Walk on the Wild Side." The *New Sensations* tour did well, and the shows were impressive—he'd asked Quine to rejoin the band for the tour, Quine figured what the hell, and the men's animosity played out spectacularly in their guitar duels for one last run. At the Capitol Theater in Passaic, New Jersey, in September, Reed was over the moon to host the Chantels—the girl group he adored as a teenager— who joined him onstage to sing their big hit, "Maybe," and add backup vocals on "Rock & Roll," as Reed traded twisted Chuck Berry riffs with Quine and sang "it's all right" with conviction.

* * *

Meanwhile, with perfect synchronicity, the Velvet Underground were finally getting their due. A new generation of bands deeply inspired by them were suddenly everywhere. R.E.M., based in the college town of Athens, Georgia, released the Velvets' "There She Goes Again" as the B side of their breakout single "Radio Free Europe" and spent much of 1984 opening their concerts with tender readings of "Pale Blue Eyes." (The band had also been inspired by their southern kin Big Star, whose frontman, Alex Chilton, recorded a crushingly beautiful "Femme Fatale" in the '70s.) In New Jersey, there was the Feelies, a twin-guitar vortex who'd caught the tailwinds of the '70s CBGB scene (they'd soon be touring with Reed), and a young band named Yo La Tengo, with the drummer-singer Georgia Hubley and feedback-loving writer-guitarist Ira Kaplan (they'd be cast as the Velvets in the film *Who Shot Andy Warhol?*). In California, a neo-psychedelic scene dubbed the Paisley Underground was spearheaded by the Dream Syndicate, named with a nod to La Monte Young. Susanna Hoffs of the Bangles, another group from the scene, recorded a superlative "I'll Be Your Mirror" for the Paisley Underground side project Rainy Day. Women musicians were at the fore of the Velvets' reclamation. In the U.K., the wistfully brooding folk-rock singer Tracy Thorn recorded a stunning "Femme

Fatale." The Raincoats were informed by gender studies and Vicky Aspinall's dissonant, droning, Cale-style violin (which turned a cover of "Lola" into a sort of Velvets-Kinks mash-up). A concurrent wave of British bands drew on the Velvets' noisier, more aggressive side: Joy Division covered "Sister Ray," Echo and the Bunnymen did "Heroin," Bauhaus and Orchestral Manoeuvres in the Dark both did "I'm Waiting for the Man." In New Zealand, the Flying Nun label launched numerous groups mining the VU's brighter latter-day sound: the Clean, the Chills, the Bats, and the Verlaines. The Go-Betweens charted similar ground in Australia, while their countryman Nick Cave, first with the Boys Next Door, then the Birthday Party and the Bad Seeds, would plumb the Velvets' darker regions. Bands even borrowed from their associated iconography—The Smiths used a photo of Little Joe Dallesandro's nude torso, from Warhol's *Flesh*, on the cover of their debut LP, and used an image of Candy Darling on the single sleeve of "Sheila Take a Bow."

To some extent, the Velvets' co-founders got in on the action. Tucker found time between raising her five kids to release solo records—covering "Heroin" on her '82 debut *Playin' Possum*, recorded in her living room—and play live. Nico toured doggedly while maintaining a fearsome heroin habit, singing VU repertoire alongside her originals. She'd relocated to the punk hub of Manchester, an industrial city famous for its gloom; she godmothered the growing goth scene, and reconnected with Cale, who produced her 1985 *Camera Obscura* LP. After working with the Stooges and Patti Smith, Cale embraced the punk aesthetic he'd seeded, promoting his mid-'70s trilogy (*Fear, Slow Dazzle,* and *Helen of Troy*) with some notorious stage antics, including the beheading of a chicken; he'd also issue an album recorded at CBGB, *Sabotage/Live*. By the time he released the powerful *Music for a New Society*, a stripped-down, brooding set of songs in 1982 that per usual did not sell well, Cale was in a bad place financially and personally, overindulging in drink and too many drugs. He took a dim view of the Velvets' posthumous canonization, as he was committed to making new work. But he did release a version of "I'm Waiting for the Man" in 1984 on *John Cale Comes Alive*, and he began setting his life in order the following year, when he became a father. Sterling Morrison, who'd been bouncing between teaching gigs in Austin and working on a tugboat in Houston, occasionally capitalized on his VU tenure, playing with local bands and contributing to records by Tucker and Cale.

VU alumni benefitted in more tangible ways when, in response to renewed interest, Verve reissued the first three LPs—the debut had been out of print in the States for more than a decade. On separate albums, Verve also issued many of the studio outtakes the group had amassed before disbanding. Reed was lukewarm on the latter idea, feeling the old songs should be left for dead, especially given degraded master tapes that, by his account, had been improperly stored in a New Jersey warehouse. His resistance was no doubt rooted in his perfectionism, along with lingering bitterness regarding his old label and bandmates. But it likely also had to do with his ambivalence over rebooting a version of himself he'd been competing with for over a decade. Either way, the songs had long been circulating as bootlegs, and an official release was a way to both improve the sound quality and earn money, so Reed ultimately signed off.

When the first outtake collection, titled *VU*, was released in February 1985, it landed at number 85 on the *Billboard* charts—an all-time high for the band. Many of the songs were familiar from Reed's solo albums—"Lisa Says," "Ocean," "I Can't Stand It," "Andy's Chest," "She's My Best Friend"—but to a one, these originals were more direct and compelling. *VU* was a secret history of a band that coined the sound and spirit of the moment some fifteen years prior, and was effectively the best "alternative rock" record of the year. Even the reissued albums did well. In short order, Verve issued *Another View*, exhuming more tracks; it was a strong set, too, though the pickings were thinner.

With the help of a lawyer, Reed and his former bandmates formed a partnership to sort out conflicting interests over the group's changing membership and multiple label contracts. When things were finally sorted, the royalties didn't amount to much; Cale said that, by 1986, he was receiving checks for roughly $1,500 a year. But he welcomed the money, as did Morrison and Tucker, who, raising a large family in Georgia, certainly put it to use. She also enjoyed the renewed fame.

"One of my kids would come home and say, 'Oh, my history teacher, Mr. So-and-So. He's really excited! He couldn't believe that my mom was in the Velvet Underground!'"

The obvious question raised by all this was the possibility of reuniting the band. But Reed wasn't interested, not yet.

* * *

Around this time, Andy Warhol also found his profile renewed through young artists who demonstrated their aesthetic debt to him. He'd always kept on eye on competitors, and liked keeping company with younger people, sometimes to a fault—e.g., his weakness for Studio 54 hot boys, who would often break his heart. Sniffing out new ideas and connections, he haunted downtown clubs in the wake of Studio 54's shuttering in 1980: the Mudd Club, the Palladium, Area, and the Pyramid. And his fraternizing with rising stars such as Julian Schnabel, Kenny Scharf, Keith Haring, and Jean-Michel Basquiat refreshed his profile as a godfather of modern art, just as '80s indie/alt-rock culture lifted Reed's profile as one of its godfathers.

In late 1985, spurred perhaps by the more activist company he was keeping, Warhol published *America*, for him an unusually explicit political work. It spoke to the moment. Ronald Reagan had been sworn in for a second presidential term in January, continuing to push a conservative agenda that criminally failed to address the AIDS pandemic, which by then had killed thousands of Americans; he'd resisted even mentioning the disease publicly until that fall. Warhol's book was filled with pictures he'd shot over a decade of traveling and illuminated by essays (written, per usual, with his team of ghostwriting collaborators) that departed from his trademark cryptic deadpanning, targeting hollow politicians ("all I see are guys scared to lose their jobs just trying to talk for 30 minutes without getting fired"), industrial agriculture ("our farmers are using all these drugs in the soil . . . the topsoil is getting worn out"), and economic discrimination. Ever mindful of his brand and still largely closeted as a public figure, Warhol didn't directly address queerness or AIDS, but the gay community certainly figured in the book's closing meditation on national identity: "I guess it's part of every country that if you're proud of where you live and think it's special, then you want to be special for living there, and you want to prove you're special by comparing yourself to other people. Or maybe you think it's so special that certain people shouldn't be allowed to live there, or if they do live there that they shouldn't say certain things or have certain ideas . . . But that kind of thinking is exactly the opposite of what America means."

Warhol's book may have figured in Reed's growing activism, along with his new financial stability and the collective anger of fellow progressives. In September, Reed played Farm Aid, the benefit concert for struggling family farmers organized by Neil Young, Willie Nelson, and John Mellencamp. He also participated in "Sun City," an all-star protest song organized by "Little" Steven Van Zandt, who'd just left Springsteen's E-Street Band to pursue solo work and activism; the single responded to musicians violating the United Nations cultural boycott of apartheid-era South Africa to perform at the lavish Sun City resort ("I ain't gonna play Sun City!" was the song's collective pledge-chorus).

Reed's cameo in the song brought him together with Rubén Blades, the Panama-born salsa star who was as much an icon in the city's pan-Latin community as he was in the rock world. The two became fast friends; Reed asked him to add some backing vocals on his next album, *Mistrial*, and shortly after attending Blades's wedding that winter, invited the newlyweds out to his Jersey place, where the men rode snowmobiles and did some co-writing. "He had the best, most honest laugh," Blades recalls. "He was always clear about what he wanted the result to be, and open to ideas on how to get there. He was, from my experience, a joy to work with. If you weren't an asshole, or trying to bullshit him, it was all good." They did good work, and Reed contributed to Blades's English-language debut, *Nothing but the Truth*. A standout was the co-written "Letters to the Vatican," a New York story with a Latin-rock undertow and a cast drawn from Blades's immigrant community. The cultural diversity widened Reed's lens on New York, and it would shape his songwriting.

Another input came via hip-hop. By 1985, rap had proved more than a fad. The Queens-based Run-DMC released the prescient *King of Rock*, which planted itself on the charts for more than a year; singles like Schoolly D's "PSK What Does That Mean"—a first-person street tale delivered in a menacingly stoned flow about buying coke, fucking "a whore," and holding a gun to the head of a "sucka-ass" rapper who bit his style—did urban noir better than Reed had. (Notably, Schoolly's debut LP also included "I Don't Like Rock and Roll.") As a forty-three-year-old Long Island Jew who'd made his name as a premier musical-poetic storyteller of uncensored New York City street life, speak-singing rhymes over beats, Reed was definitely paying attention.

The most obvious result, if hardly the most impressive, was "The Original Wrapper," written in the social-commentary vein of "The Message," the 1982 landmark Grandmaster Flash and the Furious Five single, but with the comic schtick of the Beastie Boys, a hard-rock-loving New York crew with Jewish roots whose debut LP would be released in late 1986. Reed's track referenced abortion, Ronald Reagan, Jerry Falwell, Louis Farrakhan, and New York City's anti-gay hardliner Cardinal John O'Connor, calling out religious hypocrisy and the "politics of hate" amid condom puns and gay cruising code. It also addressed the pandemic, an inescapable subject at the time, and one he'd return to. But it's notable that like Warhol—and probably for similar reasons, among them both personal fear of a then incurable disease and its radioactive effect in the '80s cultural arena—Reed would never commit to AIDS activism as he did to other causes.

As rap, the song didn't suggest Reed needed to rethink his day job, and its video got little traction on MTV (which the song accused of pumping out "violent fantasies" for kids), with a goofy parody attempt that downplayed the lyrics, featuring Reed in a fedora à la Michael Jackson, shedding glitter while roller-disco dancers zipped through the streets outside El Internacional, the Tribeca tapas restaurant and artist hangout that'd become an '80s update of Max's (in fact, Warhol and the rising star Jean-Michel Basquiat stumbled on the shoot one evening that September).

More memorable was the creepy clip for *Mistrial*'s "No Money

Down," directed by Godley and Creme of the pop group 10cc, who'd become in-demand music video directors, and were best know at this point for their award-winning work on Herbie Hancock's "Rockit." Reed's clip similarly featured a robot, in this case reciting the lyrics through a rictus mask cast from Reed's face, which he/it soon peels off to reveal a mechanical skeleton that self-destructs, first breaking off his jaw, then gouging out his eye. It certainly got noticed, but didn't last long on MTV, supposedly due to complaints from unsettled viewers.

Mistrial was Reed gamely competing in the landscape of '80s commercial pop ("We gotta sell some records!" Saunders recalls him saying during the sessions) but, again, coming up short. He was hardly alone among '60s rockers attempting reboots—Neil Young had released his similarly playful synth-rock opus *Trans* in late 1982—but *Mistrial*, its title a parting shot in the recently settled lawsuits, mostly sounded halfhearted. But when Reed sang "I know you're disappointed . . . You're thinking I misread the times" over electronic beats on "No Money Down," his laser-like lyrical insight felt on point. The self-loathing robot may have been a metaphor.

* * *

His RCA contract fulfilled, Reed upped his engagement with activist projects, leveraging his dark-knight celebrity. He did a convincing spot for MTV's Rock Against Drugs campaign, staring down the camera from behind mirrored shades. It was just six words long: "Drugs. [Pause.] I stopped. [Pause.] You shouldn't start." He also got involved with the human rights group Amnesty International, signing up for the Conspiracy of Hope tour, a superstar revue aimed at raising money and consciousness, writing a gospel-rock song, "Voices of Freedom," in solidarity with its mission. "It's one thing to read about things," Reed said at a press conference, "but when someone's sitting right in front of you telling and articulating some of these gruesome, unbelievable things that happen to people who do things that we take for granted every day. I mean, some of the records that I've made, I'd [have been] rotting in jail for the last ten years."

Reed needed to position himself in the best light for negotiating his next record deal. From a major label's point of view, his career as a solo artist was decidedly checkered—with notable successes mixed with punts; any company would know it was taking a risk. Given his situation, the interview Reed sat for on March 20, 1987, came at a perfect time. Joe Smith was a career music biz macher—president of Capitol Records, former head of Warner Bros. Records—who had begun an oral history of rock and current pop. The project was massive, with two-hundred-plus participants including Little Richard, Joni Mitchell, Al Green, Paul McCartney, Dylan, and Bowie. Reed seemed at ease with Smith, dispensing minimal attitude, content to set records straight and prove he wasn't commercially toxic.

But Reed was performatively frank about his tastes. He called the Beatles "garbage" and claimed he never liked them, while the Doors were "painfully stupid and pretentious." He expressed dislike for Stephen Sondheim ("Broadway music I despise") but admiration for Randy Newman, despite the singer-songwriter "[trying] too hard in his lyrics for my taste." He called *Astral Weeks* "one of the great albums of all time . . . in the top 10." He spoke of liking country music and "the repetitive chords" of African music. Among younger musicians he praised Tom Waits ("[he] really tries lyrically to do stuff"), Cindy Lauper ("she has this amazing emotion in her voice"), David Byrne, and Elvis Costello. He admired U2's new album *The Joshua Tree* ("amazing passion . . . very moving"). Speaking more generally, he said music getting airplay on radio was "despicable," and the only place in 1987 to find "interesting lyrics was, and is, rap music."

Nevertheless, Reed was effusive about Dylan, whom he praised a half-dozen times during the conversation, in marked contrast to his blanket dismissal of him in a 1976 *Rolling Stone* feature. Reed might've been responding to the liner notes of Dylan's recent compilation *Biograph*, in which Reed's model-cum-secret-rival name-checks him among his "secret heroes" of songcraft, alongside Leonard Cohen, John Prine, Tom Waits, Paul Brady, and David Allan Coe. When Smith mentions Dylan just got a luxury apartment in the new Trump Tower, Reed defended the need to move among wealthy people who are less likely to hassle you, noting the "college kids" who'd made the pilgrimage to his N.J. country home and walked right up onto the porch. (Reed responded by walking outside with his newly acquired shotgun.)

Reed was largely dismissive on the topic of Bowie. He talked, reluctantly it seemed, about working with him in the early '70s, claiming his own glam-rock turn was basically bandwagon-jumping, "trying to be part of whatever was going on," that he'd "watch what David did" and "do my version of it." Smith asked if Reed had "ever looked at [Bowie] and thought there was some promise there, or some things that you liked?" Reed said flatly, "No," waiting a beat before adding, "David's very bright, he knows what he wants and how to do it, he's doing what he wants to do—I think."

Things began going south when the topic turned to business. Reed spoke about the lawsuit with Dennis Katz, how it went on for nine and a half years, and how broke it left him; he noted how the bad reviews for *Berlin* were used against him in court, to suggest he was incapable of making decisions about his own production. He talked about having "practically a blanket contempt" for the press ("particularly the English, who I absolutely despise"), conceding he'd fabricated stories—in one, he claimed to have a Harvard PhD in music theory—while holding back certain opinions so as not to alienate people. Reed began sounding like a worried penitent in a confessional, expressing regret over his "terrible rep," how he was still trying to repair relationships with radio stations and trying to not say "bad things" in interviews. His guard dropped, Reed fretted how this one would sound transcribed. "I don't get along with a whole lot of people," he told Smith sulkily. "I am telling you what I really think, just for the hell of it. But I don't want it to come out snide and condescending . . . I don't want to come off Frank Zappa–ish."

Reed asked Smith to see the interview before it ran, and Smith agreed. ("I am asking for some discretion," Reed told him.) When Reed saw the transcript, he withdrew his permission for Smith to use it in his book. It's unclear what his reasons were. But the notion of legacy was surely on his mind, given the unexpected death of Andy Warhol.

Warhol had been busy as usual that winter. He'd made a series of silk screens based on Leonardo's *Last Supper*, and optioned Tama Janowitz's zeitgeist story collection *Slaves of New York*. He'd been suffering for quite some time from a diseased gallbladder, born of an inherited condition, and had been urged to get it removed. But he steadfastly refused, treating it instead with non-Western medicines, dietary changes, and thousands of dollars' worth of new age crystal therapy. His longstanding fear of hospitals was magnified by the AIDS pandemic. In September, his live-in boyfriend Jon Gould had died, presumably of HIV-related causes. It was a harrowing death; between Gould's hospitalizations, Warhol had instructed his housekeepers to wash his boyfriend's clothes and dishes separately from his own.

When Warhol was compelled to get the organ removed in February 1987, it was so gangrenous, it fell apart during the operation, and his abdominal wall, badly damaged from the shooting, needed to be repaired. While his post-op condition seemed stable, Warhol's heart stopped in the early hours on Sunday morning, February 22, 1987, at New York Hospital, near his town house on the Upper East Side. (The official cause of death was listed as "ventricular fibrillation," though the Warhol estate would file a medical malpractice suit.)

Reed didn't attend the family funeral in Pittsburgh, but he was at the memorial in April at St. Patrick's Cathedral. It was a media frenzy, and the old gang was there, along with Warhol's more recent friends and associates: Basquiat, Schnabel, Liza Minelli. Brigid Berlin read from the scriptures, and a eulogy was given by Yoko Ono, who became a widow in 1980 when John Lennon was killed in a scenario not unlike Warhol's shooting in '68.

Reed was with Sylvia, and had not been invited to speak. Sylvia recalls him being emotionally "devastated" about his friend's death, though he presented at the memorial in what she calls "the 'Lou' way— seeming very cold on the outside." After the event, select mourners mingled at a private luncheon nearby, the scene something of a dark mirror of Max's backroom. People networked, trading art ideas; Warhol would've certainly enjoyed it. At one point, according to Cale, Julian Schnabel buttonholed him, suggesting the two of them collaborate on a Warhol tribute of some sort. Then Schnabel saw Reed and called him over.

Cale hadn't spoken to Reed in years—Cale chalked it up to Reed's trying to stay clean while Cale was still partying prodigiously. But after celebrating his daughter's birth with a gram of coke, Cale had recently decided to get clean and sober, too. The estranged friends broke the ice, Schnabel backed off, and a seed of a collaboration was planted, which both Sylvia Reed and Cale's wife, Risé, worked together to facilitate. Reed returned to New Jersey on fire with ideas, and began to write. Back in the day, Warhol goaded him about his work ethic, asking how many songs he'd written that week. Now Reed was laying into it, waking up daily around 5 a.m. to put pen to paper.

* * *

On November 25, 1987, the photographer Peter Hujar died of HIV-related pneumonia at Cabrini Medical Center. Among his most famous pictures was the one of his friend Candy Darling on her death bed, surrounded by flowers, in the same hospital. Two days later, in the Church of the Holy Trinity in Toronto, a young Canadian band with a sensationalistic name—the Cowboy Junkies—arrayed themselves in a circle around a Calrec Soundfield microphone to record a set of originals and covers. Among them was "Sweet Jane," which they played at an exquisitely slow tempo, basing it on the *1969: The Velvet Underground Live* version. Michael Timmins strummed woozy changes like it was last call in Calgary, and his sister Margo sang the "heavenly wine and roses" bridge in her intoxicating low soprano, vowels blossoming lushly, the group reverberating inside the church as if they were huddled in the body of a cello. The recordings, which cost around two hundred dollars, were issued virtually unchanged by Reed's former label, RCA. *The Trinity Session* was a magnificent mood piece, and a striking rejection of the Syndrum-driven mainstream rock sound Reed had lately been chasing. It charted and eventually went platinum. Reed certainly liked the recording of his song, and the album was sold with a promo sticker quoting him, saying it was "the best and most authentic version of 'Sweet Jane' that I have ever heard."

It was high praise—especially given that, presumably, this included all of his own released versions. The song had become one of the most iconic in rock, covered by countless acts, and its status among young bands reached a sort of apex in 1986 in Austin, Texas, when a five-hour "Sweet Jane" marathon competition was staged in a local club. One of the top finishers was Two Nice Girls, a self-described "dyke rock" band who transformed "Jack" into "Jacky" in a brilliant medley mash-up (with Joan Armatrading's folk-soul "Love and Affection") that helped land them a record deal with the esteemed indie rock label Rough Trade.

With the Velvets revival as backdrop, Reed, now a free agent, connected with Seymour Stein, whose taste-making Sire Records had launched the Ramones and Talking Heads, important U.K. post-punk bands such as the Smiths, and various young dance-pop acts, notably Madonna. For Stein, like Clive Davis, it was a chance to work with a legacy artist likely worth more in terms of label cred and bragging rights than actual sales. "As a rule, I never signed established stars, but Lou Reed was the one guy you'd make an exception for," Stein noted. But the label chief would end up being surprised.

Near the end of 1987, Reed and Cale went into a rehearsal room on Ninth Avenue and Fiftieth Street to work up ideas for a song cycle about Warhol. At first, they just played for fun, cautiously feeling out whether they could recapture their chemistry—they hadn't made music together since the '72 Bataclan concert with Nico. The friends reminisced, and Cale discovered things he'd never known—among them, startlingly, the fact that Reed had fired Warhol as their manager ("So stupid!" Cale later reflected). The men discussed format; Cale wanted strings on the project, perhaps instrumental pieces. But Reed insisted on just songs with vocals, to be performed onstage by just the two of them. It would be a tribute to their initial creative partnership, working on folk songs in their crap apartment on Ludlow Street, playing as street buskers in Harlem. But in a strategic sense, it would also give Reed a control of the project he might not have had if something more musically sophisticated was involved.

Cale eventually conceded, and the collaboration was like sparring. "There was this amazing energy," Cale observed; "it was aggressive." He was impressed at how much Reed allowed him into the writing process, which rarely happened in the Velvets. "It's difficult for him to collaborate on that level—it's difficult for him to collaborate period. And he admits it." The work was relentless and efficient; within the first ten days, they had fourteen songs. One, "Work," hinged on Warhol's challenge about Reed's productivity.

In the months following Warhol's death, Reed had taken that challenge to heart, creating material for both the tribute project and his next solo album. That record would be finished and released first, setting the stage for the reflective *Songs for Drella* with an album fully grounded in the present.

* * *

It's possible that *New York*, a record that raged outwardly against a rotted society, took the shape and direction it did because *Songs for Drella* dealt with such personal material. Reed had already been revisiting the social commentary of his brief mid-'60s folk phase: on "America," the "Star-Spangled Banner" reimagining he recorded during the *Growing Up in Public* sessions, and "The Original Wrapper." For *New York*, he channeled the sentiment, invective, and wordplay of rap into his signature style and tore into current events, assuming that after nearly a decade of regressive American politics, fans would appreciate his literate spleen-venting.

New York's "two guitars, bass, and drums in a room" sound harked back to the Velvets, especially the clean sound of the third LP, and was a well-timed return to basics as guitar-centered "alternative" rock was getting major commercial traction: the previous year, U2's *The Joshua Tree* spent nine weeks at number 1, and the East L.A. band Los Lobos had a long-running Top 10 hit with their unfussy revival of Ritchie Valens's 1958 rock 'n' roll landmark "La Bamba."

Reed's new band was grounded by his co-producer Fred Maher's drums and the bassist Rob Wasserman, a genre-catholic San Francisco virtuoso who studied with the composer John Adams and made a name playing jazzy bluegrass with David Grisman. The guitarist was Mike Rathke, a Berklee student who became Reed's brother-in-law when he married Sylvia Morales's sister. The day before the men first met, Rathke's Boston apartment had been robbed and all his guitars stolen. Backstage after Reed's concert in town, Rathke admired a blue Fernandes Strat copy Reed had just been playing, sitting in an open case on the floor. "He looked at me with those steely eyes and said 'You can keep it if you use it,'" Rathke recalls.

It was the beginning of a long creative partnership. Their guitar interplay was remarkable, less about the warring pyrotechnics of Reed and Quine than the hypnotic weaves Reed achieved with Sterling Morrison, and more in step with the approach of young bands who avoided grandstanding solos. Their collaboration brought out aspects of Reed's sound he hadn't revisited in ages, and explored fresh ones: "Endless Cycle" was shimmering country rock with a melody that faintly echoed Johnny Cash's version of "Ring of Fire," while "Sick of You" had a Texas swing swagger. Reed's playing showed new focus: his minimalist solo on "Strawman" was a model of efficiency, a handful of sustained notes that climbed and resolved with perfect attack.

As compelling as the music was, *New York* hung primarily on Reed's words, pre-social-media rants delivered with poetic clarity. "I realized that these songs were what I really wanted to talk about . . . there wasn't much choice to it," Reed admitted. "It's like what my friend said to me: 'This is what eight years of Reagan does to you.'" The words were thrown into relief by Maher's production, partly inspired by Leonard Cohen's recent recordings, making Reed's enunciation sound close enough to smell the cigarettes on his breath (usually low-tar, low-nicotine Carltons, as he was trying to quit). Some songs were straight tirades. "Strawman" seethed with disgust at income disparity, racism, and various hypocrisies—religious, political, rock-cultural—its verses hollered so passionately they were nearly unrecognizable as coming from Reed, master of the sing-speak sneer. "Sick of You" was an absurdist litany of fever dreams with notable prescience; among Reed's visions were the ordination of the Trumps (then merely a boorishly unscrupulous local celebrity real estate magnate and his soon-to-be-ex-wife) and a run-in between a Wall Street inside trader and Rudy Giuliani (then a sketchy federal attorney and mayoral hopeful). Other songs were closer to character studies. The single "Dirty Blvd." opens on Pedro, an abused kid living in a welfare hotel, and flips lines from the Emma Lazarus poem inscribed on the Statue of Liberty's pedestal: "Give me your hungry, your tired, your poor," Reed snarls, "I'll piss on 'em." On "Xmas in February," a heartbreaking ballad with rolling arpeggios, he described the plight of a disabled Vietnam vet, while "Romeo Had Juliette" moved through an updated *West Side Story* scenario, its cast refracting Reed's oeuvre: there's a girl in a vest, like Sweet Jane, and a guy named not Little Joe but Little Joey Diaz. "The streets were steaming, the crack dealers were dreaming," Reed sang, imagining Manhattan sinking "like a rock into the filthy Hudson" as internal and end rhymes jostled across the stereo spread.

Speaking to the moment, the album also engaged the politics of race and identity. "Good Evening Mr. Waldheim," was an op-ed screed drawn straight from headlines. A former UN secretary-general elected president of Austria in 1986, Kurt Waldheim had been a Nazi intelligence officer during World War II, a history he'd unsuccessfully tried to bury, but which might in fact have helped him win. The song's main target, however, was the Reverend Jesse Jackson, the civil rights leader who ran a progressive campaign for the '88 Democratic presidential nomination and was criticized for his stance on the Palestine Liberation Organization, his alliance with Minister Louis Farrakhan (lighting-rod leader of the African-American Nation of Islam movement), and for having referred to New York City as "Hymietown" in a conversation with a Black reporter (what Reed called a "racist slip" in the song).

Given his standing as bard of America's most Jewish city, it's surprising Reed had barely addressed Jewish identity in his work. "The Original Wrapper" rhymed "Black against Jew" with "1942," referring to tensions between Black and Jewish communities in Brooklyn's Crown Heights in the '80s. He again invoked the Holocaust on *New York*'s "Busload of Faith," describing "goodly hearted" people who "made lampshades and soap."

The local politics of race was also on Reed's mind, as for many New Yorkers. In Howard Beach, Queens, five days before Christmas 1986, a mob of white teens chased down twenty-three-year-old Michael Griffith and his companions with clubs and bats after their car broke down nearby, for the evident crime of having brown skin. Griffith was killed trying to escape, hit by a car on the Belt Parkway; his stepfather, Cedric Sandiford, was caught and beaten with a tire iron and tree branches. In the wake of protests and international media attention, three high school students were convicted of manslaughter. On "Hold On" Reed invoked the incident explicitly, alongside other acts of racist violence, but complicated the narrative with allusions to the subway vigilante Bernie Goetz and the 1986 shooting of a white police officer by a Black boy, suggesting a near-hopeless cycle of bloodshed.

Another key theme of *New York* was the pandemic. Echoes of "Walk on the Wild Side" coursed through "Halloween Parade," in which Reed recast the celebratory pageant as a reggae-tinged funeral procession. Subtitled "AIDS" on the album's inner sleeve—though tellingly not on the jacket, a reflection of the horrific silence around the pandemic—the song name-checked Reed's buddy Rotten Rita, the trans legend Brandy Alexander, and other figures, real or invented. But the song's main presence is an unidentified "you," which Reed rhymed with "I was afraid it might be true." Approximately ten thousand people in New York had died of HIV/AIDS by the end of '87, and it's hard to imagine Reed writing those lines without thinking about Rachel Humphreys, who at the time of the 1987 Halloween parade was in prison at Lincoln Correctional, a minimum-security men's facility on 110th Street, serving a two-year minimum for criminal sale of a controlled substance, fifth degree, a Class D felony.

New York ended with "Dime Store Mystery," dedicated "To Andy-honey." The song looked at an unnamed dying man, comparing him with Christ, Buddha, and Vishnu. Reed would later describe it as "a supreme love song." And in the Great American Novel of his solo catalog, the finale of the *New York* chapter would segue perfectly into his Warhol tribute.

* * *

New York was released in early January 1989, to deserved critical praise. But to everyone's surprise, it also became Reed's most successful album yet, cracking the Top 40, selling half a million copies, and being certified gold. In part, this was thanks to Reed's learning to compromise and work with his new label. He'd even offered to record a broadcast-friendly version of "Dirty Blvd." with "piss" and "suck" deleted, so Sire's promo staff wouldn't "feel defeated before they ever went in" to pitch the single to radio programmers. It worked, and the song got significant airplay.

Moreover, *New York*'s topicality spotlighted Reed's writing like never before. The album "captures its historical moment like a cockroach in amber," wrote Jon Pareles in *The New York Times*, whose op-ed editors were so impressed with Reed's accomplishment, they printed the lyrics to "Hold On" as a standalone opinion piece. *Life* magazine commissioned a poem from Reed to accompany a photo-driven feature on "can people"—struggling New Yorkers, many of them homeless, who scavenged empty cans for rebate cash. (Reed submitted a four-stanza poem, titled "Cans," though to his displeasure the magazine printed just the first and part of the second.)

Reed was exceptionally open with journalists while promoting *New York*. Jonathan Cott engaged him on Walt Whitman and Federico García Lorca—queer poets who found epiphanies both ecstatic and horrific in New York City—and on the plague. "How many people have to drop dead from AIDS?" Reed raged. "Why do they think that's not going to spread? Do they have to wait until AIDS works its way to the suburbs before the great middle class rises up and says, 'Ohhh!'? Well, everybody should be saying 'Ohhh!' right now."

Reed also pointed out with pride in interviews that, on *New York*, "the Lou Reed image doesn't exist, as far as I'm concerned. This is me speaking as directly as I possibly can to whoever wants to listen to it." He explained his drug-addled '70s persona bluntly: "I was really fucked up. And that's all there is to it. It's like I really encouraged it. I did a lot of things that were really stupid . . . I thought, 'Fuck it, I'll give it a little push that way, a little street theater.' Getting involved in all that was like [pandering to it]. I don't think it brought out the most attractive features in me."

That past followed him still. David Fricke, preparing a feature for *Rolling Stone*, attended a Boston show where the wistful "Halloween Parade" was interrupted by someone yelling "This sucks! Play some rock and roll!" Reed stopped the show to answer the heckler: "This *is* rock 'n' roll. It's *my* rock 'n' roll . . . If you don't like my rock 'n' roll, why don't ya just split? Get a refund, motherfucker."

* * *

New York made Reed culturally relevant again, which allowed him to take more pleasure in being an éminence grise. At the fourth annual Rock and Roll Hall of Fame ceremonies, staged at the Waldorf Astoria on Park Avenue, he appeared in a suit and tie to deliver a heartfelt, over-the-top induction tribute to his fellow New Yorker Dion DiMucci, testifying that the opening line of Dion and the Belmonts' "I Wonder Why" was "engraved in my skull forever," alongside other early rock 'n' roll lyrics, "like Shakespearean sonnets with all the power of tragedy." (Dion, a guy who'd battled his own demons, including a longtime heroin habit, thanked Reed sincerely before pivoting to crack jokes about Bruce Springsteen's income.)

Just weeks prior to the ceremonies, Reed had been playing Velvet Underground covers on a Long Island radio station with the Feelies, among the best of the new Velvets-inspired rock bands. Reed subsequently hired them to open shows on the New York tour, but it raised the question of why Reed didn't reunite the Velvets, who deserved induction into the Rock and Roll Hall of Fame themselves. He'd enlisted Tucker to play on *New York* (she appeared on both "Dime Store Mystery" and "Last Great American Whale"), though Cale demurred a similar invitation, uninterested in anything that smacked of a Velvets reunion under Reed's marquee.

And Cale already had his hands full working with Reed on *Songs for Drella*. Reed continued to wrestle with the lyrics. His writing was clearly affected by the publication of *The Andy Warhol Diaries* in mid-'89—Reed had gotten an early manuscript—a book in which Reed often appears in an unflattering light. He admitted his resentment directly on "Hello, It's Me," which became *Drella's* final track: "You hit me where it hurt I didn't laugh," he intoned, addressing Warhol directly, "Your *Diaries* are not a worthy epitaph." Even the title telegraphed Reed's ambivalence: "Drella" was Warhol's nickname, but not quite one of endearment, a contraction of Cinderella and Dracula that was rarely if ever used in his presence.

The LP narrative followed Warhol's life more or less chronologically. "Smalltown" addressed his upbringing in Pittsburgh—a "small town" only by comparison with New York City—with Reed's approximation of Warhol describing himself ("bad skin, bad eyes—gay and fatty"). "Open House" recounts the artist's early days illustrating shoe advertisements, and connects the evolution of the Factory to his mother's "Czechoslovakian custom" of inviting people in for tea and "little presents." Cale name-checks Warhol's Brillo box, his films *Kiss* and *Empire*, and "a rock group called the Velvet Underground." Reed recounts the anecdote about Warhol challenging his songwriting productivity, and their falling out when Reed fired him, on "Work." On "It Wasn't Me," the men animate Warhol's defense against those who accused him of allowing his Factory acolytes to kill themselves. "I'm no father to you all," Reed insisted, giving voice to Warhol with a sentiment he no doubt shared with regard to his own fan base. "I never said stick a needle in your arm and die."

But it's on the album's keystone, "A Dream," where Reed stares down his complicated relationship with Warhol in greatest detail. A short-story-style piece like *White Light/White Heat's* "The Gift," written at Cale's suggestion, was cast in Warhol's voice, and its lines seem fully informed by the *Diaries*, paraphrasing Warhol's complaints about Reed—including his declaration "I hate Lou"—followed by a powerful section where Warhol sees blood seeping onto his shirt from the bullet wounds that never fully healed, his real-life stigmata.

It was brave, empathetic writing. But it was also a way to control the narrative. As he had with the "The Gift," Reed had Cale deliver the song, and coached him on the delivery. "When John was doing the reading, I kept telling him that when we get to that line, 'I hate Lou,' you gotta say it like a kid," Reed later told a journalist, stressing the line's importance. "It's like the way a little kid would say it. It's not like, 'I fucking hate Lou Reed, I really hate that son of a bitch.' It's more like [he puts on a whiny, sing-song voice], 'Oh, I hate Lou; oh no, I reeeeally do.' You know?" That may or may not have been true. And Warhol was in no position to clarify.

Reed and Cale renewed their admiration for each other during the project. But it was hardly stress-free. Reed wanted things his way; according to a chilly fax memo sent to Cale, Reed threatened to scrap the project outright unless Cale accepted his choices. Premiering the work at the Brooklyn Academy of Music Opera House, following a warm-up production at the nearby St. Ann's Church, the two men delivered the songs unadorned, with just guitar, keyboards, and viola. During a filmed performance, Cale delivered the "I hate Lou" line with hurt and regret—not at all, it appeared, the way Reed had lobbied for. As Cale's words landed, what seemed a flickering wince of pain blew across Reed's stoic face like a storm cloud before he turned away from the camera.

* * *

There'd apparently never been any serious discussion of involving Nico in the project. But any lingering question ended on July 18, 1988, when, biking in Ibiza, supposedly en route to buy hashish, Nico fell, hit her head, and died of a brain hemorrhage.

It was a cold irony. After years of trading on her reputation as rock's goth heroin queen, roughing it on sketchy club tours, and stuffing condom-wrapped plugs of dope into her orifices when approaching border checks, Nico had finally gotten off junk and onto methadone. She'd even begun work on an autobiography, and was taking time off on the Balearic island with her now-grown-up son, Ari, who'd spent a portion of his childhood scurrying about the Factory. His mother was cremated and buried on the outskirts of Berlin at Grünewald-Forst, a cemetery once known as a burial site for suicides and alcoholics; its former name was Friedhof der Namenlosen, "Graveyard of the Nameless." None of Nico's bandmates in the Velvet Underground attended, though some of her recent sidemen showed up, playing a benefit concert to help cover her funeral expenses. Nico's son attempted to sell her remaining bottles of methadone toward the same end.

* * *

Songs for Drella came out in April 1990, with a cover echoing that of *White Light/White Heat*: a Billy Name Warhol portrait printed black-on-black, overlayed with a shot of Reed and Cale. While the music also echoed the Velvets, *Drella* was an austere LP, and it would sell just a fraction of what *New York* did. But a brief show Reed and Cale did in France to promote the album, on the afternoon of June 15, would finally reunite the Velvet Underground

The performance was commissioned as part of a Warhol retrospective at the Cartier Foundation for Contemporary Art in Jouy-en-Josas, an arts compound set in a nineteenth-century chateau about ten miles north of Paris. "There was this underground bunker from World War I that they'd built to keep the Germans out," recalls Billy Name. "They'd transformed [it] into the Factory." The foundation had flown Name in for the event; they also flew in Maureen Tucker and Sterling Morrison.

Cale was nervous, given the years of bad blood, but the bandmates all slipped more or less comfortably into their old social roles, including Name, who acted as peacekeeper, den mother, and go-between. "Without Billy's genteel attention we would have been at each other's throats," Cale noted, impressed at how the "tongue-tied fright of Lou's persona would melt away as Billy gave voice to what it seemed Lou was thinking—and I could not help but wonder at how such a mental inhabiting of another's mind was so easily achieved—but it did happen."

By the end of the welcome luncheon, ice broken, the four bandmates agreed to perform one song together. And so, on an outdoor stage that breezy afternoon, after Cale and Reed played a handful of *Drella* songs, Tucker took the stage, then Morrison, and for the first time since 1968, the quartet eased into "Heroin." In a high-fashion black leather jacket and aviators, Reed picked out the signature notes on a red, ultramodern Steinberger guitar; Cale, hair cut into a severe art-school pageboy, in a double-breasted suit-jacket and necktie, drew a bow across his viola; Tucker, resembling the suburban mom she was, in a purple blouse, black slacks, and sunglasses, pounded the hell out of her bass drum; and Morrison, looking like the career academic he more or less was, in a rumpled sports jacket, oxford shirt, and jeans, added flourishes on a guitar borrowed from Reed, since he hadn't bothered to bring his own.

"They sounded so rich and authentic—the same setup, with the same tones and everything," Name says, visibly moved by the event decades later. Following the performance, Cale left the stage on the brink of tears. "I did not know why," he'd reflect.

But it was obvious. A young woman in the audience spoke to a TV newscaster covering the event. "C'est un grand moment," she said, beaming. "We can all die now."

10.

UPPER WEST SIDE > WEST VILLAGE

(1990s)

DISCUSSED: The death of Rachel Humphreys, the death of Doc Pomus, *Magic and Loss*, *Between Thought and Expression*, Laurie Anderson, the Velvet Underground reunion, the death of Sterling Morrison, the Rock and Roll Hall of Fame, *Set the Twilight Reeling*, David Bowie's fiftieth birthday, *Trainspotting*, some intense fan mail

---

The memorial tone of *Songs for Drella* struck a chord in the AIDS era. Warhol's friend Robert Mapplethorpe died from HIV-related illness in 1989, leaving behind a final, indelible image of himself gripping a skull-tipped cane, sick and wizened. The graffiti artist and cultural engine Keith Haring, also a friend of Warhol's, died similarly in early 1990. Reed lost friends around this time, too. After a lifelong struggle with his mental health, his Syracuse roommate and co-conspirator Lincoln Swados died in 1989. And on January 31, 1990, at age thirty-seven, Rachel Humphreys died.

Paroled in the summer of 1988, Reed's ex-partner and muse was arrested again that November, convicted of second-degree robbery, and sent to Shawangunk Correctional, a maximum-security prison upstate, where she was evidently housed in the men's section. At some point, she'd been transferred to St. Clare's Hospital on West Fifty-second Street, one of the main facilities treating AIDS patients. Humphreys was buried anonymously in a mass grave being used for AIDS victims on Hart Island in the Bronx. Her parole hearing had been scheduled for

December. Reed didn't discuss her publicly, but his former partner would evidently remain a muse in absentia.

In April, Reed performed at a Farm Aid benefit concert, his third appearance at the fundraiser. The 1990 lineup included Elton John, Iggy Pop, Jackson Browne, and Guns N' Roses, whose "One in a Million," with lyrics that included racist and homophobic slurs, had triggered a firestorm of criticism. But the concert organizers refused to cancel one of the world's biggest bands. Outraged, Reed found Mellencamp, a friend from earlier Farm Aid events, in his dressing room, and he stepped to him. "He was worked up about it," said Mellencamp, who implied the author of "Heroin" was a hypocrite. Reed played the concert, but he and Mellencamp never spoke again.

*   *   *

Reed had to face yet another death of a friend around this time, albeit not to AIDS: Doc Pomus, who like Warhol had become a sort of father figure for Reed. A Jewish kid from Brooklyn, Pomus contracted polio as a child—with cruel irony, at an out-of-town summer camp his parents hoped would shield him from it. He attended Brooklyn College, fell in love with the blues, and became an unlikely club singer, a heavyset white kid on crutches who adopted the stage name Doc Pomus because it sounded "hip" and "mysterious." He soon left performing to focus on writing music, and with his partner Mort Shuman he became a celebrated songwriter, co-authoring Dion and the Belmonts' "A Teenager in Love," the Drifters' "Save the Last Dance for Me," assorted Elvis Presley signatures, and more. By the '80s, however, Pomus was past his prime and wheelchair-bound, and could often be found holding court at the Lone Star Cafe, a lively music venue on the corner of Fifth Avenue at Thirteenth Street. He'd abandoned most of his vices by then, even dumped his last box of filterless Chesterfields, after a lifelong smoking habit that hit four packs a day. He lived for music.

Pomus was a devoted friend to many, always willing to help someone with their career. He became an advocate for reparations to R&B artists swindled by unfair publishing agreements. He wrote music with Mac "Dr. John" Rebennack when the latter was struggling with a heroin addiction. When Pomus discovered his old pal Jimmy Scott—one of the most singular, magnificent vocalists in American music—singing in a crappy Newark club, he wrote a letter to *Billboard*, excoriating the music industry for letting huge talents wither then showing up to their funerals "in hip mourning clothes [to] talk about how great" they were. Pomus also conducted songwriting workshops at his apartment, for both rising talents and veterans. In 1986, Bob Dylan came knocking at the door of his two-room flat on West Seventy-second, hoping for a mojo transfusion during a spell of writer's block. In the years that followed, Reed became a regular there.

Visiting Pomus was, for Reed, like making a pilgrimage to sit at the feet of a streetwise New York City song guru, a man who'd written lyrics that had been burned into Reed's heart as a kid. The men connected on many levels. Both got screwed by the music industry early on. Both were sons of men they felt were unsympathetic to them. They shared a sense of oppression.

The relationship, sadly, didn't last long. In early 1991, Pomus was diagnosed with lung cancer. Having hurt Warhol by not visiting him in the hospital, Reed didn't make the same mistake with Pomus, checking in with him at NYU Medical Center nearly every day. Reed even offered to bring him a fancy color TV to replace the hospital room's small black-and-white set. His friend told him not to bother; Pomus was a black-and-white guy.

The memorial service was held at Riverside—the Carnegie Hall of Jewish funeral homes—up on West Seventy-sixth Street. In his eulogy notes, Reed reflected how great Pomus was to talk to, especially about music and boxing, how Pomus always cheered him up, and how they'd had plans to go to Katz's Deli so Reed could try the grilled beef knoblewurst, which Pomus insisted would change his life. Jimmy Scott sang Pomus home with a devastating rendition of George and Ira Gershwin's "Someone to Watch Over Me," Rebennack backing him on piano. It so deeply moved Sire Records' Seymour Stein, there to pay his respects, that he gave Scott the record deal Pomus had long been stumping for.

* * *

Two weeks later, Reed was recording at the Magic Shop on Crosby Street, a new studio with vintage gear and a Neve console, perfect for the state-of-the-art traditionalism he had in mind for his next record. He'd been writing steadily through Pomus's convalescence—on one hospital visit, he'd brought his friend an upbeat number called "What's Good," written with him in mind—and had arrived at a suite of songs tethered around themes of mortality. Like *The Blue Mask*, *Magic and Loss* would open with a thunderhead of electric guitars; it then settled into polished, measured pop-rock, with sung-spoken verses high in the mix. On "Power and Glory," Reed imagines meeting God as he observes the death of a friend on a cellular level; the man's voice fails, and radioactive isotopes enter his lung to try to "stop the cancerous spread," nuclear instability being harnessed to save life rather than destroy it. "Dreamin'" conjures Pomus resignedly smoking a cigarette and declining Reed's color TV offer ("I guess this is not the time for long-term investments"). "No Chance" channels Reed's survivor's guilt, noting how strange it is that, after all he'd subjected himself to over the years, he's the one left alive. "Harry's Circumcision," a spoken-word piece recalling "Lady Godiva's Operation," deals with aging, its title character so horrified to find he's physically "turning into his parents" that he takes his shaving razor to his body. "Gassed and Stoned" was a hard-rock shirt-rending involving a postmortem phone call that seemed to allude to both Pomus ("the *New York Times* obituary") and Rachel Humphreys ("no grave to visit").

Pulling narrative threads together was Jimmy Scott, who Reed brought in to sing on the album. His crying, pleading tone, flickering between young and aged, male and female, was tremendously powerful. Throughout his life, Scott had been "teased and tortured" as a result of Kallmann syndrome, a genetic condition that inhibits hormone production. But he learned to see his condition as a gift. "When I sang, I soared. I could soar higher than all those hurts aimed at my heart," he told his biographer David Ritz. "I've been called a queer, a little girl, an old woman, a freak and a fag . . . But early on, I saw my suffering as my salvation. Once I knew that, I understood God had put me in this strange little package for a reason. All I needed was the courage to be me."

Reed considered Scott a "singer's singer," likening him to "a performing heart." The engineer Roger Moutenot recalls Scott's arrival at the studio: "Lou was just like, 'Oh my God, I can't believe he's here. I can't believe he's going to sing on my song. I'm so honored.' He really treated him with respect." Scott admired Reed, too, telling him his poetry was filled with "the totality of life," and praising his Geiger-counter sensitivity, telling him "no one has more emotion than you do." Reed was committed not just to working with Scott, but giving him exposure, and even invited him to join his touring band, where he was a compelling presence, a wizened angel who found sly ways into the music, scatting off the backing vocals of "Walk on the Wild Side" and improvising from the "I wanna fly away" reprise during "Dirty Blvd." Reed would claim Scott changed him as a singer: "He was tutoring me in the art. I learned more about vocalizing during that tour than any time before or since."

As usual, Reed had high hopes for his new LP. "He thought *Magic and Loss* was gonna be another breakthrough, like *New York*," says Bill Bentley, a musician who was Sire Records' publicist at the time. It wasn't, although it got very good reviews and Sire put significant money into its promotion—partly because *New York* did well, partly because Madonna, Reed's megastar labelmate, was keeping the coffers filled. Reed's new music was a hard sell in the pop arena, and per usual, in his refusal to compromise or glad-hand, Reed could shoot himself in the foot. Unwilling to perform live on the hugely popular early morning *Today* show, one of U.S. TV's most powerful platforms, Reed prerecorded his segment, which wound up shelved. According to Bentley, who regrets a subsequent and probably counterproductive "letter war" with the show's producers, the material was deemed too much of a downer for the morning broadcast, and there was some worry that Scott's unconventional image might upset viewers.

Sadly, Reed's tour plans with the singer also turned out to be fraught, and Scott finished only a portion of the European *Magic and Loss* tour. "The story Lou told me," recalls Bentley, "was that Jimmy—I don't know if he was drinking that day or what—came up behind Lou and kinda got him in a choke hold or something. It was probably just Jimmy's way of goofing around. But it scared Lou, because he cut off his wind, and Jimmy got sent home. Lou always liked Jimmy, never turned on him; he just didn't feel safe with him [after that]."

A Velvets fanatic of the first order, Bentley would be Reed's biggest supporter at Sire. He'd first met Reed as a teen in 1969, in an Austin, Texas, record store when the Velvets were in town for a gig Bentley missed, thanks to an arrest for a single marijuana cigarette. He later befriended the Austin transplant Sterling Morrison, who joined Bentley's band the Bizarros for a while, and after a stint as a music journalist, Bentley took the Sire Records job, and was so thrilled to be working with Reed, he wrote him a letter introducing himself.

Bentley's first meeting with Reed in his new job was instructive. "Lou goes, 'Come with me,'" Bentley recalls. "We go in this little room in the [recording] studio, and Lou just looks at me, and his exact words were 'Let's get one thing straight. Sterling remembers everything. I remember nothing. Do you understand?' I said, 'I absolutely understand, Lou.' It was his way of telling me he did not want to revisit any Velvets bullshit, any questions, any memories. I think one of Lou's ways of coping with life was, when things were done, he would just seal them in a box and put the box on the curb for the trash man to pick it up. He did not like to live in the past at all. He'd always say he didn't remember the past. I think it was just that a lot of the past was painful to him." As Reed's publicist, it was Bentley's job to oversee press interviews, and if questions veered into the personal, reformed attitude notwithstanding, Reed would terminate them immediately, whatever the agreed-upon time. "Lots of interviews ended early," Bentley says.

That didn't happen when Reed sat for an interview with Robert Hilburn of the *Los Angeles Times* and confessed "I still feel vulnerable during interviews . . . Maybe I'm too sensitive, so what can you do? If I wasn't that way, I probably wouldn't be able to do what I do in the first place." Asked if he worried about his ability to match his Velvets work, Reed replied, "Most of my life." But when Hilburn asked him about the dedication of *Magic and Loss*, which read, "To Doc and especially to Rita," Reed declined to discuss the identity of "Rita" beyond saying they "wouldn't have wanted to be known." If the reference was to Rachel Humphreys, as it doubtlessly was (Rotten Rita, possibly a stand-in for Humphreys in "Halloween Parade," was evidently still alive), he wasn't copping to it. However much Humphreys's passing haunted Reed, that part of his life was over and sealed up.

* * *

If all these deaths—Warhol, Nico, Humphreys, Pomus, Swados—didn't trigger a change in Reed's outlook, they did seem to coincide with one, as the title track, ending *Magic and Loss*, suggested. In it, Reed appears to address himself, a man of towering ambitions stuck with his limitations, rage, self-doubt, and "caustic dread," who had survived his own wars and passed through metaphoric fires, after which, he declared, "you cannot remain the same."

Indeed, he did not. What some might cast as that most quotidian of middle-class afflictions—the midlife crisis—Reed manifested as a genuine reinvention. In the coming years, he'd fully assume the mantle of an artist emeritus. He'd publish, finally, his first book. He'd turn fifty, begin reconnecting with his family and Jewish heritage, end his marriage of ten-plus years, and begin a transformative new relationship. He'd even reunite, albeit very briefly, the Velvet Underground.

Reed also began to explore the role of mentor with younger artists, as Pomus and Warhol had mentored him. Around this time, he went to see Jonathan Richman perform at the Lone Star Roadhouse, an uptown version of the club where Pomus once held court. The Boston kid who adored the Velvets, seeing them by his own estimate more than sixty times, and who played his first proper concert set opening for them in 1968, had built an idiosyncratic career, writing songs with a steel-willed naivety that celebrated the simple joys of rock 'n' roll. Among his latest, which he'd release on his 1992 album *I, Jonathan*, was titled "Velvet Underground." It paid tribute to a group that was "wild like the U.S.A. / A mystery band in a New York way," breaking into a verse of "Sister Ray" as object lesson midway through. Reed had come to the show with the magicians Penn Jillette and Teller, and the three joined Richman afterward for a bite. "We all went out together afterwards to one of those big late-night midtown delis," he recalls. "Lou and I sat next to each other at a table of about eight people. I can't describe to you exactly how it felt to have my boyhood art hero tell me that he was proud of me. But if you consider that that band, all four of them, more or less gave me my way of expressing myself through sound, and that he in particular perhaps gave me my voice in music, perhaps you can imagine how I must have felt."

*   *   *

Nearly two decades after Reed first shopped a poetry manuscript, he completed *Between Thought and Expression: Selected Lyrics of Lou Reed*. Published in late 1991, with a title lifted from his playfully polymorphous "Some Kinda Love," the book was a validation of Reed as a Writer. *The New York Times* considered it so notable, it printed the lyrics of "Heroin" and "Chelsea Girls" as a standalone item in the Arts & Leisure section.

Reed had great anxiety about the project, and Sylvia, who collaborated on the design, recalls it as "one of the hardest things" they ever did together—making, pulling apart, and remaking mock-ups of the book he imagined, over and over. "He had great reverence for the type of poet that Delmore was, the more established method of becoming a poet," she says. "He had a really high [minded] idea of what the art should be. It was *extremely* important. It scared him to think that [this] was going to be another chance for him to be shot down. He was assuming everyone was going to say it was pretentious. He was really afraid."

Reed's relationship with his wife had become more complex when she began functioning as his default manager, after Reed, following a familiar pattern, fell out with and parted ways with Eric Kronfeld, the man most responsible for pulling him out of his financial troubles. The temporary arrangement with Sylvia became permanent—maybe not the best move from a personal or business perspective, despite the former art student being a quick study and fiercely devoted to her husband. In a letter dated December 4, 1991, he confirmed her new role as vice-president of Sister Ray Enterprises, overseeing all his projects.

Reed dedicated *Between Thought and Expression* to his family: Sid, Toby, Bunny, and, "most of all," Sylvia. In the short introduction, he explained the logic of the collection's mix of lyrics, poems, and interviews (with two men he admired, Vaclav Havel and Hubert Selby Jr.), noting that his lyrics were always rooted in "an experienced reality," and that the act of writing, for him, revolved around "life and how you live it." Bolstering a notion of encoded memoir in his songs were footnotes to many of them, written with varying degrees of truth. He noted that "Pale Blue Eyes" was written for someone whose eyes were in fact hazel (Shelley Albin's eyes are brown). He cited his love for after-hours bars and fancifully described how he once saw "someone beaten to death" in one, after Nico threw a glass that "shattered in a mob guy's face." He wrote that Warhol's funeral was the second he'd ever attended, Delmore Schwartz's being the first, and he reflected on some shared wisdom: "Andy said, 'You don't have to tell them the truth.' And so sometimes I don't." The lyrics included in *Between Thought and Expression* spanned Reed's career, including nearly all his important songs. Notably missing, however, was "Coney Island Baby," along with any mention of Rachel Humphreys.

Reed's conversation with Havel, the new president of Czechoslovakia, had been arranged by *Rolling Stone* in late 1990. The men had a surprising connection. Havel explained to Reed how he'd visited New York for six weeks in 1968, witnessed the student protests at Columbia, and purchased a copy of *White Light/White Heat*, which he brought home to Soviet-era Prague. Impressed, he played it for friends, among them Mejla Hlavsa, founder of the Plastic People of the Universe, a rock band that was highly influenced by the Velvets, and whose members were arrested in 1976 and put on trial for making subversive art. A campaign organized to free them led to the formation of the so-called Charter 77 human rights movement, which, in turn, fueled the country's historic democratic overhaul. In that sense, as Havel told Reed through an interpreter, "one record by a band called Velvet Underground played a rather significant role in the development in our country."

The interview with Selby, whose work Reed had admired since college, was warm, chatty, and dealt mainly with the writing process. Reed mentioned his surprise that Havel, a dissident playwright, had become president of a nation. "This is the only country where only bad actors have power," Selby offered ruefully, a reference to the B-list film star President Reagan. "Not men of imagination."

* * *

Sid Reed wrote his son a letter, dated June 19, 1992, thanking him for his "unusual" Father's Day gift, which was likely a copy of *Between Thought and Expression*, with its dedication to the Reed family—Sid's name listed first—and its apparent, less-than-wholly-flattering lyrical references to him in "Families" and "My Old Man," the latter idolizing, then recoiling from a "bullying" parent who insists, "Lou, act like a man." Between the lines of Sid Reed's brief note seemed decades of miscommunication and regret. "Maybe I don't say it very well when we are together," he wrote to his son, "but in a letter I can tell you how extremely proud I am of you and how much I love and cherish you."

* * *

Lou Reed walked onstage at Madison Square Garden that fall to perform at an all-star tribute concert for Bob Dylan, commemorating the thirtieth anniversary of Dylan's debut LP. Reed played an obscure Dylan tune, "Foot of Pride," a cryptic blues stomper about hypocrisy, religious and otherwise, that opens with a line about a woman who "passes herself off as a man." Reed laid into the song with gusto. However, for the all-in finale of "Knockin' on Heaven's Door," dominated by Neil Young and Eric Clapton, Reed stood on the sidelines looking skeptical, thumbs in his pockets and singing half-heartedly, probably feeling a bit snubbed.

Singing beside him was a fellow singer-songwriter, Rosanne Cash. The daughter of Johnny Cash had just separated from her husband, the country music outlier Rodney Crowell, and moved to New York City. After the performance, Reed asked for Cash's phone number, with clear intent. Cash was a fan of his work; she'd seen him do *Magic and Loss* at Radio City in May, and was so moved she wept. But dating Lou Reed? That was another matter. "I think we both realized at the moment he asked that even a single date would have been a disaster," she said. "We were so, so different."

Reed's relationship with his wife was growing rockier, in large part due to her desire for a child, which he did not share, not to mention from the stress of being business partners. He'd begun looking for an off-ramp, rekindling a relationship with Erin Clermont, his old Syracuse friend. Suzanne Vega, a New York singer-songwriter profoundly influenced by Reed's music, recalls him being "very flirtatious" at a dinner with Reed and his wife that Sylvia had in fact invited her to.

None of these relationships would pan out. But around the time of the Dylan tribute, Reed connected with another New York City woman whom he found tremendously captivating, and with whom he had a great deal in common.

* * *

When Laurie Anderson was a kid, she was showing off on the high board of a swimming pool. She sprang up, did a flip, but missed the water, landing on concrete and breaking her back. She spent months in the hospital, paralyzed, in the children's burn and trauma ward. "I remembered the ward and the way it sounded at night," she recounted years later. "The sounds of all the children crying and screaming—and the muffled sounds that children make when they're dying. And then I remembered the rest of it: The heavy smell of medicine, the smell of burned skin. How afraid I was."

A doctor told Anderson she'd never walk again. But she was

convinced, with the unshakable confidence of youth, that he was wrong ("This guy is crazy," she recalled thinking). He was indeed wrong; after two years of wearing a heavy metal brace—which pressed against her lungs and made it difficult to speak—she regained mobility. But it's likely the physical experience sharpened her inclination toward the life of the mind.

Anderson was raised in the wealthy Chicago suburb of Glen Ellyn, Illinois, one of eight children in a large house designed by her mother. It was a building filled with stories. Her maternal grandmother was a Baptist missionary who took her to see Billy Graham preach. Anderson's mom, Mary Louise Rowland, eloped as a teenager with her horseback-riding instructor, Arthur Tyler Montgomery Anderson, and raised her brood like a theater director: staging family pageants, sewing costumes, organizing performances at public events, encouraging their education. Her daughter Laurie took classes at the Art Institute of Chicago, and played violin with the Chicago Youth Symphony.

"I was forced to play the violin; not at gunpoint or anything," Anderson recalled. "We had a family orchestra and we needed violins. We were eight kids and we all played—flute, cello, clarinet, piano and violin. It was like the Von Trapp family. We wore matching outfits: red turtleneck sweaters and navy pants for the boys, navy skirts for the girls." Commanding attention in a family of ten took some doing, so Laurie Anderson honed her storytelling skills. By her account, her father was never critical of her, and "sort of idealized me"—understandable behavior from a parent who nearly lost a child, then watched her make a miracle recovery. "It was always a strain to live up to this image," she confessed in an early performance piece. "So sometimes I just lied. I pretended things were fine when they were really falling apart." Her mother, meanwhile, was somewhat the opposite. When asked if she felt her mother loved her, Anderson responded, "She was not someone who really knew how to do that . . . She taught me other things. She taught me how to love books, music."

Anderson also learned to listen well, not just for decorum but to gain knowledge. In middle school she decided to run for student council president, so naturally, she wrote a letter asking for advice to Senator

John F. Kennedy, whose campaigning for the presidential nomination impressed her. He, or at least a staffer writing on his behalf, responded, with a generous letter suggesting Anderson find out what the other students wanted and pledge to do that. When she won, she wrote back to thank him, and soon received a telegram of congratulations with twelve red roses. After word got out, the front page of the small local paper, the *Glen Ellyn News*, trumpeted, "LOCAL GIRL RECEIVES ROSES FROM JACK KENNEDY." Anderson had a way of making things happen.

She briefly attended Mills, a pioneering women's college in Oakland with a modernist-leaning music program, but soon moved to New York City to make art. She sat in on classes at Barnard, painted, sculpted, and made Super 8 films. Storytelling and music became central to her work. For one project, she played violin busker-style, wearing ice skates that were frozen into blocks of ice; the performance concluded when the ice melted. Ice seemed to have an appeal, perhaps via her Swedish roots. In 1974, during a very hot New York summer, she decided to hitchhike to the North Pole, starting on Houston Street near her East Village apartment. It was a challenging trip and when she returned, three months later, she found a hole chopped through her apartment wall, and most of her belongings stolen or destroyed, artwork included. In her backlog of mail, she'd received an invitation to work at the ZBS Foundation—the acronym stood for Zero Bull Shit—a media art center and commune in upstate New York near Saratoga Springs, launched by the radio DJ and producer Tom Lopez and his audio engineer friend Bob Bielecki.

"That changed my life," Anderson says. "It was a commune, which I eventually joined . . . I went there to work on some stories that had sound effects, and Bob asked me, 'What kind of sound are you looking for?' And I said, 'Well, I don't know if it has a sound, but if there was sand under your contact lens, it would be the sound of it grinding against your eyeball.' The next time I come into the studio, he has these eighteen really beautiful vintage microphones, with a two-mic setup around this piece of glass, and he's dropping grains of sand onto various materials. And I thought: 'Oooh, I'm in love! This is, like, the greatest person I've ever met.'"

ZBS went through every phase a commune goes through, according to Anderson—including drugs, organic farming, and ultimately kids. "That's when it began breaking up, because the kids started going to school, and people needed a different thing. But it was a really great experience to be part of that group. I loved it . . . The first time I worked [on a recording] there, they said 'you can do it exactly the way you want.' I'd never, ever been in that situation before, and it was terrifying— because then you had to really know what you want. And they did that with everything. With cooking, with their personal relationships— everything was 'let's make it really the way we want it to be, not the way you think it should be, or whatever, but the way we want it to be.'" Anderson seemed to carry this attitude with her.

* * *

Anderson's leap into the music business began with making 7-inch records for a 1977 art installation called *Jukebox*, loading discs pressed from her ZBS recordings into a functioning jukebox at the Holly Solomon Gallery. Some years later, she released a standalone 7-inch for One Ten Records, a tiny label run by her friend Bob George. "Walk the Dog" was a surrealist avant-folk piece that poked fun at Dolly Parton. On the flip side was "O Superman," based on themes by the French romantic composer Jules Massenet, with Anderson's sung and spoken passages processed with a vocal pitch-shifting device. Wistful, philosophical, charming, ominous, and remarkably catchy, the 1981 pressing caught the ear of the intrepid BBC radio DJ John Peel, who aired it, and in a cultural moment increasingly defined by slick technology and smooth-talking authoritarians, it struck an immediate chord. "One day I got a call from London, an order for 20,000 copies of the 'single' immediately, and another 20,000 by the end of the week," recalled Anderson, who'd pressed only 1,000 copies, a seemingly extravagant quantity made possible by a $500 NEA grant. "I looked around at the cardboard box of records and said, 'Listen, can I just call you back?'"

Before long, she found herself teleported from the rarified SoHo art world into the front lines of highbrow pop culture, a pixie avatar of future shock with a freshly inked eight-album Warner Bros. deal.

The transition took some getting used to. "I quickly found out that in my world (the New York avant-garde) this was considered 'selling out,'" she recalls. It was not that far removed from what Lou Reed experienced in his transition from Warhol-sponsored art terrorism to corporate-sponsored rock star, who was now contracted via his Sire Records deal to the same entertainment corporation Anderson was.

Their formal meet-cute didn't occur in a Warner's boardroom, however, but at the 1992 Munich Art Projekt, an experimental music festival with multiple performer-curators, among them John Cale, Ornette Coleman, Arto Lindsay, and John Zorn. Lindsay, a downtown scene fixture since his days with the no-wave noise-rock band DNA in the late '70s, invited Anderson. Zorn—a rangy, ambitious avant-garde sax player and composer who'd seen the Velvets at the Dom as a twelve-year-old—invited Reed. Zorn was another downtown new music fixture, and had been exploring ways to incorporate his Jewish heritage into his art practice; he conceived a two-day program within the Munich Art Projekt titled "The Festival for Radical New Jewish Culture." To Zorn, aware of Reed's Jewish roots, it seemed like a perfect fit.

Reed's relationship with his own Judaism was unclear, perhaps even to him; he rarely alluded to his heritage in his work, and it had never been part of his public persona. His attitude may have been shaped at the Factory, where most everyone was Catholic, Warhol first and foremost. "There were very few Jews," said Danny Fields, "and you felt that you could never really be in with the [in crowd] . . . but Lou was a weird Jew." Reed knew Zorn's work through the rangy producer Hal Willner, who included both of them on his 1985 Kurt Weill tribute *Lost in the Stars*. Reed loved Zorn's contribution, so he agreed to play the festival.

Zorn introduced Reed and Anderson at JFK Airport, as a group of festival-bound musicians waited for their flight. In a jazz-improv spirit, he suggested the two musicians collaborate. "Lou asked me to read something with his band," Anderson recalled. "I did, and it was loud and intense and lots of fun." The text was "A Dream," from *Songs for Drella*. Anderson channeled Warhol through Reed's text, and he was wowed. "That was great!" she recalled him telling her afterward, "that was just how I would do it!" It was like she was his mirror.

The two made loose plans to reconnect in New York, where they lived near each other—although as touring performers, neither was home very often. Reed would make good on them.

* * *

In December, Denis Johnson published *Jesus' Son*, a slim collection of interconnected stories that took its name, epigram, and spirit from Reed's "Heroin." The book, which was met with great acclaim, disrobed the mind of an addict with chilling, poetic vividness. Its main character—known only by his nickname, Fuckhead—and his cohorts had voracious drug appetites, consuming random pills and gulping double whiskeys while violence descended like weather.

The same month, the Velvet Underground—Reed, Cale, Tucker, and Morrison—were rehearsing in New York City for the first time in nearly twenty-five years. They were still feeling out the viability of a reunion, which wasn't a done deal. But it looked promising. Cale, touring on an anthology of his solo work, got things rolling during a show at New York University, inviting Reed and Morrison to join him. Cale also performed with Morrison on *The Tonight Show*, where he teased the reunion. When the host, Jay Leno, boasted that he'd seen the Velvets in 1969, Cale eyed the floor, declining to point out he'd left the band by then.

> **Leno:** I hear rumors you guys may play together again, yes?
> **Cale:** Yeah, we've had a lot of good meetings about it. And, uh, I guess if we can keep all the spontaneity and enthusiasm of those first days together, it'll be great.
> **Leno:** So how long has it been?
> **Cale:** About twenty-five years.
> **Leno:** Wow. So why, all of a sudden now, you decide . . . ?
> **Cale:** Money?
> **Leno** (over audience laughter): Money! Yes. Money would be a good motivating factor.
> **Cale:** A motivating factor, absolutely.

Cale wasn't joking; he'd just moved into a pricey Greenwich Village home with his wife and child, and was struggling to maintain a comfortable New York lifestyle, which included a Hamptons summer rental. Money remained an issue for Reed, too. But Sylvia Reed still had his back. Among other duties as manager, she helped oversee licensing of his back catalog, increasing revenue while navigating his mercurial objections. The prior summer, Reed had issued a directive to EMI Publishing indicating he didn't want his songs used in advertising "of any kind," a stance likely triggered by a parody recording of "Walk on the Wild Side" that turned up in a corny ad campaign for Colman's Mello & Mild Mustard ("take a walk on the mild side").

But with his wife's encouragement, Reed soon relented, and began making serious money from licensing, something he'd done piecemeal since his Honda and Amex ads in the '80s, but never systematically pursued. As the prospect of significant record sales dimmed, he saw how ad collaborations could actually support his artistic integrity, enabling him to make uncompromising records without worrying much about sales and airplay. "I don't have to be a big shot, or rich," he said, regarding the paradoxical freedom ad work conferred. "All I want to do is more." Sylvia Reed helped negotiate deals and chased down uncleared usages, which cropped up frequently—an instrumental "Sweet Jane" snippet on MTV, a "Dirty Blvd." stem in a newsmagazine story on urban blight, a "Wild Side" cutaway bump during a Phillies–Blue Jays game.

To be sure, "Walk on the Wild Side" remained Reed's most valuable property, especially given the object lesson of his Honda ad, and how easily the song's transgressive shine could be decoupled from its actual context. Advertisers of all sorts lined up in the '90s to get a taste of it. Documents suggest Levi's offered him $25,000 to use "the 'do-do-doo' chorus" in a Canadian TV ad for a one-year period, with another $30,000 for a one-year extension. Reed evidently agreed on $20,000 to allow use of a cover version in an Italian makeup commercial, and greenlighted usage in ads for the Discovery channel ($125,000) and a European ice cream brand ($20,000). The song even made bank in print ads. A '92

Reebok request to reproduce a page of "Wild Side" sheet music apparently got a go-ahead (albeit with the word *colored* removed from the lyrics). Reed was offered $150,000 from Piper-Heidsieck just to use the song title in a series of ads—"Take a Walk on the Red Side," a reference to its signature red label champagne—despite the fact that, strictly speaking, titles aren't copyrightable, and this one was lifted by him in the first place ("in the current climate many ad agencies are being cautious + paying for uses such as this," an EMI rep cheerily advised him in a memo). In addition, there were numerous film and TV usages. In 1992 alone, Reed evidently approved it for use in *The Simpsons*, *Beverly Hills 90210*, a Dennis Rodman documentary, and a promotional campaign for the Boy Scouts of America. Whatever the context, his publisher advised asking for top dollar, and by all indications, he usually got it.

Still, Reed was protective of his signature hit and exacting in his taste. He'd cut or even waive usage fees for artists or causes he wanted to support, and deny usages he thought unethical, unenlightened, uncool, or otherwise in poor taste, regardless of fee. Documents suggest he nixed "Wild Side" licensing requests for a European airline (potentially $275,000), an Israeli beer company ($8,500), a Puerto Rican oil company ad ($35,000), an episode of an animated comedy series where a character dresses in drag ($7,500), and a request by a tabloid news show to use it during a segment about "Marky" Mark Wahlberg and Natalie Smith's 1993 *Penthouse* spread.

Maybe the most memorable commercial use during this '90s bonanza was in a British ad for Dunlop tires. With no voice-over, the original recording of "Venus in Furs" accompanied a collage of hallucinatory images—half-naked figures in alien getups, a head in a bondage hood-mask festooned with nails, a grand piano falling off a bridge, a car making sharp turns through a landscape of flames and explosions—culminating in a final shot of the brand name on the side of a tire. The award-winning ad became so notable in the U.K. that London's Capital Radio proposed a spoof ad, which meant another £5,000 in licensing fees for Reed, who apparently scrawled "APPROVED" in big blue Magic Marker letters above his signature on the deal memo, no doubt with an explosive cackle of laughter.

Delmore Schwartz might have told Reed not to "sell out." But War-hol, an adman from the get-go, saw inserting himself into mainstream ad culture as a legitimate part of his art practice. When Reed riffed on Warhol's "business is art" concept on the mid-'70s *Philosophy Songs* cassette, it was with a whiff of sarcasm and condescension. But by the '80s, when he discussed his financial woes for Joe Smith's oral history, Reed wondered how his own business sense had gone so wrong. "My father owned corporations," he said ruefully. "I should have that in my blood somewhere." Now Reed seemed to embrace "business art" wholeheartedly.

"[Lou] would say 'Call my office' to everybody, I don't think it mat-tered who it was," recalls his office manager Beth Groubert, who saw him using the line as both protective shield and badge of credibility. "Lou really liked having that office. That was his business . . . and I think he definitely liked being a businessman, in addition to an artist. Absolutely."

Some of his business decisions, though, were questionable. Among the most lucrative "Walk on the Wild Side" windfalls would come from the song "Can I Kick It?" by a group of teenaged NYC rapper-producers who called themselves A Tribe Called Quest. They'd built the song's beat by looping an easily identifiable sample of the "Wild Side" bass line, alongside less obvious elements from Eugene McDan-iels, Lonnie Smith, and Dr. Buzzard's Original Savannah Band. These were still the semi-lawless early days of sample-based music, and by the time Reed received the sample clearance request in 1990, the song was a done deal, a month out from being released on the group's de-but, *People's Instinctive Travels and the Paths of Rhythm.*

When Reed refused to clear the sample, he received a letter from Barry Weiss, VP of Jive Records, pleading his artists' case, noting Tribe's "creative and innovative" work, and the "critical acclaim" for the group. He urged Reed to consider making a deal that would ensure him a "sizable" cut of the publishing, noting an irony: Weiss's father, the storied music bizzer Hy Weiss, had cut a deal with the Velvets af-ter the release of "Foggy Notion," a song that, sans permission, lifted lines from the Solitaires' "Later for You Baby," a 1955 B side released on

Weiss's Old Town label. Barry Weiss pointed out his father's willingness to recognize the Velvets' creative appropriation, and hoped Reed would share the same "positive spirit" in making a deal with the Tribe.

Reed was largely unswayed, and claimed 100 percent of the publishing and writing credit for "Can I Kick It?," establishing the copyright as entirely his, in turn agreeing, in effect, to license the group's own song back to them. Issued as a single, the song became a rap touchstone, inspiring other artists to sample "Wild Side" and generating plenty of ad agency action. The irony that Reed's cash cow song had originally "sampled" the title of Nelson Algren's novel, and was informed by the life stories of other artists, most of them struggling, was perhaps not lost on him. But business was business.

* * *

On February 19, 1993, Reed participated in a songwriter round-robin at the Bottom Line with Rosanne Cash, David Byrne, and Luka Bloom. The show was hosted by the WNEW-FM DJ Vin Scelsa, an interviewer with whom Reed got on well. Reed veered between seriousness and stand-up in his banter. Introducing "Heroin," he noted: "I like this song [because] it only has two chords. And I really thought you ought to be able to write a really good song with one chord. Two chords is really pushing it. Three, you're getting into jazz." Though there was no drummer, you could almost hear a rim shot. Later, Scelsa asked Reed about Delmore Schwartz's vow to haunt him if he ever sold out. "I'm the one who *said* he said that," Reed responded drolly. "It sounded good at the time. I was being interviewed, and I needed something to get them to stop." It was impossible to know if he was being serious about inventing this long-standing creation myth, or just messing with people's heads.

What Reed didn't say was that the Velvet Underground reunion was a go. "Everybody was feeling a bit nervous at first," Tucker recalled of the first tentative rehearsal that month. After five or six hours, however, the four musicians were all "extremely happy." Rehearsals continued through the spring, in preparation for the band's first full shows in twenty-five years, scheduled to take place in Edinburgh, Scotland, on June 1 and 2.

Starting overseas made sense. For one thing, the Velvets had never played outside the United States, and their reputation in Europe loomed even larger than at home; by one estimate, the European market accounted for roughly 80 percent of the total sales of *Songs for Drella*. It also gave the Velvet Underground a chance to warm up away from home and the U.S. media, though the stakes remained high. Even devoted fans—especially devoted fans—had mixed feelings about the reunion. "The group's unique godhead status will begin to diminish almost from the moment they start their first number," predicted David Sinclair in *The Times* of London.

The band booked twenty-two European dates; four were arena shows opening for U2. Luna, a young American guitar band representing the Velvet Underground's numerous offspring, opened for them. The Velvets' first show in Edinburgh began with "We're Gonna Have a Real Good Time Together," and it was clear that subverting the air of reverence was on the agenda. Cale played a synthesized orchestral string overture before "I'm Waiting for the Man," which, in another pivot, he sang. On the second night, Reed radically changed the cadence and melody of his vocals on "Venus in Furs," and knocked out an apparent freestyle "Velvets Nursery Rhyme," declaring, "We're the Velvet Underground, we want no part of this / That's because we think it is pretentious shit!"

A more fully formed new song, "Coyote," channeled wistful melancholy over Tucker's bass drum pulse, with harmonized vocals by Cale and Reed. It would not have sounded out of place on the third VU album. Fans roared with pleasure, as Reed laughed with delight.

After the first show, *The Times*'s David Sinclair exhaled with some relief, noting that "the rest of the world has only just caught up with [the Velvets]." *The New York Times*'s John Rockwell hedged, mostly reporting on the reunion, although he did praise the "distinctiveness" of Reed's vocals and the "solidity" of Morrison's guitar. He saved his enthusiasm for Tucker's drumming, a "tom-toms-of-doom sound that

inspired straight-ahead punk drumming for a generation" and that remained "rocklike in the granitic sense of that word."

In London, at Wembley, Chrissie Hynde and Peter Gabriel turned
out, alongside other famous fans. At the Olympia Theatre in Paris,
when Reed delivered the line "like a dirty French novel" from "Some
Kinda Love," the French crowd cheered, Cale attacking his piano like he
was trying to crack the song open. Sometimes the tension between the
men seemed palpable. When Cale sang "Femme Fatale" as proxy for his
late comrade Nico, one could imagine him addressing "little boy, she's
from the street" to Reed, her ex-lover, relegated to singing backup with
Morrison. The frisson sometimes bore sweet fruit. The deep-catalog
"Hey Mr. Rain," unreleased until the 1980s vault raid, turned into a kinetic jam akin to the evidently retired "Sister Ray," moving into free-jazz
territory, Reed's sonic vocabulary on guitar more varied and nuanced
than it was in the '60s. The jamming didn't always gel—on one night,
Reed grinned through one section, and stuck his tongue out in comic
distaste at another. During these brief, welcome moments, they were no
longer a legend, but just a band, flying by the seat of their pants.

As a verbose Irish punk with an empathetic pop heart, U2's front
man Bono naturally revered the Velvets, Reed in particular. During U2's
1992 *Zoo TV* tour, Bono mastered a cover of "Satellite of Love" so thor-
oughly with his graceful falsetto, it became an almost definitive version.
But at the group's shared arena dates, the Bono-Lou love fest did not
help the Velvets' precarious chemistry. According to the journalist Lisa
Robinson, Cale complained that Reed was treating his bandmates like
sidemen, ditching them to ride in Bono's limousine. For Robinson, who
came of age in Manhattan in the '60s, whose husband produced Reed's
debut, and who saw Reed and Nico rehearse in her living room, the
show was a disappointment. For her, the magic was not there.

She was not the only one disappointed. Tucker found things had
changed as well. Reed "became way more of a perfectionist when
he went solo," she observed. "His show was a much, much different
thing than we did. Not even musically, but money-wise and roadie-
wise . . . [In Europe we] had sound check one time and it went seven
hours. I swear to God, it was like, are you out of your freaking mind? . . .

I really wished when we went on that tour that we just got some amps like we had when we were poor, no lighting, no bullshit, just get out and play like we used to."

After the final show on the tour, opening for U2 at a stadium in Napoli on July 9, Reed and his bandmates flew back to the States and went their separate ways.

There were plans for American dates, and MTV invited the Velvets to do an acoustic set, which would've been a hugely lucrative proposition. But there would be no *Velvet Underground Unplugged*. Reed, needing to be in charge and in control, found it hard to accept the role of mere group member during the brief European tour. At rehearsals he'd explode; one particularly vicious outburst was directed at Morrison, though Reed later apologized. The stakes were high—the Velvets' iconic greatness haunted the proceedings, as it had always haunted Reed's solo work—and his stress levels equally so. He tried to insist the shows were for "fun," to bring playfulness to bear, like in the old days. But it wasn't just about fun. It appeared as if the band's entire legacy was at stake. The money he could take or leave, especially since he owned the publishing on most of the catalog anyway. For his bandmates, however—especially Tucker and Morrison, who'd led more-or-less hardscrabble lives since Reed bailed on them in 1970—the money was a very big deal. Reed was well aware of this; Sylvia Reed recalls that her husband's desire to help Tucker buy a house was a primary factor in agreeing to the reunion in the first place. This didn't make his situation any easier.

Reed generally staged breakups from a remove, as when he'd tasked Morrison with Cale's firing in '68. Now Sylvia Reed—who, though she declined the title, was the Velvets' de facto manager by default—became the intermediary, along with the press. By late September, *NME* reported the end of the reunion and Reed's vow to never work again with Cale. Letters from Cale, faxed to Reed, veer between his offense at being dealt with this way, and pleas that Reed not end the band again. Cale's attempts to change Reed's mind while keeping his dignity were heartbreaking. In one fax, Cale invoked the thousands of Velvets fans who'd still love to see them perform, adding that Reed may even know two or three of them, i.e., himself and his bandmates.

When Reed insisted on full production control of any *Unplugged* project, along with the accompanying producer fees, it may have been less a power grab than a hand grenade tossed intentionally into a situation destined to remain beyond his control whatever his "official" role. Cale predictably refused the terms. In short order, he received a fax from Reed and his wife ending things and coolly wishing him "good luck in his future career."

Maybe saddest was the damage to Reed's friendship with Tucker, who'd long endured the intercine rivalries of the men. In the years leading up to the reunion, Reed and Tucker had stayed in touch. Sylvia considered her a friend, too, and they both helped Tucker with her modest solo career. Reed played guitar on her 1989 *Life in Exile After Abdication* and sang backing on her homespun recording of "Pale Blue Eyes." ("Moe, there is no D-minor in 'Pale Blue Eyes,'" he told her during the session; "there is in my version," she retorted.) They regularly exchanged holiday cards, Tucker invariably addressing Reed as "Honeybun" and generally signing off with "love and hugs."

She addressed him the same way in a handwritten letter faxed on September 14, in which she gently noted that she agreed with Cale and Morrison that it was a bad idea for Reed to produce the Velvets, reasoning with clear concern for him that he'd drive himself crazy (along with the rest of them) and it would destroy the fragile friendship that they'd just rebuilt. She wished him good luck with his efforts to quit smoking and signed off, "Love, Moe." Reed's three-page typed response, fired off the next morning, was brutal. While he made fair points about his production credentials, he also called Tucker "naive" and "thankless," accused her of looking a gift horse in the mouth, dryly noted "the blue collar thing is a little boring," and fumed about working with "delusional people" with "inflated visions" of their role. He complimented himself for taking only 25 percent of the concert earnings when he could've played all the bookings solo, disparaged Tucker's showmanship, and, in reference to the help he'd provided with her modest solo projects, told her not to ask him for studio advice anymore.

The next day, a memo was drafted to Tucker and Morrison confirming that there'd be no more Velvets shows because Reed and Cale "could not see eye to eye." Cale held out hope, faxing Sylvia in October asking hopefully about the MTV project. But when he got wind of Reed's nasty memo to Tucker, he went through the roof. "I wanted to say to him: 'While you were making holes in your arm, Maureen was raising four children single-handedly, so fuck you,'" Cale reflected. He faxed Reed a nine-page eruption of his own, a final nail in the coffin of one of the century's great musical collaborations.

* * *

When Reed became aware that the author Victor Bockris was writing a biography of him, he and his team went into crisis mode. Bockris had orbited the Factory and St. Mark's Poetry Project scenes for years; he'd interviewed Reed a number of times, had plenty of relevant contacts, and had already published a frank, well-regarded biography of Warhol. Reed had his lawyers send Bockris threatening letters, and personally reached out to friends and associates, past and present, urging them not to participate.

If there was ever a time Reed would want to avoid a writer nosing into his business, it was now. He was tending to a precious new relationship with Anderson, who he surely wanted to spare the spectacle of his dirty laundry. And his life was messy: along with the wrecked Velvets reunion, Reed was in the final throes of splitting with Sylvia. According to a note in his address book, he fired her as his manager via fax on March 4, 1994, "at 1:08 PM," effective in three days. Reed soon fired his personal assistant, and changed his legal representation. The timing of all this upheaval probably had nothing to do with Reed's turning fifty-two that month. But he might've noted he was the same age that Delmore Schwartz was when he died.

* * *

That summer, Laurie Anderson trekked to the Himalayas, since she "hadn't been in a crazy place for a while." For years, she'd been a student of Buddhism. "We were going to see a lake way up in the mountains where the next Dalai Lama's name was said to be written in code on the surface of the water," she explained. At around 22,000 feet, Anderson fell ill with severe altitude sickness; her temperature hit 104 and she began hallucinating. Fearing for her life, the guides put her in a body bag, strapped her to a donkey, and sent her down the mountain with two members of the party. The descent, parts of which involved near-vertical drops, took three days. "I was never terrified of death," she said months later, describing the experience of passing in and out of consciousness, indeed on the brink of death. "I was lucky to see how beautiful it is."

The experience would profoundly inform her next record, *Bright Red*. One song would be a duet with Reed, who'd given up the Upper West Side apartment he'd shared with Sylvia and moved back downtown—first to 45 Christopher Street, then into an impressive penthouse on West Eleventh Street, a short walk from Anderson's place on Canal Street.

The couple's first date, though Anderson hadn't initially recognized it as one, was attending the huge Audio Engineering Society Convention at the Javits Center. She soon suspected he had more on his mind than microphones. The pair nerded out, talked shop, went for dinner afterward, then to a movie, then for a walk. "From then on," she said, "we were never really apart."

The attraction was understandable, and informed a different sort of relationship for Reed. For starters, there was little power disparity. Anderson did what Reed did, and was every inch his creative equal—a ferociously smart lyricist and storyteller, an inspired musician and technophile with a multimedia orientation, respected in both the high-art and pop culture worlds. Like Warhol, she was an open fire hydrant of ideas, a big-picture conceptualist who could make compelling conversation on virtually any topic. She was also very beautiful, in a strikingly androgynous way, with an electric and beatific smile that resolved in deep dimples. Like Reed, she interrogated and played with gender roles, from her maternal captain on "O Superman" to the pitch-shifted, masculine voice of authority she later named "Mr. Bergamot." Both Anderson and Reed had complicated relationships with family; neither had children.

As their matchmaker John Zorn put it, accurately: "It's the love affair of a lifetime."

* * *

Soon, Reed's public image began softening, and his new girlfriend seemed to be a big part of it. Speaking to *The New York Times*, Reed praised Anderson as "the most astonishing musician" and "the kindest person I've ever met." He added, "She's also incredibly sexy, vibrant and beautiful." The couple loved going out—to films, concerts, restaurants, gallery openings—so the relationship was constantly on display. "The pair have become so visible around New York recently," the *Times* journalist Stephen Holden noted, "that they have begun to acquire the aura of a kind of First Couple of downtown Manhattan."

Around this time, the famed portrait photographer Annie Leibovitz shot the couple in black and white on the Coney Island boardwalk—the boardwalk of Delmore Schwartz's "In Dreams Begin Responsibilities," where the young man proposed to his girlfriend; the Coney Island that Reed visited as a child growing up in Brooklyn and where, twenty-odd years earlier, Anderson had lain on the beach in midwinter, in a turtleneck and a watchman's cap, trying to sleep, part of a performance art piece, coincidentally enough, about dreams. She was twenty-five then. Now in her late forties, she faced the same ocean, eyes closed again, nestled against Reed, who stared into Leibovitz's lens, cigarette dangling from his fingers—two black-clad figures merging into one, Reed's wild curls and Anderson's spiked crop outlined against the gray sky, their faces a blissful Janus mask, as the waves of the Atlantic Ocean gently rolled in.

* * *

In the summer of '95, Sterling Morrison died of non-Hodgkin's lymphoma in Poughkeepsie, New York. His life had changed radically after Reed left the Velvets in 1970. Morrison returned to school, married his longtime girlfriend, Martha—Moe Tucker's best friend back in their Long Island days—fathered two kids with her, and completed his PhD in medieval studies at the University of Texas in Austin. His dissertation, "Historiographical Perspectives in the Signed Poems of Cynewulf," was a study "very much concerned with history, but not with historical 'facts' per se," he explained, one that explored "medieval ideas (both Christian and classical) concerning the meaning of history and of the historical process itself, the nature and purposes of historiography, and the relationship between historiography and hagiography as genres." Morrison taught writing classes off and on, but eventually left teaching; he found better-paying work on a tugboat in the Houston Boat Channel, setting himself up in the city where he'd resigned from the Velvet Underground years earlier. Some believed his tugboat work exposed him to toxins that led to his cancer. He'd mostly abandoned playing music, notwithstanding scattered pickup gigs, until the Velvets reconvened, and largely stopped again when the reunion imploded. His last public performance had been the previous November at the opening of the new Warhol Museum in Pittsburgh, playing with Cale and Tucker—what would've been a Velvets gig, had Reed not declined to participate. The disease had progressed quickly; Morrison's bandmates were shocked to discover how sick he was.

When Reed learned that Morrison was dying, he took the train up to Poughkeepsie, where Sterling and Martha now lived, in the shadow of the silver-painted Mid-Hudson Bridge that once inspired their neighbor Billy Name. Reed detailed the trip in an essay that ran in *The New York Times Magazine* on New Year's Eve, thirty years from the day he and Morrison had watched themselves on the CBS nightly news, shirtless and covered in body paint, playing music in Heliczer's loft.

"Sterling said the cancer was like leaves in the fall, a perfect Morrison description," Reed began. Both men were lovers of the English language. Reed wrote about Morrison's eye for detail, and how he once saved Reed from likely electrocution via an ungrounded microphone onstage. Reed saw Morrison as "always the strongest one," the "warrior heart" of the Velvets, envisioning him as a "mythic Irish hero," describing his contradictory gauntness that day in Poughkeepsie, the remarkable clarity of his eyes, and the scene of the men sitting beside each other, holding hands, suggesting that in that moment all their past differences were resolved. Like many writers, Reed was most valiant on the page. Real life was more complicated.

But the next day, Moe Tucker faxed Reed a note—addressed, as ever, to "Honeybun," despite the rancor of their recent exchange. She wished him a Happy New Year, told him the essay he'd written made her cry, and that Morrison would've been proud.

Reed didn't attend his friend's funeral; he was playing a gig on that date ("as the chords to 'Sweet Jane' swelled up," Reed noted in his remembrance, he hoped Morrison heard them and "got a laugh"). But Reed paid homage to him again when the Velvet Underground were inducted into the Rock and Roll Hall of Fame in early '96. Reed had long been courted by the institution—something of a *Rolling Stone* franchise, co-founded and captained by its editor in chief Jann Wenner—and had gamely courted them in return, agreeing to give induction speeches for Dion and, rather shockingly, in early 1995, Frank Zappa. (In the heat of the Velvets' rivalry with their labelmates, the Mothers of Invention, Reed had called Zappa "probably the single most untalented person I've heard in my life" and "a two-bit, pretentious academic [who] can't play rock'n'roll," though he'd revise his opinion.)

Now Reed was finally joining the club. Fittingly, Patti Smith delivered the Velvets' induction speech in the form of a poem, with an extended metaphor linking the band with Warhol's Mylar balloons, praising how they connected poetry, rock, and the avant-garde, and slyly salting in lyrical references to "Heroin" and "Street Hassle."

"They opened wounds worth opening, with brutal innocence, without apology, cutting across the grain, gritty, urbanic," Smith declaimed. "And in their search for the kingdom, for laughter, for salvation, they explored the darkest areas of the psyche." Statuettes were distributed, Smith and Reed embraced, and speeches were brief. Martha Morrison, smiling shakily, said she knew her husband "would have loved this party." Tucker said she was "very proud and honored." Reed thanked "all the people who worked so hard to get us in." Cale pointed out that

Nico and Warhol rightfully shared the award. He added that it should be seen as a lesson to young musicians that "sales are not the be-all and end-all of rock and roll," and that artistic freedom was the music's cornerstone. In a black-tie ballroom of industry money-shifters, it was a fitting note to end on.

The Velvets, now a trio, played just one song, written for the occasion, and dedicated to Morrison: a '50s-style ballad titled "Last Night I Said Goodbye to My Friend." It was less a celebration than a mourning, and each musician sang a verse, trading harmonies. When Cale flubbed a line, Reed smiled fleetingly, and played a simple guitar solo that conjured Morrison's lean tone. The song lasted under three minutes, and was the last time the Velvet Underground ever played music together.

*   *   *

With his signature band consigned to history, Reed returned to his post of rock's transgressive literary emeritus, a role for which he'd be increasingly celebrated in the coming years. The role would offer him opportunities to pursue multiple creative paths, much as Anderson did. He'd publish new writing, explore filmmaking, dabble in branded product design (his Lou's Views eyewear line), and finally, after decades of thwarted attempts, engage his songwriting in musical theater. He'd also build, with Anderson, an extended family of choice, creating a community with echoes of Warhol's Factory clan that would be a devoted support system.

In another reflection of Anderson's approach, he also rethought his day job, building a home studio, dubbed "The Roof," in his new apartment. It was there he'd record the bulk of his next solo LP, *Set the Twilight Reeling*, with a scaled-down band of two virtuosi dedicated to his creative vision: the bassist Fernando Saunders and Tony "Thunder" Smith, a powerhouse Oakland-born drummer with jazz-fusion roots. The album was a scattershot set that surveyed scenes spanning Reed's life. "Egg Cream" was a praise song to the signature New York City concoction of seltzer water, milk, and chocolate syrup—U-Bet brand, as Reed mandates, and of course no eggs whatsoever—which had Reed shouting out haunts from his Brooklyn childhood, including the legendary Coney Island pizzeria Totonno's (mispronouncing the name, perhaps intentionally). "Finish Line (for Sterl)" again paid tribute to Morrison, while Reed considered his own mortality.

But above all, *Set the Twilight Reeling* was an album about Reed's relationship with Anderson, who'd prove the most lasting of his muses. "The Adventurer" was Arabic-tinged hard rock addressing "a queen reborn" who climbed the Himalayas and survived a brush with death, declaring her "my one true love." On "HookyWooky," the narrator meets his lover's ex at a rooftop soiree and plays it cool, despite wanting to hurl them into the traffic below. More telling were songs that explored the desire for self-transformation and rebirth through love. The title of "Trade In," which might seem a cruel allusion to Reed's ex-wife, refers mainly to the narrator himself—"I met a new me at 8 a.m./ The other one got lost," he begins—while praising the woman "with a thousand faces" he wants to marry, rhyming "wife" with "a fourteenth chance at this life." And the intimate "Hang On to Your Emotions" rues a tyrannical inner critic, "the demagogue in your head" who recounts a "litany of failures" and evidently treats people like shit—at one point, Reed tragicomically asks the voice in his head where it "got the right to speak to anyone that way."

One outlier track recalled Reed's *New York* political seething with a vengeance. "Sex with Your Parents (Motherfucker) Part II" was apparent chum for the notorious Parents' Music Resource Center, aka the PMRC, a censorship-minded pop music watchdog group led by Second Lady Tipper Gore. Reed announced himself "sick of this right-wing Republican shit" with a snarling, literal-minded riff on "motherfucker," dedicated to the thieving "old fucks" who "go and pass laws saying you can't say what you want." As he explained to a journalist, "To debate political objectives, views, and goals is the most American thing conceivable. And those people are despicable. They are traitors to the democratic ideal. They are disgusting. It's right to make fun of them, and this [song] is gentle fun."

* * *

Reed's new life included the public renewal of one of his most significant creative relationships. The occasion was David Bowie's fiftieth birthday concert.

Staged in Bowie's adopted hometown of New York City, the Madison Square Garden show featured the predictable ritual parade of special guests—predictable but for the fact that Bowie chose, almost to a one, musicians younger than him, whose careers were still in the ascent—his replacements, basically. This wasn't out of character, which was part of what subsequent generations admired about Bowie. He always kept up: he'd recently finished a tour with Nine Inch Nails, and was completing *Earthlings*, an electronic pop record powered by the rapid-fire snare beats and low-end rumble of drum-and-bass, the current state of the art in U.K. club music. For this show, Bowie framed himself as part of an ever-evolving cutting-edge rock continuum. Sonic Youth, the New York City art-punk band born of the downtown scene the Velvet Underground seeded, joined Bowie for "I'm Afraid of Americans"; Frank Black of the alt-rock Dadaists the Pixies came out for "Scary Monsters"; the post-punk glam acolyte Billy Corgan of Smashing Pumpkins sang "All the Young Dudes."

But the concert's main event was Reed's four-song cameo near the end. Estranged for years after the London dustup in '79, the pair had buried the hatchet. Bowie saw no reason to perpetuate a feud spurred by the substance abuse he and Reed had forsworn, and in part from his new relationship with Anderson, Reed's capacity for apologizing and moving on had grown. Plus, neither had many intimates left. Bowie's older brother, Terry Burns, had killed himself in '85, leaving a psychiatric hospital to lie down on nearby train tracks; Bowie's good friend John Lennon was murdered by a crazed fan. By strength of character and luck of the draw, both Reed and Bowie had survived.

There was no mass roar of recognition as Reed walked onstage—just a handful of old-schoolers shouting "Loooooouuuuuuu." But Bowie, playing both cheerleader and schoolmaster, joined in the chant, introducing his friend as "The King of New York himself, Mr. Lou Reed!" Bowie strummed the opening chords of "Queen Bitch," the song he wrote in tribute to Reed a quarter-century earlier that suggested a nonbinary love triangle. And when Reed joined Bowie to shout-sing the reprise—"It could have been me, yeah, it could have been me!"—he might have been thinking any number of things: of the slippery, changeable psychology of sex and gender; the vagaries of the artistic life; of failure and fleeting triumph; of dropping the ball, losing the thread, becoming irrelevant history; the allure of being sucked into a whiskey bottle, or the hollow tip of a hypodermic; of ending up deranged like Delmore Schwartz, or dead from an overdose, a heart attack, an imploded liver, or a self-administered "shotgun wound to [the] head," as a Washington State public health document described the death of Kurt Cobain, after he'd put a 20-gauge Remington model 11 in his mouth two years prior, the latest example of how fame's wildfire still consumed artists like kindling. Or maybe—in the face of the familiar screaming darkness, blinding lights, and hungry fans—Reed thought nothing, feeling only the river-rush anticipation of the next chord change and verse, and a glow of satisfaction.

Bowie and Reed covered "I'm Waiting for the Man," grinning and beaming at each other; they laid into "Dirty Blvd." and "White Light/White Heat," with Reed churning out power chords as Bowie hyperventilated like a speed freak in cardiac arrest. During the rave-up, Reed slipped offstage unceremoniously, leaving Bowie to close his party with "Moonage Daydream," singing with high-camp heart: "Don't fake it, baby, lay the real thing on me / the church of man love is such a holy place to be!"

* * *

Two months later, coincidentally, Reed got a licensing request for *Velvet Goldmine*, a glam-rock fantasia by the writer-director Todd Haynes. With a title lifted from a Bowie B side, the kaleidoscopic script involved Oscar Wilde, a journalist of uncertain sexual orientation reporting a story on an extremely Bowie-ish English rock star (Brian Slade), and his American counterpart (Curt Wild), a clear cross between Reed and Iggy Pop. Bowie reportedly disliked the script, and nixed usage of his music. Reed was apparently flattered, but not so much that it clouded his business sense—he asked for double the $25,000-per-song offer to use "Rock & Roll," "Vicious," and "Satellite of Love." (In the end, the film used just Reed's original recording of "Satellite," instead leaning heavily on songs by Roxy Music and Brian Eno, some performed by an all-star pickup group dubbed the Venus in Furs.

Reed was a recurring film presence in the '90s, sometimes as an actor. He had a cameo as himself in *Faraway, So Close!*, the sequel to Wim Wenders's acclaimed *Wings of Desire*, which also featured music by Reed and Anderson. He also played himself, more or less, in *Blue in the Face*, a New York City meditation shot by Wayne Wang and Paul Auster as an adjacent prequel-sequel-footnote to *Smoke*, their 1995 art-house drama involving the idiosyncratic characters who pass through a Brooklyn cigar shop. Reed bullshits about the Brooklyn Dodgers and his designer hinged-lens eyeglasses, and disses Long Island, slipping into his old Lenny Bruce cadence. "My childhood was so unpleasant that I absolutely don't remember anything, I think, before age thirty-one," he kvetched. Reed also had a cameo—as a nerdy john soliciting a hooker—in Auster's directorial debut, *Lulu on the Bridge*, a surreal romantic noir involving a struggling actor (Mira Sorvino) and a jazz saxophonist (Harvey Keitel) who helps her score her big break: the lead role in a remake of *Pandora's Box*, the scandalous 1929 silent film that mapped a femme fatale's downward spiral, and immortalized the actor Louise Brooks as the dazzling Lulu. Reed was intrigued by the character, the libertine antiheroine of two fin de siécle plays by the German dramatist Frank Wedekind, a figure who, as Vanessa Redgrave suggests in *Lulu on the Bridge*, "isn't a real character" but "an embodiment of primitive sexuality."

Reed made attempts to work with Martin Scorsese—the dean of New York City dirty realism, film division—whom he'd met in 1980 at a *Raging Bull* screening and bonded with over their shared admiration for Delmore Schwartz's "In Dreams Begin Responsibilities," which Scorsese had been thinking seriously about filming. The director unsuccessfully tried to develop a project based on Reed's "Dirty Blvd.," advocating in a letter for Johnny Depp to play the lead character, "Mambo." Scorsese had also invited Reed to audition for Pontius Pilate in *The Last Temptation of Christ*, which would've been brilliant casting, though Bowie ultimately got the part.

Reed's greater impact on-screen, however, was through his songs, as a new generation of filmmakers, screenwriters, and music supervisors raised on his work came of age and returned the favor. A watershed moment was in *Trainspotting*, the director Danny Boyle's 1996 film based on the Irvine Welsh novel about a bunch of Scottish ne'er-do-wells. As the antihero Renton injects himself with heroin, then ODs, "Perfect Day" unspools in its entirety, soundtracking Renton's dealer ("Mother Superior") dragging him down the steps of his flat into the street and dumping him in a cab; the cabbie depositing him in front of a hospital, where he's revived; and finally his release to his disgusted parents. Reed also comes up in conversation between Renton and his pal Sick Boy, who invokes Reed's career to support his nihilist theory of life, maintaining that "at one point you've got it, then you lose it," after which it's gone forever. ("Lou Reed? Some of his solo stuff's not bad," argues Renton. "No, it's not bad, but it's not great either, is it?" counters Sick Boy. "And in your heart, you kind of know that although it sounds all right, it's actually just shite.")

In many ways, Reed's lack of commercial success worked in his favor. While much of the Beatles catalog and other '60s–'70s touchstones became frozen in cultural amber, Reed's work was comparatively fresher, allowing for broad interpretive play and carrying the charge of a shared and exciting secret. The Velvet Underground catalog saw a lot of action: "Who Loves the Sun" and "Oh! Sweet Nuthin'" were used in the adaptation of Nick Hornby's record clerk drama *High Fidelity*; Wes Anderson used "Stephanie Says" in *The Royal Tenenbaums*. The Kills' reading of "I'm Set Free" was used in *Free Jimmy*, a Norwegian animated film involving the friendship between a drug-addicted elephant and a moose who helps him get clean.

And, of course, "Walk on the Wild Side" remained shorthand for an astonishing range of transgressive scenarios, transgender and otherwise. Reed approved its use in the film version of *Hedwig and the*

Angry Inch, John Cameron Mitchell and Stephen Trask's musical about the genderqueer rock singer who suffered botched transition surgery. That Reed was a fan is unsurprising; when it first opened at the Jane Street Theatre, he and Anderson were there, making out in their seats. ("I took it as a compliment," Mitchell said.)

But "Perfect Day" was Reed's big earner in the mid-'90s. After Duran Duran's synth-pop cover hit number 28 on the U.K. charts, and *Trainspotting* put the original on international screens, the BBC produced an all-star charity recording of the song for its Children in Need appeal in 1997. It featured Reed, Bowie, Anderson, Bono, Elton John, Dr. John, Emmylou Harris, Joan Armatrading, Shane MacGowan, Tom Jones, and other strange bedfellows, and charted across Europe, hitting number 1 in the U.K.; soon after its release, Reed asked his publisher to wire $345,000 to Children in Need, his mechanical royalties from the first month and a half of the single's sales. Reed himself benefitted financially from the "Perfect Day" advertising boom market that followed: among many requests, contracts indicate Reed approved use in a South African bank commercial ($30,000), an Irish anti-drunk-driving campaign ($10,000), and a French PSA to educate viewers about the country's refugee crisis (which Reed allowed gratis).

* * *

Another by-product of Reed's '90s renaissance was more invitations to write for the page. *The New Yorker*—the magazine Reed coveted in college, still the nation's highest-profile outlet for literary writing—asked him for a summer tour diary for the August '96 music issue. It was assigned at 2,000 words, but the assistant editor Andrew Essex recalls Reed filing something on the order of 12,000.

"Dear Lou, Here is another edit . . . You are not going to be pleased," Essex began one communiqué. Indeed, Reed was not, and was ready to withdraw the piece. But Essex talked him down, making an analogy to how album tracks were shortened for AM radio play back in the day. Reed accepted the cuts, and the finished piece was very good, funny and self-deprecating, highlighting the road-life absurdities of an aging, mid-tier rock star. Out on the tour circuit, he crossed paths with Bowie ("David wears these great costumes. I wish I could, but I always end up in black T-shirts and stretch jeans from Trash and Vaudeville") and Iggy Pop ("How does he stay in such great shape? I was doing crunches every day, but that's how I threw my back out"). Reed kvetched about substandard massages, lavish hotel suites that dwarf his New York apartment, and how a damaged packet of freeze-dried breakfast powder destroyed one of his contact lenses.

That spring, Reed had also heard from Rosanne Cash, who invited him to contribute to an anthology she was editing called *Songs Without Rhyme: Prose by Celebrated Songwriters*; the idea was to have contributors write a story informed by a song they'd written. Cash agreed to consider Reed's offer of a story untethered to a song, which made an impression. Praising it in a letter to Reed as "smart," "compelling," and "disturbing," she noted one editorial concern: a passage involving fist-fucking that she hoped might be "toned down."

Eventually they got on the phone to weigh options, though Reed would ultimately bow out. "I just, kindly as I could, said, 'Lou, I can't put this in the book with my dad's story. I think it would offend him, and I just can't do it. It's not Johnny Cash—it's my dad,'" Cash explains. "And Lou was so kind about it. He said, 'I totally understand, but I just can't edit the story. It's fine to just leave it out.'"

* * *

Lou Reed: Rock and Roll Heart was one of the more surprising entries in the prestigious PBS series *American Masters*, profiling great American arts and culture figures. The one-hour documentary, which aired nationally on April 29, 1998, was directed by Timothy Greenfield-Sanders, a celebrated portraitist who connected with Reed at a photo shoot and became a close friend. Reed pledged not to insist on final approval over everything. But he had input: commentary on a list of possible interviewees, written in what appears to be his trademark scrawl, was pointed regarding Beck, whose mom, Bibbe Hansen, was a Factory regular ("Beck?!!"); Garland Jeffreys, who knew plenty about Reed's college days ("NO!!!"); Bruce Springsteen, re his *Street Hassle* contribution ("means nothing"); Dennis Rodman ("oh please"); Leonardo DiCaprio ("Bullshit"); Jonas Mekas ("YES"), and others. Greenfield-Sanders used vintage Reed footage alongside elegantly lit talking head commentary by his co-conspirators and acolytes, filmed with a nod to Warhol's Screen Tests. Cale recalled playing "I'm Waiting for the Man" for tips on 125th Street in front of the Baby Grand, Tucker talked about being fired from Cafe Bizarre. Holly Woodlawn and Little Joe Dallesandro recited lyrics to "Walk on the Wild Side." There was almost no footage of the Velvets; little of adequate technical quality existed. But there was a glorious Sterling Morrison solo from a Velvets reunion show, and a glimpse of Reed at Bowie's Madison Square Garden birthday bash. The most compelling bits, though, were often the least flattering, in particular a rivetingly twitchy performance circa *Rock 'n' Roll Animal*, Reed decked out in fetish-gear leathers and a close-cropped blond dye job. Reed's legendary nastiness is largely glossed over but for an illuminating comment by David Byrne, who attempted to square the perpetual disconnect between those at the receiving end of Reed's displeasure, and his friends. "The mythic Lou that one reads about in magazines and newspapers, it doesn't quite jibe with the person that I know. I read something in the last year, I think in some European magazine, and the whole article was about what a strange, peculiar, cantankerous, ornery person this was. And I started thinking: 'Has this person ever been to New York before? Have they ever met a New Yorker before? Or talked with anyone here?' A conversation in New York is often a little bit of a sparring match."

Near the end, an interviewer asks Reed if Delmore Schwartz, were he still alive, might think Reed is now—finally, after thirty-some years spent creating one of the most poetically ambitious song catalogs in popular music—a "real writer." Rather than exploding, as one might imagine his response in a different setting, Reed chuckles amiably. "That would be a very pleasant thought," he says. "I think at this point I could hold my head up to him, and say: 'There ya go, Delmore.'"

* * *

Reed's perfect storm of honors reached a surreal pinnacle that fall when he was invited to perform at the White House for a state dinner with President Clinton and Václav Havel. He'd already tasted Washington largesse in 1993 when he played the Tennessee Ball (at the behest of the rock fan VP Al Gore, or one of his staff) during the Clinton-Gore inauguration. On that occasion, Reed met Gore's moral-crusader wife, Tipper, who, by Reed's account, asked him, "How can we communicate with our children better?" Reed's first thought was to tell her to shit-can the PMRC, her pop music policing organization. "And then I thought, 'This is a pointless conversation. She doesn't mean the question; I'm not here to give her a fucking answer,'" Reed later told a journalist, recalling that he told the Second Lady something like "We'd have to sit down and discuss something like that for a while over a bottle of scotch and, maybe, some crack."

Now, it was Havel who pushed for Reed's invite, which was interestingly timed, as the Monika Lewinsky scandal was in full swing—America had learned of the cum-stained blue dress, seen Lewinsky's Marilyn Monroe–style glam shots in *Vanity Fair*, and read excerpts from the Starr Report, which had dropped six days before the event. For what it was worth, Reed had the president's back. "I think what's being done to him is terrible," Reed told a reporter from *The Washington Post*. "Your private life should be your private life. I think it's a smear campaign."

On September 16, 1998, Reed performed for a small audience: Havel, the Clintons, the Gores, Henry Kissinger, Stevie Wonder, Mia Farrow, Kurt Vonnegut, Anderson, and some others. The White House asked for his lyrics in advance, to vet them, but according to Saunders, on bass that evening, Reed ignored the request for cuts, singing "Dirty Blvd." as he recorded it—observing America's appalling inequity playing out on New York streets in the shadow of the Statue of Liberty, and deadpanning before the president of the United States: "Give me your hungry, your tired, your poor, I'll piss on 'em."

* * *

Reed enjoyed his fame insofar as he could trade on it, and when it boosted his self-image. But as a Manhattanite who liked to move about freely—walking his dog, or going to a show with Anderson—he often found it irritating at best, threatening at worst. He could be brusque and flat-out rude to fans. But on some occasions, he was strikingly generous. Beth Groubert recalls an encounter with a large group of South American fans who'd come "over the hills" from Uruguay to see Reed perform in Buenos Aires. A waiter at his hotel restaurant asked if he would meet them, and he held court with each, one by one, at his table.

Other encounters could be more predatory: even in his fifties, Reed drew an intense breed of wannabe groupies. "I was on tour with him where these superfans were definitely creepily propositioning him," one assistant says, noting that, in their experience, he "never showed even a moment's interest."

Then there was the fan mail. Reed heard regularly from admirers affected by his work, and his management kept numerous file folders stuffed with cards and letters. Many were amiable and mild, asking for photos and autographs. Others revealed the disturbing obsessions of an army of Stans. Some mused on his sexual tastes. One note testified, "I would have married you at 15½" and "I'll fuck you or die at 35½." Another threatened "I'm definitely suicided [sic] soon if you can't phone . . . I am sick and worn out and severely alone." Another described an unnamed person who "sexually tormented you for 30 years and gave me a clitorectomy." Some prowled the boundaries of stalking. A Swedish fan wrote an epic series of communiqués in the mid-'90s, including a postcard of a Robert Mapplethorpe photograph titled *Contact*—a muscular, shirtless man in profile, holding a knife as if about to stab someone. Its message announced: "Kill your fathers and mothers and possibly brothers and sisters. I've gone through the Oidipuss [sic] complex with you Lou." Another, written a month later and postmarked in New York City, had a return address from a Times Square hotel, not far from his apartment. In the shadow of Warhol's shooting, it was unnerving stuff. (At one point, Reed's management called his labelmate Madonna's team asking for advice, figuring they'd seen and heard everything.)

Reed's intermittent fear and loathing toward fans surely had roots in these file folders, which surveyed a deep valley of human suffering. Yet much of the fan mail was heartening, sharing intimacies with an artist whose songs, by laying bare feelings and circumstances normally hidden, compelled them to share their own. Many, unsurprisingly, involved struggles with substance abuse. Others merely shared admiration for his music. A high school teacher described having his students read T. S. Eliot's "The Hollow Men," then playing them "Some Kinda Love" for comparison. Many wrote to praise the Velvet Underground, but it seemed just as many wrote about Reed's more recent work. Quite a number of fans wrote how *Magic and Loss* helped with their grieving; one described humming the D-A-G progression of "Cremation" while caring for his father, who was dying of cancer. A woman thanked Reed for his music on behalf of her son, who'd drowned in an accident; the young man, named Louis, was such a huge Velvets fan, his friends called him Lou Reed. It's unclear how many letters received responses, but in this case, Reed wrote back, with condolences and gratitude that "my music brought pleasure into his life."

Many of the letters Reed received were handwritten; many began with some variant on "This is the only 'fan' letter I've ever written." Many were long. Many used "Love" in the signature. Reed's fans were smart, sensitive, lonely, combative, troubled, damaged. In many cases, kindred spirits. And in their letters, Reed could see the full reflection of a lifetime's work. A young Australian trans person wrote with striking candor of their struggle to realize their identity in a narrow-minded town, and how, if they "had not had [your] songs to keep me company," they "would either be dead today or very, very, very unhappy."

11.

WEST VILLAGE > LONG ISLAND

(2000s)

DISCUSSED: *Ecstasy*, Hal Willner, Robert Wilson, *Time Rocker*, *POEtry*, 9/11, *The Raven*, Anohni, working in Europe, photography, Julian Schnabel, *Berlin* redux, Metallica, *Lulu*, "Junior Dad," writing, Reed's final days

Here come the planes. They're American planes.
—Laurie Anderson, "O Superman"

It was not a street anymore but a world, a time and space of fallen ash and near night.
—Don DeLillo, *Falling Man*

If I was half drowning an arm above the last wave / Would you come to me
—Lou Reed, "Junior Dad"

On January 8, 1999, Laurie Anderson's father, Arthur Anderson, died. He was eighty-eight years old. "My father's name is Art, and everything I've ever done seems to be tied to him," she declared, pun intended, in an early performance piece. On the 1994 song "World Without End," she intoned, "When my father died / it was like a whole library burned down." A friend heard the piece and offered condolences; at the time, Anderson explained her dad was in fact fine—she'd discussed the piece with him, and he didn't mind her fictionalizing his death. Perhaps, the friend thought, Anderson wanted to explore what the loss would feel like before it actually happened, telling stories to allow for control in processing reality, to outline space for grief, perhaps to exercise a Buddhist practice Anderson would often refer to: how to feel sad without being sad.

Later that year, Reed began having health problems, and was diagnosed with a severe diabetic condition. His mood swings, never insignificant, were magnified by it; he'd arrange to have a dietitian on hand when he traveled, or at least an alert assistant, to monitor his food needs. But he kept working, and in his creative practice, still unflinching, he began considering his own mortality anew. It fit the turn-of-the-century zeitgeist: a widespread mood of taking stock, reflecting, and summing up, with evangelical predictions of end-times and a low-simmering panic about the Y2K "millennium bug" people feared would cause computer meltdowns and societal chaos when the clocks tipped 1999 into 2000.

Reed would've noted that summing-up spirit in John Cale's memoir, *What's Welsh for Zen*. Cale's book was written with Victor Bockris, a fact that must've stung Reed before even opening the book—Bockris's Reed bio, published in 1994, had not made its subject happy. *What's Welsh for Zen* was at times brutally frank regarding both Cale and Reed. Cale sent his old bandmate a copy, along with a warm note, hoping the flashback on their shared experience would provide "at the very least, a distant smile of amusement. After all, it really was the most outrageous fun, wasn't it?"

Reed's only autobiography would be one he continued to weave through his songs. The title of his latest album, *Ecstasy*, came with irony from a rock elder—it was slang for the drug of choice of a new scene, rooted in electronic dance music, that posited rock 'n' roll as largely irrelevant. But Reed wasn't chasing trends on *Ecstasy*, just doubling down on signature sounds and obsessions. The focus was on relationship psychodramas and sexuality, echoing *Set the Twilight Gleaming* the way *Legendary Hearts* had *The Blue Mask*. Themes of jealousy, disloyalty, and the fear of abandonment loomed. "Mad" is a combative semi-apology to a lover ("I know I shouldn'ta had someone else in our bed") whose narrator seems mainly to regret getting caught. The first-person voice in "Paranoia Key of E" suggests his sexual unfaithfulness is "worse than Clinton in prime time," while confessing his own jealousy. Especially vivid is the character voicing the title track, with a "stud through my eyebrow" and "Domain" evidently spelled out in scar tissue over the tattoo of an ex-lover's name; Reed channels their reveries over minor-key cello and chattering flamenco/North African rhythms. Failed relationships abound. The troubled couple of "Tatters" sleep separately, backdropped by crying Chicago blues licks. And on "Baton Rouge," in a scenario that recalled his recent breakup, a divorcé painfully second-guesses his refusal to have a child with his ex, forsaking a rich family life (including a daughter's quinceañera and "two fat grandsons I can barely carry"), instead worn out and "back in the big city" with "a bad aftertaste." Reed's relationship with Anderson seems mirrored in "Turning Time Around," a poignant conversation about the meaning of love with a slow-build crescendo suggesting Otis Redding's "Try a Little Tenderness." The album also interrogated extreme forms of need and desire. "White Prism" unpacked the psychology of a sexual submissive like a first-person FetLife post. "Like a Possum," an eighteen-minute lava-flow blues jam, conjured working girls backdropped by used condoms floating in the Hudson, while "Rock Minuet" unspooled a gruesome cavalcade of coke-fueled backroom hate-fucking and hook-up that ends with a man's throat getting slit, as Reed's guitar and Anderson's violin waltz hauntingly in the shadow of his ugliest imaginings. Even the album cover, created with the designer-photographer Stefan Sagmeister, suggested sexual obsessiveness as unflaggingly unruly life force: Reed's face captured in a self-pleasuring selfie that, with equal tenderness, conjured both Saint Teresa of Avila and an old dude watching porn in a Show World video booth.

* * *

Ecstasy was notable as Reed's first album-length collaboration with the producer Hal Willner, an encyclopedic pop culture scholar who'd fashioned a successful career in the more-or-less mainstream by indulging wildly eclectic and esoteric musical tastes. The men first crossed paths in the '80s when Willner pitched Reed on the Kurt Weill covers project

Lost in the Stars. Discussing it on the phone, Reed suggested he sing "Pirate Jenny." When Willner countered that "September Song" might be a better choice, Reed hung up on him, incensed. But then he thought better of it and called back, agreeing with Willner, and telling him with a laugh that he was evidently "a real producer." Thus began a friendship that would last the rest of Reed's life. And though some years younger, Willner became another of his great mentors.

Hal Willner was born and raised in Philadelphia, where his dad and uncle, Holocaust survivors, ran a deli called Hymie's; Willner spent his youth escaping into a world of records, movies, and TV. He moved to New York in the '70s, worked with the jazz producer Joel Dorn, and, while still in his twenties, landed a job with an experimental comedy show called *Saturday Night Live*, where he'd work for more than twenty-five years. He acquired and eventually kicked a drug problem, and made a name for himself as a visionary auteur of concept records and concerts, casting diverse musicians in unusual song arrangements and basically inventing the modern notion of the "tribute album." His projects explored the work of the film composer Nino Rota (*Amarcord Nino Rota*) and jazz legend Charles Mingus (*Weird Nightmare*), the early Walt Disney songbook (*Stay Awake*), and eventually, that of the Velvet Underground.

Willner and Reed worked hard on *Ecstasy*, one of Reed's best-sounding records ever, in terms of both clarity and arrangements. Its steely guitar tones were microscopically vivid; its swaggering horn charts, by Willner's go-to Steve Bernstein, used Stax soul machismo and boozy New Orleans jazz flourishes as both halos and punchlines. Reed was thrilled with how the record turned out, as was Willner, who thought it "just wonderful, in every way, and it was a total joy, from beginning to end, for me to do it." Both men were crestfallen when it sold poorly and got very mixed reviews. *Pitchfork*, the upstart Chicago-based website that was becoming an important outlet for music criticism, published a smart but fairly savage one by Kristin Sage Rockermann, who dismissed it with a 6.5 out of 10, singling out "Like a Possum" ("bloated" and "unbearable") along with "Future Farmers of America" ("cringe-inducing" and "overwritten"). In *Rolling Stone,*

Robert Christgau—like Reed, a fifty-something dyed-in-the-wool New York City rock aesthete—gave it four out of five stars, lauding its tenderness, calling it "a complex, musically gorgeous synthesis of the obsessions that powered Reed's failed 1973 *Berlin* and his great marriage albums of the early Eighties, especially *The Blue Mask*."

* * *

Ecstasy was Reed's last attempt at a traditional rock LP; his future recorded output would consist of live LPs, repackagings, one-off cover songs, and repurposed soundtracks for avant-garde theater projects. The latter grew out of three separate collaborations with Robert Wilson, a hugely ambitious and uncompromising mainstay of the downtown New York avant-garde scene who'd found more receptive audiences, and more generous funding, in Europe. A friend of Anderson's about the same age as Reed, Wilson was raised in Texas, coming to New York City in the '60s to pursue a career in the arts. He made challenging theater that might be considered "difficult"—abstract, slow-moving, often of extremely long duration; an early breakthrough was the seven-hour-long "silent opera" *Deafman Glance*, featuring the deaf actor Raymond Andrews. Music became central to Wilson's work after *Einstein on the Beach*, the groundbreaking opera he produced at the Met in 1976 with the composer Philip Glass, another friend of Anderson's, whose amplified ensemble writing gave La Monte Young's "minimalist" compositional approach a more marketable form. In the early '90s, Wilson began a trilogy of rock-scored "art musicals" with the Thalia Theater in Hamburg, Germany. He enlisted Tom Waits for the first two, and invited Reed to collaborate on the third, which commemorated the centenary of H. G. Wells's *The Time Machine*.

Wilson and Reed were well-matched. The experience reminded him of working with Warhol—Wilson was a bona fide creative genius, in a medium other than music, whose direction Reed was happy to follow. *Time Rocker* premiered that summer in Germany, followed by a Paris run and ten performances at the Brooklyn Academy of Music. Reed's involvement was limited to that of composer and songwriter; a

German rock ensemble served as pit orchestra. In a wise move, given his temperament, Reed delegated Mike Rathke to direct the group's rehearsals and ensure the playing would be up to par.

The production opened with searching electric guitar, performed solo—an approach Reed hadn't explored much since *Metal Machine Music*—reprised throughout the show in various shades: drones and arpeggios, clean sustained notes and washes of guitar synthesizer. Some music was recycled. "Cremation," the existential sea shanty from *Magic and Loss,* was sung by an actor whose phrasing conjured Nico, while "Disco Mystic" was interpolated with alternate lyrics in a dance scene. "Master and Slave," a duet for two men, recalled the Ramones in its sonic assault and borderline-comic tone. "Future Farmers of America," named for the government-sponsored youth leadership group, outlined a slave-emancipation narrative echoing a current film, *White Man's Burden,* an alternate-reality drama playing on race anxiety that starred John Travolta and Harry Belafonte. As the *Time Rocker* band roared, five actors in radiation suits moved in slow motion, as if working a postapocalyptic wheat field. "I Don't Need This" was a heavy metal stomp that memorably rhymed "gay sonatas" with "persona non grata." The production also featured two of Reed's greatest ballads: "Turning Time Around," which would reappear on *Ecstasy,* and "Talking Book," the latter imagining love as a portable volume that contains a lover's touch, scent, and breath.

The work got mixed reviews abroad and at home; *The New York Times*'s pop music critic Jon Pareles found things to praise, but concluded that it "ends up uncomfortably close to late-night MTV," while the paper's classical critic Bernard Holland, who also reviewed it, praised its formal innovation, invoking Alban Berg's *Wozzeck.* Nevertheless, by avant-garde theater standards, *Time Rocker* was enough of a success to occasion another Wilson project with Reed, based on the writing of Edgar Allan Poe. This time, Wilson told Reed he should write the play's book as well as the songs.

"I've never written anything *like* that before," Reed protested.

"You were *made* for this," Wilson assured him.

So Reed got to work, literally rewriting selections from Poe that appealed to him. ("I figured if Bob says I can do it," Reed concluded, "I can do it.") *POEtry* premiered in February 2000, again with Wilson's beloved Thalia Theater. It deepened their friendship. "He scared me a little bit," Wilson reflects, laughing. "But we connected. Sometimes late at night we would speak with each other. The relationship was a very touching one." As with Willner, Reed was rediscovering the pleasure of collaboration. He even trusted Wilson enough to let him make changes to his music: when Reed had to return to New York during scheduled rehearsals, Wilson asked the musicians to radically slow down an up-beat piece, and when Reed heard the result, he was thrilled. Wilson says Reed was so moved, he wept. "I didn't know I had that in me," Reed said. "Thank you, Bob."

Poe, who lived in the Bronx for a while, was drawn to dark themes, struggled with his drinking, was wildly romantic, had a questionable moral sensibility (he married his thirteen-year-old cousin), and was often treated harshly by critics. Walt Whitman considered him "almost without the first sign of moral principle"; Ralph Waldo Emerson dismissed him as "the jingle man." That Poe resonated for Reed is unsurprising. "The psychology that he is so fascinated with, I am also fascinated with," Reed told a Dutch TV journalist, citing how Poe's "The Imp of the Perverse" expressed one of Reed's animating notions—inquiring, as Reed puts it, "why do you find yourself so attracted to commit something that you know is wrong?" Discussing the same idea with *The New York Times*'s Jon Pareles, he said, "Obsession and guilt are reasons people write in the first place. They are big continents to explore. For Poe, and for me too."

While developing the project in Germany, Reed began smoking again. He still exercised, and he played basketball whenever he had a chance, especially when he had an opponent. (Pearl Jam's Eddie Vedder was one—Reed admired his "murderous" jump shot.) Given his health issues, Reed knew he had to take care of himself. He understood he'd survived his substance abuse and the AIDS pandemic in part by luck. "I've put my dick in every hole available," he told the German musician-journalist Max Dax. "But in a way, I haven't lived a different life compared to many others. I mean, most of us have experiences with drugs, many of us smoke and drink too much. I am no different except for the fact that I have always been in the limelight."

* * *

In May 2001, Lou Reed died from an overdose of Demerol—at least that was the story reported by a number of news outlets around the country. They'd gotten the information from a bogus press release, credited to Reuters, that turned up in their inboxes: Reed's body was allegedly discovered at approximately 10:45 p.m. in the apartment he shared with his "wife, avant-garde pop artist Laurie Anderson"; David Bowie was quoted by CNN testifying, "In the last several years, Lou and I had the opportunity to rekindle a friendship that has seen many ups, downs, and corners." Reed was out of the country when the fake news broke, and phone calls came pouring into his management office asking if he was okay.

The same sorts of calls came in on the morning of, and in the days following, September 11, 2001. Reed was home at his apartment, just over two miles north of the World Trade Center. After the first plane hit, he went up to the roof, which provided an unobstructed view of the burning tower. Jeremy Darby, a friend and sound engineer he'd worked with, rang him from Toronto; the second plane hit while they were talking. Reed shrieked, then began sobbing. Bill Bentley reached him later that morning. "I think he was actually in shock. But he said, 'Billy— it's New York. Shit happens.'" Not wanting to be alone, Reed finally ventured down to the street and, by one account, walked to Pastis—one of his regular haunts, at the corner of Ninth Avenue and Little West Twelfth Street, a trendy bistro in a neighborhood once known for its sidewalk sex trade, now a center for well-heeled art stars. He took a seat at an outdoor table, as he might any other day, as the sirens wailed.

Anderson was on tour, and kept her gig that night at Park West, near her hometown of Glen Ellyn. Her cryptically avuncular songs resonated powerfully. She sang "Strange Angels," about a day "larger than life" that ended with friends who stayed over and "cried all night." She sang "Statue of Liberty," with its couplet "Freedom is a scary thing / Not many people really want it." And she sang "O Superman," the gist of its ominous reprise—"Here come the planes / They're American planes"— changed irrevocably. In the aftermath of the attacks, Reed and Anderson would choose to remain in New York. "After the shock and mourning comes the adjustment to real life," Reed said days later.

And so he and Anderson continued doing what they did. Later that month, Anderson played at Town Hall where, eighty years prior, in the fall of 1921, Margaret Sanger had been arrested for speaking about birth control, dragged off by police while the audience followed them through the streets in protest, singing "My Country 'Tis of Thee." Speaking from the same stage, Anderson said, "We want to dedicate our music tonight to the great opportunity we all have, to begin to truly understand the events of the past few days, and to act upon them— with courage and with compassion—as we make our plans to live in a completely new world." And as the body hunt continued at the crash site, Reed went into SIR Studios in Chelsea to record a twelve-minute version of the folk-blues staple "See That My Grave Is Kept Clean" for a Martin Scorsese documentary series. He also wrote a poem about the attacks, "Laurie Sadly Listening," that ran in *The New York Times*. The standout lines were:

You were all I really thought of
As the TV blared the screaming.

* * *

POEtry opened in November at the Brooklyn Academy of Music, performed again by the Thalia Theater company with a group of German musicians, with music, lyrics, and book written by Reed. It entailed irreverent revisions of Poe, to sometimes dubious effect ("The Raven" was infused with modern drug references, and rhymed "Quoth the Raven, 'Nevermore'" with "framed from flames of downtown lore"). But the music was powerful, and Wilson's visualizations were hallucinatory and often magnificent: free-floating eyeballs, torsos parading their severed heads, and a giant abstracted raven, with costumes and choreography that drew on silent-era German horror films such as *Nosferatu* and *The Cabinet of Dr. Caligari*. In collaboration with Willner and his legendary Rolodex, built from years of record-making and *Saturday Night Live* work, Reed also produced an all-star album based on the production—retitled *The Raven*, at the behest of his label's marketing staff.

With his voice as a framing device on the album, Reed performed Poe in old age, reflecting back on his life, wishing he could converse with his younger self, and pondering the elusiveness of memory. Reed described a writer who was "not exactly the boy next door," and hollered at the indignities of age ("Your ass starts to sag / your balls shrivel up!"). The cast of voice actors and musicians was remarkable; among the former were Elizabeth Ashley, Amanda Plummer, Steve Buscemi, and Willem Dafoe. In a take on "The Cask of Amontillado," the latter threatened the character of Fortunato with a promise to "fuck him up the ass and piss in his face." The Blind Boys of Alabama crowned the gospel-style "I Wanna Know" with a startling held note. "Guilty" featured Reed's longtime hero Ornette Coleman, weaving an alto sax narrative over a funk jam as Reed channeled the '50s southern R&B Coleman played as a young man. And recalling his early-'80s Broadway run as Merrick in *The Elephant Man*, David Bowie animated "Hop Frog," based on Poe's fable about a courtier with dwarfism who exacts spectacular revenge on his tormentors.

The most arresting performance on *The Raven*, though, was by the singer Anohni (whose name was then Antony Hegarty), who transposed "Perfect Day" into the voice of Lenore, a figure representing Poe's late wife. Born in England and raised in the United States, Anohni was inspired by a lineage of gender-fluid New York City art, including the work of the filmmaker Jack Smith. In that spirit, Hegarty cofounded the short-lived Blacklips Performance Troupe (later Cult), and soon began making records delivered in a remarkably agile, frequently dazzling voice. When Reed discovered her 2001 EP *I Fell in Love with a Dead Boy*, he was bowled over by the technique and emotion, and he brought Anohni into the *Raven* project. When Anohni invited Reed to perform with her group, the Johnsons—a sort of experimental cabaret act with a large queer following—both singers "seemed shy, awed in each other's presence," recalled the writer Samantha Hunt. Reed sang "Candy Says," the exquisite ballad which, in this context particularly, conjured a trans woman's transmogrification. It was a song Reed almost never performed live. "People held their breath to hear," recalled Hunt. "Reed seemed very small and worried on stage. And then he was absolutely magnificent."

Anohni would soon join Reed's touring band, and they'd often duet on "Candy Says." Sometimes Reed sang lead, tenderly, pushing the top of his register. But in time Anohni would assume the lead, singing with astonishing passion, Reed playing the changes on guitar, joining in on the chorus, and beaming—"both of them," Anderson recalled, "in a state of rapture, sweetness and love."

* * *

The Raven was a tremendous achievement, a mess and a tour de force, and it didn't come cheap. Knowing the record would be a hard sell, Reed's team brainstormed marketing strategies. They planned a premium double-disc set to sell at events, with a single-disc version for general release; they considered mailing the CD to journalists with a copy of Poe's collected works; live-streaming a stage production; pushing for an HBO or BBC documentary on the project, with readings by Dafoe, Ashley, and Buscemi; releasing "Perfect Day" as a single, yet again; promoting it alongside the thirtieth anniversary of *Transformer* and Reed's sixtieth birthday. They planned to get him back on Letterman, with couch time to talk about Poe; have him interviewed on progressive radio outlets such as KCRW and WXPN. They considered another best-of compilation and a back-catalog reissue campaign. They stumped for covers at *Rolling Stone* and *Vanity Fair*. They worked to position Reed for a Grammy Lifetime Achievement Award. They pushed for his induction as a solo artist into the Rock and Roll Hall of Fame.

Still, by major-label standards, the record arrived dead in the water. Warner Brothers' Bill Bentley was convinced it was a masterpiece. "But then, what do you *do* with that record?" he says ruefully. "I'm realistic enough to know the pop world, the rock world. Whatever that record is, it's almost unsellable."

* * *

What press attention Reed did get was, increasingly, less about the project at hand than Reed's irascibility, a story hook he'd play to dutifully. Publicist in tow, he showed up late for one British magazine interview in full rock star regalia—black leather pants, fur-lined black leather jacket, Mandarina Duck man-purse—and offered the journalist his trademark dead-fish handshake.

"You turned sixty during the making of this record," the writer noted. "Was that a major landmark?"

"No."

"You didn't mark it in any way?"

"Nope."

"Do you feel blessed, lucky to be alive?"

"Do you? This is not what I want to talk about."

Reed brusquely parried questions involving his history ("I've lied so much about the past I can't even tell myself what is true anymore"), but eventually thawed, sharing his thoughts on Eminem ("He's very funny"), the state of rock 'n' roll, and the narrow commercial appeal of his current work, wondering if *The Raven* would be his last album. It "might be a nice way to say 'goodbye,'" Reed said.

Things would play out differently. But for the next decade, Reed largely abandoned studio recording, and after a live album, *Animal Serenade*, he parted ways with Sire/Warner Brothers.

* * *

Reed found plenty to keep him busy, much of it in Europe. The market for what he did was stronger there than in the States, as it was for Wilson's work, and, to an extent, Anderson's as well. On the spring-summer *Ecstasy* tour, Reed's American guarantees ranged from $35,000 to $65,000, whereas he could pull more than $100,000 for a European appearance (he grossed $130,000 in July for his appearance at the Roskilde Festival in Denmark). The market for his back catalog licensing remained healthy there, too, which his live gigs helped fuel. A French insurance company offered $200,000 to use "Sunday Morning" in a series of ads; a telecom company offered $50,000 for "I'll Be Your Mirror"; offers came from banks, car companies, clothing chains, and more.

Club music being more central to pop culture in Europe than it was yet in the States, Reed considered a remix project of his back catalog in the early 2000s—Junior Vasquez and Moby were among those proposed to helm it—though it didn't pan out. However, the Parisian singer Vanessa St. James (née Quinones) convinced Reed to add vocals to her Italo-disco version of the Velvets' "Sunday Morning," a good match given her resemblance, vocally and physically, to Nico. He even appeared in the video, looking out over a dance floor, maybe thinking about a similar scene at the Dom three decades earlier.

Reed found support for all sorts of esoteric projects in Europe. The Berlin experimental music ensemble Zeitkratzer joined Reed to premiere a chamber version of *Metal Machine Music* as "scored" by the composer-performer Ulrich Krieger and the accordionist Luca Venitucci, who managed to transcribe the LP after Krieger perceived the "orchestralness" in its four-part structure. The finished score, largely noteless, featured numerous indications to perform "more noisy," with each section sketched in proportional time notation, to be played to a clock timer like John Cage's arrangement of Satie's *Vexations*, or *The Well-Tuned Piano* by La Monte Young, whose work inspired Reed's LP in the first place. At the other end of the "classical music" spectrum, Reed joined Luciano Pavorotti to sing "Perfect Day" at a benefit in the Italian tenor's hometown of Modena. Nothing seemed too far-fetched.

In the summer of 2002, Reed and Anderson did a handful of duo shows in Italy and Spain in which Reed—mirroring the spirit of Dylan's left-turn rearrangements of classic songs in concert—recited familiar lyrics over abstracted soundscapes, melodies largely stripped away. At an outdoor performance in Venice, the musicians sat on separate platforms surrounded by their electronic rigs, Reed with his guitar in his lap, Anderson with her violin. When somebody yelled "Rock and roll!" Reed responded tartly: "This is a reading. Or couldn't you read?" The performances were challenging for two artists used to running their own shows, and who had very different ways of doing things— Anderson's approach was lean and DIY, Reed's micromanaged and lavish. But weary of struggling to compete in the pop marketplace, and perhaps a bit envious of Anderson's talent and highbrow reputation, Reed enjoyed recasting himself as a paid-in-full avant-gardist, with Anderson beside him as ambassador. The pair came to signify in European cultural circles much as they did in New York, as a First Couple of Pop Art. When President Nicolas Sarkozy of France came to New York with his wife, the chanteuse Carla Bruni, they scheduled a meal with Anderson and Reed at his preferred brunch joint, Sant Ambroeus, a tony but low-key Milanese bistro near his apartment. Later, the visiting dignitaries caught Woody Allen's New Orleans jazz band at Café Carlyle. Like Times Square and the Statue of Liberty, Reed was a New York landmark.

* * *

Increasingly, Reed focused on pursuits outside music-making. One was photography, which he began getting serious about in 1996, when he and Anderson vacationed in East Africa. Reed got some pre-trip lessons from his accomplished friend Timothy Greenfield-Sanders, the portraitist-filmmaker, keeping a set of notes on exposure tips. A centerpiece of the trip was a safari, and Reed photographed both landscapes and animals, notably a visceral series of a lion feasting on bloody prey. In the animal world, as in the human, he was drawn to extremes.

Reed captured images any amateur might've framed. But at home, he began abstracting the photos, the way he might distort a D chord. His first photo book, *Emotion in Action*, juxtaposed the images with others from Reed's West Village neighborhood: sunsets over the Hudson's decrepit piers; shots of the city skyline, lit like a Christmas display; isolated black and whites of the Empire State Building, recalling

Warhol's *Empire*, which Reed once claimed was the greatest film ever made. (Some of the abstractions also echoed Warhol, specifically the latter-day Shadows and chance-composition Exposures series.) *Emotion in Action* contained scarcely any text, and images were not titled, identified, or dated. Reed enjoyed creating in a wordless medium for a change. Two more photo books followed, *Lou Reed's New York* and *Romanticism*, also reflecting his taste for direct expression with minimal mediation. As with guitars, though, Reed was a tech fetishist; he was a fan of ultra-high-end Alpa and Leica cameras, and an early adopter of pro digital gear. Reed found gallery support for his photo projects at home and abroad. But speaking to a writer about his new passion, he imagined what the haters would say: "'Lou's just a guy with money who can afford to take pictures, but it's bullshit.'"

Reed worked to silence or at least muffle his inner and outer critics through another nonmusical passion: the martial arts practice he'd begun in the late '70s with Michael Fonfara and Peter Morales. For someone bullied as a kid and who often felt unsafe as a public figure, Reed was drawn to martial arts for the physical confidence. But as someone who struggled with anxiety, addictions, and a hair-trigger temper, he was also attracted to the rigor and self-discipline involved. The gracefulness appealed to him, too: kung fu moves in sequence, sometimes compared with musical progressions, emphasize flow, power, and minimalist efficiency, qualities Reed valued in his art. He sought health benefits in his practice, given his diabetes and advancing age. And there was a spiritual dimension to it that became increasingly important. When he did tai chi, Anderson said, he was "looking for magic."

Reed had begun studying Eagle Claw–style kung fu with Grandmaster Leung Shum at his Twenty-eighth Street studio, and pivoted to tai chi, which combined elements of kung fu with Buddhist practice—a big part of Anderson's life—in a sort of moving meditation. He studied the combative Wu style, but when he turned sixty, shifted toward the more restrained Chen style, after watching Master Ren Guang Yi on a videotape. Reed was wowed by the formal beauty of his movements and the power of his *fajin*—the explosive issuing of physical energy, generated with minimal external movement. "From the minute I saw [him] do *fajin*, I thought I will study this forever," Reed said.

For someone even friends described as arrogant, teachers were always hugely important to Reed. "He spent a lot of time studying," said Anderson, who introduced him to the Tibetan author Yongey Mingyur Rinpoche. "He teaches Buddhist philosophy. So I'm a student of Buddhist philosophy," Reed said of Mingyur, with reverence. "If he was teaching table tennis, I would learn that." Reed's practices hastened the transformation in his personality and countenance that had begun when he began his relationship with Anderson. "We were really trying to change ourselves," Anderson recalled. "And he did."

It was visible on Reed's face in photos of him practicing tai chi, or posing with classmates, often with a startlingly out-of-character grin plastered on his face. Reed bonded with fellow students—the group Willner called his "tai chi mishpucha"—in ways that circumvented his celebrity, a great relief, and the tai chi studio became a safe space where he could stop being "Lou Reed." He practiced devotedly; he did leg stretches every day to maintain the ability to do high kicks. In a short film by a fellow student, Reed spoke in the loving tone of an initiate sharing hard-won knowledge. "You're constantly told by your teacher to do [the tai chi sequence] slowly," Reed said. "And the tendency is, because we're all living in this frenetic city, is to do it quickly. But if you do it quickly, you're usually skipping over a lot of moves that are the ones that protect your knees, and back, and ankles. And eventually you start learning from the form: to slow down, and pay attention."

As always when he embraced a new interest, Reed was all-in. According to Anderson, he did tai chi every day during the last six years of his life. He collected martial arts weapons—an array of broadswords and long knives were hung on his apartment wall over the fireplace— and he grew a home library of martial arts titles: some by Master Ren, a volume of Bruce Lee's letters, a book on qigong, a copy of *Wushu!: The Chinese Way to Family Health & Fitness*. Reed kept files on guided meditation, and notebooks of sketched forms and sequences. He disliked gyms, so when he was on the road, he rented yoga studios, or practiced wherever he could find a quiet space. At home, weather permitting, he practiced on the roof of his building, or Anderson's, looking out over the Hudson. He even recorded a soundtrack for his practices, titled *Hudson River Wind Meditations,* an amorphous set of ambient instrumental music that conjured the placid swells of a calmed sea. Released through a small spiritual-music company, it was the antithesis of *Metal Machine Music*—and yet not so far removed from it.

In his later years, Reed's Buddhist and tai chi practices became as central to his life as his art, helping him move toward a higher self— "someone good," as he'd put it in "Perfect Day." And of course, as he told one journalist, "[tai chi] keeps your dick really big. Haven't you figured that out yet?"

* * *

Reed still had problems controlling his anger. Mutual love and respect notwithstanding, he and Anderson did argue, sometimes in restaurants, where, like many Manhattanites, they were constantly. She was no pushover, Buddhist calm notwithstanding; she'd grown up claiming space in a large family, and, after all, had spent nearly a decade as Reed's partner. Reed also took out his frustrations on restaurant workers, shop clerks, and other service workers. To an extent, it was perhaps a performative demonstration of his high standards and New York attitude, and a general disinclination to suffer fools. But it was also a privileged celebrity's sense of entitlement. Reed craved the freedom of anonymity, but still wanted his perks.

Sometimes his targets earned his respect simply by standing up to him. A clerk at the Issey Miyake store in Tribeca, responding to Reed sneering, "Why is this belt so expensive?" snapped "Maybe it's because the person who made it is really good at what they do?" A long conversation ensued about belt design, and Reed wound up spending a bundle on clothes, including the belt, and gifting the clerk the heavy grommeted one that he'd been wearing.

But Reed's temper created professional problems. His longtime association with Marsha Vlasic, one of the most powerful booking agents in the music business, was sometimes challenged by it. "He would get kind of unreasonable—I'm saying that kindly," she recalled. After one incident, she threatened to stop working with him, and was moved by how upset he became; they smoothed things over, at least for a while. Reed's lack of self-control did long-term damage to his music business relationships across the board. Illustrative was the furious phone call from Reed received by a Warner Brothers executive, at home on a Sunday afternoon, regarding radio promotion for *Set the Twilight Reeling*; Reed insisted the label push the unairable "Sex with Your Parents (Motherfucker) Part II" as a broadcast single, and send copies to programmers packaged with a copy of the First Amendment. Not a bad idea, in fact—but it wasn't well received.

Reed's office manager, Beth Groubert, worked with him from the mid-'90s through the early 2000s, and the two often locked horns. "Things weren't always great between us," Groubert says. "But I've got a big New York mouth and I wasn't afraid to use it. And I think he liked that." Boundaries were essential for anyone in Reed's employ; he would overwhelm assistants with requests day and night. More than one associate spoke of him being "out of control," especially when his blood sugar dropped. (Despite his work in AA, Reed still drank on occasion, so alcohol was sometimes in the mix, too.) Hotels could be war zones if his desires weren't met. In one, a concierge was reduced to tears for daring to move his luggage to a new room he'd requested. In another, when his assistant failed to solve a problem with his accommodations, he grabbed her roughly by the arm and marched her to the front desk, demanding she assert herself. His behavior could walk a razor's edge between "tough love" and abuse, with shaming and humiliation part of the mix.

"I think to a certain degree he probably felt he was lazy, and he was trying to challenge himself," Groubert says, "and so he expected nothing less from you." As she understood it, Reed was waging a battle with himself, a concept not alien to the practice of tai chi. "I mean, there had to be an aspect to [being nasty] that he enjoyed, 'cause he was really brilliant at it, his way with words . . . But ultimately, I think he just really wanted to be a kind, good person where he could. He had a really kind heart. I think he struggled with whatever was going on in his head. There was clearly this huge struggle that he had internally."

In almost all situations, however, the presence of Anderson changed Reed. Colleagues breathed a sigh of relief when she joined him on tour. Things immediately became more familial: group dinners were more common, and hierarchy slackened. "He worshipped the ground she walked on," says a former employee who feels that Reed, quite literally, "would have died for Laurie."

* * *

On January 18, 2005, Sidney J. Reed passed away. A brief paid obituary notice in *The New York Times* identified him as the "loved husband of Toby. Devoted father of Bunny and Lou. Loving grandfather to Jill, Jeffrey & Lesley. A man of integrity and dignity for 91 years." Following a brain cancer diagnosis, he was briefly hospitalized, and by the time his son arrived to see him in hospice, Sid Reed was in a coma. His son Lewis did not speak at the funeral. To be sure, his feelings for his father—a man he'd battled with, and who even those he was close to conceded was "difficult"—remained complex.

The death of Reed's dad triggered, or at least coincided with, a burst of creative activity. Later that year, Reed enlisted a new manager: Tom Sarig, a music biz pro roughly thirty years his junior, a tall, bearlike man with a quick laugh and a disarming smile. Sarig was young enough to be Reed's son, but also fit the role of father figure. Reed was soon calling him at all hours, predictably, whenever his mind was on fire with an idea or problem, which was often. (Sarig convinced him not to call his home before 9 a.m., but Reed still called almost daily.) The two had a standing weekly breakfast date at Sant Ambroeus, and the conversation for much of 2006 revolved around Reed's idea to finally stage the *Berlin* LP, in the spirit of the rock opera-musical he'd envisioned thirty-some years prior.

Reed's collaborator was Julian Schnabel, whom he'd met around the time of Warhol's death and became close with later in the '90s, after moving in across the street from Schnabel's self-designed pink condo-palazzo. They were both Brooklyn Jewish kids made good, with personalities that veered between extremes of aggressive and tender; both were outspoken, had sizable egos, made art as much from gut as head, and had noticeably fraught relationships with critics. Schnabel recognized their kinship straightaway. "He was so familiar to me—and me to him—that we became very, very close," he said.

Like Warhol, Schnabel had pivoted into filmmaking; his first film, *Basquiat*, based on the life of his friend and fellow painter, featured David Bowie as Warhol and a soundtrack featuring John Cale. When Reed asked Schnabel to design the staging for *Berlin*—one of Schnabel's all-time favorite albums—the men decided to make a film of it, too, kicking in $50,000 each to self-fund it. Schnabel painted stage-set panels and worked on Exploding Plastic Inevitable–style projection reels with his daughter Lola and the actor Emmanuelle Seigner, who played Reed's Caroline, reveling boozily in abstracted scenes from *Berlin*'s verses.

Reed's initial idea was to have Anohni sing the entire album live, but the flattered singer convinced Reed to sing it himself; Anohni joined a group of backup singers that included the dazzling soul revivalist Sharon Jones and the Brooklyn Youth Chorus. Reprising his guitar parts from the original album, Steve Hunter joined an expanded version of Reed's touring band featuring a horn section led by Steve Bernstein and the producer, Bob Ezrin, who "conducted" the group wildly in a lab coat with the word "BERLIN," painted by Schnabel in block letters, down the back.

"You've got a nice yiddishe kop there," Schnabel said to Reed's mom, Toby, who was seated up front with her daughter on opening night, playing emcee and referring to his friend's Jewish smarts. "If he was my son, I'd be very proud of him."

The music began: Fernando Saunders played electric counterpoint to Rob Wasserman's upright bass, Hunter soloed magnificently, Tony Smith attacked his drums with explosive joy, and Reed, in an orange T-shirt, grinned with delight. The show crested with "Caroline Says II," *Berlin*'s most beautiful song, Reed near-weeping in the delivery—gripping the mic with both hands, grabbing his hair, singing about the abused girl who's not afraid to die, who put her fist through the windowpane, and whose children were taken away, as washed-out Super 8 images flashed on the screen. And then "The Bed," with Reed recounting the razor and cut wrists, singing "Oh, what a feeling," the Brooklyn Youth Chorus answering him, extending the song's coda. Then came the finale, "Sad Song," and its horrific threat to assault a woman already dead, as Steve Hunter gently played the melody on acoustic guitar.

The performance was frequently gorgeous and a bitter pill: magnificent, overwrought, pretentious, full of thematic misogyny. But in the wake of the final-note applause, in a juxtaposition that couldn't have thrown the contradictions of Reed's art into sharper relief, Anohni stepped to the mic to sing "Candy Says" with Reed, the young singer delivering the verses in a riveting sustained tremor, writhing like a pupa emerging from a chrysalis, conjuring Candy Darling, Little Jimmy Scott, and so many who reached for transcendence in the face of hatred. When they finished, Reed looked at Anohni with pride, awe, and love. Whatever critiques one could level at *Berlin* as a narrative, Anohni's "Candy Says" neutralized them in a benediction of exquisite tenderness and empathy. In this staging, decades after its release, *Berlin* became a triumph. As the realization of the theatrical project Reed never managed with Warhol, it's a shame the latter didn't live to see it.

The response to the production, which toured Europe, was deeply satisfying for Reed. "It was a big full-circle, for him to take this record back in on his own terms, and to present it in a way that he was happy with, and for it to be so well received," Anohni said. Hal Willner recalls introducing Reed onstage at the Royal Albert Hall in the summer of 2008. "It was one of the greatest moments ever for me," says Willner. "There was a picture of redemption."

*   *   *

Earlier that year, on April 12, Lou Reed and Laurie Anderson were married in Boulder, Colorado. Reed set the date, although Anderson steered him to it. "I was complaining—I'm always complaining about something," she says. "I was in California and talking to Lou on the phone about how I was going to do so many things with my life. And look at all the things I didn't do. I was going to go live in Rome for a year, and I'm probably not going to do that. And I was going to learn physics, and I'm probably not going to do that. And we were going to get married. And he said, 'Well, how about tomorrow?' And I said, 'Doncha think tomorrow is a little . . . soon?' [laughs] He said, 'I'm going to come out tomorrow and we'll get married.' So we did. We met in Boulder, Colorado, and we got married the next day."

The ceremony was performed by Nick Forster, a bluegrass musician and radio host. It took place, Anderson recalls, "in a backyard, with a big tree, and a guy who'd never done a ceremony before, and we wrote our names in a big book in the Boulder County Clerk's office. And then we were married." Reed wrote a song for Anderson, "The Power of the Heart," as a wedding gift.

"I think it's so different to marry your best friend," she adds. "There should be a different name for it, for that kind of a ceremony."

* * *

Reed deepened bonds with other friends, too. He did several projects with John Zorn, including a musical arrangement of the biblical Song of Songs—the Shir Hashirim—in which Reed and Anderson recited the lovers' text. Reed also enlisted Schnabel for further adventures, including an episode of *Spectacle*, a music show hosted by Elvis Costello, during which Reed discussed his dyslexia ("I've always had trouble reading—anything with long paragraphs," he said. "I reverse things. I thought I was unemployable"), and the "Sweet Jane" chord progression. Schnabel, kissing Reed's hand, recited the complete lyrics to "Rock Minuet" from memory.

With Willner, Reed began hosting a show for Sirius Radio, the satellite network, called *New York Shuffle*, using Ornette Coleman's "Lonely Woman" as its opening theme. On one episode, the pair lamented the disappearance of record stores in New York City; talked about restaurants in the Asian diaspora of Flushing, Queens; and savored records by the Staple Singers ("one of the sexiest voices in the history of music,

Mavis Staples," Reed noted) and June Edwards, whose smoldering take on Loretta Lynn's "You Ain't Woman Enough to Take My Man" set Reed to praising the "great women writers in country music," among them Lynn and Dolly Parton. (Another episode considered records by Feist, Ty Segall, and James Blake, whose "beautiful" single "The Wilhelm Scream" prompted Reed to wonder: "How do the English do such amazing takes on their American soul brothers?") The show, which the men recorded in Lou's home studio, gave Reed the opportunity to reclaim an old pleasure: hanging out with a friend and listening to records, a rewind to 1959, when he co-hosted *Happy Art and Precocious Lou's Hour of Joy and Rebellion* with Artie Littman at the NYU campus station.

Reed remained active into his late sixties. He'd be out with Anderson most nights of the week when he wasn't working, attending gallery openings, plays, films, and concerts. But as his health issues increased, so did his irritability, accompanied by a decrease in his stamina. He'd often fall asleep at events—from boredom, exhaustion, or both. On at least one occasion, this happened during a performance, when he was invited to do live narration for Guy Maddin's experimental film *Brand upon the Brain!* After berating the production team on the night of his appearance, Reed nodded off onstage in the middle of it, at points snoring loudly.

In 2009, Reed and Anderson bought a house in East Hampton, roughly twenty miles from Warhol's old summer estate, Eothen. Theirs was a modest three-bedroom affair, with a pool and a guesthouse. He'd once called Long Island, with privileged hyperbole, "the worst place on the planet." But that was the suffocating suburb of Freeport in the 1950s. East Hampton, a summer resort community for the rich and famous, signified something altogether different. The second home allowed Reed and Anderson to slow the New York City paddlewheel of workdays and social engagements, to entertain close friends and focus on each other. Given their frequent touring, they spent much of their time apart; many thought it was the secret to the success of their relationship. When they were in New York, they were generally working. Their respective Manhattan apartments had become personalized live-in creative spaces, a lifestyle to which Anderson had long ago become accustomed. But at the East Hampton house, they could press pause together.

* * *

Besides spending time with Anderson and his family of choice, Reed reconnected with his cousin Shirley Novick. Growing up, Reed hadn't seen her much. She'd lived in the same Chelsea apartment for decades, and frowned on his parents' suburban lifestyle, rarely visiting them on Long Island. "[Our parents] were about as middle-class as you could humanly get, and she was so much about not succumbing to the bourgeoisie," his sister recalled, referring to Novick as her brother's "spiritual grandmother . . . that person in your life who always makes you feel like a shiny penny." She kept up with Reed's career; in the '90s, he arranged for her to attend a concert, after which she sent him a thankyou note, complimenting his stage presence and "superb" musicians, praising him as "a great artist." It was a compliment he could trust.

Like Reed, Novick did not suffer fools. In her late nineties, she remained quick-witted, and her rapid-fire banter with him was remarkable and reliably comic, in a Yiddish tradition. Reed admired her intelligence and charisma, seeing her as "an amazing, indomitable force." She was also a connection to his history minus the baggage of his immediate family. "Shirley could share stories of his father with him that meant a great deal [to him]," said Sylvia Reed. Novick remembered Sid Reed as an idealistic young man wanting to fight in the Spanish Civil War, as Ernest Hemingway did. "If you knew [our father] later, this is not something that you would *ever* have imagined," Reed's sister said.

As Novick neared her hundredth birthday, with his own health struggles mirroring hers, Reed got the idea to make a film about her. He titled it *Red Shirley*, in tribute to her union-organizing nickname. Less a formal documentary than a verité snapshot of a conversation—

Warholian, in its way—between himself and Novick, it seemed as much a family keepsake as a commodity. His cousin was enthusiastic, but according to production notes, certain topics were off-limits (among them, her political beliefs, deemed "too complicated"). The finished twenty-eight-minute film, Reed's first and last, premiered at Lincoln Center during the New York Jewish Film Festival. Shirley was seeing the film for the first time, and Reed was nervous about it. When it ended and the applause died out, he learned some of the challenges of biography when his cousin looked up from her wheelchair and said to him, scoldingly, "You left a lot out!"

* * *

Reed was also making music with new collaborators, looking for creative transfusions, continued relevance, and the satisfaction of mentoring young artists. He formed a musical and personal bond with Kevin Hearn, a multi-instrumentalist who worked with the hit-making Canadian rock band Barenaked Ladies. Reed also convened the Metal Machine Trio, a noisy, free-form side project with Ulrich Krieger, the saxophonist-composer who'd transcribed *Metal Machine Music*, and Sarth Calhoun, an electronic musician Reed met through his tai chi practice.

Reed also connected with Damon Albarn, the polyglot frontman of Blur, who invited Reed to contribute to his "virtual group," Gorillaz, which showcased a rotating cast of singers and rappers. Albarn was weaned on the Velvets and adored Reed's work, but the collaboration was a bumpy ride. Initially, Reed rejected every track Albarn sent him. Finally, one clicked, and they met in a New York studio to discuss the approach. Midway through, Reed had to leave for a dentist appointment; he returned a few hours later with a full set of lyrics he'd written in the cab ("a very Lou Reed thing to do," Albarn thought). When it was time to record vocals, Reed ordered everyone out of the studio, including Albarn, who snuck into the control room to listen, hiding behind the mixing desk. The result, "Some Kind of Nature," was a perfect fit for the environmental-crisis concept LP *Plastic Beach*, Reed sounding like a gravel-voiced survivor of a toxic dystopia, which wasn't far from the truth.

Reed planned to perform with Gorillaz for their headlining set at the Glastonbury Festival, a highlight of a busy 2010 summer. Then his health took a downturn.

The trouble began in Australia, where he and Anderson had been invited to curate the Sydney Vivid Festival. They'd invited Willner, Emily Haines, the Blind Boys of Alabama, and Master Ren Guang Yi, who gave free outdoor tai chi lessons; Anderson performed a low-frequency outdoor concert composed primarily for an audience of appreciative dogs. ("They barked for five minutes," she recalled. "That was one of the happiest moments of my life.") At a press conference, Reed answered questions patiently, in marked contrast with one at Sydney Airport thirty-some years prior. When asked about plans for his next album, he hedged. "I haven't figured out just what would be a great thing to do right now, that would make a difference—for me, for you," he said, noting that he was trying to come up with something "really astonishing." In fact, he would. But at the moment, Reed seemed tremendously frail. Along with his diabetes, he'd begun interferon treatment for his hepatitis C. But it was painful and terribly debilitating. He'd fallen on a moving sidewalk in an airport, assistants had to physically help him out of chairs, he dozed off during a presentation by Anderson, and in rehearsals was even having trouble recalling his own songs.

Most performers would have withdrawn from public view. But Reed pushed on. In June he managed to play Glastonbury with Gorillaz—on the festival's iconic main stage; he was backdropped by a giant cartoon image of himself as a sort of anime punk yakuza, in a motorcycle jacket, shades, and elaborate headphones, eating guitar cords with chopsticks like they were ramen noodles. The real-life Reed, however, was a small, ailing old man, in a windbreaker, baggy shorts, black socks, and beige shoes. His hands trembled as he played, and the bassist Paul Simonon recalls him losing the thread; at one point in the song, "he was supposed to be singing, but he wasn't; he was looking at me, with a bemused look." Reed ultimately rallied, croaked out the verses, unleashed some mighty feedback, and raised his hands in the air, while tens of thousands roared.

* * *

Reed finally came up with the "really astonishing" album idea he'd referenced in Australia. It was born of his third Robert Wilson project, which reimagined the "Lulu" plays of Frank Wedekind.

Like Poe, Wedekind was a writer with whom Reed had a spiritual kinship. The son of a gynecologist, Benjamin Franklin Wedekind was born in Germany in 1864. He loved winding up the bourgeoisie—Wedekind was jailed in his thirties for publishing satirical poems insulting the wrong people. His plays addressed teen sexuality, queer desire, and bogus morality; the posthumously published memoir *Diary of an Erotic Life* chronicled the gourmandizing author working his way through a brigade of cocottes and sex workers. (An entry dated September 6, 1893, prior to the scandalous premiere of his play *Frühlings Erwachen* (*Spring Awakening*), found him kvetching after an epic night of cunnilingus. "I can hardly speak because my tongue is fearfully sore. It's at least a centimeter longer than it was.") His breakthrough works *Erdgeist* (*Earth Spirit*) and *Büchse der Pandora* (*Pandora's Box*) centered on Lulu, an amoral femme fatale whose affections destroy her lovers, male and female, one by one. Lulu is both victim and monster, the product of a misogynist, homophobic culture, and the embodiment of its worst fears. The "Lulu plays" became part of the bedrock of modern German theater, as well as opera (Alban Berg's *Lulu*, the *Wozzeck* composer's final work) and film (*Pandora's Box*, the 1929 silent film starring the American actor Louise Brooks). The Lulu narrative was an obvious choice for Wilson, given his German audience, and a perfect fit for Reed, who'd worked on Paul Auster's *Lulu on the Bridge* and whose nickname back in the Factory days was, in fact, Lulu.

Reed laid into the writing. By then, his failing health was being mirrored in his dog, Lolabelle—the rat terrier he and Anderson doted on so intensely, who was dying of pancreatic cancer and undergoing increasingly elaborate treatments (for a time, the couple had her set up in an oxygen tent). Torn up over it, and surely frustrated by his own infirmities, Reed created extreme music, alternately raging and tender. "He was going through a difficult period," recalls Wilson, who marveled at the intensity of Reed's work, swinging from the "very aggressive and loud" to "the softest, quietest sound one could make . . . These two extremes, to me, is what Lou was all about."

Lulu premiered on April 12, 2011, in Berlin. The same month, Reed began recording an album with Metallica in Marin County, California.

The collaboration was highly unlikely. Metallica was one of the biggest rock acts in the world, just coming off its largest tour—a two-year run that packed global sports arenas and grossed over $200 million. The hyper-butch thrash-metal was far from Reed's approach to rock music, but the group had broad tastes, and wasn't averse to experimentation. They'd recorded an album with Michael Kamen and the San Francisco Symphony, and as they prepared to celebrate their thirtieth year as a band, they were thinking about legacy. For an all-star concert celebrating the Rock and Roll Hall of Fame, they backed Reed on a fierce pair of Velvet Underground covers: a bludgeoning "White Light/White Heat," and a "Sweet Jane" that suggested the guitarist Kirk Hammett had, like most hard-rock guitarists of his generation, been weaned on *Rock 'n' Roll Animal*. The musicians all enjoyed the experience, and when the idea was floated to do a full album of Lou Reed songs in the same vein, everyone was on board.

Then Reed suddenly changed his mind, and decided that instead, he wanted to record material from *Lulu* with Metallica. The idea was not well received, even by his own management. "I remember to this day how viciously angry he got with me, that I thought the greatest hits was a better idea," Tom Sarig says. "To him it was like disrespecting his *Lulu* songs." After a couple of uncomfortable days, Sarig gave in and endorsed Reed's idea. The band had reservations, but similarly went along with it. They gave Reed a royal welcome when he arrived in the Bay Area to begin recording, and set up a portion of their studio building as his exclusive domain, dubbing it "Lou's Lounge," a private space where he could retreat to do tai chi, deal with his medications, and nap, which he needed to do regularly. The men let Reed take the creative lead, since the songs and lyrics were his. But they expected to have input as well, and there remained doubts about the material.

The sessions were not stress-free; according to the drummer, Lars Ulrich, Reed challenged him to a fight after a disagreement (Ulrich declined). Reed's health had stabilized since Australia, but he was still dealing with tremendous pain, and was often foggy; weeks into the sessions, he was still referring to the front man, James Hetfield, as "Hatfield." Reed was reaching for maximum freedom in his vocal delivery—"just kind of acting it and singing it at the same time," as he put it—and his delivery could feel disconnected from the band. And even by Reed's standards, the *Lulu* lyrics were often shocking, with Reed's gruff, croaking delivery conjuring Lulu's voice. "I would cut my legs and tits off / When I think of Boris Karloff," the record began. Reed's explicit additions to Poe's work in *The Raven* were mild compared with lines in "Pumping Blood," where Lulu, bleeding to death at the hands of Jack the Ripper, begs the killer to do his worst: "I swallow your sharpest cutter / Like a colored man's dick." Equally startling is a section where Reed yells for "James" to "top" him (a sly echo of Reed's "Whip it on me, Jim" outro on the Velvets' "Sister Ray"). Images of fisting and coprophilia flash through "Mistress Dread." On "Iced Honey," he yells in a parched voice over Metallica's roaring din, "And me, I've always been this way / Not by choice."

But the finale, "Junior Dad," was something else. The album's quietest song, with lyrics written roughly two years prior, it was delivered with a tenderness that had scant precedent in Reed's work. The verses moved through a Freudian minefield of parental failure and childhood fears. The singer asks to be saved from drowning, to be kissed on the lips, and envisions their dead father driving a boat. Awakening from a dream, the singer sees how time had "withered him and changed him," perhaps both of them, invoking the "greatest disappointment." A father's disappointment in a child, a child's disappointment in the father, the child realizing they'd *become* the parent: take your pick.

Listening to the playback, the lyrics cut Reed's bandmates to the core. Hetfield's dad abandoned him when he was thirteen; Hammett's had been physically abusive toward him and his mother, then abandoned them, and had died just a month prior. "I had to run out of the control room," Hammett said; "I found myself standing in the kitchen, sobbing away. James came into the kitchen in the same condition. He was sobbing too."

Reed shed his share of tears, too. One night during the sessions, he took a break to catch U2 in Oakland with Willner and their friend Jenni Muldaur. When the band paused and noted his presence—Bono calling him "a great man," Larry Mullins Jr. singing the chorus of "Perfect Day" a capella and shouting "We love you, Lou!"—Reed wept.

* * *

The recording was rapid fire by Metallica's usual standards—there were rarely second takes—and was done in a couple of months. Any doubts about the project were pushed aside.

The day before the album was released, Reed received the insignia of Commander of the Order of Arts and Letters; Antonin Baudry, cultural counselor of the French embassy, described Reed as "one of the major American writers of our time." In that honor's wake came the response to *Lulu* in the press, which was as harshly polarized as the reception to *Berlin*. Old-guard critics were mostly measured, but on the internet, the new guard let loose. *Pitchfork* gave it a 1.0 on a scale of 10, finding parts "laughable" and the full work "exhaustingly tedious," while Consequence of Sound gave it an "F" and declared it "a complete failure." Fan reactions online ranged from enthusiastic to baffled to nasty to hilarious; parody videos abounded. At least one clip featured a cat having a panic attack triggered by the music. Another sampled the 2004 German film *Downfall*, about Hitler's final days, grafting on subtitles that show him sputtering in rage at news of the Metallica project: "LOU FUCKING REED? That cunt from Velvet Underground? That ancient sack of shit wouldn't know metal if it bit his shriveled cock off!"

Reed and Willner had a hearty laugh over that one. But in general, the response to *Lulu* wasn't amusing. Press events were hair-trigger.

At the album release in New York, Reed's bitchiness toward reporters led to Hetfield storming out of the event. "I understand that to some thirteen-year-old in Cape Girardeau, Missouri, it can all seem a little cringe-worthy," Ulrich told a writer for *Spin*, "but to someone raised in an art community in Copenhagen in the late '60s, that was expected." In public, the musicians gushed over the project and one another. "They are my spirit brothers," Reed told another journalist, with Hetfield and Ulrich beside him. "Every time I listen to the record, I pray to God I was so lucky to meet these guys."

Still, there'd be no collaborative tour, and no U.S. production of Wilson's *Lulu*. The truth was that the album was a difficult listen at best, especially given the disconnect between Reed's delivery and the band's (like they're "barely . . . on the same planet, let alone in the same room," as *Pitchfork*'s Stuart Berman put it). And disconnected from Wilson's stagecraft, the songs were strange, often unpleasant and incoherent things. Except, however, for "Junior Dad." Shape-shifting like "Sister Ray" over its nineteen minutes, the finished recording was powerfully emotive. Its sound and imagery conjure the sea that enraptured Reed as a kid, roiling in a groove as hypnotic as the Velvets' "Ocean," cresting in majestic stumbles that one observer likened to recurring heart failure, as Reed begs to be saved, to be loved, it would seem, by a father who taught him only "meanness" and "fear," the singer savoring the sibilant salt of the phrase "psychic savagery" as the song drifts into a warm string coda. "Junior Dad" took its place among Reed's finest work, and as the last song on the last studio album released in his lifetime, one might consider it the closing passage of the Great American Novel he'd often suggested was serialized in his LPs, his "So we beat on, boats against the current, borne back ceaselessly into the past."

* * *

Reed devoted much of his final two years to writing. He published a preface to a new edition of Delmore Schwartz's *In Dreams Begin Responsibilities and Other Stories*. There were also plans for books of his own, including a volume on tai chi, possibly even a memoir. He also revived the notion of turning the *New York* album into a narrative work, this time as a stage musical, one more mainstream than his Wilson collaborations, and which could be rooted in his hometown. "We were working with CAA's Broadway Department on a sort of a remake of the plot of *West Side Story*—Jets versus Sharks—set to the songs," says Sarig. "Eric Bogosian was committed to writing the book, and Bill T. Jones was going to direct it. We were putting the whole team together when he passed. It would have been great."

In a turning of the tables, Reed took a stab at music criticism, reviewing Kanye West's *Yeezus* LP for the artist-centered website Talkhouse. At the time, the two could almost be seen as kindred spirits, artists who subverted the status quo, with sometimes questionable tactics, while becoming consequential enough to be acknowledged by sitting presidents. Reed felt West was essentially daring his audience to like his creative choices, and much of what he said of *Yeezus* might be said of his own albums. "Very perverse," Reed concluded.

There were recording projects on deck, too, including a standards set with Willner, for which they'd begun selecting songs. Reed also played a handful of what turned out to be his final shows in Europe, enlisting a brilliant young guitarist, Aram Bajakian, and a violinist, Tony Diodre, who doubled on guitar. Reed was in rough shape, but the shows were among the most powerful he'd ever played.

He hadn't done a proper U.S. tour in nearly a decade, and booked a string of California dates for the spring, including one at the prestigious Coachella Festival in April. Kevin Hearn was making the set list—a "greatest hits" of sorts—when he got a call from Reed.

"Kevin," he said, "I've got bad news."

Reed was dying, and his last hope was a very risky liver transplant. Years prior, Hearn had been through a near-death battle with blood cancer, and Reed frequently noted that his bandmate had come back from a place few ever see. In the coming weeks, the two spoke frequently. In one conversation, Reed described an extravagant new speaker system he'd just bought. "If I'm going to kick the bucket," he told Hearn, "I'm going to do it while listening to the best possible sound."

* * *

Reed's final public musical performance was in Paris, at the Salle Pleyel, a classical-music concert hall. On March 6, 2013, he sang "Candy Says" with Antony and the Johnsons, and given his condition, the "hate" of the main character for their body, and all it required, took on a very particular meaning. Reed sang the opening lines in a ravaged voice, reaching for the key as the band played hushed changes. Anohni stood in shadow, head bowed, hands clasped in a sort of prayer, as Reed sung-spoke his words according to his own metrical sense, improvising with a Jimmy Scott–style playfulness. And as he began the "doo-doo-wah" coda, Anohni joined him, quietly, gracefully, in a voice barely there until it was, rising to meet Reed's. They traded and finished each other's lines, both asking what they'd see if they could walk away from themselves, and Reed repeating the line "maybe when I'm older," which was now an invocation of great faith.

* * *

In May, Reed flew to the Cleveland Clinic in Ohio, chosen for its reputation with organ transplants. "It's medical tourism," Anderson, the Midwesterner, conceded wryly. "You send out two planes—one for the donor, one for the recipient—at the same time. You bring the donor in live, you take him off life support . . . I was completely awestruck. I find certain things about technology truly, deeply inspiring." According to Reed's transplant surgeon, the liver was "less-than-perfect." But Reed understood his situation, and didn't hesitate. "It's good enough for me," he said. "Let's go."

His new liver began working immediately, and Reed was soon doing tai chi, kvetching about the hospital food, and getting his strength back. Family and friends came to visit. His sister talked about seeing the Velvet Underground in Cleveland when she was in college. When it was quiet, you could hear the helicopters nearby, taking off and landing, transporting organs and patients.

Reed was soon home and, though weak, returned to work. There was optimism, even opportunities to laugh. The satirical news publication *The Onion* ran an item titled "New Liver Complains of Difficulty Working with Lou Reed." ("'It's really hard to get along with Lou—one minute he's your best friend and the next he's outright abusive,' said the vital organ, describing its ongoing collaboration with the former Velvet Underground frontman as 'strained at best.' 'He just has this way of making you feel completely inadequate.'")

In June, Reed commuted near-daily to Masterdisk, the recording facility on West Forty-fifth Street, to work with Willner and his co-producer Rob Santos on remastering his early solo catalog, a project Reed had long wanted to do. Reed savored and scrutinized much of his life's work. He swooned over Bowie's backing vocals on "Satellite of Love." He pumped his fist to *Berlin*'s "Lady Day." He time-traveled through the binaural space of "The Bells." "He took so much joy from rediscovering these records," Wilner says. "And being able to sit there in the room with him while he was doing it? Whew. I felt like the luckiest person in the world."

After the final day of mastering, Reed and Willner went to record their radio show with a guest: the actor Natasha Lyonne, a friend of Willner's and a huge Reed fan (Reed was a fan of hers, too, admiring her work in the new series *Orange Is the New Black*, which he watched while he was in the hospital). Discovering they'd just finished Reed's back catalog remastering, Lyonne suggested they listen to some songs. As a rule, Reed never played his own recordings on the show. But they made an exception. Willner recalls Reed saying, "I can't believe we're getting to do this while I'm alive."

Reed also managed a trip to Europe in June, where he attended the Cannes Lions International Festival of Creativity, the world's premiere ad industry gathering. In a public dialogue with the creative macher Tim Mellors, Reed groused about MP3s and the digital distribution of music, praised Kanye West ("The only guy really doing something interesting"), and thanked the ad industry, from which he'd earned a small fortune. "In a world of downloading, the only people who will pay you for what you do is you guys," Reed said. "Ad people play fair with you."

Reed got involved in a major ad campaign that fall, in fact, for high-end headphones developed by a French company, Parrot; he helped design an app optimizing the headphone EQ for rock music. A photo shoot for the campaign, scheduled with Jean-Baptiste Mondino for September 30 in New York City, included a filmed interview conducted by Farida Khelfa. Reed, wearing a distressed black leather jacket over a skull-motif T-shirt, appeared diminished, and spoke with a faint tremor in his voice. The interview got off to a typically testy start: when asked if his father had gotten him a guitar when he was young, Reed snapped, "My father didn't give me shit." Deadpanning, he claimed he never went to school, and that he slept with his amp. But soon he softened, waxing poetic about the magic of aural perception, about being in a hospital and hearing your blood flow during an ultrasound.

Asked about his earliest sound memories, Reed said his was the same as everyone's: his mother's heartbeat.

"And that's why we love PPWHOH, PPWHOH, PPWHOH," he said, beatboxing the primal rhythm. "It's so simple." He also described the sound of love, which he conjured by pursing his lips and softly blowing, as if to dislodge the fluff of dandelion seeds.

* * *

On October 4, Reed joined the photographer Mick Rock at the John Varvatos clothing store—located on the Bowery in the building that had formerly housed CBGB—for a book-release event. *Transformer* was a coffee-table volume assembling many of Rock's iconic images of Reed—images that defined him as an artist. Nico appears in several, as do Bowie and Warhol. Rock's photos of Reed with Rachel Humphreys didn't make the cut.

Nearly a decade earlier, Reed wrote a short essay for a small-circulation art magazine. It considered a black-and-white photograph by Robert Frank, a death meditation that showed the phrase "sick of goodbye's" [*sic*] written in paint that drips like blood on the surface of two mirrors, one reflecting a hand gripping a skeleton figurine. "To wish for the crazy times one last time and freeze it in the memory of a camera," Reed observed, "is the least a great artist can do." There was a bit of that spirit in Modino's final ad image: Reed's face in a close-up, jowls succumbing to gravity, laugh lines like trenches, hair and eyebrows streaked with white, eye bags puffy. But within them, Reed's eyes are full-bore, staring down the lens, while in the foreground, in soft focus, is his clenched fist—an expression of street-fighter strength at a moment when Reed was about as weak physically as he'd ever been.

In the months, then weeks, before his death, Reed fretted about his legacy, worrying that time would erase him. Schnabel recalled rewatching the *Berlin* film with Reed, and his friend wondering at what impact he'd made. "He always felt, in a way, unappreciated," Schnabel said. "He never felt like people really got it." Reed's sister recalls him saying point-blank: "I don't want to be erased."

* * *

When Reed's body began rejecting the liver, he was flown back to Cleveland for follow-up care. But little could be done. When the doctors told him they were out of options, Anderson recalls, he fixated just on the word *options*. Kevin Hearn flew out to help with what, at this point, was hospice care.

"It became very personal," Hearn says. He recalls Reed speaking to a doctor, parsing the difference between the words *faith* and *hope*. ("'Hope' leaves room for failure," Reed explained, "but 'faith' is the belief that things will be a certain way.")

One day, mirroring his New York routine, Reed had Hearn take him up to the hospital roof. Reed lay down on the tar paper in his gown and looked up at the sky.

"Kevin, aren't you coming down here with me?" Reed asked.

Hearn lay beside Reed. He recalls Reed yellow from jaundice, face thin, body wasting.

Reed began to weep, and thanked Hearn for coming. "You mean so much to me," Reed told him. He kissed his friend.

The next day, Reed flew back home to die.

* * *

In the end, not even Lou Reed wanted to die in New York City. He and Anderson went out to the house on Long Island, near the ocean he was raised by and that had informed his imagination for a lifetime. He spent his last days with friends, listening to music and floating in the heated pool. Willner and their friend Jenni Muldaur stayed overnight. "We didn't talk much," Willner recalled, "we just lay there with him, and he had me DJ. And as we were [listening], he sat up and told us that 'I am so susceptible to beauty right now' and just lay back down . . . I can still see the goosebumps on him." Willner's playlist included the Shangri-Las' "Remember (Walking in the Sand)," Frank Ocean's "Forrest Gump" and "Sweet Life," Radiohead's "All I Need," Valerie June's "Tennessee Time," Nina Simone's "When I Was a Young Girl," Big Joe Turner's "Lipstick, Powder and Paint," Roberta Flack's "Ballad of the Sad Young Men," Jonathan Richman's "Roadrunner," and unsurprisingly, Ornette Coleman's "Lonely Woman."

Reed and Anderson stayed up all night that Saturday, talking and doing breath work. When daybreak came, he asked to be helped to the porch. "Take me into the light," Reed said—his final words, spoken on a Sunday morning.

"As meditators, we had prepared for this—how to move the energy up from the belly and into the heart and out through the head," Anderson said. "I have never seen an expression as full of wonder as Lou's as he died. His hands were doing the water-flowing 21-form of tai chi. His eyes were wide open. I was holding in my arms the person I loved the most in the world, and talking to him as he died. His heart stopped. He wasn't afraid."

Anderson made the appropriate calls, but wanted to spend some final hours in the house with Reed. That night, Willner, Hearn, and others joined her, listening to music, talking, and crying alongside Reed's body, laid out and surrounded by things he loved, among them a tai chi sword and a guitar.

Ten days after her son's death, Reed's mother, Toby, died. She'd been in a nursing home for a while, and Reed had spent time with her in 2011 when his health was better, creating closure he didn't get to have with his dad. But his mom had deteriorated and was now in an unresponsive state. Reed's sister had been hesitating to break the news to her. Finally, she did, telling her mom "about the accolades, the world's reaction to Lou's death." Merrill Reed recalls her mom "sat up straight, opened her eyes wide, said a sentence of gibberish with great emotion, and fell back against the sofa." She's sure their mom understood, and Toby Reed passed very soon after. "She knew—and she left to join him."

EPILOGUE

The child must carry / The fathers on his back.
> —Delmore Schwartz,
> "The Ballad of the Children of the Czar"

Reed's lyrics probably do come closest to poetry as any in rock and roll.
> —Richard Hell

"The things he wrote and sang and played with the Velvet Underground were for me part of the beginning of a real revolution in the whole scheme between men and women, men and men, women and women . . . a diversity that extends to the stars."
> —Lester Bangs, "Untitled Notes on Lou Reed, 1980"

"I've spent time with a lot of artists near the end of their lives. I never met anyone who was so angry about dying— who so wanted to live."
> —Hal Willner, 2015

News of Reed's death triggered one of the earliest mass memorializations on social media. (In death, as in life, Reed was a few steps ahead of David Bowie, who passed in 2016.) Facebook had just introduced hashtags, which snowballed topics quickly, and for days, then weeks, it was a space of public mourning. Fans wrote of the Reed songs that meant the most to them; favorite concerts were recalled, Reed sightings cited, intimate stories shared. Fernando Saunders, who'd been living in Prague, learned of Reed's death from a Facebook post, initially thinking it was another prank ("He'd been 'dying' for twenty years," he says with a chuckle), but realized it was no joke when hundreds of fans flooded his Facebook page, to commiserate, mourn, and pay tribute. Saunders had witnessed the intensity of Reed's fan base over the years, but he was still stunned by the scale and depth of the devotion to Reed's music.

High-profile tributes came fast and thick. Some were unlikely, like one from Cardinal Gianfranco Ravasi, the Vatican's seventy-one-year-old culture minister, who tweeted a lyric passage from "Perfect Day" (followed by a caveat stressing he was not condoning drug use). Many were from musicians. Chrissie Hynde noted the Velvet Underground's vast influence on generations of bands that followed. "Lou, you were the schoolteacher we wish we had and the rocker we emulated," the Pretenders' frontwoman wrote. Courtney Love testified that *Berlin* "changed my worldview and made me realize that anything I believe in is art, it's not about what other people think." Michael Stipe, who reflected on finding *Loaded* and *1969: The Velvet Underground Live* "in the 8-track cutout bins of Grandpa's Hardware store in Cahokia Mounds, Illinois," praised Reed as a "queer icon," and marveled how, in the late 1960s, he had "proclaimed with beautifully confusing candidness a much more 21st century understanding of a fluid, moving sexuality." The singer-songwriter Jana Hunter of Lower Dens wrote of how, as a teenager, "his music found me out in the suburbs and woke me up," and how, years later, "I can lie on a floor stone cold sober and listen to his records, doing nothing else, and I am at the height of being. Now, same as when I was 15."

In the tradition of elegies from Shelley's "Adonais" and Whitman's "O Captain! My Captain!" to Frank O'Hara's "The Day Lady Died," poets responded to the death of a fellow traveler who "pull[ed] melodies out of the dissonance of what Yeats called 'this filthy modern tide'" as the Irish bard Bono put it.

I knew him better than I knew my own
father, which means through these songs, which means
not at all. They died on the same day . . .

          —Nick Flynn, "The Day Lou Reed Died"

I'll miss that smart-ass New York whine
blatancy and inference
symphonies of simple rhyme
passion and indifference.

—Lawrence Morrill Glass,"Lou Reed Died"

Critics for whom Reed had long been a muse rose to the occasion. Dave Hickey lauded him as "a bullshit detector in a scene nose-deep in it." Ann Powers praised his music for the demands it made, among them that "a listener sit with the ugliness of a moment and really grasp the fatal mistakes and collapses that go hand-in-hand with the risks that bring humans to life."

The most moving paeans came from Reed's friends, some of whom paid tribute by not sugarcoating his memory. In *The New Yorker*, Patti Smith noted his "devotion to poetry," and that he died on the birthday shared by Sylvia Plath and Dylan Thomas; she praised Reed as "our generation's New York poet, championing its misfits as Whitman had championed its workingman and Lorca its persecuted." But she also considered Reed's mercurial moods and how he'd alternately encourage her in her early days, then provoke her "like a Machiavellian schoolboy." Rosanne Cash remembered, "He was always so sweet to me. He couldn't have been more of a gentleman. I saw the other, difficult side of him in glimpses, but he just seemed like a really sensitive guy who hated pretension and who found it intolerable to compromise on anything that was important to him, whether it was the sound of his monitors or the meal he had ordered." Especially striking was a lengthy post by Peter Gabriel on his website:

You could be so difficult, narcissistic and intransigent, but anyone you allowed beyond that leather-jacketed protective and sometimes-poisonous veneer got to meet a special man that was sweet, tender and exceptionally loyal. Watching you and Laurie finding each other was like watching teenage sweethearts.

*   *   *

Reed's body was cremated, and his immediate family sat shiva. Per Buddhist tradition, the soul remains in the liminal space of the bardo for forty-nine days following a death. During this bardo period, Laurie Anderson hosted Sunday memorial gatherings for friends, family, associates, collaborators, tai chi students, and neighbors at their apartment on Eleventh Street. Upon the culmination of the bardo period, fifty days after her husband's death, she held an invitation-only memorial event at the Apollo Theater on 125th Street. Hundreds attended, and many of Reed's friends spoke. Paul Simon played "Pale Blue Eyes," Patti Smith freestyled during "Sister Ray," Debbie Harry tore into "White Light/White Heat," Emily Haines intoned "All Tomorrow's Parties," Anohni sang "Candy Says." John Cale did not attend; Moe Tucker read aloud from a statement he'd prepared, in which he considered "how much I gained from my friendship with Lou," adding, "I really miss my friend." And Anderson invoked "Lou's beautiful record *Transformer*, which has a new meaning with his transformation from a living person into pure energy."

There were many other tributes. Saunders convened one in Prague with the Plastic People. Kevin Hearn staged another in Canada. Two of the largest were presented as free events at Lincoln Center, the high-art omphalos where Reed played his first New York City solo show in 1973. For the first, held two weeks after his death, Hal Willner programmed an all-Reed playlist, which was cranked through a state-of-the-art sound system at startlingly loud volume in Hearst Plaza, beneath the turning autumn sycamores next to the Metropolitan Opera House. People chatted, danced, or sat with eyes closed, listening deeply. The set began with the thunderstorm guitar intro of "The Blue Mask," Reed's unsparing portrait of a soldier and his relationship with pain—"There was war in his body," Reed raged, "and it caused his brain to holler"— and unspooled over three hours, through "Candy Says" and "Street Hassle," "Pale Blue Eyes" and "Sunday Morning," cresting with the noise-groove ekstasis of "Sister Ray" and a closing blast of *Metal Machine Music*. It was a very New York scene, with Anderson at its shifting center, handing flowers out to people.

In 2015, Patti Smith again inducted Reed into the Rock and Roll

Hall of Fame, this time as a solo artist apart from the Velvets. Anderson joined her and offered a glimpse into her bond with Reed. "I'm reminded of the three rules we came up with, rules to live by," she said. "And I'm going to tell you what they are, because they come in really handy . . . One: Don't be afraid of anyone. Now, can you imagine living your life afraid of no one? Two: Get a really good bullshit detector. And three: Be really, really tender. And with those three things, you don't need anything else."

The week of Reed's death, his album sales took a predictable spike, up 600 percent, with digital sales up nearly as much; "Walk on the Wild Side" and "Perfect Day" both made the iTunes Top 50, a significant metric in 2013. A more lasting one has been how, year in and year out, musicians continue to cite his influence and cover his songs. The L.A. trio Haim recorded "Summer Girl," a gorgeous song interpolating "Walk on the Wild Side" that credits Reed as co-writer. Joseph Arthur, who became a friend of Reed's after moving to New York from Atlanta, recorded a full album of his songs, the heartfelt *Lou*. Karen O of the Yeah Yeah Yeahs covered "Perfect Day" and "Vicious." Emily Haines, who like many peers looked to the Velvets as a model of "what it is to be a band," credits Reed with showing her ways to escape conventions—"sounding pretty" as a singer, writing solely about your "feelings"—that can be traps, especially for women artists. "Lou laid the groundwork for how expressive you can be with your voice without that conventional [approach to singing]," she says. The Kansan singer-songwriter Kevin Morby feels similarly; he too covers Reed songs, among them "What Goes On," "After Hours," and "Pale Blue Eyes," which he considers "one of the best songs that's ever been written, a play-at-my-funeral kind of song." Alynda Segarra, of Hurray for the Riff Raff—a nonbinary Bronx-raised songwriter who grew up "obsessed" with the Velvet Underground—likely spoke for many peers when they conceded with a laugh that, no matter what they do musically, "there's going to be Lou Reed rip-offs." Even after his death, the reverence for Reed still invites parody: see Liz Phair's 2021 "Hey Lou," an appealingly bratty bit of sacred-cow-tipping Reed might've gotten a chuckle out of.

No less important are the countless, less-limelit lives Reed helped transform. A park ranger who identifies as a trans woman told an NPR reporter about the effect of hearing "Walk on the Wild Side" on the radio. "The first character in that song was Holly. 'Holly came from Miami, F-L-A . . . hitch-hiked her way across the USA.' I wanted to be Holly. I wanted to be that girl who just owned her identity and took her life in her own hands and went off and lived it. And that was what I thought I was going to do." Even Reed's partnership with Anderson was an inspiration to the nonconforming. One starry-eyed writer described them admiringly as being "queer as a 'het' couple could be."

* * *

Reed also left an impression on his hometown. New Yorkers of a certain age and orientation all seem to have an indelible Lou Reed story. The comedian Amy Poehler recalled serving him in the late '90s when she was a waitress at Aquagrill, and when he strolled by her as she smoked outside Theatre 80 in the East Village. "He was like a robin in spring. He was like the guy who told you you lived in New York. I always assumed that Lou Reed just walked up and down St. Marks all day long." Henry Goldrich, owner of Manny's—the most famous music store in the city—had memories of Reed going back years. Two pictures of him hung among the hundreds lining the walls at 156 West Forty-eighth Street. One is a 1968 promo shot of the Velvets, sitting on the grass at the Merce Cunningham Glass House benefit, signed, "To Henry, the best and nicest music man in the cities [sic] only music store."

Reed remained a regular. "When Lou was on drugs, I let him charge stuff," Goldrich recalled decades later. "And he owed me about a thousand dollars for a couple of years. He never forgot me for that. Now he spends a few thousand every month, and he always pays his bills." The director Allan Arkush recalled a story Reed told him about buying guitar strings at Manny's, and watching a geeky young teen plug in a Telecaster with trembling hands, crank up the amp volume, and play the opening chords of "Sweet Jane." Reed told Arkush dryly, "*That's* when I said to myself, 'Hey. I'm Lou Reed!'"

In 2016, Sony Legacy finally issued the remaster project Reed and Willner had been working on, a magnificent retrospective with a photo-filled book: Reed leading a group at his high school talent show; mugging with Bowie and a wild-eyed Iggy Pop in the early '70s; conferring with Warhol. A series of archival releases issued the demo tape Reed made with Cale in 1965 and mailed to himself to secure "poor man's copyright." Hal Willner's final project, a multi-artist rerecording of *The Velvet Underground & Nico*, was finished without him; he died of Covid-19 in the early days of the pandemic, when its American epicenter was New York City. Todd Haynes, who fictionalized Reed in *Velvet Goldmine*, completed *The Velvet Underground*, a beautiful documentary on the group that doubled as homage to the New York experimental film community that helped birth them; with little surviving footage of the Velvets to work with, they remained as mysterious at the film's end as at its beginning. The sensation of 2019's Art Basel, the billionaire-magnet art fair in Florida, was a re-creation of the album cover of *The Velvet Underground & Nico* by the Italian prankster Maurizio Cattelan, a Duchampian gesture in Warhol drag: a ripe yellow banana duct-taped to a white wall.

* * *

Reed also left an estate and, as with many lifelong New York apartment dwellers, multiple rented storage units packed with accumulated stuff. The former was easier to deal with; in his will, Reed divided it between Anderson and his sister. Anderson also inherited Reed's company, Sister Ray Enterprises, and most of his earthly belongings—albums, books, artwork, clothing, musical instruments, sound recordings, videotapes, photos, photo gear, and boxes upon boxes of business documents.

"He left no instructions; none," said Anderson, who described the dawning responsibility for Reed's archive as "like a 15-story building falling on me." The couple had once imagined a collaborative archive/performance space in Brooklyn called the L&L Art Ranch—the initials, for Lou and Laurie, fashioned into an X, like a cattle brand. "Lou always wanted to have a club where he could play every night, and musicians could drop by," she recalled. After his death, she had "a moment of like, 'O.K., I'll build it.'" But that moment passed, and after weighing her options, Reed's archive went to the New York Public Library. In 2022, the institution mounted *Lou Reed: Caught Between the Twisted Stars*, an impressive exhibit of the holdings. It featured a high-tech listening room and a re-creation of the video wall from the *Rock 'n' Roll Heart* tour; it also showcased Reed's LP collection, an autographed copy of Delmore Schwartz's *Vaudeville for a Princess*, a contract from the Velvets' April 1968 run at La Cave in Cleveland, and Bridgit Berlin's cassette recording of the Velvets' last stand at Max's, all mounted in vitrines like holy relics. A dive into the archive's more than two hundred boxes—accessible to anyone with a library card and time to burn—reveals myriad stories. The holdings recall Warhol's "Time Capsules": cartons filled with jettisoned keepsakes and emptied file cabinets, junk vibrating with the history of a life and a culture. The Reed Archive's contents date largely from the late 1970s forward, when Reed, with Sylvia Morales's help, pulled his life together. As much as anything, they're a testimony to Lou Reed as businessman, and the pride he took in running a successful company, a pride he doubtlessly got from his father, and from Warhol.

Anderson was pleased by the outcome. "I feel like it's really what I wanted, that people will get to [see and] hear it and it wouldn't be hidden away," she said, excited that the archive would be available to young musicians, and noting that it documented more than just Reed's triumphs. "It also gives a picture of somebody who didn't always make fantastic things. I love having that available to people, because it gives people courage to see, wow, Lou Reed made that thing? That was horrible. This is great for all of us who know how hard it is to find a style, find a voice."

* * *

After Reed's death, Anderson continued her own work with vigor, forging new alliances and renewing older ones. She did multiple residences at the Experimental Media and Performing Arts Center (EMPAC) at Rensselaer Polytechnic Institute, a laboratory for cutting-edge stage and sound technology just under an hour away from ZBS Media, the radio-art commune where she began her recording career in the '70s. In 2015 she installed a "film sculpture" at the Park Avenue Armory that involved live-streaming video of a former Guantánamo prison detainee, projecting it onto a monument-scale replica of himself, in an echo of Daniel Chester French's Lincoln Memorial sculpture, seated in the former U.S. military drill hall. She mounted retrospectives featuring new work; one, at the Massachusetts Museum of Contemporary Art, included a virtual reality installation (*The Chalkroom*) and a series of huge charcoal-on-paper drawings titled *Lolabelle in the Bardo*, a hallucinogenic, monochromatic imagining of the dog's postmortem journey.

Reed and Anderson's beloved rat terrier Lolabelle was also a presence in Anderson's 2015 film *Heart of a Dog*. A gorgeously abstract meditation on life and storytelling, it ends with a dedication "to the magnificent spirit of my husband Lou Reed." Under the credit roll, her late husband sang "Turning Time Around," describing love as a sort of time machine. Anderson would later reflect: "I got to spend twenty-one years with Lou. I married him. It wasn't until a lot later that I fell in love with the young bad boy Lou. He was dead by then and I read his poems. Now he is my muse. What a complicated situation!"

* * *

On October 22, 2016, Anderson performed at the Stadsschouwburg in Amsterdam. In the shadows of sparse stage lighting, she dueted on violin with the cellist Rubin Kodheli, triggering sounds from an electronics rack. She closed her eyes, and a voice rose up from the audio mix, humming a wordless melody. It soon became clear the voice was Reed's. "Would you come to me," he began singing, "if I was half drowning."

And in the wash of words and sound, it was possible to see Reed's life flash by in moments: waves slapping the Coney Island shoreline as Toby Reed's water breaks; young Lewis Reed on the beach, reaching out to hold his father's hand, and his father slapping it, not wanting his son to be a sissy; Lou Reed in the immersive drone of his electric guitar and the tidal rush of a high-dosage Desoxyn injection; in the panic attacks of "Waves of Fear"; in the fantasy of Manhattan sinking into the polluted Hudson River, as Reed envisioned it in "Romeo Had Juliette"; of meeting a partner obsessed with Herman Melville's *Moby-Dick* and the terrible glory of the human experience; and of Reed's final days in East Hampton, floating in his pool, not far from Jones Beach, where he'd worked one summer as a bathhouse attendant, wearing a sailor's suit and cap—and then in bed, his wife beside him; his hands moving through air as if through water, salt in the breeze.

Dressed entirely in black, Anderson played on for the audience in Amsterdam, a city of water, carved by canals, clouded by hash smoke and a history of war and occupation, all manner of human joys and suffering bobbing on waves of sound, as the voice of Anderson's husband filled the room, her bow moving across her strings, the cellist watching her with a look that suggests he's about to burst into tears. But he doesn't; he just plays, mournful and true, as Reed's voice whispers "state of grace." And then Anderson began singing, in a dialogue of sorts with Reed, mirroring his words, adding her own, asking if he would come to her if she were drowning, pleading with him to pull her up by her hair, her voice betraying a slight tremor, and noting a radiant light.

She let the last note of the song decay slowly. And with a pizzicato, she began the next.

NOTES

PREFACE

ix *"There's no reason to get into autobiographical"*: Lou Reed in Jonathan Cott, *Back to a Shadow in the Night: Music Writings and Interviews 1968–2001* (Hal Leonard, 2002), p. 184.

ix *"Life is hard enough"*: Reed, letter to David Bowie, November 24, 1992, Lou Reed Archive, New York Public Library for the Performing Arts.

x *"I think he'd always fought the idea"*: Don Fleming in Miss Rosen, "A Guide to the Poetry of Lou Reed," *AnOther Man*, April 17, 2018.

x *"make it for adults"*: Reed in Bill Flanagan, *Written in My Soul: Conversations with Rock's Great Songwriters* (Contemporary, 1987), p. 329.

xv *only thirty thousand people*: Brian Eno in Kristine McKenna, "Lots of Aura, No Airplay," *Los Angeles Times*, May 23, 1982; Jeff Gold, "Lou Reed & Exactly How Many Records the Velvet Underground Sold," recordmecca.com, November 10, 2013. Eno's quote had legs, though it was not wholly accurate—*The Velvet Underground & Nico* in fact sold 58,476 copies in the United States between its release in March 1967 and February 1969. But by 1982, before the revival of interest in the band really got traction, it likely hadn't sold too many more.

xviii *"a heavy resentment thing"*: Reed in Stephen Demorest, "Lou Reed & the Secret Life of Plants: Cross-Pollination at the YMCA," *Creem*, March 1979. This interview is hardly the whole story, but its evident exasperated candor makes it a touchstone.

xviii *"the first queer icon"*: Michael Stipe, "Remembering Lou Reed," *Rolling Stone*, November 21, 2013.

xviii *"the non-binary trickster"*: Anne Waldman in Lou Reed, Laurie Anderson, Stephan Berwick, Bob Currie, and Scott Richman, eds. *The Art of the Straight Line: My Tai Chi* (HarperOne, 2023), p. 183.

xviii *"The division between artist"*: Sasha Geffen, *Glitter Up the Dark: How Pop Music Broke the Binary* (University of Texas Press, 2020), p. 9.

xx *"he cared so much"*: David Marchese, "The SPIN Interview: Lou Reed," *SPIN*, November 1, 2008.

NOTES ON PROCESS, MYTH PARSING, AND PRONOUNS

xxiii *"number of different personalities"*: Reed in Victor Bockris and Andrew Wylie, unpublished interview transcript c. 1974, Victor Bockris and Andrew Wylie Collection, Harry Ransom Humanities Research Center at the University of Texas, Austin; see also Victor Bockris, *Transformer: The Lou Reed Story* (Da Capo, 1997), p. 4.

INTRODUCTION

3   *"I think it's important"*: Reed in Victor Bockris and Gerard Malanga, *Up-Tight: The Velvet Underground Story* (Omnibus, 2002), p. 203.

4   *"my hand in his hand"*: Reed quoted by Julian Schnabel, Lou Reed memorial, Apollo Theater, December 16, 2013.

1. BROOKLYN > LONG ISLAND > THE BRONX

5   *"relatable living representative"*: Guy Debord, *The Society of the Spectacle* (1967; Unredacted Word, 2021), https://unredacted-word.pub/spectacle.

5   *"when I was 9 years old"*: Reed, "Spectacle and the Single You," *Crawdaddy*, July 4, 1971.

6   *a rebellious young woman*: Lou Reed and Ralph Gibson, *Red Shirley* (2010); "Red Shirley: Tenement Talk from May 2016," YouTube (Tenement Museum), May 16, 2016, https://www.youtube.com/watch?v=3mk0gdudQFo; photographs, Lou Reed Archive; author interviews.

10   *35 Oakfield Avenue*: Nassau County Land Records, nassaucountyny.gov.

10   *"were terrific people"*: Allan Hyman, author interview, 2014.

11   *Freeport was an oystering village*: Cynthia J. Kreig and Regina G. Feeney, *Freeport: Images of America* (Arcadia, 2012), pp. 8, 23–44.

11   *"Movies didn't do it"*: Reed in liner notes, *Peel Slowly and See* (Polydor, 1995).

12   *"teach me to play the chords"*: Reed in liner notes, *Between Thought and Expression: The Lou Reed Anthology* (RCA/BMG, 1992), p. 2.

12   *"Lou spoke of being beaten up"*: Merrill Reed Weiner, "A Family in Peril: Lou Reed's Sister Sets the Record Straight About His Childhood," *Medium*, April 13, 2015, https://medium.com/cuepoint/a-family-in-peril-lou-reed-s-sister-sets-the-record-straight-about-his-childhood-20e8399f84a3.

13   *He feared he'd never hold a job*: Reed spoke about his dyslexia and fears about employment to Elvis Costello on *Spectacle*, Episode 104, recorded April 16, 2008.

13   *"I resent it"*: op. cit., Reed in Demorest.

14   *sold near a million copies*: "Work with Me, Annie" answer records and knock-offs came hot on its heels: Etta James's potent "Wallflower," aka "Roll with Me Henry"—which hit number 1 on the R&B charts—simply changed the verb, as did Georgia Gibbs's whitewashed "Dance with Me Henry," an even bigger hit. Before the year was out, the Midnighters recorded two follow-ups: "Annie Had a Baby" (she "can't work no more") and "Annie's Aunt Fannie." Little Richard cut "Annie's Back," Lynda Hayes did "My Name Ain't Annie," and, in a sort of final word, a group called the NuTones released "Annie Kicked the Bucket."

14   *It soon joined Reed's teenage repertoire*: Hyman, author interview. See also Richie Unterberger, *White Light/White Heat: The Velvet Underground Day-By-Day* (Jawbone, 2009), p. 13.

15   *a teen dance show*: "The Chantels—Maybe," *Seventeen* (WOI-TV, Ames, Iowa), YouTube (Russ Johnson), September 30, 2012, https://www.youtube.com/watch?v=ZZylQj5zwTw.

16   *"There would be this guy in the back"*: Reed to Geoffrey Cannon, audio recording, 1971. Reed spoke to this journalist for the U.K. magazine *Zig Zag*.

16 *"engraved in my skull forever"*: Reed, Rock and Roll Hall of Fame induction speech for Dion, 1989.

16 *a Gretsch hollow-body electric*: Shiroh Kouchi et al., *Lou Reed Guitar Archive*, web .archive.org/web/20111003123233/http://ww21.tiki.ne.jp/~wildside/gear.htm, 1997–2010.

17 *"we didn't hesitate to sign"*: Phil Harris in liner notes, *Rockin' on Broadway: The Time Brent Shad Story* (Ace Records, 2000).

17 *"I can't sing black"*: Reed in liner notes, *Between Thought and Expression*.

18 *a check for 67 cents*: Reed, WPIX radio show/interview, 1979.

21 *Operation Alert 1959*: Philip Benjamin, "H-Bomb Test Raid Stills Bustling City," *The New York Times*, April 18, 1959.

27 *"ROTC was required"*: Reed, WPIX interview, 1979. See also RCA publicity poster, early to mid-1970s, in *The RCA & Arista Album Collection* (Sony Legacy, 2016).

28 *"Doctor Gordon was fitting"*: Sylvia Plath, *The Bell Jar* (Faber and Faber, 1963), pp. 181-82.

29 *"electrodes on your head"*: Reed in Demorest.

29 *ECT to treat anxiety*: Peter Breggin, *Toxic Psychiatry* (St. Martin's/Griffin, 1991), pp. 52, 69–70, 184–89, 197.

2. LONG ISLAND > UPSTATE

30 *"Hubert Selby, William Burroughs"*: Reed in Marchese.

31 *"This school is intolerable"*: Undated letter from Reed to Arthur Littman, circa January 1961. An envelope that likely contained the handwritten letter was postmarked in Syracuse, N.Y., January 6, 1961.

31 *Syracuse University was founded*: Jerome Karabel, *The Chosen: The Hidden History of Admission and Exclusion at Harvard, Yale and Princeton* (Mariner, 2006), pp. 172–73, 246, 253–54. Karabel believes Harvard had a Jewish quota into the 1940s, and that anti-Semitic admission policies continued into the 1950s. See also John Robert Greene, *Syracuse University: Volume IV: The Tolley Years 1942–1969* (Syracuse University Press, 1996).

32 *"the most amazing experience"*: Reed in Demorest.

33 *"The first sound I ever heard from Lou"*: Morrison in Bockris and Malanga, p. 17. See also Mary Harron, "The Lost History of the Velvet Underground: An Interview with Sterling Morrison," *New Musical Express*, April 25, 1981; Unterberger, pp. 16–17; "Velvet Underground," *The South Bank Show*, April 27, 1986.

34 *Baldwin, who found it*: James Baldwin, "The Black Boy Looks at the White Boy," in *Collected Essays* (Library of America, 1998). Louis Menand, *The Free World: Art and Thought in the Cold War* (Farrar, Straus and Giroux, 2021), pp. 609–13.

34 *"philosophical psychopath"*: Norman Mailer, "The White Negro," *Mind of an Outlaw: Selected Essays* (Random House, 2013), pp. 42–43.

35 *Vahanian recalled Reed*: Gabriel Vahanian in Rob Enslin, "Doin' the Things That He Wants To," *Syracuse University Magazine* (Winter 2007).

35 *"The wrath of the faculty"*: Barr in Dylan Segelbaum and Erik van Rheenan, "'Excursions on a Wobbly Rail': Alumna Remembers Lou Reed's Time at WAER," *The Daily Orange*, November 4, 2013.

36 *spending time at the Hayloft*: Gary Comenas, "Candy Darling," warholstars.org,

2020; Mark Krone, "Rudy Kikel: Boston Poet Who Influenced How a Generation Saw Itself," historyproject.org, April 1, 2018, reprinted from *Boston Spirit Magazine*, January/February 2013.

38 *Swados grew up in Buffalo*: Elizabeth Swados, author interview; Elizabeth Swados, *The Four of Us: The Story of a Family* (Plume, 1993), pp. 16–24; Elizabeth Swados, "The Story of a Street Person," *The New York Times Magazine*, August 18, 1991.

40 *"she made your teeth drop"*: Bob Dylan, *Chronicles: Volume One* (Simon & Schuster, Kindle Edition, 2004).

40 *"he didn't play it in public"*: Shelley Albin in Bockris, *Transformer*, p. 49.

40 *a bluesy version of Dylan's*: Recording, mid-'60s, Lou Reed Archive, New York Public Library. See also Lou Reed, *Words & Music, May 1965* (Light in the Attic, 2022).

40 *"In those days he was 'Lewis Allan'"*: Felix Cavaliere in Ron Wray, *History of Syracuse Music*, ronwray.blogspot.com, December 20, 2011. See also Chris Baker, "Lou Reed's Lasting Legacy at Syracuse University: A Criminal, a Dissident and a Poet," syracuse.com, October 31, 2013.

41 *first issue of* The Lonely Woman: Alan Millstein, "New Literary Magazine Started by Five Sophs," *Syracuse Daily Orange*, September 11, 1962.

45 *Schwartz stepped off a train*: James Atlas, *Delmore Schwartz: The Life of an American Poet* (Welcome Rain, 2000), pp. 72, 129, 137, 231–23; Eileen Simpson, *Poets in Their Youth: A Memoir* (Farrar, Straus and Giroux, 2014), p. 3.

47 *"We drank together"*: Reed in liner notes, *Between Thought and Expression*, p. 4.

47 *Schwartz reading* Ulysses *aloud*: David Yaffe, "Lou's Gift: The Magic of a Rock 'n' Roll Poet," *Tablet*, October 28, 2013.

47 *At the National Poetry Festival*: Delmore Schwartz, recording, 1962 National Poetry Festival, poetryfoundation.org.

49 *"Your Love" and "Merry Go Round"*: Unterberger, pp. 20–21.

50 *"Who am I to edit"*: Hubert Selby Jr. quoted by Reed in *Hubert Selby Jr: It'll Be Better Tomorrow*, directed by Michael W. Dean and Kenneth Shiffrin (Squitten Pix, 2005).

52 *uneasy with homosexuality*: Atlas, pp. 37–38.

52 *"I will haunt you"*: Reed quoting Schwartz in preface to Delmore Schwartz, *In Dreams Begin Responsibilities and Other Stories* (New Directions, 2012), pp. vii–viii.

53 *"The Day John Kennedy Died"*: Reed in Flanagan, p. 337; Reed in Bruno Blum (interview recording, 1981).

54 *"If I had been a voting man"*: Dylan, p. 231. Dylan's reflections on the assassination are on vivid display in his sixteen-minute-plus 2020 song "Murder Most Foul." Would that Reed had lived to hear it; having written his own account in song, it would be fascinating to hear his take on Dylan's.

54 *Delmore Schwartz off the rails*: Atlas, pp. 361, 371.

54 *"Rockefeller's spies"*: Sterling Morrison in Harron, "The Lost History of the Velvet Underground."

55 *Alban Berg's dark, war-scarred opera*: Alex Ross, *The Rest Is Noise: Listening to the Twentieth Century* (Farrar, Straus and Giroux, 2007), 206–12.

56 *"At the time I wrote 'Heroin'"*: Lou Reed in Lester Bangs, "Dead Lie the Velvets, Underground," *Creem*, May, 1971.

3. LONG ISLAND > QUEENS (COMMUTING) > LOWER EAST SIDE

58 *"Let the musicians begin"*: Delmore Schwartz, "At a Solemn Musick" in Ben Mazer, ed., *The Collected Poems of Delmore Schwartz* (Farrar, Straus and Giroux, 2023).

58 *had a miserable homecoming*: "Students Protest U.S. Aid in Vietnam," *The New York Times*, May 3, 1964.

58 *"I said I wanted a gun"*: Lou Reed, *Between Thought And Expression: Selected Lyrics of Lou Reed*, p. 72. See also Lou Reed, "Fallen Knights and Fallen Ladies," in Robert Somma, ed., *No One Waved Goodbye* (Fusion/Outerbridge & Dienstfrey, 1971), p. 83.

59 *Pickwick marketed LPs*: John Broven, *Record Makers and Breakers: Voices of the Independent Rock 'n' Roll Pioneers* (University of Illinois Press, 2009), pp. 87–88.

59 *"He was this insecure guy"*: Aidan Levy, *Dirty Blvd.: The Life and Music of Lou Reed* (Chicago Review Press, 2015), pp. 79–83.

59 *"next stage of his career"*: Reed's ex-manager soon had bigger fish to fry; by the mid-'70s, he'd negotiated the sale of the Spirits of St. Louis to the NBA, once considered "the greatest sports deal of all time."

60 *"three or four albums"*: Reed in Bockris and Malanga, p. 19. The arrangement would seem not unlike those sponsored nowadays by companies who produce pseudonymous tracks by "fake artists" to paper playlists on streaming platforms.

61 *guitar strings to A#*: Branden W. Joseph, *Beyond the Dream Syndicate: Tony Conrad and the Arts After Cage* (Zone Books, 2008), p. 226. Joseph suggests the tuning was A#, which Conrad confirmed, though others have identified it as D. Reed would use "ostrich tuning" for other songs, including "Venus in Furs."

63 *"when I die"*: Rob Tannenbaum, "Minimalist Composer La Monte Young on His Life and Immeasurable Influence," *Vulture*, July 2, 2015.

64 *a fond farewell*: John Cale and Victor Bockris, *What's Welsh for Zen: The Autobiography of John Cale* (Bloomsbury, 1999), pp. 23, 28, 43–48.

64 The *Vexations review was mixed*: Harold C. Schonberg, Richard F. Shepard, Raymond Ericson, Brian O'Doherty, Sam Zolotow, Anon., Howard Klein, and Marjorie Rubin, "Music: A Long, Long, Long Night (and Day) at the Piano," *The New York Times*, September 11, 1963.

65 *the landmark experimental film*: A young German actor, soon to be known as Nico, was considered for the lead in *Last Year at Marienbad*, though it ultimately went to the French actor Delphine Seyrig.

65 *a year and a half*: The *South Bank Show*. Cale talks about using a bass bow.

66 *a true "multimedia artist"*: Johan Kugelberg, ed., *The Velvet Underground: New York Art* (Rizzoli, 2009).

67 *with calligraphic credits*: Zazeela's gorgeous, finely rendered line drawings illustrated the ads and program handouts for Young's performances throughout his career.

67 Flaming Creatures *was confiscated*: Menand, *The Free World*, pp. 579–600. See also J. Hoberman, *On Jack Smith's* Flaming Creatures *and Other Secret-Flix of Cinemaroc* (Hips Road, 2001); John Cale, *New York in the '60s* (Table of the Elements, 2004).

67 *"These tools can be used"*: Young in Keith Potter, *Four Musical Minimalists: La Monte Young, Terry Riley, Steve Reich, Philip Glass* (Cambridge University Press, 2000); Billy Name, John Cale in Cale and Bockris, pp. 59–60.

67   *"O was for opium"*: Cale and Bockris, p. 64.

68   *To Cale's ear*: K. Robert Schwarz, *Minimalists* (Phaidon, 1996), pp. 38–39; Bockris and Malanga, p. 13.

68   *showed up with Walter De Maria*: Walter De Maria, oral history interview, Archives of American Art, *Smithsonian* (aaa.si.edu), October 4, 1972.

69   *"That drone stuff"*: Reed in liner notes, *Between Thought and Expression: The Lou Reed Anthology*, p. 6.

69   *a wee-hours rehearsal*: Joseph, pp. 217–22. A cleaned-up version of "Won't You Smile," credited to Reed, Cale, Vance, and Phillips, would be recorded as "Why Don't You Smile Now?" by the Syracuse-based band the All Night Workers; it would be covered again by the U.K. garage-pop revivalists the Delmonas in 1986.

70   *The band's debut performance*: Conrad in Bockris and Malanga, pp. 20–21, and Jim Condon, "Three Interviews: Tony Conrad, Henry Flynt, Terry Riley," in Albin Zak III, ed., *The Velvet Underground Companion: Four Decades of Commentary* (Schirmer, 1997), pp. 38–40.

70   *"I really didn't pay"*: Cale in Legs McNeil and Gillian McCain, *Please Kill Me: The Uncensored Oral History of Punk* (Grove, 1996), p. 4.

71   *"an ease with language"*: Cale and Bockris, p. 69.

71   *"at first heroin makes you"*: Ibid., p. 73.

71   *"few sexual nudges"*: Ibid., p. 74.

71   *"my religious sensibility"*: Ibid., p. 20.

72   *"obsession with risk taking"*: Ibid., p. 73.

72   *Reed typed a lengthy*: Letter from Lou Reed to Delmore Schwartz, 1965. Delmore Schwartz papers, Yale Collection of American Literature, Beinecke Rare Book and Manuscript Library. As reprinted in *The Velvet Underground Experience* (2016; Hat & Beard, 2018), p. 43.

73   *56 Ludlow Street apartment*: Given how much significant culture emerged from 56 Ludlow Street, the building deserves landmark designation.

73   *A demo tape made*: Recording, 1965, Lou Reed Archive. Most of the demo was released on *Lou Reed: Words & Music, May 1965*.

74   *the folk-revival style*: *Gibson & Camp at the Gates of Horn*, the 1961 LP by the duo of Bob Gibson and Bob (né Hamilton) Camp, was influential among folkies in the early '60s, and Reed surely encountered it; its mix of sincerity and sarcasm would've been right up his alley. He was probably also familiar with *Tear Down the Walls* by the Greenwich Village fixtures Vince Martin and Fred Neil, released the previous spring.

74   *A more fleshed-out version*: Don Fleming and Jason Stern, "Archival Notes," *Lou Reed: Words & Music, May 1965*. Dialogue from unreleased recording of "Heroin" played by Hal Willner at Reed's memorial at the Apollo Theater, December 16, 2013.

76   *"this guy Rick's place"*: Morrison in Bockris and Malanga, p. 23. See also Jim DeRogatis, *The Velvet Underground: An Illustrated History of a Walk on the Wild Side* (Voyageur Press, 2009), p. 172.

77   *"I don't think of you"*: Reed quoted in Cale and Bockris, p. 73.

77   *two white folk musicians*: "1964—Harlem, New York City—Pt2 221120–15,"

YouTube (FootageFarm), December 11, 2013, https://www.youtube.com/watch?v=07X5Ux8uO18.

78 *"That was an education"*: Cale on *WTF with Marc Maron*, podcast, July 29, 2013.

78 *introduced herself as Elektrah*: Elena W, *Weirdland*, April 25, 2017.

78 *Lobel also played guitar*: Allan Jones, "John Cale on *The Velvet Underground & Nico*," *Uncut*, August 2006.

78 *a "ritual happening" organized*: Bockris and Malanga, p. 20. Morrison and Cale suggest *The Launching of the Dreamweapon* was the first show that the group played as the Velvet Underground; others date it to a subsequent iteration of MacLise's work, titled *Rites of the Dreamweapon: A Seven-Part Manifestation of the Presence*, presented at the Film-Makers Cinematheque on November 1. (A program from the event indeed notes "music by The Velvet Underground"). Cale also noted that the band was briefly known as the Velvet Hermaphrodite Jug Band. See also Olivier Landemaine, "The Velvet Underground: Live Performances and Rehearsals: 1965–66," *The Velvet Underground Web Page* (olivier.landemaine.free.fr), October 23, 2022; Unterberger, p. 50.

79 *Mekas was born*: Jonas Mekas with Adolfas Mekas, *I Seem to Live: The New York Diaries 1950–1969* (Spector, 2019). See also Jonas Mekas, *I Had No-Where to Go* (Spector, 1991), and Menand, *The Free World*, pp. 580–87.

79 *"center of the stage"*: Morrison in Kugelberg, p. 31.

79 *Broadway Central, a dilapidated*: The Mercer Arts Center became a petri dish for punk rock, video art, and other things in the early '70s, until its literal collapse in 1973, likely due to architectural supports having been knocked out by boundary-challenging.

80 *"through Surrealism, Dada"*: Allan Kaprow in Jeff Kelly, ed., "Happenings in the New York Scene," in *Essays on the Blurring of Art and Life* (University of California, 1993), p. 15.

81 *believed it was Angus MacLise*: Another version of the naming has Tony Conrad finding the book in the gutter on the Bowery.

81 *"the sexual corruption of our age"*: Michael Leigh, *The Velvet Underground* (1963; Wet Angel, 2011), pp. 18, 69.

82 *The title* Venus in Furs: Piero Heliczer, *Venus in Furs* in *The Velvet Underground*, directed by Todd Haynes (Criterion Collection, 2022); Roger Ebert, "Great Movies: *Bride of Frankenstein*," RogerEbert.com, January 3, 1999; Tom Raworth, "Obituary: Piero Heliczer," *The Independent*, August 11, 1993.

82 *"on the Hempstead Turnpike"*: Tucker in Legs McNeil, "Moe Tucker: On the Velvet Underground," pleasekillme.com, November 21, 2017.

82 *the Beatles' "This Boy"*: Tucker in Corbin Reiff, "View from the Drummer's Seat: Moe Tucker Remembers Her Time in the Velvet Underground," *Uproxx*, March 15, 2018.

83 *"purity of spirit"*: Reed in Johan Kugelberg and Will Cameron, curators, *Dreamweapon: The Art and Life of Angus MacLise (1938–1979)*, exhibit, Boo-Hooray gallery, 2011.

83 *"I came to love Lou"*: Tucker in Legs McNeil, "Moe Tucker—Snapshots of the Velvet Underground" *Vice*, January 21, 2014.

84 *"like some transcendent creature"*: Amy Taubin with Chuck Smith, "She Picked Up a Camera and Decided to Be a Filmmaker: Amy Taubin on Barbara Rubin," in Jonas

Mekas, ed., *Film Culture 80: The Legend of Barbara Rubin* (Spector Books, 2018), p. 41. See also Ara Osterweil, "Absently Enchanted: The Apocryphal, Ecstatic Cinema of Barbara Rubin," in Robin Blaetz, ed., *Women's Experimental Cinema: Critical Frameworks* (Duke University Press, 2007).

85   *"one of my gurus"*: Richard Foreman, *"Christmas on Earth*: An Overwhelming Great Experience of My Life," in Mekas, *Film Culture 80*, p. 53.

85   *"most idealistic human"*: Ibid., p. 5.

85   *"posing as poets"*: Al Aronowitz in Mike Miliard, "The Go-Between," *The Boston Phoenix*, December 3–9, 2004. See also Al Aronowitz, "The Origins of the Velvet Underground," *The Blacklisted Journalist*, December 1, 2002.

86   *"barricaded themselves"*: Ibid.

86   *"I liked a couple"*: Robbie Robertson, *Testimony* (Three Rivers, 2016), p. 208.

87   *"like a groupie"*: Carole King, *A Natural Woman* (Grand Central Publishing, 2012), p. 133.

87   *from nearby Berkeley Heights*: Mia Wolff, author interview, 2015; Rob Norris's "I Was a Teenage Velveteen," Kugelberg, p. 43.

88   *"how violent America is"*: Lou Reed in Mick Rock, "Penthouse Interview: Still Walking the Wild Side," *Penthouse*, May 1977.

89   *"a nervous wreck"*: Tucker in McNeil, "Moe Tucker: On the Velvet Underground."

90   *"stick to your surfboard"*: "Susie Surfer" column in *East Brunswick Sentinel*, December 16 and 30, 1965, excerpted in Bart Bealmear, "A Mysterious Army of Angry Velvet Underground Fans Respond to Negative Review of First VU Show, 1965," *Dangerous Minds*, February 9, 2018.

90   *"all those East Village junkies"*: Ruskin in John Grafitti, "Lower East Side Funk," *East Village Other*, February 1, 1966; Daniel Kane, *All Poets Welcome: The Lower East Side Poetry Scene in the 1960s* (University of California, 2003).

91   *"Donald Judd lived"*: Ruskin to Danny Fields, 1974, in Steven Kasher, ed., *Max's Kansas City* (Abrams Image, 2010).

91   *"three nervous breakdowns"*: Andy Warhol, *The Philosophy of Andy Warhol (from A to B and Back Again)* (Harcourt, 1975), p. 21. See also Blake Gopnik, *Warhol* (Ecco, 2020), p. 23.

92   *two dozen times*: Gopnik, p. 312.

93   *filmmaker Naomi Levine*: Gary Comenas, "Notes on Naomi Levine," warholstars .org, 2014.

93   *upped the provocation ante*: Gopnik, p. 381; Bob Egan, "Lou Reed—The Velvet Underground," *Pop Spots* (popspotsnyc.org). For the record, the curved Art Deco furniture star of Warhol's porny film *Couch*—the crimson velvet sofa that Billy Name salvaged off the street—was not the one on the cover of the third Velvet Underground LP. The red one was stolen when the Factory moved downtown.

93   *"people to notice me"*: Andy Warhol and Pat Hackett, *POPism: The Warhol Sixties* (Houghton Mifflin Harcourt, 1980), p. 59.

94   *his criminal portraits*: Douglas Crimp and Richard Meyer, "Imagine the Police Raiding a Film Called *Blow Job* and Finding a Forty-Minute Silent Portrait of a Man's Face!" in Gilda Williams, ed., *On&By Andy Warhol* (MIT Press, 2016), pp. 239–41.

94   *a rough upbringing*: Gopnik, pp. 423–24.

95   *"hard to define"*: Warhol, *Philosophy*, p. 91. See also Mary Harron, "Pop Art/Art

Pop: The Andy Warhol Connection," *Melody Maker*, February 16, 1980, as reprinted in Barney Hoskyns, ed., *The Sound and The Fury: 40 Years of Classic Rock Journalism* (Bloomsbury, 2003), p. 362.

95 *Edith Sitwell's* Façade: Edith Sitwell and William Walton, *Façade* (Columbia Masterworks, 1949). The recording, with Sitwell reciting nonsense verse over music by Walton, also featured Constant Lambert, the British conductor-composer whose son Kit would manage the Who.

95 *art-star supergroup*: Gopnik, pp. 297–98, 415. La Monte Young, the most musically accomplished of the Druds, was the first to quit. But he and Warhol stayed in touch: in the fall of '64, Young provided an aggressively loud drone soundtrack to a "screening" of Warhol film segments on video monitors at the third annual New York Film Festival at Lincoln Center.

96 *The Fugs, a band*: Reva Wolf, *Andy Warhol, Poetry, and Gossip in the 1960s* (University of Chicago Press, 1997), pp. 55–61.

96 *"six nights a week"*: Morrison in Clinton Heylin, *From the Velvets to the Voidoids: The Birth of American Punk Rock* (Chicago Review Press, 2005), p. 14.

97 *to finally kiss him*: Andy Warhol, letter to Gerard Malanga, March 20, 1963, *Gay Gotham*, exhibit, Museum of the City of New York, 2016.

97 *"cultural cosa nostra"*: Ed McCormack, "Lou Reed: Revising The Legend," *Fusion*, September 1972, reprinted in Heath and Thomas, pp. 21–26.

97 *bring his bullwhip*: Ara Osterweil, "Absently Enchanted: The Apocryphal, Ecstatic Cinema of Barbara Rubin," in Blaetz, p. 132.

97 *never-completed epic*: Mekas, *Film Culture 80*, p. 105. Rubin's fabulist list of "DESIRED STARS & HEROES, HEROINES" for *Christmas on Earth Continued* included Reed, Cale, Dylan, the Beatles, Bing Crosby, Brigitte Bardot, Jean Genet, Groucho Marx, Jean-Luc Godard, and dozens of others.

97 *"hyperactive young man"*: Victor Bockris, *Warhol: The Biography* (1989; Da Capo Press, 2003), p. 231. See also Gary Comenas, "Paul Morrissey," warholstars.org.

98 *"dazed and damaged"*: Warhol and Hackett, p. 180.

98 *"oil and water"*: Malanga in Bockris, *Warhol*, p. 229.

98 *Reed surely knew*: Thomas Meehan, "Not Good Taste, Not Bad Taste—It's 'Camp,'" *The New York Times Magazine*, March 21, 1965. Given his circle, one imagines Reed was aware of the Pop Art movement and had a grasp of camp aesthetics, whether or not he read the touchstone *Times Magazine* piece or Susan Sontag's defining '64 *Partisan Review* essay "Notes on Camp."

98 *"He was hot shit"*: Tucker to McNeil, "Moe Tucker: Snapshots of the Velvet Underground."

99 *"bunch of junkie hustlers"*: Aronowitz.

99 *"The exact words"*: Reed in John Wilcock, *The Autobiography and Sex Life of Andy Warhol*, ed. Christopher Trela (1971; Trela, 2010), p. 178.

99 *"usually pretty quiet"*: Morrison in Stephen Shore and Lynne Tillman, *The Velvet Years: Warhol's Factory 1965–67* (Thunder's Mouth, 1995), pp. 89–90.

100 *The segment began*: "The Making of an Underground Film—CBS News 1965," as posted in Colin Marshall, "*CBS Evening News with Walter Cronkite* Introduces America to Underground Films and the Velvet Underground (1965)," *Open Culture*, January 6, 2016.

100 *"we had rats"*: Reed, "My First Year in New York," *The New York Times Magazine*, September 17, 2000.

4. LOWER EAST SIDE

103 *Lee Strasberg Studio*: Jennifer Otter Bickerdike, *You Are Beautiful and You Are Alone: The Biography of Nico* (Hachette, 2021), pp. 392–93.

103 *Poitrenaud's 1963* Strip-Tease: *Strip-Tease* was alternately released under the titles *Sweet Skin* and *La Ragazza Nuda*.

103 *Serge Gainsbourg's debut*: Liner notes, *Le Cinéma de Serge Gainsbourg: Musiques de Films 1959–1990* (EmArcy, 2001). Nico's 1962 demo of "Strip-Tease" was included on the compilation.

104 *"I'll Keep It with Mine"*: Robert Shelton, *No Direction Home: The Life and Music of Bob Dylan* (1986; Da Capo, 1997), p. 336; Bickerdike, pp. 67–68.

104 *wine-soaked oranges*: Warhol and Hackett, p. 182. The "Mexican" restaurant where Warhol and Nico first met may well have been El Quijote, the Spanish restaurant in the Chelsea Hotel.

105 *LSD-fueled night*: Aronowitz. "It was very romantic but after she took off her clothes and got into the motel bed, she wouldn't give me any," he wrote ickily. Nico maintained she'd seen the Velvets before Warhol did, suggesting that at least part of Aronowitz's account is accurate. Ignacio Juliá, *Linger On: The Velvet Underground: Legend, Truth, Interviews* (Ecstatic Peace, 2023), p. 99.

105 *"had no lead singer"*: McNeil and McCain, p. 7.

105 *"we had a chanteuse"*: Reed in *American Masters: Lou Reed: Rock and Roll Heart* (PBS, 1996).

106 *got stoned with Dylan*: Bruce Spizer, "The Story Behind the Beatles on Ed Sullivan," *The Internet Beatles Album* (beatlesagain.com), 2006.

106 *"invited to speak"*: Warhol and Hackett, p. 183.

107 *10 billion amphetamine tablets*: Nicolas Rasmussen, *On Speed: The Many Lives of Amphetamine* (NYU Press, 2008), p. 177, and Nicolas Rasmussen, "America's First Amphetamine Epidemic 1929–1971: A Quantitative and Qualitative Retrospective with Implications for the Present," *The American Journal of Public Health*, June 2008.

108 *President Kennedy got*: Rasmussen, "America's First Amphetamine Epidemic 1929–1971."

108 *"bowl of amphetamines"*: Danny Fields in Shore and Tillman, p. 111.

109 *"just a big joke"*: Tom Doyle, "Lou Reed—Cash for Question," *Q*, May 2000.

109 *Mekas would eventually*: Jonas Mekas, *Scenes from the Life of Andy Warhol* (1990). Mekas's footage of the Delmonico event, alongside some of the Velvets performing at the Dom later that year, was used in this film; sadly, the Delmonico footage evidently had no sound, and the Dom audio is so distorted it's nearly unlistenable. The Delmonico footage also circulated as a three-minute short under the misleading title *Velvet Underground's First Public Appearance* (1966).

110 *motion picture "wallpaper"*: Andy Warhol and Paul Morrissey, *The Velvet Underground and Nico: A Symphony of Sound* (1966).

110 *the police show up*: The verité scenario of cops breaking up the rehearsal would be echoed in both Michael Lindsay-Hogg's *Let It Be* (1970, the Beatles performing guerrilla-style on a London roof), and Jean-Luc Godard and D. A. Pennebaker's

(One A.M.) One P.M. (1972, with Jefferson Airplane doing the same on a New York City roof).

110 *Edie Sedgwick, "Femme Fatale"*: Bockris, *Transformer*, p. 107.

111 *"that's our conversation"*: Shelley Albin, author interview.

111 *a coughing fit*: The Velvet Underground, *All Tomorrow's Parties* (bootleg, March 1966). The Factory rehearsal recording is the earliest known version of "Mirror."

111 *"very soft and lovely"*: Nico in Jean Stein, *Edie: American Girl*, ed. George Plimpton (Grove, 1982), p. 220.

111 *"kind of abstract concept"*: Morrison in Steven Watson, *Factory Made: Warhol and the Sixties* (Pantheon, 2003), p. 257. Cutrone in McNeil and McCain, pp. 18–19.

111 *"Lou liked to manipulate"*: Nico in McNeil and McCain, p. 10.

113 *"loved him on sight"*: Reed in Gopnik, p. 480.

113 *the four Screen Tests*: Andy Warhol, Screen Tests, 1964–66. In ST268, Reed slowly eats an apple, Eve-like; in ST270, he nuzzles a Hershey's chocolate bar. In another, he stares straight at the camera, motionless and sans props. Warhol evidently didn't tire of looking at Reed's face.

113 *"Andy's Mickey Mouse"*: Billy Name in Howard Sounes, *Notes from the Velvet Underground: The Life of Lou Reed* (Doubleday U.K., 2015), p. 71.

114 *"the hottest, sexiest thing"*: Fields in McNeil and McCain, pp. 10, 15.

114 *"work very, very hard"*: Reed in Kugelberg, p. 86.

114 *"like a hawk"*: Reed in Gopnik, p. 466.

115 *"first Mrs. La Monte Young"*: Cale and Bockris, p. 74.

115 *"queen bitch and spit"*: Cale in McNeil and McCain, p. 9.

115 *"me, Edie, Andy, everyone"*: Fields in Stein and Plimpton, p. 220.

116 *"rigid and paranoid"*: Cutrone in Watson, p. 259.

116 *"used to make tapes"*: Reed in Kugelberg, p. 86.

117 *"Nico kept insisting"*: Morrison in Bockris and Malanga, p. 53.

117 *the Velvets' heroin costs*: Gopnik, p. 494.

117 *no mention of Reed*: Archer Winsten, "Reviewing Stand: Andy Warhol at Cinema-theque," *New York Post*, February 9, 1966.

117 *"whines, whistles, and wails"*: Wilcock and Trela, p. 164.

118 *"just couldn't care less"*: Nico in Jim Condon, "The Perils of Nico," in Zak, p. 44.

118 *oversized pink plastic syringe*: Mary Woronov, *Swimming Underground: My Time at Andy Warhol's Factory* (Montaldo, 2013), loc. 243.

119 *upstairs ballroom was rented*: Ada Calhoun, *St. Marks Is Dead* (Norton, 2015), pp. 131–56. Another good overview of the Dom's history, including its later incarnations as the Balloon Farm and the Electric Circus, appears in the excellent New York City music history blog *All the Streets You Crossed Not So Long Ago*.

120 *Colored slides projected images*: Among the East Coast light show precedents, in addition to Jackie Cassen and Rudi Stern, La Monte Young's Theater of Eternal Music began performing with Marian Zazeela's "light sculptures" in December '65. See also Robin Oppenheimer, "Maximal Art: The Origin and Aesthetics of West Coast Light Shows," *Rhizome*, April 15, 2009.

121 *"There wasn't anything"*: Woronov in Gopnik, p. 492. In a bit of poetic history, the Velvets would begin recording their debut LP that month in the same building that would house Studio 54 a decade later.

121 *priestess in a pantsuit*: Joe Coscarelli and Larry C. Morris, "Never-Before-Seen

Photos of the Velvet Underground in 1966"/"One Night at the Dom: History in the Making," *The New York Times*, March 14, 2017. See also Marilyn Bender, "Black Jeans to Go Dancing at the Movies: It's Inevitable," *The New York Times*, April 11, 1966. John Wilcock, "'High' School of Music and Art," *The East Village Other*, April 1–15, 1966.

122 *"magnificent god realm"*: Anne Waldman, "Foreword: WORDS ONLY HAVE WORDS OF MEMORIES," in Lou Reed, *Do Angels Need Haircuts?* (Anthology Editions, 2018), p. viii.

122 *John Ashbery turned up*: Tony Scherman and David Dalton, *Pop: The Genius of Andy Warhol* (HarperCollins, 2009), p. 233; Kane, p. 72.

122 *"your living room"*: Tucker in McNeil, "Moe Tucker: On the Velvet Underground."

122 *"halfway knew them"*: Warhol and Hackett, p. 204.

122 *the Mattachine Society*: Thomas A. Johnson, "3 Deviates Invite Exclusion by Bars," *The New York Times*, April 22, 1966.

123 *"jars of Vaseline"*: Warhol and Hackett, p. 203.

123 *Its all-text cover image*: Vahanian's startlingly successful 1961 book, *The Death of God*, helped brand a theological scholarly movement that the *Time* cover package distilled. Pre-social-media clickbait of the highest order, the "Is God Dead?" cover of the April 8, 1966, issue, along with the accompanying article by *Time*'s religion editor John Elson ("Toward a Hidden God"), is said to have triggered more reader response than any piece in the magazine's history.

123 *turned to Norman Dolph*: Dolph in Unterberger, pp. 85–93; Joe Harvard, *The Velvet Underground & Nico* (Continuum, 2004), pp. 79–91; *The Velvet Underground: Under Review*, directed by Tom Barbor-Might (Sexy Intellectual, 2006).

124 *"He argued against restraint"*: Morrison in Harron, "Pop Art/Art Pop."

125 *horrors personal and cultural*: Jon Stratton, "Jews, Punk, and the Holocaust: From the Velvet Underground to the Ramones—the Jewish-American Story," in *Popular Music Volume 24/1* (Cambridge University Press, 2005), pp. 79–105.

125 *"a sound in mind"*: Dylan in Jann Wenner, "Bob Dylan Talks: A Raw and Extensive First *Rolling Stone* Interview," *Rolling Stone*, November 29, 1969.

125 *"curiously empowering"*: Van Dyke Parks in Michael Hall, "The Greatest Music Producer You've Never Heard of Is . . ." *Texas Monthly*, January 2014.

126 *"didn't bat an eye"*: Cale in David Browne, "Remembering Bob Dylan and Velvet Underground's Pioneering Producer," *Rolling Stone*, November 4, 2015.

126 *"money broke Andy's relations"*: Woronov in Cale and Bockris, p. 97.

127 *Blue Cheer–brand LSD*: Dennis McNally, *What a Long Strange Trip: The Inside History of the Grateful Dead* (Broadway, 2002), p. 138.

127 *"We were like, great"*: Cale on *WTF with Marc Maron*.

127 *club's financial problems*: unbylined item, *Variety*, May 17, 1966.

128 *"to go to church"*: Tucker in McNeil, "Moe Tucker—Snapshots of the Velvet Underground.

128 *"I couldn't hear shit"*: Tucker in *The Velvet Underground: Under Review*.

129 *"worst piece of entertainment"*: Bill Graham to Leonard Feather, "Rock Palace King Cools It with Jazz," *Los Angeles Times*, March 10, 1968, reprinted in Alfredo García, *The Inevitable World of the Velvet Underground* (Self-published, 2011), p. 229.

130 *"They were homophobic; we were homosexual"*: Mary Woronov in Martin Torgoff, *Can't*

Find My Way Home: America in the Great Stoned Age, 1945–2000 (Simon & Schuster, 2005), pp. 158–59.

130 *"all the bum trips"*: Ralph J. Gleason, "The Sizzle That Fizzled," *San Francisco Chronicle*, May 30, 1966.

131 *"better wear earplugs"*: "Wild New Flashy Bedlam of the Discothèque," *Life*, May 27, 1966.

131 *decadent, pill-popping*: Amy Fine Collins, "Once Was Never Enough," *Vanity Fair*, August 26, 2013.

131 *dirty amphetamine shot*: Sounes, p. 85; Jon Savage, *1966: The Year the Decade Exploded* (Faber and Faber U.K., 2016), p. 227.

131 *nightclub called Poor Richard's*: Ron Nameth, *Exploding Plastic Inevitable (aka Andy Warhol's Exploding Plastic Inevitable with the Velvet Underground)* (1966); Juliá, p. 39.

131 *obituary in* The New York Times: "Delmore Schwartz Dies at 52; Poet Won 1959 Bollingen Prize," *The New York Times*, July 14, 1966.

132 *"Delmore was Jewish"*: Clara Colle in Atlas, pp. 374–79; Unterberger, p. 108.

133 *Williams was never found*: Esther Robinson, *A Walk into the Sea: Danny Williams and the Warhol Factory* (Chicken & Egg, 2007).

134 *"The kids know that"*: Richard Goldstein, "A Quiet Night at the Balloon Farm," *New York World Journal Tribune*, October 16, 1966.

134 *"I make it all up"*: Gretchen Berg, "Andy Warhol: My True Story," *The East Village Other*, November 1, 1966. As reprinted in Williams, pp. 31–39, 226.

134 *a flexidisc single*: Christophe Levaux, "Loop," *Rock Music Studies* 3:2 (2016), pp. 167–79. The flexidisc also featured music by the raga-loving guitar virtuoso Peter Walker, credited as the "musical director for Tim Leary's touring psychedelic celebration."

134 *"music was so beautiful"*: Reed in "A View from the Bandstand," *Aspen* 1, no. 3 (*The Fab Issue*), December 1966.

135 *"a very sexy, groovy banana"*: Reed in Watson, p. 296; Olivier Landemaine, "Going Bananas," *The Velvet Underground Web Page*.

135 *"uhh, exciting rock'n'roll"*: Nico in Savage, p. 191.

136 *shorter films shot over*: Greg Pierce, *"The Chelsea Girls* Exploded: The Films Within the Film," in Geralyn Huxley and Greg Pierce, eds., *Andy Warhol's* The Chelsea Girls (Andy Warhol Museum/DAP, 2018), pp. 199–227.

136 *"so paranoid anyway"*: Reed in Mick Rock, "Lou Reed", *Rolling Stone*, October 26, 1972; Unterberger, p. 116.

137 *Yardbirds and the Velvets*: Jimmy Page in Julian Marszalek, "Glitter and Hypnosis: Jimmy Page Interviewed," *The Quietus*, November 6, 2014.

137 *"tentacles around my mind"*: David Bowie, "Bowie Rules NYC," *New York*, September 18, 2003.

5. LOWER EAST SIDE > UPPER EAST SIDE > LOS ANGELES > BOSTON

138 *move, mentally and spiritually*: Morrison in Bockris and Malanga, p. 142.

138 *"aggressive going to God"*: Reed in David Fricke, liner notes, *White Light/White Heat: 45th Anniversary Super Deluxe Edition* (Polydor/Universal, 2013).

139 *at the Garrick Theatre*: Frank Zappa with Peter Occhiogrosso, *The Real Frank Zappa Book* (Touchstone, 1989), p. 91.

140   *tiny, noisy, bug-infested*: Reed, "My First Year in New York: 1965."

140   *"So she photographs great"*: Bockris and Malanga, p. 105.

140   *"the most beautiful woman"*: Cohen in Jeff Burger, *Leonard Cohen on Leonard Cohen: Interviews and Encounters* (Chicago Review Press, 2014), p. 68.

140   *"that kind of shit"*: Reed in Scott Cohen, "The Portable Leonard Cohen," *SPIN*, August 1985. See also Kris Kirk, "As a New Generation Discovers Leonard Cohen's Dark Humour, Kris Kirk Ruffles the Great Man's Back Pages," *Poetry Commotion*, June 18, 1988.

141   *Warhol contributed "Cock"*: Intransit (The Andy Warhol–Gerard Malanga Monster Issue) (Toad Press, 1968), pp. 50–54. The readymade text of "Cock" was expanded in Andy Warhol, *a: A Novel* (Grove/Atlantic, 1968).

141   *a Be-In at the Sheep Meadow*: "BE-IN 1967 Central Park, New York—The Lost Ektachrome Footage, Easter Sunday," YouTube (Eidolon Media), August 25, 2015, https://www.youtube.com/watch?v=37yTkaZM_u4.

142   *"my bass player"*: Jarrod Dicker, "Interview with Danny Fields," *Stay Thirsty*, July 2009.

143   *"It was awesome"*: Chris Stein, author interview. Stein would form Blondie with Debbie Harry some years later.

144   *"Everybody was liberated"*: Cutrone in Bockris and Malanga, p. 124.

145   *the Venice Biennale*: Gopnik, p. 511.

146   *"offers me a joint"*: Reed in David Fricke, "Lou Reed: The Rolling Stone Interview," *Rolling Stone*, May 4, 1989.

147   *"He was really mad"*: Ibid.

147   *with God singing solo*: Hunter S. Thompson, "The 'Hashbury' Is the Capital of the Hippies," *The New York Times Magazine*, May 14, 1967, pp. 29, 120–22.

148   *"Teenage ninnies flocked"*: Morrison in Bockris and Malanga, p. 138.

149   *at the Leather Man*: Warhol and Hackett, pp. 281–86, 308. See also Gary Comenas, "*Glamour, Glory and Gold* by Jackie Curtis," warholstars.org. Warhol recalled that the production starred an impressive young actor named Robert De Niro, making his stage debut. Another account has Warhol meeting Darling for the first time at Max's around the same time, which doesn't seem implausible; see Gopnik, p. 637.

149   *hot-rodded his Gretsch*: Bozrahindrid, post, *The Gear Page*, October 24, 2009; Jonathan Richman in Bockris and Malanga, pp. 138–39.

149   *film of the Velvets*: Ryan H. Walsh, *Astral Weeks: A Secret History of 1968* (Penguin, 2018), pp. 118–19.

150   *"angry at Lou"*: Cale and Bockris, p. 106.

151   *"pure white light"*: Alice A. Bailey. *A Treatise on White Magic* (Lucis Trust, 1951; 1979), p. 161. Reed from interview on KVAN radio, Portland, Oregon, November 1969. Reed was likely introduced to Bailey's writing via Angus MacLise, who gave him a copy of *The Morning of the Magicians*, the occultist history volume by Louis Pauwels and Jacques Bergier that popularized "new age" ideas in the mid-1960s.

151   *"was very emphatic that"*: Norris in Walsh, p. 123.

152   *Reed referred to it*: Reed to unknown interviewer, Lou Reed Archive (recording 560544), 1967. See also Fricke, liner notes, *White Light/White Heat: 45th Anniversary Super Deluxe Edition*, and Bangs, "Dead Lie the Velvets, Underground."

152   *Cecil Taylor and Ornette Coleman*: Bangs, "Dead Lie the Velvets, Underground."

A less successful song from this period was titled "Ondine," a jam that fittingly sounded like a bunch of speed freaks noodling away at cross-purposes; see "Ondine," recording, Lou Reed Archive, 1967–68.

153 *"great deal of chemicals"*: Cale and Bockris, p. 108.

154 *"a really good crotch"*: Johnson in Sheila Weller, "A Role Model, Still," *The New York Times*, February 15, 2015.

154 *Debbie Harry played it*: Debbie Harry, author interview, 2013.

155 *thirty-nine-minute slow-jam*: The languorous opening-up of "Sweet Sister Ray" was not unlike what the Grateful Dead did with "Dark Star," which was issued that month as a single. Morrison has referred to an unreleased song, "Sweet Rock'n'Roll," that was an occasional preamble to "Sister Ray;" this seems like a variation of that combo. See Juliá, p. 69 and Landemaine, "The Velvet Underground: Lost Songs," *The Velvet Underground Web Page*.

155 *"a lot of tension"*: Tucker in Bockris and Malanga, p. 149; Morrison in Bockris, *Transformer*, p. 161.

156 *"a cherry bomb exploding"*: Warhol and Hackett, p. 343.

157 *wasn't the first time a gun*: Gopnik, pp. 416–17, 527, 549–51.

157 *as an assassination*: Fricke, liner notes, *The Velvet Underground: 45th Anniversary Super Deluxe Edition* (Polydor, 2014), p. 41. According to Doug Yule, the shooting was "an important event for [Reed], something he absorbed for years."

158 *"most incredible musical experiences"*: Bangs, "Dead Lie the Velvets, Underground."

158 *"the trust was gone"*: Cale in *The Velvet Undergound*, directed by Todd Haynes.

158 *time for a change*: Unterberger, pp. 202–203.

159 *"a brother-sister relationship"*: Moe Tucker, author interview, 2021.

159 *"do his dirty work"*: Bockris, *Transformer*, p. 167.

160 *"incredible pissing match"*: Kaus in M. C. Kostek, Alfredo García, and Ignacio Juliá, eds., *The Velvet Underground: I Met Myself in a Dream . . . That's the Story of the Third Album* (Velvet Underground Appreciation Society, 2019), p. 273. See also Nancy Friedman, "The Hollywood Studio Proudly Named for an Arabic Swear Word," *Slate*, June 1, 2016.

161 *devices were stolen*: Bockris, *Transformer*, pp. 172–73. Yule doesn't recall the gear theft Morrison mentioned, and maintained the band was already playing live without any distortion boxes when the LP sessions began.

161 *the atmospheric* Astral Weeks: Walsh, pp. 124–27. NB: Also issued in early 1968 was the Band's *Music from Big Pink*; its spare, dry, pointedly unpsychedelic approach would have an outsized influence on the sound of the era's rock music going forward.

161 *"best song I've written"*: Reed in Bangs, "Dead Lie the Velvets, Underground."

162 *genitals as "my flaw"*: Warhol and Hackett, p. 282. See also Richard Avedon, *Andy Warhol and Members of the Factory, New York City, October 30, 1969* (1969), a Factory family portrait in which Darling stands naked and radiant.

162 *"look in the mirror"*: Reed in liner notes, *Peel Slowly and See*.

163 *character named Jenny*: *The Velvet Underground/La Cave 1968: Problems in Urban Living* (October 4, 1968; Keyhole, 2012).

163 *"Her eyes were hazel"*: Reed, *Between Thought and Expression: Selected Lyrics of Lou Reed*, p. 23.

163 *mash note to Warhol*: Gopnik, p. 640.

164   *like silver light beaming*: Brian Eno discusses Reed's "inspiring" guitar playing in Kristine McKenna, "Before and After Silence," *Arthur*, July 2005.

164   *"fun with words"*: Reed and Morrison, liner notes, *Peel Slowly and See*.

6. NYC > SAN FRANCISCO > MAX'S KANSAS CITY > LONG ISLAND

167   *threatened Warhol, demanding*: Gopnik, pp. 685–86.

168   *"for stealing a car"*: Reed in Wilcock and Trela, pp. 184–85.

168   *"the closet mix"*: The LP was issued in the U.K. and elsewhere with a plusher mix by Val Valentin.

168   *issue of* Harper's Bazaar: The issue Reed is holding, as Name's original photos show, has cover blurbs trumpeting metaphysical themes: a haute-couture spread titled "The Cult of the Zodiac," and features billed as "Beauty Sorcery," "Astrology & Wall Street," and "A Glossary of the Occult."

169   *"the most important lesson"*: Lester Bangs, review of *The Velvet Underground*, *Rolling Stone*, May 17, 1969.

169   *"can't get your record"*: Tucker in Bockris and Malanga, p. 176.

169   *"other side of us"*: Reed from a June 1994 interview, in Fricke, liner notes, *The Velvet Underground: 45th Anniversary Super Deluxe Edition*.

170   *"think it's just fantastic"*: Reed from interview with DJ Mississippi Harold Wilson on WBCN-FM, March 3, 1969.

170   *"We had vast objections"*: Reed in Bockris, *Transformer*, p. 136; "The Velvets and the Dead," *Grateful Dead Guide*, deadessays.blogspot.com, September 7, 2010.

171   *"for like an hour"*: Doug Yule in Sal Mercuri, "Head Held High," *The Velvet Underground* fanzine vol. 3, Fall/Winter 1994.

171   *accidentally ingested some LSD*: Scott Richardson, author interview; see also Steve Miller, *Detroit Rock City: The Uncensored History of Rock 'n' Roll in America's Loudest City* (Da Capo, 2013), p. 26.

171   *"all in a row"*: Reed in David Fricke, "Lou Reed: The *Rolling Stone* Interview."

171   *"a bridge between"*: Morrison in Unterberger, p. 237.

173   *"life on this planet"*: Reed in Fricke, liner notes, *Peel Slowly and See*.

174   *program of gay porn*: Gary Comenas, "Andy Warhol's 'Porn Movie-House,'" warholstars.org.

174   *forty-five-minute "Sister Ray"*: Bob Kachnycz, "Philadelphia 1969, 1970," in *What Goes On* #5, referenced in Unterberger, p. 241. The account of the forty-five-minute version in 1969 remains apocryphal; no recording seems to exist.

176   *were booked in Austin*: The Velvets' three-night run at the Vulcan, October 23–25, was a watershed for the nascent Austin music scene, which would become a center of unconventional roots music; see Barry Shank, *Dissonant Identities: The Rock'n'Roll Scene in Austin, Texas* (Wesleyan University Press, 1994).

176   *"It was insane"*: Reed in Lenny Kaye, "Lou Reed," *New Musical Express*, January 24, 1976. Tucker in Fricke, liner notes, *The Velvet Underground: 45th Anniversary Super Deluxe Edition*. See also Olivier Landemaine, "The Velvet Underground: Live Performances and Rehearsals 1969," *The Velvet Underground Web Page*.

177   *"bug his eyes out"*: Aral Sezen, *What Goes On* vol. 5, 1996.

178   *installed a four-track*: James Sullivan, "Velvet Underground Had a Hippie Side," *San Francisco Chronicle*/*SFGATE*, November 18, 2001. See also David Fricke, liner notes

to *The Complete Matrix Tapes* (Universal, 2015). Some of the San Francisco shows were also recorded on a portable recorder by Reed's superfan and future bandmate Robert Quine.

178   *"be on your toes"*: Doug Yule in Fricke, liner notes, *The Velvet Underground: 45th Anniversary Super Deluxe Edition*; Unterberger, p. 257.

179   *"a form of yoga"*: Reed from interview at KVAN, Portland, Oregon, November 19 or 20, 1969.

179   *four or five people*: Robert Quine, liner notes to *The Velvet Underground Bootleg Series Volume One: The Quine Tapes* (Polydor, 2001). Reed quotes from various live recordings made at the Matrix, November 1969.

182   *"something about Jonathan"*: Reed and Morrison in Tim Mitchell, *There's Something About Jonathan* (Peter Owen, 1999), pp. 22–24.

182   *a "student" of the band*: Richman in *The Velvet Underground*, directed by Todd Haynes.

182   *"They saw how important"*: Richman from radio interview, WYEP-FM, Pittsburgh, October 28, 2015.

183   *"maybe a touch of archness"*: Richman, fax correspondence with author, 2016.

183   *"man-dresses"*: In the States, Bowie's LP was initially released with cartoon cover art—of a man holding what looked like a rifle—presumably less likely to disturb transphobes.

183   *Chicago's Quiet Knight*: Lynn Van Matre, "The Savage Sound of Velvet," *Chicago Tribune*, January 16, 1970.

184   *it had lost $17 million*: Jim Nash and Ben Fong-Torres, "MGM: 'We Inherited a Very Sick Company,'" *Rolling Stone*, March 7, 1970. The magazine described MGM's music wing as "falling all over itself for the past three years. The company had been mishandled from top to bottom, and employees were involved in everything from petty pilfering to outright forgery."

184   *"excellent rock sensibilities"*: Morrison in liner notes, *Peel Slowly and See*.

185   *"I was so fat"*: Tucker in Bockris and Malanga, pp. 186–89.

185   *beat of Babatunde Olatunji's*: Jason Gross, "Maureen Tucker Interview," *Perfect Sound Forever*, May 1998.

186   *"shaved his head completely"*: Warhol and Hackett, p. 290.

188   *"I loved that lick"*: Reed to Costello on *Spectacle*. See also Reed, liner notes, *Peel Slowly and See*.

188   *the "Hah!" he spits out*: Marc Spitz, "The Real Genius of 'Sweet Jane': The 2 Little Letters out of Lou Reed's Mouth That Say So Much," *Salon*, October 25, 2015.

188   *"in front of his past"*: Yule in Pat Thomas, "Doug Yule interview," *Perfect Sound Forever*, October 21, 1995.

189   *cult grown "almost religious"*: Lenny Kaye, "The Velvet Underground," *New Times*, April 20, 1970.

189   *"fantastic to dance to"*: Patti Smith, *Just Kids* (Ecco, 2010), pp. 159–60. See also Patti Smith, Rock and Roll Hall of Fame induction speech for Lou Reed, 2015.

190   *"scene in Star Wars"*: Yule in Thomas. See also Richard Nusser, "No Pale Imitation," *The Village Voice*, July 2, 1970; Mike Jahn, "'Velvet' Rock Group Opens Stand Here," *The New York Times*, July 4, 1970; Tom Mancuso, "Kansas City in the Summertime," *Fusion*, September 8, 1970; liner notes, *The Velvet Underground Live at Max's Kansas City* (Atlantic/Rhino, 2004).

191 *"have been terribly wrong"*: Tucker and Morrison in Bockris and Malanga, pp. 189–92. Yule in Thomas.

195 *the bourgeois adolescent*: Delmore Schwartz, "Rimbaud in Our Time" and "The Fabulous Example of Andre Gidé," reprinted in Donald A. Dike and David H. Zucker, eds., *Selected Essays of Delmore Schwartz* (University of Chicago Press, 1970), pp. 53–57, 246–54. David Holzer, "Chasing the White Light: Lou Reed, the Telepathic Secretary and Metal Machine Music," *Ugly Things*, February 13, 2023.

196 *"You had to have a hit"*: Yule in Thomas; John Tobler, unpublished interview with Reed, December 1971; Bangs, "Dead Lie the Velvets, Underground."

197 *the issuing of singles*: The history of single releases from *Loaded* is fuzzy; in addition to "Head Held High"/"Train Round the Bend," there's evidence of an April 1971 U.S. release of "Who Loves the Sun"/ "Oh! Sweet Nuthin'." The future rock standards "Sweet Jane" and "Rock & Roll," a no-brainer pairing in hindsight, wouldn't earn release as a single until 1973, once Reed was an established solo act.

197 *Mount Sinai Hospital's psychiatric ward*: Bettye Kronstad, author interviews, 2014; Bettye Kronstad, *Perfect Day: An Intimate Portrait of Life with Lou Reed* (Jawbone, 2016), loc. 3764–83.

199 *"a very secure ego"*: Lou Reed, "Fallen Knights and Fallen Ladies," in Robert Somma, ed., *No One Waved Goodbye: A Casualty Report on Rock and Roll* (Fusion/Outerbridge and Dianstfrey, 1971).

200 *"he didn't object"*: Robert Somma, author interview, 2016. See also Reed, "Spectacle and the Single You." The *Crawdaddy* essay recycled themes from Reed's *Fusion* essay, adding a snarky song lyric parody titled "Janis, Jimi and Me" and a glancing riff on *The Society of the Spectacle*, Guy Debord's touchstone 1967 tract about direct living being replaced by its representation. "How can an individual compete with this awesome display?" Reed asked, regarding rock's sex-and-drugs bacchanal. "The answer is simple: get drunk . . ."

7. LONG ISLAND > LONDON > UPPER EAST SIDE

203 *his "gay poems"*: Lou Reed, poetry reading, St. Mark's Poetry Project, 1971 (recording), Lou Reed Archive; Reed, *Do Angels Need Haircuts?*, pp. 23–25. Reed liked *City of Night* so much, he had a bookseller's promo poster for it hung on his bedroom wall in college, a friend recalled.

205 *"He felt totally rejected"*: Kronstad, loc. 723–31; see also Anne Waldman in Reed, *Do Angels Need Haircuts?*, pp. vii–ix.

206 *the company's "house hippie"*: Lisa Robinson, *There Goes Gravity* (Riverhead, 2014), pp. 79–80.

206 *cut a woman's face*: Bickerdike, pp. 218–29. By one account, the assault on singer/ actor Emmaretta Marks, a woman of color, was racially motivated.

208 *"Lou did kinda fall"*: Kronstad, author interview, 2014. It was Bowie and Reed's first meeting, though when Bowie caught a set by the post-Reed Velvet Underground on an earlier New York visit, he chatted up Doug Yule effusively after the show, thinking he was Reed.

209 *slipped into a back room*: Kronstad, loc. 2494, 2567, 2594–612; Lisa Robinson, "Rebel Nights," *Vanity Fair*, February 14, 2014, and "Bowie," *SPIN*, August 1990; Mick Wall, *Lou Reed: The Life* (Orion, 2013), loc. 1179–206, and Tony Zanetta, "The Week David

Bowie Met Lou Reed, Iggy Pop and Andy Warhol: An Inside Look," *Bedford + Bowery*, January 11, 2016.

210 *"sat in our room"*: Robinson, *There Goes Gravity*, pp. 84–85.

210 *"listen to the Stones"*: Tobler, unpublished interview for *Zig Zag*, 1971.

211 *soul singer Mitch Ryder*: Best known for his '66 hit medley of "Devil with a Blue Dress On" and Little Richard's "Good Golly Miss Molly," Ryder later addressed queer sexuality in his 1978 song "Cherry Poppin'" and his memoir *Devils & Blue Dresses: My Wild Ride as a Rock and Roll Legend*.

211 *"every conceivable way"*: Reed, BBC interview, 1972, posted as "Lou Reed Discusses First Album and 'Straight Rock n' Roll,'" YouTube (Morgan Blythe), September 16, 2016, https://www.youtube.com/watch?v=AZD4pFh3pCw.

214 *"respect and abuse"*: Kronstad, loc. 2200–209.

214 *A striking home recording*: "Songs [Home Recordings with Bettye Kronstad]," recording circa 1971–72, Lou Reed Archive. The couple also sing "Too Many People on the Ground," evidently another Reed original, a playful coffeehouse folk strut about crowded sidewalks that recalls Tucker's and Reed's vocals on "I'm Sticking with You."

215 *"I'm gay, and always"*: Bowie in Michael Watts, "Oh You Pretty Thing," *Melody Maker*, January 22, 1972.

217 *"I was petrified"*: Bowie in "David Bowie on Lou Reed, Writing and New York," from *American Masters: In Their Own Words*, outtake of interview with Timothy Greenfield-Sanders for *American Masters: Lou Reed: Rock and Roll Heart* (PBS, 1997), YouTube (American Masters PBS), January 13, 2016, https://www.youtube.com/watch?v=P4kUmYoc1rE.

217 *"pure and beautiful"*: Reed in *Classic Albums: Transformer* (Isis/Eagle Rock, 2001).

217 *"I re-wrote it"*: Ibid.

217 *"everybody from the Factory"*: Reed on Martin Perlich's "Electric Tongue" interview show, KMET-FM Los Angeles, 1973, transcribed in Michael Heath and Pat Thomas, eds., *My Week Beats Your Year: Encounters with Lou Reed* (Hat & Beard, 2018).

218 *motel in New Brunswick*: Holly Woodlawn, *A Low Life in High Heels: The Holly Woodlawn Story* (St. Martin's Press, 1991), pp. 49–51.

218 *LSD while shooting the film*: Warhol and Hackett, p. 159; Randy Shilts, *The Mayor of Castro Street: The Life & Times of Harvey Milk* (St. Martin's, 1982), pp. 17–20, 72–73.

218 *"write the play"*: Reed, preface to Lou Reed, *Pass Through Fire: The Collected Lyrics* (2000; Da Capo, 2008), p. xxi.

219 *Bowie's sax tutor*: see Ross's contribution to the Beatles' "Savoy Truffle," among other notable appearances.

219 *wistfully literary song*: The titular lines of "Goodnight Ladies" echo Ophelia's near the conclusion of *Hamlet*, though Reed may have recalled them from "The Waste Land," the magpie tour de force by Delmore Schwartz's fave T. S. Eliot.

219 *"kind of nodding off"*: Visconti in Andy Greene, "Tony Visconti Remembers Lou Reed," *Rolling Stone*, November 1, 2013.

220 *creative control to Bowie*: The two men would speak little about the making of the album, at least initially, perhaps for obvious reasons—the pridefully self-doubting Reed because he knew exactly how much he owed Bowie for his breakthrough record, Bowie because he was a gentleman and a caring friend.

220 *intentionally blurred shot*: Lou Reed and Mick Rock, *Transformer* (Genesis, 2013), p. 4. "When I made the first test print, I didn't notice the negative slip out of focus in the enlarger," Rock recalled, "but when I saw the result taking form in the developer, I knew that something special was stirring." Rock would become Reed's most important photographic collaborator.

220 *Reed's masklike face*: Bowie's short 1969 promo film, *Love You Till Tuesday*, involved an artist who achieves success and fame by donning a mask, only to discover, to his horror, that he's unable to remove it. Perhaps inspired by Oscar Wilde's essay "The Truth of Masks," it was an interesting parable for Bowie, who cycled through various masks during his career, shedding each quickly, and for Reed, who found his masks tougher to lose.

220 *shot by Karl Stoecker*: Karl Stoecker, author interview, 2022. According to Stoecker, Reed saw both sides of the mirror images as identities coexisting within him.

221 *"lame, pseudodecadent lyrics"*: Ellen Willis, "The Return of the Dolls," *The New Yorker*, January 13, 1973; see also Henry Edwards, "Freak Rock Takes Over?" *The New York Times*, December 17, 1972.

221 *"forget this artsyfartsy"*: Nick Tosches, "Review of *Transformer*," *Rolling Stone*, January 4, 1973.

221 *jump in bed together*: Kronstad, loc. 1067–268.

221 *"just a phony cocksucker"*: McCormack, "Lou Reed: Revising the Legend."

222 *"a sad, ageing whore"*: Richard Williams, "It's a Shame Nobody Listens," *Melody Maker*, October 25, 1969, and "Broken Reed? Lou Reed, Duncan Browne: Sundown Theatre, Edmonton, London," *Melody Maker*, October 7, 1972.

222 *nothing but Velvet Underground*: The show, at Leicester University, included leading a tender audience singalong on "Pale Blue Eyes." Bootlegs of the gig have long circulated; it's among the most touching Reed performances ever.

222 *a manuscript of poems*: Typescript rejection re: Lou Reed, *We the People*, dated December 14, 1972, and January 8, 1973; Lou Reed, *All the Pretty People*, undated manuscript, Victor Bockris and Andrew Wylie Collection, Harry Ransom Humanities Research Center at the University of Texas, Austin. There seems to be no surviving copy of the *We the People* typescript; Lou Reed archivist Don Fleming has dated a later manuscript, titled *All the Pretty People*, to 1974. It seems likely there were multiple iterations of Reed's collection, and that it evolved over some years.

225 *painted on their backs*: Kronstad, loc. 3965.

226 *"I dig the gay people"*: Jude Jade and Glenn O'Brien, "Lou Reed: Subway to the Stars," *Andy Warhol's INTERVIEW*, March 1973, reprinted in Heath and Thomas.

227 *"Drugs are bad"*: Reed in Bangs, "Dead Lie the Velvets, Underground." Reed did have a yoga practice, evidently, and was, for a time at least, flexible enough to sit in full lotus position, as documented in a Mick Rock photo circa 1974.

228 *"vaguely unpleasant fat man"*: Lester Bangs, "Lou Reed: A Deaf Mute in a Telephone Booth," *Creem*, July 1973, reprinted in John Morthland, ed., *Mainlines, Blood Feasts, and Bad Taste: A Lester Bangs Reader* (Anchor, 2002), pp. 194–201.

229 *"I still do shoot it"*: Bangs, "Lou Reed." See also Nick Kent, "Lou Reed: The Sinatra of the 70s," *New Musical Express*, April 28, 1973.

229 *"vitamins laced with amphetamine"*: Kronstad, loc. 3636–50. "The first time Lewis took me to see him," Kronstad wrote, "we waited for two hours, corralled in one

tiny waiting room after another—there must have been at least five of them—until we finally made it to the great man's inner sanctum. It was like waiting to see God. After we chatted for a bit—him in his thick Austrian accent—he bent down and smiled at me, flourishing a huge hypodermic needle . . . 'I am going to make you feel like no man has ever made you feel in your life,' he said."

230 *"claw my eyes out"*: Reed, quoted in Dave Thompson, *Your Pretty Face Is Going to Hell: The Dangerous Glitter of David Bowie, Iggy Pop and Lou Reed* (Backbeat, 2009), p. 160.

230 *"'Holly! Turn on the radio!'"*: Holly Woodlawn, author interview. Woodlawn didn't bother with "Walk on the Wild Side" at her Reno Sweeney's debut, but did do "Perfect Day" alongside the Carmen Miranda signature "I, Yi, Yi, Yi, Yi (I Like You Very Much)" and Fanny Brice's "Cooking Breakfast for the One I Love," which Woodlawn performed with a spatula and a frying pan.

231 *"Lou as a poet"*: Bob Ezrin in "Bob Ezrin, Lou Reed: Rock and Roll Heart," *American Masters Digital Archive (WNET)*, June 26, 1997.

232 *"Court composer? No."*: Reed speaking with Martin Perlich on KMET's "Electric Tongue," April 1973, recording; partial transcription in Heath and Thomas, pp. 62–71. See also Kent, "Lou Reed: The Sinatra of the 70s."

233 *both had black eyes*: Kronstad, loc. 3985–4056.

234 *all works that churned*: Bowie was an evident fan of Doblin's book and Isherwood's *Mr. Norris*; judging from his touring library in the exhibition *David Bowie Is*, he owned copies of both, and his Berlin years in the late '70s were surely informed by them.

234 *She made Reed coffee*: Kronstad, loc. 3985–4263; Kronstad, author interview.

236 *as if kissing*: Bowie in Adrian Deevoy, "'God, I Remember This': David Bowie, This Is Your Life," *Q Magazine*, May 1993.

236 *"White Light/White Heat" among them*: The VU cover didn't make the final cut of Bowie's *Pin Ups*.

236 *having Bowie watch him*: Ezrin in "Bob Ezrin, Lou Reed: Rock and Roll Heart."

236 *"between Lou and life"*: Ezrin in Jim DeRogatis and Greg Kot, *Sound Opinions*, September 30, 2011.

237 *"a heroin rebound"*: Ezrin in Rob Bowman, liner notes, *Between Thought and Expression: The Lou Reed Anthology*.

237 *the album's myth*: Bettye Kronstad, author interview; also Sounes, p. 167.

237 *Begun in the 1950s*: Seth Rogovoy, "History of the Music Inn," musicinnarchives.org.

238 *the song's signature riff*: The September 1, 1973, show is the source of one of Reed's tastier bootlegs. There was also a tender solo acoustic "I'll Be Your Mirror" and a "Pale Blue Eyes" beautifully embellished with country-rock dobro.

239 *"a needle sticking out"*: Lisa Robinson, "Elegant: How You Gonna Keep 'Em Down in Paris (Once They've Seen Lou Reed)?" *Creem*, January 1974.

239 *talked Reed down*: Sounes, pp. 170–72.

240 *"so patently offensive"*: Stephen Davis, *Berlin* review, *Rolling Stone*, December 20, 1973.

240 *"washed-out"*: Robert Christgau, "The Christgau Consumer Guide," *Creem*, February 1974, reprinted at robertchristgau.com

240 *"the strongest, most original"*: John Rockwell, "Pop: The Glitter Is Gold," *The New York Times*, December 9, 1973. Lester Bangs, *Berlin* review, *Creem*, December 1973.

241   *"get into this zone"*: Steve Hunter in "Episode 11—The Extras," *Rock-N-Roll Animals*.

241   *"my little David Cassidy"*: Reed in Duncan Hannah, *Twentieth Century Boy: Notebooks of the Seventies* (Knopf, 2018), p. 176.

242   *"Life isn't that way"*: Reed in Steven Gaines, "Lou Reed and the Pain of 'Berlin,'" *Daily News*, January 6, 1974.

242   competition *with Bowie*: David Bowie, unpublished notes for *Hunger City/Diamond Dogs*, displayed in *David Bowie Is*, exhibit, Brooklyn Museum, 2018. Like *Berlin*, Bowie's project might also have drawn from real life. His notes for it described citizens that subsist on a substance called "mealcaine," a hybrid food/stimulant. "Generations of this powdered lifegiver," he wrote, "has produced a crazed, highly strung, otherwise numb amnesiatic [*sic*] proletariat."

243   *notion of Warhol producing*: Judith A. Peraino, "I'll Be Your Mixtape: Lou Reed, Andy Warhol, and the Queer Intimacies of Cassettes," *The Journal of Musicology* 36, no. 4, Autumn 2019. Peraino sleuthed out a wealth of information on attempts at a Reed-Warhol musical collaboration in the Andy Warhol Museum Archives; I'm indebted to her work.

243   *"I want you, Andy"*: Reed in Bob Colacello, *Holy Terror: Andy Warhol Close Up* (HarperCollins, 1990), pp. 82–83. Colacello considered the idea for a Broadway *Berlin* to be Warhol's. But with Warhol, idea provenance was always a dodgy business.

243   *"all the young beauties"*: Reed in Colacello, pp. 182–83. Reed would later claim he was in talks with a dancer from Merce Cunningham's company, who imagined *Berlin* could be a small-scale opera production. But he ultimately pulled back. "She got together with me and she wanted to go over every character and really talk about this motivation and that and I just couldn't do it," he said. "So I had to drop out. The thing pretty well speaks for itself. You don't have to sit there and analyze it." Liner notes, *Between Thought and Expression: The Lou Reed Anthology*.

243   *"for connoisseurs of the truly bad"*: Clive Barnes, "'Man on the Moon,' Warhol Musical," *The New York Times*, January 30, 1975.

244   *Velvet Underground reunion*: David Sheppard, *On Some Faraway Beach: The Life and Times of Brian Eno* (Chicago Review Press, 2008), pp. 164–66; Richard Cromelin, "The Inmates Have Taken Over: Kevin Ayers, John Cale, Nico, Eno & the Soporifics," *Creem*, December 1974. Morrison and Tucker might've been game if the concert would have been part of a larger tour, which wasn't in the cards. Eno also began having reservations once word got out. "They said I was going to replace Lou Reed! . . . We weren't going to call it the Velvet Underground, and I didn't want to go on stage to be judged as Lou Reed's replacement. People would come along and expect me to sing 'Heroin.'"

8. UPPER EAST SIDE > WEST VILLAGE

245   *Yule soon ceased trading*: Jennifer Yule, "The Artist Formerly Unknown as Doug Yule," *The Velvet Underground Web Page*. Various stories suggest the Reedless "Velvet Underground" played its final show at a ski-town bar in Vermont, or at My Father's Place in Roslyn, Long Island. But Yule recalled the last gig taking place on May 27, 1973, at a Boston club called Oliver's; the lineup was Doug Yule, his brother Billy, George Kay, and Don Silverman.

246   *"a chord so direct"*: Patti Smith, review of *1969: The Velvet Underground Live*, *Creem*,

September 1974. Chrissie Hynde, review of *1969: The Velvet Underground Live,* *NME,* April 27, 1974.

248   *"New York City is Lou Reed"*: Bowie in Craig Copetas, "Beat Godfather Meets Glitter Mainman: William Burroughs Interviews David Bowie," *Rolling Stone,* February 28, 1974.

248   *like a baby bird*: Colacello, pp. 191–92.

249   *"highest form of morality"*: *Beautiful Darling,* directed by James Rasin (Corinth Films, 2010).

249   *Hodes, a clothing designer*: Barbara Hodes, author interview.

250   *the look's shock effect*: The hairdo looks fresh in a picture of Reed and Hodes taken on February 11 at the pre-opening party for a new nightclub, the Bottom Line, at 15 West Fourth Street, soon to become an important live venue and music biz schmoozatorium. In the wake of *Cabaret,* Nazi semiotic play was a thing in both leather bars and New York art circles that season. Posters of the sculptor Robert Morris—shirtless in a Nazi-era helmet, aviator shades, spiked metal collar, and wrist manacles—were plastered around downtown that spring, advertising his April show at the Castelli-Sonnabend gallery. The image was used for an ad in *Art-forum,* too, in an issue that also contained a nude photo of his collaborator Lynda Benglis sporting a unisex hairdo and a huge dildo between her legs; the latter seemed to cause more of a fuss than the Third Reich conjurings.

250   *"dancing with a guy"*: Reed in Ed McCormack, "A Last Waltz on the Wild Side," VanityFair.com, January 13, 2014.

250   *Butchie and Tommy*: Jay Shockley, "Club 82," *NYC LGBT Historic Sites Project,* November 2021; Frank Mastropolo, "'We'd Found This Cave out of Time': A Look Back at Glam Rock's Club 82," *Bedford + Bowery,* January 28, 2014. See also JD Doyle, "Club 82 . . . also called '82 Club,'" QueerMusicHeritage.com; Signed D.C., "Eighty-two'ed," *It's All the Streets You Crossed Not So Long Ago* (streetsyoucrossed .blogspot.com), November 27, 2014. The Club 82 rock shows were inaugurated by the glammy also-rans Another Pretty Face.

251   *"Rachel's something else"*: Reed in Rock, "Penthouse Interview: Still Walking the Wild Side."

251   *the fourth of five siblings*: Cece and Gail Garcia, author interviews. I'm grateful to the Garcias for sharing their memories.

251   *"three to live together"*: Reed in Rock, "Still Walking the Wild Side"; Barbara Hodes, author interview.

251   *"wanted to be a girl"*: Warhol in Gopnik, pp. 437, 637, 771–73. The near-million-dollar commission came from the Italian art dealer Luciano Anselmino after Warhol took him to the Gilded Grape, a Times Square club that drew a trans and cross-dressing crowd. See also Zagria, "The Gilded Grape," in *A Gender Variance Who's Who* at zagria.blogspot.com, November 6, 2019.

252   *soul and funk*: The LP's musical approach was timely: in '73, Al Green released *Call Me* and *Livin' for You,* two of the greatest soul albums ever made, and there was more than a little of Green's signature sound in Reed's new live band. Years later, Reed would cite Green's *Belle* among his all-time favorites. See also Lou Reed, *Ride Paris Ride* (bootleg), Olympia, Paris, May 25, 1974; Josh Jones, "Lou Reed Creates a List of the 10 Best Albums of All Time," openculture.com, May 22, 2017.

253 *self-aware cartoon*: the back cover model was credited as "René De La Bush," and the drawing was supposedly based on a photo of Reed's.

253 *a thirty-second TV ad*: Details from author interviews. The spot's announcer was Don Pardo, the disembodied voice of the game show *Jeopardy* who'd soon sign on to the fledgling New York–based comedy show *Saturday Night Live*. See also Richard Metzger, "Amusing TV Commercial for Lou Reed's Sleazy 'Sally Can't Dance' Album, 1974," Dangerousminds.net, February 25, 2014.

254 *"tied his arm off"*: Cale and Bockris, pp. 150–51; Leach, author interview.

254 *"tell me what to say"*: Warhol in Alan Solomon, introduction to *Andy Warhol*, Institute of Contemporary Art, Boston, 1966, noted by Reva Wolf in introduction to Kenneth Goldsmith, ed., *I'll Be Your Mirror: The Selected Andy Warhol Interviews* (Carroll & Graf, 2004), p. xviii.

255 *"Are you a transvestite"*: Reed and various Australian journalists, from broadcast footage of press conference, Sydney Airport, August 19, 1974, linked in "Revisit Lou Reed's Infamous Interview at Sydney Airport, 1974," faroutmagazine.co.uk, August 22, 2020.

255 *"I used to read"*: Reed in interview, Radio JJ, Sydney, Australia, August 1974.

256 *"then you hop out"*: Reed in Charlie Frick, "Lou Reed Interview," *The Aquarian Weekly*, October 5, 1974, as reprinted in Heath and Thomas. Reed also praised Sam Peckinpah's *Straw Dogs* and trash-talked Alejandro Jodorowsky's *El Topo* ("the lowest kind of hippie shit").

257 *"reprocessed form of decadence"*: Lester Bangs, "Let Us Now Praise Famous Death Dwarves, or, How I Slugged It Out with Lou Reed and Stayed Awake," *Creem*, March 1975, reprinted in Lester Bangs, *Psychotic Reactions and Carburetor Dung* (Knopf, 1987). However genuine or playacted Bangs's transphobia was—he was to some extent likely pandering to *Creem's* imagined knucklehead middle-American hard-rock readership, just as Reed was to his imagined audience—his portrayal of Rachel was shameful.

258 *at the Felt Forum*: Diana Clapton, *Lou Reed and the Velvet Underground* (Bobcat, 1987), p. 86; Wayne Robins, "Lou Reed: Felt Forum, New York," *The Village Voice*, October 17, 1974; Levy, p. 224.

258 *a practiced pantomime*: Lou Reed, performance video footage from Houston Music Hall, Houston, Texas, November 13, 1974, reposted in Richard Metzger, "Lou Reed Shoots 'Heroin' Onstage in Houston, 1974," DangerousMinds.net, May 19, 2014.

259 *"pseudo-gay choreography"*: Philip Elwood, "Music Rocks, Stomach Rolls," *San Francisco Examiner*, November 23, 1974.

259 *"That's why he's 'Rotten'"*: Warhol and Hackett, p. 199.

259 *Still saw Dr. Freymann*: Canceled checks, Lou Reed Archive; see also Watson, p. 49.

260 *"record tracks of guitar"*: Reed in David Fricke, liner notes to *Metal Machine Music: 25th Anniversary Edition* (Buddha/RCA, 2000).

261 *"heavy metal, no kidding"*: Reed in Bangs, "Let Us Now Praise Famous Death Dwarves . . ."

261 *One recording, likely made*: "Electric Rock Symphony #1 Part 1," Lou Reed Archive. There remain questions about this recording, initially dated to the mid-'70s and thought to be a *Metal Machine Music* work tape. But the presence of piano ele-

ments (maybe Cale), and a voice (maybe Nico) uttering the word *naughty* in response to some off-color comment near the tape's end, suggest it may have come out of the band's early experiments circa Warhol's *Symphony of Sound* in early 1966.

262 *Another button-pusher*: "I Wanna Be Black," *Lou Reed—New Songs* (acoustic demo), September 10, 1974, Lou Reed Archive. The early draft lyrics here, which include a string of racial epithets, is even more extreme than the later released versions.

262 *demoed in December*: "Coney Island Baby," unreleased recording with Steve Katz, December 1974.

263 *the Velvets' back catalog*: Sounes, p. 178; Yule, "The Artist Formerly Unknown as Doug Yule."

263 *"impossible to work with"*: Steve Katz, author interview. While he's credited on the January Electric Lady sessions, Katz has no memory of being around for them, and claims he'd asked RCA to be released from working on the record, a request it apparently granted. "Since I was contracted to be the producer, my name was [still] on there," Katz explains.

264 *"worst things we've ever heard"*: Reed in David Fricke, liner notes, *Lou Reed: The Definitive Collection* (Arista, 1999).

265 *zippered nipple cutouts*: Reed and Rock, *Transformer*; see also Dean Moses, "Rockabilly Business Owner Hopes to Rebuild East Village," *AM New York/The Villager*, February 9, 2021; Larry Baumhore, "Enz's," vanishingnewyork.blogspot.com, November 4, 2019. Marlowe, a New York City legend, rebranded Ian's as Enz's and moved it to the East Village, first to St. Mark's Place, then to 125 Second Avenue, and in 2021 to 76 East Seventh Street.

265 *the* autoriduttori *movement*: Robert Lumley, *States of Emergency: Cultures of Revolt in Italy from 1968 to 1978* (Verso, 1990); liner notes to Lou Reed, *The Milan Riot* (The Swingin' Pig, 1989); "Milano: guerriglia al Palalido contro un organizzatore ebreo" ("Milan: Guerrilla at the Palalido Against Jewish Promoter"), *La Stampa* (Turin), February 14, 1975. Guy Debord's Milan-based comrade Gianfranco Sanguinetti was still active in early '75, completing what would be his notorious prank-pamphlet *Truthful Report on the Last Chances to Save Capitalism in Italy*.

266 *A similar scene*: Roman Waschko, "Rome Concert by Lou Reed Results in Riot, Injuries," *Billboard*, March 1, 1975.

266 *a new contract*: Dennis Katz, letter to Lou Reed, February 20, 1975; Lou Reed Archive. The letter, which laid out the terms of Katz's management proposal, was co-signed by Reed, confirming and agreeing to the arrangement.

267 *brought a cassette recorder*: Reed quotes and scene description based on author interview with Richard Lloyd, 2017.

268 *"What was your intention?"*: Reed and Smith in David Fricke, "Lou Reed: 1942–2013," *Rolling Stone*, November 21, 2013.

269 *undated BASF C-90*: Peraino. Prior to Peraino's 2018 discovery of this tape at the Warhol Museum, its existence was largely apocryphal. My description here, limited by copyright restrictions, is drawn from Peraino's writing and my own research in both the Warhol and NYPL archives. Reed evidently kept a copy of the tape for himself; a demo cassette in the NYPL archives contains what seem to be segments of the recording cut up and run through various distortion effects. See

also Will Hermes, "Lou Reed's Lost Tapes and Back Pages," Rolling Stone.com, December 19, 2019.

269   *"making money is art"*: Andy Warhol, *The Philosophy of Andy Warhol (from A to B and Back Again)* (Harcourt, 1975), p. 54.

269   *Reed offers an apology*: Peraino; Gopnik, pp. 548, 696. The nastiness toward Warhol wasn't out of character for many Factory characters; in fact, it occasionally received validation in Warhol's art. In *a: A Novel*, Ondine apparently coins Warhol's perjorative nickname Drella, a contraction of Dracula and Cinderella, to capture a persona many considered vampiric. *The Andy Warhol Story*, an autobiographical film shot in late '66 but never released, evidently featured the amphetamine-gobbling poet Rene Ricard as Warhol, alongside Edie Sedgwick, in what would be her final Warhol film role. In it, the pair savaged Warhol for his callousness and what Ricard called his "passive exploitation." Reed must have heard about it, even if he never saw it, and may have been making direct reference to it in *Philosophy Songs*, creating a biographical hall of mirrors that must've amused him, and perhaps he thought would amuse his friend. Reed thought plenty about self-representation in his art, and his ideas on it were greatly informed by Warhol. See Gary Comenas, "The Andy Warhol Story (1966)," warholstars.org; Rene Ricard in Stein and Plimpton, p. 285–87.

269   *musical with David Cassidy*: Scott Cohen, "Lou Reed: 'Coney Island Baby'—Rock & Roll in Drag," *Circus*, March 23, 1976.

270   *"fascinated, but horrified"*: Reed in Rock, "Still Walking the Wild Side."

270   *"not even your friends"*: Danny Fields and Lou Reed, liner notes, *Lou Reed: The RCA & Arista Album Collection.*

270   *breach-of-contract suit*: *Lou Reed v. Fred Heller*, Supreme Court of New York, County of New York, case 4692–1973, decision filed June 1, 1975; Sounes, pp. 198–99.

270   *building down the block*: Rent check for $575, April 8, 1975. Sub Series II B, Lou Reed Archive.

271   *wall of noise*: Kaye, "Lou Reed." Reed told Kaye "one of the basic tapes" for the *Metal Machine Music* project was made roughly ten years prior at Piero Heliczer's loft, while crafting abstract music with Cale for underground film soundtracks.

272   *contextualize* Metal Machine Music: Joe Smith, "Off the Record Interview with Lou Reed" (recording, Library of Congress, loc.gov/item/jsmith000151), March 20, 1987.

272   *Eno released* Discreet Music: Michael Bonner, "An Interview with Brian Eno: 'I Didn't See Bowie and Lou as My Peers,'" *Uncut*, January 2017. Eno would later describe the kindred LPs as "two ends of a spectrum of possibilities that not many other people had explored then."

272   *"this magic genie bottle?"*: Reed in Anthony O'Grady, "An Afternoon with Lou Reed and *Metal Machine Music*," *RAM*, August 9, 1975. Describing their time together, the unnerved writer also noted: "[Reed's] mind can also cruise in circles with the intent of a shark cruising for food. Right now, for instance, he is carving me into small pieces. It was probably the most terrifying afternoon of my life."

272   *truly hit the fan*: Court documents, *Dennis Katz v. Lou Reed, Transformer Enterprises Limited, and Oakfield Music Limited*, Supreme Court of the State of New York,

County of New York, case 19748–1975, suit filed September 30, 1975; Barbara Fulk, author interview; Sounes, pp. 198–99.

273 *"in debt to everyone"*: Reed in liner notes, *Coney Island Baby (Expanded Edition)* (RCA/Legacy, 2006).

273 *breach of contract*: Court documents, *Dennis Katz v. Lou Reed, Transformer Enterprises Limited, and Oakfield Music Limited*; Sounes, pp. 199–201.

274 *"ok, pick a studio"*: Reed in liner notes, *Coney Island Baby (Expanded Edition)*.

274 *slashes a man's throat*: Jean Genet, trans. Anselm Hallo, *Querelle* (Grove, 1974), p. 203.

275 *deeply grieving partner*: Garcia, author interview.

276 *"enraged by his critics"*: Louis Simpson, "The Ghost of Delmore Schwartz," *The New York Times Magazine*, December 7, 1975.

276 *a gender-outlaw icon*: Camille O'Grady, author interview. See also August Bernadicou, "Camille O'Grady," *The LGBT History Project* (lgbtqhp.org); O'Grady, @camilleogradymultimedium (Instagram).

277 *"stop that plant's production"*: Charlie Messing, "Why I Have Lou Reed's Old Sunglasses," *Rogue Boomer*, charliemessing.blogspot.com, October 28, 2013; see also Binky Philips, "I Ignore Lou Reed, but My Friend Charlie Winds Up in Lou's Apartment," *Huffington Post*, November 1, 2013.

277 *"needles neatly arranged"*: McCormack, "A Last Waltz on the Wild Side."

278 *a short-lived 'zine*: *Punk* (student magazine), University of Buffalo, May 7, 1973, digital.lib.buffalo.edu/items/show/37135.

279 *"worst dreams come true!"*: Reed, embedded recording in Charles Curkin, "He Was Present at the Birth of Punk, and He Took Notes," *The New York Times*, December 26, 2014.

280 *"This was heady stuff"*: Chris Frantz, *Remain in Love* (St. Martin's Press, 2020), pp. 106–109. The Heads "felt a little sad" that they couldn't work with their hero. "We continued to visit Lou and still respected him and his work," Frantz noted, "but we would never again think of doing business with him."

280 *"isn't in Smith's league"*: John Rockwell, "The Pop Life: Imagery by Patti Smith, Poet Turned Performer," *The New York Times*, July 12, 1974.

281 *"years of his farthood"*: Charles Shaar Murray, "Lou Reed: *Coney Island Baby*," *New Musical Express*, January 24, 1976.

281 *"master of psychopathic insolence"*: James Wolcott, "Lou Reed Rising," *The Village Voice*, March 1, 1976.

282 *"I created Lou Reed"*: Reed in Kaye, "Lou Reed."

282 *"a call from Clive Davis"*: Reed in Mikal Gilmore, "Lou Reed's Heart of Darkness," *Rolling Stone*, March 22, 1979.

283 *"just a Jewish guy"*: Clive Davis, *The Soundtrack of My Life* (Simon & Schuster, 2012), p. 221. See also Clive Davis, *Clive: Inside the Record Business* (William Morrow, 1975).

283 *"That's bullshit"*: Court documents, *Dennis Katz v. Lou Reed, Transformer Enterprises Limited, and Oakfield Music Limited*. On "Leave Me Alone," a stomping glam-rock outtake from the *Coney Island Baby* sessions, Reed appeared to reference the lawsuit, calling out people who "can make it so your music isn't much fun."

284 *"Maybe they're child substitutes"*: Reed to Rock, "Still Walking the Wild Side."

It's notable that Warhol also had a dachshund, Archie, and later got a second, Amos, to keep Archie company. In his *Diaries*, the artist wondered if Reed was copying him.

284   *presumably predatory power bloc*: McNeil and McCain, pp. 276–77, and Bangs, "Who Are the Real Dictators?" unpublished, 1976; accessed 10/29/22 at www.jimdero .com/Bangs/Bangs%20Punk.htm. See also Darryl W. Bullock, *The Velvet Mafia: The Gay Men Who Ran the Swinging Sixties* (Omnibus, 2012).

285   *marijuana shortage in town*: Frank Lauria, "The Grass Is Gone," *Soho Weekly News*, July 8, 1976.

286   *"my most memorable lines"*: Reed in Lisa Robinson, "New York Telephone Conversation," *Hit Parader*, March 1977.

287   *press the play button*: Corky Stasiak, author interview, 2018, provided details for this scene.

287   *emerging video artists*: Kitchen Center 1975–76 program catalog, accessed at vasulka .org, October 28, 2022.

287   *"I got 60 TVs"*: Reed in Reed and Rock, *Transformer*.

288   *his essay on dead rock stars*: Peter Laughner, Don Harvey from *The Ann Arbor Tapes* (1976) in *Peter Laughner* box set (Smog Veil, 2019).

288   *the capsules*: "Black beauties" was the street term for 20 mg biphetamine capsules, or their supposed equivalent—a gold standard for speed.

288   *"puking and pissing myself"*: Peter Laughner, "If You Choose, Choose to Go," *Creem*, March 1974.

289   *a sort of shrine*: Adele Bertei, *Peter and the Wolves* (Smog Veil, 2020), p. 30. Bertei's memoir is in large part a vivid and moving portrait of Laughner.

289   *to hook Reed up*: Todd McGovern, "Peter Laughner: An Unfinished Life," pleasekillme.com, May 23, 2019.

290   *"made me cry"*: Reed in Timothy Ferris, "Lou Reed's Regenerative Degeneration, or: What Happens When Your Average Introvert Meets the Glass Coffee Table Queen,"*Rolling Stone*, April 8, 1976. According to Jonathan Richman, Reed was also wowed by Young's guitar solo on Crosby, Stills, Nash & Young's version of "Woodstock."

290   *"thirty-two hang-ups"*: Erin Clermont, author interviews.

291   *"One layer for each year"*: During the couple's stay in London, Reed spoke to Capital Radio about "Walk on the Wild Side" ("part of my unceasing campaign to corrupt") and the supposed influence of his songs. "There are people from Ohio who come running up and say, 'Oh, it was because of you I came to New York and I'm not ashamed anymore,'" he noted with apparent pride. "And there they are, prancing around, flying off the tables. And *I'm* ashamed." Per usual when speaking with the press, Reed blurred sincerity and sarcasm. "What do you think about being known as 'The Godfather of Punk Rock' and all of that?" the interviewer asked. "I love being titled that, I just think it's fantastic," Reed said drolly. "To be blessed with thousands of punks. I hope they keep going for a couple more months."

291   *"gentle and happy"*: Furmanovsky, email exchange with author, 2019. NB: On April 30, Konigsdag (Queensday), and the actual birthday of Queen Juliana, whose reign had been shaken by the recent Lockheed bribery scandal—Reed played Chuck

Berry's "Little Queenie," with Humphreys making a rare onstage appearance, hollering backing vocals. (The Sex Pistols' "God Save the Queen" was already generating a cultural furor in the U.K., though it wouldn't be released officially until May.) The next day, Reed debuted a new song in Groningen, Netherlands, a thirteen-minute guitar grinder that found him snarling in what seemed the voice of a street-walking sex worker baiting a cop ("Patrolman Number 99 / I'd like to make it with you sometime!"). The speed and veiled violence of the song, "Affirmative Action (PO #99)," similarly echoed the punk zeitgeist. And while Reed never recorded or released it, he'd soon find a use for the song's shouted chant of "Street hassle!" and, some years later—on his *New York* LP—for the image of sex workers baiting cops. See also Reed, *Pass Thru Fire*, p. 406.

292   *"Rachel had gotten kicked"*: Andy Warhol, *The Andy Warhol Diaries*, ed. Pat Hackett (Grand Central Publishing, 1989), p. 11.

292   *Humphreys's desire to transition*: Jayne County, author interview, 2015. County notes that Reed "liked that [Rachel's] boy parts worked."

292   *"get some fucking dope"*: Reed, "560556-Demos/Recorded Conversation" (recording circa 1977), Lou Reed Archive.

293   *how Morales met Reed*: Sylvia Morales, author interview, 2018. Bockris's account in *Transformer* (p. 334) has Reed and Morales meeting at the Eulenspiegel Society, a social group of BDSM and leather enthusiasts that advertised its monthly gatherings in the *Village Voice* classified section. Another version has Morales and Reed meeting after a concert.

294   *"Everybody's gone to sleep"*: Laughner in *Peter Laughner* (Smog Veil, 2019).

295   *"wanted to be Lou Reed"*: Bangs, "Peter Laughner Is Dead," *New York Rocker*, September–October 1977. Bangs's writing was burning hot at this point; see his vivid chronicle of traveling with the Clash, "Six Days on the Road to the Promised Land," serialized in *New Musical Express*, December 10, 17, and 24, 1977. The musician Jeff Tweedy observed, "It may be the single best piece of writing about rock music ever . . . it still makes me cry every time I read it." Jeff Tweedy, *Let's Go (So We Can Get Back)* (Dutton, 2018), p. 27.

296   *used the live recordings*: Schunke's concert recordings were the basis of "Gimme Some Good Times," "Leave Me Alone," and "Shooting Star" on *Street Hassle*. See also Stephan Paul, "Binaural Recording Technology: A Historical Review and Possible Future Developments," *Acta Acustica*, 2009.

296   *Similarly self-referential*: The *Coney Island Baby* outtake "Downtown Dirt" also got remade on *Street Hassle* into a song that suggested Reed's ongoing legal battles, quoting Bobby Fuller's 1965 hit "I Fought the Law." The Clash would record the latter not long after Reed issued his album; it's unclear if Reed's recording inspired it. Reed, *Between Thought and Expression*, p. 60.

296   *herself as "a singing playwright"*: Robert Hilburn, "Joni Mitchell: Both Sides, Later," *Los Angeles Times*, December 8, 1996.

297   *"a little Raymond Chandler"*: Reed, introduction to "Street Hassle" at Wiltern Theatre, Los Angeles, 2003, on Lou Reed, *Animal Serenade* (Sire/Reprise, 2004).

297   *"top and bottom" doo-wop*: The Ink Spots' Bill Kenny is generally credited with orginating this vocal approach, in which a bass-baritone voice speaks over upper-register group harmonizing.

297 *voiced by Springsteen*: Damien Love, "Babe, I'm on Fire: The Making of Lou Reed's *Street Hassle*," damienlove.com. The sound engineer Rod O'Brien recalled this scene in Love's piece.

298 *"I'm one of them"*: Reed in Gilmore.

298 *"Lou was crushed"*: Davis, p. 222.

298 *award Reed received*: Bockris, *Transformer*, p. 315; Peraino, p. 417.

299 *"not nihilists but moralists"*: Ellen Willis, "Velvet Underground," in Greil Marcus, ed., *Stranded* (Knopf, 1979). This anthology of music writing had A-list American critics answer the question "What rock and roll album would you take to a desert island?"

300 *"I'll chew you up"*: Josh Alan Friedman, "Lou Reed: Ugly People Got No Reason to Live," *SoHo Weekly News*, March 15, 1978; "A Foul and Bitter Interview with Lou Reed," *Tales Of . . . with Josh Alan Friedman* (Apple podcasts), November 15, 2018.

300 *residency at the Bottom Line*: John Rockwell, "Lou Reed Appears at Bottom Line," *The New York Times*, March 13, 1978.

300 *"he's not copying anybody"*: Warhol in Warhol and Hackett, *The Andy Warhol Diaries*, p. 121.

300 *"animals throwing beer cans"*: Reed on Lou Reed, *Live Take No Prisoners* (Arista, 1978).

301 *shows Reed recorded*: The album title paid tribute to a deranged fan at a show earlier that year who apparently bellowed "Take no prisoners, Lou!" while slamming his head energetically into the lip of the stage.

301 *Schunke and his binaural*: Damien Love, "I'm Set Free: The Making of Lou Reed's *Take No Prisoners* (An Oral History)," damienlove.com.

303 *"he's so sweet"*: Warhol and Hackett, *The Andy Warhol Diaries*, pp. 159–60.

303 *tenderest images ever*: Andy Warhol, contact sheet, "At 860 Broadway, Barry Landau and Polly Bergen, Vincent Fremont, Andy Warhol, Christopher Makos, others; Lou Reed, Fran Lebowitz, Susan Blond watching David Johansen perform at the Bottom Line." 2014.43.127, AWF FJ78.00121, Job 98975, July 20, 1978. Iris & B. Gerald Cantor Center for Visual Arts at Stanford University, copyright the Andy Warhol Foundation for the Visual Arts, Inc.

303 *"so adorable, so sober"*: Warhol and Hackett, *The Andy Warhol Diaries*, p. 165.

304 *money to take to Humphreys*: Lydia Sugarman, author interview, 2016.

304 *protect his new relationship*: Love, "I'm Set Free." The bassist Moose Boles recalled an incident in which Morales got roughed up in a Chicago bar during the tour; to the extent that it's true, Reed must've feared for his girlfriend's safety and their future together, should she decide a relationship with him was not worth the personal risk.

305 *"deluded creatures"*: Reed in Demorest.

305 *response to the assassination*: "Milk Left a Tape for Release If He Were Slain," AP wire story, reprinted in *The New York Times*, November 28, 1978. Due to his activism, Milk suspected he might be killed by homophobes, and in preparation, he left a taped message with his lawyer, to be released upon his death.

306 *hired a young guitarist*: Chuck Hammer, author interview, 2018.

306 *"thirteen complete sets of lyrics"*: Lofgren in liner notes, *Blue with Lou* (Cattle Track Road, 2019).

307 *"Disco is pro-sex"*: Reed to John Ogle, "Radio Radio," WPIX-FM, January 1979. As guest DJ, Reed spun "Sexy Ways" by Hank Ballard and the Midnighters, the Robins' 1955 "Smokey Joe's Cafe," "Want Ads" by Honey Cone, Bobby Short's reading of Cole Porter's "Miss Otis Regrets," and "Oh My Soul" by his "dear dear friend" Garland Jeffreys.

307 *"I wonder at its meaning"*: Liner notes, Lou Reed, *The RCA & Arista Album Collection*.

307 *"into a dark well"*: Liner notes, *Between Thought and Expression: The Lou Reed Anthology*.

309 *"are these my people?"*: Reed to John Ogle, WPIX-FM, May 27, 1979.

309 *he was using again*: Peter Morales in Reed, *The Art of the Straight Line*, pp. 61–62.

310 *"mouth that never sleeps"*: Davis, p. 223.

9. NEW JERSEY > UPPER WEST SIDE

312 *"in bed reading a book"*: Reed to Bruno Blum, interview, Montcalm Hotel, London, 1979 (recording); Bruno Blum, *Electric Dandy* (Hors Collection, 2008).

312 *"Dead Rock Stars Night"*: Warhol and Hackett, *The Andy Warhol Diaries*, p. 250.

314 *"It's a small arc"*: Reed in Reed and Rock, *Transformer*.

314 *asked him for storm windows*: Robinson, *There Goes Gravity*, pp. 99–100.

315 *"drugs are the single worst"*: Reed to John Tobler, BBC Radio 1, June 5, 1980. Transcribed in Heath and Thomas, p. 199.

315 *fans stormed and trashed*: "Graves incidentes tras un frustrado recital de Lou Reed en Madrid," *El País*, June 22, 1980; Hammer, author interview.

315 *"skeleton's brief aria"*: Angus MacLise, "Description of a Mandala," *The Cloud Doctrine* (Sub Rosa, 2003).

316 *"Good-bye, Barbara"*: Jonas Mekas, "From the Diaries: On Barbara Rubin" (1980–1983), *The Velvet Underground Experience*, pp. 86–87.

316 *"the reason I took heroin!"*: Jim DeRogatis, *Let It Blurt* (Broadway, 2000), p. 210.

316 *"recharge the battery"*: Reed in David Fricke, "A Refugee from Rock's Dark Side, Lou Reed Says Goodbye Excess, Hello New Jersey," *People*, March 30, 1981.

317 *"some revisionism"*: Ibid.

317 *"these desperate feelings"*: Warhol and Hackett, *The Andy Warhol Diaries*, p. 381.

318 *"a little sexy girl"*: Ibid.

318 *contact sheet sequence*: Warhol, "New York street scenes around the West Village; Lou Reed and Sylvia Morales." Contact sheets; 2014.43.965, AWF FJ81.04042, and Job 93771; April 16, 1981. Iris & B. Gerald Cantor Center for Visual Arts at Stanford University, copyright the Andy Warhol Foundation for the Visual Arts, Inc.

318 *"outbreak is unknown"*: Lawrence K. Altman, "Rare Cancer Seen in 41 Homosexuals," *The New York Times*, July 3, 1981.

318 *producing other artists*: Kristine McKenna, "Eno: Voyages in Time & Perception," *Musician*, October 1982; Nelson Slater, author interview, 2014. In addition to his recording career, Carroll wrote the acclaimed and powerful memoir *The Basketball Diaries*.

319 *"they couldn't play"*: Jason Gross, "Interview with Robert Quine," *Perfect Sound Forever*, furious.com, November 1997.

320 *with whom he explored*: Brian Eno, "Robert Quine," *Perfect Sound Forever*, furious .com, July 2004. Eno and Quine often talked music at the latter's St. Mark's Place apartment. "I don't think I ever visited Quine without him digging out some

obscure doo-wop song or old jazz record and getting me to listen to a genius piece of guitar playing by some long-forgotten craftsman," Eno recalled. "He was a sort of archaeologist of popular music, deeply knowledgeable and with a phenomenal memory for detail." Among other things, Quine turned him on to "He Loved Him Madly," the half-hour-long Miles Davis modal meditation on the death of Duke Ellington. That recording led directly to Eno's exploration of extended, drone-based melodies in recordings he branded as "ambient music." Quine contributed to some of Eno's recording sessions, though the results rarely made it to record. See Brian Eno, "Juju Space Jazz," *Nerve Net* (Opal/Warner Brothers, All Saints, 1992).

322   *Delmore Schwartz occupying*: Sylvia Reed, author interviews. The vision of Delmore in Reed's house was partly the result of a Ouija board encounter he and Sylvia were convinced they'd had with his spirit; Reed had also taken his wife to Schwartz's New Jersey grave site to "meet" him.

324   *"perverse and doomed forever"*: Reed to Blum, interview, 1981; see also Blum, *Electric Dandy*.

324   *recorded a "rock masterpiece"*: Robert Palmer, "The Pop Life," *The New York Times*, June 2, 1982; December 22, 1982. Upon its release, *Rolling Stone* gave the LP a rare five out of five stars, and decades later, the magazine's Rob Sheffield would hail "Waves of Fear" as "the 'Sister Ray' of suburban-husband angst." Rob Sheffield, "Happy 30th Birthday to *The Blue Mask*, Lou Reed's Solo Masterpiece," *Rolling Stone*, February 24, 2012.

325   *"attack on Lester"*: Quine in Jim DeRogatis, "Robert Quine: Such a Lovable Genius," *Perfect Sound Forever*, furious.com; see also DeRogatis, pp. 230–37.

327   *"mixed me off the record"*: Gross, "Interview with Robert Quine."

327   *tension between the men*: *A Night with Lou Reed* (Image, 1991). Given the feud with Quine, it was amusing, and telling, when Reed randomly paraphrased Clint Eastwood's memorable .45-magnum-gripping "Feeling lucky, punk?" challenge from the 1971 film *Dirty Harry*.

327   *"guy changed my life"*: Gross, "Interview with Robert Quine." Reed returned the sentiment in Quine's *New York Times* obituary, describing him as "an extraordinary mixture of taste, intelligence and rock 'n' roll abilities, coupled with major technique and a scholar's memory for every decent guitar lick ever played under the musical sun." Ben Sisario, "Robert Quine, 61, Punk Rock Guitarist," *The New York Times*, June 8, 2004.

327   *the advent of MTV*: Among the first day's programming were the Pretenders, the Cars, and Pat Benatar; heavier, *Rock 'n' Roll Animal* spawn like Iron Maiden and .38 Special; and a smattering of vets, including the Who and Rod Stewart.

328   *a number of films*: One Trick Pony (Warner Bros., 1980); *American Pop* (Columbia, 1981); *Rock & Rule* (MGM/United Artists, 1983); *Get Crazy* (Embassy, 1983). The latter featured the ex–Exploding Plastic Inevitable dancer Mary Woronov as Violetta, the nightclub's fierce house tech.

329   *recalled Quine coining*: Sounes, pp. 251–52. Additionally, "I Love You, Suzanne" borrowed its spoken-word intro and dance floor courtship theme from the Contours' 1962 hit "Do You Love Me?," a song revived notably by the Blues Brothers in 1980.

329 *into video-game arcades*: Defender and Robotron 2084 were the gold-standard video games created by Eugene Jarvis, gaming's Chuck Berry.

330 *roughly two thousand cases*: "New York City HIV/AIDS Annual Surveillance Statistics," HIV Epidemiology and Field Services Program, NYC Department of Health and Mental Hygiene, nyc.gov, 2014.

331 *"get a good laugh"*: Interview, New Zealand TV, 1984, posted on *Slydogmania!*, YouTube.com, https://www.youtube.com/watch?v=8ehTB6EBS8M.

331 *"never even looked over"*: Warhol and Hackett, *The Andy Warhol Diaries*, p. 608.

331 *upstart ad agency*: Randall Rothenburg, *Where the Suckers Moon* (Knopf, 1994); see also Lawrence Bridges, lawrencebridges.com; "LB Honda Scooter do Doc Elements of Film." In one fleeting shot in the ad, a marquee advertises *Desperately Seeking Susan*, a new film featuring another transgressive New York pop star, Madonna, who'd have her first number 1 hit with "Like a Virgin" by the year's end.

332 *no qualms taking commissions*: Warhol's TV ad for the "Underground" ice cream sundae featured at Schrafft's restaurant chain, a commission he accepted not long after the Solanas shooting in 1968, was the first of many that yoked his avant-garde sensibilities to products wanting an image upgrade, an arrangement that often proved win-win for all.

332 *deal with American Express*: According to file documents re the American Express ad dated January 9, 1987, Reed was offered $25,000 for participating in a three-hour-long (maximum) photo shoot, along with his granting permission for the company to use his image, name, and signature in print ads in the United States (plus territories) and Canada for a period of one year, with an option to extend it to two for an additional $25,000. Documents, Lou Reed Archive.

332 *a children's TV series*: The long-running show would launch the careers of the Black Eyed Peas' Stacy "Fergie" Ferguson, the dance-pop diva Marta "Martika" Marrero, and the actor Jennifer Love Hewitt.

332 *His lawsuits*: Bockris, *Transformer*, p. 339; Sounes, p. 253.

333 *new generation of bands*: "I'm staring at a record shelf filled with their albums and bootlegs," Ira Kaplan said; "their importance to me is huge." Alan Reder and John Baxter, *Listen to This! Leading Musicians Recommend Their Favorite Artists and Recordings* (Hyperion, 1999), pp. 193, 211.

334 *in a bad place*: Cale and Bockris, pp. 200, 207–209.

335 *Reed was lukewarm*: Reed to Smith, "Off the record interview with Lou Reed."

335 *roughly $1,500 a year*: Cale and Bockris, p. 209.

336 *"Oh, my history teacher'"*: Tucker in Reiff.

336 *company with younger people*: Gopnik, pp. 854–55. It's worth noting that the Velvet Underground revival irked Warhol, who'd played an important role with the band, insofar as it excluded him. "Polygram wants to buy our tapes for $15,000 which isn't enough," he noted in an April diary vent. "I mean, I just don't understand why I have never gotten a penny from that first Velvet Underground record. That record really sells and I was the producer! Shouldn't I get something? I mean, shouldn't I?" Warhol and Hackett, *The Andy Warhol Diaries*, p. 655.

337 *"opposite of what America means"*: Andy Warhol, *America* (1985; Penguin Classics, 2011), pp. 11–14, 223.

337 *did some co-writing*: Among other Reed-Blades co-writes were "The Calm Before the Storm," a mid-tempo lament with a Springsteen vibe inspired by an upsetting conversation between the two men about their respective backgrounds and upbringings; "We heard our screams turn into songs and back into screams again," sings Blades. Sounes, pp. 258–59.

338 *Basquiat stumbled*: Warhol and Hackett, *The Andy Warhol Diaries*, p. 771. El Internacional was formerly a German restaurant, and later a Rat Pack hangout called Teddy's Steak House; in the '80s it was distinguished by its black-and-white camouflage paint job and a near-full-size replica of the Statue of Liberty's crown on the roof.

339 *"'we gotta sell some records!'"*: Fernando Saunders, author interview, 2019.

339 *"gruesome, unbelievable things"*: Reed to Conspiracy of Hope press conference, from "1986 a Conspiracy of Hope Tour and 1988 Human Rights Now!—Amnesty International," video report, source unknown, *Dose*, YouTube.com, March 29, 2012 https://www.youtube.com/watch?v=CbLcgAYPupU.

340 *"painfully stupid and pretentious"*: Reed to Smith, op. cit. "Off the Record Interview with Lou Reed." The exchange, just over an hour long in edited form, is a fascinating listen. Reed made a point of mentioning that Dylan once told him "you never made a bad record." ("[That] was really nice of him," Reed said, sounding pleased.) Dismissing Bowie's music, he conceded he liked "The Bewlay Brothers" from *Hunky Dory*.

341 *withdrew his permission*: Joe Smith's *Off The Record: An Oral History of Popular Music* would be published the following year, without Reed's interview. But Reed, or perhaps his management, kept a copy of the typescript in his files. A note attached to it read: "LOU HATED THIS." It's too bad. Elvis Costello, a sharp student, quipped early on that while he wasn't well-versed in Reed's music, he'd "never miss reading [his] interviews." Costello in Nick Kent, "D. P. Costello of Whitton, Middlesex, It Is Your Turn to Be the Future of Rock & Roll," *New Musical Express*, August 27, 1977.

342 *a diseased gallbladder*: Gopnik, pp. 891, 897–901.

342 *presumably of HIV-related*: Warhol and Hackett, *The Andy Warhol Diaries*, p. 580.

342 *Warhol's heart stopped*: Blake Gopnik, "Andy Warhol's Death Not So Routine After All," *The New York Times*, February 21, 2017; Daniel E. Slotnik, "Bjorn Thorbjarnarson, Surgeon to Warhol and the Shah, Dies at 98," *The New York Times*, October 10, 2019.

343 *decided to get clean*: Cale and Bockris, p. 216; Mark Kemp, "15 Minutes with You: Lou Reed and John Cale Perform a Requiem for the Late Andy Warhol," *Option*, July/August 1990; Sylvia Reed, author interview, 2022.

343 *a young Canadian band*: Tom Doyle, "Cowboy Junkies: 'Sweet Jane,'" *Sound on Sound*, October 2015.

343 *certainly liked the recording*: Dave Bowler, "Cowboy Junkies Mainline *The Trinity Session*," *Mojo*, March 2021. When Reed met the young band, according to the guitarist Michael Timmins, "he was real friendly. The first thing he said was 'Fire your manager, don't trust your record company, and don't talk to journalists.'" And when Reed performed "Sweet Jane" in concert around that time, he would often thank the band for restoring the "heavenly wine and roses" bridge.

344 *five-hour "Sweet Jane" marathon*: Mitch Myers, "The Basement Vapes, Volume Seven: By Popular Demand—Lou Reed's Exquisite Jane," *Magnet*, July 8, 2019; "Two Nice Girls Sweet Jane 1986 18 Sept," KLRU-TV news broadcast, September 18, 1986, https://www.youtube.com/watch?v=iIwl5VrqEfw (posted on twonicegirlsmusic, YouTube.com, October 2, 2009).

344 *"make an exception for"*: Seymour Stein with Gareth Murphy, *Siren Song* (St. Martin's, 2018), p. 256.

344 *Cale discovered things*: Cale and Bockris, p 216.

345 *"for him to collaborate"*: Cale in Kemp, 1990.

346 *"'You can keep it'"*: Reed, as quoted by Mike Rathke, author interview.

346 *a long creative partnership*: Lou Reed [with Mike Rathke], "The Room," U.K. B side of "What's Good" (WEA, 1992). You can hear the musicians locking in on Reed's very first recording with Rathke, an improvised instrumental captured on a Walkman cassette recorder with a plug-in button microphone; Reed was so fond of it, he released it years later.

346 *"'eight years of Reagan'"*: Reed, Sire Records press release, 1988; Kemp, 1990; Fricke, liner notes, Lou Reed, *New York (Deluxe Edition)* (Rhino/Warner Bros, 2020). Reed dutifully smoked Carltons, though he thought they tasted terrible; he'd break off the filters so he could get a proper hit.

347 *Reed called a "racist slip"*: Milton Coleman, "A Reporter's Story," *The Washington Post*, April 8, 1984; Rev. Jesse Louis Jackson, "Address by the Reverend Jesse Louis Jackson," July 19, 1988. Posted at *Frontline*, pbs.org. Coleman wrote about the context of Jackson's notorious remark. It's worth noting that Reed watched, and was moved by, Jackson's 1988 "Common Ground" speech at the Democratic National Convention, a striking piece of oratory. "What makes New York so special?" Jackson asked, in his stentorian tenor. "It's the invitation of the Statue of Liberty: 'Give me your tired, your poor, your huddled masses who yearn to breathe free.' Not restricted to English only. Many people, many cultures, many languages—with one thing in common, they yearn to breathe free. Common ground!" It's not clear whether Jackson's use of the Emma Lazarus poem inspired Reed's paraphrase of it in "Dirty Blvd.," but it's likely.

347 *Black and Jewish communities*: Lydia Chavez, "Racial Tensions Persist in Crown Heights," *The New York Times*, April 10, 1987. Reed's decision to address Jewish politics may have been influenced by Bob Dylan's 1983 "Neighborhood Bully," an apparent defense of Israel against various slurs, including criticism of its 1981 attack on an Iraqi nuclear reactor.

348 *Reed invoked the incident*: "Hold On" also invoked Eleanor Bumpers, a sixty-six-year-old Black woman killed in her home by a police officer with a shotgun in 1984, and the artist-model Michael Stewart, killed in a 1983 police altercation after graffiti-tagging a wall in the First Avenue subway, where he was waiting for the L train after a night at the Pyramid Club. The 1986 Central Park shooting of a white New York City cop, Steven McDonald, by Shavod "Buddha" Jones, a Black fifteen-year-old (though Reed refers to a "ten-year-old kid"), was widely reported, as were the acts of Bernard Goetz, a white subway vigilante who shot four Black teens on an IRT number 2 train for allegedly trying to mug him the same year. For "Hold On," using second-person address, Reed conjured an unnamed character

riding the subway "with a black .38" and thinking about Goetz. The song did offer a glimmer of hope for change via collective action: the invitation "I'll meet you in Tompkins Square" referred to that summer's Tompkins Square Park riots, stemming from a repressive curfew, nodding to kindred uprisings in 1863 and 1874 in the park, a nexus of New York City labor and immigrant rights activism. The 1986 Howard Beach incident would also inform "Howard Beach" by the Brooklyn metal band Biohazard, "Black with NV" by the Queens rappers Black Sheep, and, reportedly, a song of apology written to Michael Griffith's mother by one of the attackers, Jon Lester, after he learned to play guitar in prison.

348   *thinking about Rachel Humphreys*: "New York City HIV/AIDS Annual Surveillance Statistics," HIV Epidemiology and Field Services Program, NYC DOHMH, 2014; New York State Department of Corrections and Community Supervision documents; Kim Christy, "Brandy Alexander: A Special Friend Who Needs Our Help!" *Female Mimics International* 12, no. 3, issue 11, 1982 (Posted in Digital Transgender Archive, archive.org); Randy Shilts, *And the Band Played On: Politics, People and the AIDS Epidemic* (St. Martin's, 1987), pp. 157–58. Brandy Alexander was evidently among the first New Yorkers to die from HIV infection. A 1982 editorial in *Female Mimics International* asked readers to support the Club 82 regular, unable to pay bills after being "stricken with cancer" that January, directing them to send cash and letters of encouragement to Brandy Alexander's East Village address, while Shilts's bestselling book described the artist covered with Kaposi sarcoma lesions at Sloan Kettering Cancer Center. (NB: The performer should not be confused with peers who also used the moniker "Brandy Alexander," including Danny Leonard and Gayle Sherman.)

348   *"supreme love song"*: Reed in Cott, p. 182.

349   *"defeated before they ever"*: Reed in Fricke, "Lou Reed: The *Rolling Stone* Interview."

349   *"a cockroach in amber"*: Jon Pareles, "Images of New York, in Anger and in Sorrow," *The New York Times*, January 22, 1989; Lou Reed, "Anarchy in the Streets," *The New York Times*, May 10, 1989. "Some of the songs, revolving around topical references, could become dated within the year. But the spirit of [the album], brittle and desperate and furious, may well sound current for decades to come," Pareles wrote, a prediction largely borne out. The edits made to Reed's poem "Cans" were evidently done without informing him, to judge by a letter in his archives—apparently smoothed out after Reed crumpled it up in disgust—explaining with faint condescension how magazines are edited.

349   *"drop dead from AIDS?"*: Reed to Cott, pp. 182–85.

349   *"I was really fucked up"*: Tom Hubert, "Lou Reed," *Q Magazine*, Spring 1989; quoted in Nick Kent, *The Dark Stuff* (Faber and Faber, 1994), p. 184.

350   *"Get a refund, motherfucker"*: Reed in Fricke, "Lou Reed: The Rolling Stone Interview."

350   *"engraved in my skull"*: Reed, "Lou Reed Inducts Dion into the Rock and Roll Hall of Fame—1989," dailymotion.com. The Feelies collaboration happened for a holiday radio broadcast on Long Island's WLIR/WDRE-FM.

352   *"that line, 'I hate Lou'"*: Reed in Kemp; Warhol and Hackett, *The Andy Warhol Diaries*, pp. 635, 771. Reed's line seems lifted directly from the September 21, 1986, entry in Warhol's *Diaries*: "I hate Lou Reed more and more, I really do, because he isn't giving us any video work." Reed denied overt cribbing from

Warhol's book in *Between Thought and Expression: Selected Lyrics of Lou Reed*, p. 140. "I wrote this trying to capture the love of the Andy I knew both inside and out," Reed noted.

352   *a filmed performance*: *Songs for Drella* by Lou Reed and John Cale (Initial/Lou Reed & John Cale/Channel Four/Sire, 1990); Cale and Bockris, p. 225. At the BAM Opera House, the song cycle was unspooled by just Reed and Cale, seated on an empty stage set with projected photos by Billy Name, in an echo of the Exploding Plastic Inevitable.

353   *remaining bottles of methadone*: James Young, *Nico: The End* (Overlook, 1994); pp. 199–207; Bickerdike, pp. 377–91. Young, Nico's keyboard player for a time, wrote a grimly comic account of touring with her toward the end of her life; it's a modest masterpiece of first-person literary journalism.

353   *"Billy's genteel attention"*: John Cale, foreword to Billy Name, *The Silver Age: Black and White Photographs from Andy Warhol's Factory* (Reel Art Press, 2014).

354   *"C'est un grand moment"*: Unknown concertgoer, "Velvet Underground—Andy Warhol, France 1990," news clip, *Fashion TV*, June 1990 (posted by oldTOtaper, YouTube .com, June 8, 2011), https://www.youtube.com/watch?v=YtfbfeQQlvY.

10. UPPER WEST SIDE > WEST VILLAGE

355   *Rachel Humphreys died*: New York State Department of Corrections and Community Supervision documents; Swados, "The Story of a Street Person." Lincoln's sister Liz, a successful playwright, published an excerpt of her memoir in *The New York Times Magazine* focusing on her brother. She wrote about the basement dorm room he shared with Reed, with pizza stuck to the ceiling; her brother's writing in *The Lonely Woman Quarterly*; and how their dad came to Syracuse and took Lincoln home after his breakdown.

355   *anonymously in a mass grave*: Corey Kilgannon, "Dead of AIDS and Forgotten in Potter's Field," *The New York Times*, July 3, 2018; hartisland.net. Kilgannon's reporting revealed that Humphreys was among the unknown number of AIDS victims buried anonymously on Hart Island in the '90s, though the specific cause of Humphreys's death remains unknown. By Kilgannon's estimate, the total number of bodies in the mass graves on Hart Island "could reach into the thousands, making it perhaps the single largest burial ground in the country for people with AIDS." According to the Hart Island Project website, the count tops 75,000. Richard "Rachel" Humphreys was buried in section I, plot #205, on February 16, 1990.

356   *"He was worked up"*: Mellencamp in Anthony DeCurtis, *Lou Reed: A Life* (Little, Brown, 2017) pp. 309–12.

357   *"in hip mourning clothes"*: Doc Pomus, *Call the Doctor: The (Unpublished—and Unfinished) Autobiography of Doc Pomus*, quoted in Peter Guralnik, *Looking to Get Lost: Adventures in Music & Writing* (Little, Brown, 2020), p. 255; as quoted in Mitch Myers, "Jazz Singer Jimmy Scott Remembered at Harlem Memorial," *Billboard*, October 26, 2014; Alex Halberstadt, *Lonely Avenue: The Unlikely Life* (Da Capo, 2008), pp. 219–27.

357   *shared a sense of oppression*: Doc Pomus, "The Journals of Doc Pomus (1978–1991)," *Antaeus: On Music* 71/72, Autumn 1993, p. 178. See also *AKA Doc Pomus* (Clear Lake Historical, 2012). In an undated journal entry, Pomus wrote: "To the world, a fat crippled Jewish kid is a nigger—a thing—the invisible man—like Ralph Ellison

says." Reed read this passage aloud, along with other sections of Pomus's journals, in the *AKA Doc Pomus* documentary.

358   *the record deal*: Reed, notes on Doc Pomus, Lou Reed Archive; Halberstadt, p. 223. Speaking at the memorial, Rebennack shared a fact publicly for the first time: he'd finally kicked his longtime heroin addiction and he credited Pomus with inspiring him to quit.

359   *"suffering as my salvation"*: Scott in David Ritz, *Faith in Time: The Life of Jimmy Scott* (Da Capo, 2002), p. xv. "[It] was little understood when I was coming up," Scott told Ritz, discussing his Kallmann syndrome struggles with striking candor. "It afflicted me and two of my brothers. My mother felt for us, but when the hospital wanted to use us in experiments, she said, 'No child of mine will be a guinea pig.' Then Mama, bless her heart, was killed in a terrible car accident. Happened when I was thirteen. The syndrome was on me, but Mama wasn't there to help me through. My testicles never descended. My penis stayed small. My voice stayed high. Facial and pubic hair never grew. Kids can be cruel. Boys especially . . . [and] adults can be as cruel, maybe crueler, than kids."

359   *"treated him with respect"*: Roger Moutenot, author interview, 2018; Ritz, p. 209.

359   *"tutoring me in the art"*: Lou Reed, interview with Jimmy Scott, *Interview*, October 1996.

359   *"gonna be another breakthrough"*: Bill Bentley, author interview, 2018. When pressed on their reservations about Scott's appearance, according to Bentley, the show producers cited "some of his hand movements."

360   *"'I remember nothing'"*: Reed per Bentley, author interview. By his account, Bentley was busted for a single joint—a felony in Texas, before the 1970 Controlled Substances Act reduced mandatory minimums—and managed to get off with five years' probation. So he felt it prudent to skip the 1969 Velvets show in Austin, sure to be rife with narcs.

361   *over and sealed up*: Robert Hilburn, "Lou Reed talks to Robert Hilburn: 'God protects fools and drunks,'" *Los Angeles Times*, January 22, 1992.

362   *"my boyhood art hero"*: Jonathan Richman, author correspondence, late 2016. By 1992, the shuttered Lone Star Cafe had rebranded itself the Lone Star Roadhouse and relocated its forty-foot rooftop iguana into a larger space at 240 West Fifty-second Street. Penn and Teller's friendship with Reed led to his cameo in their Sega home video game, *Penn and Teller's Smoke and Mirrors*, in which Reed's cartoon doppelganger murders the duo, exploding them in a shower of blood and body parts. (The game was never released.) Mike Vago, "Wiki Wormhole: Penn & Teller's Maddening Unreleased Video Game Became a Cult Sensation Online," *AV Club*, December 18, 2019.

362   *printed the lyrics of "Heroin"*: Lou Reed, "The '60s According to Lou Reed," *The New York Times*, November 3, 1991. In a telling juxtaposition, Reed's lyrics were positioned as a small item beneath a feature on the young rap group Digital Underground.

364   *"a rather significant role"*: Václav Havel in Lou Reed, "To Do the Right Thing," in *Between Thought and Expression*, pp. 151–52, 159–61. As Havel explained, the Czech "Velvet Revolution" got its name not from Reed's band per se, but from Western journalists, who thought it a catchy moniker for a largely bloodless uprising that culminated in the election of a rock fan playwright as president.

364 *"only bad actors have power"*: Hubert Selby Jr. in Reed, "A Scream Looking for a Mouth," in *Between Thought and Expression*, p. 164.

364 *"I love and cherish you"*: Sid Reed, letter to Lou Reed, June 19, 1992, Lou Reed Archive.

364 all-star tribute concert: Bob Dylan, *30th Anniversary Concert Celebration (Deluxe Edition)* (Legacy, 2014). "Foot of Pride" was an outtake from Dylan's 1983 *Infidels* sessions first released on the 1991 rarities set *The Bootleg Series Volumes 1–3*, where Reed likely discovered it.

365 *"would have been a disaster"*: Rosanne Cash in "Various Artists (Rosanne Cash, Courtney Love, Michael Stipe and more) Talk Lou Reed," *Talkhouse*, September 6, 2014; Rosanne Cash, author interview, 2019. See also Reder and Baxter, p. 70.

365 *"very flirtatious"*: Suzanne Vega, author interview, 2021. See also DeCurtis, p. 388.

365 *"How afraid I was"*: Laurie Anderson, *All the Things I Lost in the Flood: Essays on Pictures, Language and Code* (Rizzoli/Electa, 2018), pp. 271–72.

366 *"This guy is crazy"*: Anderson in Sarah Sweeney, "The Introspective Laurie Anderson," *The Harvard Gazette*, March 27, 2015.

366 *"like the Von Trapp family"*: Anderson in Ed Stocker, "Laurie Anderson: Diverse Dish," *Monocle*, May 2016.

366 *"really falling apart"*: Laurie Anderson, *In the Nick of Time*, performance piece, 1974, quoted in Roselee Goldberg, *Laurie Anderson* (Abrams, 2000), p. 50.

366 *"taught me other things"*: Hermione Hoby, "Interview: Laurie Anderson: 'I See Lou All the Time. He's a Continued Powerful Presence,'" *The Guardian*, January 15, 2017. Anderson was responding to a question about her 2015 film *Heart of a Dog*, in which she shares her feelings about her mother.

367 making things happen: Anderson in "Laurie Anderson Interview: A Life of Storytelling," video, Louisiana Museum of Modern Art, Denmark, May 2016 (posted at Louisiana Channel, YouTube.com), https://www.youtube.com/watch?v=dUo-dqMriY8.

367 *"That changed my life"*: Laurie Anderson, author interview, 2010; see also Will Hermes, *Love Goes to Buildings on Fire* (Farrar, Straus and Giroux, 2011), p. 213. Anderson spoke with me about her pre-Reed years for my book on the 1970s New York City music scene. Mills was a crucible for new music in the 1960s; its music department was led by the composer Darius Milhaud, joined in 1966 by Pauline Oliveros, who headed up the Mills Tape Music Center (formerly the San Francisco Tape Music Center, now the Center for Contemporary Music). Steve Reich took classes at Mills in the mid-'60s, as did the Grateful Dead's Phil Lesh; Maryanne Amacher, John Cage, Annea Lockwood, Terry Riley, Wadada Leo Smith, and many other major composers taught there.

368 *"can I just call you back?"*: Laurie Anderson, *Stories from the Nerve Bible* (Harper-Perennial, 1994), p. 155. "O Superman" embodied a historical moment defined by dubious technology: answering machine voices, high-profile military system failures (the explosion of an ICBM missile in Arkansas, an aborted airborne hostage-rescue mission in Iran), space-probe photographs of Saturn, and, maybe most of all, the media-sculpted persona of Ronald Reagan. As far as anyone can recall, the vocal pitch-shifting device used on "O Superman" was an Eventide H910 Harmonizer.

369 incorporate his Jewish heritage: John Zorn and Marc Ribot, program notes for Radical Jewish Culture (RJC) festival, Knitting Factory, April 1993; see also Tamar Barzel,

New York Noise: Radical Jewish Music and the Downtown Scene (Indiana University Press, 2015), pp. 57–58; Joachim-Ernst Berendt and Günther Huesmann, *The Jazz Book: From Ragtime to the 21st Century* (Chicago Review Press, 2009). Celebrating "radical new Jewish culture" in the country that engineered the Holocaust was a major event in Zorn's creative life, and the Munich event reverberated back to the downtown New York scene in numerous ways, beginning with the five-day Radical Jewish Culture festival at the Knitting Factory, a jazz-minded new music venue located on Houston Street on the Lower East Side, home to many of the city's Jewish immigrants during the first half of the twentieth century.

369 *"There were very few Jews"*: Danny Fields in Shore and Tillman, p. 111.

369 *"just how I would do it!"*: Reed, quoted by Anderson in Mark Paytress, "He Was Very Smart. Too Smart," *Mojo*, November 2016. Anderson would use her voice to conjure Warhol again, narrating Ric Burns's four-hour 2006 *Andy Warhol: A Documentary Film.*

370 *the mind of an addict*: Susannah Hunnewell, "The View from Good Grief," *The New York Times*, December 27, 1992. Johnson's tales were drawn partly from memory, partly not, though he maintained "almost everything in there actually happened to someone I know or heard about."

371 *a corny ad campaign*: Legal correspondence, Lou Reed Archive. One draft of a letter in Reed's files argued the "parody lyric" in the ad "utterly subverts the character and artistic integrity of the composition," and that the soundalike singer "compounds the damage." The situation was eventually resolved, though it took a while. In one impatient fax, Reed scrawled, "What ABOUT ME AND MY SONG! Goddamnit."

371 *"big shot, or rich"*: Reed in Cott, pp. 182–85.

372 *nixed "Wild Side" licensing*: As a rule, according to Sylvia Reed, Lou didn't license his work for alcohol or cigarette ads, given his own struggles with addiction, though documents suggest he made exceptions.

373 *"My father owned corporations"*: Reed in Smith; see also Gopnik, pp. 869–73.

373 *A Tribe Called Quest*: correspondence between Lou and Sylvia Reed and Barry Weiss, April 1990; letter of agreement between Metal Machine Music Inc. and Zomba Enterprises Inc., July 19, 1990, Lou Reed Archive. Tribe's debut album was issued on April 10; on March 6, a letter was apparently hand-delivered to Reed's lawyer asking if Reed would clear the sample. In Reed's files, a copy of that note, like countless faxes and letters, had "NO" scrawled across it in what appears to be his handwriting. Weiss's letter, sent directly to Reed, was dated April 24. The final writing credits for "Foggy Notion," per the 2014 "Super Deluxe Edition" of *The Velvet Underground*, omit Reed's name; they read "Sterling Morrison, Maureen Tucker, Douglas Yule, Hy Weiss." Though Phife Dawg claimed in 2015 that his group had "[never seen] a dime from that song," the late rapper couldn't knock Reed's hustle, blaming his own label for not clearing the sample up-front. "It's his art; it's his work," Phife reasoned. "He could have easily said no. There could have easily been no 'Can I Kick It?' So you take the good with the bad. And the good is, we didn't get sued. We just didn't get nothing from it." See also Jason Newman, "Tribe Called Quest: 'Lou Reed Got All the Money' for 'Can I Kick It?'" Rolling Stone.com, November 17, 2015. Archive documents suggest Reed stuck to the 100

percent demand for "Wild Side" samples, though he'd go lower for rerecordings or interpolations. And Tribe's "Can I Kick It?" inspired a number of hip-hop producers to sample it in turn.

374 *"a bit nervous at first"*: Tucker in Bockris, *Transformer*, p. 435.

376 *"rocklike in the granitic sense"*: John Rockwell, "Older But Still Hip, the Velvet Underground Rock Again," *The New York Times*, June 5, 1993. Among the most vivid accounts of the reunion performances was by the Scottish singer-songwriter Roy Møller, who saw both Edinburgh shows, astonished at his all-time favorite band's reunion a half-mile from where he grew up. YearZeroFilmaking, "The Velvet Underground in Edinburgh: Roy Møller," *The Sound of Young Scotland Project* (at big golddream.com), May 31, 2018.

376 *the French crowd cheered*: Velvet Underground, *Velvet Redux Live MCMXCIII* (Warner Strategic Marketing, 1993); Dean Wareham, "Velvet Underground Tour Diary," *Alternative Press*, November 1993 (posted at fullofwishes.co.uk).

376 *Bono-Lou love fest*: Robinson, *There Goes Gravity*, p. 242. Bono first met Reed during the "Sun City" project, reconnecting with him on the Amnesty International Conspiracy of Hope tour and going total fanboy, singing "Sweet Jane" in hotel bars after hours and pushing Reed on at least one occasion to join him. In a Polaroid Reed saved, his arm is around Bono, who kisses his cheek as Reed beams—it's one of the most demonstrably joyous images of him ever captured.

376 *"out of your freaking mind?"*: Tucker in Reiff.

377 *no* Velvet Underground Unplugged: MTV's flagship program *Unplugged* was a major platform at the time. When Eric Clapton released an LP of his *Unplugged* episode, it swept the 1993 Grammy Awards, including Album, Song, and Record of the Year, and by summer the LP had sold five million copies; even the video went platinum. And Nirvana's appearance was one of that band's greatest moments.

377 *reported the end*: "News: VU Peel Sessions," *New Musical Express*, September 29, 1983; fax correspondence between Lou and Sylvia Reed and John Cale, September 28–October 4, 1993, Lou Reed Archive.

378 *"Moe, there is no D-minor"*: Reed quoted by Moe Tucker in David Koen, "Heroes and 'Heroin': New Rumblings from the Velvet Underground," *New Times*, January 11, 1989; greeting cards, Lou Reed Archive.

379 *"'making holes in your arm'"*: Cale in Cale and Bockris, p. 252. Lou Reed and Maureen Tucker, fax correspondence, September 14–15, 1993; Lou and Sylvia Reed, John Cale, fax correspondence, September 28–October 4, 1993, Lou Reed Archive.

379 *well-regarded biography*: Peter Schjeldahl, "In the Footsteps of Cocteau and Dracula," *The New York Times Book Review*, November 12, 1989. The art critic distinguished the book from its competitors as "the one to read for knowledge of Warhol the man."

380 *"never terrified of death"*: Anderson in Stephen Holden, "Pop Music: To the Mountaintop and Back," *The New York Times*, February 5, 1995.

380 *"never really apart"*: Laurie Anderson, "For 21 Years We Tangled Our Minds and Hearts Together," *Rolling Stone*, November 21, 2013.

381 *"love affair of a lifetime"*: Zorn in Bill Milkowski, "John Zorn: The Working Man," *Jazz Times*, May 1, 2009.

381 *"First Couple of downtown Manhattan"*: Holden.

382 *"the meaning of history"*: Sterling Morrison, description for dissertation, "Historiographical Perspectives in the Signed Poems of Cynewulf," University of Texas, Austin, 1986 (Texas ScholarWorks, repositories.lib.utexas.edu/handle /2152/68629).

382 *"mythic Irish hero"*: Lou Reed, "The Lives They Lived: Sterling Morrison: Velvet Warrior," *The New York Times Magazine*, December 31, 1995. See also Chris O'Connell, "What Goes On," *Medium*, August 26, 2015, medium.com/the-alcalde/what -goes-on-524982f49915.

383 *"two-bit, pretentious academic"*: Reed in Bockris and Malanga, p. 65. It's not clear that Reed's opinion of Zappa's music had changed entirely since then. In fact, on a copy of his Hall of Fame ballot in 1995, voting for eight of fifteen eligible acts, Reed evidently didn't vote for Zappa, though he did vote for the Grateful Dead. But when the call came, Reed agreed to give the Zappa tribute, delivering a brief, sincere-seeming speech, declaring Zappa among the people "whose vision and integrity was such that it moved the world a bit," noting Zappa's close relationship with Reed's friend Václav Havel, and his articulate testimony to Congress against the then notorious Parents Music Resource Center, the censorship-minded pop music watchdog group. "Of the many regrets I have in life, not knowing [Frank] a lot better is one of them," Reed added.

383 *"opened wounds worth opening"*: Patti Smith, Martha Morrison, John Cale, Lou Reed, and Moe Tucker, Rock and Roll Hall of Fame Induction Ceremony, August 4, 1996. See also Legs McNeil, "Sterling Speaks! Sterling Morrison's Last Interview with Legs McNeil, 1995," pleasekillme.com, October 11, 2018. Months before he died, Morrison lamented the group's ongoing snub by the Rock and Roll Hall at length.

385 *Coney Island pizzeria Totonno's*: The correct pronunciation is "Tuh-TOE-nose," though some pronounce it "Tuh-TAH-nose." Reed pronounces it "Tuh-TOE-knee-ohs," which might've been a first take/best take flub, an intentional vernacular mispronunciation, an artistic license exercise to add a syllable for flow, or some combination thereof. Also worth noting are Anderson's siren-call backing vocals on "Hang On to Your Emotions," and the rapturous title track, where Reed describes a soul singer collapsed onstage "growing hard" while the horn section conjures vintage Stax-style charts—an amusing metaphor from a fifty-something man in a new relationship with a younger partner.

385 *"traitors to the democratic ideal"*: Reed in Ray Rogers, "Lou Reed," *Interview*, March 1996.

386 *Reed's capacity for apologizing*: David Bowie and Lou Reed in David Bowie, *Live in New York 1997—50th Birthday Concert* (bootleg DVD, 1997); Barney Hoskyns, "A Dark Prince at Twilight: Lou Reed," *Mojo*, March 1996. The reconciliation with Bowie prompted Reed to be more open about his creative debt to him. "Odds are that if Bowie and Ronson hadn't produced ["Walk on the Wild Side"], it wouldn't have been a hit," he told Hoskyns, conceding that, at the end of the day, he was a one-hit-wonder. "*My* way, there wouldn't have been a string part, especially since it's a string part I didn't write. I'm enough of an egotist where I get pleasure out of playing my own lines—not someone else's. And that's just the truth."

387 *request for* Velvet Goldmine: Licensing memos, March 11–13, 1997, Lou Reed Archive. Haynes did his research. One scene mirrored Bowie and Reed's apocryphal early '70s bedroom tryst at Lisa and Richard Robinson's apartment; another restaged the famous Mick Rock photo of Reed and Bowie's faux kiss in a London club; a number of Curt Wild's declarations echoed actual Reed interview quotes: and it's noted the character had been subject to electroconvulsive therapy as a youth to curb his queerness. (With nice symmetry, the character was played with amphetamine explosiveness by Ewan McGregor, who'd recently OD'd to the sounds of Reed's "Perfect Day" in *Trainspotting*.) "Satellite of Love" accompanied a romantic segment with Slade and a lip-synching Wild riding rocket ships on a carnival ride, an earthbound intergalactic romance. The Venus in Furs band featured Thom Yorke and Jonny Greenwood of Radiohead, while Wild's backing band in the film featured the New York rockers Thurston Moore and Steve Shelley (Sonic Youth), as well as Don Fleming (Half Japanese, Gumball), who'd later become the archivist for Reed's estate.

388 *immortalized the actor Louise Brooks*: Auster's *Lulu on the Bridge* had a splashy opening at Cannes, but never got a theatrical release in the States. Reed developed a friendship with Auster, a novelist and kindred spirit who, in his signature *City of Glass*, might've been channeling Reed when he wrote, "I have come to New York because it is the most forlorn of places, the most abject . . . The broken people, the broken things, the broken thoughts. The whole city is a junk heap. It suits my purpose admirably." The German director Wim Wenders was a longtime Reed fan who'd used "What's Good" in his 1991 film *Until the End of the World*; in his *Faraway, So Close!*, Reed sat on a backstage couch idly updating the lyrics to "Berlin."

388 *shared admiration for Delmore*: Martin Scorsese, introduction to Lou Reed, *I'll Be Your Mirror* (Faber and Faber U.K., 2019), pp. 5–6; letter from Martin Scorsese to Lou Reed, March 30, 1993, Lou Reed Archive. The "Dirty Blvd." project had a script written by the acclaimed playwright Reinaldo Povod, a product of the Lower East Side's Nuyorican Poetry Club, and a wish list for actors included Robert De Niro, Mickey Rourke, Lisa Bonet, Lou Diamond Phillips, and Rubén Blades. Years earlier, Reed wrote something of a fanboy mash note to Scorsese in *New Sensations*'s "Doin' the Things That We Want To."

390 *"I took it as a compliment"*: John Cameron Mitchell in Helen Eisenbach, "Pretty Boy," *New York*, May 11, 1998.

390 *"Perfect Day" advertising boom*: Licensing memos, Lou Reed Archive. The BBC released a second all-star version of "Perfect Day" after a live simulcast of the song in 2000.

391 *"I just can't do it"*: Rosanne Cash to author, June 18, 2019; correspondence between Cash and Reed, June 5–July 24, 1998. The singer-songwriter had just published her debut short story collection, *Bodies of Water*, which was very well received. Reed's lyric-writing around this time was as unflinching as his unpublished story submission. In a *New York* magazine piece that spring, Reed mentions "Justice and the Stick," a song he'd written about Abner Louima, a Black man subject to horrific acts of police brutality, which included being raped with a broomstick, in the summer of 1997. Lou Reed (interviewed by Ethan Smith), "Lou Reed: Wild Side Survivor," *New York*, April 6, 1998.

391 *The one-hour documentary*: Lou Reed, David Byrne, et al., *Lou Reed: Rock and Roll Heart, An American Masters Special* (PBS, 1998). Reed's family, upbringing, and personal relationships were scarcely addressed in the film, though Laurie Anderson did appear briefly, rehearsing "Hang On to Your Emotions" with Reed in Paris. Per Reed's usual demand of journalists, the focus stayed on the music.

393 *"scotch and, maybe, some crack"*: Reed in Jim Sullivan, "On the Wild Side," *Rock's Backpages*, October 2013. The short set Reed did with Rob Wasserman and Mike Rathke at the Tennessee Ball included a lean "Walk on the Wild Side" (Reed changing "colored girls" to just "girls") and "One for My Baby (and One More for the Road)," a signature of the reliable Republican Frank Sinatra. "He's not here, because they got voted out," Reed noted.

393 *"it's a smear campaign"*: Reed in Roxanne Roberts and Libby Ingrid Copeland, "International Velvet," *The Washington Post*, September 17, 1998.

393 *performed for a small audience*: At the event, Reed posed for photos with a beaming Hillary Clinton and, before starting his set—alluding to the Beatles' 1963 Royal Variety Performance—quipped, "I think John Lennon said, 'Don't rattle your jewels.'"

395 *reflection of a lifetime's work*: Fan mail, Lou Reed Archive.

11. WEST VILLAGE > LONG ISLAND

396 *"My father's name is Art"*: Anderson in Rose Lee Goldberg, *Laurie Anderson* (Abrams, 2000), pp. 28, 50. In a 1970s performance piece, *In the Nick of Time*, Anderson tells stories about her father.

397 *Reed began having health problems*: draft of letter to Ludwig von Otting, December 15, 1999, Lou Reed Archive.

397 *"the most outrageous fun"*: John Cale, letter to Lou Reed, January 5, 1999, Lou Reed Archive; see also Sarah Larson, "Lou Reed Archive Coming to the New York Public Library," NewYorker.com, March 2, 2017.

398 *a self-pleasuring selfie*: Stefan Sagmeister, email interview, 2019. See also Kylie Boltin, "Film Fix: Lou Reed Revisits His Epic Song-Cycle, *Berlin*," *SBS* (sbs.com .au), December 1, 2008. To get the cover image Sagmeister had to convince Reed to jerk off behind a curtain in order to get images of his face in orgasm. "He laughed and said that is a fabulous idea for someone else, certainly not him," the designer recalls. "[But] when I told him about a special Polaroid studio in Soho that incorporated the world's largest Polaroid camera and the possibility to have him be there, by himself, shooting himself with just a technician as support, he very much warmed up to the idea." Reed later arranged for his parents to come to the studio and sit for portraits in front of the same backdrop. Toby and Sid dressed for the occasion, and the resulting pictures, near life-sized, were stunning, loving and merciless in their detail, a son literally and figuratively drawing his aged parents close: his mom's matrix of wrinkles and bloodshot blue eyes, his dad's leathery skin and turkey neck. Reed's niece Jill, Sid's granddaughter, cherishes her print of one shot; she thought her grandfather looked as happy in it as she'd ever seen him, which she attributes to his affection for the photographer and his gratitude for the time together.

399 *notion of the "tribute album"*: The Willner-produced *I'll Be Your Mirror: A Tribute to*

the Velvet Underground and Nico was released following his death from complications of Covid-19 in 2020. But his entire catalog, as sui generis as they come, is a wonderland of inspired and surprising music, well worth exploring.

399 *a 6.5 out of 10*: Kristin Sage Rockermann, "Review of *Ecstasy*," *Pitchfork*, May 31, 2000; Robert Christgau, review of *Ecstasy*, *Rolling Stone*, April 13, 2000.

400 *He enlisted Tom Waits*: Wilson's *The Black Rider* was a collaboration with Tom Waits and William S. Burroughs; *Alice*, inspired by Lewis Carroll's *Alice's Adventures in Wonderland*, was another Wilson-Waits collaboration, as was *Woyzeck*, based on the Georg Büchner play that informed Berg's *Wozzeck*. Waits was a fellow traveler whose work Reed had long admired, as he told Joe Smith in 1987.

400 *composer and songwriter*: Reed's timing was good, as it was the start of legacy rock acts pivoting into musical theater. Paul Simon was producing *The Capeman*, whose soundtrack *Songs from the Capeman*, featuring Reed's pal Rubén Blades, was released the same month as *Time Rocker*, though the musical would not open until 1998. Costing $11 million, an extraordinary budget at the time, it would flop, a Broadway disaster pretty much unrivaled at the time until U2's *Spiderman* project decades later.

401 *"close to late-night MTV"*: Jon Pareles, "Echoes of H. G. Wells, Rhythms of Lou Reed," *The New York Times*, November 14, 1997; Bernard Holland, "Is It Opera? Maybe, but Who Cares?" *The New York Times*, November 23, 1997.

401 *"You were made for this"*: Reed quoted by Robert Wilson, author interview, 2018; Reed and Wilson from *Live at the NYPL*, staged dialogue at the New York Public Library, September 30, 2011. Wilson's Poe project was well timed: Reed had recently participated in Hal Willner's *Closed on Account of Rabies: Poems and Tales of Edgar Allan Poe* at St. Ann's Church, reading "The Tell-Tale Heart."

402 *"something that you know is wrong?"*: Reed in "Lou Reed POE-try in the News," VPRO newscast, May 7, 2001 (bakabana1966 YouTube post, July 12, 2007, https://www.youtube.com/watch?v=0sieUMNpbFE).

402 *"every hole available"*: Max Dax, "From the Vaults: An Interview with Lou Reed (2000)," ElectronicBeats.net, October 28, 2013. See also Dan Ouellette, "Lou Reed High on 'Ecstasy' / Rock Veteran Says New CD Meets All His Artistic Goals," *SFGATE*, April 16, 2000. Reed's frank statement to Max Dax was in response to a question about the "last man standing" line in "Like a Possum."

403 *the second plane hit*: Jeremy Darby shared his account in a Facebook post on September 11, 2015. See also Howard Thompson, "Lou Reed, Rubén Blades," *North Fork Sound*, July 19, 2008.

403 *songs resonated powerfully*: Greg Kot, "Laurie Anderson 9/11 Concert at Park West Revisited," *Chicago Tribune*, September 11, 2013.

404 *"After the shock and mourning"*: Reed in "9/11 Remembered: Musicians' Reactions," *Rolling Stone*, September 8, 2011; Laurie Anderson, *Live at Town Hall New York City September 19–20, 2001* (Nonesuch, 2002); Jill Grimaldi, "The First American Birth Control Conference," *Margaret Sanger Papers Project*, November 12, 2010; *Martin Scorsese Presents the Blues* (PBS, 2003); Lou Reed, "Songs for the City: Laurie Sadly Listening," *The New York Times*, November 11, 2001.

404 *irreverent revisions of Poe*: Ben Brantley, "Lou Reed, Exploring Poe's Plutonian Shore," *The New York Times*, November 29, 2001; Jon Pareles, "Lou Reed, the

Tell-Tale Rocker," *The New York Times*, November 25, 2001. Brantley, the *Times*'s theater critic, described the play as "a disjointed gray mass."

405 *Bowie animated "Hop Frog"*: There's some irony in the fact that Hop Frog is triggered by alcohol, given Reed and Bowie's alcohol-soaked fallout so many years ago.

406 *"People held their breath"*: Samantha Hunt in Sean Manning, ed., *The Show I'll Never Forget: 50 Writers Relive Their Most Memorable Concertgoing Experience* (Da Capo, 2007), pp. 253–57; Anohni, author interview, 2010; Diane Solway, "Mourning Glory," *W*, July 1, 2011; Anohni and Marti Wilkerson, *Black Lips: Her Life and Many, Many Deaths* (Anthology Editions, 2023). The nonbinary Blacklips crew, in which Anohni found her singing voice, wreaked avant-garde havoc at the Pyramid Club on Avenue A during the early-to-mid-'90s. Anohni's singing reminded Reed of Jimmy Scott. "I have access to masculine and feminine aspects," explained the singer, "although obviously there's a limitation to both of those things. I have an experience that's unique to being me, which isn't just being stranded between two things. It's another frontier, with its own expansive possibilities." NB: a standout among the rare recordings of Reed singing "Candy Says" solo is one captured in Paris on April 2, 1979, during the *Bells* tour, with Marty Fogel skywriting lovely countermelodies on flute as Reed worked the lyrics like a jazz singer for more than ten minutes.

406 *"in a state of rapture"*: Anderson in Mark Beaumont, "Laurie Anderson's Playlist Reveals the Real Lou Reed," *NME*, October 10, 2016; John Hodgkin, "Antony Finds His Voice," *The New York Times*, September 4, 2005. Reed would have a cameo on Antony and the Johnsons' LP *I Am a Bird Now*, which used Peter Hujar's iconic deathbed photo of Candy Darling on its cover. The duet "Fistful of Love" might be about an abusive relationship, or one where beatings and body markings are elements in consensual love; Reed's recitation at the head suggests the aching confessional opening of a love song by the Shirelles or the Shangri-Las, as he describes lying in bed looking up at "a ceiling full of stars . . . I just have to let you know how I feel." The album also featured Anohni's duet with Boy George, "You Are My Sister," which they'd perform at a concert in New York that Reed attended, listening with tears in his eyes.

407 *"I've lied so much"*: Reed in Gavin Martin, "Lou Reed: 'I've lied so much about the past, I can't tell what is true any more,'" *Uncut*, March 2003.

408 *chamber version of* Metal Machine Music: Amanda Petrusich, "Lou Reed," *Pitchfork*, September 17, 2007; Amber Frost, "Luciano Pavarotti Sings 'Perfect Day' with Lou Reed, 2002," Dangerousminds.net, November 20, 2013. On November 17, 2009, Reed reprised his Pavarotti duet with the classical soprano Renee Fleming at a state event in Prague to commemorate the Velvet Revolution; Fleming's performance may have helped inspire the Scottish pop sensation Susan Boyle's decision to cover the song a year later on her chart-topping album.

409 *First Couple of Pop Art*: Reed had collaborated on music with Bruni, a European beauty who, like Nico, abandoned a lucrative modeling career to pursue the arts. It worked out well: her first LP, *Quelqu'un m'a dit*, was an airy set of poetic folk-pop in the Françoise Hardy tradition that debuted at number 1 on the French pop charts. For her second LP, *No Promises*, a musical setting of nineteenth- and early-twentieth-century English poetry, she invited Reed to recite Yeats's "Those Dancing Days Are Gone." The poem, from Yeats's 1933 volume *Words for Music, Perhaps*,

ponders the aging body and invokes the spirit of a man who may sing "until he drop." At brunch, the neighborhood streets around the restaurant were "on lockdown," according to Reed's manager Tom Sarig, who sat at a side table with the French secret service while the couples dined. "Lou loved stuff like that," Sarig says.

410 *creating in a wordless medium: Emotion in Action* was published in 2003. The format—a small book of zoomed-in images, titled *Action*, inset into the die-cut cover of a larger volume, *Emotion*, containing landscapes and skylines—echoes of the twin-image penetration of Barbara Rubin's *Christmas on Earth*. Many shots were of the Hudson, the body of water Reed spent most of his life flanking—a river that flows both into and out of the Atlantic Ocean, in a freak of potamology that's a metaphor for the humanity that's long lined its banks. Reed didn't bother with written didactics. "The visuals speak for themselves," he wrote of the book's untitled images in an introductory paragraph. "I have no interest in the where and when of it all."

410 *"just a guy with money"*: Reed in Mitch Myers, "Sound and Vision: The Music and Photography of Lou Reed," *Stop Smiling*, 2004, reprinted in Heath and Thomas, p. 264; Hannah Duguid, "Lou Reed: Photographer," *The Independent*, November 10, 2009.

411 *"I will study this forever"*: Reed in Martha Burr, "Lou Reed: A Walk on the Wild Side of Tai Chi," *Kung Fu Magazine*, May/June, 2003; Laurie Anderson, talk at Brooklyn Public Library (Grand Army Plaza) on Lou Reed International Tai Chi Day, August 3, 2019. Rod Meade Sperry, "Listen as Laurie Anderson Gives Voice to 'Songs from the Bardo,'" *Lion's Roar*, July 31, 2019. One could draw a line from Reed's bond with the theologian Gabriel Vahanian at Syracuse to his connection, nearly half a century later, with Masters Ren and Mingyur.

411 *"trying to change ourselves"*: Anderson in Annie Armstrong, "'When Lou Did Tai Chi, He Was Looking for Magic': Laurie Anderson Hosts Lou Reed Martial Arts Session at Brooklyn Library," *ARTnews*, August 7, 2019.

411 *"constantly told by your teacher"*: Reed in *The Art of the Straight Line*; Bill O'Connor, talk at Lou Reed International Tai Chi Day, Brooklyn Public Library (Grand Army Plaza), August 3, 2019. One of Reed's closest martial arts buddies, O'Connor was an interesting character about Reed's age, a poet who spoke of an early career as a federal investigator specializing in international money laundering. O'Connor introduced Reed to Master Ren, and helped him wrap his head around the idea of aging with grace. "It doesn't have to be martial arts, but you have to pursue something," O'Connor said. "As you get older, you have to work on getting older. You can't rely on what you were when you were younger. And whatever system you choose has to have some type of philosophical and spiritual aspect to have any lasting benefits. Because most of us just go through life, you know, 'I have no idea what I'm doing. I have no idea why I'm here. What's the meaning of it all?' The fact is, there's no 'meaning of it all'—the meaning of it all is what you invent. This is the kind of stuff Lou and I used to talk about."

411 *did tai chi every day*: Anderson in Reed, *The Art of the Straight Line*, p. 304.

412 *antithesis of* Metal Machine Music: Lou Reed, *Hudson River Wind Meditations* (Sounds True, 2007). "I first composed this music for myself as an adjunct to meditation, Tai Chi, and bodywork, and as music to play in the background of life,"

Reed wrote in the liner notes," "to replace the everyday cacophony with new and ordered sounds of an unpredictable nature . . . I hope you find as much use for this music as I have in both writing and listening to it and exploring inner spaces." It's a long way from his "my week beats your year" liner notes to *Metal Machine Music*.

412   *"keeps your dick really big"*: Martin.

413   *"I'm saying that kindly"*: Marsha Vlasic in Dee Lockett, "Women and Power: Marsha Vlasic Told Lou Reed 'I Can't Do This Anymore,'" *The Cut*, October 16, 2018.

413   *"expected nothing less from you"*: Beth Groubert, author interview; Aram Bajakian, "Looking at Trees with Lou Reed: Reflections on Playing Guitar with a Master," blog post, Arambajakian.com, June 29, 2015. Reed drove many away, but many colleagues felt their tour of duty with him pushed them to become better and more exacting in their work. "When he ripped on people, it was only because he was trying to wake them up," reflected Aram Bajakian, who played guitar in Reed's band during his final tours, "to make their art alive and to make them play with this level of attention."

415   *"He was so familiar to me"*: Julian Schnabel in Andy Battaglia, "The *ARTnews* Accord: Laurie Anderson and Julian Schnabel Talk 1970s New York, How Art Connects People, and More," *ARTnews*, March 6, 2020. Schnabel's Lester Bangs equivalent was Robert Hughes, whose 1984 *The Shock of the New* cemented him as a consequential arbiter of the new art movement Schnabel represented. Schnabel parodied Hughes in his memoir *CVJ: Nicknames of Maitre D's & Other Excerpts from Life*, describing an encounter with a writer named "Robbie Huge" who asked to be chained up. Reviewing the book for *The New Republic*, Hughes in turn compared Schnabel's work to Sylvester Stallone's acting in *Rambo*. Robert Hughes, "Julian Schnabel," in *Nothing If Not Critical: Selected Essays on Art and Artists* (1990; Penguin, 1992), pp. 300, 302.

415   *to make a film of it*: Battaglia. Lola Schnabel directed the filming of the *Berlin* scenes, some of which were shot on the upper floors of the Old Homestead Steakhouse in Manhattan's Meatpacking District. Seigner was co-star of the film Schnabel was finishing, *The Diving Bell and the Butterfly*, an adaptation of the memoir by the French magazine editor Jean-Dominique Bauby about his life after a stroke left him paralyzed with locked-in syndrome. The film earned Schnabel the Best Director prize at Cannes; Seigner would later star in *Venus in Fur*, a metatextual take on Sacher-Masoch's novel directed by her husband, Roman Polanski.

415   *kicking in $50,000 each*: Schnabel in Reed, *The Art of the Straight Line*, p. 193.

415   *have Anohni sing the entire*: Anohni in "ANOHNI on Lou Reed's *Berlin: Live at St. Ann's Warehouse*," promotional video (Matador Records, March 2, 2009). Matador released the performance on LP and CD.

416   *"a picture of redemption"*: Hal Willner, author interview, 2015; Anohni, author interview, 2015. Reed was disappointed Sharon Jones couldn't travel with the *Berlin* production; besides her other contributions, she did a fiery duet with him on "Sweet Jane" for the encore set. "She so genuinely loved Lou, and he really connected with her on a musical level," a former Reed assistant notes.

417   *wrote a song for Anderson*: Anderson in Reed, *The Art of the Straight Line*, p. 306.

417   *"to marry your best friend"*: Anderson, author interview.

417   *"I've always had trouble reading"*: Reed to Costello on *Spectacle*; Milkowski; Michael

Dorf, "Lou Reed: The Wise Child," *New York Jewish Week*, October 28, 2013. Sylvia Reed notes her ex-husband's astigmatism, which compounded his visual disability and seemed to worsen over time. She often read to him on plane flights; one of his favorites was the NYC history *Low Life* by her friend Lucy Sante. Schnabel shared a story about his father's passing, and how, moments after he died in a room with family and friends, Schnabel asked Reed to hold his father's still-warm hand, as Schnabel cued up *Magic and Loss*. "We all loved Jack," Reed noted. Reed envied the close relationship Schnabel had with his dad. The "Song of Songs" performance with Zorn took place in New York at the Abrons Art Center, February 23, 2008.

418   *"their American soul brothers?"*: Reed in Lou Reed and Hal Willner, "Lou Reed's New York Shuffle," BBC Radio 6 (bbc.co.uk), August 12, 2012. See also Andrew M. Goldstein, "Lou Reed Wants to Talk About His New Radio Show, Does Not Want to Talk About Money," *Vulture*, June 6, 2008; *Other Music* (Production Company Productions/Factory 25, 2020). The men were devoted to the Fourth Street record shop Other Music, a highly curated temple for myriad sounds. One morning shortly after Reed's death, staff found a memorial banana waiting for them on the ground in front of the door when they opened, with "R.I.P. LOU" written on it in Magic Marker.

418   *invited to do live narration*: Christopher Bell, "Interview: Guy Maddin on His Criterion-Selected 'My Winnipeg,' Career, Film Vs. Digital, Superhero Movies & Dental Troubles," *IndieWire*, January 28, 2015. Maddin's *Brand upon the Brain!*, staged at the Village East on Second Avenue and Twelfth Street, was an autobiographical work with a format that recalled the tradition of women "benshi" performer-lecturers in the presentation of early Japanese silent film, using live foley artists and musicians; it also recalled the multimedia "happenings" and Cinematheque screenings Reed once participated in. "It was so nerve-racking," Maddin said of Reed's difficulties during the performance; "I crushed a molar from clenching my teeth so hard."

419   *"would ever have imagined"*: Merrill Weiner, panel discussion on Shirley Rabinowitz, Tenement Museum, May 2016. Shirley passed away sitting on the couch in the apartment on West Twenty-fourth Street that she'd lived in for nearly half a century. She was 102.

420   *"You left a lot out!"*: Shirley Novick, quoted by Lou Reed, interview, Marfa Public Radio, May 9, 2010. *Red Shirley* premiered in New York on January 15, 2011.

420   *music with new collaborators*: Emily Haines, "Metric's Emily Haines Pays Tribute to Lou Reed's Integrity and Humor," *Rolling Stone*, October 28, 2013; Danny Eccleston, "It's an Anglo-Saxostentialist Crisis . . ." *Mojo*, December 2018. "I don't obey the verse-chorus rule. I ignore that," Reed told Albarn. "All I do is write words and perform them as if I was speaking them naturally. And if they fall in different places, I'm happy with that." Albarn would apply those strategies to his own work going forward.

421   *"barked for five minutes"*: Anderson in Joshua Barone, "Laurie Anderson Puts On a Concert for Dogs in Times Square," *The New York Times*, January 3, 2016.

422   *"with a bemused look"*: Paul Simonon, author interview. "I think he might've been having some weird flashback," Simonon says of Reed's hesitation, and wondered if his outfit had been triggering: "I was wearing a sailor's hat and might've looked in some aspect like the guy on the back of the *Transformer* cover."

422 *"my tongue is fearfully sore"*: Frank Wedekind, *Diary of an Erotic Life* (Basil Blackwell, 1990), p. 194.

422 *undergoing increasingly elaborate treatments*: Jada Yuan, "Making House Calls with Elisabeth Weiss, New York's Most Musical Dog Trainer," *New York*, July 28, 2014; Jonathan Romney, "Laurie Anderson: 'My Dog's Character Was Pure Empathy. I Tried to Express That,'" *The Guardian*, March 27, 2016.

424 *dealing with tremendous pain*: Hal Willner in Reed, *The Art of the Straight Line*, p. 190.

424 *"acting it and singing it"*: Reed in Dimitri Ehrlich, "Loutallica," *Interview*, October 27, 2011. See also Edward Helmore, "'It Has So Much Rage': Metallica and Lou Reed Talk About Their New Album," *The Guardian*, October 20, 2011.

425 *"in the kitchen, sobbing away"*: Kirk Hammett in Billy Dukes, "Lou Reed Makes Metallica Members Cry," *Ultimate Classic Rock*, August 25, 2011. See also Rob Tannenbaum, "Metallica: The Playboy Interview," *Playboy*, April 2001; David Fricke, "When Metallica Met Lou Reed," *Rolling Stone*, September 30, 2011.

425 *"the major American writers"*: Antonin Baudry, presentation to Lou Reed of the insignia of Commander of the Order of Arts and Letters, October 30, 2011. See also "Hitler Reacts to Metallica Recording with Lou Reed," YouTube (616Dragonlady), June 19, 2011, https://www.youtube.com/watch?v=x9LcJwX9dnE.

426 *"my spirit brothers"*: Reed in Ehrlich; Ulrich in Jon Weiderhorn, "Metallica's Lars Ulrich on Orion Fest, 'Lulu' and a 'Black Album' Regret," *Spin*, May 2, 2012.

426 *"ceaselessly into the past"*: F. Scott Fitzgerald, *The Great Gatsby* (1925; Project Gutenberg, 2021), p. 236. Svante Karlsson, "Svante Karlsson Talks About 'Junior Dad,'" *Musicians' Corner*, February 12, 2014. There were a few promotional performances by Reed and Metallica, including a beautiful one on German television. It's worth noting another of Reed's final recordings, made around this time: a powerful version of "Solsbury Hill," Peter Gabriel's anthem of transformation. Given Reed's circumstances, its imagery was resonant—a pounding heart, a man being called home.

427 *"Very perverse"*: Lou Reed, "Lou Reed Talks Kanye West's *Yeezus*," *Talkhouse*, September 3, 2014. President Barack Obama famously called Kanye West a "jackass" in the wake of the latter's dust-up with Taylor Swift at the 2009 MTV Video Music Awards.

427 *among the most powerful*: Lou Reed, "Junior Dad—Lou Reed in Dresden," YouTube (LaubeTV), August 18, 2014, https://www.youtube.com/watch?v=7dQ3P8knPDw. Reed's June 30, 2012, show in Dresden, Germany, is one worth noting; the finale, as it was for many shows on his last tour, was "Junior Dad."

428 *"It's medical tourism"*: Anderson in Tim Teeman, "Wild Side Catches Up with Lou Reed," *The Times* (London), June 1, 2013.

428 *liver was "less-than-perfect"*: Charlie Miller in Reed, *The Art of the Straight Line*, p. 279.

429 *"'strained at best'"*: "New Liver Complains of Difficulty Working with Lou Reed," *The Onion*, June 3, 2013.

429 *actor Natasha Lyonne*: Jenna Marotta, "Natasha Lyonne and the Broad City Girls Talk Lou Reed, Hangovers, and Pocket Pussies," *Bedford + Bowery*, April 18, 2014.

429 *"Ad people play fair"*: Reed in Matt Creamer, "Cannes Rewind: Lou Reed, Once a Scooter Pitchman, Still Likes Ad People," *Ad Age*, June 20, 2013. An amusing

photo from the event showed Reed posing against a backdrop patterned with the logo for *Breaking Bad*, the popular TV series about a high school science teacher who becomes a methamphetamine chemist.

430   *"freeze it in the memory"*: Lou Reed, "Sick of Goodby's, Mabou, 1978," *Tate Magazine*, no. 2, Autumn 2004. The short essay was about Robert Frank's photo of the same name.

431   *"I don't want to be erased"*: Reed in Merrill Weiner, "About My Brother Lou," in "The Power of the Heart: A Celebration of Lou Reed," loureed.com, undated; Julian Schnabel in Bockris, *Transformer*, p. 503.

432   *"still see the goosebumps"*: Hal Willner in "The Power of the Heart: A Celebration of Lou Reed."

432   *"never seen an expression"*: Laurie Anderson, "Laurie Anderson's Farewell to Lou Reed," *Rolling Stone*, November 21, 2013.

433   *"she left to join him"*: Weiner, "About My Brother Lou."

EPILOGUE

434   *The child must carry*: Delmore Schwartz, "The Ballad of the Children of the Czar," in Mazer, *The Collected Poems of Delmore Schwartz*; see also Schwartz, "The Vocation of the Poet in the Modern World," 1951, reprinted in Reginald Gibbons, ed., *The Poet's Work: 29 Poets on the Origins and Practice of Their Art* (University of Chicago Press, 1989).

434   *come closest to poetry*: Richard Hell, "The Rolling Stones vs. The Velvet Underground," in Sean Manning, ed., *Rock and Roll Cage Match* (Three Rivers, 2008).

434   *"diversity that extends to the stars"*: Lester Bangs, "Untitled Notes on Lou Reed, 1980," in *Psychotic Reactions and Carburetor Dung*, p. 167.

435   *not condoning drug use*: "Vatican's 'Culture Minister' Tweets Lou Reed Song," Reuters, October 28, 2013; Chrissie Hynde, Facebook post, October 28, 2013; Courtney Love, Michael Stipe, and Jana Hunter in "Various Artists . . . Talk Lou Reed," *Talkhouse*, September 16, 2014; Stipe and Bono in "Remembering Lou: Tributes from Close Friends and Followers," *Rolling Stone*, November 21, 2013.

436   *"a bullshit detector"*: Dave Hickey, "We Have Lost the Master of the Mundane and the Malicious," *SPIN*, October 2013; Ann Powers, "What Lou Reed Taught Me," NPR.org, October 27, 2013.

436   *"our generation's New York poet"*: Patti Smith, "Postscript: Lou Reed," *The New Yorker*, November 11, 2013; Rosanne Cash, *Talkhouse*; see also Tobias Grey, "Patti Smith on Famous Friends and Simple Songs," *The Wall Street Journal*, June 18, 2014. Reed and Smith "had a complicated relationship," she told Grey. "He was always supportive but also liked to provoke." She recalled seeing him a week or so before he died and realizing he was not well. "We spoke and as he was leaving he said 'I love you, Patti' and I said 'I love you, Lou.' I realized that might have been the first time we expressed that level of our feelings and friendship to each other."

436   *You could be so difficult*: Peter Gabriel, "Oh Lou, Where Have You Gone?" Peter Gabriel.com, October 28, 2013.

437   *"his transformation from a living person"*: Laurie Anderson, Lou Reed memorial, Apollo Theater, December 16, 2013; Jon Pareles, "Lou Reed's Spirit Invoked at a

Reunion of His Inner Circle," *The New York Times*, December 17, 2013. Anderson spoke about the Sunday apartment memorials: "During the last seven weeks I've heard literally hundreds of stories mostly about Lou's kindness and generosity— 'he put me through college'; 'he gave me two cameras'; 'he listened to my problems.' But most of all the stories were: 'he changed my life—by making me do whatever it was better: music, writing, planning."

437 *free events at Lincoln Center*: Sarah Larson, "Goodbye, Lou!" *The New Yorker*, November 20, 2013; Will Hermes, "Laurie Anderson, Anohni Lead Stirring Lou Reed Tribute at Lincoln Center," *Rolling Stone*, September 1, 2016. The second event, "The Bells: A Daylong Celebration of Lou Reed," was held in August 2016; it included memorable performances by David Johansen ("Oh! Sweet Nuthin'"), Lenny Kaye ("Sweet Jane"), and a sound installation reimagining *Metal Machine Music*.

438 *"Be really, really tender"*: Anderson, speech at the Rock and Roll Hall of Fame, April 18, 2015; Chris Payne, "Watch Laurie Anderson & Patti Smith Induct Lou Reed Into Rock and Roll Hall of Fame," *Billboard*, April 20, 2015. "He was my best friend and he was also the person I admired most in the world," Anderson said. "In the years we were together, there were a few times I was mad and there were a few times I was frustrated, but I was never ever bored."

438 *cite his influence*: Joseph Arthur, "Joseph Arthur Remembers Lou Reed," *American Songwriter*, October 28, 2013; Victoria Segal, "Power Up—Alynda Segarra Is Back with Hurray for the Riff Raff's Seventh LP," *Mojo*, March 2021; Emily Haines, Kevin Morby, author interviews.

439 *"I wanted to be that girl"*: Robbi Mecus in Emily Russell, "Wild Side: How a Trans Forest Ranger Found Herself in the Adirondacks," *NPR Morning Edition* (north countrypublicradio.org), January 19, 2021; Josh Jones, "Lou Reed & Laurie Anderson: Buddhist Power Couple," *Engage!* June 30, 2016.

439 *"like a robin in spring"*: Alex Scordelis, "Amy Poehler Is One Busy Lady. But She'll Still Make Time for You," *Paper*, December 9, 2013; see also Amy Poehler, *Yes Please* (Dey Street, 2015), p. 213.

439 *"When Lou was on drugs"*: Henry Goldrich and Holly Goldrich Schoenfeld, *The Wall of Fame: New York City's Legendary Manny's Music* (Hal Leonard, 2007), pp. 132–33, 157; Allan Arkush in Anne Thompson, "Lou Reed on Lou Reed," IndieWire.com, October 30, 2013.

440 *issued the remaster project*: Lou Reed, *The RCA and Arista Album Collection* (Sony Legacy, 2016); *Words & Music, May 1965*; Neil Vigdor, "A $120,000 Banana Is Peeled from an Art Exhibition and Eaten," *The New York Times*, December 7, 2019.

440 *also left an estate*: Last Will and Testament of Lewis Reed, signed and notarized April 3, 2012; Julia Marsh, "Lou Reed Takes Care of Wife, Mom & Sister in Will," *New York Post*, November 4, 2013.

440 *"He left no instructions"*: Anderson in Ben Sisario, "Lou Reed Archives Head to New York Public Library," March 2, 2017; Ben Sisario, "Laurie Anderson on Lou Reed's Love, Work and Retirement Plan," March 3, 2017; Ben Sisario, "'You Don't Become Lou Reed Overnight.' A New Exhibition Proves It," June 6, 2022; *Lou Reed: Caught Between the Twisted Stars*, exhibit, New York Public Library for the Performing Arts, 2022.

441 *"Lou Reed made that thing?"*: Anderson in Sisario, "Laurie Anderson on Lou Reed's Love, Work and Retirement Plan."

442 *installed a "film sculpture"*: Laurie Anderson, "Bringing Guantánamo to Park Avenue," *The New Yorker*, November 23, 2015; Will Hermes, "A Body, Transformed," NPR.org, October 6, 2015. Notwithstanding brief segments of prerecorded commentary, the film sculpture of Mohammed el Gharani was silent, but for a near-ambient swarm of electronic noise-data churning in a mass of guitar-generated feedback—a piece titled "Drones," based on Reed's design for *Metal Machine Music* and performed, as it were, by his former guitar tech Stewart Hurwood.

442 *"Now he is my muse"*: Laurie Anderson, "This Is Where the Chorus Comes In," in Reed, *Do Angels Need Haircuts?*, p. 72. The collection of Reed's early poetry is drawn in part from his 1971 reading at the St. Mark's Poetry Project.

443 *she began the next*: Laurie Anderson, "'Junior Dad' (Lou Reed)—Stadsschouwburg Amsterdam—22 October 2016," YouTube (info4allat), October 23, 2016 https://www.youtube.com/watch?v=F1VyWW5hnXY.

ACKNOWLEDGMENTS

This is not an "authorized biography." But many shared their memories generously. Deep thanks to Lou Reed's family, friends, associates, and admirers who informed this book: Merrill Reed Weiner (Bunny Reed), JillAllison Opell, Laurie Anderson, Sylvia Reed (née Morales), Liz Kronstad (Bettye Reed), the Humphreys/Garcia family, Hal Willner, Jenni Muldaur, Shelley Albin, Erin Clermont, Barbara Hodes, M. Allan Hyman, Rich Sigal, Judy Titus, Arthur Littman, Liz Leyh (Liz Annas, née Sutkowski), David Weisman, Richard Mishkin, Patricia Volk, Peter Locke, Karl Stoecker, James Gorney, Garland and Claire Jeffreys, Liz Swados, Maureen "Moe" Tucker, Martha Morrison, Billy Name, Gerard Malanga, Danny Fields, Jonathan Richman, Rob Norris, Chris Stein, Debbie Harry, Holly Woodlawn, Jayne County, Robert Wilson, Rubén Blades, Guy Maddin, Stefan Sagmeister, Lorenzo Mattotti, Tom Sarig, Genya Ravan, Penny Arcade, Joey Freeman, Camille O'Grady, Elliott Murphy, Steve Hunter, Steve Katz, Vin LaPorta, Michael Fonfara, Mike Rathke, Fernando Saunders, Fred Maher, Tony "Thunder" Smith, Suzanne Vega, Emily Haines, Kevin Hearn, Aram Bajakian, Larry Packer, Jeff Ross, Chuck Hammer, Michael Suchorsky, Beth Groubert, Elis Costa, Brie Gentry, Cat Celebrezze, Ramona Jan, Corky Stasiak, Victoria Williams, Richard Lloyd, Lenny Kaye, Joseph Arthur, Richard Barone, Rosanne Cash, Damon Albarn, Paul Simonon, Eric Andersen, Kevin Morby, Ralph Thayer, Barbara Wilkinson (née Fulk), Kerri Welsh, Andrew Essex, Jim DeRogatis, Joe Concra, Jim Fouratt, Reva Wolf, Matt Leach, Spencer Drate, Scott Richardson, Rob Santos, Kate Simon, Robert Somma, Dana Spiotta, David Yaffe, Aral Sezen, Jehu Martin, Joe Kruppa, Harvey Goldberg, Billy Altman, Lydia Sugarman, Steve Philp, Mia Wolff, and the many others who shared their Lou stories, prompted and not, on record or background, apocryphal and otherwise. R.I.P. Billy Name, Holly Woodlawn, Michael Fonfara, Liz Swados, and Camille O'Grady. In memory of Hal Willner, whose encouragement, through multiple interviews, inspired this work immeasurably.

Gratitude to the MacDowell Colony, Virginia Center for the Creative Arts, and Corporation of Yaddo for community and support essential to completing this project.

Shout-outs: For research and transcription assists, Jack Conway, Jonah Furman, Daniel Goldstein, Kurt Karlson, Sarah Paolantonio, Ethan Scholl, Max Stahl; John McGhee, Nancy Elgin, Chris Peterson, and Ian Van Wye for copyedits; Robert Polito, Karl Bryant, and Anne Galperin for manuscript notes; Rodrigo Corral and Gretchen Achilles for the hot design. The New York Public Library of the Performing Arts team, especially those involved with the Lou Reed Archive; Don Fleming and Jason Stern at Sister Ray Enterprises; Matt Wrbican (R.I.P.), Matt Gray, and Charlene Bidula at the Warhol Museum; Judith Peraino and Katherine Reagan at Cornell; Johan Kugelberg at Boo-Hooray; the Harry Ransom Center at the University of Texas; Irina Reyn and Peter Trachtenberg at the University of Pittsburgh Writers Series; Eric Weisbard and the great minds behind the Pop Conference; Christian Fevret and Sylvie Sergent; M. C. Kostek; Alfredo García; Gordon Lyon; Jay Reeg; Elizabeth Finkelstein; Adam Ritchie, Bob Gruen, Forrest Scholl, Pati Rock, and all the photographers who shared their work; Bettina Der Fuchs and the Let's Talk About Lou Reed Facebook group. Thanks to Keren Poznansky, Maria Malta, Matt Sullivan, Blake Zidell, Steve Martin, Michele Hug, Jessica Linker, and Sam McAllister for recordings and other resources. *Grazie mille*: Michele Piumini for translations and Italian connections; Sloss Eckhouse Dasti Haynes and Henry Kaufman for legal; my agent Paul Bresnick for lighting the fuse; my editor, Alex Star, for acuity and admirable patience.

Fist bumps: The many writers and other creators who've illuminated Reed's work over the years. My editors and colleagues past and present, including Charles Aaron, Jon Bernstein, Bob Boilen, Nathan Brackett, Jon Dolan, David Fear, Jason Fine, David Fricke, Caryn Ganz, Christian Hoard, Jeremy Larson, Alan Light, Sia Michel, Marissa Moss,

Puja Patel, Rob Sheffield, Hank Shteamer, Richie Unterberger, Simon Vozick-Levinson, Alison Weinflash, and Christopher Weingarten. For leads, advice, and/or random acts of kindness: Beth Barusek Cohen (R.I.P.), Todd Chandler, Mirah, Barbara Lerner, Jon Stahl and Betsy Salwen Stahl, Judy Salwen, Andy Battaglia, Ginger Dellenbaugh, Seth Larkin Sanders, James Rasin, Tyler Wilcox, Kim Beck, Andrea Elliott, Jesse Jarnow, Jason King, Sarah LaDuke, John Leland, Dale Maharidge, Elaina Richardson, Guinevere Turner, Jenn Pelly, Amanda Petrusich, Mark Richardson, Lucy Sante, Sharon Tomasic, Matt Weiner, Matt Weissman, Susan Greenfield, Leslie Fuchs, Jason Gross, and the Kingston Writers' Studio gang, particularly Sari Botton, Sara Franklin, and Ryan Chapman. Extra special thanks to anyone I've failed to mention who lent a hand.

Support LGBTQ+ rights in your community. A donation from this book's proceeds has been made to the Transgender Law Center (transgenderlawcenter.org) and to Trans Lifeline (translifeline.org), a grassroots hotline and microgrants 501(c)(3) nonprofit offering emotional and financial support to trans people in crisis—for the trans community, by the trans community.

* * *

For Lou Reed fans worldwide, and all who believe art can transform us.

INDEX

A NOTE ABOUT THE AUTHOR

Will Hermes is a contributing editor for *Rolling Stone*, a longtime contributor to NPR's *All Things Considered* and *The New York Times*, and the author of *Love Goes to Buildings on Fire*. He also writes for *Pitchfork* and other publications, and was coeditor of *SPIN: 20 Years of Alternative Music*.